THE MATING DANCE

By Rona Randall

DRAGONMEDE
WATCHMAN'S STONE
THE EAGLE AT THE GATE
THE MATING DANCE

The Mating Dance

Rona Randall

Coward, McCann & Geoghegan
New York

Library of Congress Cataloging in Publication Data

Randall, Rona, pseud.
  The mating dance.

  I. Title.
PZ3.R1587Mat 1979   [PR6035.A58]   823'.9'12   78-31724
ISBN 0-698-10961-9

PRINTED IN THE UNITED STATES OF AMERICA

For Christopher Sinclair-Stevenson

THE MATING DANCE

One

Lucinda

1

I was literally born to the smell of greasepaint, inhaling it with my first breath in the dressing room of the great Bernadette Boswell during a matinee on June 16, 1880, an indiscretion for which she never wholly forgave my mother. It was not the privilege of dressers to give birth in star dressing rooms, leaving the leading lady unbuttoned all the way down the back and the callboy shouting "Beginners, please!" outside the door.

"Of all moments to choose, five minutes before curtain-up! I only just made my entrance on time, thanks to my understudy, who was standing in the wings when I came rushing down crying for help."

"For my mamma, Lady Boswell?"

"Of course not, gel! For myself. *Someone* had to button me up."

By the time I was ten I was familiar with the story and never in the least embarrassed by it; not even by the fact that the great Bernadette's husband, the legendary Sir Nevill, actually helped to bring me into the world. Of course, the story was hushed up. If the press had heard that London's leading actor-manager had performed the task of midwife to his wife's dresser, the headlines would have shrieked about it next morning. I gather that Bernadette shrieked enough as it was, returning to the scene at the precise moment that I made my hurried entrance and uttered my first piercing cry.

I was always very proud that Sir Nevill helped me make my debut. Perhaps it was that, or the smell of greasepaint, or the star on the dressing-room door that instilled into me a yearning for the stage. Certainly no theatrical ambitions were inherited from my mother, who never set foot upon the boards nor ever wanted to. Whether they came from my father's side I had no idea, because I had no knowledge of his identity, nor even wondered about him during the early years of my life. Sir Nevill became a father figure to me from the moment of my birth, and I had no desire for any other.

Of course, he never referred to the event, and after that brief confidence from his wife when her normal quota of rum happened to be doubled because she had "one of her colds coming on," she never referred to it either. Her colds, under the influence of her favourite medicine, often made her garrulous, and because I was sitting quietly in my customary place, right there in a corner of her dressing room, I was a ready-made audience. At such moments I frequently became the recipient of her more lacrimose confidences, most of which I failed to understand. But not this one. This was a revelation, a wonderful story in which I was the central figure. I marvelled to think that if I had not chosen to be born in this very room, at the very moment that Sir Nevill came through from his adjoining dressing room and found my mother in such a plight, the whole exciting drama would never have happened. I would have been born in that top room of the Boswells' house in Portman Square in the most conventional and unexciting way, without attracting any attention at all.

"He heard your dear mamma's cries and went to her assistance at once. A noble gesture from a noble actor, but hardly necessary, I thought. There would surely have been time to call another woman dresser, or even that stupid wardrobe mistress, Ethel Piper—"

"But Wardrobe is so far away—right up near the flies, and all those stairs to climb!"

And perilous stairs at that, made of iron and partially unprotected, leading up to a dark and terrifying world from which Sir Nevill might never have returned had he ventured there. To my child's mind the circular staircase, winding round a deep central well and haunted with tales of tragedy, was wholly menacing.

The great Bernadette scoffed, "I am aware of that, gel, and of course I was proud of his presence of mind—*and* of his compassion for an unfortunate woman. But it amazes me that he knew what to do, though nature does most of the work of course. Oh, dear, I suppose I shouldn't talk of such things to a child like you—"

"Please do!" I begged as she sipped her medicine again and seemed likely to forget me. "Please tell me more, Lady Boswell."

"No more to tell, really. Thank heaven I was onstage, and so was almost the entire company. A crowd scene, and one of the longest in *The Only Way, or: A Far Far Better Thing* . . . and about the only scene in which Sir Nevill, playing Sydney Carton, didn't appear—which was perhaps fortunate or unfortunate, depending on which way you look at it."

"Fortunate, I should think. For Mamma and me, at any rate."

The great Bernadette came as near to sniffing as her dignity would allow, then continued, "By the time I reached my dressing room again, there you were. By then one or two female understudies had gathered and Piper was fluttering around with garments from Wardrobe to wrap you in, and the stage doorman had hurried off to fetch a doctor. Never has my dressing room been so crowded except after a first night, and you, child, stealing all the limelight!"

She said it good-naturedly, but I always felt that had riled her most of all. That, and Sir Nevill's concern for my mamma.

My mother was Miss Gertrude Grainger, commonly known as Trudy, and I was therefore Miss Lucinda Grainger, commonly known as Lucy, though as I grew up I refused to answer to that abbreviation. I liked the name Lucinda, the more so because my mother had chosen it especially for me, and all by herself. As for the surname, I disliked it only because it was inherited from a stuffy family who claimed that my birth had besmirched it and therefore refused to have anything to do with either of us. But everyone had to have a surname of some kind and I could see no reason why there should be any disgrace attached to it just because it came from a mother instead of a father. But the Graingers could. They had been a respectable chapel family for generations, and the daughters of nonconformist ministers didn't break the seventh commandment. (Or, if they did, they had the good sense never to be found out.)

Of course, when I was small I was unaware of any stigma. It wasn't until Clementine Boswell called me a bastard, on my seventh birthday, that I learned one of the facts of life, and even then I thought it was a compliment. Clementine was eleven and full of knowledge, so when she burst into her mother's dressing room at the Boswell Theatre and thrust a badly wrapped package at me, singing "Happy Birthday, Bastard!" I thought she was calling me by some noble title from one of the classical dramas the Boswells had made famous.

"Mamma said I should give you a present, so that's it," she said, already at her mother's dressing table and fiddling with her sticks of Leichner. Alongside them stood pots of cream and rouge and a jar of lampblack (used only when playing Lady Macbeth, all white-faced and hollow-eyed and bloody-handed), also some blue stuff for her eyelids when playing other parts, and bottles of wet white for her voluptuous arms, chins, and bulging breasts.

Bernadette Boswell was the greatest tragedienne of her day. I knew this because she often said so. I also knew that her young stepbrother, Gavin Calder, the company's handsome juvenile lead, on whom she doted and who frequently dropped into her dressing room, did not agree. Behind her back he would wink at my mother, who pretended not to notice, and then at me, who didn't. I enjoyed that wink. It made me feel that I shared a secret, and a secret shared with a grown-up was much better than one shared with a child—even a knowledgeable child like Clementine. Then he would stoop and whisper in my ear, "In *her* opinion, darling!" after which he would stroll nonchalantly from the room, bowing to her in mock homage from the door.

Even at that age I sensed that Lady Boswell was supremely satisfied with herself; even with her large pink body which she never attempted to hide from Clementine and me, although my mother always tried to screen her with a wrap. "Trudy, dear, don't *do* that! You'll have me undressing behind that screen next, and you know there's scarcely room. What a Puritan you are!" Then would come the arch glance, the meaningful smile. "Not that you have always been. We have dear little Lucy as evidence."

I remember once piping up, having heard something about the Puritans and religious reform, but not understanding much about either, "Mamma isn't a Puritan, Lady Boswell, she's a nonconformist," at which the famous Bernadette laughed richly.

"That is true enough, my pet, or *you* wouldn't be here, would you?"

"Bernadette—please!"

"Don't worry, Trudy, the child can't understand. Anyway, I don't blame you. I remember when we were girls together and that saintly family of yours tried to repress you. (My goodness, the rules and regulations in that household!) Well, I knew even then that one day you would cease to conform in ways other than religious. Thank God I married into the theatre! We have our own laws—"

"And very often just as strict. Some for actors and others for actresses, even backstage."

"Well, darling, that's necessary. If we were allowed to mix freely we would have all sorts of goings-on in the dressing rooms. I know other theatres are more lax than ours—music halls and suchlike—but the Boswell Theatre has a reputation to uphold. *We* do classical drama, and don't forget that dear Nevill is *Sir* Nevill now. We are above the theatrical hoi polloi."

I didn't know what "hoi polloi" meant any more than I knew what "bastard" meant, but from Lady Boswell's eloquent sniff I knew it must be something that smelled bad—like her gowns, which my mother sprayed with perfume to kill the odour of perspiration. ("No woman could be more fastidious about her toilet than I,'' the great Bernadette would boast.)

But Clementine's "Happy Birthday, Bastard!" sounded like a conferred honour, so I thanked her for it.

"For what?" she scoffed. "For that cast-off bonnet? Well, so you should. It cost a lot of money when new. Mamma had it made for me by a Bond Street milliner."

I had unwrapped the present by then and declared, "It's a lovely bonnet, truly it is." And so it was, even though some of the flowers were missing. "Indeed I thank you for it, but really I was thanking you for the new name. It means something, doesn't it?"

She stared at me in the big unframed mirror surrounded by glaring gas jets. "Don't you know, stupid? Don't you *know* what it means?"

I had to confess my ignorance. "I haven't reached that word in the dictionary yet." My mother was teaching me the way the famous Ellen Terry had been taught in childhood when travelling from theatre to theatre with her parents. A dozen words memorized from the dictionary each day were more educational, her father had declared, than half a morning's tuition in the three R's.

Clementine aped her mother's trilling stage laugh, and scoffed, "I'm sure your mamma will skip *that* word when she comes to it. As to what it means, I'll give you a guess and I'll help with a clue. It has to do with the bar sinister."

So then I asked what the bar sinister was, which made her laugh even more.

"It appears on family escutcheons when a member has been born on the wrong side of the blanket—which, stupid, means outside marriage. That's what a bastard is. It's a disgrace. And you're one. I found out today."

"I don't believe you."

I took the bonnet off and laid it aside. I was lucky enough to be the recipient of most of Clementine's cast-off clothes, on which her doting mother spared no expense, but this time I felt no gratitude. I also knew that if I could avoid it, I would never wear this bonnet at all. My Bastard Bonnet.

Because my mother, even in my babyhood, would never leave me in the care of anyone else, I had to be taken to the theatre for every performance, so I grew up mainly in that star dressing room, where my child's mind registered everything that went on. I learned later that the privilege of having her child constantly with her had been one of the things my mother had stipulated even before I was born; in fact, it was the only thing because she had been in no position to demand more when her life-long friend, Bernadette Smith, now elevated to theatrical limelight and a title along with it, came to her rescue at a time when no one else would.

" 'I will gladly work as your dresser, but when my baby comes I must take it to the theatre with me. I will never be parted from it. That is my only stipulation.' That is what she said, my dear, and that is what she meant, and being a mother myself, who could understand better? Though of course dear Clementine was born in wedlock, which is a very different thing." This information was imparted to me by Lady Boswell when I was considered old enough to understand why Clemmy was superior to myself.

But on my seventh birthday I had no knowledge of this. I was seated in my corner as always, waiting for my mother to return from the offstage dressing room where the great Bernadette did her quick change in Scene 3, Act 2, of *The Huguenot Count, or: The Maiden Deceived.* I had occupied this corner all my life, carried here in a basket only forty-eight hours after my birth, graduating to a heap of cushions barricaded by chairs where I could kick my legs in safety, from the cushions to a high baby chair, and now to a child's which my mother had picked up for a shilling in the Caledonian Market.

"So long as she behaves herself, she can stay here, Trudy, but the minute she becomes a nuisance, out she goes to Wardrobe and Piper can look after her, and remembering how that woman looked after *me* during the two days you were resting after the baby's birth, I would pity the poor mite, really I would."

So my mother made sure I was never a nuisance. Perhaps her care of me, which was always devoted, ensured that I was a placid and contented child. I accompanied her to the theatre an hour before curtain-up, and sometimes earlier if she had sewing to do, clutching my precious rag doll (another hand-down from Clementine) and, later on, the even more precious rag book which my mother saved pennies to buy for me one Christmas, and I would head straight for my corner and stay there.

There was no hardship attached to this because it was the star dressing room, distinguished by the glittering symbol on the door which Sir Nevill so disliked. He called it vulgar, but his wife refused to take it down. In those days, silver stars on the doors of lead dressing rooms were not customary. It was believed that Bernadette herself set the fashion one Christmas after a party onstage, when she seized it from the top of a Christmas tree and carried it away triumphantly, waving it gaily in one hand and a glass in the other and singing "Rule, Britannia!" while the stagehands sniggered behind her back and her husband pretended that his wife had not lost her dignity and nothing was amiss. And on reaching her dressing room she called loudly for a hammer and nails and fixed it on the door herself.

At any rate, that was the story Gavin Calder told me years later, but as a child that star had no association in my mind with a tipsy actress, only with glitter and magnificence. I was proud to be admitted into the room with the silver star, and when everyone else in the company complained of freezing dressing rooms and icy draughts, I snuggled in my corner, appreciating the warmth of Lady Boswell's oil stove, and not even the odour of it could overcome the exciting smell of theatrical makeup and the attar of roses which Clementine was now splashing on herself.

"Mmmm—gorgeous!" she breathed, quite unaware that only a moment ago she had dealt me a mortal blow. "When I grow up I shall pour perfume in my bath, like Cleopatra."

"She used milk," I put in, anxious to score.

"Horrible. No smell about it except cows."

"Asses. She bathed in asses' milk."

"Even worse. She was a heathen, of course, so knew no better."

"Oh, but she did. She knew a lot of things. And she knew that milk made her skin soft and men mad about her."

"I won't need milk to make men mad about *me*." Clementine stood sideways before the mirror, puffing out her chest like a pouter pigeon. "Look, I'm growing bosoms."

The dressing-room door opened and my mother swept in, the immortal Bernadette's discarded costume over one arm. Then she stood still, sniffing.

"And what have you two been up to?" She softened the words with a smile. My mother had the most beautiful smile in the world. It lit her grey eyes until they sparkled, and curved her gentle mouth in a way which made everyone smile back.

Clemmy said angelically, "Don't be cross, Trudy dear. And please don't tell Mamma. I would hate Lucy to be punished for making me steal her perfume."

"I did *not*! You helped yourself!"

"Only because you dared me. You called me a coward. 'If you don't, you're a coward!' you said, and nobody likes to be called that."

"I didn't call you anything of the sort, but anyway, it's better than bastard."

My mother looked at me quickly, then put the costume on a hanger and placed it with others on a long rail covered with a dust sheet; then she turned and said to me quietly, "Where and when did you learn that word?"

"Just now. Clemmy taught me. She says it's what I am."

Clementine was aghast.

"Lucy Grainger, you're a liar!" She turned large and innocent eyes on my mother. "Trudy dear, I don't even know what such a word means."

"I am glad to hear it." My mother's face was expressionless. "Would you like to run along to the prompt corner and watch your parents from the wings? I am sure the stage manager would let you."

"He'd better!" Clementine muttered darkly, and raced off, not bothering to shut the door. My mother closed it, then said, "Now you and I can have tea together, Lucinda. This scene takes a whole half-hour, so we won't be interrupted."

She took a paper bag from her shopping basket and opened it. Inside were two ha'penny Chelsea buns. Then she took out a clean cloth and spread it on Lady Boswell's theatrical skip, a large wicker basket in which costumes were stored. Then two cups, two saucers, two spoons, and two plates, which she set on the skip as if it were a table, with the Chelsea buns in place of honour.

"And come out of that lonely corner, my darling, and be happy with me. This is your birthday party and we are going to enjoy it. We'll pretend this room belongs to me and therefore you can sit wherever you wish, because whatever I have in life is as much yours as mine, and will always be. That's the way it is with people who love each other. And there's something else, too—loving someone makes you know when the other person has been hurt, so you want to comfort and protect them. Clemmy hurt you when I was out of the room and I cannot allow that. Sometimes people can hurt more with the truth than with lies, though it's important to be able to tell when people *are* lying."

"You mean about stealing perfume, Mamma, and things like that?"

She nodded, smiling at me through the steam as she poured boiling water into an earthenware teapot. "And other things, Lucinda. Like a bastard being something to be ashamed of. It isn't. I will tell you what a bastard really is. It is a child born of love. So that is what you are—my very own love child. Can you think of a nicer thing to be?"

The Boswells had moved into a splendid house at Number 47 Portman Square when Nevill received his title. They lived abovestairs and my mother and I lived below. That was by day. By night we slept right at the very top of the house, in the largest attic of all. Here my mother and I had our own private world, shared with no one, and when, at the age of five, I was given a room of my own, my mother acquired (on Sir Nevill's intervention) a table and chairs and an old settee when the staff room was at last being refurnished. With these she turned the attic into a bed-sitting room so that our private world still existed and we could retreat to it whenever we had the opportunity.

I never knew what unexpected impulse made Lady Boswell agree to my having a room of my own, but I was not overgrateful for it. I had enjoyed the large attic with the big brass bedstead and I felt cooped up in the six-by-four with the narrow bed just across the landing, but at least we were still separate from the rest of the household and before long we privately called our attic quarters "home," and sometimes, when playacting for the fun of it, even "the royal apartments."

Downstairs in the basement our daily life was spent with Hawkins the butler, Mrs. Wilson the cook (who was really Miss, but cooks were always given the courtesy title of Mrs.), Giles the footman, who also served Sir Nevill as valet, Kate the housemaid, who also did parlour duties, Daisy the kitchenmaid, Tommy the pageboy, and the between-maid Tweeny, whose real name I never found out and who seemed to spend all her life doing the most menial jobs, after cleaning out grates and lighting fires before the household was astir. For this she was more highly paid than many Tweenies in Portman Square, receiving as much as ten pounds a year and a Christmas box of ten shillings from Sir Nevill, who always insisted on these extra rewards for the staff despite his wife's insistence that it was overindulgence.

"Do you realise that the butler at Number 10—an earl's, no less—receives exactly half of what you pay ours? Forty pounds a year, my love, forty pounds—and you paying Hawkins eighty!" I heard this protest clearly one night from behind her ladyship's bedroom door as my mother led me upstairs.

It was a long time before I found out just how much, or how little, my mother earned, and that Sir Nevill discreetly supplemented it with gifts from time to time, which his wife knew nothing about. I frequently overheard things which grown-ups believed I paid no attention to, listening unashamedly to conversations which were carried out in front of me and to remarks which they imagined I could not understand. Many lingered in my memory, becoming significant only in later years, particularly those which Lady Boswell delivered in a pointed fashion, as if they were key lines in stage dialogue and therefore to be stressed.

"Don't forget, Trudy dear, that we are supporting both you *and* your child, feeding, housing, and clothing you both, which was more than your respectable family was prepared to do."

"I appreciate that, Bernadette."

"And that is another thing. I don't mind you calling me by my Christian name in private, because after all we did grow up together and attend your father's dreary chapel and that equally dismal school (and let no one ever say I am not loyal to my friends!), but the fact remains that we are no longer socially equal, so do try to remember my title when in company and in front of the servants."

That was my first acquaintance with humiliation, and even now I can recall my mother's painful flush. She was brushing Lady Boswell's hair at the time. When returning from the theatre, her duties were not ended until she had helped her to prepare for bed, waiting up for hours when late entertaining was going on, or husband and wife had supped at the Savoy or Romano's after the evening performance. Putting in regular appearances at the right restaurants was an essential ritual amongst the theatrical hierarchy of London, and the great Bernadette had a healthy respect for doing the right thing at the right time, in the right place and in the right way.

"I am the Mrs. Siddons of today and, like her, a stickler for etiquette. I know, as she knew, what my public expects of me, and, like her, I will never disappoint it. In fact, I resemble the renowned Mrs. Siddons in most things, I suspect."

"In girth, at least," Gavin Calder would whisper with his mocking smile—making sure, as always, that she did not hear. It only occurred to me in later years that he made these remarks *sotto voce* to ensure that her good nature was not soured toward him, or that his brotherly visits, which invariably resulted in a generous handout, were not terminated in one of her rages.

But it was only in later years that I recognised the menace which could lie behind a mask.

By the standards of our Portman Square neighbours, the Boswells' household staff was small. Mrs. Wilson combined the services of cook-housekeeper, there was no senior housemaid, and Lady Boswell had no lady's maid—but she had no need of one with my mother living in the house.

Even when a child, I knew that my mother never really fitted in below-stairs, though she was always on good terms with the staff and everyone liked and respected her. She was always addressed as Miss Grainger, never by her Christian name. This subtly elevated her. "We are above the domestic hoi polloi," I thought proudly, "and I am a very special kind of bastard." For the first time in my life I felt superior to Clementine, who had certainly not been born of love. I knew that with the unerring instinct of childhood.

Besides, from my ringside seat in the leading lady's dressing room, I was a silent beholder of many scenes, including some between husband and wife. Sir Nevill did not open that dividing door very often, and even more significant was the fact that they did not share a dressing room, as did many married couples in the theatre in those days. But when he did open that door, and if my mother was present at the time and not running some errand for his wife, she would take me by the hand and draw me into the draughty corridor outside, shutting the door carefully behind her. Even this sometimes failed to cut off the sound of raised voices, and as I grew older I marvelled that the facade of one of the most famous stage partnerships in London could conceal two personalities so diametrically opposed.

When I was thirteen I asked my mother how such a marriage had ever come about, at which she smiled a little sadly and said, "Believe it or not, they were in love, my dear. I knew it was happening, right from the start, because Bernadette took me into her confidence about everything in those days. Nevill Boswell and his parents came to live near us in Richmond, and of course they became the most renowned family in the district. His parents and grandparents and all their forebears had been famous, acting with Kemble and Garrick and Kean and all the great theatrical names of their day. You can imagine what a stir it caused when the Boswells bought a house in Maid-of-Honour Row. Since their time, Richmond has become a popular district with theatrical folk, but they were the vanguard. Picknickers on Richmond Green would linger outside the entrance to the Old Palace, pretending to gaze up at the window above the gateway from where Queen Elizabeth's ring was dropped to a waiting messenger, to be raced off to James in Scotland as proof of her death, but in reality they would be hoping for a glimpse of the Boswells in their nearby house. Meredith Boswell, Nevill's father, was as much a matinee idol as his son is now. Nevill was then eighteen and had been acting with his parents since the age of twelve."

"And you met him then, Mamma?"

"No, but Bernadette did. The Smiths occupied the old Judge's House on the opposite side of Richmond Green. Joseph Smith was a leading Q.C., so of course they moved in higher social circles than the Graingers. We lived more humbly on the Sheen Road. But Bernadette and I went to school together and were close friends. I heard all about her love affair with Nevill, which was a whirlwind one. They were married when he was twenty and she eighteen, and I was a bridesmaid, though my parents didn't wholly approve because it was High Church, the Boswells being Roman Catholics."

"So you met Sir Nevill at a wedding? How romantic!"

"Romantic?" my mother echoed. "Why do you say that?"

"Because weddings are romantic. What a pity he was the groom instead of best man, who is usually unattached."

"Not always." My mother's tone was dismissive, and she would have changed the subject had I let her.

"I cannot imagine a man falling in love with a woman like Lady Boswell. So big and so loud."

"She was not always so. When she was young she was very pretty. Not unlike Clementine. Boys were attracted to her from a very early age."

I pondered awhile, then asked, "If they were in love when they married, why didn't it last?"

"Who can say why love doesn't last?"

"Sometimes it does, surely?"

"Oh, yes, sometimes it does."

"Do you know what I think, Mamma? *I* think that if it dies, it cannot be very much alive in the first place."

My mother had looked at me a little sadly then and murmured, "Out of the mouths of babes . . ." and, this time, changed the subject firmly.

In time, I learned a lot about Gavin Calder, whose widowed mother, Charlotte Calder, had married Bernadette's father, a widower, when Gavin was three and Bernadette fifteen.

Sometimes Gavin would come belowstairs to the sitting room, which was the exclusive territory of Mr. Hawkins and Mrs. Wilson, my mother and myself—though I knew that these two senior servants disliked sharing their sitting room with a child. It placed too much restraint on conversation. "Little people have big ears," Mrs. Wilson would warn when Mr. Hawkins was tempted to relay upstairs gossip, which she loved to hear because the only time she ventured there was to present the week's menus to her mistress. So I learned when to make myself scarce, slipping away to the kitchen to listen to the prattle of Kate and Daisy, whose tongues were always unrestricted.

It was from Kate, who had been with the Portman Square household ever since it was established, that I learned how "young Master Gavin" had come to live here when his mother "followed his stepfather into the world beyond." Kate had a liking for elaborate phraseology, particularly with a touch of mystique.

"Not that the master wanted him here, I can tell you. 'That young man is old enough to stand on his own feet,' I heard him tell the mistress. 'He is twenty now. Isn't it enough that I have taken him into the company to please you, although he's no actor nor ever will be unless he works harder, without your insisting that he lives with us?' Oh, yes, that's what the master said. I heard him with my own ears."

"Well, y' couldn't've 'eard wiv anybody else's, couldya?" Daisy had quipped, eager to listen but determined to hide her envy. Nothing did this more effectively than apparent indifference to Kate's knowledgeable gossip, gossip which stressed the fact that her superior duties admitted her into that elegant world abovestairs which no mere kitchen maid could hope to enter—especially if she dropped her aitches, which Kate had mastered diligently.

But however Gavin Calder had become part of the household was of no matter to me. All that did matter was that he was here, and that I occasionally saw him at Portman Square as I did at the theatre, and that he never passed without a smile and a greeting and sometimes even a chat. From babyhood I adored him, and the feeling grew with the years. By the time I was fourteen he was my idol, and I envied Clementine's rounded bosom and curving hips, hating my own skinniness, my almost flat chest, and my long thin legs—straight up and down like one of those new ironing boards which were coming into use these days; that was how I appeared in the discoloured cheval mirror in our top-floor bed-sitting room, and never did I feel more conscious of my physical inferiority than when Clemmy came home from the exclusive French convent which her parents had selected as a finishing school for the two years prior to her "coming out."

That convent wrought a change in Clementine which no one learned about but me. On the surface she returned from France supremely lady-like and poised, but with me she soon slipped into the intimacy of child-hood (or some degree of it), inviting me to her room for heart-to-heart sessions which consisted mainly of casual references to titled schoolfellows and a clothes parade which I genuinely revelled in. I would perch on her bed while she dressed and undressed, displaying everything for my benefit. Never had I felt a more gauche fourteen in comparison with her assured seventeen. Never had I seen such bonnets, such cloaks, such gowns, such underwear (which she now called lingerie with a fine French accent), nor such scandalous nightwear.

"Of course, Mamma doesn't know I have *those,* and what my dear Papa would say if he saw them I dread to think. That is why I am keeping them locked up, and if you ever tell anyone about them, Bastard—"

"Don't call me that. My name is Lucinda."

"All right, Lucinda-bastard—"

"Just Lucinda, if you please."

"My, my, we *are* hoity-toity nowadays! No, don't go, Lucinda—I'm sorry. I was only teasing. Stay and see what else I have to show you."

The eagerness, the covert elation in her voice brought me back. From the big drawer at the bottom of her wardrobe, from which she had taken the secret nightwear, she was withdrawing a parcel wrapped in plain brown paper, and the very air with which she did so awakened my curiosity.

It contained a book, also covered in plain brown paper. The text was in French, but the illustrations needed no interpretation. They shocked me profoundly. I had never seen anything like them, nor imagined that such things were printed.

"Wherever did you get *that?*"

"From the same source as the nightwear."

"But I thought that school you went to was a convent!"

"So it was. But there was a gardener there named Pierre. He could get all sorts of things. He taught me all sorts of things, too. Half the fun of being at a convent was pulling the wool over the nuns' eyes. So I developed a passionate interest in horticulture, which pleased the mother superior, who saw nothing wrong in letting half a dozen girls talk to the gardener and watch him at work, accompanied by Sister Theresa. So long as she was there he would never speak unless spoken to, and always answered questions in the most gentlemanly and respectful way. Each of us was given our own garden plot, and Pierre would advise us on what to plant and when. He would take us to the hothouse to make our selection. Sister Theresa never stayed there long; all those robes and all that heat were too much for her. So we were left to make our choice and to do the planting and then return to the main convent building later." Clementine giggled excitedly. "Those sessions in the hothouse were best of all. Right from the beginning Pierre let the other girls choose first, and when they went off to do their planting . . . well . . . he taught me other things. Exciting things. And later, when they were doing dreary tasks like hoeing and weeding, and Sister Theresa merely supervised the start of the work and then left us to get on with it, I would slip away and join him there."

Memory made her pupils dilate and her breathing quicken. "It was wonderful. All that heat and perfume—and the screen of a high trellis at the far end, completely covered in vines. 'I erected that to hide disused plant pots,' Pierre told Sister Theresa. 'It helps to keep the place tidy. I take a great pride in my hothouse.' I remember how Sister Theresa nodded her head approvingly, and never glanced toward that area again. But *I* knew what was behind it and that the glass walls beyond were painted a dense white so that no one could see through, though he said it was to control the light. He must have taken lots of girls there before me. It was a secret arbour he had built, with a bank all covered in moss, very soft and yielding. He used to lock the hothouse door, of course, and if anyone came along, all they could see was an empty place as far as the vine-covered screen, so of course they always went away. I loved those moments, lying very still, holding my breath with excitement, and Pierre laughing very quietly and whispering, 'They will think I have locked up and gone home, *cherie*—we have time to do it just once more.' And we always did. And that last time would be the best of all because we had to hurry, knowing someone was looking for me. It was a dare, a challenge, and I would think, 'If only they knew what I am doing right now!' which made it even greater fun. And when Pierre hurried, it was wonderful because he would thrust hard and fast and cover my mouth with his hand to stifle my cries—oh, yes, I used to cry out, but only because it was so marvellous. I could never have enough."

"Of what?" I gasped. "Of *what?*"

She didn't even hear me. Her eyes were half-closed.

"Normally he would start very slowly, lingeringly, then faster and faster building up to a climax, and when we had reached it and it was all over we would lie very still, but not for long. He knew just what to do to rouse me again and taught me what to do to him. Then we could both scarcely wait to start again, and every time after that it would be more passionately, more impatiently, building up to that last wild frenzy because time was running out and he prided himself on never failing. And he never did, no matter how many times he took me. Frenchmen don't. But the nights were best, because we had longer then."

"*Nights!*"

"Of course. It was as easy as pie to slip out at nights, a convent being such a pure and unsuspecting place and the nuns so innocent. They never imagined that young girls weren't innocent too."

I gasped again, "You mean . . . you let this man *seduce* you?"

"What else do you think I've been talking about all this time!"

"And you went *on* letting him?"

"Why not? If you've done it once you might as well do it again. Besides, you want to."

"But the other pupils—surely you shared a dormitory? Didn't they even know when you left it?"

"Naturally, but think what trouble they would have got into had they dared to breathe a word. They would have been punished for keeping quiet, so the longer I swore them to secrecy, the more guilty they became, the more compromised, and the less willing to tell tales. 'You will all be expelled for conspiring,' I told them, 'and *I* will say that you all kept quiet because you were doing it too—or something very similar.' That was another card up my sleeve. 'I could reveal what some of you girls do together, and *that* is even worse. And those of you who don't take part but like to watch, and even those who bury their heads beneath the sheets and pretend not to know what is going on, all of you will be considered just as guilty and you will all be punished.' That terrified them, so I had nothing to worry about, though I did feel sorry for them because I knew that what they did was a poor substitute for what they couldn't have and I was getting as often as I liked. I would slip away to the hothouse two or three nights a week."

"But what about your faith? You were committing adultery."

"Nonsense. That applies only to unions outside marriage, so *I* wasn't the one committing adultery, since I was not the one who was married."

"And he was?"

"Of course. I would never get involved with some tiresome boy who expected me to marry him just because I had slept with him—not that I went to Pierre for sleep!" She giggled again, that proud excited giggle which hinted at great superiority. "Pierre was thirty-four. That was why he was such a good lover. Experienced. A man who is a virgin is no use at all. He can teach a girl nothing. Imagine being a guinea pig for a man to experiment on!"

I retreated to the door.

"You make it sound crude and ugly—secret and ugly and wrong. And you, who go to confession regularly!"

"What has that to do with it?"

"I hope you confessed to your priest?"

"How silly! Why should I? Had I started that, I would have had to confess every time, and think how monotonous that would have become. All those Hail Marys and promises not to do it again when I had every intention of doing so! Besides, it's only a venal sin, not a mortal one. And *I* wasn't the one to blame, it was he. A married man with children, and I a virgin not yet sixteen! I used to remind him of that, just to make sure he didn't take me for granted or decide to put an end to things until I was ready to. Also for . . . other things." Her glance slid toward the drawer where the brazen nightwear was hidden, and then down at the book in her lap. "He had to get them for me if he wanted to go on having me, which, my goodness, he did, and although I would never have reported him to the mother superior, it did no harm to let him fear that I would. It gave me power over him, which added to the fun."

She was curled up on the floor like a cat—complacent, satiating herself on memory. I could imagine her, when the house slept, taking out those tiny black chiffon things and stroking them on her naked body before her long mirror . . . gloating, remembering, wanting. . . .

I said briskly, "I don't believe a word of it. A gardener could never afford things like that. Not the clothes, at least. They may be scrappy, but I can tell they were expensive. I have no idea about the book, because I don't know what French books cost, particularly that kind, but I do know that gardeners the world over earn very little."

She gave a secret, knowing smile. "That depends on what other things they do to supplement their wages. Pierre had a rich lady customer every Wednesday afternoon. That was his half-day. He went to her house. She would have employed him more often, but what with me and having to give *some* time to his wife so that she didn't become suspicious, he could only spare one visit a week, and then only for an hour unless she wanted more, which she always did. He charged overtime for longer periods, of course. So if I wanted something costly, he had to prolong the hours accordingly, which delighted her, because she believed he just couldn't have enough of her. He used to say, 'God knows, I deserve that overtime pay—she is one of those sex-starved *mesdames* who cannot get it any other way, and for the services of someone like me she knows the price has to be high.' Compensation money, he called it.''

Clementine subsided into peals of laughter, but I could only stand there staring at her. This was not the Clemmy I had grown up with, the Clemmy I thought I knew. This was a seventeen-year-old as ripe as a peach.

"How could you love a man like that?" I reproached.

"Who said I loved him? You don't have to love a man to enjoy doing that with him. I do declare you are a prude, Lucy Grainger. Never was there such an age as this for hypocrisy, so dismiss it before you grow up, otherwise you will be a repressed virgin forever and there are far too many of those in this day and age—in respectable circles, at least. Not in others. Do you know the things that go on right here in London? You would be shocked if you went to certain places, and you must have seen things on your way home from the theatre when dear Papa has been unable to bring you back in the carriage with himself and Mamma.''

"He orders a hansom for us then. He will never let us walk alone through the streets late at night.''

"Indeed? And does my dear mamma know that?''

"I suppose so.''

"Well, *I* don't. Knowing dear Mamma, I cannot see her permitting such extravagance.'' She changed the subject. I had a feeling that she was anxious to air her worldly knowledge and enjoyed telling me things about which I knew nothing. ''Just wait until the old queen dies—if she ever does. There will be less covering up of things then, though even in these Victorian days London's vice dens are notorious. That is why the place is known as the whore shop of the world. You should have *seen* the prostitutes selling themselves at Victoria Station when I arrived back! And worse besides, though you are too young to learn about that yet. Personally, I would hate to sell my body for money. Giving it to a man for enjoyment is another matter, as I am sure your dear mamma could tell you.''

It seemed to me that there was little difference between money and gifts, but I was too enraged by her last remark to bother with that thought.

"Never dare talk of my mother like that! She gave herself for love, real love. I know. She told me. That is why she calls me her love child.''

"Stupid. Bastards are always called love children in polite circles.''

I flung myself out of the room, but before the door was half-closed she seized my wrist and pulled me back.

"If you dare breathe a word about anything I have told you, Lucy Grainger, I will swear you made it all up, and then neither you nor your mother will last long in this house. And if you have any idea of talking about my treasures, the things Pierre gave me, I warn you that I intend to find a hiding place for them that no one will discover, and then you will be unable to prove a thing."

"If you have any sense, you will get rid of them."

"How?" she mocked. "Give them to Kate to dispose of?"

"Of course not. You could burn them."

"Right here, in my bedroom grate? Do you take me for a fool?"

"There's an incinerator at the bottom of the garden."

"The garden of a town house is the size of a pocket handkerchief, and to get to it I would either have to go down the flight of steps leading from the drawing-room French windows, from where I could be seen by my parents, or out through the kitchen belowstairs. I can imagine the servants' faces if I did that, especially carrying a parcel which I then set alight outside. They would soon be ferreting amongst the ashes to find out what I had burned. Particularly Kate, the nosiest of them all."

"Then give it to me. When the dustmen come I will meet them at the top of the area steps and make sure they take it."

"Dustmen could be curious too. They would very likely unwrap a parcel deliberately smuggled out of a house. Do you think I would run the risk of being blackmailed? That book has my name on the flyleaf."

"Tear it out. Anyway, is it likely that dustmen would be able to read?"

"I shouldn't think so, but those pictures are very graphic. Some unscrupulous rogue might seize a chance to blackmail the famous Sir Nevill Boswell if such a book came out of his house. Books like this are supposed to be banned in this country, though I've heard they are sold quite openly on pornographic bookstands only a few steps from Exeter Hall in Holywell Street. What fun it would be to go along there one day and see for ourselves, though I daresay only men can do that. . . . Anyway, if this book *was* brought to Papa's attention he would know at once where it came from, being in French, and who had smuggled it in. I wouldn't run the risk of exposing the poor darling to such a shock." She reached out a hand to me, patient and indulgent now. "Dear Lucy, forget you ever saw those things. Forget all I told you. There is no need to worry about *me*. I know how to look after myself—Pierre taught me. I couldn't have had a better tutor than a Frenchman, and that book is packed with information. I am not going to part with it, any more than I am going to part with that lovely nightwear before I ever have a chance to wear it.

Not that it will stay on for long once I am in bed, nor before I get as far as
that, I imagine, once a lover sees me in it. But I shall find out. Romantic
and earthy and warm as the hothouse was, I don't intend that all my experiences shall take place on a bank of moss! That was why I would never
wear those things for Pierre's pleasure. They were too lovely to spoil. I
just used to bring them back as trophies to show the girls.''

She was laughing again, confident and happy.

"But you will never be able to go to bed with him now," I pointed
out. "You will never see him again."

"I know that, stupid, but there are sure to be others. I am certainly
not going to stop doing *that*, whether you think it sinful or not. I only
hope the next lover I have will be as satisfying as dear Pierre was, and,''
she finished generously, "that Pierre enjoys the next convent girl he se-
duces as much as he enjoyed me. He loved initiating virgins and could
pick out those with the best potential. He knew at a glance how satisfying I would be. He told me so. 'And you a leetle English mees!' he used
to say. 'They are usually much too ladylike!' 'And how do you expect me
to be ladylike in *this* position?' I said to him once, and my goodness, how
he laughed! Dear Pierre . . .''

She touched a moist corner of her eye as she turned back to her wardrobe to lock up her treasures. I would have felt sorry for her had I not
known instinctively that she had already half-forgotten him—and if she
had not made everything seem so squalid and underhand and cheap, with
not a trace of romance about it.

Outside I came face to face with Gavin. He took one look at me,
glanced at Clementine's door, and then said, "What has she been doing
to you?"

"Nothing."

"Saying to you, then. You've had a shock.'

"No . . . no . . .''

He took me by the hand and led me downstairs, past the doors leading
to family rooms, which I always hurried by, and down to the basement
sitting room. I was glad of that, because on the private "family" floors I
always felt an intruder, and not without reason. If I were discovered
there, Lady Boswell would freeze me with a glance or, if in a more kindly
mood, point out that the only domestic regions I was allowed to inhabit
were those belowstairs or high above, but never here. Consequently I
never lingered, afraid of discovery—as indeed I had experienced when
passing Sir Nevill's study one day when the door was open and I heard
his voice raised in anger.

"What the devil are you doing at my desk?"

I was so startled by this unaccustomed note in a voice which was normally quiet and controlled that I had stood stock-still and heard Gavin's voice reply, "Looking for a copy of the new play script, brother-in-law—I have lines to learn and fear I have mislaid my own." What Sir Nevill said in return I failed to hear, because the great Bernadette appeared at that moment and demanded to know why I was loitering, at which I had promptly fled.

Finding the basement sitting room empty, Gavin led me inside.

"Now, let's hear all about it." He waited. "So you're not going to tell, little Lucy? You're a loyal soul, though that bitch upstairs doesn't deserve it. Why look so shocked? There are worse names a man can use. But she's not wholly to blame for what she is. There's a lot of her mother in her, and we cannot choose our parents."

"Lady Boswell is very good to *you*," I reminded him, at which he shrugged.

"So she should be. She's my stepsister and twelve years my senior. Would you think she was only thirty-seven, with those matronly measurements? She'll soon be confined to character leads if she gets any stouter—girth cannot be disguised by flowing robes forever." He finished thoughtfully, "I should think she hates your mother's guts."

"My mamma! Never! She has said to me many times that no actress could have a better dresser."

"Nor a prettier one, nor a more slender one, nor one men notice more, which is enough to make any woman hate her guts. Shall I tell you something, little Lucy? You are going to be your mother's double in no time at all. You already have her big grey eyes and her blonde colouring and her tiny waist." He slipped an arm about it, drawing me close and then releasing me. He touched my cheek with a gentle hand. He ran a fingertip over the outline of my short straight nose and then across my too-wide mouth, but not once was his touch anything more than affectionate and brotherly. I wondered how I would react if he were to touch me the way Pierre had touched Clementine in the hothouse arbour, but I could never imagine him doing anything so dishonourable. There was nothing underhand or disrespectful about Gavin Calder.

He asked abruptly, "How old are you, little Lucy?"

"Fourteen and a half." The half was important, making me much more grown-up.

"You will soon be ready for it," he said.

"Ready for what?"

"For . . . life." He seemed to pull himself together and went on quickly, "What are you going to do with it? What do you want to be? Not a theatrical dresser, I hope—you would be wasted, as your mother is. An actress, perhaps? I know you have a hankering to be. I have seen

you onstage after the curtain has come down, secretly acting while waiting for your mother and the great Bernadette. You think no one knows
that you slip down there, acting to unseen audiences? You're wrong. *I*
know, and so does my worthy stepbrother-in-law. I once saw him in the
wings, watching and listening to you. He must have been attracted by the
voice coming from a deserted stage, as I was, and decided to investigate.
He let you run through the whole of Portia's speech on mercy, and then
went away quietly. Since then I know for a fact that he has done it again
several times. He has his eye on you, as I have, little Lucy, but not, I
imagine, in the same way—though one never knows, of course. Men in
their forties have been known to fancy pretty fourteen-year-olds, and
even younger."

"Not Sir Nevill!" I was receiving many shocks today and being angered by them. "He is like a father to me. Kind and considerate." I refused to have my picture of him destroyed.

Gavin merely smiled, but as always his smile dazzled me. He had the
most fascinating curve to his mouth, the whitest of teeth, and was incredibly handsome. The great Bernadette would often say, "My stepbrother
may not be the world's greatest actor, but his looks will pack in a female
audience all his life." And I knew it to be true. Gavin's dark good looks,
his crisply curling black hair growing long in the nape of his neck, his incredible profile, which always reminded me of a Greek god, and his compelling voice—all would make up for any lack of talent, and I thought it
rather hard of Sir Nevill to criticise him, as he so often did.

Gavin Calder had not been born and bred in the theatre, nor steeped
in acting since early childhood, as Nevill Boswell had been. Nor had
Bernadette, though she had been passionately addicted to acting all her
life, playing leads in many drawing-room productions until she married
into the profession and proved that she could not only carry that talent
into her new life, but absorb everything her husband could teach her.
She might overact sometimes, but present-day trends leaned that way.
Sir Nevill himself had the grandiose, declamatory style Victorian audiences loved, and his wife had worked hard to achieve a matching profes-
sionalism, which, combined with a striking stage presence, had helped
form a theatrical partnership now so well established as to be unbreak-
able.

That Sir Nevill was the strength of it and the main star attraction, Bernadette was blissfully unaware—nor would have acknowledged, had she
known. She firmly believed that she was "the immortal Bernadette, the
finest tragedienne of her day," and to disillusion her would have been
cruel.

Loyalty compelled me to acknowledge all I owed to the Boswells; not
only food, clothes, and a roof over my head, but a certain amount of edu-

cation too, though I doubted whether Lady Boswell was aware that her husband paid my fees at Miss Templeton's Academy for Young Ladies in the Bayswater Road, which I had been attending daily for the past six months, enrolling for a three-year course on my fourteenth birthday. There I was learning all the requisite accomplishments—French, music, singing, a little painting, and more than a little needlework and housewifery, plus social etiquette—and very tedious it all was, though gratitude compelled me to hide the fact.

I could scarcely wait for the final release on my seventeenth birthday and harboured totally different ambitions from my fellow pupils, who anticipated only one kind of future—marriage to some eminently respectable young man of whom their parents would wholly approve. And very dull those young men were. I met them on occasional visits to friends' houses and for the life of me could scarcely tell them apart. All spoke the same way, thought the same way, moved and walked and talked the same way, and all unanimously seemed to regard me as something of a novelty.

"You're not *really* connected with the theatre, are you? I have never met anyone with a theatrical background!"

Like something from a zoo.

But on this particular afternoon I was able to forget about that sedate school. It was the Easter recess and I was back in the world of the theatre full-time, helping my mother to prepare Bernadette's clothes and doing other tasks before curtain-up, after which I would hurry down to the prompt side to watch every performance. I had long since graduated from the leading lady's dressing room; I was a young woman now, too big to be relegated to a corner, due to put up my hair once schooldays were over, and ready and willing to do any backstage chore because to be actively involved was my greatest ambition. I loved the atmosphere behind the scenes and was accepted by every member of the company as one of them. Understudies uncertain of their lines found a willing listener in me. Props appreciated my help in the absence of his traditional aid, the callboy, who had graduated to a full-time props job at a rival theatre, and the ASM frequently let me relieve him of the cue copy when he wanted to slip outside for a smoke.

No task was too menial for me, no chore too exacting. I was learning from the ground up, absorbing everything as I had done from babyhood, but not in the confined space of the room with the silver star where quarrels and tantrums had mainly tutored me in theatrical behavior.

Gavin said to me now, "If you really want to become an actress, little

Lucy, I will coach you; teach you how to express yourself, how to move and walk. Your diction is naturally good, but you must learn breath control. We could meet onstage when it's not in use."

"I don't think I will go there anymore. Not if Sir Nevill knows, though it is kind of him to pretend he doesn't."

I was well aware that only the manager of a company could give permission for even established members of a cast to make use of the stage outside rehearsals and performances, when it was always left ready for curtain-up, every piece of stage furniture and every prop in place for the opening scene. Any use of it betweentimes had to be under the diligent eye of the stage manager, and woe betide any trespassers. But I had been trespassing for a long time now, blissfully unaware that my secret was known. I think I loved Sir Nevill even more for pretending it was not.

"All right," Gavin agreed. "I will coach you at home. Upstairs in my room."

"I think not," said my mother's voice from the door.

He turned and laughed at her.

"Do you doubt my intentions, Trudy dear?"

"Yes," she answered blandly, and to me she added, "It is a beautiful afternoon, Lucinda, and I am free for a couple of hours. Shall we walk in the park?"

Delighted, I hurried away to get ready. For my mother to have any free time at all was a rare treat, and as we stepped out across Portman Square in the direction of Hyde Park I forgot everything but the pleasure of exercise and the joy of being alive on a sunny day. Even Clementine's shocking confessions slid from my mind, and Gavin's suggestion about visiting his room seemed to have slipped from my mother's, since she said no further word about it. I wished she would, because I knew she had misunderstood him, and anxious to exonerate him from any possible doubt, I said, "You were wrong, Mamma. About Gavin, I mean. He was being kind."

"In what way, my love?"

"In offering to coach me for the stage."

She made no answer, and at Marble Arch we crossed the road to Soapbox Corner, where already the street orators were being harangued by cockney audiences. Although Sunday morning was the accepted day and time, because only on Sundays were workers free, the habit was spreading. The unemployed, plus political agitators, were now beginning to gravitate daily to this area, which had once been part of Tyburn Hill and seen many a public hanging where the famous arch now stood. Tourists, mostly American, because London now attracted more than a hundred thousand of them annually, and the number was ever increasing, regarded Soapbox Corner as one of the free entertainments of the metropolis, and so did Londoners themselves. Our footsteps slowed automatically as we approached, but before my mother's voice was drowned in the babel I heard her say anxiously, "You are not really wanting to go on stage, are you, Lucinda?"

"More than anything in the world, Mamma."

I thought she was not going to reply, but as we merged into the crowd she said, "It isn't a life I would choose for you, but if your heart is really set on it, I won't oppose you. But the person to coach you is Sir Nevill, not Gavin, who is hardly qualified. It is presumptuous of him to imagine that he is."

"Presumptuous! But he is a fully fledged actor, romantic lead of the company!"

"With a great deal to learn as far as acting is concerned, but not in other ways, I fear."

"Mamma! It sounds as if you dislike him."

Her reply was lost in the welter of shouting voices. All I saw was the shake of her head, which could have meant denial or confirmation. I chose to take it as denial, because I failed to see how anyone could dislike a man like Gavin Calder.

My mother pushed her way through the crowd, heading toward the wide expanse of grassy park beyond. I followed automatically, fascinated by the medley of characters shouting from their soapboxes, by the barrackers, by the urchins dodging barefoot in and out of the crush, by the mixture of races and colours flocking round the speakers, by the shouts and the derision, the cheers and the catcalls. "Remember the Chartists!" a man was yelling. "They put 'em down once, but they'll rise again and it'll take more than seven thousand troops to stop 'em *this* time!" Jeers and cheers echoed simultaneously and a voice yelled above the din, "Better 'urry up then, mate—the Chartists marched in forty-eight! Most of 'em were deported and the rest are pushing up the daisies by now!"

The crush was thickening. I stood on tiptoe, searching for my mother, and caught sight of her tulle-swathed hat pushing ahead of me. As always, she was an elegant figure, despite lack of means. As with me, inheriting Clementine's castoffs, my mother inherited Lady Boswell's, skilfully unpicking them, cutting them down, renovating and restyling them until they looked like new and frequently earned the great Bernadette's envious and regretful glances, but I knew that however much the famous actress might wish she had not parted with them, it was my mother's skill alone which made them so much more elegant now—that, and her slender figure. Her waist was so small that lacing was superfluous and she only submitted to it because fashion dictated.

My mother was a very fashion-conscious woman and I was becoming so. I appreciated her poise and her carriage, and as she retreated from view I appreciated the colour harmony of amber velvet with her honey-coloured hair, and the wide-brimmed Bangkok straw swathed in amber-coloured tulle. For a fleeting moment I saw her in profile and was glad I had inherited her short straight nose. I hoped that one day it would appear as delicately chiselled as hers and less snub than it now looked in my fourteen-year-old face.

Was Gavin Calder right when saying that one day I would be my mother all over again? I prayed so. I could think of nothing more desirable than to match her delicate loveliness, her creaminess of skin, her slender curves—not straight up and down as I was at the moment, with such small and immature breasts that they were scarcely discernible beneath my school blouse. My mother was beautiful and I was never surprised when eyes followed her; envious in women and openly desiring in men. Yet she remained unaware of stares, oblivious of admiration, ever loyal to the memory of my father, whom she had loved totally and for all time.

She disappeared from sight. I elbowed my way after her, past a man shouting about the evils of drink and hoping in vain for an audience; past a strident woman crying, "Franchise for women! This country is unfair to women! But one day, my friends, *one* day . . . ." What women were going to do one day was lost in a sudden burst of cheering nearby. My way was blocked by a knot of people surrounding a dais on which two men, stripped to the waist, were boxing with bare fists. One was a dark-haired thug who looked a very ugly customer to me.

"Ten to one on Joe!" someone was shouting. "Ten to one 'e beats the Toff!"

There came a crack on the jaw of the thug, who crashed to the canvas amidst further jeers and cheers. The victor raised his arms above his head. "Anyone who bet on Joe has lost!" he cried, laughing and exultant. "Who wants to take his place? Sixpence a bout, and every penny for the Stepney Mission!"

He was magnificently tall, his hair copper-brown, his face and neck and hairy chest gleaming with sweat, his muscles rippling. At some time his nose had been broken, which didn't surprise me, and his biceps were enormous.

He stooped and helped the other man to rise.

"All right, Joe? Want to carry on?"

The thug shook his head, grinning.

"You won, Toff, an' a fair fight. Gotta 'and it to yer. Them little buggers at yer mission'll know 'ow to take care of 'emselves if yer teach 'em that right 'ook!"

His mouth was bleeding, but he was unworried. The Toff helped him into his shirt and was about to do the same with his jacket when he paused midway, examining it. It was in rags.

"With pockets like these, Joe, *you'll* never be any temptation to your fellow buzzers."

"'Owdya know I were a buzzer, gov?"

"How else did you come by sixpence? Not by honest labour. I know you, Joe." The Toff was smiling broadly. "I'll keep your tanner, but you can take my jacket." He tossed his opponent's ragged one to the crowd and the next moment was helping him into a good piece of Harris tweed. "If you swill less beer, Joe, it will fit you like a glove." He smoothed the shoulders, laughing. His teeth were very white, shining in his glistening face, but the thing that surprised me most was his voice, a strong contrast with his rough audience. What was a cultured man doing here, challenging all comers in bare-fist fighting and obviously enjoying it?

The crowd parted slightly as Joe, preening in his new jacket, pushed his way through, calling over his shoulder, "Thanks, Toff—next tanner I pinch I'll take yer on agin, see if I don't."

I smelled sweat and beer as the man passed me; then suddenly he stood still and yelled, "Jerry! Jerry, lad, where are yer? Now, where's that blarsted little cove? *There* y'are, young devil! I 'opes as 'ow y've bin 'ard at work wile pore ol' Joe's bin takin' punishment from a bleedin' gent?"

"Sure, gov! Sure I 'ave!"

A small fist was outthrust before me, clutching a woman's purse. I gasped, "Give that to me!" and then, "Mamma! *Mamma!* You've been robbed!"

"*Git,* sonny!"

Joe gave the boy a shove, but I was quicker. Seizing the child's collar, I hung on tight. "Police! *Police!*"

Joe's hand shot out, grabbed the purse, and fled.

"Grab that man!" I cried.

The boy kicked me. "You leave Joe alone, missy!" He was wriggling like an eel, but I hung on even tighter.

"Fight as much as you like, Jerry—your father may have got away, but *you* are not going to. Mamma! *Mamma!*"

The small bundle of skin and bones gave a desperate twist and eluded me. I saw a pair of angelic blue eyes dance with triumph, heard his gleeful chuckle, and then saw him crash to the ground as the silver handle of a man's umbrella hooked him round the ankle. I flew to the child's aid, shocked by blood streaming from his nose and his wild cry of pain. Enraged, he struck out, and a man's elegantly gloved hand descended on his shoulder and remained there.

"Stop that caterwauling, boy. What is your name?"

"Jeremy 'Awks, gov."

"Sir."

"Sir."

"Cease wriggling. No one is going to hurt you—"

"And that includes you, Durbridge. Take your hands off him."

It was said so quietly I was amazed that anyone should hear, but the man called Durbridge did, and so did I. The Toff was standing there, his shirt half on, no longer smiling, no longer challenging. With the minimum of movement he dislodged the hand in the doeskin glove. "I will take care of Jeremy Hawks."

The crowd was silent, watching with undisguised enjoyment. A confrontation between two people of quality was an unexpected bonus; better than a scrap between a couple of costermongers.

Durbridge shrugged and hooked his immaculately rolled umbrella over a sleeve of his immaculate frock coat, tailored in dove-grey velour and worn with a shining top hat. His moustache was curled and waxed at the ends. A monocle fell from his eye as he surveyed the Toff, and he laughed very quietly.

"Well, well, so it actually *is* you, Steel. There I was, out for a constitutional, and thought I recognised you, despite your appearance. Couldn't believe my eyes, dear chap. Heard things, of course. Who hasn't? Some mission or other in the East End, I believe?"

"You believe rightly."

"For boys?" Durbridge drawled.

"To help boys. To protect them."

"From pickpocket fathers?"

"And from men like you."

Durbridge slowly replaced his monocle. "Don't think I care for that remark very much, Steel. Could be . . . misinterpreted. I would advise you to choose your words more carefully."

"And I would advise you to confine your attentions to stage doors."

Durbridge laughed.

"Not nearly such fun, my dear fellow. Actresses are two a penny."

"And needy urchins less?"

"I help them, as you do. I could help this little devil." He touched the begrimed face with one fingertip, lifting the chin so that the cherubic countenance looked up into his. "A pretty boy, or would be if bathed and fattened up a bit."

The Toff drew the child away. "Come along, Jerry. You can have some food at the mission and then I'll take you home."

"Ain't got none now, gov. Chucked out yestiday, we were."

"So it's the workhouse again?"

"For Ma and the kids, but not for Joe 'n me. 'Jerry,' 'e sez, 'it's up West fer us. We'll earn enough there to bail yer ma an' the kids out.' An' I were doin' orlright until missy 'ere grabbed me."

"Which was very commendable of her," drawled the man called Durbridge. Turning to me, he doffed his hat and with a slight bow continued, "Did I hear you say that your mother had been robbed, young lady? This is a matter for the police."

I didn't want to answer because I disliked him, though this dislike could only be due to his disparaging reference to actresses. I thought the Toff, or Steel as Durbridge called him, was wrong to condemn a man who wanted to help an unfortunate small boy. Obviously, Durbridge had money. Perhaps he could have proved more beneficial to this urchin than a man who had to challenge the public for sixpences, and since I could see no other motivation than compassion, I failed to understand the Toff's attitude.

Thankfully, I saw my mother approaching. "Lucinda, *there* you are! I thought you were behind me . . ." She broke off, glancing from one to the other of us, the anxiety she always felt when any stranger accosted me showing plainly in her face. "What is going on? Come away, my love."

Durbridge bowed again. "Madam, I congratulate you on having a very diligent daughter. Are you aware that you have been robbed? She tried to apprehend the thief, but failed, unfortunately."

The urchin broke into a wail. The Toff gave him a kindly shake and told him to be quiet. "If I may know how much was in your purse, ma'am, I will see it is refunded. You live in Portman Square, I believe. So do I. I hope you won't press charges against this boy. I intend to make myself responsible for him."

"He does have a father," said Durbridge.

"Not exactly. I know the Hawks ménage. Jerry's real father is dead."

"Killed in a fight down on the docks," angel-faced Jerry announced proudly, "but I like this new bloke wot me ma's took up wiv—'e's a bit of orlright, is Joe."

My mother looked at him compassionately. "Did you really steal my purse?"

"Look in yer reticool, ma'am. Betcha never even felt me touch it!"

"An artful little dodger," commented Durbridge. "Do you really intend to make yourself responsible for him, Steel?"

"And what were you intending to do?" the Toff murmured. I thought the remark unnecessary, since Durbridge plainly considered this whole thing a matter for the law. There seemed to be an undercurrent of mistrust in the Toff's voice which I failed to understand.

"There was little in my purse," my mother said. "A few coppers, no more. I think we should let him go."

"And I agree, Mamma. But promise never to do such a thing again, Jeremy Hawks."

"A bloke's gotta live, missy."

"Not that way,"

"Wot uvver way is there?"

"I will teach you." The Toff was buttoning up his shirt, suddenly aware that his chest was naked in the presence of a lady. I didn't blame him for not worrying about that until my mother came along. At fourteen and a half one only hoped to be taken for grown-up.

As he fastened the garment, I saw again the thick thatch of copper-brown hair on his chest and the ripple of muscles in arms and shoulders. No real gentleman would make such an exhibition of himself in public, that I knew, and I could well understand the disdain of the man called Durbridge. But I liked the Toff's attitude to the street urchin, even so.

"Give me a hand with this thing, Jerry." He was heaving the wooden dais up from the ground. "It dismantles into sections."

Space was widening around us. The crowd, disappointed because the scene had not come up to expectations, was drifting away in search of better entertainment—all except Durbridge, whose heavy-lidded eyes were fixed on my mother appreciatively. I had often seen men look at her like that, and ignored it as she did. But not now. Clementine's voice was suddenly echoing in my mind. *"Giving it to a man for enjoyment is another matter, as I am sure your mother could tell you. . . ."*

(Did you, Mamma? Was that all it meant to you—illicit pleasure like Clemmy's? Was I really born of lust, not love? And who was he? Can you remember, *do* you remember?)

Shocked by such thoughts, I tried to thrust them aside. Never before had I doubted my mother in any way, least of all in this. The fact that she had remained a spinster had always confirmed, in my mind, her loyalty to my dead father, the one great love of her life. But was he dead? She had never actually said so. That she referred to him in the past tense, when she referred to him at all, and then only when I asked some childish question about him, had merely suggested that he was, and so I had believed it, taken it for granted. But now all sorts of unanswered questions thrust themselves forward, questions a more curious child, or a less contented one, would have asked long before the age of fourteen and a half.

It was evidence of the security my mother's love had provided, and the sufficiency of it, that only now did I actually think of my father as a living person equally responsible for my existence, and not as some long-dead, almost mythical figure from a romantic legend, to whose memory she would remain eternally faithful. That speculative glance of the man called Durbridge, skimming over her high breasts, narrow waist, curve of hip, and shadowy outline of thigh beneath swirling skirts, was wholly sensuous and reminiscent of Clementine's secret relish when talking of the things her French gardener had taught her. It occurred to me that Clemmy would have liked Durbridge very much. I did not. He was a disturbing and somehow threatening figure who, I hoped, would never cross our paths again.

Something else about him troubled me, though I could not define it. The Toff's attitude to the man had held an indefinable undercurrent which, even more strangely in recollection, had suggested a determination to get a hapless small boy away from him. To me, that didn't make sense. If the Toff had something to do with an East End mission, he should be glad of a rich man's interest, yet it seemed that he disliked Durbridge's attention to Jeremy Hawks, even to the extent of withdrawing the boy from him when an elegantly gloved finger had tilted up his chin the better to study his face. *"A pretty boy—or would be, if bathed and fattened up. . . ."* Apart from thinking that the word "pretty" was an effeminate one to apply to a boy, I considered that cleanliness and food were surely commendable things to desire for a half-starved, neglected scrap of humanity.

My mother said, "Come, Lucinda. We must go home."

Durbridge stepped forward.

"I understand from my friend Steel that you live in Portman Square, madam? Allow me to escort you."

The dismantled dais, now piled in sections one on top of another and carried at each end by the Toff and his small charge, suddenly formed a barricade between my mother and the man. Durbridge frowned and tried to step round it, only to find it laid on the ground at his feet, ready to trip him up. The Toff ordered, "Fetch that handcart from over there, Jerry—you'll find it easier to handle than this thing."

The lad streaked off to a rickety vehicle propped in a nearby gutter.

"Good God, Steel—you're not trundling a thing like that across the streets of London, a man in your position?"

"What has my position to do with it? In any case, I doubt if anyone considers that I have one left. But as you see, I have to transport my boxing stand somehow, and this is the most effective way. Thanks, Jerry—hold the cart steady while I lift these sections onto it."

My mother smiled and so did I. There was suddenly a comical side to the whole situation—the lofty disdain of the man-about-town and the total lack of self-consciousness with which the Toff heaved the wooden boards of his improvised boxing booth onto a handcart which any costermonger would use for selling jellied eels or winkles. With a casual nod of his head to Durbridge and an indication to my mother and to me that we could all be on our way now, Steel, with Jerry's grubby hands assisting, began to wheel the barrow across Park Lane to the top of Oxford Street, dodging wheels and horses' hooves, with my mother and I following as if it were the most natural thing in the world.

I don't know what made me look back as we waited on the corner of Park Lane to cross to the other side of Oxford Street, but I was surprised to see Durbridge following at a discreet distance, and I don't know what made me feel that I had taken my last walk to the park as a young and innocent girl, and that the recent encounter marked a stepping-stone in my life, and a frightening one—worse than the illicit knowledge Clementine had passed on to me only a few hours earlier. I had tried to forget her confidences, even to disbelieve them, but somehow I knew that though I might be able to do so, I could never forget Durbridge's striking figure, or his smooth voice, or his leisurely walk, or his darkly appraising glance, or his overfull, loose-lipped mouth, or the strange suggestion of menace in his heavy-lidded eyes. It was there as he halted beside us again, letting his glance run up and down my mother's slim back, which seemed to fascinate him.

Fashion now dictated only the hint of a bustle, a feature many people considered the most tantalising ever designed. It certainly caught the eye of this man in a way which puzzled and repelled me. It also reminded me of an illustration in Clementine's shocking book. I had caught only a glimpse of it as the pages flickered fanwise through her hands, and surely, I had thought, I could not have seen aright. A man and a woman would never conduct themselves in such a way. I was as certain of that as I was that love between a man and a woman, real love, could never descend to the obscene, and I was not grateful to Clemmy for trying to tarnish my ideals. But watching this man as he studied my mother's figure awakened a strong distaste in me. I knew instinctively that he had travelled strange pathways in his lifetime and as a result was different from most men, and that he would never be satisfied with the conventionally amorous activities of men who haunted stage doors.

For the most part, Stage Door Johnnies were silly but harmless. One or two had even begun to pay attention to me as I emerged with my mother after the nightly performance, chucking me under the chin and laughing when I pulled away. "Rather young to be an actress, aren't you, dear? Still . . . in a year or two . . ."

Not even in a year or two, not ever, would I cheapen myself by allowing Stage-Door Johnnies to pick me up, harmless as most of them were. Just occasionally, and only occasionally, did a member of them try to buy an actress for what the wise old hands in the theatre called "abnormal practices" (taking good care that I should never learn what those practices were), but such men were made short shrift of, not only by members of the company like dear Bramwell Chambers, who played character leads and who acted as self-appointed father to all the female members of the company, but by George, the stage-doorkeeper, who kept a list of the regulars and irregulars.

Ethel Piper often declared that George could have blackmailed half the titles in London with the aid of that book. In it he recorded details which would have frightened most of them away, the very least of which was how much they tipped him for conveying flowers and gifts to the ladies of their fancy. George possessed far more intimate knowledge than that: where they livrd, how they lived, and who their associates were of both sexes. Whether their pockets were well-lined; the size of bets they placed on the Derby and the Oaks; whether they could afford to attend Ascot in the proper manner and if they were admitted to the Royal Enclosure or not; how many Gaiety Girls they had dallied with before turning their attention to actresses at the Boswell Theatre, situated nearby along the Strand; their parentage, family scandals, secret escapades, scraps with the law, even the amount of money they spent on gifts for their lady-loves and the shops where they ran accounts, places like Asprey's earning star ratings; what type of apartments they set them up in, the class of rooms they took them to after wining and dining, the restaurants which accepted them and those which blacklisted them—there was nothing George didn't know about London's Stage Door Brigade.

"Ask him how long a particular johnny has been on the beat—that's the nightly parade, dear—and George'll know, and if any one of them isn't good to a girl, he'll know that too. If they're mean, if they're married or not, if they've got a girl into trouble and helped her over it or ditched her there and then—George'll know. It's part of a stage-doorman's job to be a watchdog. No actress in this theatre needs to get involved with a johnny that's no good, or has nasty habits, or isn't likely to treat her well. At some theatres they can buy their way in easily, particularly the music halls, but not here, thanks to George. It would be more than his job is worth, Sir Nevill being Sir Nevill. . . ."

I had never seen the man called Durbridge on the stage-door parade and knew instinctively that I was never likely to. Such as he would never line up with other top-hatted and bespatted swains awaiting the favours of their elected, or vainly hoping to catch the eye of one not already booked. He would do his own wooing. He would curry no favour with George, nor ever allow him to be a stumbling block in his path, and George would be out of his depth with such an unknown quantity.

Standing there on the corner of Park Lane and Oxford Street, with carriages and hansom cabs and horse-drawn omnibuses driving haphazardly all over the road, with barefoot scavenger boys scooping up horse dung right beneath oncoming wheels and drivers crisscrossing at a tangent to deposit elegant ladies upon pavements on either side in order to avoid soiling their skirts in the road's filth, I was desperately anxious to get away from this man who seemed to cast a dark and menacing shadow over us.

Beside me, the Toff said quietly, "Don't worry, we will get away from him."

He had mopped and cleaned his face now and his wide-sleeved shirt was buttoned to the neck. It was made of fine cambric, though the quality was somewhat obscured through being thrown on the ground during the fight.

"How many opponents did you take on?" I asked.

"A round dozen this afternoon."

"And did you win every time?"

"My dear young lady, if I wasn't sure of winning I wouldn't do it. This is hard-earned mission money, so I cannot afford to miss a penny of it."

"Six shillings seems poor reward for such an afternoon's work."

"It swells the coffers but, more importantly, it makes people aware of the Stepney Mission. Tourists have often thrown money into the kitty; far more than the sixpenny challenge. Right . . . off we go. No, wait! This damned cabby isn't going to halt for anyone." Turning to my mother he finished, "Your pardon, ma'am—such language isn't meant for the ears of yourself and your daughter. One has to use oaths in Stepney to make oneself understood, and unfortunately it becomes a habit. I even slip up occasionally with my own sister, but since she works at the mission too, she takes it in her stride."

We stepped back onto the pavement, but he left the handcart projecting into the road, gently inching it forward so that horses were forced to step round it and drivers cursed, but despite giving all his attention to forcing a way through the traffic, I knew he was still aware of Durbridge's lurking presence.

Now the man asked, "What do you propose to do with this boy, Steel?"

The Toff answered, without glancing over his shoulder, "Find him gainful employment, to use a lofty phrase. Work, in other words. Unfortunately, after the age of ten even the London School Board cannot make education compulsory, though I am fighting for it and so are others."

"Garn!" snarled young Jerry. "I've 'ad enough of school! I'm eleven, I'd 'ave yer know, and that's growed-up, that is."

I couldn't believe that a boy so stunted could have reached the age of eleven, though beneath his grimy face there seemed to be knowledge beyond his years. I felt an abounding pity for the child, and my mother did too. I could see it in her large, grey, gentle eyes and the sweet curve of her mouth. She was always at her most beautiful when moved by pity for others. That was the only kind of pity she was capable of feeling—never for herself.

"What kind of work have you in mind, Mr. Steel?" she asked.

"Any kind where he can make himself useful, learn something, have a worthwhile future. The mission has fixed up many a boy, given him a start in life—at any rate, a better start than the one he was born to."

"Sir Nevill!" I cried. "We must take Jerry to see Sir Nevill! We are without a callboy at the theatre just now."

"Sir Nevill Boswell?" echoed Durbridge. "Are you acquainted with that eminent actor, madam?"

My mother nodded, but she had eyes only for Jeremy Hawks. "What an excellent idea, Lucinda! Don't you agree, Mr. Steel?"

"Please do," I begged. "He would love the theatre, wouldn't you, Jerry?"

"Dunno, missy. Ain't never bin in one, but I know a busker wot does the pubs. Same thing, ain't it?"

"Not exactly, Jerry."

We were following the Toff and his handcart across the road now, zig-zagging beneath horses' heads and reaching the other side unscathed but for a splash of mud thrown onto my upheld skirt. I stopped to wipe it off and saw that the man called Durbridge had remained on the other side, as the Toff had known he would. A man such as he would never walk along with a man pushing a coster's barrow, nor would he risk his neck or his shoes, or the immaculate turn-ups of his trousers, or his dove-grey spats, by forcing his way through traffic. He would cross the road only at the appointed places where crossing-sweepers kept the path clean and expected to be tipped by the gentlemen. There were over eleven thousand cabs on the streets of London, employing twenty thousand horses, which, added to the hundreds of cart animals hauling drays and number-less horses drawing trams and omnibuses, made the roads hazardous for pedestrians in more ways than one, so crossings were essential for people on foot, and indeed we ourselves would have used one had we not been accompanying a man pushing a coster's cart. It suddenly struck me as both odd and amusing that my mother and I had instinctively elected to follow his lead.

But the thought was driven from my mind as I paused to brush my skirt, for across the dividing space Durbridge's glance met mine and held it, and without rhyme or reason I experienced a sudden conviction that this man was not to go out of the lives of my mother and myself, and that we were both endangered by him. I had never felt threatened in such a way before, but I felt so now, and I didn't like the taste of it, rising like nausea within me.

2

The sight of a coster's barrow being pushed into fashionable Portman Square by a man in fine, if soiled, cambric shirt and tight-fitting boxer's breeches, a man of striking height and noticeable looks for all that he was not in the least handsome, with a shock of copper-coloured hair blazing in the sun, and accompanied by a grubby urchin on the one hand and an elegant young woman and her daughter on the other, must have attracted and puzzled the eye of many a passerby. Although my mother and I walked on the pavement and the Toff and his companion trundled the barrow in the gutter, where barrows should be, we made no attempt to disguise the fact that we were all together. Conversation between us never flagged. My mother was telling Mr. Steel all about the Boswell Theatre and Sir Nevill's theatrical company, of which he had heard but never seen perform.

"My work leaves little time for social affairs, ma'am, but if there are prospects for Jerry, I shall certainly call on Sir Nevill. It is kind of you to want to help the lad."

"It was Lucinda's idea, remember."

The man smiled down at me. "Thank you, Miss Lucinda. Say thank you, Jerry."

"Wot for? 'Ow do I know as I'll like being a flippin' caller or wotever?"

"Callboy," I corrected. "Many stage directors have started as such. It is frequently a first step backstage. How many steps you take after that, and in which direction, is up to you. Who knows—you might even become house manager one day."

"Wot kind of an 'ouse?" Jerry asked suspiciously.

I laughed. "The theatre itself. It is always known as 'the house.' The house manager is in charge of staff, both back and front of the theatre, and the maintenance of the entire place. He engages box-office staff, the housekeeper, or 'chief char' as she is known to everybody, also the commissionaires and the heads of departments backstage, such as the master carpenter, the property manager, who is known as 'Props,' and even the wardrobe mistress. And he leases the bars to brewers. And then there's the stage manager—he is the stage director's assistant—and the man in charge of lights. He is simply called 'Lights' by everyone. And so on right down the scale. Every job is important, and starting as callboy can lead to many of them."

"Provided he gets the job," said the Toff. (Mr. Steel, I reminded myself.) "We will have to spruce you up first, Jerry."

He halted outside the Boswell home. "I believe this is where you live, ma'am. I have seen you coming out and going in many times."

"I must confess your face is not unfamiliar."

"No doubt. I live on the other side of the square, at Number 20." He nodded north of the central gardens, to a house with shining windows and an immaculate Georgian front door set beneath a splendid fanlight. I had passed it many times and recalled seeing a brass plate there, though what name it bore I had never paused to notice.

"Then you are the man who runs that notorious gymnasium."

"Notorious, ma'am? Famous, I hope—or that it will become so."

"I meant 'notorious' in the sense that the whole square is up in arms about it."

"The square will have to get used to it. A man may do what he likes with his own cellars, and a gymnasium cannot be closed down on moral grounds since it contributes to a healthy society and does not disturb the peace. The only objection the more snobbish residents can have is that any man can attend, providing he can afford to, and therefore the tone of the square runs the risk of being lessened if one measures it by such values."

"And do you extend your activities to Hyde Park in order to bring in new customers?"

"Far from it, ma'am. My gymnasium not only pays for itself, but helps to support an even more worthy scheme—which is my main object in running the place. I presume you arrived in the park when I had finished sparring, otherwise you would have heard my challenge and known the reason for the public booth. Sixpence a round, and double to the man who knocks me down."

"Wich nobody ain't niver done," Jerry declared, "not even Joe, an' 'e's blacked more eyes down on the docks than any other bloke."

"He was off form today, Jerry, which was lucky for me."

"Aye, but just you wait until 'e's *on* form agin, an' 'e'll lick the bloody 'ide offya."

"I'll keep up my training," the Toff promised solemnly. "Meantime, mind your language in front of ladies."

The sound of wheels slowing down beside us caught my attention. They belonged to the Boswell carriage, and from it descended Sir Nevill and his wife. At the sight of a street barrow outside her front door, Bernadette's eyebrows rose, and at the sight of my mother standing beside it, they rose even higher.

"My dear Trudy, are you *gossiping* with this costermonger?"

My mother burst out laughing, and the Toff smiled broadly.

"This is no coster," said my mother. "This is a neighbour from the other side of the square."

Lady Boswell's disbelief was evident. Owners of Portman Square properties did not push street barrows, but before she could comment further, her husband had taken charge. Holding out his hand to the Toff, he said, with that gentle amiability with which he met the highest and the lowest, "I hope you were coming to call? We met at the Cavalier Club two Sundays ago—the charity exhibition fight between Gentleman Jackson and the Frenchman, du Cros. Remember?"

"I remember your face, but not your name, for which I apologise. I was introduced to so many people that night. Being Sunday, it was particularly crowded, and the fact that it was on private premises, and therefore could not fall foul of both the gaming and the ecclesiastical laws, made it even more popular."

"Of course. You organized the event, I recall, in aid of an East End mission." Sir Nevill was never in the least perturbed if people failed to recognise him. "After all," he would say, "not *all* people are theatregoers," but his wife felt differently. That anyone could possibly fail to recognise so famous a man as her husband filled her with outrage. Only the ignorant or the stupid could be unacquainted with a face which adorned not only the entrance to the Boswell Theatre, but newspapers and often hoardings. Theatres were also beginning to advertise on the side of horse-drawn trams and omnibuses, the Gaiety featuring blurred photographs of their well-contoured chorus line, and theatres like the Boswell the distinguished features of their leading actors. In this, Sir Nevill was aggravatingly modest. He saw no reason why he, as actor-manager, should dominate these newest playbills; whoever was playing current lead should be billed from time to time, so he rang the changes with pictures of his wife, as was her due, and of the company's male character lead, Bramwell Chambers, and of Chrystal Delmont, who was playing more and more leads like Mrs. Tanqueray and Lady Teazle, which did not please the great Bernadette at all.

"But an actress in your position can afford to be generous to one less fortunate," her husband would point out. "Everyone knows that poor Chrystal's husband is a struggling musician. Giving her a chance now and then can only be a tribute to your own graciousness, and your public will admire you for it." Sir Nevill was always the soul of tact when his wife complained. Sometimes he succeeded in pacifying her and sometimes not. I even thought she regarded him with faint suspicion occasionally, though he met her questioning glance with his usual benign one. Sir Nevill could disarm most people with that glance, and he did so now as he turned to her and said, "My dear, I don't believe you have had the pleasure of meeting our new neighbour, Dr. Steel?"

"A doctor?" she echoed, looking expressively at his unconventional attire. The surprise in that glance reflected my own. Apart from the fact that doctors usually wore frock coats, top hats, and pin-stripes, they never indulged in bare-fist fighting in public nor pushed coster barrows through the streets, and if Lady Boswell's pained expression suggested that his appearance was a betrayal of a respectable profession, I hardly blamed her. She would have been even more pained had she known the reason for the laden cart and what he had been doing at Soapbox Corner.

Further comment was forestalled by the appearance of Clementine, who emerged from the house at that moment. I saw her pause on the top step, the door still ajar behind her, so that she was framed against the dark interior of the hall. She wore a gown of white lace and pink Pompadour foulard, trimmed with rose-pink ribbons. The skirt was covered with lace flounces across the front and the corsage tapered to a point, subtly emphasising the curve of her waist and leading into the more voluptuous curve of her hip. On her head was a bonnet of English straw, trimmed with pink posies and a modest ostrich plume of *écru*. The whole effect was of a chic Parisienne aping an English rose and succeeding so well that she seemed to have stepped straight out of an English garden, fragrant and unsullied.

She looked ravishing and knew it, holding the pose as if she had just made her entrance onstage—that skilful, professional halt which lasted no more than a second or two, but which always made an impact on an audience.

"An actress should never rush straight into her lines the moment she steps from the wings, unless, of course, the part demands it. A brief pause on entering gives the audience time to study her, and builds up anticipation. Remember that, my darling gel. A halt, a questing glance into the air—splendid, splendid, that angle of the head is most provocative—and now a light, indrawn breath and straight into your opening lines. . . ."

That was a lesson I had heard Bernadette instil into her daughter when rehearsing her for a youthful stage appearance at the age of thirteen, and, like all lessons in acting on which I had eavesdropped, I remembered it well. So did Clementine apparently, for nothing could have faulted her appearance now, pausing briefly on the top step as she looked down on us, and then following with a leisurely descent, unfurling her pink parasol as she did so and placing it prettily behind her head like a befrilled frame which cast a delicate and becoming glow onto her face. I was not surprised by Dr. Steel's frank appreciation of her. He watched in silence and scarcely seemed to hear her mother's greeting.

"My darling, you are *not* going out unescorted, surely? Nevill, my love, you cannot allow your daughter to venture on the streets of London alone, even at this hour of the day!"

In a flurry of rustling skirts, Clementine slipped her free arm about her mother's shoulders and kissed her lightly.

"My dear Mamma, I am off to take tea with Penelope Driscoll, Lord Driscoll's daughter, who was at the convent with me, and *of course* I shall not walk to Grosvenor Square! I heard the carriage arrive, so hurried out to save Curtis the trouble of putting it away only to get it out again." She threw Curtis, the coachman, a considerate glance, at which the man touched his cockaded hat respectfully and appreciatively. Curtis was new and had only met the daughter of the house since her return. "A most considerate young lady," I had heard him call her to Mrs. Wilson when he came up from the mews to the kitchen for his midday meal. "Considerate and quite an eyeful, for all she's so ladylike and mannerly. Makes a man wonder what she's like underneath."

Cook had shushed him quickly, indicating my presence and making me all too aware that as soon as I disappeared a great deal of confidential gossip and speculation would be indulged in. I found myself speculating even now, finding it hard to reconcile this demure and ladylike vision with the outspoken young woman who had shocked me earlier today. I must have dreamed that half-hour, I decided. Not in reality could this pure and unsullied beauty have admitted to such experiences, nor revealed such relish in doing so. Nor could I now imagine her lying naked on a bank of moss while some unknown Frenchman did whatever he liked with her body, but when she related the story it had all been vivid enough. Too vivid, as had been her sensuous nostalgia and her knowledge of things at which I could only guess, transforming her lustful young face into that of an insatiable and greedy woman.

None of it had ever happened, I told myself as she smiled at us all, shaking hands demurely with the man whom I could no longer think of as "the Toff," but only as a suddenly enigmatic figure whom I could not sum up. I saw her eyes appraise him, as he appraised her, and I wondered whether he too hid another personality beneath the surface—a doctor on one hand and a prizefighter on the other, a professional man and yet a wholly animal one? I had been liking him until this moment. I had felt at ease with him, but no longer. He was a man much older than myself, and I was nothing but a fourteen-year-old, immature, inexperienced, shut out of the adult world. I wanted to run up those steps and into the house and shut the door on both of them.

But my mother was speaking. She was saying, "We were on our way to see you, Sir Nevill, with Jeremy here. Jeremy Hawks. We are hoping you will engage him as callboy.''

Bernadette raised her lorgnette and looked at the lad, quite obviously disliking what she saw.

"The child is filthy! Where *did* you find him, Trudy?''

Dr. Steel put in, "I introduced them and am most grateful to Miss Lucinda and her mother for bringing him to see Sir Nevill. The boy won't remain filthy, I promise you. He needs work and he needs to be with people who will see that he sticks to it. If you could give him a start . . .''

"Bring him indoors," said Nevill Boswell, not sharing his wife's displeasure, nor apparently noticing her glance of distaste, first at the boy and then at the handcart which the doctor left unashamedly beside the curb. I was aware of Curtis handing Clementine into the carriage and of her gentle smile in thanks, the polite acknowledgment of a servant but no more than that. Or so it seemed. If she was aware of Curtis's good looks, she showed no sign of it, but he was certainly a well-set-up young man and wore his uniform well. Lady Boswell had chosen that uniform herself, in the same colour as the footman and pageboy—dark green with gilt lapels and fawn breeches, dark green top hat with gilt cockade. Similarly the female staff wore dark green dresses with beige aprons for afternoon wear, Kate's befrilled and elegant so that she created a good impression when serving afternoon tea.

Only Hawkins, a traditional butler in every way, declined to be "decked out in some fancy costume just to please her ladyship," her idea of butler's wear being dark green frock coat with beige waistcoat and trousers and even gilt edging to lapels, at which he promptly threatened to give notice. Being indispensable to Sir Nevill, he got his own way and wore the traditional butler's dark and discreet frock coat with pin-stripe trousers. The result was one of tremendous dignity and I was as frequently awed by him as were the staff. Hawkins could quell with a glance and silence with a stare. He had that effect on Jerry now, striking terror into the boy's heart as we trooped into the house.

This being the footman's half-day, Hawkins had had to demean himself by opening the door for Clementine on her way out and holding it ajar for us on our way in. It was an even greater indignity for him to admit a street urchin, whether accompanied by the master of the house or not. I felt sorry for the boy. The Boswell establishment was awe-inspiring enough without the addition of a lofty butler's intimidating eye, and I was not surprised to see the lad's footsteps falter, or his frantic look at the closed door behind him. That glance said all too plainly that he wanted to do only one thing—dive through it to the outside world and take to his heels.

But the Toff's hand was on his shoulder, assuring him that he had nothing to fear. The boy relaxed a little then, but his native suspicion made him wary. Life in the East End had taught him to fear authority, to believe that society was against him and that there could be no future for him anywhere outside the slums into which he had been born. The Toff he could accept because he had met him against his own background, but he had never visualised the man against such a background as this, and the ease with which he entered it erected a barrier between them for the first time.

Jerry cast the doctor a bewildered, suspicious, questioning glance. What are you bringing me here for, what are you up to, what are you trying to do—sell me to these people? Suddenly I realised how a person felt when being led into bondage, and I did the first thing that came into my head.

"Come and look at this, Jerry." I drew him into the long drawing room. I had rarely entered here myself, and then only when invited, but that didn't deter me now. I knew Sir Nevill's model theatre stood in pride of place beside the tall French windows. He had built it personally and used it for trying out scale sets for newly planned productions.

"Don't let the boy touch that!" The great Bernadette's voice was sharp as I led him across the room. She was displeased with her husband for bringing him indoors, and she was certainly displeased with my audacity.

"He will do no harm, my love. Lucinda will see to that."

I was grateful to Sir Nevill and smiled at him in thanks. His smile in return warmed me, as always, and when he came over and joined us, pointing out the various part of the theatre, young Jerry's manner eased gradually.

"These are the wings, and the area down front of the stage is called the apron. Actors come down there to speak their most important lines; no one can upstage them there—that means to mask them, conceal them from the audience, cut off their lines; and up above are the floats, galleries of lights which shine down on the stage, suspended from this maze of iron"—he pointed to a reproduction of an area known as the grid, spreading high above the entire stage—"and even higher are the flies, so known because scenery can be drawn up there, hoisted into the air."

I put in, "Now you see how a theatre differs from a pub, Jerry. Your busker friend wouldn't be at home on a stage like this; he would be happier in the open air, entertaining queues. But the theatre is a whole world of its own—a wonderful, exciting world—and when you belong to it you will feel so proud that you will never want to belong to any other."

Sir Nevill said, "Lucinda really loves the theatre, don't you, my dear?" But his words were silenced by his wife's declaration that we were stuffing the child's head with a lot of dreams which would do him no good, since he was never likely to enter the theatre anyway.

"Give the boy something to eat and send him on his way. Doctor . . . we respect your interest in him, but to expect us to employ him is quite out of the question. Callboys come from the ranks of stagehands; children of scene-shifters and carpenters and propmen—"

"I don't see why an accident of birth should debar Jerry from undertaking the simple duties of a callboy," her husband interrupted firmly, "and the reason we are without one at the moment is that none of the stage crew has a son of the right age." He turned and looked compassionately at the boy. Sir Nevill's kindness was well known. He had all the warmth of heart which characterised his profession. Theatricals helped each other instinctively and without question, all too aware that life could be hard and success elusive, that an actor could be at the top one day and at the bottom the next. Rogues and vagabonds they might be, and as such they were known, but there was honour of a kind amongst them, a camaraderie, and a bond born of hardship and struggle.

Only comparatively recently had morning performances, in addition to afternoon and evening ones, been dispensed with in many theatres, the Boswell being one which now gave matinees only on two afternoons a week. At most out-of-town theatres actors were expected to perform from eleven o'clock in the morning, rehearsing the next show between afternoon and evening performances, followed by more rehearsals after the final curtain-fall, so that a seventeen-hour day was an accepted thing, their whole waking hours being spent within the theatre walls.

Despite being born into a successful theatrical family, or perhaps because of it, Nevill Boswell was in a position to understand and observe the strains and stresses of an insecure life. This was something of which his wife, marrying straight into the hierarchy of it, had no conception. She had never witnessed an actor's struggles, never had to share his long spells of "resting"—the polite term for being out of work—never known failure or insecurity, and as a result she had neither sympathy for, nor comprehension of, the grimness of poverty. To her, an urchin was an urchin, a guttersnipe a guttersnipe, corrupt from birth and therefore a danger to society, but to her husband he was a human being deserving of compassion, someone potentially promising.

He looked down at young Jerry now with that smile for which he was famous and of which he was quite unconscious, as he was of his good looks—though it was mainly due to these looks that he had become a matinee idol. Without them he would have been a highly competent actor upholding an illustrious theatrical name; with them, he was something more memorable. I never tired of studying his classic features and noble bearing; I would stand in the wings, listening spellbound to his fine voice, so deep and resonant that it reached the back row of the gods with ease.

Middle age was adding to his distinction, touching his dark hair with silver and etching lines which merely emphasised his character; the mouth was wide, the eyes deepset and surrounded by a network of delicately pencilled creases, and he had the large, high-bridged nose which seemed to characterise prominent actors throughout history.

"You are a bright-enough boy, aren't you, Jerry?" he said. "You are capable of understanding orders and of climbing endless stairs backstage to knock on dressing-room doors and to summon actors for their entrances five minutes before their cues come up—that is the time allowed for them to get down to the wings in readiness, and the stage manager will tell you when to go and whom to call, and in between helping the stage crew, you can run errands for the cast and at the end of the week pick up tips from them in addition to your wages."

At the mention of tips, the boy's face lit up. "If there's money in it, gov, I'll do it good'n proper!"

Lady Boswell shuddered. "*Sir*," she corrected. "You must always address Sir Nevill as '*Sir*.'"

"Yes'm. Sir."

She turned to her husband again. "My dear Nevill, you surely cannot be serious? You don't even know where the boy comes from or what his background is."

"No, but I can guess, and I am sure the doctor would confirm my guess. All the more reason for helping the lad. And of course I am serious. Why not? Provided he wants the job and will work hard, I will accept Dr. Steel's recommendation and he can start at once. The house manager will be only too pleased to engage him on such recommendation, also to be relieved of the headache of finding another lad. Lucinda, my dear, will you bring Jerry with you to the theatre tomorrow morning and introduce him to Gregory and Willard? I will give you a letter, confirming everything. Mr. Willard is our stage director, Jerry, and you will take most of your orders either from him or from his stage manager, Mr. Gregory."

"I gotta let me ma know. She's in the work'ouse an' I'm dossing down wiv Joe in the Rookeries, so I'll git back there an' tell 'im, so's 'e can git a message to 'er. O'course, not bein' 'er 'usband 'e ain't allowed to visit 'er, but anyways, 'usbands'n wives ain't allowed to be togevver in the work'ouse, nor are their kids, but Joe 'as a pal in the Rookeries wot can git a word to Ma."

"The Rookeries!" wailed Bernadette. "Great heavens, the boy comes from a den of thieves and worse!"

"And would you leave him there?" her husband asked. He turned to Steel. "Can you shelter the lad and get a message to this man Joe? I cannot let Lucinda enter the Rookeries to collect the boy tomorrow morning. It wouldn't be safe for her."

"I will see to all that. I am taking Jerry home with me now and counting on my sister to lay her hands on clothes for him."

My mother said eagerly, "I am sure Tommy the pageboy would have spare garments—"

"Only to lend!" declared Lady Boswell. "I do *not* equip my servants for the benefit of others."

Sir Nevill protested, "Of course we will provide what we can for the lad," and I promised to see what could be produced and to bring the garments to the doctor's house. Lady Boswell then demanded that the boy be bathed.

"*And* disinfected too, from the look of him! Hygiene and cleanliness are things I am *most* fastidious about!"

I thought of the perspiration stains beneath the armpits of her gowns, and my mother's constant replacing of dress shields, which the great Bernadette always ripped out, complaining that they made her hot and uncomfortable, and of the many times I had seen her husband turn slightly away when in close contact with her, and although I disliked her very much at this moment I also found myself feeling obscurely sorry for her—a woman no longer loved, no longer really beautiful, and tragically unaware of either—and with a daughter who was anything but the pure and virginal creature she believed her to be, a daughter she adored.

Dr. Steel assured Lady Boswell that she would not recognise Jerry when his sister had finished with him.

"You don't know Helen—when she sets her mind to a thing, no one has a chance. So I warn you not to put up a fight, young Hawks, because my sister will have you in that tub whether you resist her or not. And I will tell you something else—when Miss Lucinda calls for you tomorrow morning you will have had a good night's sleep in a comfortable bed and plenty of good food under your belt."

Jerry, who had looked mutinous at the mention of being bathed, now hesitated, and I saw the last flicker of defiance fade. Perhaps it was due to the prospect of sitting down to really substantial food instead of foraging for scraps, or to the thought of earning money, or to the recognition of a stronger will than his own (and if the will of the doctor's sister was as strong as her brother's, she must be very intimidating, I thought). Whatever the cause, the Toff had won another round, and the idea that I had helped indirectly gave me satisfaction.

I remember that moment as being a very happy one, suddenly clouded by Jerry's final comment before the doctor led him away. Looking up at the man, he said bluntly, "That cove in the park, does 'e belong to the theatre, too?"

"He does not," I said quickly. "You are never likely to see him again."

"Then that's orlright, cos I don't take to *that* sort an' if the likes of 'im were part of the setup, you could count me out an' that's the bloody truth."

The great Bernadette gave an even more horrified gasp, but I scarcely heard it. This sudden reminder of the strangely sinister Durbridge drove all my pleasure out of the moment.

Helen Steel proved to be far from intimidating. I liked her at once. With frank appreciation she inspected the clothes I had brought over for Jerry, while the boy protested loudly that never would we see *him* in them there things. "Sissy, that's wot. Blarst me eyes if I'll wear 'em. They'll laugh at me in Stepney, orl dressed up like a pansy. None of me pals'll know me!"

"Perhaps that will be a good thing," remarked Helen. I liked her good-natured smile and humorous tone of voice. I liked her pleasant face and the obvious self-will in eyes, mouth, and chin. I liked the way she carried Jerry away with kindly determination, laughing at his protests, and when she rejoined me in the first-floor drawing room and announced that she had left him in the bathtub declaring *he* wasn't going to be bossed around by any woman, she finished triumphantly, "But *I* was the victor, as I meant to be!" She then flopped on a couch, put up her feet, and urged me to do the same. "Though I won't persuade you to sample one of these," she added, helping herself to a cigarette.

I stared. I had seen many a super smoke in the secrecy of their dressing rooms, but never imagined that anyone so ladylike as Helen Steel would do the same. At my expression, she laughed.

"Do I shock you? My dear, it is absolutely *comme il faut* to smoke nowadays. The Marlborough House Set does it all the time."

"Is that why you do? Somehow, I cannot imagine you aping the Marlborough House Set."

"I don't, though I am not surprised by many of their antics, which I am sure are merely goaded by the old queen's disapproval. Teddy and Alexandra must have a lean time of it, constantly frowned on as they are, so who can blame their defiance? I sympathise. My brother sometimes makes me feel the same. I lit this cigarette in the hope that he will walk in at any moment, not because I enjoy it." She grimaced distastefully, puffing in and out energetically so that the room became filled with smoke.

"Is he so prudish? I am surprised."

"Why? Because he strips to the waist and boxes with riffraff in public? You don't know Magnus! The things a man can do and a woman cannot are separate and apart. He has absolutely no regard for his own position, only for mine. At the same time, he will drag me into his schemes without compunction when necessary—as with young Jerry." She smiled. "And I will tell you something more—I thoroughly approve and am more than willing to be dragged. Imagine what my life would be like, running this household and receiving a lot of dull females on At Home days, and returning dull visits on theirs! Social chitchat bores me as much as it bores Magnus. We were brought up with it, you see. Dear Papa was a most respected bishop and dear Mamma his most respected wife. Consequently life was infernally dull for my brother and me. He was the first to rebel because, being the elder *and* male, he was able to. He refused to enter the Church and chose medicine instead. He claimed it could have more practical applications, but only when it was finally accepted as a respectable profession did our relatives begin to acknowledge him again. I must admit that dear Papa put no opposition in his way once he saw that Magnus had made up his mind—or perhaps because he knew it was useless to oppose him. Of course, Mamma fell in with Papa's views, as always, it being unseemly for a wife to disagree with her husband, which is probably why I have never been able to bring myself to marry—well, as much for that reason as for the fact that I would never accept any husband chosen for me and never met one I would choose for myself. I really cannot see what disgrace there is in being an old maid."

"But you are not old!"

"Twenty-seven, my dear. Two years younger than my brother, which is old in a woman but not in a man—another of life's unfairnesses."

"Are you a suffragette?" I asked curiously. "You sound like one."

"Of course I am a suffragette, as any right-minded woman must be. Perhaps it's a good thing dear Mamma is dead, because she would certainly not have approved. Papa too. He outlived her by only a year, poor man. Never were two people so devoted, nor so dependent on each other. Had he preceded her, dear Mamma would have gone into a swift decline. Another reason for not marrying, in my view. To rely so completely on a male, not only for one's existence but for one's thoughts and opinions, is carrying dependence to the point of subservience, to my mind."

"She must have loved him very much," I ventured.

"Oh, she did, and I would greatly like to love a man to such a degree, but not to sell myself to him body and soul. The body part is expected, of course, and I have heard that women can even enjoy it, though it is considered shocking if they do, and highly suspect into the bargain. Only immoral women are supposed to enjoy that sort of thing, which is why many wives pretend to find it distasteful. But I meet and talk with mothers of boys at the mission and *their* viewpoint is vastly different. Some say it is the only fun they have because it is the only one that's free, and others, poor creatures, that they do it not to please the customers but because it guarantees them a living. Those are the ones I really feel sorry for, forced into prostitution to keep a roof over their heads and to feed their children. But to get back to the subject of respectable marriage, I realise the physical side is necessary in the interests of motherhood, but a woman's mind should remain her own, I always think. But only Magnus seems to agree with me—and of course Dr. Maynard, who helps at the mission. But *he* is a man in a million. As soon as most men discover I have opinions of my own, any opinions on any subject whatsoever, and that they don't always agree with theirs, their male vanity is immediately injured. But the day will come . . ." She stubbed out the cigarette. "There, now, the place reeks sufficiently to let my brother know what I have been up to." She beamed at me with satisfaction.

"Since he apparently concedes that a woman's mind should be her own, why should he object to your smoking, since that is your own decision?"

"The inconsistency of the male, of course. Why else? I like my brother, Miss Grainger, but see his faults as ably as he sees mine. He believes that smoking is injurious to health, a view no one else subscribes to, but to which he stubbornly adheres simply because, like myself, he won't be opposed."

"Perhaps he is right."

"He will have a hard job proving it. Meanwhile, Magnus being Magnus, he simply refuses to listen to argument. He always says that if Prince Teddy would give up those infernal cigars, he would not suffer with his chest so much. 'Filling his lungs with smoke, what else can he do but cough and wheeze?' Well, say I, they are his lungs and his cigars, so why can't he do what he likes with either? Because other people have to inhale his wretched smoke too, says Magnus, which isn't right or fair. And, as always, he wins the argument."

"I can tell you are fond of him, all the same."

"We-ell, proud of him," she conceded. "He knows what he wants to do, and does it, and in all fairness to him I admit he encourages me to do the same."

"Which is?"

"Helping at the mission. He warned me that Stepney is no place for a lady, in which case, I told him, I was quite willing to cease being one, and life has been a great deal less boring ever since. Ladies don't smoke, or cycle through London wearing bloomers, but if Mrs. Bloomer could do it, so can I—and bless the woman for inventing garments so practical. I was pedaling down Park Lane the other day when our dear Aunt Agatha went driving by in her most impressive landau, so I knew she was entertaining someone special, and I was right. I hailed her, of course—not because I like her, but because I wanted to shock her, cycling along like any servant girl *and* wearing bloomers. Not that servant girls, poor dears, can afford either. Anyway, shock her I did. I thought she was going to have a heart attack; her face went quite puce. That notorious Durbridge was with her too—you won't know who he is, of course, and a good thing too, but he has the ability to deceive any woman over the age of forty and possibly less. But not me. When Aunt Agatha recovered from shock, I saw her holding forth at length and fanning herself as she did so—telling him a thing or two about her unconventional niece and nephew, no doubt. I could tell *her* a thing or two about that man's lack of 'convention.' Not that she would believe me. 'Lord Durbridge *that* kind of a man! What appalling slander against one who donates generously to charities and is received in all the best houses! Never!' I can hear her saying it, and have no doubt she had invited him to drive with her in the park for the sole purpose of persuading him to support one of her own charities—not undesirable ones like my brother's mission, but genteel charities like her Gentlewomen's Sewing Guild, unsullied by East End grime and crime. And no doubt he donated a handsome cheque, laughing up his sleeve as he did so, and she, poor soul, totally unaware of his own penchant for vice. I do chatter a lot, don't I? But you will get used to it. You won't let it dissuade you from coming here again, will you? I like you, Lucinda Grainger. I like your name, too. I hope you don't let anyone shorten it to Lucy? And don't stop calling here once we have found a suitable home for Jerry. He can't go back to the Rookeries, of course.''

''Sir Nevill suggests that we fix him up with one of the scene shifters who lives off the Edgware Road and whose wife takes in quite a number of stage crew from various theatres in London, then he will be able to go home with someone every night, though I imagine Joe may well interfere. He seems to have his own ideas about the best way for Jerry to make a living.''

Magnus Steel's voice spoke from the door. ''No need to worry on that score. I have squared things with Joe.'' The man entered the room as he spoke, dominating the place with his great height. ''I have been to see him in that horrifying dive which he and Jerry have been dossing down in. Fourteen lodgers of both sexes sharing three makeshift beds, and other things besides, and the youngest no more than five. Even Joe admitted that it wasn't what Jerry's mum would want for him, so it was easy to persuade him the boy would be much better off elsewhere. In fact, I think he was impressed by the fact that Jerry had landed a job. If and when he sets up any sort of a home for Jerry's mother again, the picture may change. In their rough way, they make up a devoted family and Joe seems genuinely attached to Jerry's mother. But in the meantime, the boy is one less worry to him, though I imagine the man will miss the lad's pickpocket propensities. 'A real promising buzzer,' he called him."

"He will learn a better trade in the theatre," I said confidently, "and stage crew are sharp-eyed, so he won't have much chance to pick anyone's pockets."

"I am also sharp-eyed." Magnus Steel eyed his sister's stubbed-out cigarette. "My sense of smell is equally good. You really don't have to puff so hard to betray your activities, Helen, and if you hope to shock me, you must know by now that I am virtually shockproof."

"A mere gesture," she answered airily.

"To indicate your independence, I suppose. In fact, that is your only reason for smoking. You don't even know how to do it properly. All puff and blow!"

She laughed. "Confound you, brother—you win, as always."

I had certainly never met a young woman like Helen Steel before, but I certainly wanted to meet her again, and when, before leaving, she urged me once more to call at any time, I was only too pleased to agree.

Before leaving, I saw young Jerry looking quite transformed; clean and well-clad and wolfing a good square meal in the big kitchen of Dr. Steel's house.

The doctor saw me home across the square. He looked very different now, clad in a respectable suit, but one which looked as if it had been pulled on haphazardly, without regard to sartorial elegance. Even his socks didn't match. He saw me glancing at them and, looking down, asked what amused me, so I told him.

"You don't really care how you look, do you, Doctor? Few men would dream of appearing in public wearing odd socks."

"Few men have as little time as I to think about such things." His deepset eyes twinkled as he smiled at me. "Don't worry, I promise to pay attention to such details when visiting the Boswell establishment in the future. I could see Lady Boswell was shocked by my appearance today."

"You must admit that few gentlemen would be seen in public so unconventionally attired."

"I admit few men would indulge in prizefighting in public, so the necessity to dress the part wouldn't arise. I hope the daughter of the house was not equally shocked."

"Clementine? I am sure not." All I was really sure was that Clemmy would observe what lay beneath a man's clothes, or, if not as apparent as the doctor's physique had been today, at least she would speculate upon it. I recalled her comprehensive glance running up and down Magnus Steel's casually clad figure, and his own appreciation of her.

"Is she also an actress?" he asked.

"She has done a certain amount already, and I know she intends to continue, although her mamma has set her heart on her doing the Season. Her coming-out ball is to be held a few weeks from now, and all the necessary strings have been pulled to have her presented, a rarity in the theatrical profession."

"As far as the old queen is concerned, I can believe it, but once she became a widow, the rigid laws controlling debutantes relaxed considerably. It is common knowledge that the prince adores a pretty face, and particularly actresses. Miss Clementine will enchant him."

We were nearing the other side of the square now. I saw Curtis driving round to the mews and guessed he had only just brought Clementine home from Lord Driscoll's house. Had Penelope Driscoll known of Clemmy's extracurricular activities? I wondered, and thought it more than likely. I could imagine them, two spoiled and indulged young women, exchanging reminiscences over the teacups until long after it was time for Clementine to depart. It would mean nothing to her that Curtis had sat outside waiting, or had patiently exercised the horses in the park to keep them fresh. Nothing would mean anything to Clemmy but the opportunity to hold forth about her illicit triumphs. I had no doubt Penelope Driscoll had been the audience, wide-eyed and envious, and Clementine the centre of the stage.

"And if you dare breathe a *word* of what I have told you, Penelope . . ." Would she threaten a rich friend the way she had threatened an impecunious one?

"Well, here you are—safely home. Thank you for bringing the clothes for Jerry, Miss Lucinda, and thank you for proving his salvation this afternoon. But for you, God knows what would have happened to him."

"That man Durbridge would have looked after him. It was plain he was willing to. Perhaps Jerry would have fared even better with him than as a theatre callboy."

Magnus Steel said abruptly, "I think not. Good night, and thank you again, Lucinda Grainger, little angel of mercy. I will see that young Jerry fulfils your faith in him."

"Sir Nevill's faith too," I pointed out. "He had no hesitation in employing him."

"Unlike his unhappy wife."

"Unhappy! Lady Boswell can be far from unhappy, married to such a man and being a famous actress into the bargain!"

Magnus Steel made no answer. He merely smiled again and urged me to go indoors because the afternoon was drawing in and the air becoming nippy. As he walked away I felt that he had forgotten not only me, but the great Bernadette and even Jeremy Hawks, because there was an air of preoccupation about him. Perhaps he was remembering Clementine as she descended the steps looking like an English rose, pure and unsullied and divinely pretty. If so, I couldn't blame him. But when I thought of him becoming her lover—and why not? he was attractive in his rugged, individual way—I found the idea outrageous and disturbing.

Two

Clementine

3

That first sight of Magnus Steel, gazing up at me from the foot of the steps, was gratifying though not surprising. I knew how ravishing I looked in that foulard gown and had taken my usual pains in making the most of it. If a young woman has looks, she should exploit them with confidence, and I see no sense in pretending (to myself) to be unaware of mine, or having any hesitation about wielding one of woman's most powerful weapons. The other is her body, but that can be used later—it is her looks that make the first impression. With beauty she can enslave anyone, male or female, and although I have always had a predilection for the male, I must admit that members of my own sex have had their uses too.

I learned that lesson as soon as I entered my convent school, where the nuns, bless their frustrated motherly hearts, promptly succumbed. "The *dear* child—have you ever seen one so pretty and yet so unaware of it, Sister Cecilia?" The words were not meant for my ears, but as I left the mother superior's study following Mamma's departure, they came floating out to me before the door finally closed, and I knew then that if I went the right way about it I could have these nuns eating out of my hand.

Even the novice delegated to show me to the dormitory which I was to share with several other girls kept stealing sidelong glances at me as we went on our way, and it amused me to disconcert her suddenly by asking why. She blushed furiously, stammering that God had made me so pretty, so unlike any of the other girls. She touched my dark green velvet

61

travelling coat and sable muff with a shy and guilty hand, then hastily withdrew as if ashamed of giving way to envy. That revealed a weak spot which might come in handy, I reflected. It was certainly worth bearing in mind. So I gave her a dazzling smile which completely won her over. The poor thing, so plain and repressed; she looked as if no one had ever smiled at her before. Certainly no man. Then, horror of horrors, I saw immediate adoration in her eyes and realised that a smile from me would mean more to her than a smile from any man, and *that* sort of thing I had no time for at all.

Still, it taught me that women could also succumb and therefore prove useful if manipulated the right way, and when I saw the bunch of girls I was to share a dormitory with I knew that this pathetic creature had spoken nothing but the truth when saying I was unlike any of them. And thank God for that! Pious and disciplined backgrounds were stamped on each and every one; provincial French, Italian, and German, with one or two Spanish thrown in, and only one girl with an English look about her—the aristocratic look of a well-bred horse. Titled, no doubt, but painfully respectable.

I could imagine Gavin's expressive glance should he see this lot, his raised eyebrows, his mock horror, his wicked grin which would tell me precisely what he saw beneath their painfully similar exteriors, and promptly I felt amusement bubbling up inside me. I would take a leaf out of my wicked uncle's book and find out for myself—which, in time, I did to my complete advantage.

But why remember that now? Why remember my doting mamma accompanying me to Paris, chaperoning me so diligently that bold male eyes were instantly quelled, then being mercifully seasick when crossing the Channel and lying prostrate in our cabin while I took advantage of the fresh air on deck and the advances of a charming young Frenchman who, poor thing, looked completely baffled when I pretended not to know him once dear Mamma rallied on reaching Calais. She kept her eye on me from that moment and had even reserved a compartment on the train. All the poor young man could do was saunter up and down the corridor outside, gazing at me wistfully until Mamma slammed down the blinds. I hated her for that. I hated her for being there at all. Without her I could have enjoyed that exclusive, reserved compartment very much indeed, especially with the blinds down. At that time I was still a virgin and tired of it. I was eager to experience bodily love and I had always heard that Frenchmen were the best tutors in that respect—which, of course, turned out to be true later on.

So when Magnus Steel was attracted to me on sight, it came as no surprise. I had learned by now to consider male adulation as wholly my due, and coming from such a man, garbed in that unconventional attire and looking like no gentleman should look, it had a spice of originality and the unusual about it. I must find out more about him, I mused idly as Curtis handed me into the carriage and I cast a brief glance backward to see Lucinda hurrying into the house ahead of everyone, as if wanting to escape.

A funny girl, Lucinda. When I had emerged she had been smiling, happy, chatting to the grubbiest urchin I had ever seen while Mamma examined the child through a lorgnette, disgust written plainly on her face. A stranger tableau I could not have imagined— coster barrow and stately carriage, distinguished actor and autocratic wife, elegant Trudy (and how *did* she manage to look that way in renovated castoffs?) and a man who caught the eye, not because he was handsome or well-dressed, but because there was something about his looks which proclaimed his masculinity even without that revealing shirt of fine cambric and tight boxer's breeches clinging to muscular thighs and calves. I knew he was as palpably aware of me as I was of him. Had Lucinda realised this too, and was that why her smile suddenly switched off? Surely a gauche fourteen-year-old couldn't have been jealous?

I dismissed the thought and turned my mind back to Dr. Steel, only to be interrupted by Curtis asking where I wished to go. I had scarcely heeded the man as he handed me into the carriage and then climbed onto the box. Now he looked down at me over his shoulder, his eyes questioning. But they were doing more than that. They were looking straight down the cleft between my breasts. How *dare* he! My cheeks flamed and I hoped he realised it was in anger— or thought it was. The last thing I wanted him to recognise was my pleasure. One couldn't allow a servant to be so familiar; even less could one allow him to guess that one enjoyed it.

But this new coachman really was a handsome devil. In contemplation of him I forgot the intriguing Magnus Steel; he could come later. Meanwhile I wondered why I had never noticed Curtis's chiselled features before and concluded it was because, when driving with my parents, I sat facing them with my back to the box. This was the first time the new coachman had driven me alone, and since I was not acting with the Boswell company at present, nor would be until I had been presented at Court and enjoyed what my mother hoped would be a highly successful Season (which meant a marriageable one), all my outings seemed to be with Mamma on shopping expeditions, or for fittings in preparation for my coming out, six months ahead, or calling on the mammas of other debutantes on their At Home days. On these occasions Curtis drove us stolidly and dutifully, never daring to stare at the daughter of the house. But he stared now, not even trying to conceal his admiration, and the man's amazing good looks suddenly registered.

There was something else about him too; a tanned, outdoor look, and a strong back beneath his well-fitting uniform. How did a London coachman, usually elderly, bowed, and pallid, come to be so young, with a physique like that?

Perhaps it was because I had been talking about Pierre and confiding in Lucinda my delectable secrets that I was now in a particularly responsive state—the restless and frustrated state of wondering how, and with whom, I was going to replace him. Perhaps for this reason I had observed Magnus Steel's muscular thighs, and now Curtis' broad shoulders. Pierre had left me with a hungry body and an observant eye. Both needed to be satisfied, and this handsome coachman certainly pleased the eye. To me, it was natural to wonder what he would be like as a lover; Magnus Steel, too, who was really more in my class, despite those appalling but fascinating clothes. It was perfectly normal to speculate upon a man's sexual prowess; I had soon found out that those repressed girls at the convent also had their secret thoughts, *and* their secret practices as consolation, for which I had both despised and pitied them. For me it had to be a man, and a virile one too. I would settle for nothing less.

My feigned anger gave way to feigned hauteur as I gave Curtis the Driscoll address, adding casually that he need not exercise the horses whilst waiting because I would be remaining for only a short time, after which he could drive me to the park.

"An afternoon like this is too good to waste indoors," I finished negligently, with which he solemnly agreed.

Penelope Driscoll still looked like a thoroughbred horse, but now she was a well-groomed one. We had become friends partially because we were the only English girls at the convent and partially because she had been one of the most appreciative members of my audience when I slipped back into the dormitory after my interludes with Pierre. Actually we had little in common, but my theatrical background had intrigued her and she knew, of course, who my father was. She had been taken to see his *Macbeth* on her last birthday, and now she was awed and impressed by meeting the daughter of so famous an actor and more than willing to become my disciple because of it. I had used her to carry secret messages to Pierre, and never would she have dared to betray me or she would have betrayed her own collusion.

It was she who contributed to my further prestige amongst the girls by revealing that my father was one of the greatest actors in London ("*The* greatest," I had corrected sharply), and from then on an aura of glamour had surrounded me. I found this both flattering and surprising in view of the fact that her own father's title was inherited and of far higher rank

than dear Papa's conferred one. The Driscoll family went back for generations, ancient titles bespattered amongst the lot of them, but, being
born to all this, she took it for granted and deemed my own background
far more interesting—which it probably was, despite their family estates
in Gloucestershire, Yorkshire, and far-flung Devon, and the Scottish
branches with their castles in Ayrshire and Fifeshire and their miles and
miles of moorland with shooting rights and fishing rights and all the rest
of it, and every branch of the family having its own London house in Park
Lane or some other fashionable Mayfair street or square.

To Penelope, I represented a world unglimpsed, a world which was
gossiped about—scandalous and therefore fascinating. She expected me
to behave immorally, believing I had been brought up amongst immoral
people, and in this I made no attempt to either disappoint or disillusion
her. Not for the world would I have confessed that my parents, particularly Papa, were so respectable as to be positively dull. I could imagine
neither of them ever doing anything scandalous. Both worked to preserve the good name of Boswell and of the theatre, and Mamma, I knew,
considered us the aristocracy of the theatrical world. The nearest she had
ever come to touching the fringe of immorality was in condoning Trudy
Grainger's adultery by sheltering her and her child. Mamma had frequently emphasised that the Graingers' good fortune was due solely to
her kindness of heart, and I naturally shared her belief that they should
be eternally grateful.

Not that Lucinda always showed it. She had a streak of independence
which was increasing. It had been very evident today when she sharply
corrected me for calling her Lucinda-bastard. There had been reprimand
in her voice, taut and angry, as she turned away to the door, forcing me
to call her back and apologise. Why had I yielded? I should have
shrugged and let her go, but the desire to shock her had been stronger. I
knew she had never seen a book like my French one in her life, nor ever
glimpsed indecent French nightwear. The look on her face! I laughed secretly at the recollection of it, for it reminded me of the time I had parad-
ed in the convent dormitory wearing nothing but those fragments of
black lace, a couple of loops uplifting my breasts so that they protruded
nakedly and voluptuously, a lace fig leaf my only other covering, every
girl goggling in surprise and horror and secret envy, with the exception
of Penelope Driscoll. She had gazed at me for a long time and then exclaimed, "My goodness, Clementine, but you're beautiful! No wonder
Pierre can't have enough of you."

I liked her for that, though something beneath her horselike gaze
made me wonder if there wasn't a streak in her similar to that novice, or
those two scandalous Scottish women whose private boarding school in
Edinburgh had been closed down a few years ago because of their dis-

gusting relationship. It had shocked the whole of Britain, and all because
a small pupil had overheard sounds from their bedroom and told her
adoring grandmamma, innocently asking what caused them. . . .

But if Penelope had gone through a schoolgirl crush on me, it had
passed and all that remained was the bond of shared schooldays and now
the additional bond of an imminent Season. Six months could pass in no
time, and Mamma was already in a whirl of preparation. She was also determined that on no count should Penelope's coming-out ball outshine
my own, and had therefore urged me to find out all I could about the
coming plans for Penelope's debut, but Penelope always shrugged when
I questioned her, saying the whole thing would be a frightful bore anyway. She recalled her sister's coming out as terribly tedious.

"Let's talk about more interesting things," she would say, but there
seemed to be few interesting things to talk about apart from the social
round. I knew she hoped that I would then confess to some scandalous
secret love affair. She seemed positively nostalgic for the convent dormitory and bitterly disappointed because I had nothing new to relate. I,
who had started so young, *not* behaving immorally now? But all actresses
did, surely? That was why the old queen disapproved of them and the
Prince of Wales adored them. . . .

Sometimes she contrived to take me upstairs to her room, confident I
was holding something back which could not be revealed in front of her
mother, and she would probably do so today I decided as Curtis stopped
outside the Driscoll mansion in Grosvenor Square, unable to halt precisely in front of the steps because another carriage was there already—a
very impressive carriage with crests on both doors. That indicated other
visitors from whom Penelope would want to escape for a tête-à-tête with
me as soon as the tedious ritual of tea was over, for the visitors would
surely be stuffy friends of her parents or the mother of yet another of this
year's coming debutantes, accompanied by her daughter.

I could anticipate the conversation, for it always followed the same
pattern: the weather, servant problems, the latest Parisian or London
fashion house, the coming Season, the royal family, the poor dear
queen, the scandalous goings-on of the Marlborough House Set ("They
do say the Prince of Wales secretly visits *Babylon!* Pray God his dear
mamma does not know!"), which always intrigued me and made me long
to hear more, whereupon the topic would immediately be switched back
to the Season, the cost but the importance of it, and eligible bachelors
who still seemed unwilling to be snapped up. (Gavin would say there was
something wrong with men like that.) Then back to the dear queen's
health and her rakish son's goings-on, which were never detailed in front
of "the dear young girls," then on to Princess Alexandra's increasing
deafness, which she refused to acknowledge, not to mention her appall-

ing unpunctuality, both of which Prince Teddy did at least tolerate with unending patience, one had to say *that* much for the man. . . .

I decided that today's visit would be boring indeed and one which I would terminate as soon as possible.

Curtis lodged the reins, leapt down from the box, and opened the carriage door for me.

It was the first time he had ever touched me physically. Oh, he had handed me in and out of the carriage often enough, but it had been no more than an immaculately gloved hand taking hold of my immaculately gloved fingertips—not a human touch at all. This afternoon was different. I had unbuttoned my long silk gloves at the wrists and tucked them back for coolness during the drive, and when he saw my bare hand he imperceptibly removed his own glove so that our flesh made contact. And what contact! No light touch of the fingers, but my hand grasped in his so that I felt the strength and the span of it, wholly encompassing.

He had no right to do such a thing, of course; no right to remove his glove, no right to help me down so slowly in order to prolong the moment, no right to retain my hand as long as he did, but I was suddenly so conscious of him that I could utter no reprimand, and I found myself descending very leisurely, lifting my skirts to prevent them from brushing the steps and thereby displaying ankles of which I had every right to be proud. I saw Curtis's eyes upon them and at once I was back in that greenhouse arbour, with Pierre kissing them and then moving his mouth upward, upward . . . to knee and thigh and beyond . . .

It was a bad moment to remember such ecstasy, because it brought the colour flooding to my face and I had no doubt that bold Curtis believed it was caused by the clasp of his hand.

I pulled away sharply and swept up the steps to the Driscoll front door, refastening my gloves as I went, because no lady would arrive with them unbuttoned. Concentration on the task gave me time to compose myself, and when the butler admitted me I was cool and unflustered. Thank heaven for an actress's training, which taught her how and when to control her emotions in public as well as onstage!

All the same, I knew I would go for that drive in the park later on, and experienced a faint tingling of excitement at the thought of it.

To my surprise, the Driscolls' visitor was a man, unaccompanied and very striking, though by no means good-looking with those heavy-lidded eyes and overfull red lips, but fascinating because he was unlike any man I had ever met. I knew instinctively that a world of experience lay behind him and that I would welcome an introduction to it. I was always eager to explore new regions, eager for new experiences, provided I profited by them or derived pleasure from them, and somehow I knew that here was a man who could open many unexplored doors and that his immaculate appearance (obviously produced by the best tailor in London), not to mention his impeccable manners, hid a dual personality, and that the hidden side would be the most interesting.

Lady Driscoll was hanging admiringly on his every word. Not for the first time I thought how blatant middle-aged women could be in their reactions to men, and what fools they could make of themselves in the process. This man was shrewd enough to see through his hostess's gushing charm—and so, to my surprise, was Penelope, who remarked caustically that Lord Durbridge had just agreed to donate a thousand pounds to dear Mamma's favourite charity, and wasn't that generous of him? Having dismissed that, she insisted, "And now you must meet my friend Clementine Boswell, daughter of Sir Nevill Boswell, the famous actor, of whom I am sure you have heard. . . ."

"Not only heard, but seen perform many times," Lord Durbridge replied, bowing over my hand and totally unaware that Lady Driscoll found my arrival unwelcome and ill-timed.

"Penelope, my love, I am sure you two girls would like a tête-à-tête upstairs? They were at finishing school together," she added to her guest, "and you know how school friends love to chat about old times, so we will excuse them, will we not?" She crossed to the fireplace and pulled an embroidered bell rope. "I will order fresh tea to be sent to your room, my darling."

Her darling looked pleased, but I had no intention of being despatched like that—not from the company of a man I found so intriguing. Besides, his name was familiar. I recalled Gavin once referring to Durbridge as one of the wealthiest men in London: "But I won't tell you how he comes by it. You're too young to know about such things."

That was an irritating trait in dear "Uncle" Gavin. He would hint and then withdraw, always saying I was too young to know about this and that, mocking me, making me feel that he could see right through me and knew that I was not the virtuous maiden dear Mamma believed me to be. He would tease and tantalise me, then go on his way, laughing. One day, I vowed, I would get even with that so-called uncle of mine, and right at this moment I felt that to meet Lord Durbridge might be one step toward it. Then I could casually let drop that I knew the man and watch Gavin's face when I did so.

"Dear Lady Driscoll," I cooed, "pray do not trouble. I have already taken tea with dear Mamma and am on my way to another appointment with half an hour to spare."

I sat down and spread my skirts with all the grace I had ever been taught, and my hostess could do nothing but accept the situation, reseat herself, and allow Lord Durbridge to do the same.

I saw a glint of amusement and speculation beneath his heavy lids and knew that I interested him. I also knew he was examining me both critically and intimately, mentally stripping me without Lady Driscoll or Penelope having the slightest suspicion he was doing so. A clever man, a fascinating and strangely alluring man, but a baffling one too, because that penetrating glance, assessing my body beneath my clothes, had no desire in it, a fact which I found both unflattering and challenging. Why the interest, if he was not bent on seduction? That veiled, assessing glance was the kind a collector focused on a work of art—critical, dispassionate, calculating its value. No man had looked at me in such a way before.

"Lord Durbridge is London's most generous supporter of charities," Penelope's mother was saying with a tight smile. "We were just discussing a most worthy project when you—"

"Interrupted?" I finished sweetly. "Pray forgive me, but do feel free to continue." I sank demurely back in my seat, refusing to meet Penelope's beseeching glance. She wanted to get away from the boring conversation of these two; her mother's talk invariably ran along charitable lines because she prided herself on being known for her good works and had scarcely any other topic of conversation. London abounded with hostesses such as she, competing against each other for renown in the charitable stakes.

"Mamma," said Penelope harshly, "you know perfectly well that you had finished and all you are waiting for is Lord Durbridge's promised cheque."

The man laughed, showing very white teeth between thick red lips. "The frankness of the young!" he commented. "I am quite sure that in *your* youth, Lady Driscoll, you would never have dared to be so bold. But even so, your daughter is right—my promised cheque is our only unfinished business, so here it is." He drew out a chequebook, wrote with a flourish, and laid the slip of paper on a Pembroke table between them. "And now, alas, I must take my leave."

He rose, and his hostess could do nothing but extend her hand in farewell. He lifted it to his lips, brushing it lightly, and then turned to me. I made no attempt to rise, merely holding out my hand, clearly indicating to my tart hostess that I had no intention of departing at the same time as her precious guest and thinking as I did so: *That should please you, ma'am, because I know full well you don't want me to further my acquaintance with this man. You want him for your daughter exclusively, and she is not in the least interested in him, nor attracted by him. I have never known Penelope to be attracted by any man. You poor thing, you are going to have an old maid on your hands for life, if you did but know it. An elegant old maid, good-looking in her horsey way, but only capable of deriving a vicarious enjoyment out of the love affairs of others; quite incapable of experiencing one herself. Poor Lady Driscoll, you are wasting your time and money in giving a lavish ball for your unwilling daughter and in lining up all the eligible men you can think of. She is no more interested in them than they are in her, so leave her alone, she is happy as she is. . . .*

I felt Durbridge's thick lips against my fingers, and to my astonishment they were quite cold, almost sexless, although I knew instinctively that sexually he was vastly experienced. Dear Pierre had taught me a lot, but some things he had left me to find out for myself, and there was much I wanted to find out about this man and his unfathomable ways.

"Pray give my regards to your talented parents, Miss Boswell. I have seen them act many times, but never had the pleasure of meeting your mother. Sir Nevill I was once introduced to, briefly, when an acquaintance took me backstage on a first night, but alas, your father curtailed the meeting, and no similar opportunity has come my way since."

"Then I will see that it does, if that is your wish. I am sure dear Mamma would be delighted to meet you."

"No doubt they will do so, in passing, at Penelope's coming-out ball," Lady Driscoll said dismissively, ringing firmly for the butler to escort her honoured guest to the door. I had broken up a profitable meeting and she was angry, which indicated either that she had yet another charity for which she hoped to make an appeal or, more likely, that she viewed the man as a possible suitor for Penelope's hand and resented my intrusion because I outshone the girl. I enjoyed the woman's reaction very much. I also enjoyed her determination that any meeting between Lord Durbridge and my mother would only be "in passing." The jealousy of these ambitious mothers, the scheming, the manoeuvring! I wanted to laugh aloud because I knew full well just how Lord Durbridge was going to meet Mamma. He would be invited to my own ball. I would see to that.

Meanwhile, I could wait, and it could do no harm to let him wait too. There was hidden motivation behind the veiled inspection he had given me; to deprive him of an opportunity to repeat it in the immediate future could serve to whet his appetite, and I acted on that instinct when he remarked, "Did I hear you say that you had another appointment, Miss Boswell? My carriage is outside—may I convey you there?"

I thanked him and declined, explaining that my own carriage was waiting. I was thankful for that. It would have been difficult to invent an appointment when none existed, and I had the uncomfortable feeling that this man had somehow guessed as much, because amusement hovered beneath those heavy lids, coupled still with that secret awareness of me which was so hard to interpret but so very satisfying. The admiration there told me full well that he appreciated my looks even though it was, at the moment, merely in the detached way of a connoisseur. I was vexed, but flattered; intrigued and challenged. There were dark depths here to be plumbed.

"Your coachman could follow, thus giving me the opportunity to enjoy your company for a little longer, Miss Boswell."

Oh no, I thought, *you don't win me over with flattery! Not at this stage of our acquaintance. I don't like being studied as if I were an* objet d'art, *m'lord. I will get to know you, and you me, in my own good time—not yours.*

"But I came to see Penelope and she has had no opportunity to enjoy my company at all, sir. Besides which, I still have fifteen minutes to spare."

That, at least, pleased Penelope's mother, although when the door closed upon Lord Durbridge she remarked dryly that I could have been enjoying her dear girl's company from the moment of my arrival, had I wished to, whereupon she retired, bearing Lord Durbridge's generous cheque to lock within her escritoire, and I managed to terminate my visit within ten minutes because suddenly that drive in the park with handsome Curtis became too tempting to postpone any longer.

After we had been bowling along the outer perimeter of Hyde Park for a while I reached up, tapped Curtis on the shoulder with the ferule of my parasol, and ordered him to halt beneath the shade of some trees.

"It will refresh the horses. They were standing too long in the sun in Grosvenor Square. The poor things are feeling the heat, I fear."

There was no sign that the poor things were, but I could hold no discourse with the back of a coachman high upon his box.

Curtis half-turned his head and smiled down at me—the respectful and subdued smile of a servant, no more. He didn't make the mistake of glancing at my low neckline this time, which pleased me even as it disappointed me. All he said was, "Thank you, Miss Clementine. That is very considerate of you."

The horses drew to a halt, their driver's implacable back remaining erect and disciplined. Unless spoken to, he could not turn and look down at me again. This at least gave me the opportunity to study those averted shoulders more closely, and the back of a well-shaped head beneath his coachman's cockaded hat, but I soon had my fill of both and wanted to see his well-cut features again. Even so, I had to take things slowly; one could not appear to deliberately attract the attention of a servant.

A servant! This man would not remain one forever. I was certain of that, and when he turned to gaze out across the wide span of grass and trees to our left, I saw his profile sharply etched—strong, determined chin, resolute mouth, proud nose, intelligent forehead. Then the head was averted again, staring straight in front with the discipline of a coachman who knows his place.

What was going on inside that head? What thoughts, what dreams, what speculations, what ambitions? And what had made a man who possessed the stamp of an outdoor life turn to so menial and confined a job as this, accommodated in miserable quarters in the mews behind a London house, bare rooms above the stables? I guessed they were miserable because my dear mamma did not believe in pampering servants; to her, bed and board meant, literally, palliasse and bare floor, though she could deny the servants little in the way of food, since catering, by tradition, lay in the hands of Cook, and Mrs. Wilson knew how to look after her allies—which included Hawkins and the rest of the household staff. There was no doubt about it, servants in good houses ate well below-stairs, but they could hardly expect luxuries in their accommodation as well.

"Are you ready to drive on, Miss Clementine?"

"No, Curtis. I find it very pleasant sitting here in the shade and seeing the world go by, and the riders in the Row, and the dear little children, watched by their nannies, playing on the grass. Do you not agree?"

He had to turn then, but his eyes again avoided the neckline of my gown. I knew then that that first glance had disturbed him too much to risk another. I felt a warm rush of pleasure and excitement stir in the most vulnerable part of my body, just as Pierre had made it. How long ago that seemed!

Too long.

"If you would care to descend from the box to stretch your legs, Curtis, I would have no objection."

"I must attend the horses, miss."

"You can attend them standing on the ground just as well as sitting up there."

He tipped his hat, thanked me, and descended. Still holding the reins in a gloved hand, he stood on the verge beside me, his eyes on the horses but not on me. I opened my parasol and twirled it negligently behind my head, humming lightly beneath my breath. *"Three little maids from school are we . . . tum-tiddle-tum-tum, tum-tum-tee . . ."* What fun it would be to play in Gilbert and Sullivan instead of Papa's classical dramas! Would there be any hope, ever, of persuading him to try a light musical production in which I could look as fetching as any Gaiety Girl? Very little, that I knew. D'Oyly Carte at the Savoy, almost across the road from the Boswell Theatre, presented too much opposition. Besides, operettas were not my father's forte. If I ever hoped to shine in that sphere, I would have to strike out on my own, and that didn't appeal to me. I was too accustomed to the security of the Boswell Theatre and its productions, which would always keep me in the public eye.

When the Season was over, I would go back to the theatre. Already I was missing the limelight. Mamma would be disappointed, of course. I knew her greatest ambition for me was a rich husband, preferably titled, but I was not sure that it was mine. One man, one bed, *forever*? What an appalling thought! In time I would get to know the tone and pitch of every snore; even worse, the routine physical approach, because husbands could never be the same as lovers. Within the bounds of respectability there could be no wild abandon, no eroticism. For that sort of thing Victorian husbands kept mistresses, because no well-brought-up wife could be expected to tolerate such degradation.

"The physical side is a sacrifice a woman must make in order to bear children, my dear, distasteful to delicate sensibilities, but to be tolerated as a wifely duty."

I knew this was the only premarriage advice respectable mammas gave to their daughters on the eve of their wedding day, making no further reference to the subject. How infernally dull marriage would be, I thought, with everything done prosaically beneath the bedcovers, the gaslight extinguished, the wife conventionally on her back, nightdress lifted to oblige her husband, and the act performed with decorum, but no passion, on his side, and patient submission on hers. Good God, did they even try to pretend it wasn't happening? Was that why they did it in total darkness, covered up, as if hiding something shameful or embarrassing?

How could it be otherwise when most marriages were arranged with an eye to financial betterment or social convenience? *Affaires* were different. My initiation with Pierre had taught me that, and nothing less would ever satisfy me now. So when *I* married I would choose my husband with care, making sure he was stupid enough to be wholly trusting and rich enough to own at least two establishments, well away from each other in town and country, and, above all, he must be sufficiently gullible to be easily duped. This seemed, to me, nothing less than plain common sense.

"What made you become a coachman, Curtis? You have not always been one, have you, despite the fact that you know how to handle horses?"

He looked surprised. "I didn't know you had observed me so closely, Miss Clementine."

"It doesn't take much observation to tell the difference between a townsman and an outdoor man. Were you brought up in the country?"

My tone was deliberately casual, indifferent, denying him the pleasure of believing that I had studied him with interest.

"No, Miss Clementine, I'm cockney born and bred."

I couldn't hide my surprise. There was a cockney intonation in his voice, but not that of the real East Ender.

"Then where did you learn to handle horses, and where did you get that outdoor tan?"

"My father was coachman to a wealthy Hampstead merchant. My mother was Cook. The house was on the edge of Hampstead Heath and we lived in the coach house until my father died and my mother married again and moved to Devon. I was sixteen then, too young to be retained as coachman, good as I was with the horses. They offered to keep me on as a stable lad, but I didn't like the idea of sleeping with the horses, not after the home my mother had kept. My father had been replaced, my mother too, so the coach house was needed. There was nothing for me but to go to sea, which I did. I was cabin boy, deckhand, and then an ABS. That accounts for the tan, Miss Clementine. I was an able-bodied seaman for eight years on merchant vessels, which gave me the chance to see the world, but no further opportunity for promotion, so I quit."

"And you think being a coachman will take you further?"

He laughed. "Not in a lifetime, missy, but it's a good stopgap."

"So you mean to leave us when something better comes along?"

"I . . . did."

The hesitation was significant. I refused to look at him now. I closed my parasol and, apparently intent on adjusting its folds, repeated negligently, "You . . . did? That sounds as if you have changed your mind."

He made no answer, and when I looked at him I saw his intent gaze and knew why his plans had changed. *You* changed them, his eyes said, which was audacious, but pleasing. I liked audacity, though I believed in keeping it in its place. Pierre had been audacious, seducing a wealthy pupil at the convent, but I had handled him skilfully. I could do so again.

Changing the subject, I remarked coolly that I hoped his present quarters were as comfortable as the coach house in Hampstead.

"Well, as to that, Miss Clementine, they can't really be compared. At Hampstead the horses were kept in separate stables; we didn't live above them. In a mews, a coachman has to, though I sleep in the room above the carriage part. Less smell there, and in time I mean to cover the floor with linoleum, which will help."

I was aghast.

"You mean the floors are absolutely bare?"

"Not entirely, miss. Mrs. Wilson let me have a rug from the staff room. I put my palliasse on that, which makes it warmer."

I knew well enough that kitchen maids slept on palliasses; such things were expected, but a *coachman?* I felt a sudden fury against my mother because she never troubled to inspect the servants' quarters—nor had I ever thought of doing so myself, but such a responsibility was hardly mine. I was not mistress of the house; Mamma was. She was conscientious enough about their immaculate uniforms, and I knew that Curtis's distinctive clothes had been designed with an eye to creating an impression. ("The Boswells have a reputation to uphold, and a well-dressed coachman, well-groomed horses, and a fine carriage contribute to it.") I had heard her say that often enough. But would she keep this excellent coachman if she housed him badly? The thought made me quite anxious.

Curtis was saying, "Please don't concern yourself, Miss Clementine. There was an old iron bedstead there which I'm repairing, then I can put the palliasse on that and have the rug beside, to step onto. I'm a handyman. I can knock up shelves and repair cupboards; in time the place will be as comfortable as I can get it. I'm making no complaints, so please don't say anything to her ladyship."

I had no intention of doing so because Mamma would be sure to ask how I knew that the coachman's quarters were inferior, and if I revealed that he had implied as much, Curtis would go. That was the last thing I wanted to happen. I wanted other things. . . .

"Curtis," I said, "drive me to the mews at once. I will inspect your quarters myself."

I knew how and when to make an order sound like an order. Without a word he climbed back onto his box and turned the horses' heads; without hurrying, he headed toward Portman Square and the mews at the back of Number 47; without a word he handed me down, opened the door between those of the stables and carriage house, and revealed a bare staircase running straight up between two narrow walls. Above the stables and carriage accommodation ran the coachman's rooms, but never having visited them in my life, I had no idea what they were like. Even as a child I had kept away from the mews, disliking the smell of horses myself, though Curtis groomed them well and, I guessed, kept their stalls cleaner than many neighbouring ones. Even the bare stairs were well scrubbed, with a deckhand's skill, but they struck a chill into me as I ascended, my Louis heels echoing hollowly on every wooden tread.

When I reached the rooms above, I stood stock-still. I had emerged into one containing no more than a table with a couple of wooden straight-backed chairs, a sink with a cold-water tap and dilapidated wooden drainer, cupboards above already in a partial state of repair. There was a shabby armchair with the stuffing sagging out beneath, a few shelves on which were faded sepia photographs of a man and a woman (his parents, no doubt), and some startling souvenirs from overseas—

primitive wood carvings and things which had an Eastern look about them. Something advised me not to look too closely at those, for everyone knew that all sorts of strange and obscene objects came from the East, and I refused to be embarrassed at this precise moment. Later, I would not be embarrassed at all.

Even then I knew there was to be a "later" between this man and myself, for how long a duration only I would decide. Even as I entered the room which served as a bedroom, more sparsely furnished than the other, I was aware of that. Repelled though I was by the inadequacies, the bare windows and floors, the coldness of the place, and above all, the permeating odour of years of neglect combined with the one filtering through the floorboards, I knew I had found the man who would temporarily replace Pierre—and even the place where he would do so, but only when I chose and in conditions that I chose and for as long as I chose.

"The place needs fumigating!" I exclaimed.

"I have done my best, Miss Clementine."

"I can tell that. Your seaman's best, with plenty of deck scrubbing."

"And disinfecting," he said defensively. "If you had come here when I took over, you wouldn't have been able to walk up them stairs."

"Those stairs," I corrected automatically, and saw a dull flush mount his cheeks.

"You don't have to rub it in, that I don't speak right, Miss Clementine, because one day I will. I'm learning." He nodded toward an orange box which acted as a crate. "I've books in there. Books I've picked up for a few pence second hand, and books on grammar from my Board schooldays that I pinched the day I left—they belonged to the school but I reckoned they wouldn't miss them. Of course, they only taught the basics there—reading, writing, and 'rithmetic. I've picked up books that've taught me more than that, and one of these days they'll take me far and *then* you won't be able to talk down to me."

My goodness, but he was angry! He had a temper, this man. Perhaps he could even be violent, as Pierre had been sometimes. The thought excited me. I liked violence in a man when making love, but outside that I knew how to cope with it, how to hold my own. Woman's wiles could be just as effective, so I used them now, opening my eyes wide in distress and putting my hand on his sleeve in pleading. "Forgive me, Curtis— pray do forgive me. I didn't mean to hurt you—"

He cut in roughly, "I reckon a woman like you could hurt a man real deep. Why did you want to see this place? To patronize me, shame me? D'you think I don't know it's a dump, but that's not my fault, is it? A man has to take the accommodation provided and, by God, it won't be a dump by the time I've finished with it. The bloke who lived here before me must've been a tramp to leave it in such a mess, but perhaps the heart had been knocked out of him, or perhaps he'd never dreamed of anything better.''

The anger was still there, and I couldn't wholly blame him. I was angry myself, but with Mamma for not caring how her servants lived. No wonder old Baxter, coachman here since we moved to Portman Square, had died of influenza at the end of last winter. I guessed that neither of my parents had ever visited the coachman's quarters, because had Papa done so he, at least, would have insisted they be made more habitable, with essential facilities installed and existing ones improved.

My hand was still on Curtis's sleeve, and although angry, he had not shrugged it off, so I increased the pressure very gently and sympathetically as I said, ''I don't see how you can possibly afford to improve these quarters on a coachman's wages, nor why you should. I shall do it myself, and no one but you and I will know. Rest assured I shall not breathe a word to my mamma that you brought me here, or so much as hint that you are dissatisfied—''

''Now, look, Miss Clementine, did I say I was? And I didn't bring you. You ordered me to.''

He was on the defensive again, and perhaps a little afraid of losing his job even though he did regard it merely as a stopgap, but beneath his apprehension I sensed something equally strong—an awareness of me, of my nearness, my perfume, my body. He was much taller than I, and when his eyes lowered they settled on my breasts again, then turned away swiftly, his colour deepening.

I was immediately triumphant, so I let my hand fall away, satisfied.

Turning toward the stairs, I said over my shoulder, ''I am glad you changed your mind about leaving us, though I admit a man of your promise deserves something better than a coachman's job. Meanwhile, I shall take this place in hand. There is a lot to be done. Handyman or not, you cannot replace inadequate plumbing, or buy floor coverings—good, warm floor coverings—nor curtains and essential comforts such as decent furniture and a good feather bed.''

His hand fell on my shoulder, spinning me round.

''Now, you listen to me, miss. One thing I won't do is take gifts from women. Are you trying to buy me?''

''For what purpose?'' I opened my eyes wide in surprised innocence. ''And they are not gifts. When you leave, at least your successor won't be able to accuse *you* of being content to live like a tramp.''

I had scored, and enjoyed it. It was a delicious game, this tempting him and then rebuffing him, and it would continue to be delicious whenever I visited here to see how the improvements, which I would put in hand immediately, were progressing. He would be alternately tantalised and hopeful, then cast down and disappointed, then yet again tempted and provoked, until he was on tenterhooks and the right moment had come—and *I* would choose that.

And how delightfully it would while away these pre-Presentation weeks!

4

I was later in returning home than I would have been had I merely taken tea with Penelope. Curtis drove me there sedately, handed me down with appropriate courtesy, then went on his way back to the mews, his mind awhirl, no doubt.

As I waited on the steps for Hawkins to admit me, I thought I saw Lucinda and that extraordinary doctor walking across the square, but could not be sure because this time the man was decently dressed and therefore not so eye-catching. And they were some distance away, and it was growing dusk.

The first person I saw when I entered the house was Gavin, pulling on his overcoat preparatory to leaving for the theatre.

As soon as Hawkins was out of earshot, he warned, "Don't go near your dear mamma. She is recovering from a scene with your father, and all because he agreed to employ some filthy little urchin whom Lucinda picked up in the park. The brat is to be our new callboy, and what there is to make such a fuss about, goodness only knows. 'If he stinks, disinfect the lad,' I told Bernadette, 'and then he won't stink anymore,' but on she went about *her* views not being considered and *her* wishes not being consulted, and to employ a waif-and-stray without suitable investigation was madness, so I walked out and left them to it. Of course, my dear stepsister may be right. I didn't see the lad because I wasn't around, and Lucinda, I gather, is out." His eye ran over me. "And what have you been up to, niece? You look like a cat that's been at the cream."

"I wish I had. Tea with Penelope Driscoll and her mamma. I'm bored, Gavin. Bored with the life of a debutante before I've even made my official curtsey. I'll be glad when it's all over and I can get back to the theatre."

"Don't tell your mother that. It would ruin all her dreams. She is already visualising a wedding at St. Margaret's, sooner than any other and eclipsing any other." His mouth quirked. "And doesn't such a thing appeal to you? I thought every girl longed to get married—all that bridal

white and so forth. Virgin white, of course. So appropriate for an innocent maiden like you."

Outside, I heard Lucinda's footsteps running down the area steps. She
always came in that way, through the kitchen and up the service stairs,
unless she was returning from the theatre at night with my parents and
her mother, when she and Trudy were allowed to enter with them
through the front door. Lucinda hung around the theatre a lot these
days, school holidays being in progress. Sometimes I thought the girl was
positively stagestruck, but she would grow out of it. She would have to.
It would be domestic service for her, or dressmaking, or millinery or
some-such. Anyway, I wasn't interested in Lucinda, only in what my
dear stepuncle had said. "Virgin white, of course"—so appropriate for
me. There was sarcasm there, and a knowing look along with it, but before I could answer, he had forgotten me. He was listening to Lucinda's
diminishing footsteps and then the distant shutting of the area door.

"So she's back," he murmured, and then to me, "What did you do to
her today?"

"*Do* to her? Lucinda, you mean? I don't know what you are talking
about."

"Then think about it. You upset her, shocked her. I saw her come out
of your room. Leave the girl alone, niece. She's sweet and shy and her
innocence isn't for you to destroy."

"Meaning that task is reserved for you?" I answered smoothly. "And
let me remind you I am not strictly your niece. We are not blood relations." I sidled up to him, smiling, until we stood close together, and he
smiled back, knowing what I was up to.

"You're a minx, Clemmy. And you don't have to thrust out those inviting breasts to make me aware of them. What do you want me to do?
Kiss them? Right here in the hall? I am sure they've been kissed many
times in greater privacy."

Even so, he stooped swiftly and pressed his lips against the rounded
flesh protruding above the neckline of my gown. Then he looked at me,
laughing.

"Not such fun when it's done in a hurry, is it? But you're right—we
are not blood relations and I can't say I'm sorry about that."

"Nor am I," I whispered.

"My God, Clemmy, born in other circumstances you'd be a whore.
You have all the necessary attributes. And don't try to look outraged.
You've been up to something this afternoon that has left you in a state I
am well acquainted with—you want a man to take you to bed. Well, darling, it isn't going to be me. Not here in this house. I know when I've
got a good berth, and I don't intend to jeopardise it."

"Most men of your age have their own establishments."

"Which *I* cannot afford on the salary your revered father pays supporting actors." His smile changed to a scowl. "He seems determined not to give me the chance I deserve. Jealous of the rounds of applause I get every time I come on and go off, I suspect."

"That applause is for your looks, not your talent." I enjoyed administering that jibe. He deserved it for saying I had the makings of a whore. "And I don't need *you* to take me to bed. I met a man today who would be more than willing."

"At your friend Penelope's house? Some dull debutante's brother? Not your cup of tea, my love. You'd find that type very disappointing."

"At my friend Penelope's house, yes, but I doubt if I would find him disappointing. Nor was he some dull debutante's brother, but a man I have heard you declare to be one of the richest, if not *the* richest, in London. A man named Durbridge."

Gavin had already begun to walk to the front door. Now he spun round, stared, and burst out laughing, which was far from the reaction I expected.

"You should be impressed," I snapped. "He *is* rich. He gave Lady Driscoll a thousand pounds for a pet charity, and it seemed no more to him than the scrap of paper it was written on."

"It wouldn't be—I agree with you there. But you say he wanted to go to bed with you? How did you know?"

"I could tell from the way he looked at me. I always can. He couldn't take his eyes off me. Honestly, Gavin, I felt positively stripped. If Penelope and her mother had not been so unobservant, they would have seen it too—though perhaps," I finished thoughtfully, "Lady Driscoll wasn't *entirely* unaware, which would account for her desire to get me out of the way. . . ."

"Durbridge is a past master in the art of visualising a woman in the nude, but what makes you imagine his interest went as far as desire?" Gavin began to laugh again, quietly at first, shoulders heaving, then aloud and helplessly, shaking his head at me. At length he gasped, "My dear sweet niece, I do believe *you* are the innocent one, after all!"

I stamped my foot at him. "It's true, I tell you, true!"

"I have no doubt of it, but don't misinterpret things, Clemmy. Look deeper, or stick to less complicated men. There are plenty around."

"Such as you—slinking off to Babylon night after night?"

"Not every night, my pet. Only when I can afford to. Babylon is an expensive place, though it does cater for all tastes and all pockets. Unfortunately, only the more costly attractions appeal to me."

"Take me there!" I begged. "Oh, Gavin, take me to Babylon just once! I have heard so much about it."

"You shouldn't even know about it, a well-brought-up miss like you. Convent-trained, too! How would the poor dear nuns feel if they imagined any of their pupils visiting one of London's most notorious districts, society's underworld?"

"Don't be stupid—they've never even heard of the place. But it's useless to pretend it doesn't exist, because everyone knows it does. That is why Papa won't let us be driven home anywhere near the Haymarket or St. James's late at night. He doesn't want me to see certain things . . ."

"Or Lucinda or Trudy or even your mother, though she's been long enough in the theatre to know the ways of the world. Nevill is wise there, anyway. I wouldn't want Lucinda's innocence shattered."

I turned away from him impatiently. "You are very concerned about Lucinda's innocence, all of a sudden. Surely you cannot have a soft spot for that gawky creature?"

" 'That gawky creature' is going to be a beauty someday, and not so far off, either."

I spun round, astonished. "You can't mean it! That long, skinny thing—"

"That tall, slender, and graceful thing. She's at the coltish stage now, but just you wait! I admit she lacks the fashionable plump curves and the dimples and the ringlets, nor will she ever have them, but don't underestimate your rival, darling Clementine."

"My rival! The daughter of my mother's dresser is no rival to *me*!"

"Not yet," Gavin murmured, and closed the front door behind him.

Simultaneously, the drawing-room door opened and out came Mamma, dabbing at her eyes, and Papa, looking composed and resolute, ordering her to calm herself or she would fail to give her usual superb performance tonight. I could say this much for Papa—he knew just how to flatter Mamma when necessary, and a reference to her brilliance onstage always worked.

Seeing me, she gave one final dab at her eyes and then swooped, gathering me close.

"Oh, my darling gel, if *only* you had been here to support me! Instead, your father and that dreadful doctor calmly arranged everything, and now we are to be saddled with a criminal child from the Rookeries!"

Papa said firmly, "Nonsense, Bernadette. The lad can't be branded a criminal just because he comes from such a background. No child can choose the circumstances into which it is born. And Dr. Steel is by no means dreadful. I consider him a very fine man."

And so do I, I thought secretly, remembering those splendid thighs.

My mother made a visible effort to pull herself together, murmured something about needing her medicine—"So fortifying when life presents one with such terrible crises!''—but Papa ignored that, merely pointing out that Trudy would be waiting upstairs to help her to get ready for the theatre.

I struggled to free myself from Mamma's all-enveloping embrace, because I disliked being smothered in the folds *and* inhaling the odour of perfume and perspiration. Why couldn't she really be fastidious about her toilet, the way she claimed to be? No wonder Papa no longer shared a bedroom with her.

"My darling gel, come upstairs with me and tell me all about your afternoon. How were Penelope and her dear mamma?''

"Much as usual, though dear Mamma scarcely welcomed me, and no wonder—I arrived when she had a special guest to whom she very plainly did not wish to present me.''

"And *why* not, may I ask?'' The very idea aroused my mother's indignation.

"Because she wanted him exclusively for her daughter. Apparently he is very rich.''

"Aha!'' Mamma laughed in delight as we mounted the stairs, her tears and fury quite forgotten. "And you eclipsed Penelope, of course. You always do. Who was he, dear child, who *was* he?''

"Lord Durbridge. And he donated a thousand pounds to one of Lady Driscoll's pet charities as if it were a mere bagatelle.''

From below, Papa's voice followed us. "He may be rich, but he is also disreputable. He was introduced to me in my dressing room once, but I soon got rid of him. I hope for Penelope's sake that nothing comes of it.''

I smothered secret laughter, well aware that nothing would, and as we reached the top of the stairs and turned the corner, my mother said *sotto voce*, "Take no notice of your dear papa, child, he is a mass of prejudices, very often against all the wrong people. Tell me, are you likely to meet this Lord Durbridge again?''

"That is up to you. One shouldn't appear too eager, should one? I think an invitation to my coming-out ball would be early enough, don't you?''

"Excellent, excellent! My clever gel! I will make sure that is done.''

My mother disappeared into her room, well-pleased, and I went on to my own on the floor above, also well-pleased. The afternoon had turned out much better than expected. Little had I imagined, when Hawkins opened the front door for me on my way out, that the hours ahead would offer any more than tea and gossip with Penelope; instead, they had yielded three attractive men—Magnus Steel, Durbridge, and last but certainly to be first, because he was on the spot and available, Curtis.

Getting to know the unusual doctor would take time. I would have to create opportunities in which to meet, or wait for him to do so. For the time being, that process would have to be conducted slowly and circumspectly, a pleasant dalliance which could be very enjoyable because the cards were already stacked in my favour. His immediate attraction to me vouched for that. I could even afford to wait, and then turn to him when I felt the time was ripe.

As for Durbridge, he was another matter, an unknown quantity which had to be handled carefully. The first step I had planned was, for now, sufficient. Without a shadow of a doubt I felt he was to be very much a part of my future, but not as Curtis would be and not as I intended Magnus Steel should be. My handsome coachman would be, for me, no more than the stopgap he had intended his job to be on the way to better things. He would be an easy and convenient substitute for Pierre, an illicit lover and therefore exciting. He would also be completely under my thumb because he was a servant and therefore in no position to possess or dominate me. I had power over him, the power to summon or reject, to punish or dismiss. On his part he would be grateful, humbly adoring; we would be mistress and slave.

And somehow I knew that strong young body of his would also be eminently satisfying. Thank God for that. I needed another lover badly.

At that point in my thoughts I reached my room, opened the door and stopped dead in my tracks.

Kate was there. Kate the housemaid. She was on her knees in front of my wardrobe, with the long drawer open and my secret book in her hands.

Stunned by shock, I could only stare, then I burst out, *"What are you doing here?* No maid has the right to enter any of the bedrooms after they have been cleaned and tidied for the day, and well you know it."

She looked up at me, quite unconcerned, then nodded toward a bowl of flowers.

"I brought those up for you, Miss Clementine. Picked them myself, I did. There's not much in the garden right now, but I've made the most of them, don't you think?"

Cool as a cucumber, she closed the book and put it back in the drawer, then picked up the scraps of black ribbon and lace between thumb and forefinger, dropping them after it. Then she rose and faced me without a word, eyeing me steadily until I spluttered, "How *dare* you rummage amongst my things!"

"Oh, Miss Clementine, what an accusation! That drawer was gaping wide, and everything so untidy. I thought I'd do you a good turn and put it straight for you."

She could lie without the flicker of an eyelid. I had always suspected that, and never liked her. My mind raced. *Had* I left that drawer unlocked? I must have done, or how else could she have opened it, how else discovered what it held? Lucinda couldn't have told her, because I knew she had gone for a walk with Trudy almost immediately. I knew this because I had seen them from my bedroom window, and anyway, Lucinda rarely talked to Kate because she didn't like her either, and I have to say this for Lucy Grainger—she never betrays a confidence. Maybe she knows that if she did, Trudy would lose her job and they would be out of this household in no time, but whatever the reason, I know I can trust her.

So I had only myself to blame for leaving the key in that lock. I remembered putting the things back, planning to find a safer place as soon as possible, and had only just closed the drawer when Mamma sailed in, announcing the arrival of the fitter who was working on my coming-out wardrobe.

"And do see that she does the job properly, dear gel. Unfortunately I cannot stay to supervise because I am just off with your dear papa to visit Clarkson's, the wig-makers. *So* tiresome!"

But not for me. Mamma's fussing always made fittings unendurable. However, I couldn't deliberately turn the key with her standing there, nor thrust it in my pocket without attracting her attention. ("What have you locked in that drawer, Clementine? Why are you hiding the key?") Maudlin she might sometimes be, but never at that hour of the day, and when she hadn't been at her medicine Mamma could be lynx-eyed.

After the fittings, I had gone off to visit Penelope, quite forgetting about the unlocked drawer.

Now I resorted to anger, which wasn't difficult, because I certainly felt it.

"Pack your bags at once, Kate! You will be dismissed for this. I shall report you to my father immediately."

I turned to the door, blazing with fury and determination.

"I don't think you will, Miss Clementine." She spoke softly, but her tone halted me. "If anyone is going to speak to the master, it'll be me—knowing what I know now *and* what I can show him."

I spun round as she slipped the key into a pocket beneath her apron, and I knew there was no chance of my seizing it because she was twice my size, strong and country-bred, wiry after years in domestic service. Physically I was no match for her. I knew it and she knew it, and both of us knew she was ready to prove it.

I felt suddenly sick. No one had ever made me feel that way before, and no one had ever frightened me before, but Kate did.

I had no choice but to surrender, and she gave me back the key of my wardrobe drawer, but on her terms, which fortunately proved to be nothing excessive—merely promotion from a room shared with Daisy the kitchenmaid to one of her own. I knew it would mean putting Daisy in with Tweeny in that narrow place beneath the stairs, truckle beds end to end, because it wasn't wide enough to admit them side by side, and that neither of them would like it. The place was no more than a narrow passage enclosed as a cupboard, with no room for anything else; clothes placed on the floor by night and on the truckle beds by day, but since they had scarcely any clothes between them, that wouldn't be much of an inconvenience, would it, Kate argued logically.

"After all, Miss Clementine, *I* am parlourmaid here and therefore above a kitchenmaid and entitled to a room to myself. With Daisy out of it I'll be a great deal more comfortable and certainly more contented—if you know what I mean?"

I knew well enough what she meant—that contented people would not be prone to gossip or whisper; that contented people could be trusted.

Kate could make the most subtle implication blatantly obvious.

"The allocation of domestic accommodation is my mother's responsibility, not mine," I began.

"But it's useless for me to ask your dear mamma for a room to myself, miss. I'm sure you know why. She might promise to see about it, but she would forget, now, wouldn't she?"

That was Kate's way of letting me know that she was well aware of what made my mother forgetful, well aware of her weakness.

You nasty little blackmailer, I thought. *How often do you practice this sort of thing?*

And would it continue?

"So you will see about it, won't you, Miss Clemmy? Today, if you don't mind."

"It is too late now. Tomorrow."

"All right. Tomorrow. First thing. I'll remind you when I bring up your morning tea."

She left the room with a secret smile on her face. Sly Kate. Cunning Kate. I hated her then and I hate her now, and I have the uneasy feeling that if I'm not careful I am going to hate her even more in the future.

It's not very nice to know that there's a spy in the house.

Three

Lucinda

5

Despite my resolve to stay away from the deserted stage, I was back there the next night, drawn by a compulsion quite beyond my control. As always, I had sat near the prompt corner during the performance, in between initiating the new callboy and helping him to carry out his duties, showing him where the dressing rooms were situated and how to execute the recognised RAT-a-tat-TAT without any variation, because not only was it the traditional code, but this was the rhythm which echoed most effectively along the stone corridors, so that even before the knock sounded on an actor's door he heard its advance and was alerted.

There was also a traditional way of pronouncing the call, and a routine timing. "Half-an-hour, please! *Half-an-hour, please!*" before curtain-up, followed by the quarter and then five minutes and then overture-and-beginners, and after that the individual summonses for those who made their entrances later, and so round again to "Curtain-up!" preceding the ensuing acts.

"Always use 'Mr.' and 'Miss' before their names—don't forget that, Jerry, because it's important; unless, of course, you are calling Sir Nevill or Lady Boswell, when you address them as such. And always call the gentlemen 'sir' and the ladies 'ma'am.' In classical drama companies this is known as etiquette."

"Ettiwot?"

"Et-ee-ket. In other words, what is right and proper. So you knock on the door like this"—RAT-a-tat-TAT—"and then you call, 'Onstage, please, Mr. Chambers, sir,' or 'Miss Delmont, ma'am,' or in the case of actors who are sharing dressing rooms and due to make their entrances at the same time, 'Onstage, please, gentlemen!' (Or ladies, as the case may be.) Then again, repeat the call and knock twice to make sure they've heard—and if they don't answer immediately, repeat it yet again. Never leave a dressing room without getting an answer, even if you have to thrust your head round it and shout at them—actors have been known to nod off while waiting for their cues. You don't open the doors of the ladies' dressing rooms, of course—"

"An' wot if *they* don't 'ear me? Judging by the din in number twenty at the top o' them stairs, I'd 'ave to fire a bloody gun!''

"Persevere until they do hear, Jerry—and *no* swearing. Remember what Dr. Steel said—mind your language before the ladies.''

"I've 'eard worse from women in the Rookeries. They ain't lidies, o'course, but from the look o' some o' that there lot upstairs, I wouldn't say they were, neither.''

"They are supers, casual players employed for walk-ons. When we are doing a play which has no crowd scenes, those spare dressing rooms at the top of the stairs are empty.''

"An' a good fing, too. Y' could break yer bleedin' neck on 'em!''

I said nothing because he was right. There had been many an accident on the iron circular staircase, a perilous affair which rose from the off-prompt wings to as high as the floats, with a single handrail down the outside and an unprotected drop down the central well. Because of the danger, the topmost dressing rooms were never used except when necessary, and for the most part the dressing rooms on intervening levels, the levels onto which one stepped at intervals en route to the top, were allocated to men because of the risk of ladies tripping over their long skirts or catching fragile heels in the open treads.

These iron stairs were a traditional backstage feature, and I always marvelled at the skill with which stagehands negotiated them to and from the floats or the grid. Although I had climbed up and down them myself, I had continuously been warned about their danger and was therefore wary, remembering the tragic plunge to death of an actor wearing the elaborate costume of a French courtier, who caught a shapely Louis heel in a topmost wrought-iron tread and fell headlong down the central well. Stagehands told other graphic stories about tragedies on backstage spiralling stairs, no doubt embroidering them, but based on truth for all that, but all I said to the newest member of the Boswell Company was, "All the more reason to go carefully, Jerry. We can't have our brand-new callboy twisting his ankle, can we?''

Jerry would shape all right, I reflected as I loitered in the wings after the performance, waiting for my mother to finish helping Lady Boswell change out of her stage costume and remove her makeup, a task which took almost as long these days as did the application of it, after which we would all drive back to the house in Portman Square and Mamma would start ministering to her again once we arrived there. As I waited in the wings, and the cast left the theatre one by one, I thought how wonderful it would be to take my mother away from this servitude, to which I could see no end. So long as Lady Boswell continued to act, she would continue to need Trudy Grainger as her dresser, and no doubt after that she would take it for granted that she would remain as her lady's maid, and I supposed there was a lot to be thankful for in that. At least, so Mamma insisted.

"Think how fortunate we are, Lucinda—a roof over our heads and all found for both of us, plus regular employment for me. We have a great deal to be thankful for."

But I was not satisfied. I would never be satisfied until I could put an end to my mother's life of subservience, of being patronized by the great Bernadette, and frequently, as she grew up, by Clementine too. Although my mother chose to be amused by Clemmy's attitude toward her, I could never be, and I often wondered if Mamma didn't just assume it for my benefit. Pride, I had learned early in life, helped a person to tolerate much, or at least pretend to.

Of one thing I was certain—I would not tolerate charity, or the sense of obligation which accompanied it, longer than absolutely necessary, and there, in the darkened wings, standing behind the flats at the off-prompt downstage entrance, my dreams took flight. Somehow, someday, I would no longer be the daughter of a theatrical dresser, but an actress in my own right, speaking lines above the hiss of naked gas jets, loving the sound of words as they went soaring into that dark outer world peopled by that mysterious entity, the audience—that unpredictable, powerful entity which could make or mar an actor's career, elevating him to stardom with its approval or knocking him to the ground with a whim. One bad performance could do it, Sir Nevill always said, which was why he never gave one. Nor did Irving or Forbes-Robertson or any of the established kings of the London stage—though Irving was wise enough to back up his own talent, which many considered mediocre, with good supporting players. Nevill Boswell, in my opinion, was the greatest of all, not merely because I considered him the finest actor in London, but because his talent was tempered with humility.

"The minute a performer takes success for granted or believes his position to be inviolate, he or she starts the speedy descent into obscurity, a road which is covered more quickly than the long climb to the top."

He, for one, guarded his pinnacle by the only means open to any actor—unending hard work—but Bernadette had not been born to such dedication, and success was, for her, becoming increasingly dependent upon her husband's support, upon the Boswell name, and upon the bolstering quality of rum. Mercifully, despite blurring facial contours and ever-thickening limbs, she possessed that miraculous and wholly inexplicable thing, a stage "presence," which even now could win admirers. To see her from the other side of the footlights was to see another person— majestic, impressive, capable of moving and speaking with lightness and clarity, even though, the minute she stepped offstage, she moved heavily and slurred her words. It was all part of a mysterious alchemy which went to work the moment she became part of that make-believe world, as if only when there was she truly herself—or another person outside herself who was a great deal more likable and by no means pitiable.

But at this moment I had no thought for Bernadette Boswell or even for her husband, though subconsciously he was the greatest influence in my life. It was this influence which compelled me forward now, forgetful of my vow to Gavin Calder that never again would I slip onstage to perform in secret. I could not remember a moment in my life when that strip of apron above the orchestra pit had not called to me, and it did so now. I could see the stage already dressed for the opening scene of *Measure for Measure,* the current production, which, being one of Shakespeare's shortest plays, we were combining with a solo performance by Sir Nevill of some of his greatest dramatic speeches. After the performance, the last job of the stage crew was to reset the opening scene, with props in readiness at the S.M. corner, lighting chart to hand, and cue sheet on the prompt desk, so that all that remained was to lower the tabs and then the safety curtain before the audience was admitted, and the next performance could be off and away.

The stage was faintly illuminated now by a few remaining houselights, for after the auditorium emptied, both the safety curtain and the tabs were taken up again to comply with ventilation bylaws. In the semidarkness the deserted stage looked eerie, and soon not one flickering gas jet would remain as cleaning women finished polishing the brass rails of the orchestra pit or crawled from beneath seats in the auditorium after sweeping up chocolate wrappings and cigar bands, always hoping to find a dropped coin or two, or some trinket from a woman's hand, or even a lost pair of gloves—anything small enough to be concealed, because the management ruled that everything found should always be handed in. I remembered a cleaning woman once thrusting a lady's ermine muff beneath her skirts, and being summoned before the housekeeper, who knew full well that the sudden increase in girth must have some cause other than nature, though she chose to interpret it as such.

"And how many months gone are you, Mrs. Jones? It looks as if your time has almost come, which means you won't be working here much longer, pregnant women not being much use at kneeling jobs. . . ."

And the poor woman, faced with being hauled before the police for theft or the alternative of losing her job, had to choose the lesser of two evils and pretend to be seven months gone.

"In that case," said Chief Char, who had herself stepped up from the ranks and become power drunk on the way, "your time has come to leave, but before you go *I* will take charge of whatever is pretending to be your big belly."

So it had been the police after all, a conviction for theft, and the loss of her job into the bargain. It had been Sir Nevill who bailed out the poor woman and had her reinstated, hearing the story a few days later.

But not a cleaner was in sight now; the front of the house slept. A few dim jets spluttered beyond the pit and at the back of the grand circle, waiting to be extinguished by George on his final rounds. George had long since been entrusted with helping the house manager to check the theatre for the night, but if he should happen to wander by, it would not worry me. George never told tales, and the house manager concentrated his attentions on the bar and box-office takings, leaving George to dowse all lights finally. So George had heard me enact Portia and Desdemona and Ophelia and Rosalind and a hundred more, innacurately sometimes but ardently always, and now I glanced about the set, which was an apartment in the duke's palace in Vienna, and instantly I became Mariana revealing the truth to Angelo.

> . . . now I will unmask!
> This is that face, thou cruel Angelo
> . . . this the body
> that did supply thee at thy garden house.

My voice stumbled. In my mind I was not Mariana, but Clementine, lying with a man in a garden house, supplying him what he wanted. Then I was Mariana again, confessing to Angelo that it was she, in the guise of someone else, who had lain with him in such a place and in such a way. . . .

I trembled and started again. Ophelia now. "There's rosemarry, that's for remembrance; pray, love, remember . . ." As Clementine remembered, and as I would remember the things she had told me, the things she recalled with such intensity? It seemed that every young female character created by Shakespeare knew things or experienced things which had not yet come my way. And why did Ophelia call rosemary "rosemarry"? Did it hold some particular significance . . . marriage . . . a man's bed? "It is the false steward, that stole his master's daughter." Ophelia again; poor, mad Ophelia who seemed to know so much more than I.

All houselights had gone now; the stage was dimly lit from the wings, waiting for the last members of the company to leave. I thrust Mariana aside, and Ophelia aside, and Clementine aside, and became Juliet upon her balcony:

O, Romeo, Romeo! Wherefore art thou, Romeo?
Deny thy father and refuse thy name;
Or, if thou wilt *not,* be but sworn my love,
And I'll no longer be a Capulet.

That was better. No bodies entwined in garden houses here, no false stewards stealing their masters' daughters. My confidence returned, and into the pitch-black auditorium I let flow the liquid words, loving the music of them, forgetful of myself and the bewilderment of being only fourteen and therefore not admitted into the mystical and somehow frightening world of sexual love. My voice went on:

O, be some other name! What's in a name?
That which we call a rose, by any other name
Would smell as sweet. . . .
Romeo, doff thy name,
And for that name, which is *no* part of thee,
Take all myself.

Transfixed, I heard his answer:

I take thee at thy word;
Call me but love, and I'll be new baptised . . .

Romeo's words, but Gavin's voice. Although unable to turn my head to look at him, I gave line for line, stanza for stanza, lifted out of myself into the body of a young woman whose lover had come to claim her.

Thou know'st the mask of night is on my face
Else would a maiden blush bepaint my cheek. . . .
O gentle Romeo, if thou dost love, pronounce it faithfully . . .

Silence. I could not turn to see if he had gone. I could not face a deserted stage where he had stood, nor the shadows from where his voice had come, drawing words out of me and awakening an intensity of feeling such as I had never experienced before. There was more to playing a part than speaking a character's lines; there was the complete subjugation of self until the character's emotions became one's own emotions,

their desires one's own desires. And I desired Gavin Calder as passionately and as achingly as Juliet had desired Romeo.

"My dear little Lucinda, you mustn't be afraid."

His hands were on me, turning me round. I saw his dark head stooping
above mine, the thrust of his prominent cheekbones, the line of jaw and
curve of mouth. I knew he was smiling, although in the gloom he was
scarcely visible, and I knew that the smile was unlike any he had given
me before, that it was not the smile an adult bestowed upon an immature
girl, and the awareness quickened my blood in a way which was weakening and exciting and hot and wholly beautiful.

"Why are you afraid, Lucinda? Do you know how old Juliet was? She
was fourteen, your own age, and ready as you are for a man's bed."

He drew me gently into his arms, holding me close. I laid my head
against him, and my arms slid round him and clung there. I felt the pressure of hip against hip, thigh against thigh, and a surging sweetness
spread from the most responsive part of my body. All this was new in my
life, and I was bewildered and excited by it.

He didn't kiss me. He stroked my hair as he pressed me to him, and I
wanted to get closer and closer until we were no longer two separate
bodies, but one.

"Remember the scene between Juliet's mother and the nurse?" he
whispered. " 'Thou know'st my daughter's of a pretty age.' "

I quoted back, " 'Faith, I can tell her age unto an hour . . . ' "

" 'She's not fourteen.' So you see, little Lucinda, Juliet wasn't even as
old as you. She had more than a fortnight to go before her fourteenth
birthday." He laughed gently. "I can't call you 'little Lucinda' anymore.
For one thing, you are not little, but almost up to my shoulder, which is
tall for a woman, and for another, you are no longer a child." His lips
brushed my hair. "And you feel like a woman, don't you? *I* make you
feel like a woman."

A sound from the wings was a jarring intrusion into a moment of ecstasy. I could not move despite it, but Gavin put me aside.

"Go," he whispered. "I know that footstep."

So did I. It was Nevill Boswell's. He had come through the door leading from the main dressing rooms, his own and that of his wife being just
beyond it.

I scarcely remember leaving the stage. I was still in a trance, my limbs
moving of their own volition. I was thankful for the deep shadows offstage. I saw Sir Nevill's tall figure silhouetted against the gas-lit passage
beyond, and because I did not want the light to fall on my face, I looked
down at my feet as I approached him; better to look guilty for breaking a
rule than to let my flushed cheeks betray more.

"I thought you might be here, Lucinda." As always, he spoke kindly.

"You come down to the stage quite often, I know. Do you want to act so much?"

I nodded, unable to speak, and walked past him, not looking back. I was aware of George approaching and heard Sir Nevill ask if everyone had left the theatre.

"Yes, sir. I've checked every dressing room, so it's lights-out now."

"Better wait a moment, just in case someone should be lingering behind."

"Onstage, sir? That's not likely. I'll turn off them lights in the wings right away."

I wanted to stop him, but knew I must not betray Gavin, hiding out there on the darkened stage. No man liked to be caught in an embarrassing situation. Besides, I wanted no one to learn of our encounter, because to do so would mar it. Those moments were treasured moments, to be shared with no one and frowned on by no one.

So I walked ahead and Sir Nevill came behind me, saying, "Your mother was looking for you, my dear, but I kept her away from the stage. She has no idea that you sometimes go there after the performance, has she? But I have." He had caught up with me now and I was mercifully more composed. "I am not going to scold you for breaking the rules, but if you want to act, you must go about it the right way. That means we must have a talk. When your mother is preparing my wife for bed tonight, come to my study."

He was waiting for me beside the fire and, pulling up a chair for me, sat down opposite.

"So you want to be an actress, and you have wanted that for a long time. I know because I have heard you onstage after many a performance, as I expect Gavin Calder has already told you." When I glanced at him in surprise, he continued, "Don't be alarmed. I shall take neither of you to task, though Gavin should mind his step. He joined you there tonight and remained hiding rather than face me. If he stumbled in the dark and injured himself, it would serve him right, but I intend to say nothing to him for your sake, not his, because I know it would distress you to think that he got into trouble because of you. All I am concerned about is that you should not get into trouble because of him—and I don't mean through breaking any theatre rules."

I could not meet his eyes. For the first time in my life, I felt shy with this man whom I had always regarded as a sort of father figure.

I said lamely, "He hid for my sake. He has already reminded me of the theatre rules and I alone am to blame for breaking them."

"Still, he could have faced the music with you, had he cared to."

I could think of no further answer in Gavin's defence, and hated myself for it, but it comforted me to reflect that he had been so carried away that discretion had been forgotten.

"When I first heard you reciting down there on a deserted stage,"—Sir Nevill changed the subject—"I thought it was probably no more than a whim, a childish delight in aping your seniors. Children copy adult members of their world, and ever since you were born your seniors have spent the predominant part of their lives behind the footlights, with the exception of your mother. The theatre has never got into her blood, but you . . ."

"I suspect it has been in my blood since birth, Sir Nevill. After all, I was born in a dressing room, born to the smell of greasepaint, so perhaps it isn't surprising."

"No," he said reflectively, "perhaps not." Then he added more briskly, "Life in the theatre is hard, Lucinda. Hard and demanding; very often heartbreaking and very often shocking in ways you can know nothing about. You have been protected from all that, but once you make the stage your career, nothing can protect you."

"Shocking in what way? If you mean the gossip and the scandals, I hope I have learned sufficient wisdom to pay no heed."

He smiled a little. "Wisdom—at your age? Fifteen, isn't it?"

"Fourteen and a half," I admitted reluctantly.

The smile deepened. "That is almost the same thing, and I suspect you wish it were, that you are impatient to be sixteen and then seventeen, a woman all too soon."

How could one be anything but impatient? I wondered. Being born in the theatre, one became aware of the facts of life at an early age. Or so I thought.

Sir Nevill said now, "What a pity the young have to grow up. . . ."

"A fine state of things it would be if I remained immature forever, dependent as a child forever!" I didn't add that Lady Boswell would make quite sure I did not. I knew instinctively that she would terminate the Boswell charity, as she regarded it, as soon as I was capable of standing on my own feet, and that I would be thankful to do so.

I clasped my hands earnestly. "Sir Nevill, you can have no idea how greatly I long to act. It is no whim, no idle fancy. For as long as I can remember, I have wanted it, and nothing my mother or you or anyone else can say will make me change my mind. It is an *instinct*. Does that sound presumptuous, pretentious? It doesn't seem so to me. It just seems the natural thing to want to do. The only thing."

"I am glad, yet sorry. I fear your mother will be sorry, too. She has seen enough of life behind the scenes to know the reality of it."

"I have seen it, too. Almost every day of my life."

"But not understood all of it, or perhaps even much of it. Innocence, or ignorance, can be a great protection."

I said earnestly, "I know the life is hard and demanding, if that is what you mean."

"I don't, my dear. I mean other aspects of the theatrical world about which you can know nothing, but you are right in recognising the demanding side of it, the dedication, the need for total commitment, unending work, incessant study. Even the born actor never ceases to learn, from the beginning to the end of his career. Regular hours and a six-day week are not for him. He must be prepared to rehearse every day and to perform every night, with more rehearsing and studying and memorising of lines between matinees and evening shows. Even Sunday is not a day of rest for him. The same goes for actresses."

"But I know all this! I know the need for constant study, to attend rehearsal calls, to be ready to step into other parts when necessary—"

"—and to start from the ground up, as you were telling young Jerry Hawks in all the wisdom of your years." His smile was understanding, but regretful too. "Is there nothing I can do or say to dissuade you, to make you consider some other way of life? Nursing, teaching—women are going in for all sorts of things nowadays, even helping in offices and using typewriting machines."

I answered reluctantly, "I suppose, when I finish at Miss Templeton's, I could qualify as a governess of some kind, but I would hate it. I don't care much for school as it is. I am sorry, but there is only one thing I want to do, one thing I want to be, and I swear that I shall do it and be it."

"And nothing will daunt you. You have the courage of your mother, apparently, plus ambition."

His voice and eyes were somehow sad; then he said, as if reaching a decision, "Very well, I will do what I can, but you must obey me in all things; work when I command, study whatever I set you, take criticism no matter how harsh, accept discouragement, hide resentment when you feel passed over in favour of another actress, devote all your working time to the theatre, forgo pleasures which young women take for granted—"

"Young women like Clementine," I said without thought, "but I will never have their opportunities, their social chances, invitations to this and that. I will never move in their world. Even at Miss Templeton's I don't really 'belong.' Oh, don't imagine I am ungrateful for being sent there! It is just that I feel more at home in the theatre and more at ease with theatrical people."

"And I would have you know theatrical people less intimately. That is what I was referring to earlier. There is a side to many of them which you have not yet glimpsed, and I would prefer you not to."

"If you mean illicit love affairs, I could hardly miss them."

"They are only part of it. I have never really wanted Clementine to become an actress because there are things, experiences, certain kinds of knowledge I would wish to protect her from. We have done our best in that way, her mother and I. Similarly, your mother has done her best to protect you. I have tried to help Trudy there."

"By never letting us walk through the streets of London alone at night, I know. You have shielded both of us from unpleasantness and even danger that way."

"I would shield you from more, if I could, just as Bernadette and I shielded Clementine when choosing that select convent school."

My eyes fell, hiding the pity he must otherwise have seen. Thank God he had no idea of how little protection that convent school had afforded. Or would a girl like Clemmy have known such experiences whatever school she went to? I fancied so, for I knew now that in whatever circumstances life had placed her, such experiences would have sought her out, or she would have sought them.

Sir Nevill was saying, "You will finish your course at Miss Templeton's Academy, dislike it as you may. I can understand that much of it must seem a waste of time to you, and much may well be, but I do know that her teaching of French and elocution and deportment are good, and you will find such things great assets in your career as an actress."

My career as an actress! He had said it—*he*, the great Sir Nevill Boswell. Uttered by him, in his wonderful voice, the words came to life and brought me to life also. I leapt to my feet and flung my arms about his neck, thanking him passionately, swearing that I would work day and night to please him, and that one day he would be proud of me. "So proud!" I cried. "So very, *very* proud! You have always been kind and good to me, though I cannot imagine why, but I do want you to know how grateful I am."

He patted my hair with a fatherly hand and put me aside.

"I want no gratitude from you. As for being proud of you, I know I shall be that."

I nodded eagerly. "Indeed you will! One day you are going to say, '*There* is Lucinda Grainger—*I* made her the actress she is!' and I shall say, 'There is the great Sir Nevill Boswell—I owe it all to *him*!' Oh, please, please, when do we begin?"

"Very soon. I shall be auditioning for *The Bells*. You can sit beside me in the stalls and learn precisely what qualities I seek in a performer. That will be lesson number one."

"So you are going to rival Sir Henry again! That is one of his most successful plays."

"No, my dear, I am entering into no competition with Irving. I intend to send the play out on tour, the first Boswell Company ever to visit the provinces."

The door clicked open before he had finished. The great Bernadette stood there, a startling figure in a voluminous brocaded dressing gown with rampant gold dragons embroidered on peacock-blue satin and with curl papers sprouting from beneath swathed yellow tulle tied in an immense bow on top of her head, her face richly creamed.

"Are you not coming to bed, dear Nevill? I have been waiting."

He answered mildly, "I would have looked in to say goodnight, my dear."

Lady Boswell frowned. This reminder, in front of someone else, that he preferred his own bedroom and was content to be no more than a brief caller at hers, found little favour in her eyes. She groped for acid comment, and found it.

"And what is all this about sending the Boswell Company on tour, pray? *I* have heard nothing of it."

"I said 'the first Boswell Company,' not '*the* Boswell Company.' You and I and supporting leads will remain in London, but not others. For that you should be grateful. You have always wanted your stepbrother to be given greater opportunities, bigger roles. Now he will have them. I will tell him myself tomorrow morning."

"And when did you decide this?" she demanded, surprised and pleased.

"Tonight, my dear. After the performance. A sudden decision, but a good one, I think."

I could not look at him. I was stunned, hurt. I knew precisely when and why he had come to that decision, and in the midst of my happiness I felt suddenly bereft. He was sending Gavin Calder out of my life as quickly and effectively as possible.

And in that he succeeded. Despatching the Boswell Touring Company on the road removed Gavin not only from the theatre, but from Portman Square and therefore from all possible contact with me, but the rapture of that moment on the darkened stage was mine forever. I loved Gavin Calder with all the passionate ardour of extreme youth, and knew that I always would.

6

We had only one meeting before he left. Throughout those whirlwind weeks of excitement and preparation for his first provincial tour, Gavin scarcely had time for anything else.

I understood, of course. He had waited so long for a chance to play leads, and he had so much to do, so many new parts to learn. It had been decided to tour a repertoire of what had become known as the Boswell Classics, rather than *The Bells* alone, but this meant almost nonstop rehearsals with snatched intervals of sleep between costume fittings and lighting and set rehearsals, with which lead players had to familiarise themselves. Understudies could stand in when the stage director and his crew of technicians charted and timed the scenic changes and lighting effects, but the nearer to the opening of a show, the more essential it was for acting members of a cast to attend every call. There was more to putting a show on the road than actors learning their lines; there were all the backstage mechanics to be perfected as well, and it was essential for the cast to know precisely where to be onstage when limelights were charted to focus on particular spots.

But the one brief encounter Gavin and I had before the first train call took him from Kings Cross to the northeast was better than nothing, even though I found it humiliating to stand before him wearing the detestable straw boater with its navy-blue ribbon band and the badge of Miss Templeton's Academy for Young Ladies on the front, and the severe navy serge skirt which scarcely covered the ankles of my flat-heeled lace-up boots, and the plain white blouse with leg-o'-mutton sleeves and navy tie-bow which that worthy woman deemed ladylike and refined and which, to me, were just plain frumpy. I was aware that my thin wrists dangled beyond cuffs which could be let down no farther, and that my skirt had been lengthened with a false hem (after two previous alterations) to keep pace with my growth.

It was absurd for a girl of fourteen and a half to be so tall, and I didn't blame my school companions for calling me Beanpole. I stood a good head above any of them and, in consequence, felt gauche and self-conscious in a school uniform. I would race upstairs on returning home and scramble out of the hideous garments as fast as I could, but on the day I came face to face with Gavin, I had no time.

We met on the doorstep, he going out and I coming in. His eyes ran over me, and that slow, endearing smile which made me melt inside spread across his fascinating mouth. I could never find the correct word to describe his mouth. Years later I realised that "sensuous" was the right one, but at fourteen and a half I lacked Clementine's knowledge and therefore "sensuality" was not in my vocabulary. All I knew was that I longed to feel his mouth on mine and that his lips would be soft and warm and gentle, because that was what I imagined a kiss must be like between a man and a woman.

I knew of no other way of kissing than the pressure of mouth against mouth, though somehow Clementine had made me feel that she and Pierre had kissed in a strange and different way. Even in varied ways. But I was not thinking of Clementine now. I rarely thought of her these days because I rarely saw her; her life was too taken up with preparing for her first Season, and her Presentation, and then her coming-out ball, to spare any time for a gangling and inexperienced schoolgirl with whom she now seemed to have little in common. The confidential talks and the private dress parades in her room were gone and forgotten, perhaps because she felt she had impressed me sufficiently, or because I was merely the daughter of her mother's dresser who slept abovestairs and lived below. The social gap between us was as strong as ever and possibly stronger, since she no longer bridged it at all.

But none of this worried me. I was happier out of range of Clementine's mocking tongue. Had she seen me now, standing self-consciously before her mother's stepbrother with adoration plainly writ upon my face, even though my eyes were downcast, she would have mocked even more. I was all too painfully aware that when it came to hiding my feelings I could not act at all.

"Lucinda."

No other man could have made my name sound like that; none could have uttered it so significantly. He put a hand beneath my chin and lifted it, forcing me to look at him.

"What so shy all of a sudden? Only a child is shy, and you are no longer that." His hand ran down from my chin to my throat, from my throat to my shoulder, from my shoulder to my breast. "*That* gives you away, my lovely. A young woman parading in schoolgirl clothes—how absurd and how sweet."

No man had ever touched my breast before. I felt my nipple rise and harden, and he felt it too beneath the thin cotton of my blouse. The pressure of his hand increased, then fell away.

"Wait until I come back," he whispered, and was about to go when another thought struck him. "About that night—I remained onstage solely to protect you. You realise that, of course?"

When I nodded, saying nothing, he went on, "It would have made everything much worse for you had I been seen. It would have appeared as if we had a clandestine meeting, a prearranged meeting away from every-one, and of course it was nothing of the kind."

I nodded again, still unable to look at him.

"Nevill would have been very angry in that event, and I didn't want to involve you in any trouble. As it was, he sounded neither angry nor sur-prised, because he knows of your secret performances and is very fond of you. And now he is coaching you, which would certainly not have hap-pened had I failed to keep off the scene, so you see, I did act for the best, didn't I?"

Yet again I nodded.

"But be careful of Bernadette, my dear. My stepsister can be a very jealous woman. She hates her husband to take an interest in any other ac-tress, even a juvenile and a beginner. She was outraged when Nevill gave Lily Langtry a start because the Prince of Wales was trying to get her launched onto the stage, being anxious to get her off his hands. The woman had no talent, but she did have beauty, so nothing would per-suade dear Bernadette that her husband's motivation was solely diplo-matic. She should be thankful for that diplomacy now, because as a result of it our luscious Clemmy is being presented at Court. But our proud Bernadette cannot see beyond the end of her nose, which may or may not be a good thing in your case."

"I don't know what you mean."

Again he touched my cheek. "You don't have to, Lucinda. Not yet, anyway. So forget it, but don't forget me." His voice sank to a whisper, and the hand slid down and covered my breast again. "And remember what I said—wait until I come back."

Then he was gone, running lightly down the steps and into a waiting cab. I was vaguely aware that he carried a gladstone bag. I stumbled across the doorstep and upstairs to my room, mercifully meeting no one. Had my door possessed a key, I would have locked it, because more than anything in the world I wanted to be alone. I could still feel the pressure of Gavin's hand on my breast, and I wanted to go on feeling it and re-membering it, because the surging sweetness in my body demanded that I should.

I flung the hateful hat across the room, tore off the blouse and skirt and flung them after it. I stood before my mirror in camisole and pet-ticoat, but the glass was too small to reflect my body—a square fourteen by fourteen inches in which I could see no more than my face, so I stud-ied that instead, loosening my tied-back hair until it fell about my shoul-ders. I felt its softness on my bare skin, and the excitement Gavin had awakened in me intensified. I wanted to feel his hands there too, with no detestable cotton blouse or petticoat or anything else between us.

I didn't hear my door open, nor was I aware of my mother's presence until she said behind me, "What is the matter, Lucinda? Why are you studying yourself like that?"

I jerked round, my cheeks flaming.

"I thought I was alone! Can't I be alone in my own room?"

"Lucinda!"

Shame overcame me. I could not look at her.

"Something *is* wrong," she said.

"No . . . no . . . it's just that . . . well, I *hate* being a schoolgirl, or pretending to be one, because I am nothing of the kind. I am a woman, Mamma, and want to be treated like one and look like one and behave like one."

"Oh, my darling, don't grow up too soon."

"I *am* grown-up. You told me yourself, six months ago, why a physical change takes place in a girl, and you know it has already happened to me. So that means I am a woman, doesn't it? I could have babies already if I wanted to."

She stooped and picked up my school uniform, pulled back the curtain which hid my clothes rail, took down a frock at random, and said with a kind of false brightness, "Well, I certainly hope you won't, my love. As for these school garments, you won't be wearing them that much longer, so don't fling them across the room; just tolerate them for now. Why not wear this blue cotton for tea this afternoon? I like you in it. After that, we should have time for a walk in the park. Bernadette is upset over her stepbrother's departure and is resting. She declares she wants no one near her, and you know what that means. It is silly of her to behave that way when she has been badgering her husband, for goodness knows how long, to give that young man better opportunities in the theatre. Well, he has got them now, and I can't say I am sorry to see him go."

"The house won't be the same without him," I mumbled beneath the smothering folds of the blue dress.

"That is what I mean," she said as my head emerged.

"You have never been fair to Gavin," I protested.

This time she made no answer. She looked at me for a long moment, then said, "I hope you feel like a walk in the park, Lucinda?"

"No, Mamma, I don't."

"You never seem to enjoy it nowadays. Not since the day we met Dr. Steel, which is strange, since you have become such friends with both him and his sister."

"It isn't that."

"Then what?"

How could I tell her that I never ventured into Hyde Park without recalling Durbridge and the feeling of threat he seemed to convey? It was nonsensical, and I knew it, because we had never met the man again. Even so, I said, "Let's go to Regent's Park instead."

"But it is farther away."

"Very little. We could walk up Baker Street and across Marylebone Road and in through York Gate. Regent's Park is never so crowded as Hyde Park, because it gets fewer tourists. Nicer, I think."

"Well, just this once, but the longer walk will mean that we have less time to spend there."

I didn't mind that. Regent's Park was not associated in my mind with anyone sinister.

The Savoy was a natural choice for Clementine's coming-out ball, for apart from its traditional associations with the greatest names in the theatre, from Sir Henry Irving to Dame Nellie Melba, it was unique in being lit by electricity throughout, with a continuous supply during all hours of the day and night, the current obtained from a large installation in the basement, so that no outside source was relied on. The snob appeal of this influenced Lady Boswell as greatly as the snob appeal of the royal names which patronized the place, particularly the Prince of Wales and the Duc d'Orleans, claimant to the throne of France, who maintained a permanent suite there.

"And Ritz stages such magnificent settings for society functions! When the Duc d'Orleans' daughter, Princess Hélène, married the Duke of Aosta, he transformed a vast area of basement rooms by widening the windows and having new doors installed, linking them into one vast new suite and turning the whole thing into a bower of flowers and ferns and palm trees, with blocks of ice concealed within them, and Escoffier served a banquet which enchanted all the Bourbons and the Hapsburgs and members of the House of Savoy. M'sieur le Duc was quite *overwhelmed*!" She still gave this exiled member of the French royal house his proper title, instead of referring to him as the Comte de Paris, as he was now more popularly known.

But it was true that the Savoy's general manager, Ritz, whom many people expected to have his own hotel one day, and very likely named after him, was a genius when it came to staging glamorous events, and the great Bernadette knew exactly how Clementine's ball should be planned.

"Nothing cheaply sensational—not that Ritz himself could ever produce such a thing—but all London will expect something theatrical, and for that reason my darling's coming-out ball must not eclipse the rest of this year's debutantes merely by theatricality. Oh, dear me, no—it must be the most dignified, the most restrained, and the most beautiful of the

Season, and I know exactly what the theme must be. Purity. Virginity. Innocence. She will wear her white Presentation gown, of course, but white camellias will replace the Prince of Wales feathers in her hair, and there must be banks of white flowers everywhere. She will stand against massed white roses to receive the guests—what a picture she will make—and every man will see her as the epitome of the pure, unsullied bride.''

She was confident of a brilliant match for Clementine, and when I saw the presentation gown, I felt Lady Boswell's confidence to be justified. I already knew that more than half of London's most eligible bachelors had been invited to attend and that the guest list sparkled with titles. A social secretary, Ethel Tait, had been employed to organise the whole thing, and sometimes this snobbish creature, who liked nothing more than to boast about the titled families who had employed her and the brilliant social successes she had achieved for them, would condescend to take tea with my mother and myself in the senior-staff sitting room, but only in the absence of the cook and the butler. Rather than sit down with domestics, she would icily carry a cup of tea to her room and shut the door. My mother and I suspected that the haughty creature had anticipated being accepted into the family instead of eating apart from them, and for this reason she scorned "the *nouveau riche* and social climbers from lesser circles," by which she meant theatrical circles, of course.

But the Boswells paid well, so she remained, and without a doubt she earned every penny, not only in endless planning and correspondence and organisation, but by the most discreet espionage. Somehow she learned the most guarded secrets concerning the coming-out balls of other debutantes, and not only was every detail relayed in advance to Lady Boswell, but unfailingly proved to be right. Such events were usually held in the homes of debutantes when their families had ballrooms sufficiently large, but the rest had to compete for the most fashionable and expensive venues, unless they were able to persuade some high-ranking society matron (preferably a peeress) to officially sponsor a coming-out ball in her home under the guise of hospitality (which, everyone knew, had been paid for under the counter). It was part of Miss Tait's function to learn where and when these events were being held, the names of invited guests, and the number and names of acceptances. Without such information one ran the risk of being outshone on all counts by a rival.

No one asked Ethel Tait how she came by her information; her methods of espionage were strictly a trade secret, and only the results mattered. "I pride myself that no coming-out ball arranged by me has ever suffered in comparison with another, nor endured the indignity of being eclipsed, as an eminent earl and his wife—who shall be nameless—were once eclipsed by a lesser title. Have I told you that tragic story, Miss Grainger?" (Ethel Tait always emphasized the personal pronoun when addressing my mother, subtly stressing the disgrace of her unmarried motherhood.) "Somehow this mere baronet learned that the earl's daughter was to have her coming-out ball at the Hotel Cecil, *and* in which ballroom, whereupon he promptly booked the largest one in the same hotel, for the same night, and swept the society board clean. Of course, only a member of the *nouveau riche,* so deplored by the dear queen, could behave in such an ill-bred fashion."

Behind the story there seemed to lurk a hint that the ballroom of the Savoy was an equally presumptuous choice for a family whose title was not inherited, but only conferred. I saw my mother's eyes spark angrily at that, and I shared her reaction. Any slur on Nevill Boswell challenged our loyalty, but since only a few weeks of Miss Tait's company had to be endured, we kept silent and, by mutual consent, avoided her as much as possible.

This was not always easy. She was a tenacious creature, and since my mother and I were the only two members of the household, apart from her employers, whom she deemed even remotely worthy of her conversation, we had to tolerate it. At moments this was not wholly unendurable, because from it we learned a lot—I particularly, since I was caught up in the excitement of the whole affair. Clementine's coming-out ball was, to me, pure magic, with all the enchantment of a fairy tale in which I could take no part. I was a breathless onlooker. I knew that no fewer than two hundred guests had been invited and that Miss Tait had drawn up the guest list herself ("I know precisely who should receive invitations and who should not. . . .") and apparently it was of no matter that Lady Boswell was unacquainted with all two hundred, or that certain names put forward by her were discreetly dropped. ("The hallmark of social success is having only the *right* people on the list of acceptances. . . .") So the wrong people were carefully omitted, which seemed to include all theatricals except those with titles.

"You must be very envious of dear Miss Clementine," Ethel Tait said to me more than once.

Envious? Was I envious? If wishing I could go to the ball signified envy, then she was right, but because I knew it was impossible, I wasted no time in futile regret. In any case, I enjoyed all the attendant excitement and listened avidly to the ever-growing guest list.

"Seventy-five percent acceptances already!" the woman announced proudly one day. "What *would* poor Lady Boswell have done without me?"

When Miss Tait entered a room, I could tell, almost at a glance, whether triumph or disappointment accompanied her, though she could shake off disappointment with a shrug and a contemptuous comment. "*They* won't be missed!" or "*They* were scarcely worth inviting anyway. . . ." It became automatic for me to glance at her expectantly when she appeared, waiting to hear of the latest social catch. I did so one afternoon shortly after my fifteenth birthday, when Mamma and I were sitting down for tea with Mr. Hawkins and Mrs. Wilson, and my expectance was doubled because I knew that only something important would bring the haughty Miss Tait down to the staff sitting room at such a moment. Certainly she had not come to partake of tea with the butler and the cook.

"I thought you would be here, miss—I have something for you." With the patronage which was always reflected in her voice, she dropped an envelope onto the table beside me. "With Sir Nevill's compliments."

It was a thick gilt-edged envelope addressed to me in Sir Nevill's hand.

"I bring it only on his insistence," she added before sailing majestically out of the room.

I sat there staring at the envelope, recognising it but not daring to believe in it. It was one of the envelopes that matched the invitations to the ball, but it could not possibly contain such a thing for me.

"Well," said Mrs. Wilson eagerly, "aren't you going to open it, love? It looks to me like one of them gilt-edged envelopes *she*'s been addressing."

I scarcely remember opening it. I only remember the gilt-edged card and the accompanying note and the slip of paper which fluttered to the floor, and my mother stooping to pick it up before Cook could do so and placing it, folded, in my lap. I didn't even glance at it until I had read the note: *"Clementine's ball won't be complete without you, my dear, so buy yourself something pretty to wear as a present from me."*

I have that dress still and will never part with it, despite all that happened later. I keep it hanging in my wardrobe as my one remaining link with innocence, with days which held neither suspicion nor shock nor terror, nor knowledge of things undreamed of.

"I wish you were coming too, Mamma."

She smiled. "Lady Boswell's dresser could never be socially accepted."

"You say that without bitterness, but if that is their attitude, I don't want to go."

"It is Bernadette's attitude, not Sir Nevill's. In leaving me out of the invitation, he is being tactful. And of course you must go. It is your first ball and therefore important in your life."

"There may be others someday."

"But not this one. I want you to go and I am sure Sir Nevill would be hurt if you did not. You owe it to him to appear in the gown he has bought you.''

We were alone in her room, the room in which she slept by night and we used as a sitting room by day. I was standing in front of the faded cheval mirror, and I turned round slowly, watching the swirl of *ceil*-blue damask and lace about my feet. Never had I dreamed of owning such a gown as this. Brocaded onto the delicate blue ground was a design of flower petals in palest pink; and the low neck was festooned with lace garlanded with pearls. The damask skirt also had similar garlands of pearls across the front and was gored in parasol shape, finished with a deep flounce of embroidered lace below a narrow ruching of tulle, and the nipped-in, pointed waist suggested the hourglass figure which was speedily becoming fashionable.

"No need to lace *you*," said my mother proudly. "You have a good figure, Lucinda."

"Oh, no, Mamma. I am long and skinny and not a bit like Clementine."

"You are tall and slender and not a bit like Clementine," she corrected. "To me, you are lovelier."

I told her she was prejudiced, and I believed it because I knew full well that I could never compete with Clemmy's delectable prettiness. I envied her rounded curves, her pink-and-white skin, her dimples, her chestnut curls, her pouting mouth which was as near to the fashionable cupid's bow as nature had ever bestowed on any female. I envied the bloom about her which, since her return from France, reminded me of a peach. Luscious, Gavin had called her, which showed that he too was aware of her beauty.

No man would ever think of me in such a way, with my pale skin and long straight hair, my narrow hips and thin arms. Slender, Mamma called them, but that was because she could see no fault in me. My too-wide mouth could never be remotely compared with a cupid's bow; its only virtue was to display teeth which were mercifully even and very white, so that when I smiled my mouth looked at its best, but otherwise I could see little to commend me physically. I acknowledged that my short straight nose might have been worse; in fact, my mother's similar nose looked decidedly pretty, but in my opinion I could not compare with my mother any more than I could compare with Clementine, whose entrancing retroussé nose made mine look very ordinary. Rounded cheeks, dimples, curls, and tip-tilted noses were particularly admired in this day and age, especially when accompanied by a curvaceous body, but since I had none of these desirable features, it was stupid to waste time envying those who had.

Studying myself now, I could not help wishing that Gavin could see me. The gown made me feel magically different, almost beautiful. As my mother unhooked me, I found myself looking forward to the ball, because surely he would be there. He was back in London after months of successful touring, and his new status of leading actor had enabled him to set up his own establishment in one of these new blocks of flats on the Chelsea Embankment. I had been bitterly disappointed when he did not return to Portman Square, but, as my mother pointed out, it was natural for a man to have a place of his own.

"Not even Gavin Calder could expect to live on his brother-in-law forever," she added, stirring me to indignation. I could never understand my mother's thinly veiled criticism of Gavin and, as always, accused her of being unfair to him, to which, as always, she made no reply. Sometimes I even wondered if she knew that I had fallen in love with him and, because of her own experience, was afraid I might be hurt and therefore wanted to discourage any possible development. Poor Mamma. I could understand her anxiety, but surely she must know that I needed no protection from such a man as he.

I carried the treasured gown back to my room, wrapped in the protective holland cover provided by the modiste, and placed it reverently on my clothes rail, pushing my homemade garments as far away from it as possible. This was the first absolutely new gown I had ever had; everything else had been made from remnants, unpicked from clothes passed on by Bernadette or Clementine. Clemmy's would no longer fit me—I had outgrown her by a couple of inches already—but Mamma's ingenuity renovated them into wearable items such as blouses or chemises or jackets. As always, she kept me as well dressed as herself; no one would have suspected that she was no more than a theatrical dresser.

That thought reminded me of her claim that her occupation made her socially unacceptable, and my resentment stirred again. I was proud of my mother; proud of her elegance and dignity; proud of everything about her. Memory went winging back to that moment in childhood when I had heard Lady Boswell pointing out that despite having grown up together and gone to school together, they were no longer socially equal, and the recollection made me turn my back on the beautiful new gown which had cost more money than I had ever dreamed a gown could cost. Now I hated myself for accepting it and thought how much better spent the money would have been had I insisted on using Sir Nevill's cheque to buy new daywear for both of us. But Mamma had insisted, and Mamma had won.

"Sir Nevill intended it to be spent on you and he indicated in what way. It would be ungracious to decline such a gift and ill-mannered to refuse to attend the ball." She was right, of course. She was always right. Except where Gavin was concerned.

Dropping the curtain which covered my hanging rail, I turned moodily to the window. Of course I loved the gown and of course I was longing to go to the ball, but my desire to get my mother away from her present way of life was ever increasing. Sometimes I would be highly optimistic, sure that I would be a successful actress the moment I set foot on the professional stage, an overnight sensation, the toast of London, but at other times, such as now, optimism dwindled to despondency. I had yet to make my debut even in the smallest role, and common sense told me that Sir Nevill would not cast me as anything more important than an understudy or small-part player for a long time to come. He was an exacting tutor, a hard taskmaster, extracting the maximum in hard work and study, generous in praise when deserving but very much the reverse when not. So what hope had I of rescuing my mother from her menial existence?

I went on staring out of the window until something far below distracted me. From this height I had a good view of the square, though figures were naturally dwarfed. Being situated at the front, I could see over the heads of the trees to the roof of the Steels' house, but at this moment my glance focused on 'the Boswells' carriage drawing up at our own front door. I saw Curtis climb down from the box, lower the carriage steps, and then help Clementine to descend. There was nothing unusual about that, but surely there was something unusual in the way he took both her hands instead of only one, and surely it was unusual for a coachman to retain his hold of a lady passenger—and for the lady to permit it? It seemed to me that she paused for a moment, saying something, but from this height I could see only the top of her elegant hat, so my impression that she was looking up at him in an intimate sort of way might well be wrong.

The next minute she was turning toward the house, but instead of climbing back onto his box, Curtis remained where he was, staring after her. Then she was lost from my view, cut off by the projection of the first-floor balcony, but when he doffed his cockaded hat in the direction of the front steps, I knew she must have turned to look back at him.

A moment later he sprang jauntily onto his coachman's seat, gathering up the reins in a way which suggested he was very pleased about something, and I was turning from my window, vaguely disturbed.

Going downstairs, I told myself that I had imagined the incident, or that I had read into it something totally fanciful. I could not believe that even Clementine would encourage the attentions of a manservant. Her attitude to the domestic staff was always one of condescension, because she believed that was the way to treat them. Nor could I believe she would be so indiscreet as to look with favour on a handsome young coachman, in full view of her parents' house. Indiscretion at a convent school on the other side of the Channel was one thing, but indiscretion at home was quite another, even for Clemmy. Besides, her mind was occupied with her own social whirl these days. When we met, which was only in passing, she seemed to have departed to another planet and to be scarcely aware of the likes of me on this one. So of course I had imagined the whole thing.

But when I came face to face with her on the drawing-room landing and was about to step aside to let her pass, she paused and flung out her arms to me.

"Well, if it isn't darling little Lucy—though I can't call you 'little' anymore, can I? My dear, how tall you are! I hope you don't continue to grow at such a pace; excessive height is *so* unbecoming to a woman, I always think. A disadvantage, too, because men don't like it, and who can blame them? Propelling a tall gangling female around a ballroom floor must be very unappealing. But how are you these days, Lucinda-bastard?" Her hand flew to her mouth. "Oh, dear—you don't like being called that, do you, but it is so long since we saw each other that I quite forgot. Forgive me."

I was momentarily held in a perfumed embrace before she prattled on, "I'm afraid I have been neglecting you these past months, but with all the excitement of the Presentation, and the whirl of the Season, and the dressings and undressings . . ." She broke off, giggling. "Undressings for fittings, I mean, of course. One has to have a constantly replenished wardrobe for one's Season; one cannot appear twice in the same ball gown, or twice in anything for any occasion, for that matter. But why are we lingering here? Come up to my room for one of our gossips; it is ages since we had one."

She was going before me to the floor above, chattering as she went, confident that I would obey, but I wanted no gossip or any of her chatter.

"I'm sorry," I called after her, "but I have lines to study."

She halted and looked back. "Lines for what?"

"Merely for study, as I said."

"What are you studying?"

"Drama. Acting. Your papa is tutoring me."

"Is he, indeed? And for how long has this been going on?"

"Ever since Gavin went on tour—"

"Mr. Calder, to you," she interrupted.

"No. We have been Gavin and Lucinda to each other for a long time."

I should have bitten back the words, but her patronage had stung me. I watched her descend the stairs, her eyes on me all the time, and when she reached the bottom tread she remained there, still looking at me.

"And how long has *that* been going on?"

"Nothing has been 'going on.' Gavin has always been kind and friendly toward me. Why shouldn't he be?"

"Because *your* mother is *my* mother's dresser."

"Neither Gavin nor your father share your attitude."

"Gavin responds to any pretty face, and I'm afraid my dear papa is
overindulgent toward you and poor Trudy. He feels sorry for both of
you, and particularly for her, I suppose. He thinks she's a 'valiant little
woman,' whereas in actual fact she is a lucky one. Few women in her situation would have been taken into a household like ours, except in the
most menial position, but Trudy is treated almost like a family friend."

"She is a family friend. She grew up with your mother, went to school
with her, mixed in the same circle . . ." That wasn't strictly true; the
family of a Queen's Counsel and the family of a nonconformist minister
never moved in the same social circle, but I rushed on, "In fact, our two
mothers were such close friends that Mamma was a bridesmaid at your
parents' wedding. In the circumstances, I consider it both natural and
right that she should be treated as a friend in their household, but I shall
certainly take her away from it as soon as I am successful."

"Successful in what way?"

"As an actress."

"And is that what my dear papa is coaching you for?"

"What else?"

"And a very promising actress she is," said Sir Nevill, close by.

He was standing within the open drawing-room door.

"I heard your voices. Clementine, my dear, you look flushed. Have
you been hurrying, or are you angry? Not with Lucinda, I trust. As she
has just pointed out, her mother was Bernadette's lifelong friend and I
hope will always be. That is also my desire for you two. And now, Lucinda, I will hear your Rosalind—Act III, Scene 2."

He held the drawing-room door open for me. I didn't look at Clementine as I walked into the room, but all my despondency and all my resentment had vanished. I launched into *As You Like It* with such zest that I
was word perfect, movement and timing perfect, emotion and gesture
perfect. I was Rosalind in the Forest of Arden, Rosalind enchanted by
Orlando's verses, Rosalind flirting with him, teasing him, wooing him. I
was Rosalind in love. And when, at the end of it, Sir Nevill said, "Well
done, my dear," I knew he meant it.

There was a tap on my door. It was Clementine. I stared, because never before had she come up here. The attics were as far outside her world
as were the regions belowstairs.

She smiled endearingly. "I came to apologise."

Apologise! Clementine *apologise?* This, too, was unprecedented.

She laughed. "Don't look so surprised. I mean it. Papa did right to remind me of our family friendship, and I share his hope that it will last forever between you and me. That is why I am going to ask him to let you be my understudy."

I wanted to declare that I would be no one's understudy, least of all hers, but contented myself by saying, "So you do intend to have a stage career after all?"

"After all? What other future did you see for me?"

"Well, after being presented at Court and becoming a fashionable debutante, the logical outcome would be a successful marriage."

"Oh, that." She shrugged. "I doubt if I have a taste for marriage. It is too restricting. Of course, if I had an accommodating husband, it might be different."

"A husband who wouldn't object to your being an actress, you mean?"

Her eyelids lowered, her mouth quivered as if to check secret laughter. "Something like that."

Nothing like that, I thought. *You want a husband you can cuckold.*

She glanced about the room. "What a poky place! I had no idea you were so poorly accommodated. I shall see that you get a better room than this."

"Please don't. We are happy up here, my mother and I."

"Quietly tucked away from the household," she murmured.

"We don't mind that. In fact, we like it. It is almost like having an apartment of our own."

"Where you can discuss the other inmates of the house in private, unlikely to be overheard? Your mother's room is across the landing, I take it."

I nodded, ignoring her first words. "That room is our sitting room by day."

"I am sure that if I asked Papa, he would give both of you better quarters."

"Please don't. As I said, we are content."

"But you told me earlier you intend to take your mother away from this house one day, so I wonder if you really are content—and if she would really want to go?"

I was puzzled. I felt she was trying to insinuate something, but since I could not imagine what, I kept silent.

"Papa is very fond of you, Lucinda. That is why he wants you to come to my ball, and I am delighted about that. He has shocked that awful Miss Tait by insisting that several lesser people be invited, including that doctor and his sister from across the square, who seem to do things that shock everyone. You know them well, I believe. You visit their home, do you not?''

"Quite frequently. Helen Steel and I are good friends.''

"And what of her brother? I thought him attractive, on the brief occasion that we met; unconventional in looks and dress, and with a magnificent body, and I do like men with magnificent bodies. I thought him fascinating. I am glad they have accepted the invitation to my ball, though I wouldn't have been surprised had he declined. He doesn't look a society man to me.''

"Perhaps he accepted for his sister's sake. She could hardly go to a ball alone.''

"Nor can you, so their acceptance is doubly convenient. Dr. Steel can escort you both. But why assume that he accepted the invitation solely for his sister's sake? *I* may have been the attraction.''

That seemed distinctly possible, recalling that moment of their meeting, of her surveillance of him and his response, and his curiosity about her as he accompanied me back across the square. I wanted to urge her to forget about the man, to concentrate on the foppish young mashers who courted every Season's debutantes, but it was natural for Clemmy to be aware of every man who crossed her path and to immediately enslave them, so again I remained silent.

"Have you a dress to wear?'' she asked. "If not, I am sure Trudy could alter one of mine. It would have to be taken in, because you are so skinny, and lengthened, because you are so tall.''

I thanked her, adding that I already had a gown.

"A new one?'' she asked in surprise.

I nodded.

"And how did you come by that?''

"It was a present.''

"From Papa? Come, Lucy, you don't have to hide anything from me. I am not in the least jealous. Why should I be? You must see my coming-out wardrobe—Mamma has had additional cupboards built into a guest-room to house the overflow, so I would hardly begrudge you the gift of a ball gown from my father.'' She added casually, "By the way, have you visited Gavin's new apartment?''

"Of course not.''

"I am sure you will. I am sure he will invite you.''

I repeated the words my mother had always drummed into me. "It would be unseemly for a young unmarried woman to visit a man's bachelor quarters.''

She grimaced.

"Dear little Miss Prim." She strolled toward the door, saying over her shoulder, "We will always be friends, won't we, Lucinda? After all, we have grown up together."

"In the same house," I corrected. "That isn't quite the same thing."

"Never mind. It will be different in future. When I am a leading actress and you are my understudy, we will be closer than ever. If Papa says you have promise, it must be true, so I am sure he will think my suggestion a good one." Her hand was on the doorknob now, and she looked back at me with the sweetest of smiles. "That way we will always be together, as our mothers have been."

Never like that, I thought. *I will never be subservient to you, never your shadow.* But I said nothing. I was learning how to wait.

"And of course," she finished thoughtfully, "we can never tell when we may need each other. . . ."

7

"My dear, don't come near me—I reek of mothballs. This dress hasn't been taken from its cover since my own coming-out ball—and what a disaster *that* was!—so it is not only aromatic, but ancient."

"You should have bought yourself something new, sister."

"My dear brother, why waste good money on something which will never be worn again? How often do I go to balls nowadays? When I was coming out, I endured my share of being a wallflower, with other wallflowers and their disappointed mammas. I was presented on my seventeenth birthday, Lucinda, and this was my Presentation gown—dated, isn't it, with all this excessive back bustle, but I am no dab-hand at altering things. Poor Mamma, she spent a fortune on it, and all to no avail. I soon ran out of partners, once their duty dances had been done. I chattered too much, Mamma said, and on all the wrong subjects. I should have glided round the ballroom gazing up at them coyly or wistfully or admiringly, not wearing them out with conversation. They, alas, wore me out by their lack of it. Lucinda, you look most enchanting—that gown is really beautiful. Surely your mother didn't make it, talented as I know she is?"

Clementine's voice cut in. "Indeed, she did not, Miss Steel. It was a very generous present from my papa."

At her words, Lady Boswell raised her lorgnette and scanned me from head to foot. Its use added to her dignity, which, at this moment, she badly needed. Her eyes were slightly glazed and her cheek unnaturally flushed beneath its heavy coating of rouge. I also saw that her husband's face was tense and his smile forced as he greeted Helen and Magnus Steel, who had called at this precise moment to take me to the ball.

Nothing was going well. Curtis was late in bringing round the carriage, an unforgivable sin on such a night as this. "Doesn't that young man realise we must be at the Savoy well in advance of our guests?" Bernadette fretted. "What in the name of heaven can have delayed him? And I hope, Dr. Steel, that your carriage is not blocking our entrance?"

"I don't possess a carriage, Lady Boswell. Only a trap to get me to and from Stepney."

"Gracious heaven, you do not propose to arrive at the Savoy driving a pony trap?"

Magnus looked amused. "I don't think I would insult that six thousand square feet of courtyard opening from Savoy Hill, not to mention the Della Robbia fountain and the palms, in such a way, Lady Boswell— though I must confess I would mightily enjoy doing so. I felt a hired brougham might be more appropriate for two ladies clad in evening gowns. For myself, I would travel by pony trap or on foot if I felt so inclined." He gave a slight bow. "If you will excuse me, I will tell the driver to wait some paces from your door."

"I should think so too," the great Bernadette murmured as he departed. Her speech was slightly slurred, though she walked steadily enough. I had seen her move unfalteringly about a stage when, as now, she had obviously been at her medicine. But onstage she could also control her diction; not so when fraught with anxiety about her daughter's coming-out ball.

"And you, Clementine—even you had me worried when you disappeared this afternoon. For two whole hours! Wherever did you go? I expressly ordered you to rest, and you disobeyed me. When Hawkins told me you had just come in, I couldn't believe my ears. 'From *where?*' I asked, to which all he could say was 'From outside, ma'am,' wherever *that* might have been. Surely you did not go shopping or walking on such an important day as this?"

"No, Mamma. I was driving in the park. I had need of fresh air and ordered Curtis to take me there. Blame me if he was late returning and had to attend to the horses again." Clementine dismissed the whole business with a flick of her fan. "Do stop making a ridiculous fuss about nothing."

"But to be absent for two whole hours! You must have driven round and round the park many times!"

"I did," her daughter answered serenely.

"And the fresh air has put colour in her cheeks," her father remarked pacifically. I could see he was proud of his daughter tonight, as well he might be, for Clementine's gown by Worth justified every penny it had cost. In white French faille, with a front of matching satin richly self-embroidered, the corsage had a pointed plastron to match, and the fronts were continued down the skirt in panels, decorated with tasselled loops of Venetian bugle beads. It was an elaborate gown which somehow achieved the effect of simplicity because she had been wise enough to wear no jewels. Her rounded bosom and her soft neck were bare, crowned by her pink-and-white dimpled face. She wore her chestnut curls parted in the centre and drawn back into a high coil in which a cluster of pure white camellias nestled softly. Errant strands caressed her forehead, adding to her look of girlish innocence, but the bloom about her was not of the same quality, nor was the secret light in her eye, which, I felt sure, no one could detect but I, and which surely owed nothing to fresh air in the park. I had seen that sparkle once before when being regaled by her unbelievable experiences with the French gardener. And if not a gardener, why not a coachman? . . .

I suppressed the thought, because Sir Nevill was looking at his daughter so fondly and I hated the idea of his being deceived.

I had come downstairs assuming that the Boswells had already departed and therefore expecting to wait alone in the hall. As it turned out, I could scarcely have timed things more badly, for there they were, waiting for the carriage.

I had been about to retreat when Sir Nevill heard my step and, looking round, exclaimed, "My dear Lucinda, you look charming. Don't you agree, Bernadette . . . Clementine? I am sure Trudy helped to choose that very becoming gown. She has excellent taste."

I saw Bernadette's petulant frown, and my desire to escape had increased, but her husband had held out a friendly hand to me, saying, "Come near to the fire, my dear—it is chilly over there."

He had moved away from the marble fireplace in the middle of the hall, and I had reluctantly taken my place amongst them, aware that his wife's glance raked me thoroughly and then dismissed me. It had been then that I detected the betraying signs of her indulgence. Poor Lady Boswell, why did she need her "medicine" so much?

The thought had scarcely passed through my mind when the iron doorbell jangled, heralding the arrival of the Steels, and now, of course, the three of us would have to wait until the Boswells departed, because it would never do for guests to arrive at the Savoy before them.

"There is plenty of time," Sir Nevill assured his wife, but the impatient tapping of her fan against the back of one hand continued, and now

Clementine's announcement that my gown was a present from her father made me the focus of attention and I had to face the raised lorgnette once more.

"Sharming indeed," slurred Bernadette. "I hope you appreciate my husband's generosity, gel."

"I appreciate it greatly, Lady Boswell."

"I want no gratitude from Lucinda," Sir Nevill said curtly.

"And why not, may I ask?"

"Mamma, I think it would be a good idea if you lay down for a while," Clementine put in. "You insisted on being ready far too early."

"I think it might be wiser if your mother waited in the drawing room rather than upstairs," her father began, but at that moment Magnus returned with the news that his hired vehicle was no longer blocking the entrance and that their carriage was coming to a halt in place of it, and Hawkins was walking majestically down the hall to usher them out.

Cinderella at the ball could not have been so bedazzled as I that night, and the evening proved to be almost as momentous for me as for that legendary heroine, because one of the first people I met, after being received in the long line of guests, was Gavin.

"Lucinda."

He murmured my name in that intimate tone which I had last heard on the darkened stage; quietly, in my ear, so that I spun round breathlessly, my face betraying me. He took hold of my hand and led me onto the ballroom floor, and we glided into a waltz with ease. It was the first time I had ever danced the waltz, the first time I had ever danced with a man, but he led me so expertly that I had no time to be nervous.

"You dance beautifully," he said. "Don't tell me they taught you the waltz at Miss Templeton's select academy! That worthy soul would surely disapprove of men's arms about the waists of her pupils."

"How do you know she is a worthy soul?"

"To run such an establishment, she would have to be, but it is you I want to talk about. How much longer must you attend that school? You have grown up, my lovely. Nature has been doing her best with you in my absence."

I wasn't experienced enough to parry compliments, or to accept them without self-consciousness, and though I thrilled to his words, I evaded them even so.

"Tell me about the tour," I said. "I want to hear all about it. I know it was a great success, that *you* were a great success."

"Didn't you expect me to be?"

"Of course I did. And you will be an even greater success yet."

"Provided I discard the conventional drama which the Boswell Touring Company took on the road. Tastes in the provinces differ from London, except in certain theatres in Manchester and Birmingham and Dublin, where they still like Shakespeare and the classics. But they are in the minority. Tastes are changing. Even melodramas like *East Lynne* and *Maria Martin in the Red Barn* don't play to good houses anymore, even in the number twos. And I have no intention of playing number twos, *or* of appearing in anything but popular, fashionable, and profitable plays— plays of today."

"But Sir Nevill will choose the company's programme, surely?"

"Alas, yes, but I won't have to endure that forever. I have my own plans, and the Boswell Touring Company is merely a stepping-stone toward them."

The music whirled to a stop, cutting off our conversation, robbing me of the pressure of his arm about my waist.

"Who were the people you came with?" he asked as he led me from the floor. "Strangers, to me."

I told him about the Steels and that it was through Dr. Steel that Jerry Hawks had become our callboy. The story entertained him vastly.

"You mean that well-dressed man over there boxes for sixpences in Hyde Park?" Gavin threw back his head and laughed heartily. "My dear stepsister must surely be unaware of that, or he would never have been invited tonight."

"I believe Sir Nevill put his name and that of his sister on the invitation list, as he did mine."

We had almost reached the edge of the floor. I saw Helen and her brother leaving it too. Helen's gown was indeed rather outmoded, but her nonchalance carried it off. Helen's charm was her total indifference to appearances or opinions.

Magnus looked striking in evening clothes which might well have come from Savile Row, but he had the same lack of self-consciousness as his sister. Tonight he looked a very different person from the half-stripped man at Soapbox Corner. Fascinating, Clemmy had called him. He wasn't fascinating to me, but he was certainly very masculine and very noticeable, though I could not analyse the particular quality about his looks which made him so. But Gavin was talking again, and anything Gavin said was of more interest to me than passing reflections about another man.

"It shouldn't have been necessary for your name to be put on the invitation list," he was saying. "You are one of the family."

"No. I am the daughter of Lady Boswell's dresser. Living in the same house doesn't make me one of the family."

"I am sure it does to Nevill, and I know it does to me." He halted then, unwilling to let me go. "Not that I regard you as any kind of sister or cousin, believe me, though to be related in another way holds distinct appeal." His glance ran over me. "You have a lovely figure now. Tall and slender. You will look well onstage. When my plans materialize, as they will, you will play a big part in them. You stand out because you are different. You are no copyplate edition, therefore you are noticeable even amongst this elaborately dressed crowd. Have you observed how every woman has set out to eclipse every other, and that every man has set out to conquer every woman? And why not? Life is nothing but a mating dance, and to most people it scarcely matters who it is performed with. The important thing is not to be left out of it." He looked down at me and smiled. "Now you are bewildered, sweet Lucinda, so let us change the subject. Is Nevill still coaching you?"

I admitted that he was, and that he was working me very hard, and that I loved every moment of it.

"Clementine suggests that I should become her understudy," I added.

Gavin's mouth curved in amusement. "Understudy in what way?" he murmured.

His glance went across the ballroom to the spot where Clementine and her parents were holding court. Lady Boswell was very much in control of herself now, and the tension about Sir Nevill's face had disappeared. Clemmy was giving the performance of her life as the shy debutante, virginal as the massed white flowers behind her. The whole scene was a splendid one. The entire walls of the ballroom were hung with white silk threaded with silver, and the ceiling formed a vast canopy of white flowers through which light sparkled in thousands of prisms from immense chandeliers. Although electric lighting was no longer a novelty, and the Savoy Theatre claimed to be not merely the first theatre but the first public building in the world to be lighted entirely by electricity, it was still viewed with certain suspicion when used abundantly, and only recently a famous manufacturer of umbrellas had advertised in the *Morning Post:*

> The Electric Light, so favourable to
> Furniture, Wall Papers, Screens, etc.,
> is not always becoming to Female
> Complexions. Light Japanese Sunshades
> will be found Invaluable.

But no Japanese sunshades shielded female complexions from the Savoy's glittering chandeliers tonight. The whole scene was like something from a fairy tale, a setting for a pure white princess, against which the gowns and jewels of London's society were bedazzling and colorful, the satins and brocades and silks enhanced. But none looked so lovely or so pure as Clementine, and when her father led her onto the floor, I joined in the spontaneous applause.

I think that was the first time I ever consciously envied Clementine, the first time I thought how wonderful it must be to have a father. To be led out onto a ballroom floor by a man so proud of his daughter was an experience which would never come my way, but I got a vicarious pleasure out of watching them—particularly Sir Nevill, tall and distinguished and famous and yet so unassuming, so modest, so unaware of himself.

Clementine looked equally modest in her white gown, unadorned by jewels, her eyes downcast. I found myself looking at her with sudden detachment, seeing her in a role which was not truly hers but which she was playing admirably for her parents' sake. I respected her for that, at least. I even found it hard to believe that she had ever regaled me with stories of her adulteries, or shown me things I wished I had never seen.

"Sweet, modest little flower, isn't she?" Gavin murmured.

I looked at him swiftly. How much did he know about Clemmy, and how had he found out? Perhaps it was not knowledge, only suspicion. Perhaps men had instincts about these things. Once before, Gavin had intimated that he had summed up his stepsister's daughter pretty well.

Couples were following their host onto the floor, and Gavin took me in his arms again.

"When are we going to see each other, Lucinda? I don't mean like this, in public, but alone."

Faintly startled but distinctly pleased, I said, "Perhaps we could meet and walk in the park?"

He grimaced. "Would you be content with that?"

"We would have to be, wouldn't we?"

He smiled a little ruefully. "Not yet *quite* grown-up, are you, Lucinda? Never mind—you will be. And before very long."

I was a little out of my depth now, unaccustomed to conversation like this, so I said at random, "Tell me about the tour. It was a long one!"

"Nearly ten months—England, Ireland, Scotland, and Wales. All the leading cities, and then some lesser ones. Strenuous, but very worthwhile. I learned a lot."

"Such as?"

"Where the money is."

Both his tone and his words seemed enigmatic, and the way in which he cut them off suggested that he intended to reveal no more. But I was curious.

"You mean the cities, or the type of entertainment?"

"Both." He smiled, and I felt that he changed the subject deliberately. "That is a very lovely gown you are wearing. Not from pretty Trudy's needle, surely? That is no renovation; it's a model. Who paid for it? My stepsister's revered husband?''

"How did you guess?''

"No guesswork necessary. Who else could have bought it for you? Who else *would* have bought it for you?''

The music ceased. The encore had been short. Again we were walking back across the floor, Gavin's hand guiding me through the crush. Occasionally people bumped into us, so I paid little heed when this happened yet again. Only when Gavin halted and greeted someone did I turn, and freeze in my tracks.

I was looking at the man called Durbridge.

8

"You don't know Miss Grainger, of course,'' Gavin was saying.

"On the contrary, we met some time ago.''

The mouth was as loose-lipped as I remembered it; slightly moist, as I remembered it; the eyes as heavy-lidded, the clothes as immaculate, the manner as impeccable, the personality as distasteful. He seemed less tall than I recalled him, but I had grown taller myself since that memorable day.

The shielded glance ran over me. I felt stripped. I didn't want to accept the extended hand, but courtesy demanded it. I wasn't surprised by the soft, fleshy grasp, though I suspected it could become like iron if he so decided, nor was I surprised when he kissed my fingers. What did surprise me was the coldness of his lips, because they were the reddest I had ever seen in a man.

"Where did you meet?'' Gavin asked, surprised. He seemed in no hurry to get away, and unaware of my own desire to.

"In the most extraordinary circumstances,'' drawled Durbridge. "And how is your charming mother, Miss Grainger?''

"She is well, I thank you, sir.''

"And the boy you befriended? Is he still at the Boswell Theatre?''

I nodded, adding that Jerry was doing very well.

"It would be interesting to see how he has developed,'' Durbridge mused. "Perhaps I shall call backstage to find out. I have helped many a promising lad to better his lot.''

"So has Dr. Steel.''

"But he does it with banners flying, the banners of charity to advertise his work. I do it less obtrusively."

I could not understand why Gavin looked secretly amused at that. My own reaction was one of anger, because I disliked any disparagement of Magnus Steel. And then, to my relief, there was Magnus himself beside us.

"Supper is about to be served, Miss Lucinda. I came to fetch you."

"My dear Steel, you have a talent for intruding at moments when your company is not only superfluous but unwanted."

"So you have often intimated, Durbridge." Magnus offered me his arm and I took it gladly, though I would have preferred Gavin's. He, however, was merely standing there listening to the conversation with an attentive look on his face. Realising that he had never met Magnus, I introduced them at once, and a minute or two later I was walking into the supper room with the Steels while Gavin remained behind, talking to Durbridge. Glancing over my shoulder, I saw that they appeared deep in conversation.

The Steels may have been regarded as lesser people by the snobbish Miss Tait, but they were greeted by a great many guests, with whom they were obviously well acquainted, including a starched and bejewelled lady who descended on them as we reached our supper table, exclaiming, "My dear niece . . . and nephew, too! Why did you not let me know you were to be here? We could have come together."

She enfolded Helen in a stiff embrace from which that young woman detached herself firmly.

"Remembering how I disgraced you when cycling along Park Lane, would you really wish to be seen with me in public, Aunt Agatha?"

"My dear niece, I have drawn a veil over that painful recollection. Do you imagine I wish to recall you looking such a sight?" She inspected Helen's appearance and pronounced, "At least you look better tonight, but surely you are wearing your Presentation gown? Don't you realise it draws attention to the fact that you came out a long time ago? The style is positively dated."

Helen replied happily that she was perfectly aware of that, but did it matter? "Nobody minds, least of all the women, because I represent no competition and my gown only emphasises the modishness of theirs."

The old lady's shoulders rose and fell in a resigned shrug. She turned her attention to her nephew.

"As for you, Magnus, when I see you looking so presentable I cannot help mourning the waste of your manhood."

His eyebrows raised in amusement. During the time I had known the

Steels, I had learned that he found most things entertaining. The only time I had seen him really serious, apart from that encounter in the park when he had made himself responsible for young Jerry, was when he talked about his East End mission, to which Helen had promised to take me one day.

"And now I suppose you want me to ask in what way I am wasting my manhood," he said to his aunt now, his voice slightly mocking.

"What an absurd remark! You know perfectly well in what way. A man of your age and in your position should be married and producing a family instead of playing around as a disciple of some sort in the East End."

"I can assure you, Aunt Agatha, that what I do there is certainly not 'playing around.' Were you on your way to your table? Let me escort you."

He was suave and courteous and very, very firm, but the old lady still had some guns to fire.

"You are getting yourself talked about, nephew. I have heard that you make an exhibition of yourself in Hyde Park. Disgraceful! What would your poor mother think? Your father, too."

"My father would be no whit surprised, and my mother would be shocked but resigned."

"No doubt, no doubt. Poor things—you were always a headstrong boy, impossible to handle. But I feel it my duty to protest about your sister being dragged into your slumming activities. She will never find a husband *that* way."

Helen cut in, "I may never find a husband any other way, my dear aunt, but if I am left on the shelf it will be a very busy and well-occupied shelf, and a great deal more interesting than the domestic one I would occupy as the mistress of some man's dull household. Let me introduce you to my friend Lucinda Grainger before you leave us. My aunt, Lady Field."

I was favoured with a brief nod and then forgotten until Helen added with emphasis, "Miss Grainger is to be an actress, Aunt Agatha, and I am sure she will be a very good one. She is being trained by Sir Nevill himself."

The inspection was renewed, and not wholly with approval. "An actress, indeed? I find that regrettable. One hears such scandalous things about theatrical folk."

"Not about the Boswells, Lady Field. I have been brought up in their household, and none could be more respectable."

"And," Magnus added pointedly, "they do happen to be our hosts tonight."

I felt he did not like his aunt very much, and nor did I when she asked

if I were related to them, as if I thereby qualified for slightly more favour.

"No. I am the daughter of an employee."

"Indeed. And what kind of an employee?"

"My mother is Lady Boswell's dresser."

"And highly respected," put in Magnus. "Miss Lucinda could not
have a more charming mother. And now, my dear aunt, I insist on taking
you to your table."

There was a glint in his eye and a line of determination to his mouth.
He put a hand beneath the old lady's elbow and led her away, but as they
departed I heard him say, "There are two things in life I detest, Aunt
Agatha—one is snobbishness and the other is scandalmongering, and if it
is Durbridge who has regaled you with scandal about theatrical folk, you
should dismiss it."

Her indignant answer eluded me, but somehow I knew she was defending that titled gentleman, and I remembered Helen's avowal that he
could pull the wool over the eyes of any woman over forty and possibly
less. Certainly he seemed to be pulling it over Clementine's eyes; her
mother's, too. He was supping at their table. Miss Tait must have considered him very important, to have placed him in such a position of honour. Was it because, as Helen had told me, he donated generously to
charities and was received in all the best houses?

I wished the man were not here tonight, but Clementine obviously did
not share my view. After supper she danced with him frequently, sparing
time for Magnus even so.

"My brother seems to be as susceptible to a pretty face as the next
man," Helen commented dryly as the couple whirled past. "He is quite
enamoured of Miss Boswell, as that handsome young actor is of you.
Here he is, coming to claim you again."

After that I thought of no one else but Gavin, and he thought of no
one else but me, dancing with me as often as possible and carrying me
into a seventh heaven of delight. I went home from the ball on a cloud,
scarcely aware of Magnus and Helen and only making monosyllabic answers to his questions about Jerry and how he was acquitting himself at
the theatre, and after a while he lapsed into silence. Perhaps he was
thinking of Clementine, as I was of Gavin.

I was too alert, too excited, too wide-awake to sleep. I lay there in the
darkness, reliving the evening, and particularly the moments with Gavin,
hearing again the things he said, feeling again his arms about me, responding again to his voice and his glance and the intimacy he had estab-

lished between us. He had made it plain that he was in love with me, and even that he had plans for us.

"It won't be long now," he had whispered as we said good night. "It is going to be worth all the waiting, my lovely." That could mean only one thing—that we would be together. Married, of course. And I wanted that as much as he. I was now verging on sixteen, and many a girl had married at that age.

I lay in such drowsy contentment that I paid no heed to the creak on the landing outside. I often heard creaking floorboards at night. When I had first occupied this room as a five-year-old, the sounds had frightened me because I had never been aware of them when sharing that other attic room with my mother, but she had soon reassured me, explaining how wood expanded in the night atmosphere. But this sound stopped outside my door, and when the tap came, I groped for my candle, believing it to be my mother coming to hear about the ball, but I was wrong. It was Clementine.

She perched on the side of my bed, as wide-awake as I.

"We didn't have a chance to talk all evening, Lucy. Did you enjoy yourself? You looked as if you did; you danced with Gavin nearly all the time. You're in love with him, aren't you? Did he ask you to go to his rooms?"

"Of course not."

In the flickering light she looked as if she disbelieved me, but the next thing she said was, "I saw you talking to Lord Durbridge. I didn't know you knew him."

"I don't. We met once before, very briefly, but that was all."

"Gavin seems to know him well."

"I hope not."

"Don't you like Durbridge?"

"No."

"Why not?"

"A sort of instinct."

"But you must admit there's something fascinating about him."

"Not to me. I don't trust him."

"That is what *makes* him fascinating. Men one can trust are so dull."

"I would trust Magnus Steel, and he isn't dull."

She admitted that, adding that the doctor was fascinating because he was so masculine, which surprised me, because although I liked him, I didn't find him fascinating at all. Compared with Gavin, all men paled.

Clementine went on, "I am sure Magnus Steel would be a very good lover, but Durbridge could teach me all sorts of things."

"Don't you know enough already?"

I reached out and snuffed the candle. I was suddenly tired and in no mood for the kind of conversation which, I knew, she was leading up to. Even so, she lingered, and her voice came to me out of the darkness.

"One can never know enough or experience enough, so I hope I meet Durbridge again. So does Mamma, but not for the same reason. She only sees his family tree; I see other things. And what is more, Durbridge knows I do. . . ."

From the night of the ball, life took over at such a pace that Clementine's remarks were soon forgotten. With Gavin's return, events seemed to move swiftly, though he was in no way responsible. It was just that nothing could stand still when he was around; his vitality overflowed, infecting everything—and particularly me.

Sir Nevill had no immediate plans for another tour of his secondary company, so Gavin returned to the Boswell Theatre, playing the subsidiary roles he had previously filled. Naturally, he found this frustrating, but most of the theatres in London, particularly in and around the Strand, which was the heart of theatreland, were running established productions playing to full houses, or had stock companies such as Sir Henry Irving's at the Lyceum or D'Oyly Carte's playing Gilbert and Sullivan at the Savoy. In or near this mecca were also situated the Gaiety, the Olympic, Drury Lane, the Globe, the Strand, the Opera Comique, Terry's, Toole's, and the Adelphi, with the Boswell situated between this and Romano's famous restaurant. The only theatres in the West End at any distance from the vicinity of the Strand were the Haymarket, the St. James's, the Criterion, the Princess's in Oxford Street, which had been called after Queen Victoria before she came to the throne, the Royalty, the decrepit Prince of Wales's, which was on the verge of closing down, and a place called the Court Theatre away on the frontier of Belgravia and Chelsea.

Because these theatres were not in or around the Strand, they were all slightly beyond the pale, so it was better, Gavin said, to play secondary roles in an area of London which mattered.

Nevertheless, after being on the road as leading actor, and therefore the most important member of the company, the present situation irked him. "And Nevill doesn't really want me back. He has never liked me and seems more reluctant than ever to welcome me into the fold, but at least I am not darkening his door again at Portman Square, though running a bachelor establishment isn't easy on the salary he pays me. But I have plans, great plans. . . ."

Gavin was always talking about his plans, never revealing what they were. "You will know one day. As I told you, you are part of them, but you must wait, as I must. Meanwhile, make the most of your chances with the great Sir Nevill.''

I wished he wouldn't speak of my benefactor in such a tone, almost sneering and faintly disparaging. I always thought of Nevill Boswell as my benefactor because that was what he was, but when I said so, Gavin would merely smile and say, "Go on believing that, Lucinda. Keep your illusions," and I wanted to argue that it was no illusion.

I was torn between loyalty to Sir Nevill and love for Gavin. I wanted to go on believing that the famous actor-manager was right in all things, and yet to believe that Gavin was too. I hated the thought of any dislike or antagonism existing between them, but I could not forget that Sir Nevill had deliberately banished Gavin following our secret meeting on-stage, and that he had condemned him for remaining there instead of coming forward to support me. I felt it unreasonable of him not to realise that Gavin had taken that course solely for my sake, to protect me from censure.

But that was in the past, and the present was becoming too exciting to leave any time for worrying about things that had gone before. With Gavin back in my life, my only thought was that every passing day brought me nearer to my ambition—to get started as an actress. Yet when the chance came, I was so unprepared for it that something like panic hit me.

"*Me?*" I gasped when Sir Nevill told me. "You surely don't mean *me?*"

He laughed.

"I do indeed, Lucinda. The part is small, but the smallest part is important in any production and I will expect you to work hard and to give of your best."

"But it is midterm—Miss Templeton will never release me."

"I will write to her, explaining the circumstances and suggesting that your tuition should continue privately."

He was reviving that classic drama *The Only Way; or: A Far Far Better Thing*, and I took it as an omen since I had been born during a performance of it. I wondered if he remembered, but didn't dare to ask. The play had a large cast, needing plenty of supers for crowd scenes, and was liberally bespattered with minor roles such as the one now offered me—a young French *aristo* awaiting her turn at the guillotine as Sydney Carton nobly went to his death in place of Charles Darnay, and weeping as he delivered his noble speech of farewell:

It is a far, far better thing that I do, than I have ever done; it is a far, far better rest that I go to than I have ever known.

It would be easy for me to weep when Sir Nevill spoke those lines in his stirring voice, easy for me to cry out in defiance of the howling revolutionary mob as I stood waiting in the tumbril, and though Gavin declared that the play was outmoded, and I would never have dared to disagree with him, it moved me profoundly.

So I seized this three-line part with joy, seeing it as the start of my career and the prelude to bigger and better roles. Nor did I waste time envying Clementine the insipid part of Lucie, the heroine of the piece, for whose sake Sydney Carton gave his life to save that of the man she loved.

The great Bernadette made no demur about playing the character part of Madame Defarge, the Lady Macbeth of the piece who coded into her eternal knitting the names of aristocrats who were enemies of the Republic and therefore to be brought to the guillotine. Yielding honour to the daughter she doted on was a different thing from yielding it to a rival like Chrystal Delmont, this time (happily, in Bernadette's opinion) miscast as the unattractive but useful Miss Pross. With Bramwell Chambers as Dr. Manette and Gavin as Charles Darnay, the cast was complete and, as always, Bernadette was pleased because her stepbrother was to play the romantic lead and display his good looks to the full.

Besides, Madame Defarge gave her great scope for grandiloquent gestures and dramatic speeches. *"Tell the wind and the fire where to stop; not me!"* She declared that the citizeness was a great part, admirable for an actress of her calibre, and that she could think of none other who could do justice to it. With that, her pride was satisfied, and with the three-line French girl I was more than satisfied because it heralded the fulfilment of my dreams and, unexpectedly, my sudden release from school. Miss Templeton was so aghast at the thought of any pupil of hers appearing on a public stage that she declined to tutor me even privately.

I was overjoyed. I piled my hateful school garments in the middle of the floor and danced on them, my mother subsiding into laughter as she watched. But the sight of me putting up my hair saddened her a little.

"Darling Mamma, surely you knew I would have to grow up someday?"

"Of course, my love, but somehow it seems to have arrived so quickly."

Her voice and her eyes were so sad that I put my arms about her spontaneously, anxious to comfort her but failing to understand why she could not feel as I did—elated because girlhood was behind me at last.

I shall never forget the day I bought my first supply of stage makeup. Basic legitimate, of course, because one always began with "basic legitimate," this being the distinction between makeup for the straight, or le-

gitimate, theatre as opposed to the more bizarre circus or music-hall
makeup, the "basic" being the minimum requirements for a beginner.
Sticks of Leichner numbers 2, 3, and 5 were enough to go on with; other
shades, becoming darker by numbers, could be added later, but because
I was to play a dark-haired French girl, I added a stick of number 9 to
make my fair complexion deeper. Then there was lampblack or kohl for
eyelids and lashes, and a white liner for underlining the eyebrows, and
rouge for cheeks, lips, the palms of the hands, and inside the ears.

"Shade them very lightly," Gavin warned. "Hands look dead flat if
the palms aren't faintly emphasised, and ears can look large unless coloured lightly pink in the centre and on the lobes. And be careful with the
kohl. It can be dangerous for the eyes, and yours are too lovely to risk."

He came with me to Willy Clarkson's, the famous wig-maker in Wel-
lington Street off the Strand. On the opposite side of the street was his
rival, Fox, and both windows displayed their best wigs accompanied by
photographs of famous members of the profession wildly extolling their
virtues. At least one wig was a standard requirement in any actor or actress's wardrobe, and for the French girl I had to be dark. After trying on
a succession and enjoying the experience hugely, I settled, on Gavin's
advice, for one of thick near-black waves. Somehow my mother had
managed to provide the money for all this, but the purchase of a theatrical skip, which I passionately longed to own, would have to wait. To
have one of those coveted wicker affairs, with one's professional name
stamped on a metal disc affixed to the lid, and SIR NEVILL BOSWELL'S
COMPANY painted in large black letters on the sides, would put the seal
on my professional status, but Mamma was right in saying such a purchase could wait since I wore only one costume in the play, and that
would be kept on a hanger in my dressing room.

I wondered which room would be allocated to me and whom I would
share with. There were many minor roles in this production, so I anticipated dressing with other speaking parts. Therefore it was a shock to
find, when the day of the dress rehearsal came along, that I had been
relegated to the largest one at the top of the theatre, housing the female
supers. These itinerant players were invariably rough, particularly those
engaged for costume productions, because in modern plays the cast had
to supply their own clothes, which meant having sufficient money for
some sort of a stage wardrobe. Supers for modern productions were
therefore cleaner and more respectable as a general rule.

I had witnessed many an audition for supers, which were conducted by
Gregory, the stage manager. The queue would be waiting at the stage
door long before George arrived to open it, and onstage these casual actors would be summoned, a dozen at a time, carrying their "stage ward-

robes'' in bundles or shabby suitcases. They would then stand in line with their clothes spread out at their feet, and along the rank Gregory would go, inspecting every item and ticking them off one by one.

"One gent's lounge suit, one smoking jacket, one set of evening clothes, one hacking jacket and breeches, one brocaded dressing gown— you are well equipped, sir, so you're in. Half-a-crown a performance. And now the next—is *this* all you've got? No go, mate. Sorry. You'll have to come better fitted out next time. All right, all right—no answering back! I know this play doesn't call for riding clothes or brocaded dressing gowns, but you never know, do you? An actor has to be ready for anything. The suit you stand up in and those few things won't get you anywhere. And now to the next—what have we here? Not bad, not bad. A bit the worse for wear, so we'll have to put you at the back of the crowd, which means two bob a show instead of half-a-crown—take it or leave it. You'll take it? Thought you would. But as for *you*, sir,'' moving on to the next, "you can't expect to get into a Boswell production with only *that* lot to your name. . . .''

The hope, the anxiety, the despair in the faces of these impoverished players always tore at my heart. Sir Nevill had once admitted that for the same reason he could never attend such auditions, but at one time Bernadette had inspected the women, eventually handing the task over to Gregory when deciding that it was beneath her dignity to continue. After that, Wardrobe Mistress Piper lent a hand at the female auditions, ushering them onstage for Gregory's inspection.

"Right, ladies, on you go—no shoving, *if* you please! Twelve at a time, no more. That's right, plonk your stuff on the stage before you— no, not like that, dear. Spread it out so's it can be seen. Good luck to you. And the same with you, love—stand in line with your things on show. Hello, Daisy! Back from the road, are you? Well, I don't have to tell *you* what to do.'' Then she would join the stage manager for the inspection, making comments as they went.

"Not bad at all, that one. Two feather boas, a nice jet-beaded gown, and a good supply of hats. A fur tippet, too, and a smart coat. Oh, yes, she's got a very nice stage wardrobe, that one—no less than two tea gowns and a coupla negligeeze into the bargain. Taken care of her stuff, without a doubt, and *very* good taste.'' Then a nod and a wink to the owner of this splendid array, who would buy her a gin across the road at the Duke's Head later (if she hadn't done so already) and Gregory would pronounce, "Right dear, you'll do. A bob and a tanner for you. Top pay for women, that is.''

And so on along the line until they had all been either engaged or dismissed, and the next lot trooped onstage to lay out their clothes like stalls in a market.

Costume productions brought a different type of super altogether—poorer and rougher, because they didn't possess the money to equip themselves with any kind of stage wardrobe. In costume productions, clothes had to be provided by the management, so pay was proportionately lower. Most of the women were prostitutes whose earning powers had diminished, driven to the stage door by poverty, knowing they could pick up a maximum shilling a night, and the same at matinees, merely for walking on and making noises off. So with costume productions it was a case of first come, first served, and the fighting in the queue would be fiercer.

"Surely there must be some mistake?" I pleaded of Gregory, whose job it was to allocate dressing rooms, when I saw he had put me with the supers in dressing room number 20, but he shook his head commiseratingly.

"No mistake, love. You're the most inexperienced member of the cast, which means you're only one step above a super, and an S.M. has to dole out dressing rooms accordingly. This is a crowded show, so you'll have to make the best of it. Take my tip—grab the spot nearest the door. You won't be stuck in the middle of them then."

But I was too late to pick and choose. All places along the mirrored walls and down the centre of the room had been taken by the time I climbed the circular stairs, and only by seizing a spare chair from along the wall and pushing my way in with it did I manage to get seated at all. No one took any notice of me. They were listening to a loud-mouthed woman who seemed to be self-appointed adviser to the lot.

"It's money for jam, ducks, and you can pick up more than a shilling if you're accommodating on the side. Actors can't afford to pay much, but if you take on two or three a night you don't do too badly. 'Course, trade is better backstage in the music halls because you can use the dressing rooms there, everyone turns a blind eye and the *artistes*—that's what they call themselves, *arteestes*—don't mind doing it in a room with a dozen others. But in theatres like this, trade ain't so good because that sorta thing ain't allowed on the premises, so the actors take you back to their lodgings and that leaves you less time for other customers, but there y'are—rules is rules, and they're strict at the Boswell. Classy, that's why." Catching sight of me, she broke off. "Well, well, look who's here, girls. An *actress*, no less! Get up and curtsey to her ladyship!" She executed a mocking and very wobbly bow.

For all my embarrassment, I acted without thought, executing a deep curtsey in return.

"If you bend the knee like this, keep your back upright and just slightly incline your head, you will keep your spine in alignment and run no risk of toppling over," I said. "It's easy when you get the knack of it."

There were smothered titters, and a voice more bold than the rest shouted, "'Ow about that, Maisie Stockwell? Put you in your place, didn't she?"

"She'd better not try it again," snarled Maisie, but she left me alone after that. Even so, I knew I had made an enemy, and I regretted my impulsive action. I turned back to the mirror and concentrated on my makeup, and as soon as I was in costume I went down to the wings, preferring to wait in the draughty shadows than in dressing room number 20.

On my way down, I met Jerry. "You didn't oughta be in with that lot," he commented. "'Tain't right for the likes o' you, missy."

But I knew I had to take the rough with the smooth, and said so. "If I have to accept them, Jerry, remember that they have to accept me. It works both ways."

"That it don't. An' if any of 'em cheeks yer, yell fer me. I knows 'ow to deal wiv that kind. The Rookeries was full of 'em."

Jerry was a well-established member of the stage crew now, still acting as callboy but helping Props as well. The theatre had become his world very quickly, and when Joe had tried to entice him back to the life of a buzzer he had cheerfully declined.

"'Tain't worth the risk, Joe, not when the coppers can do yer for it. I git reg'lar money at the Boswell and I ain't goin'ta stay a callboy. I got me eye on better fings. Could be a stage-doorman one day, pickin' up tips from the gents wot 'ang arahnd after the actresses, as well as from the actors on Sat'day nights. I likes it 'ere; I likes the life and I likes the folk. Suits me fine, it does."

He was almost passionately devoted to me. "I owes yer a lot, missy, an' I ain't likely to fergit it, so if any o' that lot upstairs ain't nice to yer, they'll 'ave *me* ter reckon wiv."

But I felt that on the whole the female supers, apart from Maisie Stockwell, would accept me in time, though I knew they would have been more comfortable without me. Maisie very soon made it plain that she regarded me as some sort of spy, planted in the dressing room to report on them.

"Afraid of goings-on up here, ain't they—the management, I mean. Well, mark this, your ladyship—any tale-telling will bounce right back and that you *won't* like."

This warning was issued before curtain-up on the opening night, but I was too excited to heed it. I had other things to think about, and delivering my three precious lines was the most important. These came toward the end of the final act, but, as at the dress rehearsal, I was ready and made up long before Jerry's voice bellowed outside the dressing-room door, *"Overture and beginners, please!"* and the familiar RAT-a-tat-TAT followed.

The supers crowded out, laughing and squealing as they clattered down the iron stairs, and I was left alone in the dressing room with its odour of bodies and gin and greasepaint, an odour I found sickening when emanating from over thirty unwashed women. I only hoped that Clementine would complain about the smell of the supers when onstage with her (Bernadette, incredibly, never seemed to notice), and that orders would then be issued that they should not merely wash regularly, but make a start by visiting the public baths in the Tottenham Court Road before the next night's performance, for which admission tickets would be issued by the management instead of the required twopence per head. (Hard cash would be spent on other things.)

I opened the skylight to ventilate the room and took deep breaths of the night air which came rushing in. Cold as it was, it was welcome. It helped to steady me, though I knew it was stupid to be nervous about playing such a very minor part. But it was of vast importance to me that every sob and every cry should be strong and telling, every word clear and audible. I wanted that unhappy French girl to be memorable, a vignette imprinted on the memory of the audience. I wanted Sir Nevill to be pleased with me, perhaps even to tell me so, and I wanted Gavin to feel the same way and to tell me the same thing.

At the thought of Gavin I jumped to my feet. As Charles Darnay he would be onstage very soon, and I didn't want to miss his entrance or any moment of his performance. I heard the echo of the supers returning up the spiralling stairs and knew that the crowd scene which preceded his first appearance was over. I hurried from the room but was forced to wait at the head of the stairs to allow them to pass. I stood chafing with impatience as the women trooped by me and back into the dressing room. I heard Maisie's screech of fury on finding the skylight open and its heavy bang as she closed it.

"Gotta let the smell of us out, has she? *I'll* teach her ladyship that she doesn't own this dressing room, so she can't do what she bloody well likes in it!"

I paid no heed and hurried down to the wings. Luck was with me. Gavin was waiting up right on the prompt side, and I heard Clementine, as Lucie, speaking the lines leading to his cue. I went over to him, reached up, and kissed his cheek. "Good luck," I whispered, and he slipped an arm about me and kissed my lips in return.

"Good luck be damned, my darling. I only hope this revival folds within a week. The play has been done to death and the public must be sick of it. I have my sights on something better, and I intend to achieve it. Something tells me it will be soon."

I was forced to a mild protest about his prediction for the play, but he didn't even hear it. I felt that his mind was elsewhere, but not on his cue, which was due any minute. But he was too experienced an actor to miss it, so perhaps my first-night nerves were making me unduly apprehensive.

"Jittery, darling?" He smiled. "You have no need to be. You make a very attractive French girl, but I can think of better ways to display you. I'll do it, too, and before long, if things work out as I expect. . . ."

His cue came. He stepped onstage and straight into Charles Darnay's lines as if he had no other thought in his head, and after that I forgot everything he had said prior to making his entrance. I was caught up in the first-night atmosphere, the backstage excitement, the agony of waiting for my own brief appearance, the crush of people who came through the iron pass door from the auditorium during intervals, to Sir Nevill's annoyance and Bernadette's delight. She never discouraged these dressing-room calls from regular first-nighters, who were invariably high-ranking socialites, liberally bespattered with titles. She was enjoying playing the sinister *citoyenne*, astonishing everyone with her hideous makeup. In my corner of the wings I heard comments as they passed.

"How wonderful of Bernadette to submerge herself in such a part, to hide her looks in such a way! Only a great actress would do it, of course."

And no doubt they said the same thing, but more flatteringly, in the crush of her dressing room. I could picture my mother effacing herself, then quietly making sure that everyone left in plenty of time to get back to their seats and for Bernadette to prepare for the curtain to rise again.

It was a long time since I had visited Lady Boswell's dressing room. The days when I had sat quietly in my corner were now no more than a distant memory, faded with childhood. I preferred to be here in the wings, seated unobtrusively in shadow, or talking with other small-part players, and I chose to remain there even during the intervals that night, despite the strict rule that no members of the company should linger backstage except when awaiting entrances. I had no stomach for that overcrowded dressing room at the top of the theatre, nor for the supers' ribaldry, and I knew that Willard and Gregory would both turn a blind eye, should they have time, on such a night as this, to notice me.

If I had not chosen to avoid dressing room number 20, I would not have seen many of the guests who flocked backstage to compliment the leading players. I knew that both Bernadette's and Clementine's dressing rooms were filled with flowers. I had seen endless deliveries arriving at the stage door. Clemmy seemed to be going over well as pretty Lucie, an undemanding part in which she had only to look helpless and anguished, and I was not surprised by the number of well-wishers crowding to her door. There were even more at the end of the second act, but by that time my own fever of expectancy had risen to such an extent that I paid less heed. In a quarter of an hour the curtain would rise on the third and final act and my debut as a professional actress would be almost upon me.

I jumped when a voice said, "So there you are, Lucinda. Someone told me your dressing room was 'way up by the roof, but I determined to find you, even so. I confess I'm glad I don't have to climb those dizzy-looking stairs, all the same."

It was Helen Steel, wearing her Presentation gown again. "Getting quite a lot of use, isn't it?" she said, observing my glance. "I'm told one has to dress up specially for first nights, but never having been to one, I wouldn't really know. But I should think even an outmoded Presentation gown would be acceptable for such an occasion, don't you? My dear, how exciting it all is—seeing backstage, I mean. I can't say it's very attractive, though. So cold and so bleak and so high!" Her eyes surveyed the stark wings rising blackly into space. "Are those what you call the flies up there? And the floats—where are the floats? What funny names to use. And didn't I once hear you refer to the apron? Well, it's all very interesting, I must say. I just came round to wish you luck," she finished. "I know you come on in the third act, and I said to Magnus, 'Well, you can leave at the end of the second if you wish, but I am staying to see Lucinda.' "

I was disappointed to hear that Magnus would not be out front when I appeared.

"You mustn't mind," Helen said hurriedly. "He has a charity fight at midnight."

"Is he taking part?"

"Yes, indeed. The Toff versus Battling Bruce of Bermondsey. St. Swithun's Hall in the Marylebone Road, and bookings are good, even though it's an amateur fight. Well, I must get back to my seat. Good luck, Lucinda, good luck!"

She planted a warm kiss on my cheek, and suddenly I felt happy and unafraid. I had been wishing for a few quiet moments with my mother, for a few words of comfort and assurance from her, but her job of dresser left no time for anyone but Bernadette during a performance. Helen's unexpected appearance somehow made up for that.

She was turning to go when she said, "I suppose I should try to see Clementine Boswell to thank her for the tickets, but I am leaving that to Magnus because I know it is he she really wants to see. Those complimentary tickets would never have been sent to us otherwise. He is quite besotted with her, otherwise I doubt if he would have come at all. I hope the poor man gets a look-in amongst the people I saw crowding into her dressing room. I would surely get stuck in a corner with someone I didn't like, such as Durbridge. I saw your mother conducting him from Lady Boswell's dressing room to her daughter's, so I didn't bother to stop. That man knows I see through him, and he doesn't like it. Consequently he doesn't like me, either."

She waved an affectionate hand and headed back toward the iron pass door. Soon other visitors followed, but Magnus was not amongst them. He had obviously left by the stage door after paying homage to Clementine, though "homage" seemed out of character, Magnus Steel not being the type of man to kneel to anyone. Perhaps "devotion" would be more appropriate, I thought, for he was undoubtedly in love with Clementine. Meanwhile, members of the audience trooped back to the auditorium, and sure enough, Durbridge was amongst them. And who had sent complimentary tickets to him? Lady Boswell, I imagined, since he had paid his respects to her first.

He passed so close that a meeting was unavoidable. His heavily marked eyebrows raised in that characteristic way which seemed to convey disdain for the world and everyone in it.

"Miss Grainger, is it not? I have just discovered that your mother is Lady Boswell's dresser . . . well, well. And I also learn that you have your first speaking part in this production."

"It was nice of Lady Boswell—or was it her daughter?—to mention it."

"Neither of them. I had it from my friend Calder. I wish you success."

A heavy whiff of his cigar drifted over me. Despite huge notices forbidding smoking backstage, Durbridge and his costly Havana would never be parted. Mingled with its aroma was the smell of hair oil and expensive perfume. He wore several large rings on fingers which were thick and white and very hairy; one, with an immense solitaire diamond, on his fleshy little finger. I saw the sparkle of diamond studs in his stiff shirt-front, and he even wore sparkling buckles on his patent-leather evening shoes.

The stage manager spoke beside us. "Would you please return to the auditorium, sir? The curtain is about to rise."

Durbridge ignored him. He tapped ash from his cigar in a negligent, insulting fashion, and I saw Gregory's mouth tighten.

"If you please, sir, smoking is forbidden backstage, and all visitors must leave when requested."

Durbridge adjusted his monocle. "My good man, can you not see that I am in conversation with this young lady?"

"Miss Grainger has no right to be here, either. It isn't your call yet, Lucinda, so please return to your dressing room."

I was about to go when Durbridge's clammy fingers closed about my wrist.

"She stays. She may be the daughter of a backstage servant, but I gather she has greater ambitions for herself."

My cheeks flamed. I pulled free of him angrily, and at that moment young Jerry passed on his way to call the opening players.

"Ha! If it isn't our urchin from Soapbox Corner!" Durbridge's beringed hand fell on Jerry's shoulder, turning him round. "Let me look at you, boy." His fleshy hand tilted up the young chin and lingered there. "A distinct improvement, I am pleased to observe."

Jerry jerked away. "Thanks, gov," he said curtly, and moved on.

"That boy needs teaching a lesson," Durbridge murmured.

Gregory was waiting pointedly by the pass door, and I walked round the back of the set to the stairs on the opposite side, stepping over guy ropes and stays and angle rods, and never tripping until I was running up the twisting iron treads. For a moment the unshielded well in the middle yawned up at me, warning and steadying me, and by the time I reached the dressing room I was calm again.

The heat from rows of flaring gas jets met me as I opened the door. So did the babel of voices, the raucous laughter, the stench. There was sudden silence as I walked down the centre aisle to my cramped spot at the long trestle table. There were also titters and watchful eyes. I pulled out my chair, sat down, and crashed to the floor amidst the sound of splintering wood and a roar of satisfied laughter.

Slightly winded, I rose. The chair was a broken one, not the one I had chosen. I walked calmly round the room, found mine pushed into a corner, and retrieved it. The laughter died as I reseated myself and carefully retouched my makeup.

Maisie's taunting voice came to me. "Ready for your entrance a bit early, ain't you, your ladyship? I remember, at rehearsals, you made your entrance near the end. Late players don't have to be made up and on call until the beginning of the act they appear in. They don't even have to arrive at the theatre until half an hour before then."

"They do on first nights and until a run is established," I answered, still intent on my face.

"Well, well, it's a real pro we are! Know all the ettiket, don't we? Going to be a great star one day, ain't we?"

Her voice ran on, goading me. I was thankful when Jerry yelled outside the door, "Onstage ladies! *Jump to it, ladies!*" Jerry had added his own authoritative touches to the stage calls, and they worked. Seconds later I was alone again, and glad to be. The incident had shaken me more than I cared to admit, and it had taken all my willpower to deny those women the satisfaction of knowing it. I put my head down on the dressing table and closed my eyes, praying for the night to end, praying for my entrance to come and go, praying for help, for success, for self-confidence, for comfort—the comfort of Gavin's arms about me and the comfort of his voice.

I had not seen him since that offstage moment before his first entrance. He was a leading player and I was not. Leading players and lesser players met only onstage. They never mixed, even at rehearsals. I knew that during the intervals Gavin's dressing room had been crowded with friends and admirers, as the dressing rooms of other lead players had been, but the privilege of being amongst them was not for me. Besides, women players were not allowed to visit the dressing rooms of men players, not at the Boswell, so I could not tap on his door to seek a word of encouragement. If I dared to do such a thing, Bernadette would be sure to hear of it and I would be summoned before Sir Nevill or herself and sternly reprimanded.

I knew that for practically the whole of this act the supers would be onstage and I would be left in peace up here. This oasis of time was welcome, and I remained with my head on the dressing table, my eyes closed, following the whole sequence of the play in my mind so that I would know when my own entrance was due. It would be unnecessary to wait for Jerry's call.

Beneath this subconscious recitation of stage dialogue my thoughts ran on. Surely Durbridge had exaggerated when calling Gavin his friend? An acquaintance, perhaps, but no more than that. Then I remembered seeing them deep in conversation at Clementine's coming-out ball. But two men already acquainted would naturally talk together, wouldn't they? It could have been superficial conversation and quite meaningless. I was letting my prejudice against Durbridge become too strong. I had no real cause to be prejudiced against him, no actual cause for dislike, but both reactions were instinctive and both so sharp that I expected other people to feel them too. With every meeting I disliked him more and more, and for referring to my mother as a backstage servant I positively hated him.

My head jerked up. Beneath the mixed odours of this horrible room I detected a smell of burning. Had one of those women accidentally singed her hair when smoking? The reek of cheap cigarettes was mixed with all the other assorted smells. They would go without food rather than without their gin and fags.

I sniffed again. The smell was near at hand; acrid, like singeing hair. Then I saw the lid of my wig box slightly awry and knew that someone had moved it.

I snatched off the lid, and froze. I was faced with dark tresses, half-burned. My fingers felt numb as I picked up the wig. I could not believe that anyone could have done this diabolical thing. Then the real horror of it hit me. My wig was unwearable.

The door clicked open, and Maisie's voice echoed across the room. "Had an accident, your ladyship? Been smoking on the quiet, have you, and with your lovely wig on, too? I should have expected a real professional actress to have taken better care."

"*You did this.*"

"What an accusation! I might just as well accuse you of pinching my fags, and I bloody well will if you take stories like that to the management."

"I know you did it. I can see it in your face."

I dropped the wig and buried my face in my hands.

"Crying will mess your makeup, your ladyship. Won't make a very impressive entrance, will you?"

"Get out of here. Leave me alone."

"I will when I've got what I came for." She picked up a tattered shawl from the back of a chair. "It's damned cold down there in them wings."

So they had reached the part in the play where the mob gathered off-stage to yell at approaching tumbrils, with the property manager and stage crew manipulating sound effects of horses' hooves and rumbling wheels. That meant my own entrance was near. I heard Jerry's feet hammering up the stairs and knew he had come to call me. I made hasty dabs at my face and fought for self-control. Maisie was right—my makeup was now smeared and unsightly, but suddenly I looked more like a girl who had been shut up in a cell in the Bastille. With shaking hands I pinned up my long hair, pulled on the half-burned wig, and tousled its tattered shreds, leaving a shower of burned hair on the dressing table. The beautiful black locks were now matted and unkempt, but they were the hair of a suffering creature who had been unable to care for it during months of imprisonment. When Jerry called outside, "Onstage, Miss Lucinda! Onstage, please!" I was tearing the lace collar of my gown to shreds and dirtying the fabric with lampblack. In the mirror I saw Maisie watching me wide-eyed, and suddenly I felt triumphant.

"You may have done me a good turn after all," I threw at her, and then I was hurrying down to the stage and climbing into the waiting tumbril, and as two lines of male supers dragged the vehicle by its ropes, I forgot I had ever been Lucinda Grainger. I was a bedraggled victim of the French Revolution, going to her death. I was already sobbing as the tumbril was pulled onstage and I saw the fine figure of Sir Nevill being led up the guillotine steps.

Then his voice was ringing out the famous words—but he was not Nevill Boswell, actor, he was Sydney Carton, and in a volley of French I cried out my three precious lines and he turned his head and looked down at me. In that moment there was such awareness between us that we were not two performers, but real people bound by an inexplicable communication and an inextricable bond.

9

It was over. I had made my first appearance on the professional stage, and although the part was too insignificant to be a triumph, at least it had not been a disaster. I had averted that, and with the warm generosity of theatrical folk, those around me when the curtain fell were swift with their praise. Hands reached out and patted my shoulders as, with the su-pers, we hurried offstage, leaving it clear for the leads to take their cur-tain calls. The pats and the smiles and the handshakes were all from fel-low actors, small-part players like myself, and from the stage crew.

Even Jerry pushed his way through to me. "Cor, missy, you were great! But blimey, wot lingo was that?"

I had been as surprised as everyone when I cried out in French. The translation had been instinctive and unpremeditated. It was as if the trag-ic French girl had taken possession of me and my tongue had become hers. Perhaps it was this unexpected deviation which had made Sir Nev-ill's eyes focus on me for that tense moment. Perhaps I had imagined the rapport between us; perhaps he had not felt it at all, but only surprise be-cause a member of his cast had delivered her lines in a totally different manner from that used in rehearsal. But did it matter if an insignificant player spoke an insignificant number of lines in French? I had the ex-traordinary feeling that even though the words might not have been un-derstood by all of those unseen people in the auditorium, their meaning had been caught and their agony and intensity felt, for there had been a strange kind of stillness in the theatre—the stillness of shock and com-passion.

Gavin was beside me for a brief moment before taking his individual curtain call. The supers were all crowding back to the dressing rooms, leaving merciful space about us.

"Lucinda, Lucinda . . . how like you to steal the moment!" He was smiling at me, and his elation was evident. "Clever girl—you planned that well."

Before I had time to protest that I had not planned it at all, he was onstage and my mother was beside me.

"I came down to wish you luck, my darling, but you didn't even see me—"

"Mamma! You've been here all the time?"

"Of course. I was waiting when you came down. I had been wanting to see you all evening, but I couldn't leave the dressing room—there are always so many things to do for Bernadette, even when she is onstage. But nothing would have kept me away from *your* appearance. Besides, it is safe for me to be here now—she expects me to wait in the wings with her shawl when she finally comes off." She kissed me fondly. "Sir Nevill will be pleased with you. *I* certainly am. The way you cried those words was dramatic. I had no idea you were to deliver them in French. You didn't tell me."

"I didn't know myself. I hope Sir Nevill won't mind."

I knew I should follow the supers upstairs, but the thought of their company, particularly Maisie's, was more than I could face at this moment, so I decided to wait until most of them had left. Supers were always in a hurry to get away before the pubs closed, usually to the one nearest the stage door, because it would be patronised by many of the actors and therefore good picking-up ground. So I lingered beside my mother, counting the curtain calls and trying to judge by the volume of applause whether the production was a success. Not that first-night enthusiasm was always a good weathervane as far as the run of a play was concerned, or vice versa. Nor were the press reviews. Critics had been known to damn a production, and the public to acclaim it, so this one might run for a very long time, whatever the critical reaction. For my part, I prayed for a very long run, even though it meant enduring the company of Maisie and the rest of them in dressing room number 20.

Twelve curtain calls for Sir Nevill alone, and shouts for Bernadette and Clementine—also the usual enthusiastic reception for Bramwell Chambers, always popular. Standing down right, we could see the whole of the stage apron and the line of leading players as they took their bows. Bernadette had let her hair tumble from beneath Madame Defarge's revolutionary cap, and the audience loved her for it, shouting their appreciation of her willingness to conceal so much loveliness for the sake of her art. One of Bernadette's finest features was her hair, which she made the most of onstage. For the first time this evening it now rivalled her daughter's, and Clementine turned and kissed her mother with daughterly pride and affection. The audience loved that too.

They were out there alone now, father, mother, and daughter, and Gavin had come offstage to our corner of the wings. He said sardonically, "Don't they make a picture of family devotion? But Clemmy is hating her mother for that gesture, and Nevill's smile for his wife is forced, and as for Bernadette . . ." He shrugged. "My poor stepsister really believes she has a devoted husband, doesn't she, Trudy?"

My mother stiffened. She had grown to like Gavin no better with the years. If anything, I felt she disliked him more, and particularly at this moment. She bit her lip, saying nothing, and suddenly I felt shut out, forgotten by both of them.

And now the final call, traditionally for the entire cast except supers and walk-ons and small-part players like myself, so Gavin rejoined the leads centre stage, smiling his attractive smile and lifting Clementine's fingers to his lips, because of course he was Charles Darnay and she Lucie, the married couple, the lovers of the play, and the audience expected such gallantry. Then he did the same to Bernadette, as if in homage to a great actress, and then he bowed to Sir Nevill with the same humble respect—and beside me, my mother's fingers clenched and unclenched on Bernadette's shawl.

I said to her, "I hope they won't be home very late tonight. Waiting up for Bernadette fatigues you."

"First-night suppers always go on until the early hours."

"Where is this one to be?"

"Romano's—conveniently close. A large party hosted by Lord Durbridge, on his insistence."

"That will please Bernadette. She sees him as an eligible husband for Clemmy, I think."

"Then I hope she will be disappointed, for her sake as well as Clementine's. Durbridge is not the marrying kind, I can tell."

The final curtain descended. The actors came off, well pleased, the more ingratiating amongst them showering the Boswells with congratulations. Then I was face to face with Sir Nevill and he was looking down at me with an expression I could not read in the offstage shadows. He stood there for a moment, saying nothing, but his hand rested on my shoulder.

I said, "I am sorry I lapsed into French, Sir Nevill."

"I am not, my dear. I shall expect you to do the same at every performance, in exactly the same way."

That was all. It was as if that moment of communication onstage had never happened, but I was encouraged by the kindly pressure of his hand.

* * *

Mercifully, dressing room number 20 emptied rapidly. The first to leave was Maisie, and after her departure I waited only for her especial cronies to follow. Lingering backstage, I saw Durbridge and a group of others returning through the pass door, and I knew that by the time I had removed my makeup, changed, and come down again, the champagne served onstage after a first night would have run out and the supper party have moved on to Romano's. After that, my mother and I would return by hansom to Portman Square, where I resolved she would go to bed despite protests. I could wait up and deputise as lady's maid for once.

As the rest of the supers filtered past me toward the stage door, I glimpsed Gavin talking to Durbridge onstage, champagne glass in hand. Their conversation appeared to be light and casual, but Durbridge's hooded eyes were fixed on Gavin in a compelling sort of way. But he looked at everyone like that, except Magnus Steel. With Magnus it was different. I always felt that Durbridge had difficulty in meeting the doctor's eye and was only too pleased to avoid it. But Magnus was not so gregarious as Gavin, good mixer though he was. Gavin met everyone with friendly camaraderie; Magnus met them critically, summing them up with his frank and appraising glance.

". . . then I'll follow. You can do the honours meantime."

The words floated out to me from between the flats. It was Durbridge speaking. I could not catch Gavin's answer, but the conversation was meaningless anyway. Nor did I like eavesdropping, so I moved away. The last words I heard were, "Everything's arranged and the menu ordered . . ." Durbridge was obviously discussing his supper party and asking Gavin to hold the fort for him for some reason or other.

I climbed the circular stairs to dressing room number 20. I saw Jerry tidying the prop room, a wide space opening directly offstage, and called good night to him. His cheerful face grinned up at me, clean and cherubic now that he was well fed and well housed, but he was still undersized and always would be. I was proud of Jerry, proud that it was I who had suggested taking him into the theatre as callboy. Even his language had improved, and now his face was no longer pinched with hunger, it looked more angelic than ever.

Mercifully, the dressing room was empty, but the stench was worse than before. I opened the skylight again, and even the smoke-laden air of London seemed sweet by comparison. I felt hot and begrimed, and was thankful to see that the pitcher of cold water supplied to every dressing room had remained untouched. After removing my makeup, I filled the chipped enamel bowl which accompanied it, stripped, and began to sponge my body, thankful that I had waited for my roommates to depart. To strip and wash in front of them would have exposed me to ridicule and ribaldry, whereas now I could take my time about it without fear of intrusion.

I knew it would be some time before Bernadette released my mother, so I tipped the basin of used water into the pail provided for the purpose and refilled it with the remaining water from the pitcher. Already I was feeling clean and refreshed, and I had time to linger over this second toilet. Tension had vanished, first-night nerves had quietened, and I was relaxed and at peace until the scream from next door pierced the dividing wall.

It came from the men's dressing room, a room corresponding with this and used for male supers. I grabbed a towel, anxious to be gone, and not a little frightened. If some of the men were still there and a drunken fight were breaking out, the sooner I left, the better. My hands were shaking as I rubbed myself half-dry, but when the sound came again I knew that no men were fighting in there, because the scream was that of a boy, and it was a scream of impotent fury and terror.

I was out of my dressing room in a flash, the towel knotted about me, and without ceremony I flung open the adjoining door. What I saw paralysed me. Jerry was on the floor, kicking and fighting as Durbridge strove to rip the clothes off him.

My sudden entry caused the man's head to jerk up. The look on his face made nausea rise in my stomach, but in the same moment I came to life. I leapt forward, and Durbridge's grip on the boy slackened. Quick as an eel Jerry was away, shouting, *"You buggering bastard! You filthy, buggering bastard!"*

The next thing I heard was a crash as Durbridge lunged at me, knocking over a table which, in turn, sent me hurtling to the floor; then, his face twitching and his moist red lips trembling with frustration and fury, he bore down on me.

I struck my head as I fell, and a blinding pain shot through it. The world darkened and then came back again. I felt my arms and legs flailing helplessly and the rough wooden floor scraping my naked body, and I heard Jerry's frantic cries for help as he clattered down the iron stairs, and Durbridge's savage breath panting in my ear. Then my arms were pinioned from behind and I was rolled over, face downward, and his voice was gasping, "Damn you, you bitch—you interfering bitch—for this, *you'll* do instead." I screamed as he knelt astride my back and the realisation of what he was about to do shot through my brain. My face was pressed flat against the floor, and I jerked my head sideways for release; he struck at it, shouting obscenities, trying to force me to be still, trying to raise the lower part of my back toward him by thrusting his arm beneath my thighs to pull me into a kneeling position, and with every muscle and every searing breath I struggled and fought, rolling from side to side to dislodge him and knowing I was fighting a losing battle, that soon he would commit his foul assault and that I was powerless against his rage and his bestiality; then I saw his hand braced against the floor beside my mouth and I sank my teeth into his wrist until I tasted blood.

He gave a shout of pain, and his strength slackened. With one superhuman effort I scrambled from beneath him, snatched up my towel, and staggered to the door. Beneath my shocked senses I was aware of footsteps racing up the stairs and my mother's voice frantically calling my name. She had almost reached me, but Durbridge was quicker. They met face to face at the top of the stairs, and he lunged at her so that she retreated, grabbing the iron rail and stumbling downward because there was no other direction she could take.

"Lucinda . . . get back to your room and lock the door! Jerry has gone for help!" Her voice came up to me as Durbridge lumbered down the stairs, intent on silencing her. The echo of their footsteps diminished, then ceased abruptly. I heard an ear-splitting scream followed by a heavy thud, then I too was racing down the stairs, clutching my tattered towel around me and coming to a sudden halt because my mother was there, staring down the central well at Durbridge's body spread-eagled far below.

She said in a wavering voice, *"I* did it, *I* did it . . . I turned and struck his legs on the step above, and he stumbled . . . he tried to grab the rail, but couldn't hold it . . . his hand was wet with blood and it slipped . . ." She went on mouthing the words, *"I* did it, *I* did it . . ." until I gathered her close to silence her.

10

"He is dead," said Gavin.

He was kneeling on the floor beside Durbridge's body, and now he looked from one to the other of us, his face shocked.

"How did it happen? Jerry came racing into Romano's demanding Sir Nevill, but he was in the middle of a distant group and because the boy was gabbling some story about Lucinda needing help, I came at once . . ." He broke off, seeing, for the first time, the ragged towel covering my nakedness. "Good God, how do you come to be in that state?"

I looked down at my bare legs. They were torn and bleeding and I felt the soreness of my body also, seared by the rough floorboards. I had scarcely been aware of either until now. Gavin put out a hand and touched my face, and blood and dirt came away on his fingers. My mother gave a cry and put her arms about me, and we went on sitting there cradling each other until Gavin separated us, commanding me to get dressed at once.

"We must get out of here quickly. Hurry, *hurry!*"

But my mother clung to me, refusing to let me go, and it was then that I realised something was wrong with her.

"What the devil's the matter with Trudy?" Gavin asked at the same moment, and she began to whimper like a child.

"You're not to touch her, you're not to touch her!" she cried, like an animal defending its young.

I said gently, "Gavin is here to help us, Mamma." I disengaged her hands and repeated what I had said, but she shook her head from side to side, over and over again, until Gavin took hold of her shoulders and shook her.

"Trudy!" he commanded sharply. "Pull yourself together!"

But she couldn't. Shock had done something to her. I didn't know what it was, but it frightened me. I said urgently, "Gavin is *helping* us, Mamma. We can trust him. Come upstairs with me now. . . ."

She was not averse to that. What she was not prepared to do was to leave my side. Back in the dressing room she bathed my chafed body, her eyes filling with tears when she saw the state I was in. I was thankful that concern for me penetrated the defensive retreat of her mind.

Gavin was rapping on the door, urging us to hurry, and as I pulled on my clothes, my mother rolled up the stained towel. "I will get rid of this," she said. "No one will find it, no one." Dazed with shock in some respects she might be, but where I was concerned her thoughts were lucid and concise. I had to be protected. I must be looked after, and she was the one to do it. Beyond that basic and all-important instinct, a shutter seemed to have come down. Perhaps it was better so. Perhaps it was better that she should not recall Durbridge's attack on me. Did she even know what he had tried to do, or did she think he had merely tried to rape me?

Gavin had a cab waiting outside. "Get your mother home and call a doctor to her," he ordered as he shepherded us across the rear of the stage, giving a wide berth to Durbridge's sprawling body, assuring us all the time that we had nothing to worry about so long as we kept quiet about everything. "Say nothing to anyone. Make some excuse for your mother's shock and leave everything else to me. Neither you nor your mother will be involved in this in any way."

I remembered Jerry and asked what had become of him.

"I sent him home direct from Romano's. He knows the streets of London by night and can take care of himself. I'm glad I sent him packing, because it means that only we three know what happened to Durbridge. Not even George was on the premises, but Nevill will think he locked up as usual."

"Why didn't he? George is always the last to leave the theatre."

"Not tonight. He had a drop too much. We've a hard-drinking bunch of supers in this production, and some of them are cronies of his. He was over at the Duke's Head as soon as the last curtain fell. That's not unusual, but he always comes back after his nightly pint. That gives him time to see everyone off the premises and then to lock up." We were hurrying along the passage to the stage door now, and Gavin thrust a hand into a pocket and held up a key. "I relieved him of this when I saw the state he was in. Some of Nevill's guests were still imbibing onstage, so I took charge and sent George home. In the morning he'll keep quiet, because he won't want the management to know. But in any case, no questions will be asked. I'll see to that."

He handed us into the waiting cab. "Straight home and to bed," he ordered, "and don't worry about anything. You can tell me tomorrow what happened." His glance slid to my mother, sitting tensely in a corner, clutching her reticule in which she had stuffed the towel. She had to grip the sides to keep it shut, and as the cab pulled away I said, "You could have left that behind, Mamma. There's nothing incriminating about it. We could have dropped it in the skip for dirty linen back stage."

She didn't seem to hear me. She was staring out into the night and she remained like that the whole way home, except for one moment when the cabby took a shortcut through an alley in Soho and she reached out and threw the towel into the gutter. I heard her reticule snap shut and her sigh of relief as she leaned back.

"There," she said, as if she had been very clever. "A soiled cloth in a Soho gutter will arouse no comment at all. By morning it will be no more than a sodden rag."

I looked at her in concern and covered her hand with mine. She was the one in need of protection, not I; not merely because she had been involved in Durbridge's accidental death, but because she suddenly seemed as defenceless as a child.

She behaved even more strangely when we reached Portman Square. Instead of going straight upstairs to our rooms, she went into the Boswells' drawing room and seated herself. "We must wait up for his return," she said, and I knew she meant Sir Nevill though it was most unusual for her not to refer to him as such. Surely, I thought, she doesn't mean to tell him what happened, after all the trouble Gavin is taking to keep us out of it?

Again I tried to coax her to bed, but she answered, "No, we must wait here."

"But we have no right . . ."

The words died on my lips because I could see she was paying no heed. I became really concerned then. Her eyes seemed to have taken on a faraway look. Not an imbecilic look, but a sort of blankness, and yet I felt she was seeing something or remembering something which had nothing to do with the present, but which was real and vital and alive to her. She also seemed more at peace, as if, with our arrival home, she was lulled into a feeling of security.

"We must go upstairs, Mamma. I don't think Lady Boswell would be pleased to find us sitting in her drawing room."

"It is not hers. It is Nevill's."

I was startled, but a single note from the mantelpiece clock distracted my attention. One o'clock in the morning—how the night had flown! The curtain had risen at eight-thirty and come down at eleven, and since then so much had happened. I shuddered when I remembered it, and the soreness of my skin beneath my clothes was an aggravation which brought alive those hideous moments on the bare dressing-room floor: the rough wood, the man's rage, his savagery, his perverted lust. I shivered, though the fire was sending out plenty of heat. It was always well banked up to await Lady Boswell's return; she hated coming home to a chilly fireside.

I wondered how soon the supper party would end, how soon the carriage would halt at the front door, how soon she would come marching in here, ready to ring for her nightcap and then for my mother.

"Mamma," I said helplessly, "you really must go to bed. I can wait up."

"Oh, no, my love. Nevill would be disappointed."

She was smiling, sitting there contentedly beside the fire, but I was shaking, frightened by something I could not comprehend. "Get your mother home and call a doctor," Gavin had said, and immediately I thought of Magnus Steel. His fight with Battling Bruce of Bermondsey must be over by now; he should even be home. Without explanation I hurried from the room.

Minutes later, after running round the square because the gardens in the centre had been locked for the night, I was hammering on Dr. Steel's front door. He answered it himself. He wore a quilted dressing gown and held a lamp high, shining its light down on me.

"Lucinda!" He drew me across the threshold. "You are shaking—and in heaven's name, what have you done to your face?"

I could feel the bruising and the throbbing and the soreness from deep scratching, but I brushed all that aside.

"What has happened?" he demanded. "Has someone hurt you?"

"No, no, it's nothing. Please come to my mother. I don't know what to do with her, how to handle her . . ."

He wasted no more time. Seconds later he came downstairs, wearing street clothes and carrying a gladstone bag. His keen eyes surveyed me as if it were I who concerned him chiefly, but he asked no more questions. The streetlamps had been extinguished in the square and the detour around it hindered us sufficiently for the Boswell carriage, turning into the south side at that moment, to pull up at their front door ahead of us. In the light from the carriage lamps and from the porch I saw Curtis helping Lady Boswell down. She descended heavily, clumsy of movement and leaning on the coachman's arm until her husband was at her side and leading her up the front steps. Then Curtis was holding out his hand to Clementine and, distraught as I was, his protective custody was not lost on me. We were only a few yards away by then, and without looking at Magnus I knew that he also was watching Clementine in the mesmerised way in which a man always watches a woman he is enamoured of. I was not surprised, for Clemmy was certainly a man's woman.

It was plain that Curtis also found her so and that his attention was more than that of a respectful servant. I saw her pull her hand away as soon as her feet touched the pavement, and his frown as she swept past him to the front steps without even troubling to glance at him or to say good night. We were almost upon them by then and I could feel his resentment as he watched her go.

I wondered if Magnus had noticed the incident, but doubted it, absorbed as he was in contemplation of Clementine. As we drew level, Curtis sprang back onto the box and whipped the horses angrily, his handsome face scowling.

Curtis, I felt, could be a very ugly customer if he chose to be. Clementine had been foolish to encourage him, but male admiration was meat and drink to her; she threw provocative glances by instinct, and if these were misinterpreted she had only herself to blame.

Then I forgot Curtis as we mounted the steps to the front door, reaching it just as Hawkins was about to close it. I heard Lady Boswell's voice drifting back to us from the hall. Her husband was helping her off with her cloak and she was saying ". . . strange sort of behaviour, and so unlike Lord Durbridge to forget about his guests . . . and then Gavin disappearing too and not returning. *What* a first-night celebration!"

Her speech was again slightly slurred, but she was not intoxicated, merely angry and affronted. She lumbered toward the drawing room then and Magnus and I reached it just as the three Boswells walked into the room ahead of us and my mother, rising from her chair beside the fire, moved swiftly to Sir Nevill, crying, "Oh, my love, thank God you have come! Something terrible happened to our darling child tonight!"

11

I saw my mother's arms reach up and entwine themselves about Nevill Boswell's neck and through my shock I heard her saying, "You know I have always tried to protect her, but I failed tonight, my love . . . I failed tonight!"

He was absolutely still. The whole room was still until his wife slumped to the floor in the clumsiest and most inelegant faint I had ever seen her perform. But this was no stage faint, carefully rehearsed for grace and effectiveness. She simply collapsed and lay in an ungainly heap on the floor. All this seemed to register in an area of my consciousness made remote by shock.

Then Sir Nevill was stammering, "My dear . . . my dear Trudy . . . you don't know what you are saying."

"Oh yes, she does, Papa. She is saying that your daughter—yours and hers, not yours and my dear mamma's—met with some mishap tonight." It was Clementine, pouring out condemnation and derision. "It's a good thing we have a doctor here. At least *he* seems concerned about my mother."

I saw Magnus stooping over Lady Boswell, but I could take in nothing except my mother's words. She seemed bewildered now, puzzled and hurt because Nevill Boswell just stood there saying nothing. He was trying to detach her clinging hands from around his neck; gently, but with a touch of panic. It was that which convinced me that my mother spoke nothing but the truth and that he was desperately wishing she would be silent.

At length he burst out, "Trudy, please leave us. I will speak with you later, not now."

"Afraid, Papa? Afraid of everyone knowing what everyone must surely have guessed long ago—except my poor dear mamma, of course. I have suspected it myself from time to time and I'm quite sure Gavin has. That is why he despises you and you have always hated him for that."

"Be quiet, Clemmy."

"Why should I? Your dear Trudy seems determined not to be."

Clementine was helping Magnus to heave her mother into a sitting position now, and to me she rapped, "Can't you make yourself useful, Lucy?
My mother's smelling salts are in the bureau over there."

Jerking me to action was the best thing she could have done. A moment later I was passing the smelling salts to and fro beneath the great
Bernadette's nose. The nostrils looked pinched and her face had gone
ashen beneath its blobs of rouge. She was conscious now, staring around
with slowly dawning comprehension. Despite my own shock, I found
myself pitying the woman until she flung out a plump and beringed hand,
pointing it venomously at my mother.

"*A viper! A viper in my bosom!*" Even at this moment she dramatised every tone and gesture. I dropped the smelling salts in disgust and went to
my mother's side, remorseful because it was she I should be caring for,
no one else.

Then Bernadette began to cry in a high-pitched wail, rocking herself
backward and forward like a child until Clementine ordered her to be
quiet.

"You won't win any sympathy by making a scene, Mamma. Nothing
will alter the truth. What you have to decide is what you are going to do
about it. I take it it *is* the truth, since Papa hasn't denied it."

Magnus had got Bernadette into a chair now. He came over to my
mother then and said gently, "Let me help you to your room, Miss
Grainger. I will give you a sleeping draught and return to see you in the
morning."

"Never!" screeched Bernadette. "*Never!* Out of this house she goes.
A viper in my bosom all these years! Clementine, fetch the brandy. No,
not you, Nevill—don't come near me, now or ever!" Her screeching
turned to wailing again, and Clementine rolled despairing eyes heaven-
ward.

"What a night *this* turned out to be! My big first night, too. And apparently it's all your fault, Lucy Grainger. What have you been up to,
sparking your mother off like that? I do believe the poor thing has taken
leave of her senses. Shock, I suppose, but what sort of a shock to trigger
her off like that after all these years? From the look of you, you've been
up to something—what a mess your face is! Don't tell me you've been
brawling with those supers in your dressing room? Like takes to like, I
suppose. Did you attack them as viciously as they appear to have attacked you?"

I was about to utter a sharp retort when Magnus advised Sir Nevill to
get his wife to bed at once, but the man looked helpless and uncomfortable and made no response. At that, Clementine blazed, "Papa, don't
just stand there wishing you could escape! You can't. You've been hiding the truth very successfully all these years, but it's out now. If you

have any sense, you'll keep out of Mamma's way until she has recovered, and we'll send for our own doctor, who won't be so indifferent." Turning to Magnus, she finished, "You seem more concerned for my father's mistress than for his wife."

"I came here to attend Lucinda's mother. Your own has now recovered from her faint. Her pulse rate is affected by alcohol and anger, but very little else."

"Then kindly stop looking at Trudy Grainger as if you feel sorry for her. You too, Papa. You've kept the woman under your roof long enough and very conveniently, and she has done very well out of it considering everything. Not many women who have behaved as she has have got away with it."

I leapt to my mother's defence. "*And* she has been punished enough and endured enough. I won't let anyone say cruel things about her. Nothing she has ever done could be wrong in my eyes."

The great Bernadette, gulping brandy between intermittent wails, shouted, "Get them out of here, both of them—the girl as well! Never shall they darken my door again!"

Sir Nevill at last spoke up. "They will stay until I can find somewhere for them to go. They are my responsibility and I happen to care about them. If I have coped with things badly or wrongly, the blame is mine, but Trudy and Lucinda are not to suffer or be condemned in any way."

His glance went to my mother and then away again, as if the sight of her was a reproach. She was still silent, and a worried crease on her brow was deepening, as if she found everything too bewildering to follow. A terrible passivity seemed to have settled on her.

Then Magnus was picking up her coat from the chair on which she had dropped it and saying gently, "This is yours, I believe? Let me help you on with it and then we can go. My sister and I will be happy to have you and your daughter to stay with us for as long as you wish. Come," he added coaxingly when she did nothing but stare at him helplessly. "Helen will be glad to have your company and our house is amply big enough for all four of us. Lucinda, are you ready? The rest of your things can be sent over tomorrow. Helen will provide anything needed tonight."

We were out in the hall when the great Bernadette's voice echoed behind us with a renewed wail. "But what am I to do without a dresser? How *dare* she leave me in the lurch!"

I went back to the drawing room and halted in the open door. Nevill Boswell was standing exactly as we had left him, Bernadette was gulping brandy as if her life depended on it, and Clementine was turning away in exasperation.

I said clearly, "My mother should have left this house long ago, and had I known the truth I would have made her."

Without another word, I turned my back on the Boswells and followed Magnus Steel and my mother out into the night.

About noon the next day Helen came to me and announced that Sir Nevill wished to see me alone and was waiting in the upstairs drawing room. I was in the basement kitchen, cleaning vegetables. I was determined to help in this house and, understanding how I felt, Helen had agreed.

When I hesitated now, she said, "You don't want to see him, I can tell, but be fair to him, Lucinda. He deserves a hearing, at least."

Characteristically, she had asked no questions nor seemed in the least put out by our unexpected arrival in the early hours of the morning. She had bustled about preparing beds and finding nightgowns for us, and I had helped by lighting fires in bedroom grates and then getting my mother to bed. Magnus had given her a sleeping draught and after that he had surveyed me with a keen professional eye and tended the scars on my face, then told Helen to get me some hot milk and to let me sleep late in the morning, and though I had not expected to sleep at all, it was ten o'clock before I finally wakened.

My mother showed no inclination to rise. She simply lay there dozing fitfully, at other times staring into space. Helen was preparing broth for her and before leaving for Stepney, Magnus had examined her again, then pronounced that there was little wrong with her physically, but that her state of shock was acute.

"I don't think Nevill Boswell was entirely responsible for it, though his reaction made her finally retreat into this unhappy silence." He had looked directly at me then. "You could enlighten me, but you don't want to, do you? You will have to eventually, even so. Your mother said that something terrible had happened to you, and she was perfectly lucid about that. Adding everything up, the answer seems to be that something traumatic had happened to the pair of you."

But not to anyone could I reveal details of my encounter with Durbridge, nor the tragedy which followed, though to me it was only a tragedy insofar as it affected my mother. I could feel no reaction to the man's death other than dread in case her involvement in it came to light. The fact that it had been an accident scarcely lessened my apprehension. To expose her to police questioning in her present state would be dangerous, her confused answers even likely to condemn her.

I pinned my hope on Gavin. His determination to protect us was like a rock to lean on and, combined with Magnus Steel's care, my mother was in good hands.

"Very well," I said to Helen now. "I will go upstairs and meet my father." I said it deliberately, defiantly. "I suppose Magnus told you?"

"A little. Only enough to make me understand the state your mother was in." She touched my arm as I passed her. "Don't be afraid of this encounter, Lucinda. I fancy Nevill Boswell is feeling more nervous than you are."

I didn't believe that. I remembered his stony silence last night and his reluctance to admit the truth until finally forced to. Overnight, my view of this man had changed.

He was standing by the window, staring out into the square, and when he turned I could not see his face because his back was to the light. Instead, it focused on me and I felt that he had planned it so, subtly turning the tables so that it was I who appeared to be the supplicant and he the inquisitor. I would have none of that.

I said without preamble, "I cannot see you with your back to the light. Please be good enough to let me see your face."

His discipline as an actor enabled him to hide his surprise, but I sensed it even so. He walked away from the window and came and stood before me, and I saw that he looked taut and strained.

"Is that better, Lucinda?"

I nodded, but did not ask him to sit down.

After a moment he said, "You feel nothing but antagonism for me. I wonder why I didn't expect that."

"You should have done."

"I believed there was a bond between us."

"And what of the bond between yourself and my mother?"

"It has always been there. Ever since I met her."

"But last night you didn't want to acknowledge it."

"I was taken by surprise. Shocked."

"And cowardly."

He nodded. "That too."

"You, who once accused Gavin of cowardice!"

"The night he hid onstage, you mean? I still don't admire him for that, but now *you* don't admire *me*, do you? I can see you are determined not to make things easy for me."

"You didn't make things easy for my mother last night."

"You are right to defend her. For myself, there is no defence, but I have always loved her."

"Not enough to acknowledge her. Not enough to marry her and make her child legitimate. Though I don't mind being a bastard. It has never made any difference in my life. Possibly it has even been a source of greater happiness, because I have had my mother's undivided love."

But not wholly undivided. . . . I remembered my mother's admiration of this man, her loyal defence should anyone dare to criticise him, as

Gavin sometimes did, and her insistence always that we owed our security to him, and suddenly I felt that I had been very naive all these years.

My father answered sadly, "I have never heard you speak in that tone before. Hard and accusing. Don't be like that, Lucinda. Don't change toward me, I beg."

"I have already done so." I burst out, "What do you expect? How do you expect me to feel? She has been kept like a servant in your house—"

"Not by choice. I have tried to ease things for her in every way I could, but—"

"But not enough. It would have been kinder to provide for her elsewhere instead of housing her in a menial position. I don't admire you for that."

I knew I had hurt him and I was glad, but then, unexpectedly, I wanted to cry. Until now, I had had no desire to. I had felt shocked and angry and fiercely protective, but now I felt pain because in hurting him it rebounded onto myself.

He protested, "Do you imagine I wouldn't have obtained my freedom and married your mother, had it been possible? With the divorce laws of this country as they are, it was not. And it still is not. My wife has never been unfaithful to me, so I am in no position to divorce her, and my own infidelity would have to be accompanied by much greater offences to enable her to divorce me. The most I could have hoped for would have been a separation, which would have been no solution at all. To live with your mother outside the law would have exposed her to ostracism and humiliation. Wisely or not, I wanted to spare everyone from inevitable scandal, which, in this day and age, can be painful indeed."

"By 'everyone' you mean your wife and daughter also. Your legitimate daughter and a wife whom you no longer loved. I have been aware of many things in my life, except the most important one. That seems unbelievable now. So many things pointed to it, but I had neither the sense nor the eyes to see it."

"You accepted the situation because you were born to it and because your mother made your world secure. I hoped I contributed to that a little. I have watched with tenderness and pride as you grew up. Having you both beneath my roof enabled me to do that. You are my daughter and I love you. I also love your mother. In that I never changed, even though our relationship ended when she came to live in my house. It was her choice, and I respected it. I wanted you both near, and I wanted you to grow up in my care. That is why I am here now. I want to find out what happened last night, what had affected her in such a way, and why your face showed marks of violence. I hope Gavin Calder was not responsible?"

"Gavin! He would never hurt me."

"Then were you attacked on your way home? Surely you didn't return from the theatre on foot? You know I will never permit that."

"We came by hansom cab, as always, and I suffered no violence anywhere, in any way. I tripped over an angle rod backstage and hurt my face, that is all."

I was now anxious to change the subject, anxious for him to be gone. I wanted no questions about last night in any way at all.

He said thoughtfully, "That is what you want me to believe."

"It is the truth."

"No. You are hiding something from me, but because it is your wish, I will accept your story. Your mother is another matter. She must be cared for."

"The Steels are doing that. We are remaining here until I can make other arrangements."

"*You* make other arrangements, a girl barely sixteen?"

"I can find employment."

"You have that already."

"A minor player doesn't earn enough for what I intend to do."

He became angry.

"You heard me say last night that you were both my responsibility and that I would make arrangements for you. I insist on that."

"I don't consider you have the right."

"I claim it. I will find a home for both of you, and you will have the career you were intended for. You will justify the ability you have inherited from me and fulfil all my ambitions for you." His tone changed. "I beg you not to disappoint me in this."

"Surely you don't imagine I could come back to the theatre and continue as a member of the company? There would be embarrassment all round, and besides, Lady Boswell would never agree."

"It is I who own the Boswell Theatre and the Boswell Company, and don't forget that you have a contract for that part, small though it is. I shall keep you to it. Only the management can terminate it, never a player. To enable you to earn more money, you can also understudy the part of Lucie."

I refused point-blank. "First my mother as your wife's shadow, and now I as your daughter's? Never."

"That is not how I think of either you or Trudy."

"It is how I would feel."

I almost added that it was also how Clemmy would like me to feel, but the stricken look on his face prevented me.

"Then I shall find an alternative," he said, "though I must remind you that when you first agreed to be coached by me, I clearly pointed out that you would not only have to work when I commanded, study whatever I set you, and take criticism no matter how harsh, but that you would have to accept discouragement and hide resentment when you felt passed over in favour of another actress. If you resent understudying Clementine, remember that you will not be understudying *her*, but the part of Lucie. That is important. Remember that an actress is never understudying another actress; she is understudying the *part*, not the player. So in this you must obey. However, I will see what I can do concerning an additional small part as well. I shall take care of your future and provide for you when I am gone, as I have always intended to. And now . . . may I see your mother?''

I answered truthfully that she was sleeping, adding that Dr. Steel would decide when she was ready to face problems again.

"I haven't come here to face her with problems, but to alleviate them, and I can only pray that in time you will view me more kindly, even if you can never accept me as your father. I know I don't come out of this situation in glowing colours.''

I could think of no reply. The sight of his lined face was like a reproach. Then I remembered my mother's face when he turned away from her. Failing to acknowledge the truth until he could no longer avoid it amounted to rejection in my eyes. My lifelong view of him as a father figure died, and my pity was stillborn. He was right when saying he did not come out of this in glowing colours.

I wished he would go. The room seemed filled with discomfort. I felt he wanted to say more, but my lack of encouragement prevented him. *Go*, I wanted to tell him. Go now. Go out of my life.

"You are sorry you learned the truth, Lucinda. You are wishing I were not your father. If you cannot feel toward me as you did, can you not try to remember me as I was?''

I was on the verge of saying, "As I *thought* you were . . ." but the words remained unspoken. It was better for certain things not to be uttered.

I wished desperately that Gavin would come. Tomorrow, he had said. "You can tell me tomorrow what happened." So he would call at the Boswells' house and hear that we had left with Magnus Steel. He would trace me here and he would then come to tell me what he had done about Durbridge's body. He would have had to report the accident to the police, of course; it would appear in the press, and there would be an inquest, but Gavin would be as good as his word—he would keep my mother's name, and mine, out of it. Thank God for Gavin. Dear God, send Gavin. Make him come soon.

He came at that moment, as if summoned by the power of prayer. Helen ushered him into the room, quite unaware that it might have been better to wait until Nevill Boswell had gone. The two men stood there, not saying a word, and Helen looked from one to the other in a surprised sort of way, and then at me apologetically. The door closed tactfully behind her.

"So you called at my house," said my father without any greeting, "and then followed Lucinda here."

"Why not? I am concerned for her. I gather from Clementine that certain things were revealed last night which I believe Lucinda has never suspected. You have kept your secret very well all these years, but not from me. I guessed it long ago. If you're on the point of leaving, don't let me detain you."

My father's eyes darkened with anger. I had seen him look at Gavin like that many times in the past and attributed it solely to personal dislike. Now its motivation seemed stronger and more understandable. Any man would resent another who knew the secrets of his life and disapproved of them.

"I came to see Lucinda," Gavin said pointedly, and there was nothing the older man could do but depart.

When we were alone, Gavin put his arms around me and held me close. "My poor darling, you've come through a bad time, and it's still going on, isn't it? Your mother is in a bad state. I could see something was wrong with her last night. What happened back there at the theatre?"

I closed my eyes and leaned against him, the strength of his body seeming to wrap me round. This man would never terrify or hurt me, never abuse or misuse my body. With him I felt not only safe but alive in a warm, sweet, totally adult way. When he lifted my face and his mouth came down on mine, softly at first and then with increasing pressure, and then in a way which I had not anticipated or even suspected a man did to a woman, the experience was wholly beautiful. His embrace tightened and I forgot all the shocks I had experienced in the last twelve hours, for everything was submerged beneath a physical longing so powerful that I desired only Gavin.

His mouth left mine, and with his lips against my ear he whispered, "I am going to be your lover, Lucinda. You know that, don't you? I have watched you grow up; I have waited, desiring you. We must be together. You know that, don't you?"

I nodded, my head against his shoulder.

"You have nothing to fear, dear heart. I don't know what happened to you last night, but whatever it was, with me it will be different. Your body won't be bruised and torn. It will be cherished and you will love every moment of it." He put a hand beneath my chin and lifted my face. "What did he do to you?" he asked, his voice hardened by anger. "Did he rape you?"

"No . . . no . . ."

"You managed to avoid him, naked as you were? And why were you, by the way?"

I told him, and after that I had to tell him everything. I had to explain why I ran out of my dressing room clad in nothing but a towel, and why it was Jerry who went racing to my mother in search of help. "It was the boy he wanted, not me," I finished, sickened by the whole memory of it, "but he was ready to take my body in the same way, as punishment."

Gavin uttered an inarticulate sound and held me closer, so close that my face was buried against his shoulder again. I was thankful for that, because it helped to blot out memory. But not entirely. A question which had been hammering at the back of my mind now sought utterance. "What I can't understand," I said, "is how Jerry came to be in that dressing room next door. When I left the stage, I saw him in the props room, tidying up. You were onstage at the champagne party then, talking to Durbridge. I heard him say something about following you and asking you to do the honours in the meantime."

Gavin was shocked. "Good God, Lucinda, surely you don't imagine that I knew what the man had in mind? He told me he had to go along to White's to settle a gambling debt before midnight, and naturally I believed him. A member can get into serious trouble at White's if he doesn't honour his debts by the end of the month, and a man like Durbridge wouldn't risk his reputation by failing to. So of course I agreed to hold the fort for him. Had I known what he planned to do . . ."

"He must have tricked Jerry into going up there, though I can't imagine how. The boy has never liked him."

"We could cross-question the lad, I suppose, though I feel it would be wiser to say nothing. Did the accident on the stairs happen after Jerry had left for Romano's?"

"Yes. He ran down, shouting, and my mother came at once—"

I broke off, shaking, and Gavin said softly, "Hush, my darling. It is all in the past, and Durbridge can never come back into your life. You are safe, I promise. You and I and your mother are the only people who know that anyone was near at the time of his death; the stage-doorman had gone, the callboy had gone, and no one else was in the theatre, so no questions can be asked. And we won't arouse Jerry's curiosity by questioning him, either. He was unharmed, I take it?"

I nodded. At least my intervention had achieved that.

"And you were also unharmed, thank God. I had no suspicion Durbridge was that kind of a man."

But Magnus Steel had known. I remembered his attitude in the park, the things he had said and implied, and my failure to understand any of it.

Gavin said, briskly changing the subject, "Anyway, the doctor who examined the body confirmed that his neck had been broken due to falling from a height, and that the end was instantaneous. We needn't go into the story now; I'll tell you the rest some other time. The important thing is that neither you nor your mother has anything to worry about. The whole thing has been hushed up."

The door clicked open and Magnus entered unceremoniously. I was relieved because his face was expressionless, so I knew he had overheard nothing.

He said to me, "I have just visited your mother and am happy to say she is more like her normal self. It would be a good idea if you went to her." When Gavin made a move to follow me, he added, "Alone."

Gavin said amiably and confidently that Trudy would wish to see him. "In fact, I think she will be anxious to."

"Later."

Magnus, who had been holding the door open for me, closed it firmly as I hurried upstairs to my mother.

She was sitting in an armchair beside the fire and Helen was placing a tray before her, urging her to eat.

"If you don't, Cook will be offended, and she is too valuable to lose. The thought of having to prepare household meals appalls me as much as the thought of trying to replace her. She has been with our family longer than I can remember and rules the domestic roost superbly, so please, Miss Grainger, don't let me down."

Helen's cajolery impressed me. I was well aware that she had prepared the broth herself and that Cook had been only too willing to let her. As she sailed out of the room, leaving us alone, I stooped and kissed the top of my mother's head lightly, as if I hadn't a care in the world, but she made no response. She seemed anxious not to look at me. Confusion had been replaced by embarrassment and even shame. I knew she was remembering the culmination of last night's events and her own startling revelation and was now afraid to meet my eye, but I was relieved because the dazed look had disappeared, and to add reassurance I took both her hands and said, "Mamma, it is important that you should know the truth—Durbridge didn't rape me or seduce me or harm me in any way."

Having said that, I prayed the matter would be closed, for indeed it was the truth. I had managed to evade the man and could not keep a triumphant note out of my voice because of it. Even so, I felt sullied by the encounter. I had experienced no sexual assault in my life, and Durbridge's left an indelible impression on my mind. There could be no forgetting, no matter how hard I tried, but the last thing I wanted to do was to talk about it anymore. Confiding in Gavin had been enough; with my mother, impossible.

She lifted her head then, and her large grey eyes looked into mine.

"You are telling me the truth, Lucinda?"

"The whole truth, Mamma."

"Thank God . . . thank God . . ."

I wondered if she would now regret her own impulsive revelation, realising it had been unnecessary because the situation had not been bad enough to warrant throwing away a lifetime of silence, but fate had catapulted both of us into the present state of things. Our old life had been ruptured and we had to make a fresh start. This would be easier for me than for my mother. I was compelled to continue at the theatre, but she would never enter it again. Not the Boswell, at any rate, and the thought of her seeking work as a dresser at any other theatre was one I refused to contemplate. I said, with a confidence I did not wholly feel, "We will manage, Mamma. Somehow we will manage."

But her thoughts were elsewhere. They came stumbling through her next words.

"I . . . I didn't think he would ever be ashamed, but he turned away from me. . . ."

"He was taken by surprise, as everyone was. He didn't evade the truth in the end."

I hoped the forced note in my voice conveyed a stronger belief than I felt, but the words 'in the end' were significant. I regretted them, because my mother nodded wretchedly and said, "When he was forced to, yes. I do remember that."

I couldn't bear the sadness in her voice, but could think of no words to comfort her except the banal suggestion that she should drink her broth. "Helen made it herself," I confided, "so you wouldn't wish to disappoint her, would you?" I picked up the spoon and tried to feed her, but she lifted a work-roughened hand and took it from me. She began to sip halfheartedly, scarcely aware that she did so, and after one or two attempts she stopped and looked at me again.

"Forgive me, Lucinda. I beg you to forgive me. I was beside myself last night."

"It doesn't matter, dearest Mamma. It doesn't matter."

"But it does. It matters because I shocked you, and the truth must have hurt you. I beg you not to hate me or despise me."

"You know I could never do either. Nothing you ever did could make me. You loved my father and you loved me, and nothing can ever change that. He loved you, too. I know because he told me. He came to see me not an hour since."

"Nevill has been here!"

I nodded. "You were asleep."

"But he didn't come to see me. He came to see you."

"Only to find out how you were. He wanted to see you after talking with me."

"No . . . no . . . I shall never see him again. It is over. Even loving each other, as we have continued to, is over. I have always known the day would come, but not yet, I thought, not yet. Then I brought it on myself. But I was so sure—it seemed the only thing to do, the right thing. You needed a father last night and I needed Nevill's help and counsel. He has always given me both. He has protected and cared for us always. I thought he was the right person to turn to." Her tone changed to one of pleading. "Don't condemn us, Lucinda. Don't condemn him. He has always done his best for us—"

I interrupted. "I know. He told me." I found it hard to conceal my feelings, even so. He may have loved her so much that he wanted her beneath his roof, but was it really necessary for her to be there in a subservient position, in his wife's employ? Even though I could think of no other way in which he could have kept her so close to him, I knew I would have had more respect for him had he housed her with more dignity elsewhere.

I said briskly, "Come, drink up. We have plans to make." I had to draw her away from introspection and possible self-pity, though this last characteristic had never been part of her nature or she would have indulged it long ago. It seemed even more justified now that I knew the truth, yet still she found it possible to plead for my father. In time, perhaps, I would be more sympathetic toward him, but not yet. My concern was all for her.

She sipped the broth again because she was ordered to, docilely as a child, and as she did so, I talked—a little wildly, because I had no plans formulated. The only certain fact was that I had a contract for a minor part at the Boswell Theatre and had to fulfil it. I could even enjoy the situation in an ironical sort of way, feeling on a kind of par with Clementine and even with her mother because I was a member of the company and not the daughter of a "backstage servant" anymore.

The recollection of Durbridge's words brought the memory of him back with a sickening thrust, momentarily halting me as I chattered wildly about setting up a home together somewhere. "We can do it, Mamma, of course we can do it! I am a fully fledged actress now."

A small-part player, with a small-part player's earnings, which were precious little more than a super's. There had been no favouritism from Nevill Boswell when engaging me as a member of the company; the contract had been drawn up in the usual way, no different from the rest. There would have been veiled disapproval from Willard, who combined certain managerial duties with those of stage director and therefore handed round the pay packets when the ghost walked on Saturday nights, and there would have been more than veiled resentment from other players had they learned of any preference being shown—and since nothing was secret backstage, such favouritism would not have been hidden for long.

But how could such a minor actress as I hope to set up house on such wages? They wouldn't pay the rent of a room for two in a lodging house. My father was right, and I knew that I would accept whatever additional work he offered, not only because of the extra money, but because my burning ambition to act would make me seize all and any opportunities.

I was pleased to see that my mother had finished the broth. Now she set the bowl aside and said calmly, "An experienced theatrical dresser can always get work, and I am a very good one. I won't even need a reference; the name of the Boswell Theatre will be sufficient."

The door opened and Helen Steel walked in, a bundle of clothes under one arm.

"My brother tells me you are much improved, Miss Grainger—Trudy. I insist on calling you Trudy because I like it and it suits you, and since we are to live in the same house, formality seems very stupid." She turned her wide, warm smile on both of us as she set the clothes on a nearby table. "Also, since you are much improved, I am going to make use of you, scheming creature that I am. I abominate sewing and consequently do it badly, so I am enlisting your aid. This pile of repair work is needed at the mission, so I propose to tackle it with your assistance."

She seated herself and began to sort out the garments. "They're for children of all ages, as you can see. People are very generous, though I sometimes suspect they donate these things to get rid of me; I am very persistent. I go from door to door, and not a house in the vicinity escapes. Just look at these trousers—a patch in the seat, don't you think? Oh, *thank* you—you will do that detestable job for me? See, Lucinda, how clumsy I am in comparison with your mother; already she is threading her needle and I cannot even do that at the first attempt."

I wanted to hug her. She could not have come at a more opportune moment or used better tactics. Now she said persuasively, "I wonder if I could prevail upon you to undertake this work regularly, Trudy? You would be doing me *and* the mission the greatest service if you would. The pile never grows less, and I frankly hate it. I don't mind coping with other things; organisation I positively enjoy, being the bossy female I am, but sewing a fine seam, ugh! And I am delighted at the thought of having you in this house for another reason—when I am absent you will be here to receive things. People not only bring clothes to the door—doing that keeps me away from theirs!—but the gentlemen who patronise the gymnasium very often bring things they and their families have finished with. In fact, Barker makes sure they do, because he once benefited from a suit of clothes given to him by the mission and has never forgotten it. You haven't met Barker yet, but you will. He used to be an acrobat, formerly in a circus, but when Magnus found him he was busking in Leicester Square. Now he passes on all his training in the gymnasium belowstairs. A fine teacher, my brother says. I once went down there to watch him practice—not when the gymnasium was open to patrons, of course, these all-male establishments never admit ladies. Barker was wonderful to watch and I thoroughly enjoyed myself. He teaches physical prowess and my brother teaches boxing, and both make sure that the patrons pay well because it all goes to support the mission. My dear Lucinda, just look how your mother's needle flies!''

By the time I left for the evening performance, everything was settled without argument or fuss. We were annexed as part of the Steel establishment and somehow made to feel that it was we who were doing them a favour, not the reverse. On my way out I slipped down to the basement, drawn by curiosity as well as by a desire to see Magnus, who had come back from the mission half an hour earlier and gone straight down there. "He always puts in an hour's training before Barker opens up for the evening," Helen told me, and I suspected that she told me for a reason and looked the other way deliberately when I went below, though I couldn't think why, unless it was because she knew I wanted to express my thanks to him as well as to herself.

He was stripped to the waist and, at the moment I entered, lifting a massive bar with circular weights at each end. As he heaved, the muscles of his naked back rippled in unison with chest and arms, and as he bent the knees for the final thrust and then straightened up, his thigh muscles were taut beneath gymnastic tights. I was not a little awed by the man's strength and a thought raced unbidden through my mind: *Now I know why Clementine finds him fascinating—he is a magnificent animal.*

But there was more than animalism in Magnus Steel. As the weight crashed to the ground, I saw character and purpose in his face, also a certain relentlessness. He would achieve whatever he set out to achieve, conquer whatever he wanted to conquer, be it a woman, a problem, an obstacle, or a massive weight that would get the better of the average man.

He turned and saw me then, and I promptly felt selfconscious and a little confused.

"I came to thank you. I am indebted to you both. You have offered my mother the first real security she has ever known, I think, by employing her at the mission.''

He picked up a towel and began to dry the sweat off his body. He was as unselfconscious as he had been in Hyde Park, which told me all too plainly that, unlike Gavin, he was quite unaware of me as a woman.

"So my sister's plan has succeeded? Good. But the thanks are on our side. The mission has been needing a skilled needlewoman for a very long time."

Then he noticed my outdoor clothes and asked where I was bound for.

"The theatre. The curtain rises at eight-thirty."

"So you are still going there?"

"I am an actress," I said proudly. "I am under contract, and no actress would ever dream of breaking it."

"Won't you find it painful?"

I had been denying that to myself, but I couldn't deny it now. It could also be embarrassing were I to come face to face with the great Bernadette; Clementine, too, no matter how I might try to feel on a par with them. Fortunately there was nowhere so impersonal as behind the scenes in a theatre, where most members of the cast met only during a performance. This particularly applied to lesser players. Social divisions at the Boswell were wide. Unwritten laws prevailed, laws that ruled out any fraternising between leads, understudies, and lesser members of the cast. I had deliberately broken those laws when seeking Gavin out last night. Normally, a small-part player like myself could spend an entire evening in the theatre and only come face to face with the chief actors when behind the footlights, and that, I now resolved, was how it would be with me from now on.

"I have my living to make, Doctor, and a career to pursue."

"And how are you getting to the theatre?"

"On foot."

"And coming back? The streets of London are no place at night for a young lady alone."

I was on the point of saying that I would not be alone, so confident was I that Gavin would see to that, but Magnus Steel forestalled me.

"So long as you live in my house, Lucinda, you will not return unaccompanied. Barker will collect you with the trap; a less elegant conveyance than a carriage with a cockaded coachman, but at least he knows how to use his fists." He flexed his muscles and finished with a grin, "And so do I, so when I have other work for Barker, or it's his evening off, I will fetch you myself, or send a fly from a livery stable."

I was on the point of leaving when he added, "When I asked if returning to the theatre wouldn't be painful for you, I was not referring to human relationships, but to the pain of reminder. Something happened to you there last night, something which shocked and injured you and which made your mother distraught to a degree. Tripping over backstage scenery didn't cause those marks on your face, though whatever happened certainly happened at the theatre because between the time you left Portman Square and the time you returned, you couldn't have been anywhere else. So mark this—however much you may deny it, or make light of it, or even try to conceal it, I shall find out what it was, no matter how long it takes me."

To my consternation I was suddenly aware of this man's strength and determination, both of which I found so disconcerting that I turned and fled, forcing my movements to appear unhurried, but afraid that they were nonetheless revealing.

The supers were swarming up the circular staircase when I arrived, so it was impossible for me to look down at the fatal spot where Durbridge's body had sprawled. We scrambled up the iron steps one after another, so closely packed that all I could do was make sure where I placed my feet, one step at a time.

Everywhere seemed exactly the same as usual, the stage set for the opening scene, the tabs drawn, the safety curtain down. I knew precisely how it would look from the front, with the masks depicting Comedy and Tragedy painted large upon it and its reassuring quotation from *Hamlet* emblazoned on a gigantic scroll beneath: *"For Thine Especial Safety."* As a child, sitting breathless in the auditorium when my mother was given the couple of complimentary tickets to which every member of the company was entitled, I would be rooted to my seat, waiting to be transformed into that magic world behind the footlights which seemed so different when seated out front. For me, the magic was always there, even though I knew precisely where my mother was going, and why, when she slipped quietly out of her seat prior to every exit of Lady Boswell's, and disappeared through the iron pass door behind the stalls boxes. For this reason our tickets were always for the two seats at the end of the nearest row, and for this reason she never saw a performance right through. For her, it was constantly interrupted, because not for a single one was she released from her duties as dresser, but for me it was continuous delight from the moment that I lowered the theatre seat and felt its red plush upholstery, and an indulgent usherette, knowing who I was, placed a free programme in my hand and said, "In on comps, ducks? Enjoy yourself then. I 'spect your ma'll be joining you shortly. . . ."

Enjoyment was doubled when my mother slipped into the seat next to mine after curtain-up, but even prior to that the spell was on me. The massive safety curtain, impregnated against fire, filled me with expectant awe, and when it rose, revealing the heavy crimson velvet tabs elaborately adorned with gold braid and fringe, and the initials N and B for Nevill Boswell on each side, I could scarcely wait for them to part and the whole backstage world be transformed into fantasy. But before that happened there were other magic moments, and I would sit rigid with expectancy, awaiting each one.

First would come the gentlemen of the orchestra, creeping from beneath the stage into their brass-railed pit, and although I knew the space from which they crawled was a vast, dusty, cluttered area full of mechanical devices to release trapdoors in the stage and other effects, not to mention disused scenery and discarded props over which they had to pick their way carrying their instruments, from the front of the house it seemed as if they rose from some secret and exclusive world, some Valhalla to which no mere mortals were admitted. The enchantment could not be dispelled even by the knowledge that they sat amidst the clutter during performances, with their meat pies and bottles of stout, and stifled their yawns when they crawled out again to entertain audiences during the intervals. I had the ability to transfer myself from backstage reality to front-of-the-house unreality with ease, accepting it as a child accepts a fairy tale because that's what fairy tales are for.

The breathless sound of the orchestra tuning up before the first rise of the curtain was particularly potent; the scrapes on the fiddles, the booming into trombones, the blowing down trumpets, the rattling of drumsticks, the wailing of woodwinds—all were discordant and exciting and full of a promise which never failed to be fulfilled, and I knew precisely when that moment was to come, for from that cramped door beneath the stage, last of all, would rise the splendid figure of the orchestra conductor, and he would step onto the rostrum and immediately become authoritative and impressive, very different from the shabby little baldheaded man who slunk through the stage door in a dirty mackintosh half an hour before curtain-up and joined his team of musicians down in that dusty world below stage. When he emerged, baton in hand, his bald pate was covered with a splendid mane of hair (pulled out of his mackintosh pocket prior to crawling out of Valhalla), and the rostrum added imposing inches to his height, and the light above his music stand shone onto his starched shirtfront, patched in the sleeves as I very well knew because I had once slipped down into Valhalla myself during a performance and seen him sitting on an old packing case, minus his tailed coat.

But none of this spoiled the magic for me; instead, it enhanced it because only magic could so transform ordinary mortals. By the time he rapped with his baton on his music stand, and the tuning-in faded to respectful silence, and the fiddlers waited with their bows poised, and the brass lifted their shining instruments to obedient lips, the safety curtain had slowly risen and the magnificent velvet curtains hung majestically, so promising and so tantalizing that I would sit tautly on the edge of my seat, awaiting the crash of cymbal and drum which always heralded the overture. Productions at the Boswell were accompanied only by musical classics; Beethoven's *Leonore,* Wagner's *Meistersinger,* Smetana's *Bartered Bride,* and more besides—I knew them all. Nothing light or frivolous was ever performed by the Boswell Orchestra; Beethoven or Tchaikovsky or Mendelssohn was needed to provide the right atmosphere. Was anything more evocative than the *Manfred* Symphony or the *Pastorale?* Although I knew every overture and every shortened symphonic movement played between scenes, and exactly which would be performed before and during respective productions because the repertoire of the Boswell Theatre Orchestra never varied, the renderings never failed to catch me by the throat.

Tonight I could hear the distant shuffle of the orchestra beneath the stage as I climbed to dressing room number 20, and Jerry's voice was already echoing along stone corridors. "Half an hour, please! *Half an hour, please!*" I wanted to meet him, and yet was anxious not to because we would both remember last night and the whole ugly scene would come flooding back.

We came face to face halfway up. He was about to step onto the stairs ahead of me, pushing his way from the third level with aggressive elbows and all the authority of a callboy going about his duties, but he halted when he saw me and his cherubic cockney face looked up into mine. There was a question in his eyes, but he did not voice it because the supers ahead of me and the supers behind me would have heard. *"You all right, missy? Nuffink 'appened to yer, did it? I fetched yer ma in time, didn't I?"* I smiled and nodded imperceptibly, guessing the question rightly, and his young-old face beamed in relief.

But when I stepped off the stairs and drew him to one side and asked how he came to be in that deserted dressing room last night, he pulled away. *"'Scuse me, missy; I've gotta get on wiv me job."*

All I could do was let him go. Gavin was right, I decided. It was kinder not to question the boy.

It seemed incredible that there was no indication of anything violent happening backstage less than twenty-four hours ago. I had walked through the stage door and along the passage to the wings marvelling that everything looked so exactly the same, the backstage shadows with their maze of guy ropes and angle rods, the immense flats propped against the rear wall ready to be set as backdrops for other scenes, the smaller ones at the sides, used to screen prompt and off-prompt entrances and exits, the yawning doors of the prop room, which stood permanently open, and those of the carpenter's shop and paint shops alongside; the S.M.'s chair and table with cue copy at the ready, and Lights sitting at the controls of onstage gas jets, with signals to Number 1 Limes on the other side and to Number 2 high above by the grid. The only independent operator was Number 3 Limes up in his concealed box behind the gods, but he had only four beams to control and did them by a numbered chart. All these details, normally overlooked because they were taken for granted, succeeded in reassuring me tonight. The theatre was the same as always, therefore everything else must be the same as always. . . .

Even Maisie failed to trouble me when I fought my way to my seat at the long centre dressing table. She was intent on jellied eels, eaten out of a newspaper and washed down with beer drunk straight from the bottle, and although the smell added to the mixed aromas which, by the end of the run, would have permeated every crack in the woodwork, I was glad she was so occupied. I took out a book borrowed at the last minute from Helen Steel's shelves and focused my attention on it. There could be no escaping down to the wings tonight; I would be forced to spend my time in this room until my entrance in Act III, so my mind needed to be occupied and if I became the target for Maisie's tongue, I could then pretend not to hear. I had chosen the book without glancing at the title and was now surprised to see that it was the famous Rosa Carey's *Lover or Friend?* I could not have imagined the practical Helen devouring anything so passionate, but the pages were much-thumbed.

The note from Clementine came a few minutes later, delivered by Jerry on his quarter-hour call. *"We must have a talk, you and I. Come to my dressing room at the first interval."* It was characteristic of Clementine to put a request in the form of a command, and characteristic of me to immediately want to decline. However, I did not. I presented myself at her dressing-room door immediately the curtain descended, braced to discuss last night's events because there could be nothing else she would wish to talk about.

There I was wrong. She thrust a copy of the *Morning Post* at me without so much as a greeting.

"I suppose you are rubbing your hands with glee over *that,*" she said.

Puzzled, I took the paper. It was folded back haphazardly, but the article stood out because it was accompanied by a picture of Nevill Boswell as Sydney Carton, and a headline which proclaimed: SIR NEVILL REPEATS TRIUMPH AS DICKENSIAN MARTYR, and a lesser one which projected a weak pun: "THE ONLY WAY" PROMISES TO BE A FAR FAR BETTER THING THAN BEFORE. The opening paragraph then went on to predict a long run for this revival, so I looked at Clementine and said, "It is you who should be rubbing your hands with glee, this being your first lead role."

"Don't tell me you haven't read the rest of it," she snapped.

"This is the first time I've seen it."

I had almost forgotten that tonight was the second night of the production, and I marvelled that the atmosphere in the theatre had struck me as being the same as usual, because a second night never was. It was always an anticlimax, flat as champagne that had lost its sparkle, depressing if reviews were bad and merely relieved in a tired sort of way if they were good. It was the inevitable reaction to high tension, and it took over the theatre as surely as the individual atmosphere of a first night. Everyone was thankful when a second night passed, and grateful for the respite it offered before facing the inevitable inquest onstage following the third night's performance. By that time the daily and evening newspapers had made their comments and the call board would summon the entire cast before Sir Nevill after the final curtain.

"Now that the play is launched, ladies and gentlemen, we must get down to the task of polishing and improving the production and individual performances. There will be rehearsal calls daily at ten o'clock until I am satisfied."

That was always my father's preliminary to a merciless analysis of faults and errors and failures, individually and collectively. (Already I was thinking of him as "my father" and not as Sir Nevill.) No one would be spared, not even himself, though his approach to the immortal Bernadette would be couched in tact and even flattery.

But Clementine knew this as much as I did, and since the *Morning Post* review was obviously favourable, and the drama critic of that newspaper was renowned in his way, she should be feeling pleased, I thought, not petulant. So I dismissed her attitude with a mental shrug, and read on.

Sir Nevill had been his "brilliant self, an actor who never failed"; Lady Boswell was to be admired for her portrayal of Madame Defarge, and equally for her remarkable makeup; Gavin Calder was "a smooth and polished Charles Darnay, but handsome is as handsome does," which seemed a silly comment to me, and finally: "Miss Clementine Boswell's beauty would adorn any stage, but looks alone cannot bring a rôle to life if emotion is lacking. It is to be regretted that Miss Boswell's grief failed to match that of a lesser performer, playing the very minor rôle of a doomed aristocrat at the foot of the guillotine. The impassioned cry uttered by that unknown actress made an impact upon a blasé first-night audience."

I felt my cheeks flame with delight and embarrassment. No wonder Clemmy's greeting for me had been tart.

"Well?" Her tone was still acid. "I suppose you are feeling very pleased with yourself."

"Of course, I am pleased. No small-part player even expects to be noticed."

"Nor to eclipse the lead. Not that other critics such as Max Beerbohm even mention you, and that young man's views carry more weight today than Howard Mortimer of the *Post*, who is not only past his prime, but, as everyone knows, has a weakness for pretty young girls.''

I refrained from pointing out that my makeup must have concealed any claim to youth or prettiness.

Clementine took the paper from me and threw it aside. ''The man is a fool,'' she pronounced contemptuously. ''I only showed you that review as encouragement. Don't let it go to your head. And your name isn't even mentioned.''

''Not surprisingly, since it isn't on the programme.''

''Surely you didn't expect it to be?''

''Of course not.'' Walk-ons and minor parts were never listed. ''Is that all you want to say to me?''

''No.'' She studied her reflection in the mirror and added nonchalantly, ''So we're half-sisters. Amusing, isn't it? I wasn't wholly surprised, though it was plain that you were. What do you propose to do now?''

''Why . . . nothing. What can I do?''

Her eyebrows raised. ''Since you were obliged to leave the house, one would naturally expect you to leave the theatre also.''

''Sir Nevill will not permit it. He told me so this morning.''

''Did he indeed? He came to see you, then?''

I nodded.

''I am sure my poor mamma was unaware of that.''

I waited, still saying nothing.

''Are you remaining in the Steels' household?'' she asked negligently.

I nodded again.

Suddenly she burst out laughing. ''The situation is very amusing, don't you agree? No—I can see you don't. Come, Lucinda, you and I have to live with it, so we may as well make the best of it. And I don't blame *you* for the sins of the fathers. People do it all the time. The illegitimacy rate in London is higher than anywhere else in the world, I'm told.''

I could see no point to this conversation, unless it was to find out if her father had plans for my mother and myself. I was relieved when a tap on the door spared me an answer. Since Clementine's dresser was absent (sent from the room during this confidential chat?), she was forced to call, ''Come in,'' but not until she had given me a dismissive glance which I ignored. I was no longer the daughter of a backstage dresser, nor intended to be treated as one.

It was Gavin who entered. He had a pile of newspapers.

''I expect you have seen all these, Clemmy darling?''

She smiled sweetly. ''Including the one which encourages dear Lucinda. I have just been showing it to her.''

His mouth quirked in amusement. "Knowing your generous nature, niece, I thought you might."

"I am not your niece and you are not my uncle, Gavin dear. Do I still have to remind you that we are not really related?"

Her glance was challenging and I knew he was aware of it. Clementine was running true to form, unable to refrain from flirting with any man. I tried to edge to the door, but Gavin casually blocked my way.

"Not going, are you, Lucinda? I am sure Clemmy has been congratulating you, as I now do. Being noticed by Howard Mortimer still counts for something."

As he spoke, his eyes were on Clementine, teasing and mocking her, but she chose not to notice. Instead she said, "I am glad you have come, Gavin. I have been wanting to ask what happened to Durbridge last night. You were summoned away from Romano's, the maître d'hotel informed us. Was it by Durbridge?"

"No, it was not." Gavin's voice was smooth. "Didn't he turn up after all?"

"He did not, to Mamma's fury and everyone's disgust. I must say it was very peculiar behaviour and very ill-mannered—and no apology sent to Portman Square today."

"That's odd, but Durbridge is an unpredictable man, a law unto himself, I imagine. Men as rich as he can afford to be."

I marvelled that Gavin could be so cool. I felt very much the reverse and headed for the door again. This time Gavin made no move to stop me. As I left the room I heard him assuring Clementine that Durbridge was bound to send an explanation sooner or later, and his tone was so dismissive that anyone would have imagined the matter to be totally unimportant, but I felt shaken as I closed the door behind me. It was inevitable that Durbridge's disappearance would arouse comment. I should have anticipated it.

"Lucinda . . . wait."

Gavin came hurrying after me.

"Darling, don't give yourself away like that every time you hear Durbridge's name mentioned. Clementine wasn't looking at you, but I was. Your face was very revealing. It always is." He slipped an arm about my waist and walked along with me, and at the precise moment that we passed my father's dressing room, the door opened and he emerged. Gavin's arm fell away, but not before it was observed. I saw my father's flickering glance and the tightening of his mouth, but all he said was, "This meeting is very opportune, Lucinda. I presume you collected Willard's note on the way in?"

I was both bewildered and surprised. It had never occurred to me to glance at the call board just inside the stage door, because house messages pinned on it were never for lesser members of the company. Letters delivered by mail were put in pigeonholes on the letter rack in George's cubbyhole, but missives from the management were attached to the official call board, at which everyone glanced on their arrival. But I only read the notices, never the names on sealed envelopes.

"I see you didn't," my father remarked. "In that case, I suggest you collect it right away."

Without another word he walked on. Jerry was already banging on doors and summoning beginners for the opening of Act II and, seeing Sir Nevill on his way to the stage, passed on to the next door—Lady Boswell's. "Onstage, please, Lady Boswell, ma'am . . . onstage, please!" I beat a hasty retreat, anxious to avoid the leading lady at all costs, and anxious to read the stage director's letter, whatever news it contained. If the actor-manager of the Boswell Theatre Company had decided to terminate my contract, it would be Willard's duty to inform me.

"Don't look so apprehensive, darling. It can only be good. Your father wouldn't dare to let it be otherwise, and he has surely seen Mortimer's comment in the Post."

Bernadette Boswell's door was opening. I saw her dresser, a new woman suddenly produced from nowhere and obviously nervous, holding the door for her mistress to pass through, and heard Bernadette's plaintive command to "Stand out of the way, woman! Can't you see you are blocking my path? My goodness gracious, but you have a lot to learn!"

"Here comes the tragedy queen," Gavin murmured. His secret laughter was infectious, but alarm spurred me forward. I was gone before she emerged.

Gavin caught up with me. "Darling, I'll see you tomorrow—can't manage tonight, I'm afraid. Business. Urgent."

But I couldn't let him go like that. We were out of sight and out of earshot now. Disappointed as I was that I was not to see him after the performance, another thought was uppermost in my mind.

"What I can't understand is how you kept it out of the newspapers," I said. "About Durbridge, I mean. If his death had been reported, it would have been all over the theatre by now."

"Which proves you have nothing to worry about, my love. Didn't I tell you I would take care of everything? Good luck with the news from Willard—it's sure to be good. Couldn't be anything else."

His dazzling, confident smile left me feeling relieved and grateful and unhappy all at once. I desperately wanted to talk to him and had been counting on doing so after the curtain came down, which showed how foolish it was to take anything for granted. I would still have to wait to hear how he had managed to conceal Durbridge's death.

12

> Sir Nevill asks me to inform you that you have been chosen to under-study Miss Boswell in the role of Lucie, and to undertake the additional role of the innkeeper's daughter in Act I, Scene 3. Please attend under-study call at ten A.M. tomorrow, and for the part of the innkeeper's daughter at four P.M.

The letter also confirmed that I would fulfil both appointments in a fortnight's time and quoted the increase in salary, divided between the understudy and the additional small part. My reactions were mixed: ela-tion because of the dramatically improved state of my finances, joy be-cause I was to be given another speaking part, and reluctance to under-study Clementine. Any other actress would have been delighted on all counts, but I was averse to playing second fiddle to my half-sister, who had overshadowed me all my life. But this was obviously my father's wish, and he was forcing me to accept. This was all part and parcel of be-ing a professional actress, and he was determined to drill me into it.

I could not hate him for it, though I wanted to protest the moment he came offstage. Wisdom curbed me. I was learning fast. I had to keep si-lent about my feelings, as I had to keep silent about last night's events. I also had to control my reactions when Durbridge's name cropped up, as it surely would. In their different ways, both Gavin Calder and Nevill Boswell were managing my life, and all I could do was let them.

I had additional cause to be pleased, I reflected as I returned to dress-ing room number 20. As soon as I joined the ranks of the understudies and graduated from one minor part to two, I would be promoted to a dressing room with others of similar rank. It would be good-bye to the supers, good-bye to Maisie, good-bye to overcrowding and discomfort. I did a mental calculation—there were three female leads and therefore three understudies, and I would be one of them. Understudies were very often not cast until after a first night, so I had no idea who the others would be, but we would all share a dressing room. I had only to endure room number 20 for two more weeks. There would be the embarrass-ment of replacing the actress who had failed as the innkeeper's daughter, but such a thing could happen to any performer; it was one of the hazards of the theatre and could happen to me at any time.

I was jolted out of my complacency as I reentered the room. Maisie's voice met me. "Oh yes, something were up," she was saying. "Mark my words, girls, *something* were up. Things were going on here last night."

"*What?*" breathed her audience.

"Well, I don't know exactly what, but something did. We were coming out of the Duke's Head across the street, me and a gentleman friend, and that callboy came tearing out of the stage door as if the devil were after him. Catapulted straight into me, he did. 'Hi, young shaver,' said my gentleman friend, 'that's no way to great a lady!' 'S true, girls, that's what he called me—a lady!'' She smirked.

Someone urged, "Go on, do!" and she continued, 'Well, that's all, really, but when I asked the brat where he was going in such a hurry, he just pushed by and went pelting on down to the Strand. And the funny thing was that nobody came out of the stage door after him—not then, at least—so who the devil he was running away from, Gawd only knows. But he knew where he were off to, all right, and nothing was going to stop him. Christ, you should've seen his face—red with fury, it were! His blood was up, I could tell. Oh, yes, *something* happened here last night, and somebody in this theatre knows what it was, *and* I have a fair idea who. . . ."

"Why didn't you go after the brat and question him?" someone demanded.

"Couldn't, dear. My gentleman friend was getting impatient and I had my own business to attend to, after all. But d'you know what I learned on my way in tonight? One of the lead actors was talking to another by the stage door and I heard every word as I walked by. It were all about a big supper party at that posh restaurant down in the Strand, the place where all the mashers go, and the man who'd invited everybody never even showed up! Not that that surprised *me*—the host being Lord Durbridge. I could tell a few things about *that* noble lord if I wanted to."

To my surprise I heard myself say, "You know him, then?"

"Do I *know* him? Of course not. Gentlemen like that one don't know the likes of me."

"Then how could you reveal things about him?"

She answered with elaborate patience, "Because I've been a super on the boards for longer than you've been born, your ladyship, and when I say 'the boards' I *mean* 'the boards'; not all this highbrow stuff, but the music halls, the real entertainment places; musical shows with choruses both male and female, and it was the chorus boys his lordship used to come after, though sometimes he would use girls the same way. Not that you're old enough to know anything about *that* yet. . . ."

Long ago, Clementine had said the same thing. Now I had learned in the worst possible way. In the past twenty-four hours I had changed from a naive and semiknowledgeable girl to a young woman who could have lost every romantic illusion had she not been in love with a man like Gavin Calder, who would show me how beautiful a relationship between a man and woman could be, with nothing selfish about it, nothing merely animal. With Gavin it would be the idealistic expression of love, never to be debased. I longed for the day when he would carry me to this higher plane of experience and, in so doing, obliterate all memory of that experience with Durbridge.

Now I thrust the recollection of it aside. Durbridge was dead. He could threaten no one anymore. I had to cling to that knowledge and heed nothing of Maisie's prattle, though it had been a shock to hear her talk so knowledgeably about the man, and an even greater shock to learn that she had seen Jerry racing out of the stage door and had put two and two together sufficiently well to realise that something must have happened backstage to send him flying out into the night like that, and that somebody in this theatre must know what it was. I prayed that her curiosity would subside, but that calculating, knowledgeable face worried me. I knew now that it was going to be necessary for me to act both onstage and off, and I had to start right away. I had been right—the actions of a man so prominent as Durbridge would be sure to arouse comment; therefore his absence would also arouse comment when he was missed from the London scene.

Maisie had forgotten me and turned back to her audience.

"You know what it means, don't you, girls, that celebration supper going wrong? If anything goes amiss on an opening night, anything at all, and especially if it follows a successful show, it's a warning. An omen. It means the show will flop. Oh, yes, it does—as surely as a bad dress rehearsal means a good first night, a bad hitch after it means something will go wrong. It's a mark of doom, that's what it is. A mark of doom."

I learned later that not all the press notices had been good. In fact, Howard Mortimer's had been the only one, the generally accepted reason being that the play was a favourite of his.

"He's a traditionalist, darling. He likes the old and the tried and the conventional. The man is growing old himself and is therefore opposed to anything new. He should make way for a younger critic. Max Beerbohm will soon oust him."

Gavin told me this next day when, to my surprise and delight, he arrived at the theatre during understudy rehearsals and sat in the stalls watching. Any member of the company was free to attend rehearsals. One could learn a lot from watching other actors at work, and Nevill Boswell always encouraged this.

"But it was you I came to see, not the rest of the understudies," Gavin told me when Willard called a halt and commanded everybody to be back by two o'clock sharp.

"That gives us time to go across the road to Rule's." Gavin put a hand beneath my elbow and led me across Maiden Lane from the stage door. "We'll have a celebration luncheon, my lovely. We have a lot to celebrate, you and I—or will have. And my prediction about the current Boswell production seems likely to be right. How many reviews have you read?"

Only one or two, I had to admit, at which he shrugged and said, "You haven't missed anything. The majority were so bad they would only have depressed you. It is just as I said—the play has been done to death, people are tired of it. Nevill should move with the times. There's a whole new era in the offing, the Edwardian era. The Widow of Windsor cannot last much longer, and when she goes, times will change, tastes will change. Places like the Empire in Leicester Square will really come into their own."

"But that place is notorious!"

"Because of its promenading? My dear, *that* is the attraction, not the ballet. A couple of years ago, when that self-appointed suppressor of vice, Mrs. Ormiston Chant, led a campaign to separate the bars of the Empire from the promenade area where the ladies of the town tout for trade, a young cadet at Sandhurst, named Winston Churchill, flew to the defence of the freedom of the individual by writing his first letter to the press declaring, 'In England we have too long obeyed the voice of the prude!' " Gavin threw back his head and laughed. "No one had heard of him then, but I imagine we will hear much of a firebrand like that in the future. When a partition was erected, to Mrs. Ormiston Chant's satisfaction, that young man led a mob of three hundred to storm the barricade and tear it down. They succeeded, too, and the promenade area at the Empire has been an even bigger attraction ever since, its prostitutes the most expensive. Picking up the dancers during the intervals is another thing men go there for. That's why the intervals are longer than at any other theatre in London, longer even than its rival, the Alhambra, on the other side of the square; intervals of an hour and more, enough time for the dancers to emerge from backstage and drink champagne with the gentlemen, and to make assignations. That is what they are engaged for, not their ballet dancing, which is mediocre. And whether the elegant promenade ladies like it or not, the rivalry between themselves and the *corps de ballet* keeps trade competitive. My God, if *I* ran the Boswell Theatre I would turn the place into a gold mine!"

I knew he was joking, so paid no heed. I was walking on air, bound for the famous Rule's Restaurant, which I had often dreamed of entering one day. Little had I imagined that the event would come so soon, for Rule's was the haunt of only the greatest names in the theatrical world. Thank goodness Kate had delivered our clothes yesterday! "On Sir Nevill's instruction," she had said, eyes agog with a curiosity which I had left unsatisfied. Kate had always been too inquisitive. Often I had found her listening outside closed doors, though she had immediately pretended to be dusting when I appeared. She was an untrustworthy creature with a prattling tongue, and I had no doubt that there had been a great deal of prattling in the Boswell kitchens since our sudden departure.

But all that was behind me. For my first understudy rehearsal today I wore my best street costume. Thanks to my mother's ingenuity and skill, it was extremely elegant; made of green silk, unpicked from one of Bernadette's and therefore providing plenty of material for a whole new outfit for someone as thin as I. The skirt was of the latest godet shape, the leg-o'-mutton sleeves were enormous and the short Louis XVI coat, finishing smartly at the hourglass waist, had a cutaway front which opened widely on a double-breasted white silk vest.

This striking outfit was capped with a large cravat of white chiffon and a hat of green straw, once belonging to my mother but now retrimmed with wide matching ribbon, rising in stiffened loops high at the back.

I felt supremely confident and happy, aware that I looked my best and, I hoped, worthy of my handsome escort. More than anything, I wanted Gavin to be proud of me in such an establishment as this, where women were now admitted, provided they were escorted. Times were changing. It was no longer considered brazen for a woman to lunch or dine in public, provided she was seen in respectable places and with a man of good reputation. I felt proud and excited as Gavin ushered me through the narrow door of this small and exclusive eating house. I was an actress. A real, live, professional actress. Coming here made me feel that I had really "arrived."

Gavin's hand found mine beneath the table as we sat side by side studying the menu, but I scarcely saw a word of it. His thumb was caressing my palm in a way which set my blood running hotly. I left the ordering to him and disregarded an inner voice which told me this was neither the place nor the time to reveal my emotions. I could do nothing about my betraying face, which displayed all too plainly how I felt.

"You look adorable with your eyes glowing like that, and your lovely face flushed . . . my darling, my darling . . ." His whispered words set my blood coursing faster still, and I was forced to pull my hand away.

"I have to," I whispered, begging him to understand, but he seized it again and held it all the tighter, and his thumb began its caressing motion once more.

"When is it to be, Lucinda? Things should be easier now you have left the Boswells' house. Come to my rooms. Who's to know? There's plenty of time between matinee and evening performances, and I know you don't go home then, but stay in the theatre eating sandwiches, because the walk takes too long and you can't afford cabs. In future, I will pay for a cab to bring you to my apartment and you can throw the sandwiches to the pigeons in Trafalgar Square. We will have to leave the theatre separately and return separately, of course, but that way we can be together three times a week at least, and I promise to be gentle and never to hurt you. I love you too much for that . . . ."

He broke off so abruptly that I was forced to look up—straight into the eyes of Nevill Boswell standing beside our table.

"Willard tells me you shaped well at rehearsals, Lucinda. Keep it up."

"I . . . thank you . . . I will." I stammered to a halt and he then turned to Gavin.

"You know my rule, Calder—only the lightest of lunches when rehearsing. So why bring her here?"

"Why not? She can eat as lightly here as anywhere else."

"No wine, then. She is too young."

Gavin inclined his head mockingly. Their wills clashed, as always, and my father moved on without another word. Gavin swore beneath his breath.

"Damn the man. He is determined to interfere, but it's a bit late for him to assert parental authority over you. Don't let him, my lovely. I know he has always been protective toward you, up to a point. One would have to be blind not to see it; as blind as you were yourself, though you can hardly be blamed for that. Because of your birth, your mother kept you strictly sheltered from the truth, but now that you know it, don't let Boswell interfere in your life. He has no legal right to; only Trudy has that, as yet. Besides, you are mine. At least, you are going to be, so the sooner we marry, the better. *That* will show him."

I was breathless, giddy with joy, unable to speak. I had not looked beyond the ecstatic prospect of being lovers, nor allowed myself to hope that he intended to be my husband too. How could a girl in my position, born as I was, hope for such a thing as marriage? But now the words were spoken, Gavin became masterful, determined, repeating them with relish.

"That *will* show him! It's a brilliant idea! I will marry you, sweetheart, and no one will stop me. What's more, I will behave myself until then so no one can accuse me of trapping you by seduction."

"*You* trapping *me*?" I gasped. "How could anyone think such a thing? More likely the other way round, because I am a penniless nobody and not even legitimate, and you are a famous actor. You could take your choice—"

"I have done," he answered with quiet determination. "I have chosen you, Lucinda."

Only later did I realise that the opportunity I had been waiting for, the opportunity to question Gavin more closely about his handling of events after my mother and I left the theatre that night, had slipped through my fingers and I had been content to let it. I had had no thought for anything or anyone but Gavin and our future together. The world was an enchanted place in which no one existed but ourselves.

I was now approaching sixteen. Many girls nowadays married at sixteen or seventeen, though admittedly eighteen to twenty was considered a more mature age. Ridiculous! Maturity was an individual thing, and these boundary lines were absurd. After eighteen many young women were already young matrons, and if they had not achieved the marriage state by their coming of age they were considered failures, scorned by their younger sisters and disappointments to their mammas. I could feel nothing but impatience with these views, perhaps because I had been born of an unmarried mother and therefore the bonds of matrimony had never seemed important. Even so, Gavin's decision to wed me filled me with pride and delight. I wanted to shout it to the world, so I was disappointed when he commanded me to tell no one yet.

"They would only put opposition in our way, my love, considering you to be too young."

He was right, of course. Gavin was always right. I knew it was wise to be guided by him and so I stifled my disappointment.

A few days later my mother went to the mission with Helen Steel, the trap filled with parcels of clothing which she had repaired and renovated.

"She's a genius," Helen declared to me privately. "She makes things out of nothing and still has stuff left over for more. It was a great day for Magnus and me, and the mission too, when you both walked out of that house across the square."

"We didn't exactly walk out, we were ordered out."

"By Lady Boswell, I suppose."

"One can hardly blame her."

"One can blame her for many things, and your father too, but I will keep silent because it is no business of mine, or so my brother tells me. He was reluctant to reveal a thing about that night, but I got it out of him. Being me, I was agog to know, and guessed the reason must be something big, because a treasure like your dear mamma would never have been allowed to leave the household otherwise. And even if the famous Bernadette did not have hysterics and command you to go, I am quite certain in my own mind that you would have walked out anyway as soon as you could. I suspect you have been wanting to do that for a long time, Lucinda, if not for your own sake, for your mother's.''

She then changed the subject abruptly because her brother walked into the room.

"Of course, a talent like Trudy's is wasted on renovation jobs like this.'' She held up a little girl's dress, smocked and puff-sleeved. "She made this out of an old skirt of mine—imagine! It's for one of Jerry Hawks's little sisters. Did you know that Joe has found a steady job on the docks at last and installed Mrs. Hawks and her family in tenement accommodation with him?''

"Yes. Jerry told me.''

"But why Joe doesn't make an honest woman of her, I can't think.''

"Then you are not very bright, sister. The reason is obvious—Joe has a wife somewhere already.''

"How tiresome of him! Ah, well, so long as he treats Mrs. Hawks and her children well, it's no business of ours. What happened to his wife?''

"She ran off with a sailor years ago and hasn't been heard of since.''

"It's time the divorce laws of this country were revised,'' pronounced Helen, then turned the subject back to my mother. "Did I tell you she is now making a new gown for me? She insists that I need one and has even designed it. I declared I could never wear anything so striking, but she pooh-poohed that and insisted we should purchase the material right away; nor would she consider anything plain and sensible, which would have been a great deal more suitable for me than the fashionable faille she chose. I declare she should be in the couture trade; that is her métier. How successful she could have been with her own establishment!''

"Alas, there has never been any money for such training. She is entirely self-taught, you know.''

All this time Magnus was listening, his only comment being that he was glad his sister was to look presentable at last; then, to my surprise, he asked if all was well at the theatre.

"Of course. Why do you ask?''

"I've heard rumours that the production is likely to end. Apparently young Jerry said something of the sort when visiting his mother and Joe last week.''

"Well, I have heard nothing of it.''

I tried to convince myself that the last person to know of such things would be the theatre callboy, though I knew this to be untrue. Stagehands were always amongst the first to sense any impending change; they knew instinctively when a production was likely to run for a long time and when it was likely to fold. Coupled with Maisie's prediction, and Gavin's too, I felt uneasy, anxious to get to the theatre in the hope of learning the truth. If anyone was likely to know, it was Willard, but would he be approachable? A resident stage director was in a confidential position, aware of the management's plans and very often consulted on future productions, and for this very reason he would maintain discretion. A whisper could travel round London's theatreland as rapidly as a brush fire, so in the event of failure the cast of a play was kept completely in the dark until a termination notice was posted on the call board.

Today was Sunday—the one day of the week actors had to themselves, though not always then if rehearsals were in progress. It was exactly a fortnight since I had been elevated to an understudy and an additional small role. Tomorrow I would not only make my first appearance in the new part, but move to another dressing room. Last night I had packed my makeup and my tattered wig and carried them, with my costumes, down to the second floor and dressing room number 10, ready for my arrival on Monday, and I had done so with indescribable relief. For the last two weeks I had endured Maisie Stockwell and the rest of the female supers, refusing to rise to their bait or to be provoked by Maisie's derision, until at last they had grown tired and ignored me. I had suffered only one last jibe from Maisie before I left that stifling and odorous accommodation.

"*Good*-bye, your ladyship. Curtsey to her ladyship, girls. Now she really is too good for the likes of us, or so she thinks, but pride goes before a fall. Remember that, your ladyship, when the notice goes up."

She, too? Did she know something which no member of the cast knew? She mixed with the stagehands on more than a friendly basis, so she would be likely to hear what Jerry also heard, and pick up the same tidbits of gossip, the same rumours, the same warnings—and I had seen her scanning *The Era*, whose columns advertised vacancies for supers or announced forthcoming auditions. I had hoped this indicated her possible departure for another theatre, and interpreted her scanning of *The Era* as no more than a desire to find more lucrative employment—crowds for musical productions earned sixpence more per performance than in straight productions—but now I wondered.

I wished I could see Gavin to lull my apprehension, but although we usually met in Kensington Gardens on Sundays, today he was unable to. My disappointment had been keen when he told me.

"About tomorrow, darling—it breaks my heart, but there can be no meeting in the park. Business. Urgent."

Nothing but urgent business ever kept him away from me, though he never revealed what that business was, and somehow I knew I was not expected to ask.

It was my custom to walk along the passage to the stage door very slowly, hoping he would appear to say good night. Being one of the lead players, he had a dressing room on the ground floor; the higher in a cast one ranked, the lower in the theatre one was accommodated. He told me he knew my step and listened for it. ("Don't make it too quick, my lovely, and if I don't emerge before you reach the stage door, linger by the call board, pretend to be studying it. . . .") I had done so last night and he had strolled negligently along the passage so that anyone who saw him would not think he was coming specifically to meet me. He was making sure no one would suspect our involvement, and there had been no further suggestion about my visiting his rooms, though I knew I would have gone there without much persuasion.

But instead of the usual "Tomorrow, my lovely?" which meant lunch following morning rehearsals during the week or our usual meeting place in Kensington Gardens on Sunday, last night it had been merely the quick, light, friendly kiss which actors bestow on actresses in passing, and the casual "Good night, darling—see you on Monday," which was the customary exchange between members of the profession and therefore not to be concealed because there was nothing compromising about it, nothing to indicate that we were anything more than friends. But the words which followed had been whispered because they were for my ears alone and, as yet, any meetings outside the theatre had to be guarded.

For this reason we had never again lunched at Rule's, but went to little-known places never patronised by members of the company and certainly not by Sir Nevill Boswell. ("When we are ready, my sweet, when my plans are accomplished, *then* we will spring the news.")

My mother appeared in the middle of my conversation with Helen and Magnus. She was wearing outdoor clothes and looking a great deal better than when we first came to this house. Being kept busy had left her no time for thought. She slept well at nights and had achieved more peace of mind—or was it resignation? Life had schooled her into acceptance long ago.

We had spoken little about our last night in the Boswell establishment or about the circumstances which led up to it. Apart from intimating that the truth about my parentage made no difference in my life, I had deliberately avoided it. I could feel her gratitude reaching out to me, almost with humility, and this I found painful. I wanted to assure her that things were exactly the same between us (how could they be otherwise?) and that, if anything, I loved her all the more. I also pitied her more, though never would I reveal this, knowing she would find it galling.

I had always felt sorry for my mother because she had lost the man she loved and because, through that love, she had had to endure a stigma which I thought cruel and unjustified. I still thought it cruel and unjustified, but even more cruel was the way in which she had been forced to tolerate a menial position in the Boswell household, accepting Bernadette's charity in the name of friendship. Was there no limit to the humiliation a woman in my mother's position was forced to endure?

A child's memory could be very retentive, and mine had most certainly been. I remembered a hundred instances of the great Bernadette's slights, and my mind could summon up a hundred significant moments I had witnessed from my isolated corner of that dressing room—glances, sneers, and rebuffs. I was now convinced that Bernadette Boswell had always known, or suspected, the former relationship of her husband and her pretty dresser, despite the fact that she had fainted at its revelation.

Then why had the woman pretended? She had not been born a Roman Catholic, though she had adopted the faith, nor had she ever been a particularly devout one, so her acceptance of the situation for all those years seemed to have a nonreligious motivation—either a material one, because to break with her famous and successful husband would have meant the end of their stage partnership and without that partnership she could not have held her own, or a purely emotional one in which vanity played a larger part than wifely devotion. It was vanity which was hurt when he displayed his indifference, vanity outraged when he chose to occupy a separate room, and vanity seeking revenge when she elected to befriend the woman he had preferred to herself, and so placed her in a subservient position in which she would be constantly made aware of the need for gratitude and be constantly patronised and humiliated.

I had often felt sorry for Bernadette, but not now. Her husband's infidelity might well be laid at her door. She had apparently been very like Clementine when young—and was any man likely to remain faithful to my half-sister, any more than she was likely to remain faithful to any one man? Would she become as gross and self-indulgent as her mother when age robbed her of beauty? Both women demanded and expected admiration—easy to command when young, but not so easy when self-indulgence led all too quickly into heavy middle age.

My mother looked particularly lovely this afternoon in a dove-grey dress of serviceable calico, admirable for a visit to an East End mission, and an enormous wide-brimmed hat firmly attached to her piled-up hair with stiletto pins. I felt a sudden rush of love for her, and a sudden remorse because I had a secret from her, the first of my life. If only Gavin had not commanded my silence! I longed to tell her that he had asked me to marry him, because I still had an uneasy suspicion that she didn't wholly trust Gavin, and nothing could have assured her of his honesty more than that.

Helen was buttoning her coat; her brother, clad in his tight boxing breeches, full-sleeved shirt, and leather waistcoat, was bound for Soapbox Corner, where, on a Sunday afternoon, he could be sure of many opponents to meet his challenge. Barker was stacking the portable boxing booth onto the barrow outside at this very moment; I glanced from the window and saw his wrinkled-leather face intent on the job, his wiry form lifting the sections with ease. He was accompanying his master today, and I could imagine his cheerful cockney voice yelling to the crowd: *"Roll up! Roll up! Come'n beat the Toff!"*

Everybody was going out; the house would be empty and I would be left alone to fret with disappointment over today's lost meeting with Gavin and to worry about those disturbing rumours from the theatre, though surely there could be no truth in them, a failure at the Boswell being unprecedented. Even so, I hated the thought of being alone, and asked spontaneously if I could go along to the mission too, a suggestion gladly accepted.

Helen drove the trap and as we bowled along Oxford Street toward Tottenham Court Road, where the creation of new thoroughfares had pressed the areas of St. Giles and Seven Dials closer together until finally the Rookeries had been squeezed out completely, sending the overflow of squalor and vice farther east, she was unaware of the eyes which followed us: three women driving unescorted from the West End toward less salubrious parts made a spectacle that caught the eye, but even had she noticed, Helen would have been quite indifferent. Ribald shouts, the closer we approached the East End, left her unperturbed. They began in High Holborn, that borderline between London's East and West, but the nearer we approached that square mile known as the City, because it had once formed the whole of the City of London, the less attention we seemed to attract. Here the inhabitants were unimpressed, perhaps because they were accustomed to the sight of this suffragette female driving militantly by, and by the time we reached the area of the Tower of London we aroused no comment at all, for we were in a part where women fraternised freely on the streets, competing for male quarries.

The trap bowled down Tower Hill at an increasing speed, past a smattering of preachers haranguing indifferent flocks, people so ragged that words of religious reproach passed right over their heads, and then we plunged into the back streets of Stepney and the squalor leapt at us with the density of a fog. I felt choked by it.

I saw my mother's soft eyes mist with tears at the sight of near-naked children crawling on filthy pavements, of gin-soaked parents (because a penny would buy more gin than food and allayed the pangs of hunger), of hundreds of prostitutes waiting for sailors from the London docks, of poverty unknown in the aristocratic environs of Portman Square, and I shared her distress. Nothing could have jerked me away from self-pity more effectively than this; compared with it, my fretful brooding over today's disappointments put me to shame, and by the time we reached the mission I had been shocked right out of it.

"You won't find life pleasant here," Helen said as she reined outside a shabby building, "but the inhabitants of this neighborhood can't be said to find it pleasant, either. Unhappily for them, they can do nothing about it. Happily for us, we can."

Just how much the Steels did came as a revelation during the next three hours, when my mother and I helped to feed endless lines of hungry people with bowls of soup and hunks of bread. There were helpers from all walks of life, people who gave their time and money freely, and within the first ten minutes I knew that my mother would become an established worker at this mission. This was a task in which she could lose herself, and we returned home laden with more clothes to be repaired or renovated. By that time we had seen all over the establishment. Helen showed it to us proudly, leading us from her brother's surgery, manned in his absence by another voluntary worker, a silver-haired, rather shabby doctor whom Helen introduced as Hugh Maynard, a man with a lined face and gentle eyes who, I learned later, was not nearly so old as he looked.

"He lost his wife two years ago, leaving him with a small son and daughter and a struggling practice in the wrong end of Fulham, the kind of practice overburdened with patients who can never pay their bills. For this reason I suspect he never renders them. But still he can give up his weekends to the mission. That's the kind of person he is."

It was the first time I had ever heard Helen speak of any man with unstinted admiration; even for her brother it was tempered with sisterly criticism.

While my mother lingered behind, playing with a group of children, Helen showed me the room where women who had lost all interest in life were helped to regain a spark by learning how to sew, to cook, to look after their young, but first, all had to learn the basic rules of cleanliness and hygiene. No psalm-singing and cant met life's flotsam here, male or female; no one asked if they had been baptised or into what faith, if any. Not even their backgrounds were investigated, nor their way of life. At Magnus Steel's mission they were human beings in need, and that fact alone qualified them for help.

But ignorance and poverty were the biggest barriers to break down. The last problem was insurmountable, but the first, Helen declared, could be overcome with time. Meanwhile, suspicion was instinctive.

"Wot, orl that washin'! 'Tain't good, that it ain't—catch yer death, y'would. 'Sides, where we live we ain't got no water an' there's six fam'-lies sharin' our room, an' four rooms on each floor likeways, an' only one outside pump an' an earth-closet fer the 'ole bleedin' street—an' anyways, 't wouldn't be decent to take all yer clothes orf! Never 'ad orl me clothes orf in the 'ole of my life, I ain't. 'Twouldn't be decent!''

In time, Helen insisted, they *must* win through. "But until we have compulsory education beyond the age of ten, and free education at that—the Ragged Schools are no real substitute, though they are doing their best to combat child labour in the factories—how can anyone be ex-pected to grasp the meaning of right and wrong, or anything else for that matter? Political female though I am, I know it is no use asking these wretched women whether they care about having a vote. Taking a mid-wifery course taught me that. How can they be expected to care, when their lives are nothing but one pregnancy after another? We must deal with that problem first."

"And how do you propose to do that?"

"There are ways." She flicked her hands through a pile of pamphlets. "Unfortunately, none of these women can read—hence the need for education. Hugh Maynard and I are holding reading classes once a week, well-attended too, he for men and I for women and girls. One step at a time. We have to get through to the men as well as the women, and where childbirth is concerned I tell the women what they need to hear. What they *want* to hear, moreover. But the men are difficult. They're afraid that the things we want to teach their wives will spoil or even deny them their 'rights'—as if women don't have rights as well, and more im-portant rights than political ones. *They* will come in time, but when wom-en get the right to vote, the majority won't bother to use it, or else they will vote as their husbands tell them to because they are hidebound by male domination both mentally and physically. Eventually they will think for themselves, but I fear that when we reach that stage of female eman-cipation I shall be old indeed or possibly even gone."

I had never heard that note of despondency in Helen's voice before. I preferred her usual militancy.

I said in encouragement, "Even if you are gone, your influence will re-main and I daresay there will be even more advanced literature than this being published."

I glanced at the titles. *Population Control. A Woman's Rights in Mar-riage. The Choice of Parenthood.* Revolutionary stuff. The moralists of the day would be horrified.

"Are you allowed to teach these things? What would Mrs. Ormiston Chant say?"

"Mrs. Ormiston Chant would probably die of shock, and that would

Rona Randall

be a good thing. She is free to come here anytime. We have even invited her, but the invitation was declined. My dear Aunt Agatha is one of her followers and has no doubt hinted at our shocking beliefs. Magnus once asked our aunt for a donation of funds, but was unwise enough to reveal what it would be used for in addition to general mission work. Printing these pamphlets, which he writes himself. You can imagine her reaction."

"No wonder she disapproved of the pair of you!" I laughed.

"And yet she consorts, if consorts is the word, with Durbridge—that pillar of respectability, that supporter of good causes. The most respectable causes, naturally." Helen finished thoughtfully, "I wonder what has happened to that man."

"Happened to him?" I jerked, glad that my mother had lingered behind. "What do you mean, happened?"

"Only that he failed to put in an appearance at a supper party he was hosting recently. Some fashionable restaurant or other. Strange. Out of character, too. Durbridge is a man who likes to do things in style and never puts a foot wrong socially. To commit a gaffe like that would naturally shock London society, though it would be a great deal more shocked if it knew of other things he does. . . ."

It was time to go, I thought, and moved to the door. All the same, I couldn't resist one last comment.

"The fact that he committed a social *faux pas* doesn't necessarily mean that anything has happened to him. I expect he sent explanations and apologies."

"That's just it—he didn't. Lady Mortlake is a neighbor of ours, an inveterate first-nighter. I saw her in the stalls and she told me about the party to follow. That was when it was to be, after the first night at the Boswell Theatre."

"Only a short time ago."

"I know, but a woman like the Mortlake is a stickler for etiquette— such a bore!—and expected a prompt and elaborate apology, no doubt accompanied by flowers. She received neither, and that, too, is unlike Durbridge, famed for his grandiose gestures. Odd, don't you think? Perhaps he has gone out of town on one of his escapades—though I didn't like to suggest that to the Mortlake."

To my relief, Helen dismissed the matter, but I was troubled. First Maisie and now Helen. Others would be commenting soon, and the fact that no mention of his death had appeared in the press would increase speculation when he failed to be seen around London. All those slighted supper guests would whisper and conjecture, smarting beneath his indifference. I had no doubt at all that Lady Boswell would do the same, for I

knew how her resentment could smoulder. The insult meted out by him
on the occasion of her daughter's first lead appearance would not be forgotten.

I returned home so tired that I dropped into bed exhausted. Even so, I
did not expect to sleep. Too many questions hammered at my mind, too
many anxieties, too many needs—particularly the need to see Gavin as
soon as possible. I had to talk about Durbridge, to find out more about
his handling of the situation. He had spared me too much in his desire to
save me anxiety. I now needed and wanted to know details.

I also found myself wondering what business could possibly keep Gavin occupied on a Sunday, and this speculation was intermixed with the
inevitable nervousness which preceded any appearance in a new part for
the first time. Tomorrow was another opening night for me, and an important one despite the fact that the additional part was small. And
thrusting through all this mental turmoil were those faces at the Stepney
mission—young faces prematurely old, old faces which had never been
young. I tried not to believe that Magnus Steel might be fighting a losing
battle against poverty, ignorance, and disease, but I feared it. My anxiety
on behalf of this man, whose world was so far removed from mine in the
theatre that the two could never really meet, was surprisingly strong.

I slept suddenly and deeply, waking in the morning with an urgent desire to get to the theatre as quickly as possible because there I would see
Gavin, there I would also take my place in a new dressing room, and
there I would stand a better chance of finding out if there was any truth
in those disturbing rumours about the play coming off.

That much, at least, I did learn as soon as I walked through the stage
door, for there on the call board was the fatal notice. The management
regretted that decreasing box-office receipts compelled an early closure
of the current production, the last performance of which would take
place a fortnight hence.

That would be Saturday, June 16. My sixteenth birthday. Who had
first said that when your age matched your birthdate it was a lucky one?

There was unmitigated gloom throughout the theatre that night. A
failure at the Boswell? Impossible! Unheard of! But it had happened, despite the promising first night. The show was folding.

I was on in the first act as well as the last one now, and although I got
through the part of the innkeeper's daughter without a hitch, I knew my
performance was hardly memorable. It was not a part which held any

dramatic scope, being merely that of a flirtatious girl ogling the revolutionaries, but apart from that, had the kindly old Howard Mortimer been out front he would not have deemed me worthy of notice tonight.

But zest seemed to have gone out of everyone's performance. First-night elation was a distant memory, blotted out by an imminent last-night depression which I guessed would hang over the theatre until the final curtain two weeks hence.

Only Gavin seemed unperturbed, even cheerful. Coming offstage in the first act, I met him in the wings awaiting his own entrance.

"Oh, Gavin," I wailed, "have you *heard?*"

"That the notice has gone up? Of course. But don't worry, darling. You've no need to worry at all."

"If you mean that I may be kept on in the company, I doubt it, though of course the Boswell is sure to go into production right away—"

"I shouldn't count on that, but as I say, you've no need to worry." His cue was near, and so was Bernadette's, which meant that I had to get back to my dressing room before she appeared. I had skilfully avoided her since that terrible night, seeing her only onstage during performances and then not in any proximity because my tumbril had been banished from centre stage, on her insistence. She had claimed that it masked her, and since then I had uttered my agonised cry up left, where it was less effective but at least out of her vicinity.

As I turned away, Gavin said hurriedly, "Darling, I must see you after the show. We'll have a quiet supper somewhere discreet, and then I'll take you home. I have news, important for both of us, so get rid of that man of Steel's if he's coming to collect you. If he isn't, send the fly back to the livery stable."

There was a suppressed elation about him, but no time for questions. I nodded and hurried away—and met Bernadette Boswell face to face.

She eyed me stonily, then said, "Well, gel, you will at least be able to say you have acted professionally with the finest company in London and at the greatest theatre. That should stand you in good stead when seeking work with other managements."

The message was clear; I was not to be included in any future casting. My life at the Boswell Theatre had ended as abruptly as had my life in the Boswell home.

13

"So you see, my darling, nothing could be more opportune! We go into rehearsals two weeks hence and there'll be no tangle with the Boswell Theatre over your contract. When others in the cast are doing the rounds of the agents, looking for work, we will be packing our skips and heading for the road."

I couldn't believe it. I was to be engaged as juvenile lead in a new production which was to be tried out in the provinces prior to London production.

"It's like this," said Gavin, leaning across the table and covering my hands with his. "A married couple stands a better chance of being engaged by any theatrical company, because a joint salary is more economical. A wardrobe mistress and a stage manager, a leading actor and actress, two character supports, two juvenile leads—it doesn't matter what their rank or in what capacity they apply, as a couple they are a better proposition because they cost less. And in this instance *we* will fare even better, because I am to produce the show as well as play lead. So what do we have?" He ticked off the items on his fingers. "Producer, lead actor, and female juvenile lead—and a triple-joint salary. What do you say to that?"

I was speechless with joy.

"Of course," Gavin continued, "we have to be married to qualify for the joint salary, so I won't hear of any refusal, my darling. My whole career depends on this. I would never get the chance to produce or play leads at the Boswell Theatre and you would never be anything more than a minor player and understudy to Clementine. You don't want that, do you?"

I did not. I had vowed, long ago, to play second fiddle to her no more, and now I knew she was my half-sister, my resolve was even greater.

"You would never have had the chance to play Lucie, even if *The Only Way* hadn't folded. You realise that, don't you? Clementine is never likely to be off for a single performance, whatever she's playing in, so casting you as understudy was no more than a gesture on Nevill's part, a sop to his conscience. He announced his intention to look after you both, didn't you tell me? Well, throwing you the understudy bait was a magnificent demonstration, I must say."

"Oh, no—he didn't mean it like that, I'm sure."

Gavin patted my cheek.

"Well, my lovely, go on believing that if you wish. Far be it from me to disillusion you, but I say again that if Nevill Boswell had really wanted to be a father to you, he would have undertaken the role long ago, and more effectively. He could and should have acknowledged you legally, and my sister would have had to accept things—and *would* have accepted them, since the worst thing that could happen to her, and she knows it, would be a breakup of her stage partnership. But only a divorce could have brought that about, because there is no worse stigma in this day and age; it even bans people from the Royal Enclosure at Ascot, and could there be any disgrace worse than that?" His smile was mocking. "The hypocrisy of present-day morals—it doesn't matter what you do, so long as you do it in secret! Ninety percent of married men have mistresses, and their wives know it and have to accept it. It is almost a requisite symbol of a man's success. So acknowledging his responsibility for your birth wouldn't have brought down the Boswell Theatre or ruined my stepsister's career. Public sympathy might even have strengthened it—the noble tragedy queen bravely facing up to tragedy in real life! And people expect prominent actors to be rakes anyway. They like it, because it makes them seem more human. Look at Irving and that mistress of his! Nevill's pretence disgusts me. Providing a roof over your head and your mother with employment as his wife's dresser can hardly rank as generosity. You say it was his wife's idea, but how can you be sure? Face facts, my darling. The man could have treated Trudy better than that, and even if you were likely to remain at the Boswell Theatre, which you are not, you would remain in the background, his daughter's shadow as you have always been."

"I am his daughter, too," I protested feebly.

"But not his legitimate one. Not even his acknowledged one until the truth came out. Oh, my dear love, don't look like that. I can't bear it. Far be it from me to distress you, but we can't escape the truth. At the Boswell you would never be given the opportunity I am giving you now. You have me to thank entirely for this. I've worked for it, schemed for it, determined to get you into the company somehow. Going on the road without you would be unbearable. I had to play my cards well, and it has taken all my time and ingenuity, but I have pulled it off. I have invested in this company, bought my way in if you like, and as a result I've got the producer's job, which means a certain amount of control. Control means power, and power means being able to do what you wish. *My* wish has always been to combine producing with acting, even to have my own company one day. My revered stepbrother-in-law isn't the only man who can be an actor-manager. For now, this is the best I can do, but part of my bargaining power was being able to produce a wife already acting and trained at the Boswell—so you see, some good did come out of your life there. I am being perfectly honest with you."

"Who are the management?" I asked.

"You won't know the name; it's new. Shaftesbury Productions, so called because they have offices in Shaftesbury Avenue; Suite Number 6, Cathcart House. It's a company with all sorts of irons in the fire, but I am only interested in this one. They are very sound people, believe me. I wouldn't get involved with them otherwise, much less allow *you* to."

Excited as I was, I said, "I must have Mamma's permission, of course. She may or may not like the idea of my going on tour. You know what touring companies are like."

"I know what they are reputed to be like, which isn't necessarily the same thing. Anyway, the straight theatre can't compare with travelling music hall and third-rate melodrama, one-night stands and so forth. Trudy didn't see anything wrong with Boswell sending out a Shakespearean company under his banner, did she? But in any case, she won't be able to object. As my wife, I will be responsible for you. *I* will make the decisions."

I said painfully, because the thought was unbearable, "If she refuses to let me marry you, what then?"

Gavin's fascinating mouth curved in his fascinating smile—teasing, persuasive, sensually attractive.

"She won't be given the chance to refuse, my darling, because we are not going to tell her until after the event." Seeing my face, he rushed on, "It is by far the best way. Present the world with a *fait accompli* and, short of invoking the law because you are a minor—which *she* must have been when Boswell seduced her, anyway—there isn't a thing anyone can do. As for invoking the law, I know she couldn't raise the money for such a costly procedure, so we've nothing to worry about on that score."

"But she would be hurt."

"Knowing how much she loves you, I also know she puts your happiness above all things. So long as you are happy, she will be too."

"In that case, there's no reason why I shouldn't tell her."

He must have detected anxiety in my voice, because he said at once, "You're not sure. You're afraid. You think she would forbid you to marry me, but why should she? She knows I'm not penniless; my own father as well as my stepfather left me provided for. Oh, I know I was a bit extravagant when young, but I always cleared my debts and I've never been involved in any scandal. I don't pretend to have been a saint, but what man is? And I've been a damn sight better than many because I've prided myself on my good name. I'm a lead actor and my future is assured, and when she hears you've married a producer as well as a lead actor, she will know I am able to take care of you."

In that case, I thought, why can't we tell her? I wanted to do that. I wanted to have her blessing.

Aloud, I said, "I have never in my life done anything behind her back."

Gavin was hurt. "Of course, if you look at it that way, as if it were something to be ashamed of . . ."

I cried at once, "I don't, I don't! It's only that I can see no real reason for keeping it secret."

He answered patiently, "My darling, if we tell your mother, the Boswells will very likely hear of it. I don't care about my stepsister's reaction, though she would probably scream her head off at the idea of my marrying her husband's illegitimate offspring—she is almost as possessive about me as your dear mamma is about you—but what I won't tolerate is interference from Nevill. You know he always gets my back up. I wouldn't put it past Trudy to lose her head and rush across the square to him, seeking his help as before. You have to leave the nest sometime, though I doubt if she will ever let you go willingly, whatever your age. You have been all in all to her since the day you were born, but you can't remain that way. You have to break free, be yourself, choose your own way of life." The hurt note crept back. "Why did I imagine you wanted it to be the same as mine? Why did I think you wanted to spend it with me?"

"I do, you know I do! I have adored you since my childhood."

"And I have waited for you since your childhood—well, almost. I could always see the woman you would become." He picked up my hand and touched the wrist with his mouth, nibbling it affectionately, kissing my fingers and then my palm, until I felt myself weakening with desire.

"The thing is, sweetheart, that I don't want Boswell trying to come between us. You saw for yourself, that day at Rule's, that he didn't approve of your being with me, God knows why. And since your mother has no one else to turn to, she might well do what she did that awful night."

"About that night," I said. "What happened after we had gone, how did you cope with . . . things? You told me a certain amount, but I want to know more."

He cut me short. "This isn't the time to talk about that. I took care of everything, as I told you, and that's all you need worry your head about."

"But people are beginning to talk."

"What people?"

"One of the women supers who seems to know a lot about Durbridge—"

"Good grief, you surely don't gossip with that kind of super, the kind that makes it their business to know all they can about prominent men because such knowledge comes in useful, and what they don't know, they make up? So who else has been talking?''

"Helen Steel.''

"The doctor's sister? A frustrated spinster is always prone to gossip.''

"I wouldn't call Helen frustrated; her life is too busy. She happens to be a neighbor of Lady Mortlake, who was a guest at the supper party at Romano's and has apparently been talking about it a lot.''

"That woman! I know her well. She'll be prattling about someone else tomorrow, and someone else the day after that.''

"If a notice had appeared in the obituary columns, no one would speculate at all.''

"My dear Lucinda, do you think I would be so unwise as to draw attention to his death? Questions would be asked as to how it came about; witnesses would be sought, which means you and Trudy. As it is, his disappearance, when it is noticed, will be nothing but a nine days' wonder, and after that it will be forgotten, eclipsed by some other piece of news.''

"But surely his family—''

"He was a bachelor. A man like Durbridge doesn't marry. As for relatives, I know of none and haven't troubled to find out. The important thing is that I have covered the traces, as I promised, and I have no intention of telling you how. You have to trust me. Covering up your part in that ugly business, *and* your mother's, proves that, doesn't it? And now, let's hear no more of it. I was talking about us. If we slip away quietly and get married, appealing to Boswell to break things up won't avail your mother anything, because he can bring no pressure to bear. He has no legal right at all, since he has never legally adopted you. You are your mother's child; she and she alone is your guardian, and it is her name that you bear, not his. I don't have to hide how I feel about the man. I think he has treated your mother abominably all these years. The least a man should do when fathering a child is to look after the mother decently, provide a home for them both, and support them well.''

"He did educate me.''

"How generous!''

"And he was training me for the stage.''

"That won't continue now. I heard Bernadette's pointed remark to you in the wings.'' He added with a touch of impatience, "Darling, wake up! Let those scales fall from your eyes. Do you honestly think you stand a chance in any way at all against Clementine, the legitimate Boswell daughter? You saw his pride in her at her coming-out ball—and what did *you* get? Your first ball gown as consolation prize. Oh, my darling, don't cry.'' He leaned over and kissed my eyelids and didn't care if the whole world saw. "*I* could never be ashamed of you. I want to love and protect you, always. Please let me—please.''

I nodded, unable to speak, and he said very firmly, very softly, "That means, my precious love, that you must be guided by me and do whatever I say. Always.''

He didn't call a cab when we left the discreet little Chelsea restaurant. His rooms on the Embankment were only a short walk away.

"I want you to see the home I'll be taking you to," he said, slipping his arm about my waist and turning me toward the river. The night was dark and warm and intimate, and I went with him willingly.

I knew I would like any home he took me to, any place which would be our own private world, but the reality was more elegant than I expected—a small, tastefully furnished apartment at the top of one of the new and fashionable blocks of flats which were being built around London. I had expected a bachelor establishment to be rather bare and purely functional, but much thought and not a little money had gone into this place.

Ushering me into the hall, he lit an oil lamp and carried it high as he led me into the living room. He showed me everything, including the kitchen and the small bathroom with his dressing room leading from it. The bathroom was a note of real luxury because it contained a proper bath of enamelled iron standing on lions' feet, with taps for hot as well as cold water, a contrast with the hip bath used in most middle-class homes. Gavin was certainly a man of means; not affluent in a flamboyant way, but comfortable and well able to provide the security my mother would want for me.

I jerked my thoughts away from my mother, confident that I would be able to win her over. Gavin was opening a door and saying, "And this is the bedroom, my darling.''

I entered, compelled by a desire to see the room which would be the most intimate of all.

Close beside me he said, "I'll get rid of that couch, of course. A double bed can be accommodated well.''

He set down the oil lamp. I was glad he had not lit the gas. The cold light of hissing jets would have dispelled enchantment. Then I felt his lips on my neck and his hands on my shoulders. They were moving very slowly, very surely. I gave an inarticulate cry and his mouth silenced me, his hands still unbuttoning the neck of my gown and then unfastening my bodice. I felt them on my bare shoulders, then on my breasts, and I murmured incoherently. My voice seemed to come from far away—a sob, a whisper, a sigh—and he commanded softly, "Hush, my darling. Be still. I am undressing you."

He took my body slowly and with consideration, easing the experience with an expert touch so that there was no shock to make me flinch and retreat; then came one brief and startling thrust of pain, minimised beneath blurred senses, after which the moments seemed tireless and prolonged, with response gathering within me until it was a mounting tide, my body rocking rhythmically with his, my mind delirious, but through it all I was aware of his strength mingled with tenderness, so that instead of fear I knew nothing but delight and consuming desire, wave upon wave of incredible sweetness carrying me to a blinding climax which surged through my flesh and my blood and my senses too. I had not dreamed that my body could be filled with such ecstasy or that a woman's whole being could merge with that of a man until they were totally one.

Nor had I known that the aftermath could bring such tranquillity. When at last he drew away, we lay naked and tired, drowsy with happiness. The bedcovers had tumbled to the floor, and, lying on his side, he gazed at my body, stroking it softly as he said, "If only you could stay, if we could have the night together! I would soon be arousing you again, my love. You are so responsive. You enjoyed it, didn't you? You loved it. It was beautiful. And it will always be like that, and even better. And we will have all this for the rest of our lives."

I nodded, too happy to speak. I closed my eyes and his voice sank to a murmur. He had a wonderful voice, with the deep timbre of an actor; at this moment it had an additional vibrancy which thrilled me. I felt his hand on my thigh, then higher, sliding exploringly upward until it covered my breast, massaging, caressing, fondling. "You are beautiful, my darling. My Lucinda."

Beneath languourous contentment my blood began to stir again. I opened my eyes and saw his handsome head leaning over me. His mouth came down on mine, claiming it, as if putting a seal on his possession of me. "That is in promise," he said, then shocked me by turning away. "Now, alas, I must take you home."

I had no idea of the time. I had lost all sense of it, and in the aftermath of passion I did not care. I had no desire to leave this tumbled couch and, all unbidden, heard Shakespeare's words about Juliet being "hot from the marriage bed" echoing in my mind. That was how I felt now, with the sheets tousled beneath us and Gavin's bare limbs close to my own. I was hardly aware of turning on my side and of sliding one leg over his hip to draw him to me again until he cried, "You learn fast, my love, but no, or I shall be unable to let you go. We must wait until next time. God forgive me, I didn't mean it to happen until after marriage."

"I am glad it did."

"You agree that we must make it soon?"

"Yes, oh, yes!"

"And that we mustn't risk anyone stopping us?"

"No one. No one at all."

"They would try to, you know, because you are underage, but you are a woman now, my woman, and you are going to remain so. I can't wait to make you my wife."

I could not wait either. I would do whatever this man asked of me so long as I could make sure of that.

After he had dressed and gone out to find a cab, I also dressed, though reluctantly. I wanted nothing so much as to sleep on this couch tonight and find him there beside me in the morning, our bodies warm from the heat of the night and ready to be afire again. When I thought of those moments, I could feel again the pulsing sweetness of them and craved to experience them once more. Why was anything so beautiful regarded as sinful, and how could anyone distort or profane it? I had not thought of Clementine's cheap confessions for a long time, but suddenly I recalled them and felt sorry for her. She had had no love for Pierre, nor he for her, and the practices they had indulged in had been for animal satisfaction, nothing more. Any man's body would serve her; she had intimated that without embarrassment or shame. That was the difference between us. I loved Gavin and could have given myself to no other man, but Clementine had probably enjoyed others since her French gardener—Curtis, I suspected.

Had she slipped down to those rooms of his above the coach house in the mews, amusing herself with him, using him and then rejecting him as she would a servant? I remembered that smouldering look he had focused on her the night I had fetched Magnus Steel to my mother, a look of bitter resentment because she spared him not even a glance. Foolish Clementine, didn't she know it was unwise to play with fire? She would even have allowed Durbridge to do what he liked with her in her eager quest for experience.

Why think of Durbridge now? I had to forget him, never think of him, never recall him, much less allow him to intrude at such a moment as this, but suddenly the way he had died thrust itself into my consciousness again like a hideous shadow stalking me. I was trembling as I buttoned my jacket and went into the living room and sat down, awaiting Gavin's return.

The world was very quiet outside. How late was it? Very late? It must be. My mother would be abed by now. Surely she wouldn't wait up for me? I had told Barker that I was going to a private supper party with members of the cast and that I would be brought safely home; at least the last part of that story was not a lie and Gavin had assured me the first part was only faintly so. That had been after the curtain came down and I could think of no excuse to dismiss Barker, and begged Gavin to advise me. I was not experienced in evasions, but sometimes they were necessary, and I must have recited it all very convincingly because Barker had accepted his dismissal without the blink of an eyelid. But now the first stirring of guilt touched me; I would have to be even more convincing when I faced my mother again, and that was the part I was going to hate—pretending to her, lying to her. Would she see through me? Would tonight leave its aftermath in my face, my eyes, my expression, my personality? How could I hide it?

My heart lifted at the sound of Gavin's step upon the stair. With him, no doubts could worry me, and his smile was reassuring as he came to me, hands outstretched. "Alas, my lovely, our time together is over—I have a cab outside. Come."

We sat close together in the darkness, hand in hand, laughing in our secret enjoyment. It was a beautiful secret, a wonderful one, and nobody must be allowed to mar it.

"I will get a special licence, and since it will be necessary to lie about your age, I suggest you put up your hair and try to look older than you are when we go to the registry office. You do understand that a church ceremony is out of the question, because banns have to be called for three consecutive weeks, and I cannot tolerate such delay. We must do it as quickly as possible."

It was only when we were nearing Portman Square that I wondered how I was going to get into the house. Unmarried women didn't have latchkeys, and besides, I was only a visitor in Magnus Steel's home. When I voiced my apprehension, Gavin said, "Didn't you tell Barker to make sure the place was left unlocked for your return? Never mind—if you can't get in, so much the better; you will have to come back with me then," and the now familiar pressure of his thumb in my palm began again, suggestive, persuasive.

There was a dim light in the hall. I could see it shining through the fanlight, but when Gavin helped me down, telling the cabby to wait, I wondered how I was to open that solid front door.

I need not have worried. We had scarcely reached the steps when light flooded out into the night and I saw Magnus Steel silhouetted against the bright hall. He seemed taller and stronger than ever at that moment.

It was I who felt embarrassed, not he. He held the door wide to admit me, saying easily, "Thank you for bringing her home safely, Calder. That supper party must have gone on for a long time."

He didn't invite him in, nor did he give him time to answer, but nodded a brief good night and shut the door again.

"And now," he said to me, as if I were an errant schoolgirl, "you'd better get to bed at once. And go quietly. Your mother is asleep."

"I shan't disturb her," I answered coldly, resenting his tone. "If you had left the door unlatched, you would have been spared the trouble of waiting up."

"I didn't. I had work to do."

I noticed then that light shone from his study at the end of the hall, and there was ink on his fingers.

"Nor would I have put any servant to the trouble of sitting up for you," he continued. "The door would, as you suggest, have been left unlatched had it been necessary. Why should other people be inconvenienced just because thoughtless theatrical folk decide to keep you out later than a young woman of your age should be kept out? And if Calder had any consideration for you, he would have brought you home before the party broke up."

"You sound like a disapproving parent!"

I had reached the foot of the stairs, where I paused and looked back at him. He was wearing a much-worn smoking jacket, and the shirt beneath was open at the neck. I saw the thatch of copper-coloured hair which I had noticed that day in Hyde Park, except that then it had been beaded with sweat and now he was cool and well groomed—but just as masculine. He towered above me. He boxed in the heavyweight class, his sister had told me, and I could well believe it, for never had he seemed so powerful as at this moment. In other circumstances I could have been intimidated by him, but with the glow of Gavin's love still lingering, I felt surprisingly self-confident. Did all women gain in confidence when they lost their virginity?

"I may be disapproving," he retorted, "but I don't feel in the least like a parent. Good night to you, Lucinda."

He was angry. I shrugged, said I was sorry for being so late, and turned to go upstairs.

"You are not in the least sorry," he said from behind me. "It shows in your face. You have an expressive face, a revealing one. Perhaps it's a good thing your mother won't see you tonight."

I paused, then went on. I didn't look back, but I knew he watched my departure. Not until I reached a turn in the stairs did I hear him walk along the hall and close his study door.

I had to go carefully, I decided. Very carefully indeed if I hoped to keep any secret from this man.

14

My mother's reaction to our marriage was not what I expected. No cries, no protests, no tears. She sat down very slowly and went very white.

"We must tell her when she is alone," Gavin had said. "She is sure to take it badly, and it would be better for this to happen when others are not present." So we arrived at the house when I was sure Magnus and his sister would be at the mission and my mother sewing at home.

Seeing her reaction, I was about to rush over to her when my husband's hand detained me. *Don't fuss*, his eyes said. *That will make her worse. Let her recover in her own good time.* But after waiting, and seeing her sitting there so still, so silent, I shook his hand aside and went to her.

"Mamma . . . please. I know it is a shock, but try to be happy for me. You know I have always loved Gavin, and I love him more than ever now."

Her eyes turned to me in a slow, almost stupefied fashion, and for a moment I thought her mind had retreated as it had on that last night in Nevill Boswell's house; then comprehension seemed to take over. Her lips moved soundlessly at first, then words managed to come through.

"Who thought of this, to do it this way, I mean? To marry first and tell me later. Not you."

"Of course not, Trudy. It was I." Gavin's voice was brisk, but kind. "I take full responsibility, as I intend to take full responsibility for Lucinda from now on. You wouldn't have consented had we come to you first, now, would you?"

She shook her head. It seemed to jerk from side to side, like a puppet's.

"No. She is underage."

"But you won't try anything on those grounds, will you? As she says, she loves me, and you have always known it. Her mind never changed about that even as she grew up, so surely you must realise that it won't change now, and that no opposition can make it. The reverse, in fact. We belong together now, Lucinda and I."

She stared at him. "You mean . . . you *already* belong to each other?"

I could not look at her. She had guessed the truth. I would have spared her that.

Gavin nodded and said reasonably, "So it is better that she remains my wife, don't you think?"

"But she is so young—so very young!" There was a wounded note in that cry. I could scarcely bear to look at her. Then she took a steadying breath and said, "I cannot respect you for this, Gavin Calder. You are much older than my daughter and you seduced her with a purpose. It would be unlike you to act without one."

He laughed, making her wince, then said hastily, "I am only amused by your wrong judgment of me. You have no grounds for it. You have never really known me, but neither have you liked me. Perhaps your opinion will improve with time. I hope so, for Lucinda's sake. I don't want her to be alienated from her mother."

"We could never be alienated!" I cried. I knelt before her, taking hold of her hands and looking up into her face. "Mamma . . . dear Mamma . . . please try to understand," but she stared into space, saying nothing.

Gavin took over again.

"Trudy, listen to me. It is true that Lucinda is underage, but she isn't a child. She is sixteen and a mature young woman. She is ready for marriage. She needs to live with a man, and I am he. If you deny her this right, she will hate you for it in time, whatever she may think or say now. Things would never be the same between you again. You would be losing your daughter even more surely than you are losing her now, but you won't lose her at all if you accept the situation. And you do realise, don't you, that trying to break our marriage would cost a lot of money? I know you haven't the means."

"You banked on that, did you?"

The words came out with unbelievable bitterness. In all our life together and despite its circumstances, I had never heard bitterness in my mother's voice before.

Gavin said reproachfully, "Surely you know me better than that?"

"I think I know you very well."

"In that case, you must know how much I love your daughter."

"I know that you have been aware of her for a long time."

"Then you also know that I have waited very patiently. Did I force my attentions on her when she was too young to receive them? And didn't I prove my concern for her the night Durbridge fell down that staircase, the night you caused his death?"

"*Gavin*! It is cruel to remind her of that!"

"Well, darling, she seems to have forgotten it, doesn't she?" He turned back to my mother. "Durbridge wasn't in love with your daughter, as I am. He came across her naked in the theatre and tried to take her by force in his own particular way." He paused to let the words sink in. My mother's eyes closed and a shudder ran through her. "I am guilty of seducing Lucinda, yes, but not against her will and not in a way which means agony to a woman. And now I have married her, doesn't that right what you now seem to consider a wrong, though apparently you didn't hold that view when young? I don't see how you can disapprove of what you yourself were guilty of then, with *no* marriage in view."

He didn't mean to be harsh, but I wished he had not said that. Or other things. This meeting was not going the way I expected. Tears and reproaches from my mother would have been easier to cope with than her rigid stillness, her white face, and now her silent acceptance of my husband's words.

At length she managed to ask me how long we had been lovers.

"A few days, no more. Forgive us for not waiting, Mamma, but as Gavin has told you, we intended to marry anyway."

"In that case, a little patience on his side would not have come amiss. Or did he imagine I would refuse my consent and therefore seduction seemed a good way of forcing it?"

That angered him. "If you are going to make accusations like that, Trudy, we will leave at once."

A glance from me told him that I would not go until she was in a better state. I felt that displeased him, though he made no demonstration of it. Instead, he said persuasively, "Come, Trudy . . . accept things and be glad your daughter has married a man with good prospects. I don't intend to remain merely an actor. In fact, I have already accepted a producer's appointment as well as male lead, and I mean to have my own theatre one day. What's more, it will be a success. No flops like this recent one at the Boswell. I shall keep up-to-date with public taste. Has Lucinda told you we are off on tour together in a prior-to-London production?"

I had had no opportunity to tell her anything yet, as he must know, but I guessed he was making random conversation in order to give my mother a chance to rally, to accept and be reconciled to the situation, and this waiting could be no easier for him than for me.

Now my mother said, "Her father will not be pleased."

"Forgive me, but I fail to see what it has to do with Nevill Boswell. He isn't Lucinda's legal guardian. You are. And I know you care more for your daughter's happiness than anything else, and that you will give us your blessing and accept me as your son-in-law because I am the man Lucinda loves and wants to live with. It's as simple as that. A choice between your wishes and hers. Her father's don't enter into it.''

"He cares about her.''

"He should have demonstrated that more strongly years ago.''

"He did. He provided for her in a will drawn up when she was a child. It rescinded all former wills. He told me about it.''

"Well, I'm glad to hear he has some sense of responsibility, but so have I, and I'm not likely to back out of it as he is doing.''

"What do you mean?''

"He is not re-engaging her as a member of the company. It's true. The theatre is closing down—''

"For its annual break? That is normal.''

"Then it is reopening with *Twelfth Night*, and Lucinda's name isn't on the cast list. So I don't think it would avail you much if you went running to him on her behalf again.''

This lack of tact was so uncharacteristic of Gavin that I knew it to be unintentional, but for the first time in my life I wondered why men couldn't realise that there were moments for blunt honesty and others for hiding it.

My mother replied, "I don't believe you. Nevill told me only the day before yesterday that nothing had changed, nor ever would.''

I was startled. "You've seen him?''

"Yes. He called because he failed to see me the first time and wanted to assure me he would stand by the promises he made long ago—to look after you and to provide for your future, as, in fact, he had already done.''

"Well," said Gavin, "I'm glad to hear it. And what is he doing for you?''

"Nothing, because I refused it. I don't need his help. Dr. Steel is employing me at the mission, and accommodation here is to be part of my wages. I am well content and very comfortable, but I would refuse nothing from Nevill on Lucinda's behalf.''

"By providing for her future, I presume he means after his death, by which time she and I will be more successful than he is now, and certainly more successful than he is likely to be if he doesn't change his policy at the theatre. The public is all too familiar with stock drama, and Shakespearean audiences are shrinking. Too many managements rely on Shakespeare for their bread and butter—Forbes-Robertson, Martin-Harvey, even Henry Irving, though he does have the sense to intersperse the Lyceum's programme with plays like *The Lyons Mail* and is wise enough to recognise his own limitations as an actor and to surround himself with better players to carry him through. The public wants lively stuff these days. The starch is going out of things and will disappear altogether when the Prince of Wales comes to the throne. Nevill doesn't even *see* trends nowadays. But Lucinda and I don't have to worry our heads about that. Come, darling, it is time we left; we have a matinee to get through, which is hard after a morning wedding ceremony. You see how we put you first, Trudy dear; instead of snatching a few hours alone, we came straight here to see you. Lucinda wants your blessing, and I know you are going to give it."

She didn't look at him. All her attention was on me, and I could feel her agony of mind. I had not anticipated immediate approval of our runaway marriage, but this was worse. There was more than reproach in her eyes as she looked at me; there was sickness of heart. *Did you have to do it this way? Did you have to do this to me?*

I put my arms about her again, trying to comfort her as I had always done, but feeling that I was further away from her than I had ever been and that the hurt I had dealt would not quickly heal. How could I protest that I had not wanted to do things this way—that it had been Gavin's suggestion, Gavin's wish, that he had thought it the wisest thing to do? I owed him my loyalty, so all I could murmur was, "Forgive me, Mamma. Don't let anything change between us. . . ."

But a great deal had already changed, and it was going to take a great deal to put matters right.

"Please, Mamma . . . your blessing."

She took my face between her hands and kissed it. "You always have my blessing and I always want your happiness, so if that happiness really lies with Gavin . . ."

"It does, it does!"

"Then I pray God it will last, Lucinda."

"I knew she would come round," Gavin said, but I made no reply. I was remembering her white face, her stunned eyes, the sadness and numb acceptance in her voice. I had not wanted to receive her blessing like this, but at least she had given it.

I turned my face away in case he should see my tears, and his voice ran on. There was confidence in it, and relief. His hand sought mine, but I could not return the pressure. He turned my face toward him then and exclaimed, "Oh, my darling—tears on our wedding day?"

I was in his arms then and he was saying fervently, "Damn this matinee. If it weren't for that, I would take you straight home to bed."

In the privacy of the hansom cab we were very close. It was the final day of the Boswell Theatre production, and after this evening's performance we were to start immediately on rehearsals for the touring one.

Only tomorrow morning, Sunday, would be free; two o'clock sharp was the rehearsal call, on my husband's decree. As producer, he was eager to be started, and even half a day's idleness frustrated him. There was a whole new future stretching ahead of us and not a moment of it to be wasted. His excitement infected me. I could feel it as he kissed me, as he urged me not to fret, as he assured me that once the initial shock had passed my mother would be the same as ever.

"I have no doubt that after we left, she shed a few tears, the privilege of a bride's mother, then promptly began to revive. No doubt she is even now realising that the acquisition of a son-in-law can be a desirable thing, but even more desirable is a legalised union for her daughter. She must always have wanted that for you—a respectable marriage, a man's name, a gold band on your finger. Mark my words, Lucinda, at this very moment she is thinking to herself, '*Mrs.* Calder—my daughter, a married woman accepted by society!' And you *will* be accepted. There will be no furtive meetings, no secret ménage, no humiliation because, as a man's mistress, you could not be presented to family or friends. All this she will realise and be thankful for, and then she will get over her shock."

"There would have been no shock at all had she been at the wedding. I shall always regret that."

"Never waste time in regrets, never brood over past mistakes—not that I consider our private wedding ceremony to have been a mistake. To me, it was something deeply personal, between you and me only, and I was glad to have no guests for that reason. I thought you felt the same."

Immediately, guilt swung the other way and I was hastening to assure him that indeed I did, but I had to clamp down on the memory of that dusty registry office with its unwashed windows and its queue of people waiting to register births and deaths, and the registrar in his black frock coat sprinkled with dandruff, pin-striped trousers badly in need of pressing, stiff celluloid collar slightly greasy at the edges, and his dusty black cravat, which made him look as if he were presiding at a funeral. I also had to forget the frightening feeling I had experienced, as if I were going through some sort of hurried inquisition which had nothing to do with anything so human as love. All this had been emphasised by the man's haste as he raced through the final words, so fast it seemed he couldn't get this very unimportant piece of business finished quickly enough, and then snapping, "That'll be seven-and-sixpence, please."

The cab rumbled to a halt and Gavin said, "Here we are at the Boswell Theatre for the last time, my love. Two more performances to get through, and then we can say good-bye to the place."

As he paid off the cabby I went ahead through the stage door, and saw George, in his cubbyhole, turn to the letter rack behind him and then back to me. "I was asked to give you this personally, Miss Grainger, in case you overlooked it on the call board." The letter had an official look about it, which was not surprising, since it was from the theatre's actor-manager, summoning me to the green room at the first interval.

I don't know what made me push the letter into my pocket, unless it was the knowledge that the interview would be merely to explain why I was being passed over in the next production, a courtesy I could well do without. And coming on such a day as this, I had no inclination to meet my father face to face.

Then Gavin was beside me.

"Don't waste time removing your makeup when the curtain comes down, you can do that at home. I'll get George to have a cab waiting so that we can hurry straight off and have an hour at least to ourselves between this matinee and tonight's performance. Performance! It will be a wake, but what do we care? We're all set for the future—and you haven't seen the double bed I ordered. It was delivered yesterday, so we'll snatch an hour's honeymoon on it, and more when we get home tonight. . . ."

He flashed the smile which never failed to dazzle me and, bemused, I went on to my new dressing room, the letter from my father forgotten. I remembered it only five minutes before the curtain came down on the first act, and I knew that however reluctant I was to see him, I would have to obey the summons.

The usual notice, reserving the room for the management's use when needed, was pinned on the green-room door. I knew then that Nevill Boswell was going through the routine business of saying good-bye to actors he was not re-engaging, a courtesy few other managements bothered to extend at the end of a run. I also knew that he made personal gifts of money to those most likely to need it—"patronage money," Gavin called it—and I knew that if this was offered to me I would proudly refuse it, and that I would be equally proud to announce that I had signed a contract elsewhere. Gavin had not been tardy about getting all details signed, sealed, and settled.

Now I tapped on the green-room door and walked in head high when summoned. Nevill Boswell was sitting at a low table on which were a tea tray and a sheaf of papers. He dragged himself to his feet when I entered, and the movement was slow and heavy, unlike his usual buoyant self. The lines on his face seemed emphasised and his smile was an effort.

"Lucinda . . ."

He indicated a chair, and against my will I took it. I didn't want to be seated because it was always easier to curtail a meeting if one were standing, but to refuse would have been churlish, and there was something in his face which told me that this failure at the Boswell had gone deep.

I was glad he kept his voice impersonal, with no overtones from our previous meeting or any hint that he even remembered it.

"You will have seen the cast for *Twelfth Night* on the call board."

"I have heard about it."

"But not glanced at it? Was this because your informant, whoever he or she may have been, told you that your name was not included?"

I nodded.

"And so you assumed you were overlooked completely? A pity you didn't glance at it. You would then have seen that only the principal actors are listed; in the case of the women, Olivia and Viola. Now I have cast the supporting players, and you will play Olivia's maid, Maria, which will give you good scope for comedy and substantial lines. I have your contract here."

I was shocked into silence, which he failed to notice as he turned to the papers before him and continued, "It is useless to pretend that the failure of the current revival has not been a surprise and a setback, but the Boswell is sufficiently well established to weather it. Rehearsals for *Twelfth Night* will commence after a week's break, so I want you to start on your lines immediately, though of course you are already well acquainted with them through your training sessions with me. Those sessions will now start again. You will meet me here each day one hour before rehearsal call and remain for one hour afterward . . ." He broke off. "What is the matter?"

I had jumped to my feet, shaking my head and stammering, "No . . . no . . . I'm sorry . . ."

"What do you mean? Sorry for what? Lucinda, what is wrong?"

"Nothing! That is . . ." I blurted it out then. "I cannot accept, I cannot play Maria."

"You will play her very well by the time I have put you through your paces."

"You don't understand. I am not free to."

"Not *free*? What are you talking about? Your contract for this play expires tonight. There will be a new one for the next production."

I shook my head helplessly. "I can't sign it. I have accepted a part with another management."

"Your mother said nothing of this when I saw her the other day!"

"She didn't know."

"It is unlike you to keep things from your mother. Who is putting on this new production? I will get in touch with them and arrange for you to be released. I can do these things."

"I have signed the contract. We start rehearsals at once and go on tour three weeks from now."

This was supposed to be my moment of triumph, but it was nothing of the sort. It was painful and embarrassing and left me floundering. I stammered a final apology and headed for the door.

"Wait!"

He was on his feet, frowning.

"Who put you up to this, Lucinda? *Some*one did. You don't know the ropes sufficiently well to pull off such a thing for yourself, and although there are agents, it has never been necessary for you to use one." He gave me a sharp look. "*Did* you take it into your head to contact an agent? If so, which one? All are known to me, and I can deal with them direct."

Instead of getting easier, the moment was becoming more difficult. Why couldn't I make the announcement coolly and proudly, as I had imagined? I took a deep breath and faced him squarely.

"Not an agent," I said. "My husband."

Silence. Then he was laughing; uncertain, broken laughter. "My dear Lucinda, what sort of a joke is this?"

"It is no joke. I was married this morning. To Gavin."

His face didn't blanch, as my mother's had done. It just seemed to age, every line deepening and sharpening, the eyes going dead. At length I could stand the silence no longer and burst out, "It is true, *true*! And we are going on tour together, with the same company."

He had risen when I rose, but now he sat down again, and I saw his hands grasp the arms of his chair. They were shaking. "Why didn't Trudy tell me?"

"I've told you—she didn't know."

"She knows now?"

"Yes."

"And . . .?"

"She has given us her blessing." (But of course that wasn't strictly true; she had given *me* her blessing, not both of us.)

Suddenly my father exploded, "I don't believe it! Your mother would never condone such a thing—marriage at *your* age!" He was shaking more violently now, and this time with anger. "*I* will put a stop to it, if she cannot."

"You won't be able to. You are not my guardian."

The words jerked out of me, striking at him, and I knew I could not have hurt him more had I tried to.

The room was silent again, but shock and anger and antagonism filled it. Then he said slowly, "Did Gavin Calder point that out to you? Was it he who reminded you that I have no authority, no legal right as your father? It seems the sort of thing he would do. It has his calculation about it."

"No . . . no . . . and I won't listen to any more!"

He shook his head sadly. "My poor, foolish Lucinda, and my poor, foolish Trudy—trapped into giving her blessing. How, I wonder."

He was not talking to me, nor looking at me, but when I again moved to the door, he was aware of it and rapped, "I want to know the name of the company you have signed with."

"You won't have heard of it. It is new."

"Ah . . . I thought as much. Only a new company would entice Boswell players away. There is a certain code of ethics between managements—Irving at the Lyceum would never encroach, nor would I on his players. So . . . their name, please, Lucinda." When I made no answer, his voice rang out with that commanding note which I always obeyed. "I said . . . their name, Lucinda."

I told him, and he echoed, "Shaftesbury Productions? Situated in or near Shaftesbury Avenue, I take it. From where else would they choose such a name? It smacks of the theatre, too, which some upstart company would find very desirable."

He turned his back in dismissal, but before I could close the door behind me I heard him say, in a voice no longer taut with anger, but immeasurably tired, "And may God go with you, child. Remember I am here if you want me."

Four

Clementine

15

I don't believe it. Gavin and *Lucinda*, running off and getting married like that, without breathing a word to anyone! Gavin might at least have had the decency to tell *me*. I do believe Papa has been right about him all these years, declaring him to be unreliable and untrustworthy and more than a bit of a scapegrace, but of course Mamma has always doted on her young stepbrother, and now what a state she is in! Not even her medicine consoles her. There she is, prostrate on her bed, weeping and wailing and protesting wildly that she has always known that the gel was a schemer.

"That quiet kind always is. And remember how she looked when she came back to the drawing-room door that night, the night she and her no-good mother left this house, and had the impertinence to say she should have taken her away from it long ago! Brazen, impertinent, ungrateful! Oh, she's a schemer, that one. Revenge, that's what she's been after, and now I suppose she imagines she has won it, marrying into the family so she can thumb her nose at all of us! My poor dear Gavin, trapped by such a hussy! I have no doubt her mother put her up to it. 'Get him into your bed,' she would say—oh, I am quite sure she said it, and so the gel did it. Like mother, like daughter. 'He'll have to marry you then, Lucinda!' I can hear her saying the very words."

"Well, getting a man into her own bed didn't get *her* a husband, did it, Mamma?"

I couldn't resist that thrust as I slammed out of the room, heartily sick of Mamma's hysterics. Papa was closeted in his study downstairs; had been ever since he broke the news at breakfast this morning. Mamma had been talking about the next production and asking what part he planned for dear Gavin. "You must cast him in something worthy of his talents this time, Nevill. With all his experience, *and* playing leads on tour, he really does deserve a better chance at the Boswell."

Papa had answered quietly, "He has achieved it, apparently—or thinks he has—but not at the Boswell. With some new touring company, taking Lucinda with him."

Never had Mamma sat so bolt upright.

"What do you mean, 'taking Lucinda with him'? Surely he has not used his influence on that gel's behalf?"

That was when Papa finished drinking his coffee, laid down his cup, pushed back his chair, and rose.

"He has done more than that, my dear. He has married her. Secretly. That is the way he has used his influence where Lucinda is concerned. I've been afraid of it for a long time, afraid of him seducing her, because it was obvious he wanted to, but I have to admit that I didn't anticipate his persuading the child to run away and marry him, which, in my opinion, is a great deal worse because it means that she is his for life."

He had walked out of the breakfast room, ignoring Mamma's horrified screech, and when she lumbered after him, hurling questions and frantic disbelief at his head, he went into his study, shut the door quietly, and locked it. And there he remains.

Characteristically, Kate appeared on the scene. How near had she been hovering, making sure of overhearing, missing nothing? Keyhole Kate, who never misses an opportunity to gather knowledge and to trade upon it. And it is useless to ask Mamma to dismiss her. Kate knows how to make herself indispensable to my mother and how to keep up the pressure on me. I had been sadly deluded in believing that arranging for her to have a room to herself would rid me of her petty blackmail, though she had been well pleased at the time. I had kept my promise and attended to it promptly and discreetly. Deaf to Daisy's protests, I had had the girl moved out of their joint bedroom without consulting Mamma, who would not have cared anyway, and that, I had thought, would be that, but no—next came hints about the cold bare floor, and admiration for my bedroom hearth rug when she brought up my morning tea one day.

"How wonderful it must be to step out of bed onto something like that at six o'clock in the morning when everywhere is freezing, though of course you don't know what it's like to face cold mornings, do you, Miss Clementine, with a nice fire lit in your bedroom grate an hour before I bring up your tray . . . and the whole floor carpeted, too! That really makes a thick hearth rug unnecessary, doesn't it? Oh, dear, I didn't mean to touch you with my icy fingers! Is there any special job you would like me to do for you today, Miss Clementine? Tidy your wardrobe or your drawers, f'r instance, though of course I promise not to disturb anything strictly private. . . ."

Reminding, reminding, always reminding.

So down to her room went my lovely fur hearth rug. Next was a wall mirror, and a good one, too. "Have you seen the tiny cracked thing I have to use, Miss Clemmy? It would shock you, really it would. It's too small and discoloured for me to see if my cap is even straight."

I had tried to ignore that, determined that she would wheedle no more out of me, but she had won with a master stroke.

"It doesn't seem fair that Curtis's room should be made so comfortable and not mine, does it, Miss Clementine? Curtis must be ever so grateful to you for all you've given him—"

"And how do you know about that?" I had demanded sharply, which was just about the worst mistake I could have made. I should have looked at her with a total lack of comprehension, pretending not to know about any of the comforts in the coachman's quarters. I should have said, "If Curtis has acquired any improvements, then he can only have done so without the knowledge of myself or my parents," implying that the man must have stolen things or got them by other illicit means, but I didn't think of that until later, when the shock of learning that she knew all about my association with Curtis had subsided. As it was, I had given myself away badly, which made her smile—that knowing smile which hinted at so much.

"Well, now, Miss Clementine, there's only one way I *could* know, isn't there? From Curtis himself. Such a handsome double bed he's got, with a feather mattress, too. . . ."

That was when I began to cool toward Curtis. The man needed to be put in his place. So the next time he drove me to the park I had made it clear that it was to *be* a drive in the park this time and not a brief detour round the block and back to his door in the mews. When he looked surprised and questioning, I added nonchalantly that I was glad to hear from our parlourmaid that she shared his appreciation of my gifts to him, at which he had stared and then blurted, "That Kate's a lying bitch! She's only been to my rooms once, when Mrs. Wilson sent her with some broth when I was down with flu. Took a good look around, she did. I knew she was missing nothing."

Knowing how characteristic that was of Kate, I was inclined to believe him, but even so I added sarcastically, "Including the luxury feather mattress, I suppose?"

"Including that, Clemmy."

"*Miss Clementine.*"

"Sorry, I'm sure. You're not always so particular, not when your clothes are off and mine are too. I can call you whatever names I like then, and you love it. And if you think I could bed a servant girl after bedding the likes of you, you're mistaken . . . Miss Clementine. Kate's common and I've lost my taste for common women now, though God knows you're no lady yourself in some ways. As to how she noticed the feather mattress, how could she miss it? After sleeping on a servant's palliasse, she couldn't fail to notice the difference between that and the big fluffy thing I was lying on. And no one knows better than you, *Miss* Clementine, just how big and soft and downy it is. We fair sink into it, don't we? And we could sink into it for a couple of hours this afternoon and I'd kiss you the way you specially like and that fair drives you wild, you know it does."

But I wouldn't be swayed, though the temptation was great. I knew what it was like to be kissed in the Continental way, his mouth covering the most intimate part of my body, and it had surprised me to find a lowly coachman so expert in these matters—he had certainly learned a lot of things as a seaman in those far Eastern ports. Nevertheless, I had steeled myself and stared straight ahead and told him to get up on the box and drive me to the park instantly.

"Not until you've listened to me," he had declared. "I swear to God I didn't tell Kate who furnished the place so well. Don't blame *me* if she guessed."

But I had inadvertently confirmed her guess, which meant that henceforth she would be spying even more diligently. I knew then that I really ought to give up Curtis and confine myself to my own social level, where she was less likely to learn details of my activities. Magnus Steel was the obvious choice, but had so far proved elusive. He seemed determined not to surrender, and I was equally determined that one day he would. Meanwhile, there was still Curtis to satisfy my needs, and why should I give him up just because I was afraid of a spying housemaid? Defiance alone made me continue with the affair, but I also continued to make sure of her discretion. I had to. It was as if an awful alliance had sprung up between the pair of us, manipulated and controlled by Kate.

Now, when I left my mother weeping and wailing in her room, I wasn't really surprised to find Kate waiting outside.

"The poor dear soul, she is in a state, isn't she? And who can blame her? Shock is a terrible thing, and you must be feeling it too, Miss Clemmy."

"Me? Why me?"

"Well . . . you and Master Gavin have always been very fond of each other, haven't you?"

"As uncle and niece, naturally."

I went on to my room, but I couldn't shake her off.

"Of course, he isn't really your uncle, I know; not as far as blood goes. So you must be feeling very upset about what he has done."

I was more than upset, I was blazing, but I was learning how to hide a lot from Kate.

"I am angry, if that is what you mean, but only because he has shown no consideration for my parents, especially my poor mother."

"Of course. I know how tenderhearted you are, so naturally you feel that way. And *because* I know how tenderhearted you are, I know you'll be shocked to hear what has happened to my own poor ma. She's a widow, Miss Clementine, and now she's so bad with rheumatism she's been turned off as a cleaner at Whiteley's Emporium. She needs extra help from me, and knowing your kind heart . . ."

We had reached my room. I made a sympathetic but dismissive sound as I went to open my door, but she was quicker and had her hand on the knob, her arm in front of me, blocking the way.

"You do look upset, miss. You poor dear, Mr. Gavin and you were so fond of each other, that I know, so of course you're hurt. It's only natural in the circumstances."

She looked at me guilelessly, and when I abruptly commanded her to open my door, she complied with commendable obedience and held it open for me to pass through, but she remained holding it open after I had done so. I gave a nod of dismissal, which she didn't appear to see.

"Don't you believe my story about my poor ma being turned off, Miss Clementine? Well, it's true, but how can the likes of you know what that store is like? All the workers have to sleep in, the men under the shop counters and the women in dormitories in bare houses nearby, called hostels. They're taken there in horse-drawn vans when they've finished work, which is long after the shop doors close, and back again in the morning to start work at seven-thirty. And no marrying allowed. That might get the women pregnant and stop them from working, and the men would be asking for more money to keep their families. They'd be sacked on the spot, without wages, if they went against the rules, but when a body's past being useful, like my pore old ma, they're given a week's pay, all ten bob of it, and turned off. I'm sure a kind person like you can't bear to think of such things."

I couldn't. Not because these stories of bad working conditions upset me (one was beginning to hear so many such tales nowadays that they were really becoming quite monotonous, and besides, what could one do about them?), but because I knew what Kate was after, and had a very uneasy feeling why, so in case it were true that she had knowledge of yet another secret, I reached automatically for my purse.

No one, I thought, could be more generous than I. (Look at the things I had given Lucinda over the years, and *now* look how she rewarded me, eloping with Gavin from right under my nose!) I don't like my generosity being treated with ingratitude, nor do I like it being taken for granted or my hand being forced. And I didn't for a moment believe that the money I handed over to Kate would be passed on to her "pore old ma," if she had one, but I gave it to her just the same. Better to be sure than sorry, though there was no tangible guilt she could point to now—not even indecent French nightwear or pornographic books smuggled into the country illegally by a respectable convent pupil returning home chaperoned by a nun. Such things had outlived their interest or their usefulness to me long ago, and I had got rid of them bit by bit, items of black chiffon thrust into my reticule and dropped casually into street wastebins when no one was around. It amused me to think of vagrants foraging for scraps of food and coming across them. Would they even know what a transparent black fig leaf with loops of narrow ribbon on each side was for, or that two circles of black lace with holes in the middle were worn on women's breasts?

Then finally, still wrapped in its plain brown wrapper, my once-precious book had been tossed into the Thames from the Chelsea Embankment—and promptly the recollection of the Chelsea Embankment brought Gavin back to mind, because his rooms were situated there. Damn him, *damn him*, how could he *do* this abominable thing, and with my father's by-blow, too?

I heard Kate saying softly, "Oh, thank you, Miss Clementine. I'm sure Mr. Gavin would be pleased that you've been so generous. . . ."

My God, she did know! I had to get out of this house, away from Keyhole Kate, away from Mamma's weeping and wailing, away from Papa's silence, so I ordered the carriage to be sent round at once. It was some consolation to see Curtis waiting to hand me in, and his firm grip gave me the usual pleasure, but inside me I was feeling restless and disturbed, badly in need of a different kind of consolation. This news about Gavin and Lucinda had shaken me more than I cared to admit; I needed something to take my mind off it. A fresh love affair, another man in my life. There was nothing like a new lover to revive a woman's spirits and make her bloom again.

That was when I remembered Durbridge, and how he had secretly inspected me with those hooded eyes the first time we met, and again in my dressing room on that memorable first night—that awful first night when he had failed to arrive at Romano's for the supper party he was giving in my honour; at least, he had implied that it was in my honour, since the role of Lucie Darnay had been my first lead part, and very humiliated I had been, in front of all those guests, when he snubbed me by not arriving for it. Such a slight had been made worse by my conviction that the man had had sensual thoughts about me, secret plans even, all of which had come to naught with his strange disappearance.

What had happened to him? No one seemed to know. He had simply disappeared from the London scene; gone out of town, or abroad perhaps, on a sudden impulse which only a man so rich could afford to indulge, but at least he might have had the courtesy to fulfil his duties as host that night. Disappointment still lingered with me over that, because I had cherished such high hopes of learning all sorts of things from him. He had seemed to represent a door opening onto a whole new world of experience which I had been more than eager to embrace, but what use was it to think of that now? He was gone—for the time being, at any rate, though I certainly hoped he would turn up again someday. Meanwhile, the best thing to do was to think of someone else.

Inevitably my mind turned to Magnus Steel. Why I still hankered after a man who deliberately eluded me, I really didn't know, except that it was a challenge. Was that what he was up to? Was he trying to challenge me, to provoke me into pursuing him instead of the other way round? I had never done the pursuing in my life and had no intention of doing so now—until we turned into Hyde Park and, to my astonishment, there he was, stripped to the waist, fighting bare-fisted amongst a crowd of yelling spectators. I could scarcely believe my eyes, although I had heard rumours which I had naturally dismissed.

But I couldn't dismiss them now. Nor did I want to. The man was magnificent! Imperiously I commanded Curtis to stop.

He obeyed unwillingly, not wanting to halt at such a spot as this, and when I dismounted and ordered him to wait for me, he looked astonished and disapproving. I knew he was watching me as I went back to mingle with the crowd surrounding the boxing stand, and when I turned and saw him following, and promptly paused and commanded him to return to the carriage, he stubbornly refused to obey.

"You need someone to keep an eye on you in a mob like this, Miss Clementine." He still addressed me respectfully, except in private, when he used the most familiar endearments, but I was beginning to resent his air of proprietorship, and it was there now. "What you need is a bodyguard, and I'm making that my business. Full of rogues and buzzers and gonophs that lot is. You could have your reticule snatched without even being aware of it."

"In that case you can take it back to the carriage and stay there to keep an eye on it."

"And let you wander alone, an object for other offences?"

"Such as what? Public rape? Even that doesn't take place in broad daylight. At any rate, not amongst crowds."

"It's been known, *and* for people to stand by and watch."

"In the East End, no doubt." I held out my reticule. "Take it and do as I tell you. And remember you are my coachman, not my watchdog."

He almost snatched it, saying angrily, "You don't have to rub in the fact that I am nothing but your servant."

"On the contrary, it seems I must." When his face hardened, I said gently, "*I* didn't use the words 'nothing but a servant,' and when we have driven round the park we can go back to the mews and I will prove it to you."

"Oh, yes," he answered grimly, "I serve you that way too, don't I? Sometimes I think that's the only use you have for me, as and when you please. You drop me whenever you feel like it, then pick me up again. D'you think I don't know when you've been having someone else? A man can always tell, but it isn't my 'place' to ask who, is it? I guess it's always one of those society blokes with all polish and no guts. I daresay you find that type pretty tame after a while, being made the way you are, though I wouldn't put it past you to have more than one man at a time. As for why you cooled off me in the first place, I've never quite believed it was because that parlourmaid was suspicious, because she's still got reason to be, now you're favouring me again."

I turned my back on him and walked away, confident that I knew how to handle the man. He was under my thumb, and would stay there. The mere fact that I *was* able to summon him and then reject him whenever I felt so inclined was proof of that, so I dismissed him from my mind and concentrated on Magnus Steel, whom I could see head and shoulders above the crowd on his portable boxing stand, half-stripped in the sun, his chest covered with dark coppery hair which would be irresistible to stroke. . . .

Quite a knot of people had gathered to watch, and now I recalled the rumours I had heard and dismissed—that the pugilistic doctor was known as the Toff and that his charity bouts were one of the biggest attractions here, so much so that although some of the soapbox orators and political agitators and evangelical soul-savers were periodically moved on, the doctor from the Stepney mission never was because even the bobbies on the beat enjoyed watching. Now it seemed the rumours were right, and I should not have been surprised that so unconventional a man should behave in so unconventional a fashion. I was conscious of a quickening of interest and excitement. No man I had ever known would have dared behave in such a way, totally regardless of the opinion of society or of the circle into which he had been born. *Magnetic Magnus*, I thought, *the time has come to really get to know you.* . . .

"Never bin beaten yet, 'e 'asn't," I heard a spectator telling another as I halted on the fringe, "but always a gent to 'is opponent an' always ready with a grin an' a gag. Nice bloke, the Toff."

I wanted to push my way to the front, but unyielding shoulders blocked me. I had to content myself with remaining where I was, which, in view of the odour of unwashed humanity, was at least advantageous in one way. But the spectators were not all rough. There were well-dressed tourists amongst them, who evidently found the enjoyment worth the toleration of discomfort.

I decided there and then to arrive earlier tomorrow, and did so; also the next day and the next, determined to make the most of my time before rehearsals for *Twelfth Night* began.

I quickly established myself amongst the front ranks, not because I was interested in boxing, but because I wanted to see Magnus close up, and wanted him to see me. I knew that I drew the attention of the crowd, but it was his that I wanted, so I didn't care about the raised eyebrows which the sight of an unaccompanied and elegant lady inevitably caused, and I certainly did not care about my angry coachman, waiting resentfully beside the carriage, day after day. All I cared about was achieving my object, but to my chagrin the only person who continued to be oblivious of me was the battling Toff, who, between bouts, would gaze out over the heads of the crowd, laughingly calling his challenge and focusing his eyes only on the men.

"How about you, sir? And you, sir? And you at the back—Alf Walker, isn't it, from the King's Arms by the Watling Steps? What are you doing so far from home?"

"Out for a jaunt up west wiv me missus. We allus comes to 'Yde Park once a week when Bill looks after the bar."

"Then once a week I will take you on. That's right, Mrs. Walker, encourage him. Your wife wants to be proud of you, Alf, so come up here and let her see what guts you've got!"

And of course Cockney Alf finished up biting the dusty boards and the crowd was cheering and laughing while the Toff helped him to rise, promising to make it up to him by standing his customers a round at the King's Arms next time he passed that way, and coins flew into the box, which his man, Barker, was skilfully passing round before any spectators could disperse.

Sometimes an adventurous tourist would fling off his jacket and climb into the ring, and Americans would lavishly fling down money as bets, ignoring the bobby's admonition about street betting being illegal here in England. "The racecourse is the place for that, gentlemen. . . ." But the policeman's protest was unheard because it was not made all that enthusiastically anyway. He was enjoying the spectacle as much as anyone else, but not so much as I. No one could possibly do that because, admire the Toff as they might, they were not here for my particular reason—to gaze my fill on Magnus Steel and to bring him to heel as I had planned to do the very first moment I saw him.

Now that time had come, but never had I dreamed how difficult my final conquest of him was to be, nor how frustrating, aggravated as it was by the fact that watching him in action awakened in me the strongest sexual desire, so much so that Curtis would find me almost insatiable afterward and it was all I could do to stroll negligently back to the carriage and wave him on to drive me round the park.

Sometimes I could not even wait for that, but I would still strive to look nonchalant as I glanced at my fob watch and said, "Good gracious, I had no idea the time had flown so quickly! Only half an hour before I must return home . . . dear Mamma frets if I am late and she is needing the carriage herself, so perhaps . . . ?"

No need to say more. Curtis would head for the mews and the deep feather bed, and neither of us would care if it were half an hour or a whole one or even more before we pulled up sedately outside the front door and I stepped from the carriage looking as immaculate as when I departed, my clothes uncreased, because no matter how impatient our bodies were, I would lay my garments aside with meticulous care, so that when I dressed again I would not look like one of those crumpled whores along Oxford Street who lifted their skirts in side alleys, or for a quick lay under railway arches. Dreadful creatures! How *could* women give themselves so promiscuously or so shamelessly? To someone so fastidious and ladylike as I, the very thought was shocking.

"There's something about you when you've watched that boxing for a spell," Curtis remarked disconcertingly one day. "What does it do to you? Stir up your blood?"

We were lying hot and naked and very content after an hour of delicious satisfaction, and I was grateful to him for satisfying the hunger Magnus had aroused in me. In fact, if I had never set eyes on Magnus Steel I would certainly have found Curtis the most desirable of men because he not only had a physique which matched his handsome features, but, despite his humble birth, he could never be wholly described as uncouth. Rough sometimes, and even violent when passion rode him, but I enjoyed brute strength in a man. Perhaps it was the power behind the pugilistic doctor's punches that stirred me. Certainly it was not the sport itself. I understood none of the finer points of boxing. To me it was no more than a demonstration of one man's domination over another, of strength pitted against strength. Any skill or intelligence was lost on me, though I had gathered from knowledgeable comments amongst the spectators that a certain art was involved, and the Toff had it.

The Toff: What a delicious soubriquet, and so significant too, setting the man apart from the crowd, indicating their awareness that he was socially above them but man enough to come down to their level without in any way losing his superiority. I had never met a man like him in my life; only actors, who were always vain and narcissistic and jealous of anyone who stole the limelight. There was even a certain vanity about my father, though in all honesty (and no one could be more honest than I) I knew it to be based on his professional pride. All the same, he was well aware of that profile of his, letting the audience see it to its best advantage whenever possible.

"Your left side, Sir Nevill! Show them your left side—that's the best

one." Willard never let him forget this at rehearsals, and would even manipulate my mother's moves very skilfully, the better to display her husband's splendid features. And as for Gavin, he knew only too well how
handsome he was and would have run a mile rather than risk a flaw on his
looks. But Magnus never gave a damn for any punch that landed there;
he would laugh and fling one back.

"Did you hear what I said?" Curtis repeated. "I'm no fool, you
know. There has to be a reason for this sudden interest in those boxing
demonstrations."

"They're fun," I answered lightly. "I have never seen a boxing match
in my life, and you know perfectly well that ladies don't attend them."

"Some women do."

"I said ladies."

"And you think it ladylike to stand in that mixed crowd? I wonder you
don't draw back your elegant skirts."

"I frequently do." I yawned languidly and without effort because I
was feeling very languid indeed and hoped he would be the same and ask
no more awkward questions, but Curtis was often very vital and alive after making love, and nothing was going to silence him now.

"It does something to you," he stated bluntly. "After watching it,
you're really on heat, and that's saying something, being the way you are
by nature. You really give it to me after you've had a spell near that boxing booth; a real hungry savage it makes you."

"Then since you reap the benefit why complain? If you enjoy the results, don't scowl when I keep you waiting by the carriage in future." I
stretched luxuriously and ordered him to hand me my clothes. "And
don't crease them," I warned. "They cost a lot of money."

"And I cost you nothing," he answered bitterly.

"Quite the reverse. The comforts I bought for this place cost a pretty
penny. What more do you expect? Payment for services? What are
you—a ponce?"

He struck me then, hard across the face, so that I fell off the bed and
lay there crying.

"*That* will teach you not to insult me. You're my woman, and don't
you forget it." And to prove it, he picked me up and threw me on the
bed again and in his violent rage he came down on top of me and had his
fill once more, without mercy, and although I was hating him, my body
exulted. At the end he said, "My God, but you're wonderful, Clemmy.
My Clemmy."

He stroked my inflamed cheek and kissed my wet eyes, and I let him
think I was crying because he had ill-treated me, but it wasn't so at all. I
had enjoyed every moment.

Before we parted he said one final thing.

"I'm not stopping near that boxing booth again. I'm not even going to drive that way. If brute strength stimulates you, you can have it from me. I'm not going to be used just to satisfy a lust stirred up by another man, a man you're not in love with as you are with me. I hate to see you standing there gloating as he shows off his physical strength. I have plenty myself.''

He kept his word, as I knew he would, so I had to think of another way in which to watch Magnus draw the crowds. Next day I walked to the park, for which I had every excuse, since Curtis had driven dear Mamma to her dressmaker in Knightsbridge. I took a lot of pains with my appearance, determined that this time he really would notice me. It seemed unbelievable that I should have been in the audience every day for the best part of a week without his being aware of it, but today I was resolved to distract him somehow.

If only I could catch his eye as I had the first time he ever saw me! Alas, I had that Pompadour foulard no more; I never wore the same clothes more than a few times, because no self-respecting actress would—not if she were the daughter of a titled actor, bearer of a famous name. It was all right for actresses like Chrystal Delmont, whose renovations could never hide the fact that they *were* renovations (heaven preserve me from ever having to support a struggling musician!), but nothing advertised success so much as one's clothes. That had always been one of dear Mamma's few intelligent observations.

Today I needed something which would really catch the eye, and I took plenty of time over choosing it. A *demi-saison* gown seemed appropriate both for the day and the time of the year. It was late September, summer mixed with a promise of autumn; too warm for a coat but too cool for a lightweight gown. The trees of the park were already tinged with a faint russet, and I needed a colour to stand out against such a background, not to merge with it.

I also had to bear in mind that I would be walking, and no well-dressed woman in London would appear in the streets wearing an outfit designed for anything else. One could descend from a carriage in a promenade gown if the object of the outing was merely to promenade beside the Ladies' Mile in Rotten Row, but I would be proceeding on foot from Portman Square, and one had to observe the rules of fashion etiquette or appear to be a member of the ignorant masses.

The choice was a major problem, because I had so many gowns to choose from, which meant that each had to be tried on and discarded and sometimes tried on and discarded yet again, until my bed was piled with garments, all of which I would have to replace myself because never since the day I caught Kate prying had I allowed her to so much as hang up a garment for me, and I knew that this intensive rehearsal and this overanxious selection of a street ensemble would awaken her curiosity, because she knew well enough that I never went walking for walking's sake.

The whole business was really quite exhausting. I badly needed a lady's maid, and a trustworthy one at that, but never for a moment would my dear mamma share her latest one with me. Since Trudy Grainger's departure, ladies' maids had come and gone frequently in my mother's life, but with such a major problem on my mind as choosing a delectable outfit I could spare no thought for such tiresome domestic details. I had to get to Soapbox Corner somehow, and without Curtis' cooperation I had no choice but to go on foot.

One could not summon a hansom cab just to drive there from Portman Square, little more than a stone's throw away. Besides, Hawkins was off duty today, so it would be Kate's task to order it and to tell the driver where to take me. Why did so many problems beset a woman's life? I wondered fretfully, but my spirits rose when I finally discovered a walking dress of vivid orange, a startling colour which dear Mamma had pronounced as "rather vulgar, dear gel . . ." and had insisted that it be relegated to the back of my wardrobe.

But what a colour to set against the faintly russet background of the trees in Hyde Park! I had had it copied from a Paris walking costume by the Maison Rouff, featured in *Harper's Bazaar.* I always fell upon the journal eagerly because it displayed all the latest Paris designs as well as those from London, beautifully sketched in black and white, with colours carefully described in the text.

When at last I was ready, I surveyed myself with satisfaction. The smooth-faced cloth was braided with narrow strips of satin, a highly fashionable touch these days. The braiding was also on the sleeves and on the striking shoulder epaulettes, which were very wide and square and quite the latest thing, but the most unusual feature was a deep rounded yoke of tucked turquoise silk, crowned by a very high upstanding collar in the orange material and flaring outward in semi-Elizabethan style to reveal an inside frill of matching turquoise. The final touch was a row of turquoise-and-rhinestone buttons running down the centre of the bodice.

The whole thing was the perfect choice, and so was the hat—an enormous thing in burnt-ochre, with a magnificent sweeping brim adorned with ostrich feathers of a rich dark orange.

No one could possibly overlook me.

Suddenly happy, I thrust everything back into my wardrobe, then sailed downstairs filled with excitement and determination. Not even Kate's astonished glance when she met me in the hall so much as ruffled my composure. I didn't even give her time to open the front door for me, but left her there gaping with curiosity while I swept past her and actually opened the door myself, leaving her to shut it behind me when she came to her senses. Nor did I spare time to look back, though I knew she would hurry to check on the direction I took. Fiddle to Kate! Fiddle to Mamma and Curtis and everyone else, including that plain-looking Helen Steel, who happened to be playing in the gardens of the square with two small children. I knew she saw me over the hedge, but I didn't spare her a glance.

I had never liked that woman. She was the forthright, sensible type of female whom I could not abide. It was always a puzzle to me how a man like Magnus came to be related to a woman so ordinary and frumpish. With his broken nose and rugged features he could never be called handsome himself, but he was striking enough to be noticeable wherever he went, whereas his sister could be passed in the street without attracting a single glance—until recently, anyway, when she had begun to appear rather more modish. I suspected that was Trudy Grainger's influence.

But the worthy Miss Steel was not very well turned out today. She seemed to wear her oldest garments when romping with those children, who, Lucinda had told me, belonged to a doctor working part-time at the mission. "She adores them and they adore her," Lucinda had added. And they certainly seemed to visit her a lot. Hadn't they a mother of their own? I dismissed the thought because it was of no interest to me, and reached Soapbox Corner just in time to see Magnus take on his first opponent.

I felt supremely confident, gratified by the admiring stares I had won during the walk here and by the effect my arrival created. I had now acquired the skill of working my way to the front of the crowd, and today my appearance was apparently so startling that people just fell away and let me through. I thanked them all with a dazzling smile and then took up my stance. I was right there beside the makeshift booth; I could hear the creaking of the boards and the thud of the boxers' dancing feet. I could hear the challenger's heavy breathing and Magnus's also, deep and controlled.

Not for a moment did his eyes leave his opponent's face. His concentration was so total that he was oblivious of the rest of the world, and I knew what would happen—he would win as always, shake the man's hand, and then seek new challengers, looking right out over the heads of the crowd, including mine so close by. So I had to do something to attract his attention, and I did it. I opened my purse, took out a handful of sovereigns, and flung them onto the boards.

If lightning had struck, it could not have produced a more startling or more unexpected result. The sharp clatter of sound on hollow boards and the dancing flashes of gold about the boxers' feet halted Magnus's raised fists for a fraction of a second—his head jerked in surprise, his opponent saw his chance, landed a swift uppercut, and sent the unbeaten Toff sprawling.

The crowd yelled, caps flew in the air, the victor danced for joy and flung up his arms in triumph, but I was staring at Magnus. Not for a moment had I expected such a thing to happen. All I had wanted was to be noticed when, at the end of the round, he demanded to know the identity of so generous a patron. I was not even aware of his man, Barker, pushing me aside and scrambling into the ring to gather up the sovereigns before the challenger, and others from the crowd, had a chance to snatch them.

Then Magnus was getting up, shaking his head to clear his vision and laughing over his defeat. He seized his opponent's hand and shook it heartily.

"Give him his winnings, Barker. Double for a knockout, remember."

Barker carefully counted out the sixpenny pieces. At that the challenger became truculent.

"That's not enough. There's sovereigns there. I fought and I won."

"But not for sovereigns," retorted Barker. "That weren't part of the bargain."

"Sovereigns?" Magnus echoed. "Was it actually *sovereigns* that came pelting? I wondered what caused the clatter." He turned to the crowd and demanded to know who had thrown them, and I stood there silently until a man beside me shouted, "She did—this 'ere lidy! I saw 'er. If she 'adn't done that, you wouldn't've bin beat, gov."

Magnus looked at me then. He stared, saying nothing, and assuming a look of profound penitence, I pleaded with him not to be angry.

"They were for the mission. I didn't mean to cause a distraction. I acted quite spontaneously, really I did, but for such a good cause . . ."

I sighed and looked up at him wistfully, and that wonderful smile of his spread across his features. I had always thought his smile attractive, but at this moment it was for me alone and therefore doubly so.

"My dear Miss Boswell, don't apologise. For a fistful of sovereigns it was worth being knocked down. It was generous of you. I appreciate it, and so will the mission."

Barker was handing him a towel, which he took automatically, drying his magnificent chest as he continued to smile at me. Then he was pulling on his shirt and stepping down to my side. The crowd took this as a sign that the entertainment was over for the afternoon, but Barker was making no attempt to dismantle the portable stand and was exhorting the crowd not to go away.

"It's a break, an interval, ladies and gents, that's all! The Toff'll be ready to take on new challengers any minute now!" To Magnus he hissed, "Sir! *Sir!* You're not packing up, surely? That punch wasn't a knockout, not enough to upset the likes o' you, and the challenge is only for a knock*down*. . . ."

"I know, Barker."

"Then why are you putting on your shirt?"

"Because a gentleman doesn't converse with a lady without it. Keep calling for competitors, and I'll be back up there shortly." He put his hand beneath my elbow and drew me aside, dropping his voice to a pitch which only I could hear. "I beg you, Clementine, don't come here again. This isn't the first time, and I have been only too well aware of it, but apart from the fact that you are out of place in a crowd like this, which makes it unsafe for you, a woman so pretty distracts attention from the fight, and when I know you are there *I* am distracted too, though until today it had no dire results."

"But I enjoy coming. I enjoy watching you."

"I beg you not to." Then he said with controlled passion, "Keep away from me, Clemmy. Keep away."

"You mean you don't want me here? You don't want to see me? But why?"

"You know why."

I did, and was well pleased. I left without another word, but all the way home I was in a state of elation because indeed I knew why he wanted to avoid me. He was afraid of me, afraid of the attraction between us. He didn't want it to disrupt his well-ordered life or to interfere with his work, to which, I had heard, he was dedicated. But he wasn't the kind of man to live a monastic life, and even one so passionately devoted to his work must sometimes take moments away from it.

There had to be a chink in Magnus Steel's armour somewhere, and that it existed had been revealed in his passionate plea. It had been worth a fistful of sovereigns to discover that much, though as I passed a shop window displaying a perfectly ravishing hat I had a momentary pang because the sovereigns I had squandered could have been well spent on that.

My problem now was how to penetrate that chink in his armour. Naturally, I had not the slightest intention of keeping away from him, nor had I promised to. I had to arrange another meeting, and soon, and I was not afraid of taking the initiative, because the response had been there and I knew he would not be able to suppress it forever.

16

I was hindered in making this second approach by rehearsals at the theatre, where we had embarked on Papa's new production of *Twelfth*

Night. In any case, I considered it indiscreet to hurry the matter and decided to let a further week go by before timing my re-entrance into Magnus Steel's life. By then my daily absence from the park would let him
think that I had taken him at his word—and give him time to regret it. It
never did a man any harm to miss a woman. Meanwhile, I used Curtis to
alleviate the tedium of waiting and, in the process, forgot all about Gavin's secret marriage to Lucinda.

It was fun to plan the conquest of a man and I chose a Sunday for the
important final step. I also chose the place, knowing just when he would
be in that gymnasium of his. Beneath the brass plate on the railings of his
house, bearing his name and medical qualifications, was another indicating the sporting premises in the basement, with a sign pointing to the entrance at the foot of the area steps: "Open daily from 10 A.M. to 12 noon
and from 2 P.M. to 5 P.M. Evenings: 7 P.M. to 9:30 P.M. Tuition sessions
Monday to Saturday, and on Sundays between 12 noon and 2 P.M."

So all I had to do was stroll across the square after putting in the traditional Boswell appearance at Mass, walk down the area steps of his
house, open the gymnasium door, and saunter in—and this was precisely
what I did.

Barker was the first to see me and came hurrying across, eyes popping.

"Ma'am! Ma'am, you can't come in here! It's for gentlemen only."

"So I see," I replied sweetly, putting him aside with one gloved hand
and then letting it rest with the other on top of my parasol. For a moment
I stood there (an effective pose, giving every man in the room a chance to
observe me), and then I moved leisurely forward because the tiresome
Barker was actually tugging at my sleeve.

"If you're calling on Miss Steel, ma'am, you want the front door."

I took hold of his hand and removed it firmly. I even quelled him with
a glance which Magnus, shadowboxing before a group of men at the far
end of the room, luckily did not see. I was glad of that, because no woman's face looks its best when frowning. He seemed to be giving lessons to
the group, and it wasn't until he became aware that he had lost their attention that he halted and saw me.

I assumed maidenly confusion at once.

"Forgive me!" I stammered. "I have made the most stupid mistake,
but quite unintentionally. I saw your brass plate up above, with the sign
pointing down here . . . so silly of me . . . I was calling on your sister, so should have known better."

"In that case, Barker will show you upstairs. There is access directly
from this room." He sounded quite calm, but I knew he was not. I was
well aware that the sight of me had startled him, even shaken him, and I
knew I had the same effect on every man present. I cast a sweet and apologetic smile all round before making my exit, which I did unhurriedly. I
was not going to be banished from the place yet, so I turned the apolo-

getic smile into an awed glance and let it travel round the whole room as I breathed, "What a wonderful, *wonderful* place! I have never seen a men's gymnasium before. How strong you must all be! And do you really do things with these amazing pieces of equipment?"

A man performing on a vaulting horse had come to a halt and didn't even hear Barker say, "If you'll just continue with those exercises, Mr. Hailsham, I'll be right back." Apparently Barker was taking a class also, because other men were lined up awaiting their turn. They were all clad in tight-fitting white trousers and white short-sleeved singlets, and I included every one of them in a comprehensive glance of admiration. "How *very* strong you must be!" I breathed.

"That is what we come here for, madam." It was the man who had been performing who answered. "To keep fit."

Barker was getting restless, waiting beside an open door leading onto stairs. Magnus was holding out his gloved fists to be untied, and I saw, to my surprise, that the boy who did it was Jerry Hawks. That gave me further excuse to linger.

"Why, Jerry, I didn't know you were an athlete too!"

"I ain't, miss, though I try a bit o' this an' a bit o' that. I come along in me spare time to 'elp the doc one way an' t'other."

"And you enjoy it?"

"Wot do *you* fink? I wouldn't come if I didn't."

Disrespectful, as always—to me, at least. He was never so abrupt with others, but I could never earn from this boy any real display of good manners. But what could one expect from a street arab?

I pointed out gently that it was kind of the doctor to employ him. "A spare-time occupation, coupled with your work at the theatre, must help you a lot."

"I don't employ him," Magnus said. "He comes voluntarily, don't you, Jerry?" He ruffled the boy's hair affectionately. "And don't forget, boy, that you're taking your midday meal with us." To Barker he called, "Tell Miss Steel I'll be up shortly."

There was nothing for it but to follow the man, but I rewarded everyone present with a last lingering smile before doing so. It was tiresome having to go upstairs to visit Helen Steel, and even more tiresome to know that when Magnus did join us he would be bringing that cockney brat with him. Sometimes I suspected that Magnus' charity extended just a bit too far. After all, one did not have to offer the hospitality of one's home to the needy. There was a rightful place for everyone in this world, dear Mamma always said, and in that place one should stay. It did no good to help the poor to climb out of it, giving them ideas above their station. Luncheon, indeed! I had hoped to be invited to stay for that myself, but to sit down at the same table with one of the most menial of theatre employees was quite out of the question.

I felt discouraged as I climbed the stairs to the first-floor drawing room, where I received another surprise. Helen was not alone. Trudy Grainger was with her, and so were those two children; also a man, very tall and thin and with prematurely white hair. *"Yon Cassius has a lean and hungry look,"* I quoted subconsciously, guessing rightly that this must be the father of those children, the doctor who worked at the mission in his spare time. Didn't his wife, if he had a wife, feed him properly? And he looked decidedly shabby; not even the careful pressing of his suit, his spotless stiff collar and white shirt, or his well-polished boots disguised the fact that all had seen better days.

He couldn't be much of a doctor if he looked like that; certainly not a West End doctor, where all the best ones were situated. That meant he must practice somewhere on the outskirts; in one of the poorer suburbs, perhaps, in which case it wasn't very enterprising of him to give his services free to any deserving cause. I was a great believer in charity beginning, and ending, at home. Long ago Mamma had taught me that, declaring that Papa was foolish and indulgent to give charity performances the way he did.

"What does he get out of them? Not a penny. Just grateful thanks and comments in the press about his generosity in giving up his time at Sunday-afternoon recitals in aid of this and that. It isn't as if he needs the publicity! Not with a name like Boswell. . . ."

I was gratified by the surprise on Trudy's face, but not by Helen Steel's amiable indifference.

"How nice of you to call, Miss Boswell. Pray be seated, and do take a glass of madeira with us. And let me introduce you—you know Miss Grainger, of course, but Dr. Hugh Maynard I think you have not met."

Lean Cassius stooped over my hand politely, and I noticed that he was really quite a nice-looking man. I noticed something more—the way Helen Steel looked at him and the note in her voice when she spoke to him. Gracious heaven, the woman was in love with the man! I don't know why I was surprised, because even the plainest of females must have emotions of some sort, and it was obvious that this particular one had plenty. Her heart was in her eyes when she looked at him, and it even included his children, the boy and girl who played with her in the square gardens every now and then. Quite frequently, in fact. Now I knew why. She was after their father. Was he a widower? It seemed so, since his wife was not present.

I was not very fond of children and was grateful to Pierre and Curtis for taking care that I should never conceive. I had taken precautions myself, thanks to Pierre's book, which had taught me a lot, but birth control was a subject much frowned upon by moralists in England. I had even heard of a bookshop in the King's Road being closed down as a result of a campaign by Mrs. Ormiston Chant and members of the Church because its windows displayed pamphlets on such shameful matters as family planning. I wondered what Magnus, as a doctor, thought of the matter and what precautions he himself would take. How lovely it would be to find out. . . .

"And this is Kathy, Dr. Maynard's little girl, and Julian, his son."

"I am not little," said Kathy. "I am seven, but Julian is only four."

I thought her rather pert, but apart from that they were well-mannered children, the little girl curtseying and the boy bowing from the waist like a little gentleman.

Kathy's voice prattled on, but I scarcely listened as I sipped my madiera and wondered how soon Magnus would come to join the family party. Were all these people staying to luncheon? Apparently so, because when Kathy reached out to sneak another macaroon Helen promptly said, "No more for the moment, Kathy dear. Luncheon will be served just as soon as my brother joins us." Little Julian then demanded to know whether he could have a go on the punchball this afternoon, adding that Jerry was getting quite good at it, so he would like to get in a bit of practice too.

It was all very boring conversation until Kathy Maynard asked me, somewhat awed, "Is it true that you are an actress, ma'am? Miss Steel told us you were. She pointed you out from the square gardens one day and said you were famous, and so were your papa and mamma."

I beamed on the child and said yes, it was quite true, and then she said, "But you are not married to an actor, are you, like Miss Grainger's daughter? Haven't you been able to get yourself a husband? Everyone thinks that very surprising, don't they, Auntie Helen? I have heard you say so." The child turned back to me. "We always call Miss Steel 'Auntie Helen' because that's the way we think of her. It's the next best thing to having a mother, but of course we can't call her that because we have one already."

How very interesting, I thought, secretly amused not only by the child's candour but by the painful colour rising in Helen's face. Poor creature, in love with a married man! What a waste of time and emotion! And what was he doing here without his wife? Was she an invalid or something? Or perhaps in a home of some sort? Hadn't Lucinda once implied that he had lost his wife, suggesting he was a widower? Obviously Lucinda had not learned as much as I had learned in the last five minutes.

I immediately decided to learn more.

"And your mamma is not with you today?" I asked the little girl.

"She is away, ma'am. She has been away a long time. I remember her going, but Julian doesn't. Anyway, we've got over missing her now. All I mostly remember is how cross she used to get, and that would make us cry, and now we only do that if we fall down and hurt ourselves, and then Papa or Auntie Helen kisses the spot to make it better."

Her father cut in, "Kathy, my child, you must not talk when grown-ups are wanting to. We were in the middle of a conversation, remember?"

He was plainly anxious to silence the child because he was aware of Helen's discomfort and wanted to alleviate it, but the woman's feelings did not worry me at all. Serve her right, I thought, for implying to these children (and to how many other people besides?) that I had been unable to get a husband, indicating failure when actually the reverse was true. Naturally, someone like Helen Steel would imagine that any woman would jump at the first proposal that came her way; she would never be able to comprehend that someone like myself could pick and choose and was not ready to do so yet.

According to her ideas, no doubt, virtue should only be lost in the marriage bed, in which case, what did she think of Trudy Grainger's disgraceful past?

The child Kathy proved to be an irrepressible chatterbox. "Why don't *you* get married, Auntie Helen? Is it because Uncle Magnus would be angry, the way he was when Miss Grainger's daughter married that actor? I remember how angry he was because we came to tea that day and he had just heard the news and I have never seen *any*one so angry about *any*thing. I told him he looked as if he had had the shock of his life and *he* said, 'I have, child, I have,' and looked terrible about it. And do you know what I think? *I* think he was jealous."

What an appallingly precocious child, I thought, disliking her even more.

"Kathy, you talk too much," her father said severely, and at that moment the door opened and Magnus walked in. He had changed into a dark suit, finely tailored, but his tie was crooked, as if he had tied it without the aid of a mirror. I longed to straighten it for him, to reach up and let my fingers accidentally touch his throat. There was something endearing about this man's indifference to appearances; never slovenly, but haphazardly dressed always, as if he had no time for vanities—yet with his looks he had plenty to be vain about, unhandsome as they were. He was living proof that a man didn't have to have the features of a Greek god in order to be outstanding or attractive.

He was always completely unselfconscious, but at this moment I was maddeningly conscious of *him*, almost painfully so, because the little girl's remarks had triggered off a terrible reaction in me. Magnus, angered over Lucinda's marriage? Why should he be? The child's conclusion that it had been jealousy was silly and could be dismissed, because there had never been any sign of attraction between Magnus and Lucinda; merely friendship, the friendship of the Steels with the Graingers, which meant the girl was no more to him than the daughter of a friend. But all the same, why *anger* over her marriage?

* * *

That had been a frustrating encounter, because with so many people present—including Cockney Jerry, who came upstairs with his master and grinned cheerfully at everyone, very much at home—I had no opportunity to speak alone with Magnus, and when it became obvious that luncheon was soon to be served, it became equally obvious that I should take my leave, but when Helen rose to see me downstairs, I urged her not to trouble.

"Your brother is already on his feet—let him see me to the door."

I even kissed Trudy affectionately on both cheeks, just to show how generous-hearted I was about her shocking liaison with my father. Then we descended the stairs, Magnus and I, alone at last. I had achieved that much, at least.

Even now I can recall the drawing-room door closing behind us and the leisurely descent I made, picking up my skirts to display my neatly shod foot and shapely ankle and going carefully in a very feminine way, as if afraid of tripping. This all helped to prolong the time. His steps descended behind me, and neither of us said a word, but when we reached the hall I turned and said pleadingly, "I do hope you are not angry because I disobeyed and didn't keep away from you? But I did try. You don't know how hard I tried. Then I thought: Why should I? If only I knew the reason! Why don't you tell me? Is it because you dislike me? I can't believe that, because when you look at me it isn't with dislike."

I stood very close. So close that he could not escape my perfume or the suggestive proximity of my breasts. With every breath they lightly touched him, and he did not draw away, so then I drew closer and put up my hand and touched his cheek.

"Please, Magnus, don't be cold toward me! You don't feel that way, I know."

Then everything happened just as I had prayed it would. I was in his arms and the familiar leaping of my blood went coursing through me.

"Oh, God, Clementine, why did you have to come?"

"Because you begged me not to and I knew why. Also because I wanted to and couldn't keep away."

"It would be better if you did. Better for my peace of mind and body."

"But I can soothe both," I whispered. "You fell in love with me the first moment you saw me, and I knew it, so why keep me at arm's length?"

It was then that he burst out, "Don't you understand? I can't surrender to the way I feel for you when I am suspicious of every man you look at with open invitation in your eyes, knowing damn well you expect them to surrender and knowing damn well they do. How could I bear being married to a woman who is not only lusted after by other men, but who lusts after them in return?''

In view of the way things developed between us, it was only natural that I should not regard that as insulting until later. At the time, I could only stare at him, astonished that the idea of marriage should have entered his head, because it had certainly never entered mine.

Turning my glance from surprise to one of outraged virtue, I vehemently denied that I ever looked at men in a lustful way.

"It isn't *my* fault if they want me! It isn't *my* fault that they can't take their eyes off me! I tell you, Magnus, I have never been so embarrassed as I was today, when I wandered into the gymnasium by mistake and faced a roomful of covetous male eyes.''

He laughed then, but indulgently. "Are you so sure it was by mistake?'' he murmured, whereupon I also laughed and admitted it was not.

"You should be flattered,'' I scolded lightly. "I have already told you that I wanted to see you, and where else was I more likely to find you?'' Then I hesitated and added with becoming shyness, "I wonder, would I . . . *could* I find you there tonight? Is the door always open?''

I slid my hands over his shoulders, and his defences went down. He said, in helpless capitulation, "For you, it will be,'' and I knew then that I had won.

After that we wasted no more time in words. Our parting was brief, but passionate and full of promise. I went home knowing that I would have my way, as I always did. But marriage? That was another matter. Before I committed myself so far, I wanted to discover what Magnus was like as a lover and how long my passion for him was likely to last. I still had this reluctance to being bound solely to one man, fear of the monotony of sleeping with the same one constantly until his body became so familiar to me that it ceased to mean any more than my own limbs meant. And when it became so taken for granted as that, what happened to desire?

"When did you lose your virginity?''

The question startled me. I looked at him, standing with his back to me, his figure silhouetted against the shaft of moonlight filtering down the area steps outside and through the basement window. This had been the only light throughout our lovemaking, and the novelty of the whole setting had appealed to me enormously. Never before had I lain with a man on a pile of soft practice mats in a gymnasium, snug and warm between fleecy rugs.

I knew he had not taken me upstairs because his sister lived in the same house, and down here we were sure of privacy. It was like being shut away in some exciting world of our own, and the unconventionality of the setting added to my delight.

Consequently his question took me by surprise, and for a moment I made no answer. After loving me with such tenderness—and for so strong a man his gentleness had amazed me—the last thing I expected was an inquisition.

And it had all been so easy and smooth and effortless that I felt sure he had enjoyed it as much as I. Then, after lying still beside me for some time, saying nothing, he had risen and pulled on a robe and walked away down the long room to stare out into the shadowy area beyond.

He stayed there for quite a time, not glancing back at me once. He didn't now. He simply flung the question over his shoulder, and for the life of me I couldn't understand the tone of it.

I propped myself on one elbow and said, "Why do you ask? What went wrong? Wasn't I any good?"

"Too good," he answered curtly.

I realised then that he had actually expected to be my first lover, despite the things he had said about my glances encouraging men.

I was astonished because I couldn't really believe he was one of these late-Victorian males who expected their women to be pure and unsullied—not a man who must know so much about life and saw so many aspects of it. However, I didn't want to shatter his picture of me entirely, so I admitted shyly that I had lost my virginity way back in my convent days.

"You wouldn't think a young and innocent girl at a convent could get into that kind of trouble, would you, but that is just why it happened—my being so young and innocent and trusting."

"Good God, how could seduction take place within the walls of a convent school?"

Well, I could hardly tell him that it had happened outside them, or where, so I had the bright idea of blaming the visiting music master.

"He lived out at St. Cloud, and one day, when the school piano went wrong and I had an examination very soon, he asked the mother superior for permission to give me my final coaching at his house. . . ."

"And the mother superior allowed you to travel all the way to St. Cloud alone?"

"Oh, dear me, no! It isn't very far outside Paris, but of course I was taken in the school carriage and the driver had to wait to bring me back. Everyone at the convent had the highest regard for M'sieur le Févre, a married man with two small daughters who were day pupils at a local kindergarten, so naturally I trusted him completely. I didn't expect . . . In fact, when it happened I was absolutely unsuspecting. After he had taken me through three of Czerny's most difficult studies, he suggested I should have a rest and told me to sit on the sofa while he made some tea. It was the children's half-day from school, and his wife had taken them on a picnic, so there was no one there to make any for us. Quite naturally, I believed all he said, and he did bring some tea and he sat beside me and then started stroking my hair, saying how lovely it was and how sweet he thought me, and because I knew he was a respectable gentleman, because the mother superior would never have employed him otherwise, I thought he was just being fatherly when he sat me on his knee. I didn't dream he intended to do me any wrong, even when he somehow dislodged my garments and had me sitting astride him. . . ."

It was such a good story that I actually believed it myself, though the picture of bald-pated old M'sieur le Févre in the role of seducer had its comical side, but when Magnus made no reply I said unhappily, "Should I have told you? It happened so long ago. I was scarcely fifteen, and of course I have put the whole unpleasant experience right out of my mind. Not that one can ever really forget something so dreadful as that, but of course it has never happened since—"

He blazed, *"Don't lie to me, Clementine—don't ever lie to me.* You are a very experienced young woman indeed. Now, get dressed and I will do the same, and then I will see you home."

He turned then to the door leading to the upper part of the house, and I leapt up and ran after him and clung to his arm, imploring him not to be angry. "You must believe me," I insisted. "You have to believe me!"

He shook me off.

"I said, get dressed."

When he returned I was only half-ready, and crying piteously. He buttoned up the back of my gown and then put my cloak about my shoulders and led me toward the area door, whereupon I cried more bitterly.

"You don't love me," I sobbed. "You cannot love me or you wouldn't be so angry."

"I am angry because you fooled me and thought you could continue to. I am angry because you pretended not to have lain with any man since your youthful seduction and believed you could take me in, but alas and by God, I am *in* love with you, though from that state I am determined to recover. Now, stop crying—I don't believe you are all that heartbroken. You are an actress. I must remember that."

"I am not acting now. I love you, Magnus, truly love you."

"I would be more convinced of that if you hadn't demonstrated your sexual dexterity tonight. It must be difficult for a woman who has obviously been bedded so often to know the difference between love and lust."

"And yet you want to marry me. You said so."

"I had contemplated it, thought about it, wondered how it would work out."

"And now you think it wouldn't, just because I am not a virgin? Why should you condemn me for that, when you are obviously experienced yourself? One law for a man and another for a woman, is that what you believe in?"

"It isn't a question of law but of moral desirability. Of course I am experienced, and much of the unsavoury kind I could well have done without. I went through university and medical school learning the same things in the same way as other male students, and always with the wrong women, but one thing at least those experiences taught me—how to tell the difference between a woman who can be any man's, and one who has some self-respect. Of course I don't condemn you for not being a virgin, or for what that unscrupulous music master did to you, but I would like to forget about the rest."

"I will make you forget! And there aren't any other men now, nor will there be. Only you, Magnus. I will be morally desirable in every way, I swear, which means being yours alone, doesn't it?"

We had left his house and walked back round the square. Now we stood outside my front door, and with sudden compassion he said, "If I was harsh, forgive me. I'm an idealist at heart, I suppose, though God knows how I remain so, serving as a doctor in the particular world I practice in. Perhaps that is why I cherish certain dreams. If I let squalor and vice and the results of them blind me to everything else, I would be disillusioned indeed. And I mustn't forget that you come from a different world, the theatrical world, where standards are lax. Being brought up in it, you can hardly be blamed for following the same laws. That was why I shared Trudy's anxiety about Lucinda going into the theatre."

"Lucinda! Why should you care about Lucinda?"

"Because I want her to be happy."

"Is that the only reason why you were angry about her marriage?"

"I was angry about the way it took place, secretly and furtively and hurting her mother. It seemed out of character, too. When I got over my anger, I knew where the blame lay. Poor little Lucinda, she's so young. . . ."

But I didn't want to talk about "poor little Lucinda," nor could I resist saying, "'Like mother, like daughter,' as the saying goes. Trudy Grainger is no saint, don't forget."

"One error in her life, for which she suffered? One love, which meant the world to her? No woman should be condemned for that."

"Women should not be condemned at all," I said plaintively. "I least of all, because I went to you tonight only because I love you."

I reached up and slid my arms over his shoulders, and we stood there in the darkness holding each other, but I knew I was holding a man whom it would take me a long time to get to know. But was that so important? I had won him, and the more frequently I paid my secret visits to him, the more certain I would be of keeping him.

And so I was, and so I did, until I was obsessed by the man and he by me. In time I knew he had forgotten his determination to get over loving me. I gave Curtis no further thought and even forgot my outrage over Gavin's secret marriage to Lucinda. Neither he nor she mattered anymore, and soon I found that I could think of them with indifference, even with pity, because everyone knew that touring was a dreary life. My own was now far from dreary; as I expected, the stimulation of a new love affair revived my spirits enormously. I surrendered completely to a man who was unlike any I had known before. His lovemaking was a mixture of tenderness and passion which I found delightful, even though it lacked the violence and the touch of brutality in which Curtis often indulged and which I so enjoyed.

But I could wait. A man who could fight so fiercely as my pugilistic doctor must have an underlying brute strength which, in time, I could arouse to the pitch I desired. Apart from that, I could not complain about the degree of his ardour, nor of his physical passion. The only flaw in our affair was his strange aversion to secrecy and his increasing dislike of our place of rendezvous. Personally, I found the underground gymnasium a highly original place in which to make love, so different from Pierre's greenhouse and Curtis's now cosy quarters in the mews, not to mention the conventional bedrooms in which I had enjoyed casual liaisons with other men, slipping away from dance floors during balls in private houses, or to sofas in withdrawing rooms with the doors discreetly locked, and then, adding spice to the evening's adventure, returning unobtrusively without a hair out of place and the flush on my cheek attributable only to the heat of the ballroom, and dear Mamma, inevitably absorbed in the food and the wine, believing her darling gel had been dancing her pretty feet off all the time. . . .

So when Magnus expressed his dislike of what I considered very necessary secrecy—"I hate furtiveness," he would say; "I don't want a mistress, I want a wife"—I remembered his earlier reference to marriage and naturally thought he meant me. I had to sidestep very adroitly then, because I was becoming aware that he would never be the type of husband I sought—the blind, trusting type who could be easily duped. But I did want to keep him as a lover, so dodged the issue by begging for time to be sure, quite sure.

His quizzical look in reply baffled me. This man often made me feel that he was thinking a lot when saying nothing; I could even have interpreted that look as implying "But why should I want you as a wife now that I can have you without marriage?" had I not known how passionately he was in love with me. Every time he enjoyed my body he demon-

strated that, so I really could not understand his aversion to secret meetings in the house he shared with his sister.

To me, the idea of fooling that prosaic spinster upstairs was highly
amusing. It enhanced the whole situation, though of course I didn't let
Magnus know that. I also had the sneaking suspicion Helen Steel wasn't
all that guillible anyway and that she would respect her brother's private
life because it was her business to do so. Sisters, like wives, had to turn a
blind eye to things their menfolk did, and in any case her position in his
household was only that of housekeeper, so why should we worry about
her? But when I actually said that, he stated bluntly that it was the pretence, the lack of openness, which he chiefly disliked, at which I was
wise enough not to tell him the truth—that I only really enjoyed an affair
when it *was* illicit. Instead, I said with disarming wistfulness, "But what
if you tire of me, Magnus? Then you will wish we had continued the way
we are, with no one knowing a thing."

I expected him to declare that he would never tire of me, but he
didn't. All he said was, "You could tire, too," and he said it in that enigmatic tone which so often baffled me. Very often I failed to understand
him, but instinct warned me not to underrate him. As far as Magnus
Steel was concerned, I had to play my cards very carefully indeed, but
since I had always done that successfully, I saw no reason why I should
not continue to.

So I manipulated the affair with my customary skill and to my complete satisfaction, added to which was the feeling that in some obscure
way I was hitting back at Lucinda, because although I knew he could only
regard her as a charity child whom he had taken into his house solely
through kindness, I couldn't fail to be aware of his fondness for her. His
concern about her runaway marriage revealed that, though of course it
could be compared with the concern of a big brother for a very much
younger sister.

Except that she was not his sister and during the weeks she had lived in
his house this fondness had apparently developed. Propinquity could
create a bond between the most unlikely people. So in one way I could
now be glad that she was off the scene, much as I resented the circumstances of her departure. That resentment underlay the spice of retaliation which I now enjoyed in my relationship with Magnus. It lay beneath
every delightful moment, enhancing and colouring it. The only draw-
back was that she did not know he was now my lover.

Five

Lucinda

17

Three weeks of intensive rehearsal, and Gavin and I were on the road. Those weeks gave me little time in which to think of anything but the immediate present; of learning lines, of living with a husband, of sleeping with him, of sharing passion, of getting up in the morning and hurrying across London to rehearsal rooms which proved to be surprisingly seedy, situated above a public house in Soho.

"Not unusual, my darling. A company without a theatre of its own has to make do with whatever rehearsal rooms are available. This quarter of London abounds with them, and many are a great deal worse than this. When we do have our own theatre, it will be different."

Gavin often talked about having our own theatre. It was a dream to which I listened, but could not wholly believe in. To own a theatre, one had to have money and a great deal of it; more than it took to acquire an elegant little flat on the Chelsea Embankment.

There were no costume fittings for this new production, because it was a modern play for which the cast had to supply their own clothes, but those I had to wear were a greater shock to me than the shabby rehearsal rooms, for my part demanded that I should run around in a transparent negligee, semi-naked. I should have guessed that a play called *Bedtime Frills* could only be frivolous, but Gavin assured me that audiences would love it.

"You've been steeped in conventional stuff all your life, so this sort of thing is bound to shock you at first, but it's marvellous training in comedy, and all I ask is that you play the part as I direct."

I drove from my mind the thought that Maria, in *Twelfth Night*, was marvellous training in comedy of a much higher kind. I was in Gavin's hands now. He proved to be a good producer and soon had the cast working hard, including me, although my part demanded no great acting prowess. All I had to do was provide the romantic interest and look inviting, but it seemed to me that the invitation seemed more blatant than necessary.

"There's no *meat* to the part," I fretted on our way home one night. "I shall never become a serious actress playing this sort of thing."

I was tired. We had been rehearsing since nine in the morning and it was now after eleven at night. The opening was looming ahead and was to take place at the old Victoria Theatre in Reading. That was also a surprise.

"The first booking seems as poor as the play," I added without thought, and in the darkness of the hansom I heard my husband's sigh of impatience.

"It is good enough for a tryout. When we have polished the production, we will be ready for the number-one dates."

"Have they been booked?"

"Of course. You don't imagine we're touring the number twos, do you?"

I had learned already that fatigue made Gavin irritable, so said no more. Later, in the intimacy of our bed, it would vanish, smoothed away by our love. In such moments all thought was dispelled; all memories, too, leaving no room in my mind for other people—not even my mother, and much less Clementine, who had called me a dark horse when she heard of my marriage.

She had arrived unexpectedly at the flat one day, when Gavin was out. "I came to congratulate you, Lucinda-bastard. You've done well for yourself." She had sauntered in without being invited, making herself at home and quizzing me as if she found the whole thing vastly entertaining and a subject she expected me to discuss down to the most intimate details.

"What is Gavin like as a lover? Good, I should think. I always intended to find out someday, but I don't suppose I shall have the opportunity now. Yes, you certainly *are* a dark horse, Lucinda-bastard."

She still liked to taunt me; the habit seemed to have increased since the truth about my birth had come to light, though she still called it teasing. However, I could afford to ignore it now, and did. Nor would I give her the satisfaction of the kind of conversation she so enjoyed. The intimacy of my life with Gavin was private, not to be cheapened by confidential discussion with anyone. It was our secret world. He was my lover, my husband, the other half of my soul, and giving my body to him was a sacred thing. None of this would Clementine be able to understand, had I even tried to make her. She would have laughed and called me a sentimental idiot.

Strange that I should think of her now, when all I wanted was to get home to bed, to reach out to Gavin in the darkness and soothe his irritability. There was more to such moments than the physical, but to the Clementines of this world that was where such unions ended and all they consisted of—the satiation of physical desire, the titillation of the senses. She had learned it all in the wrong way. Being tumbled on a mossy bank by a licentious Frenchman had given her no idea of the true meaning of a relationship between a man and a woman in love. I felt sorry for her and wondered whether her affair with Curtis was still going on, or if it had petered out to its inevitable end. If she had finally rejected him, that man would not take it lightly.

The cab rumbled to a halt, and as we climbed the stairs to our flat Gavin slipped his arm about my waist and said, "God, I'm tired! But not too tired to make love to you. Nor you to me, I hope?"

Indeed I was not. I was never too tired to love him, and as our senses merged that night everything else was obliterated, including the disappointing comedy, my dislike of the part, the squalid rehearsal rooms, and the manners and behaviour of the cast, which compared very unfavourably with those of the Boswell Company's supporting players. With the Shaftesbury, leads fraternised with lesser actors, and everyone was on Christian-name terms. Gavin considered this a good thing. "It makes for friendliness," he said, "and why not?"

Why not, indeed, but when the male members of the company slipped their arms about me with easy familiarity, letting their hands stray to my breasts, I disliked it. This seemed to amuse them, and I disliked that even more. Gavin advised me to take no notice. "You'll get used to it in time, darling. It doesn't mean a thing."

But when dress rehearsal came along and I was forced to appear in a transparent negligee with nothing whatever beneath it, their roving hands angered me.

"I hate it, Gavin! I hate it as much as I hate the idea of audiences seeing me running around half naked."

"But audiences will love it. You have no idea what a beautiful body you have, and nothing could be more suggestive than a filmy covering— far more revealing than if you appeared stark naked. Do you know what I think when I see you onstage like that? 'She is mine, all mine, and nobody else can have her.' That is what I think and why I don't mind the whole world seeing you 'running around half naked,' as you put it. That's nonsense, of course. That trailing garment covers you all over."

"Clinging and transparent. All right for our bedroom at home, but not onstage. I shall wear something beneath. I insist."

"And I insist that you do not. Onstage, every scene you appear in is a bedroom one, so if that ravishing thing is suitable for our own bedroom, it is perfectly appropriate for the play. Just imagine—at the Boswell you would be strutting around in some cumbersome costume with nothing but your pretty head and shoulders to hint at what lies lower down. And remember this—*I* am the producer of this French farce, and you will play the part and dress the part as *I* direct."

The management of Shaftesbury Productions gave Gavin *carte blanche* with the play's production and did not even send a representative to rehearsals. "At my request," Gavin told me. "I stipulated no interference, no interruptions, and no comments until we're ready for the road, and if they don't like it then, it will be too late. I know what I am about, my love. When they see the box-office receipts, there will be no complaints."

"You said they had other irons in the fire. What kind?"

"Shows of all types. Musicals, vaudeville—that's what music hall will eventually give way to—and exhibitions."

"What kind of exhibitions?"

He answered vaguely, "Artistic tableaux and that kind of thing. I don't really know, because I'm not involved in that side."

I had not revealed my father's curiosity about the company or mentioned his questions and comments about it, and on the Sunday of our departure I thought it a pity he could not see the comfort in which we travelled. No expense had been spared in staging the show, and quite apart from a specially built scenic van for transporting the sets, a whole coach had been reserved for the company on the train—third class, of course, but still an entire coach. Sunday travel could be tedious, with no direct trains to anywhere and more goods traffic than passenger services. Although I had never toured, I learned much about it from others in the company, particularly the elderly female character lead, Ethel Grimsby, whose whole life had been spent on tour.

"Weekly dates aren't too bad, dear—in fact, they're the cream, because you can settle in your digs for six whole days, and if you have a good ma, you'll soon feel at home. Twice weekly isn't so good, because you have to travel all night between the curtain coming down in one place and going up in the next, and then go on before you've even got the chill out of your bones if you're opening with a matinee. Thank God morning performances in the provinces are going out of fashion! Bless the scene shifters for that—they're protesting about the hours and no extra pay. As for one-night stands, well, I wouldn't touch them unless I were really down on my luck."

"Ma," I gathered, was the universal theatrical name for landladies, and they could make your life comfortable or decidedly uncomfortable. Being married to the producer of the play, I was lucky—not only could we afford the best lodgings, but Ma would put herself out on our behalf, preparing supper for us when we returned from the theatre at night, whereas the other members of the cast had to buy fish and chips on the way home. I felt cherished by my husband, protected by his double rank of producer and lead actor. We even had a carriage to ourselves on the journey to Reading, but were invited into Ethel Grimsby's for a cup of tea when shunted into a siding because the goods part of the train abandoned us to take its load of fish on to Oxford.

"It's only a short trip to Reading, dear, but a cuppa always helps to pass the time when waiting to be hitched onto the end of another train. I still use the spirit stove my dear mamma took on tour with her. I learned the art of making tea during train journeys on many a Sunday trip with her and my father. They were in the profession too, and so were their folks before them. Circus and then pubs. They'd be proud at the way I've gone up in the world, playing character leads on tour in the legit. You're lucky to be in a production like this, dear, and if you work hard—and that husband of yours'll see you do . . . he's a slogger, that one; ambitious, too, I shouldn't wonder—well, as I say, if you work hard you can make a good steady living on tour. I once knew an actress who even got to London eventually. What experience did you have before joining this company, dear? Ever acted before?"

When I told her, she was flabbergasted. "Acting in London, and coming down to *this*? That's doing things in reverse, love! Couldn't you have stayed where you were?"

I had nothing to say to that. I wouldn't let myself remember my father's offer of Maria in *Twelfth Night*. And what did Ethel Grimsby know about things, anyway? I had already learned that the world of the theatre was divided into different levels and different factions, London rarely overflowing into the provinces, and provincial actors and actresses rarely coming into the metropolis. But Gavin would, and I with him, eventually. For the present, this was a new beginning, a new road, but it would lead us back to the theatrical hub of the world, and until then I would go resolutely forward.

The train call was for ten-thirty that last Sunday in September, and as a porter trundled our personal bags along the platform I saw the company's skips being loaded into the guard's van, ours amongst them. I had felt excited and proud when removing Gavin's personal label, for this was the hamper he had taken on the Boswell tour, and replacing it with one marked GAVIN CALDER and LUCINDA GRAINGER and, in brackets, because I couldn't resist it, "Mr. and Mrs. Calder." But now the large black letters, painted on the side, leapt out at me—SHAFTESBURY PRO-DUCTIONS—and I experienced a strange sort of pang because it was not THE BOSWELL THEATRE COMPANY, as I had once dreamed of seeing on a skip of my own. That name had been on this one originally, but had been painted out and replaced with the new one. It was ridiculous to be emotional over a small thing like that and I jerked my glance away, searching the platform in the hope of seeing my mother, who had prom-ised to come to see us off.

I had paid regular visits to my mother since leaving Magnus Steel's house, but only once had I met him. That too was an encounter I pre-ferred to forget, rejecting it as I had firmly rejected the unhappy one with my mother immediately after my marriage. However great the de-mands of rehearsal, and however late they ran, I had made a point of see-ing her as often as possible during the last three weeks, determined to regain our earlier trust no matter how long it took. But restraint still lin-gered between us, even though she welcomed me with warmth. That warmth was not extended to my husband, though I was confident that it would come in time. Meanwhile, I would tell her about rehearsals, skim-ming over details of my own part and merely describing it as a comedy role.

"Not a great part, Mamma, but very good training."

She had listened to everything, stitching away at her pile of mission garments, and then I would listen to all she had to tell me about her work there, and the people she met. One day she had said, "I do believe that nice doctor who deputises for Magnus is very fond of Helen and she of him," and I remembered Helen's praise of the man and thought how ro-mantic it would be if she found happiness with him. Beneath her plain exterior, I knew that Helen hid a romantic heart. Not only her choice of literature, as Rosa Carey's colourful romance testified, but her reaction to my marriage told me this. She had actually cried. "And you so young, dear Lucinda, so young! But Mr. Calder is an experienced man, and so handsome—I am sure he will take care of you and make you happy. Oh, dear, what a foolish woman I am, making an exhibition of myself like this!"

I loved her for it. Not so her brother, who had faced me with undis-guised anger and called me a bloody little fool, at which I had retorted, "You were right when you said your language had become that of Step-ney! And what business is it of yours who and when I marry?"

"It's *how* you have done it, how you went about it—underhandedly and cruelly, without any consideration for your mother. Hasn't she suf-fered enough? And what sort of a man is Calder, to carry you off like that?"

But I wouldn't allow Gavin to take the blame.

"Everyone misjudges him except your sister!" I had flung back, at which he had shouted contemptuously, "My sister is a fool too—silly and romantic beneath all that militancy. Sometimes I wonder how a woman so sentimental can be so efficient!"

"At least she is human and understanding."

"And I am not?"

"Human enough where the mission is concerned, but what does a man like you know about love? Although I suppose you call your infatuation with Clementine by that name."

"How I feel about Clementine is no concern of yours."

"Nor is my marriage to Gavin any of yours."

We continued to glare at each other, burning with anger and resentment. The resentment had been mine and the anger his.

"Keep away from me when you visit this house," he ordered. "Just keep away from me, that's all."

That had proved easy enough. I even suspected that it was he who did the avoiding when I visited my mother. Sometimes I had seen his study door close and heard its sharp little slam as I went upstairs or down, and of course I was pleased about that because I had no desire to meet him any more than he desired to meet me.

So to see him now, standing a little way off as she came hurrying along the station platform, was disconcerting. Across the dividing space my glance met his and must have betrayed me, because he gave a mocking little bow, doffed his hat, and strolled away. I guessed he had brought my mother here in that trap for which I had formed quite an affection. I even wished we had one; it would be useful for travelling from Chelsea to Portman Square, and I could take my mother for drives in it, but the idea had seemed to amuse Gavin when I suggested it. To him, a pony trap was quite inappropriate for sophisticated London.

But I forgot about such trivialities as I ran to meet her. She was running too, holding up her fashionable skirt in order not to restrict her steps. Dear Mamma; whatever knocks life dealt her, she would hold her head high and look elegant.

She had brought me a small bunch of roses, which must have swallowed quite a few shillings of her precious money. I think I shall always remember the fragrance of them, and the moisture on the petals which somehow seemed to match the moisture on her cheeks. This parting was to take me farther away from her than I had ever been; much farther than Chelsea.

"Good luck, darling. I shall be thinking of you on your first night." She turned to Gavin, but didn't hold out her hand. "And good luck to you also. I know how important this play is to you, and I hope it gets splendid notices wherever it goes."

He kissed her fondly. "Thank you, Trudy dear, and bless you. Don't shed tears for your daughter—she is going to be a great success, I prom-

ise. You look excited about something, and since it can't be our departure, because I know you can't bear the thought of Lucinda going away,
it must be something else. Something has happened. What is it?"

I saw then that her eyes were alight despite the hint of tears. She nodded breathlessly, and at that moment someone in the company called to
Gavin and he went to join them. I could see my mother was glad of that
and guessed she wanted to tell me her news alone. She was opening her
reticule hurriedly and taking out a folded sheet of paper. "It is this, Lucinda—see for yourself."

The letter was from a firm of solicitors, Peabody, Wainright & Waring,
of Lincoln's Inn Fields, and they "had to inform her that the sum of one
thousand pounds had been lodged in Coutts Bank, in her name, for the
financing of a modiste's establishment in premises to be selected by herself." Their client's name was to remain anonymous, "but it was his wish
that the gift should not be declined. In such an event, the money was to
remain on deposit for her in Coutts Bank, but they wished to point out
that it was their client's specific desire that she should utilise these funds
for the purpose named."

"What must I do, Lucinda? What must I *do*?"

"Accept it, of course! It is wonderful. Why hesitate? You have always
been too independent, refusing to accept help from him. Take it now."

It could only be from Nevill Boswell. I found myself softening toward
him and remembering the last time I had seen him, tired and sad in the
green room of the Boswell Theatre, telling me of his plans. I had rejected them, but I was determined my mother should not do the same.

"How would you benefit by refusing?" I urged. "He won't take it
back—the lawyers make that quite clear. It will simply remain in the
bank untouched, *so make use of it*. You know it has always been a dream of
yours to own such an establishment, and *I* know you would be a success.
Others know it too—Magnus and Helen, for instance."

"Bless them, they are good friends."

"Have you shown them this letter?"

"Not yet. The first person to see it had to be you. Oh, how I wish you
could come with me to find suitable premises!"

I wished the same. This was wonderful news and about the best thing
that could happen to my mother, and that she was not going to turn her
back on it was confirmed when she said, "I will still work for the mission, of course. I can cope with all the sewing they need in the evenings
and on Sundays, *and* enjoy it."

It was time to go. Gavin returned and helped me aboard. I waved
good-bye to my mother through a sudden blur of tears, leaning through
the open window until my husband drew me inside and firmly closed it.

* * *

Compared with the Boswell Theatre, the one at Reading was small and second-rate, but I reminded myself that it was only for a tryout and that soon we would be playing to better houses in Birmingham, Manchester, Glasgow, and other leading cities.

Preparations for the opening kept Gavin busy from the time of our arrival. He went straight to the theatre and left me to settle into our lodgings, which were something of a shock. Modest as my accommodation with my mother had been in the Boswell house in Portman Square, it had been in an aristocratic neighborhood and had prepared me for nothing like this.

Lists of theatrical lodgings were compiled by the Actor's Church Union and were therefore presumed to guarantee respectability, cleanliness, and a good Christian atmosphere, but number 322 Hardcastle Street was one of an endless chain of terrace houses badly in need of renovation and with a distinct air of seediness. I judged the house had not had a coat of paint for years, and the genteel Ma who had specified "B and S for Management and Lead Players" had very poor ideas of what constituted Board and Service, judging by the chipped teacups, the coarse bread and margarine, and the stale fly-blown cakes which looked like leftovers from a Great Western Railway station buffet. The meal was already set out to await our arrival, the tea half-cold, and when I sat down on one of the rickety chairs, springs twanged.

When I tried the bed, the response was the same, but at least the bed was accommodated in the next room, leaving us with what was proudly designated in the Actors' Church Union directory as "a superior private sitting room." The only superior thing about it was the galaxy of theatrical photographs on the mantelpiece (or the expressions on their faces), all signed with profuse curls and twirls and messages of affection.

"*Love to Ma. Never have I lived so comfortable! Gloria Starr.*" and: "*Bottoms up, Ma! We'll Have Another Pint Next Time Round! Love from Charlie Wigginsbottom (alias Charles Winchester).*" There were Mables and Daisies and Ernies and Alfs, complete with tights and spangles, or in classical poses against plaster Doric columns. There were ogling eyes round ostrich-feather fans and male profiles in rapidly fading sepia, and all so crowded together that the dust between them was almost hidden. The whole place smelled of dust and, gulping the half-cold tea, I fled to the theatre. Without my husband, I could not face another hour in those rooms.

Backstage at the old Victoria, I felt more at home. Gavin was busy with a scenic rehearsal and cursing his stage manager's inability to deal with the resident stagehands, who seemed to resent working for "London swells." I slipped through the pass door and into the stalls, and one by one the rest of the cast appeared. There was to be a run-through this evening, and all resented it.

It was not customary for a rehearsal to be called until Monday morning, after travelling on Sunday and settling into digs, but it was already obvious that the producer of *Bedtime Frills* was a driving force which had to be obeyed. By the time we left the theatre that night, I was too tired to even heed the twanging of Ma's best bed. I slept soundly and awakened refreshed, ready for the opening night and praying it would be successful for my husband's sake. Dislike the play as I might, I knew an actress had to accept the bad with the good, but for Gavin I wanted only the good. This production was important in his career as a producer, and for that reason I did my best with a part I found thoroughly distasteful. The applause and the whistles it brought only made it more so, but my husband was pleased.

"Didn't I tell you the audience would love it? There'll be no losing money on *this* production."

We were together in the wings during the last act, he having just come off and I waiting to go on again. There was a full minute before my cue came, and I found myself wishing it were over, hating the thought of flitting coyly onstage, once more holding my transparent draperies about me and trying to control their fluttering in the draught from the wings and loathing the salacious laughter when I failed. It was all I could do to stop these flimsy skirts from billowing upward, but when I said so, Gavin laughed.

"Then don't try, darling. Give the audience what they want—although you are cheating them of a lot by wearing that trailing nightgown beneath. When you've played the part a few times, I'll insist on your discarding it. This is French farce, not English, remember. As actors, we are here to please. Remember that, too."

I answered shortly, "I know what we are here for—to act, not posture. My father always said so."

"And took a heavy financial drop with that last revival."

"It couldn't have been all that heavy, or he couldn't have been so generous to my mother now."

"In what way?"

When I told him, Gavin let out a low whistle. "A thousand pounds! That's certainly a lot. Funny, though, I hear he is putting on *Twelfth Night* with the same old sets and costumes, a bad mistake. If a play is being dished up even for a second time, it has to be redressed and restaged, and a thousand pounds would have gone a long way to doing that. It doesn't make sense, with the Boswell having to exercise economy the way it is. False economy, Gregory calls it, and he's right. A useful fellow, that stage manager; never discreet like Willard, and even less so when he's had a few drinks. Prising information out of him then is easy."

I refused to believe my husband would use such methods. "Not you, of all people!"

He laughed indulgently, and told me not to be a prude. "Everybody in this business does it."

"Including Shaftesbury Productions?"

He gave me an affectionate little push. "There's your cue."

Suddenly I was onstage. The eternal draught from the wings blew icily about my bare legs and penetrated the thin chiffon of my trailing skirts. Now I heard myself prattling my lines exactly as Gavin had coached me, and it all sounded as cheap and distasteful as it undoubtedly was.

I tried to shut my ears to the catcalls and the ribald laughter as a sudden rush of air from the wings lifted my gossamer draperies, revealing my nakedness beneath. Good God—a stagehand in the wings was operating the massive wind bellows and focusing them directly onto me! This was something for which I was totally unprepared, and I fled upstage and downstage in a desperate attempt to escape, clutching the trailing chiffon about my knees and almost sobbing with humiliation as the laughter and the cheers and the whistles grew louder and louder. Suddenly I could bear it no more and fled offstage and straight into Gavin's waiting arms.

He was laughing. "All right, man, you can stop." That was to the stagehand. To me, "On you go again, my lovely!"

"No!"

He seized me, kissed me, shook me gently. "It won't happen again, I promise—*but on you go.* Can't you hear them calling for you?"

Another push, firmer this time, and I was back in the public eye. Mercifully, there was no draught and my lines came back to me, but I had to speak them loudly to drown the whistles, which met my reappearance. How would I endure a ten-week tour of this play? Would I become immune to its vulgarity and deaf to the lines I had to speak? I tried to focus my vision on the dark recesses of the auditorium where the audience was invisible. Features were clearly discernible in the front rows of the stalls, and I could not endure the salacious relish of male smiles at such close quarters.

Nor could I gaze into outer space all the time. An actress had to vary the range of her vision as she varied her lines, but if I could avoid glancing at those few front rows I would be all right, so I looked beyond them into the dark abyss of the pit, then up to the grand circle, then higher still to the gods and then sideways to the uppermost boxes—the remote boxes where light thrown up from the stage revealed no more than white blobs of faces and one could not tell whether they were laughing—and then down to the next tier of boxes level with the grand circle, where the blobs were slightly more distinct but still vague and impersonal. That way, constantly moving and unaware of the audience as anything more than unseen dummies, I could get through this performance somehow.

It was nearly over. Only a few more lines and I would make my exit. My glance slid finally to the stage box, which was always empty because few members of the audience could afford anything so expensive as two pounds to accommodate four people, so it was a useful blank space on which to concentrate, and no one was sitting there tonight.

But the space was not blank and the box was no longer empty. Out of its shadows a face appeared—the face of a man with a loose mouth and heavy eyelids. His hands were resting on the front of the box, and I was standing immediately below. The flickering gas jets of the footlights gave an upward spurt at that moment, picking out those hands, and I knew that if they came closer they would be thick with black hairs and terrifyingly familiar.

Then the face leaned forward, looking straight down at me, and it was as clear as if it were beside me on the stage. It had the reddest lips I had ever seen on a man.

It was Durbridge, come back from the dead.

18

"Ridiculous," said Gavin. "Durbridge isn't alive."

"But he is. I saw him."

My husband was laughing. He was being patient and indulgent. He could afford to be, because the first night of this tawdry play had been a success and the front-of-the-house manager predicted full bookings for the rest of the week. Gavin had talked of nothing else all the way back to Hardcastle Street, so excited that he didn't even notice the seediness of the district and the shabbiness of the house.

But the single gas jet in the dark and narrow hall cast a sinister light. I was thankful to reach our rooms and stood shivering in the darkness, waiting for Gavin to light the gas. Dear God, how I hated this place, how I longed for home! And the strange thing was that when I thought of home I didn't even see Gavin's elegant little apartment, but Magnus Steel's house. I had stayed there for a very short time indeed, but the room I had occupied remained alive to me. So did the house, perhaps because my mother lived there now and in it we had been happy, made welcome by those two good friends. *One* good friend, I corrected hastily, for my last encounter with Magnus had driven us poles apart.

I was striving to think of other things to avoid immediate fears. As I heard the flare of a match and saw my husband's hand lift it to the gas mantel, I was wondering why I was still unable to think of the Chelsea apartment as ours, but only as Gavin's. Perhaps it was because I was still a new bride in new surroundings which would, in time, become my own, but these trivial thoughts did nothing to take my mind off the matter which I had endeavoured to bring up on the way home and which I still intended to pursue.

"It was he," I said again. "Durbridge. He was unmistakable."

Gavin tossed the match into the ugly iron grate, saying indifferently, "Then the man has a double. It's not unknown." He yawned. "Thank God we went out to supper, provincial hotel though it was. If *this* is a sample of Ma's catering, I can see us bringing home fish and chips like the rest of the cast."

I looked down at the tea tray, identical to the one set out for us the night before, the tea cold, the slices of bread and margarine curled at the edges, the fly-blown cakes, and suddenly I cried, "Oh, Gavin, take me away from here!"

He took me in his arms and his love flowed out to me. "Poor darling, you've never been on the road, so of course this sort of thing is a shock to you, but believe me, many theatrical digs are worse. You'll get used to things in time. Here—this will make you feel better."

He took a brandy flask from his hip pocket and poured some into the small silver cup screwed to the top. It was a handsome flask and he patted it affectionately. "A present from Bernadette when I first went on tour. She has her faults, but, bless her, she understands a man's needs."

But not her husband's, I wanted to say as I accepted the brandy wordlessly. The fiery liquid braced me, making the chill of the room seem less penetrating, but the gloom and depression of the place refused to be banished. Gavin took an unused teacup from the tray and poured a tot for himself.

"We'll drink this in bed, darling, then you'll sleep like a log and feel better in the morning. First nights are a strain, even on tour, but at least we can be happy about this one."

He lit a candle in a cheap tin holder and turned off the gas. I waited until we were in bed before saying, "About Durbridge—you don't believe me, do you?"

"My darling, don't start that again. How *can* I believe you? The man is dead, and no one knows that better than I. I helped Stacey move the body."

"Stacey? Who is Stacey?"

"His man. Been with him for years. I had to fetch him, of course. After I'd seen you and your mother off the premises, I locked the theatre and went to Durbridge's house in Grosvenor Square. I promised to tell you everything about that night, so you may as well hear it now. I collected Stacey and drove back to the theatre. Actually Stacey drove, having the good sense to use one of Durbridge's carriages rather than attract attention by transporting his master in a hired vehicle. I warned him of the need for discretion, and fifteen years in Durbridge's service had taught him the need for that anyway. So I dismissed the hansom I arrived in and we had no inquisitive cabby to contend with, though of course we pretended that Durbridge was drunk when we carried him out of the theatre between us; not that anyone was in sight, except one lone prostitute on the other side of the street. When we got back to Grosvenor Square again and carried him upstairs between us, I told Stacey I would make sure the newspapers heard nothing about it, which is easy enough to arrange, so of course the man guessed there was something suspicious about his master's death and cooperated all he could. Next day I called, to check that he had stuck to the story I advised him to tell the doctor, and I haven't seen the man since. Taken care not to, as a matter of fact, because I don't want any questions even from him."

I had finished the brandy, but my fingers still curled about the small silver cup because it was something to hold on to. I began to feel cold again, propped up against Ma's uncomfortable flock-filled pillows.

"And what story did you advise him to tell the doctor?" I asked.

"That his master had fallen downstairs, of course. I felt it wiser to stick to the truth, since a doctor would examine the body. The only variation was that the fall had occurred in his own home. That house in Grosvenor Square has a magnificent curving staircase, so a fall down it could have been equally fatal, and fortunately he had no cuts or wounds to leave telltale marks on the uncarpeted marble treads. Oh, by the way, those teeth marks on his wrist had to be explained. I covered that well; told Stacy to tell the doctor that he believed his master had had a quarrel with a vixen of a lady friend, which lent credibility to the whole story—a seducer chasing an unwilling bedmate, as she raced downstairs, could meet with such a fall easily. Stacey was to say that he had heard, but not seen, the lady. It was hardly a doctor's function to enquire about his dead patient's amorous life. So it seemed a clear-cut case of accidental death, and was accepted as such."

"It *was* accidental."

"But your mother caused it. She made Durbridge trip and fall, don't forget."

"But not to his death. He couldn't have been in that box tonight if he were dead, so if the manservant said a doctor signed a death certificate, he must have been lying."

"He wasn't."

"And nor am I. Durbridge is here, in Reading."

"He can't be."

"He could, if the fall didn't kill him, if it only injured him and now he has recovered."

"No man could recover from a crash like that."

"Others have fallen down those stairs and sustained only injuries, and it would explain, wouldn't it, why no rumors of his death ever got about?"

Gavin grew impatient. "I've told you—I took care of all that, and you know why. Few people knew of Durbridge's habits, but they would have come to light had his death become known. You would have been dragged into an inquest, and so would your mother. Do you think I wanted to see your name in headlines because you had been in a backstage dressing room with him, naked?"

"An accidental death in his own home would surely have meant an inquest too."

"I *told* you—the doctor was satisfied and signed a death certificate." Gavin finished his brandy and placed the cup on a rickety bedside table; then he blew out the candle and said, "Of course, if you won't believe me, I am not going to waste my time trying to convince you. I did what I could and hushed up the whole thing, and that was the end of the matter. Now, let's go to sleep. It is late."

I lay down, but in the darkness I insisted, "He *is* alive, Gavin. I know he is. He must have been merely unconscious after the fall and you concluded he was dead. That would account for no funeral reports."

"And the doctor was taken in too?" He laughed indulgently. "You're letting your imagination run away with you. Come here . . ." He pulled me toward him and springs twanged loudly. "My God, what a bed to make love in!"

By the end of the week I was forced to admit that Gavin was right: I must have imagined the whole thing, because Durbridge didn't appear again, either in the stage box or the stalls or anywhere else within my range of vision, but I departed from Reading feeling relieved in more ways than one.

Gavin was well satisfied because the house manager's prediction proved right; we played to full houses for the rest of the week. And I too was satisfied because there was no repetition of the stagehand's performance with the wind bellows, though the whistles and catcalls my part always won became routine, culminating in Saturday night's noisy finale. Unaccustomed to rowdyism at the Boswell Theatre, this was a shock to me, but the rest of the cast was well pleased.

"It's a sign of appreciation," they told me. "The time to worry is when provincial audiences, particularly on Saturday nights, are *not* noisy—especially the number-two stands. Number ones are more classy and, in places like Birmingham and Manchester, the stalls and grand circle will even be in evening dress—but that won't make any difference to behaviour in the pit and the gods and the rest of the house, and the farther north we go, the noisier they will be."

But when we reached Birmingham and Manchester we found ourselves in number-two theatres, places that usually featured third-rate melodrama, never the classics.

"Well, what did you expect, my love? I told you we would play the number-one cities, but I didn't say the number-one theatres—not for French farce—nor have I ever pretended that *Bedtime Frills* was classical stuff. The important thing is that it will make money, and that's what I am after. With money we can go far, you and I." Gavin finished with a hint of impatience, "And I do wish you would appreciate the valuable experience you are getting. You'll become known more quickly by playing to nonintellectual audiences up and down the country, than to limited audiences in London, and Nevill Boswell didn't exactly get rave notices the other night. 'A tired performance,' one critic said of him, and even Howard Mortimer hinted that he wasn't up to standard. Nevill is past his peak, and should realise it."

"He will never pass his peak," I declared. "If his performance was below par, there must have been something wrong."

We had covered six weeks of the tour, with four more to go, and I was well aware that my father's opening night had passed. Now I saw the pile of newspapers my husband had brought to read during our Sunday train journey, and I was anxious to read the reviews. Gavin tossed them to me as he finished with them, one by one, and I seized them with more eagerness than was wise.

"You seem very interested in what goes on at the Boswell, my dear. In the circumstances, I wouldn't have expected you to be too enthusiastic about your father's activities."

"I spent the major part of my life in his theatre, so I suppose it is hardly surprising." I tried not to put a pleading note in my voice, but I wanted my husband's understanding above all things. His answering smile reassured me.

"Of course. Read those reviews, by all means. They will make you appreciate the success we ourselves are having."

These tedious Sunday train journeys had one virtue—they provided ample time in which to read. Once the newspapers had been devoured I would turn to Shakespeare, Sheridan, and all the great dramatists, for I travelled with a small library of books. I also caught up with correspondence, writing long letters to my mother in station waiting rooms or railway sidings, and rereading hers, which I received no less than twice a week. She had found premises for her modiste business in George Street, a short walk along Baker Street from Portman Square.

"The shop is very small, but Helen optimistically declares I will have to expand ere long. . . ." And: "Today Helen came with me to choose decorations; she has a most feminine eye, which surprised me." And again: "Magnus is wonderful, coping with workmen as I could never do, and as a result it will all be completed in record time. I do hope you will be back in London the day I open my door for the first time—it won't be the same without you." And the latest, received at the theatre just before we left on Saturday, related that she already had more than a dozen advance orders, thanks to Helen spreading the word amongst her friends and acquaintances.

I turned then to an unopened letter, which proved to be from Clementine, oozing goodwill and amiable gossip:

> . . . so much to talk about. . . . I wish you had not gone away . . . you will remember my once saying that we should always be close because we could never tell when we would need each other. . . . Well, I need you now for one of our let-your-hair-down gossips. Since you left this house I have had no one to talk to at all, and you were such a good listener—easily shocked sometimes, but I fancy you can't be anymore, married to that stepuncle of mine. I know him well. I don't mean *that* way, of course, though it wouldn't be incest, since we are not blood relations, but I could hardly grow up in the same house with him, in the same family, and not learn a thing or two about him. Mamma forgave all his sins because she doted on him, but Papa—well, you must surely know how Papa feels about Gavin!

(*Because he doesn't understand him,* I thought defensively. *Neither he nor Mamma has ever understood him.*)

> Alas [continued Clementine], men are all the same, with the possible exception of Magnus Steel, because he is rather an exceptional specimen—all that beautiful physique, too! But I think he is exceptional in other ways as well. He doesn't care for public opinion, for example, nor for all his rich and respectable relatives. Did you know he comes from a very wealthy family, very highly connected, all of whom thoroughly disapprove of the spectacle he makes of himself in Hyde Park? I went along there one day to see for myself and thought he looked absolutely *beautiful* stripped. Afterwards I asked him why he did it, because it couldn't be for the money, and he said the value was in drawing attention to that mission of his, quite unaware, I am sure, that it is *he* who draws all the attention, especially from women. Then he begged me to stay away in future because someone so pretty as I proved a distraction.

I could almost see Clemmy preening as she wrote that, and even more vividly could I hear Magnus saying the words. I knew he had always admired her beauty, and to be envious was absurd, but I felt an inexplicable pang.

I read on hastily:

As you know, we are back to dreary Shakespeare at the theatre. I wish we could perform something more modern in which I could wear delectable clothes. I read a review of *Bedtime Frills* in the touring column of *The Era*; my dear, it sounds very daring, but what fun! And fancy *you* running around half-naked! At least, that is what *The Era* hinted, and Papa was aghast. He didn't say a word, but I could see it in his face. And the critic wasn't very kind to you, darling; said you were "ill-suited to the part," which meant you lacked the looks and figure for it, I suppose. We should change places. Viola bores me immoderately. But at least we are playing to good houses again, though Mamma isn't pleased by hints that Chrystal Delmont's Olivia is an attraction.

Papa doesn't seem to be giving his usual performance as the Duke; I think perhaps he is a little off colour. He has taken to walking all the way to the theatre and back, for exercise and fresh air, he says. He has always loved walking around London, as you know, but personally I think it tires him these days. Mamma doesn't worry because it doesn't affect her; she isn't appearing in *Twelfth Night*, and if she were, she certainly wouldn't walk all the way to the Strand! Papa kept her out of the production by insisting that she had been working too hard and needed a prolonged rest, and that overcame all her rage about Chrystal replacing her as Olivia (but can you *imagine* my darling mamma lumbering on as the Duke's willowy light-o'-love?). Personally, I don't think overwork had anything to do with the state she was in. That was due to recent events, which is hardly surprising, and on top of them came her darling Gavin's runaway marriage with you. Poor dear, I thought she would never get over *that* shock.

Clementine then switched, in her inconsequential fashion, to other things: the Gaiety, as ever, was flourishing, and its girls were increasingly the rage, and she wouldn't mind being one herself:

. . . so much less demanding than acting, with no lines to learn except a few silly songs, and half the men in London at your feet just for looking pretty, wearing lovely gowns, showing your shoulders and as much of your bosom as you dare, and displaying a shapely calf every now and then, though Evie Greene goes a great deal further than that in *Les Merveilleuses*, with a skirt slit in the front higher than her thigh (or at least to the top of it) and held together only with crisscrossed pearls, and a *gorgeous* garter just below the knee—brazen, Mamma says, but I don't agree. Why shouldn't a woman with legs like hers show every inch of them, and more, not to mention her bosom, so exposed that every time Louis Bradfield leans over her shoulder you can see him looking down it. People are *packing* in, my dear; the more a woman shows of her body, the better the houses these days, I'm told. As for the Empire and the Alhambra, they continue to make more money than all the other theatres in London put together, but by even more profitable means (though it is rumored that the Alhambra may lose its dancing licence ere long). Meanwhile, at the Boswell, I must hide my legs with doublet and thigh-length boots when posing at Cesario, with a tunic coming right down to the top of them, and again with voluminous gowns as Viola. I do wish Papa were not so straightlaced about these things. I also feel that my necklines as Viola could be a little more revealing (in fact, a great deal more so), but you know what a stickler Papa is for everything being strictly in period.

However, I am enjoying life very much indeed in other ways, but with whom I am *not* going to tell you. There, now—that has set you guessing, hasn't it?

Magnus? Could it really be Magnus? I don't know why I immediately thought of him, except that I could still recall that moment when he first set eyes on her. Nor could I really understand why the idea of Clementine playing fast and loose with his affections was so painful, except that because of his kindness to myself and my mother I could not bear to think of him being hurt—which, with Clementine, he was very likely to be.

Resolutely I turned to the final paragraph of her lengthy epistle, which proved to be the most startling:

My dear, guess whom I have news of? Durbridge. He has not been seen around London since he blotted his social copybook by failing to fulfil his duties as a host at Romano's, but would you believe it, he is actually living quietly in the country! I could scarcely credit it when Penelope Driscoll told me. She had been visiting her aunt in Berkshire, and Durbridge has a country house nearby, between Sonning and Reading. The interesting thing is that he has been living like a recluse since he went there—for a rest, he has now put out, though I doubt the truth of that. Papa has always called him an unsavoury character (which makes him all the more interesting, of course). My guess is that he suddenly departed for the country because he was up to something, which means that I suspect he didn't go alone. Penelope's aunt says all sorts of strange people are his guests down there (*what* kind, I wonder!) and sometimes he shuts himself off from local society in this way, and not even his servants talk about what goes on. Penelope's aunt's butler knows Durbridge's man, Stacey, and says he is as close as a clam. All very strange, don't you think? But it is quite true, nonetheless, because dear Penelope actually saw Durbridge in person. It was at the opening meet of the Berkshire Hunt, and to everyone's surprise, he wasn't participating, even though he is MFH. He did put in an appearance, but only in his carriage, in which he sat with a rug over his knees, greeting people and partaking of the stirrup cup even though he wasn't riding. Some said he had been ill. . . .

I sat very still when I finished the letter, then folded it carefully and put it in my reticule. I don't know why I didn't face Gavin with the news. It was a golden opportunity to tell him that I had been right and he wrong, that it *had* been Durbridge sitting in that stage box at the Victoria Theatre, Reading, and he could not have been dead when my husband and the manservant conveyed him from the theatre to the safety of his home. So what had prompted Stacey to announce that a doctor had confirmed his death? Could it possibly have been on Durbridge's orders, and if so, why?

Perhaps I was silenced by fear and the knowledge that if the man had sustained serious injuries, as he must have done, my mother and I were responsible, and unless I kept the news to myself, she, as well as I, would be haunted by the memory of him and the dread of his retaliation. Hadn't I known instinctively that this man was to be a menace in our lives?

19

Gavin said, "You're very quiet. You haven't spoken a word since we pulled out of Crewe, and here we are at Colwyn Bay. Wake up, my love."

Colwyn Bay—another number-two date on a tour which I had foolishly expected to be number ones, but how *could* I have expected such a thing with such a show as this? I was rapidly losing my naivete.

I dragged myself to my feet and took the valise Gavin handed down to me. I wondered what the lodgings would be like this time; clean, I hoped. Only three more bookings to fulfill, then home.

The lodgings turned out to be better than most. Our sitting room even had a view of the bay, which was nicer to look at than the garish cabbage-rose wallpaper. I sat beside the window, chin in hand, until my husband said from behind me, "There was something in that letter, wasn't there? Who was it from, and what did it say?"

I turned and looked at him then, wondering how to tell him and how to begin, but he saved me the trouble by reaching for my reticule and calmly taking the letter out.

I waited silently whilst he read. He looked amused by the references to Magnus Steel, and irritated by those about himself.

"Surely you don't heed Clementine's prattle? Is that what worried you—her claim that I am not the saint I should be?"

"No," I said. "Read to the end."

I watched his face when he reached the important part. I saw incredulity, but no concern. When he had finished he said, "Unbelievable, but good news, of course. At least your mother was not responsible for the man's death, which is a relief." He folded the letter and handed it back, smiling good-naturedly. "Now you can say 'I told you so' and enjoy it. You were right and I was wrong, but the fact that the man is alive is splendid. Now we can both forget him."

"Can we? The thought of him being alive frightens me."

"Why, in heaven's name?"

"He might be vindictive. I think he is that kind of a man. I don't trust him."

"Nonsense. Do you think he would want anyone to know what he was up to that night? Knowing that *you* know, he is likely to be more afraid of you than you need be of him."

"But he came to the opening night in Reading and made sure I saw him. He leaned toward me from the stage box so that I couldn't miss him. Why, I wonder, and how did he know we were performing there?"

"That's obvious. Living near Reading, as he apparently does, he saw the billboards, or the advertisements in the local press."

"And would a man accustomed to London theatres patronise a provincial one like that?"

"If he were buried in the country and had been unable to enjoy any social life, very possibly. And don't forget, our names would attract him. Particularly yours."

"That is what I'm afraid of. As you point out, *I* know the truth about him."

"But you are married to me. Doesn't that make you feel safe?"

"He doesn't know of our marriage—how can he?—and would it make any difference to such a man? No wonder my father disliked and mistrusted him. He has always been very shrewd."

"Not in human relationships. He didn't handle his own very well. Nor is he being very shrewd where the Boswell Theatre is concerned these days."

I retorted defensively, "You underrate him. He is aware of all that goes on in the theatrical world." I had been about to add my father's comments about the newly formed Shaftesbury Productions, then thought better of it. I was learning that it was unwise to antagonise my husband.

Harrogate, Derby, Bedford, and we were home; all were number-two dates, but all played to packed houses and Gavin was well pleased with the financial results of our first tour. For my part, I was so glad to see an end to it that all I could say was, "In that case, perhaps the proceeds will finance something more worthwhile."

It was a bad homecoming and I knew the fault lay with me. I knew I should be the soul of discretion and compliment my husband on his success, but I could not. He had been wasted in the trivial hero part, but had been content. Gavin would be content with anything which yielded a good financial profit, and it was useless to blind myself to the fact. Remembering that this sort of thing was purely a means to an end, the end being actor-managership of his own theatre, did little to comfort me, because it would take many such tours to achieve it. When he answered shortly, "You are tired, my love. I recommend an early night," I made no demur and went to bed. He would dine at the Interval Club, he said, and left as soon as he had changed.

I was certainly tired. The short journey from Bedford to London had been taken at a snail's pace, the lackadaisical Sunday train stopping at every station and every junction, collecting and disgorging goods. Actors were never so important as the Sunday deliveries of fish, and the cast had parted company without any lingering farewells. The round of the agents would start again tomorrow morning and the intimacy of ten weeks' touring was severed with ease, a fact which all the "dears" and "darlings" and affectionate protestations of keeping in touch could not disguise. No one really cared if the future held no reunions; the only important thing was to get into another show as quickly as possible and pray for a lengthy run.

After my husband had departed, I settled down to sleep, but, tired as I was, it eluded me. I lit a candle and went into the living room to choose a book, and was running my finger along the shelves when Clementine arrived.

"I saw in *The Era* that your tour ended this week," she said without preamble, walking in before I could even invite her to, and settling herself in an armchair beside the fire as if she were already familiar with the place. "Where is Gavin?"

"Dining out."

"Neglecting you already?" She softened the taunt with a teasing smile, but her glance didn't overlook my nightwear. "Forgive me for calling late, but I thought you would still be up."

"I planned to read in bed."

She screwed up her nose at the book. "Poor company, darling. . . ." She shed her cloak of silver-grey vigogne, trimmed with darker grey passementerie and dull red velvet, revealing a matching velvet gown beneath, and then, peeling off long silk gloves of silver grey, insisted that she wasn't going to stay longer than a minute and promptly settled well into the chair so that I knew she was established there for at least an hour. "I was desperate to escape from the house. Papa is dining with dear old Bramwell at his home in Glebe Place, and I invented the excuse of driving over to collect him because Mamma is at her most maudlin tonight, harping on the impossibility of finding good dressers these days, but refusing to admit the truth—that she misses Trudy because none has come up to her. No less than three, my dear, since the pair of you walked out of the house!''

She was taking out a cigarette holder at least twelve inches long and inserting a thin cigarette.

''You're not shocked, are you, Lucy dear? Women are even smoking in public nowadays, at any rate they are in the Savoy Restaurant after dinner, however much the dear old queen might disapprove. It is quite *comme il faut*, believe me. Rumour has it that Princess Alexandra indulges in private, but I didn't come here to talk about the Marlborough House Set; I came to hear all about your tour. It must have been great fun after the dreary old Boswell.''

''Great fun indeed,'' I agreed wryly.

''All that freedom—how I envy you!''

''On the contrary, it scarcely left us any free time at all.''

''It would be freedom to *me*. Just to get away from Papa's diligent eyes would make it all worthwhile. Oh, I know theatrical digs can be squalid, Papa has warned me about that every time I have hinted at even a desire to go on tour, but *I* would stay only at the best hotels.''

''Touring actors and actresses can't afford them. Salaries correspond with the tour's grading, number ones paying more than number twos. This first Shaftesbury tour was decidedly number two.''

''Nothing will remain second class with Mamma's dear stepbrother at the helm.''

''It will with plays like *Bedtime Frills*.''

''I would pin my faith on Gavin, if I were you. He is nothing if not ambitious.'' Conversation threatened to flag then, and she continued hastily, as if clutching at a useful topic with which to prolong her visit, ''You haven't asked how our current production is going.''

''I read about it in *The Era*, so I know it is playing to good houses. I'm glad.''

''Good ones?'' She shrugged. ''Satisfactory, I suppose, in view of the fact that Papa isn't giving the performance he used to. Some critics even hinted that he should step down in favour of Bramwell, but the dear man wouldn't surrender his throne unless he dropped dead. You know Papa.''

I used to know him, I thought with sadness. *There used to be a secret communion between Nevill Boswell and myself, and I am the one who broke it, the one who turned away.*

''You are not very hospitable, Lucinda. Don't you know the duties of a hostess? Aren't you going to offer me a glass of wine?''

Clementine still had the ability to make me feel gauche at times. I answered with a touch of defiance, ''I thought you said you were only staying a minute,'' but I rose hastily, all the same, and fetched a decanter.

"Oh, Papa and Bramwell won't finish their after-dinner cigars and brandy for ages yet. Only one glass? Are you not joining me?"

"Not just now. I was on my way to bed."

"If that is a hint for me to depart, I'll take it when I have finished this. Being Gavin's wine, it is sure to be good. He keeps an excellent cellar."

If she wanted me to ask how she knew, she was disappointed. Somehow I felt there was a motive behind this visit, but could not imagine what.

I glanced through the window while she sipped her wine, which she appeared to be in no hurry to finish, and saw the Boswell carriage at the pavement and Curtis on his box. He was as handsome as ever and wore his uniform well, but there had always been something about him which worried me—a boldness, a self-confidence amounting almost to arrogance.

"So you still have Curtis," I remarked idly.

"What do you mean, 'have' him?" Her tone seemed defensive, but I paid little heed because I had seen a man pause beside the carriage and speak to the coachman, who removed his hat respectfully as they talked. I recognised Nevill Boswell's figure even from this height and said, over my shoulder, "Did your father know you were coming here?"

"Of course not. I came merely to kill time before going round to Bramwell's house; I thought it would be a pleasant surprise for Papa, having me to drive home with—and of course it was a good opportunity to see how you and Gavin were."

"Well," I answered, dropping the curtain and rejoining her, "you will be saved the trouble of going to Glebe Place, because Sir Nevill is coming to this door right now."

I was shocked when I saw him. In a matter of weeks he had lost weight. There was even a faint stoop to his shoulders which had never been there before.

"I have told Curtis to take you straight home," he said to Clementine. "I shall walk or take a cab. I came to talk to Lucinda."

Her raised eyebrows clearly asked why she should be excluded.

"I have also told Curtis that if he doesn't deliver you back to Portman Square by the shortest possible route, there will be trouble. Furthermore, I shall check on the time of your return. Hawkins is on duty tonight."

She burst out pettishly, "I am not a child and I won't be spied on!"

"Then don't give me cause. I had no idea you were going out alone tonight."

"Calling on Lucinda and Gavin—do you consider that going out alone?"

He sighed. "I am sorry, my dear, but London is no place for respectable women to take solitary drives in at night, even in private carriages."

"Curtis would protect me, and in any case, I intended to travel back with you. In fact, the object of my journey was to call for you at Bramwell's house and give you the pleasure of my company on your way home."

He softened. "That was thoughtful of you, my dear."

She pouted prettily. "And I was so lonely and bored, Papa, with Mamma in one of her 'moods.'" There was a hint of tears now, and his heart melted completely. Patting her shoulder, he murmured, "There, there . . . I didn't mean to be harsh. I will see you down to the carriage."

He picked up her discarded cloak; it hung beautifully from her shoulders and she displayed it well. Clementine seemed to grow more lush every day, a riper and riper peach for men to pluck. The thought shamed me and I bade her goodnight with extra affection by way of atonement, thanking her for coming and saying how sorry Gavin would be to have missed her.

"*Dear* Gavin," she cooed, "give him my love."

When he had seen her safely into the carriage and watched it drive away, my father returned and said, "I want to discuss something important, something which concerns you and me alone. I knew your husband was out because Bramwell's son returned from the Interval Club and mentioned seeing him there, well settled in with cronies. That should give us plenty of uninterrupted time."

He accepted some wine and settled in Clementine's vacated chair, then asked how the tour had gone and if I had enjoyed it.

"Enjoyed?" I mulled over the word. "No, I cannot honestly say that I enjoyed it."

"I didn't think you would. Touring is a hard life. It can even be really harsh for a young woman unaccustomed to its squalid side. Of course, were she appearing in a worthwhile production, playing a worthwhile part, that would make up for a lot."

I nodded, saying nothing.

"I don't imagine that was so in your case. I have read about the play."

"It was . . . good experience," I said, compelled by loyalty to my husband, but Nevill Boswell's discerning eye made me feel he saw right into my mind and knew I was being defensive for that reason.

"I would agree," he answered carefully, "were it impossible for you to get good experience any other way, but it isn't. You know that, and so does Gavin Calder, but we will leave your husband out of things because what I have to say doesn't concern him. It concerns the Boswell Theatre, with which he is no longer involved. Incidentally, I have had Shaftesbury Productions investigated as far as I am able to, and they appear to be financially sound. They have money to spend on other things.''

"I know. Gavin told me. Exhibitions, for example.''

"Did he tell you what kind?''

"Art,'' I answered vaguely. "Things like that. He doesn't really know, because of course he isn't involved with that side. He is a producer, and a good one. The profitable tour proved that.''

"So he will remain with the company and expect you to do the same, but for the moment you are free of any contract, which means you are free to accept another. New productions take time to launch, and fill-ins don't grow on trees—except the wrong trees. Which is one reason why I am here, so we'll take that first. I want you to come back to the Boswell, to take over the role of Maria which I offered you. The actress I engaged was free to play it for exactly the length of time I wanted her for, which was approximately the length of your tour. A week from now she is due to start rehearsing with Irving at the Lyceum; she was signed for that before I offered her this fill-in, so you need have no fear that you are ousting anyone.'' He leaned forward. "Come back, Lucinda. Come back to the Boswell. I have been waiting for you. You know the part; Maria was included in your training long ago. Do you remember those sessions we used to have, when you performed various parts for me alone?''

Could I ever forget them, or the bond between us, as I poured out my heart with my lines? Whatever the role, however long or difficult the speech, he had been Svengali to my Trilby, drawing the best out of me, lifting me to the skies. There had been no such moments when rehearsing for *Bedtime Frills*. I had begun to hate that part even at rehearsal, but love for Gavin had made me endure it. Love for Gavin was still there, but so was my desire to be a real actress, a good actress.

"Your talent is still at its chrysalis stage, Lucinda, and you have much to learn, but the wonderful thing, to me, is that I have produced a child capable of doing so. Much as I love my other daughter, I am aware that Clementine's greatest asset is her looks. Being her father doesn't blind me to the truth about her acting ability, which will never be above average, nor to the fact that the theatre will never mean to her what it means to you. I have known that since you were children. One of the most memorable moments of my life was when you appeared for the first time as that tragic French girl. It was worth staging that unfortunate production to enjoy that brief performance of yours. I remember hearing your impassioned cry as I mounted those steps, and turning, transfixed, to look at you. There was a communion of mind between us that I have never so totally experienced onstage. Did you feel it, I wonder?''

"Yes . . . I felt it. Nor have I ever forgotten it.''

In the silent room we looked at each other for a long moment; then he said, "I am a man with faults, I know. Cowardly sometimes. A little, anyway . . ."

(*No,* I thought, *you are a human being with human weaknesses, like anybody else.*)

". . . but your mother was the real love of my life. The unfortunate thing was that I met her too late. And I cannot blame you for turning away from me when you learned the truth."

"It is all in the past now."

"Not to me. I shall atone for it when I am gone. Meanwhile, I count on you to develop your appreciation of good plays and good dramatists. Only that way will you achieve stature as an actress. Tastes change, but the real classics go on forever. There will always be audiences for Shakespeare and Sheridan and Marlowe; other playwrights will come along to join them, and lesser ones will disappear. Melodrama is rapidly reaching its end, and what is taking its place? French farces like *Bedtime Frills* and *Nightime Frolics*—have you heard of that one?—things which make money and then vanish without trace. There will always be a theatre for rubbish, but mercifully there will be a more permanent theatre for all that is finest and best. I want you to promise to fight for that, always, even after I am gone, and to keep away from all that is third-rate."

"An actress cannot pick and choose."

"*You* will be able to, one day. In this certainty I can die content."

"Don't talk of dying!"

My throat was suddenly constricted, and he touched my cheek with a gentle hand.

"Tears, Lucinda? Tears for me? But why?"

I answered with truth, "Because the very thought of losing you makes me feel desolate."

"We must all part sometime, my child, and I shall go happily if I have your promise to uphold my dreams for the Boswell Theatre. Promise that my standards will be your standards, my ambitions your ambitions. Always."

"I promise," I said. "I do promise, Father."

I saw his eyes light up and knew it was because, at last, I had called him by that name.

"I have given my word," I told Gavin. "I open as Maria a week next Monday."

"And the actress now playing her?"

"She was signed up only for this length of time."

"Cunning of Nevill. He had it all planned, of course."

"No. She was committed to another part with Irving, in rehearsal now and opening next week."

"So it all fitted in very well, and of course Nevill knew just how long a tour we had been booked for."

"These things are common knowledge. *The Era* reports them in detail."

"He was determined to get you back, because with your lack of experience, you will cost him less."

That hurt. I was learning that Gavin's tongue could hurt very much when he was angry, though I could see no reason for his anger now.

"I am sure he would not offer me the part if he felt I was unequal to it. I have never known him jeopardise a play by bad casting."

"He is jeopardising the present one, by all accounts. Everyone is saying his performance has gone off."

"Then 'everyone' is cruel. I think he is unwell."

"All the more reason for not acting. For a while, at any rate." Gavin shrugged and dismissed the whole thing. "Well, go back if you want to. It will fill in time before we go on tour again, though I see no reason for your working at all. It is something of a slight on your husband too. People will think my wife needs to earn money."

"Nonsense! Everyone knows that acting is the breath of life to people in the theatre, and when they are not acting, they are not living." I added hastily, "Not living to the full, I mean."

It was the next morning and I was about to pay my first visit to my mother's new shop in George Street. For such an occasion it was important to look my best, and I chose a Directoire redingote of light cream-réséda twill, on which a *broché* Persian design was wrought in soft colours. With it went the long vest, the wide sash, and the short broad revers which were now so fashionable, with the back and sides of the skirt in continuous princesse breadths from neck to foot, the whole outfit crowned with a Directoire hat of cream straw, with a bow beneath the brim and darker ostrich plumes nodding over the front. As I pinned it to my upswept hair I said pacifically, "Father admired the apartment. He said it was a fine advertisement for your success."

"My work will advertise my success, but I am glad he saw this place even so. And since when have you been calling him Father?"

"Since last night, officially, though I have often thought of him as such."

Gavin was not yet dressed and wore a long quilted robe over his nightshirt. There seemed to be something more than displeasure in the way he looked at me now, a pettish quality I could not understand, and against my will I asked what was wrong.

To my astonishment he said, "You were asleep when I returned last night."

"Of course. Didn't you expect me to be?"

"I expected you to make it up to me this morning. When I wakened, you were already dressed—and look at you nqw, all ready to go out."

I stared, then picked up my gloves and reticule.

"By 'making it up to you' I presume you mean by making love?"

"Of course."

I answered carefully, "We have made love in the mornings when we have wanted to, but I have never done so merely from a sense of duty or because, as a wife, I am expected to submit to your physical desire by way of atonement or to 'make up' for anything. Nor will I. The desire has to be on both sides."

"Very obviously, it was not on yours this morning. You had other things on your mind, such as your father's visit and the part he offered you. And now your mother. You seem in a hurry to get to her. Don't let me detain you."

"Gavin, this is childish. I would have gone to see Mamma last night had we not reached home so late in the day. Naturally, I want to see her as soon as possible, having been away for so many weeks."

"A mother is not so important as a husband, and let me point out that there is nothing childish about a man's need for his wife."

Instinct warned me to say no more, and yet I still could not bear to be reproached by him. I answered in a conciliatory tone, "We will be together tonight. If any 'making up' has to be done, I will do it then."

"Perhaps I shan't feel in the mood."

"In that case, I won't complain or demand my rights."

He laughed at that. "Women don't have any rights, except to look after their husbands and their homes."

"And surrender their bodies when required?" I was stung, and was suddenly remembering Helen Steel's work at the mission and her brother's campaigning booklets. I turned on my heel without a word and was halfway through the door when he called, "Sorry, my love. Go back to the Boswell by all means. It will please your father and may well stand both of us in good stead eventually." He finished on a casual note, "Did he say anything about the future?"

"The future? Only to advise me to work hard and set my standards high."

"I didn't mean in that way, but no matter. I know what the future holds, anyway—success for the pair of us in a stage partnership. Remember that. And remember that you leave the Boswell Theatre the minute we go into rehearsal for another tour."

"Not if Twelfth Night is still running. I couldn't give up a part like Maria for the kind of thing I have been playing on tour. Surely you wouldn't expect me to?"

"I expect you to tour with your husband, whatever part you are cast in and whatever the play. A husband's career must naturally come first."

"Couldn't you tour without me? It happens in the theatre, when husbands and wives can't act together."

"But *we* can. That was part of my bargain with the Shaftesbury company. Remember? Joint salary for husband and wife."

"You would still have a joint salary as actor-producer. With me in London, that could surely be enough."

"No. A bargain is a bargain. I have to stick to mine, and so do you."

I felt as if he were slipping a noose about my neck, and protested quickly, "*I* have no contract with these people."

"No, but I have, and there is a clause in it covering the husband-and-wife team. So all you have to do is make sure that a clause is included in your new contract with the Boswell, promising to release you when required. Of course, if a miracle occurs and the future offers us greater profits there, that will be different. Contracts can always be broken, option clauses opted out of somehow. Good-bye for now, my sweet. My love to your mother."

TRUDY, MODISTE occupied a small shop with a single Georgian window flanked by white louvre shutters and a white front door with a Georgian knocker of shining brass. In the window one elegant morning gown was displayed, with a matching hat adorned with sweeping osprey feathers, and long suede gloves lying casually beside them.

A bell tinkled as I entered, and a delicate whiff of perfume drifted from a bowl of malmaisons standing on a gilt table, which also displayed copies of *Les Modes, Petit Courier des Dames,* and *Journal des Demoiselles.* Two women were poring over them. They lifted their heads as I entered, and with a cry, my mother was upon me.

After embracing as if we had not seen each other for years, she stood back and surveyed me.

"You look beautiful, my darling—thinner, perhaps, which you can scarcely afford, but an elegant slimness is very desirable to display clothes well. And your taste does me credit, or does that sound conceited?"

"Conceit is something you have never had, Mamma, nor ever will. Helen!"

The other woman was waiting with a broad and welcoming smile. I would scarcely have recognised her. From being a plain and dowdy person she had become a plain and striking one. Something had happened to Helen, and it was more than the acquisition of a street costume bearing my mother's hallmark.

But the thought was fleeting; I was back to my mother again, feasting my eyes on her. She looked younger; the valiant line of her mouth, smiling determinedly at the world, had relaxed into one of contentment. She had a fulfilled look, a zest and vitality, the air of a woman occupied with living and finding every moment of it wonderful. My heart filled with so much happiness I felt it would overflow.

Nothing would content her but that she should hear every detail of these past weeks. "I know the tour was successful because I have been taking *The Era* to find out, but was the part really to your liking, my love? It sounded . . . well . . . not quite right for you."

I dodged that by demanding to hear all her news, adding that I couldn't wait to see over the premises. "And I love the decor," I added, glancing round appreciatively and hoping to hide my regret that she had seen *The Era*, because I had no desire for her to know the truth about that play. It was behind me and I wanted to forget it. I resolved to side-step any questions by resolutely sticking to events here. Her books, I learned, were rapidly filling with orders, and she was taking on a machinist and an apprentice.

"Lucky apprentice," I said, "to start with you, even if they do spend the early weeks doing no more than picking up pins and taking out tacking threads—"

"And making tea," put in Helen. "So I will be the apprentice now. . . ."

It was mid-morning and a tactful excuse to leave us alone.

"Mamma, I am so happy for you. I have never seen you look so well."

"And what of you, my darling? You are happy too? Of course you are." She swept on, giving me no chance to provide assurances; not that assurances were needed so long as I did not recall the conversation I had had with my husband before leaving, or allow myself to contemplate a future spent touring in cheap and vulgar plays.

"I have news," I said. "I am going back to the Boswell Theatre. I'm taking over the part of Maria and open a week from today. I am due for rehearsal, privately with my father, at noon, and for the rest of the week with Willard."

Her smile was radiant. Nothing made her happier than to know that I was acting with Nevill Boswell again. "And it is good to hear you call him Father." She hesitated, then asked when I had seen him.

"Last night."

"And . . . how was he?"

"Thinner, I thought, and tired. He seems to have aged suddenly. I'm sorry—perhaps I shouldn't have told you."

"I am glad you did. I wish I could see him, but of course . . ." Her shoulders rose and fell in resignation, so I knew he had not been near her again.

"Perhaps he feels he cannot call on you without an invitation."

I had been about to add that I was now in a position to convey one on her behalf and that it was up to her to let me, when Helen appeared with the tea and conversation inevitably turned to the mission, Helen saying gratefully that Trudy still found time to deal with the problem of clothes. "She works on them in the evenings and at weekends. Consequently I have more time to help Hugh."

"Hugh?"

"Dr. Maynard," Helen answered casually, turning away with a negligent air which was obviously overdone. So, I thought pleasurably, they had advanced to Christian-name terms, a significant step in this day and age. And the new bloom about her—was that attributable to something more than my mother's well-designed clothes?

I asked politely after her brother, because courtesy demanded it. Neither of them knew of my last stormy encounter with Magnus.

"How is he?" Helen echoed. "You can see for yourself. Here he comes now."

And there he was indeed, stooping from his great height as he walked through the door. There was something incongruous about a man like this in so feminine a place, but he walked in with that air of ease which went with him everywhere. I had never seen Magnus Steel appear self-conscious against any background; people had to accept him in the same way that he accepted them. But how strongly he could react to things which outraged him, such as Durbridge's interest in boys at his mission! Memory went winging back to that first encounter in Hyde Park, when I had interpreted that interest as purely altruistic. How many years ago it seemed, and how I had grown up since then! I had been fourteen—fourteen and a half, as I had proudly insisted at the time—and now I was sixteen and already married, soon to be playing at the Boswell Theatre in a much bigger role than the one I had portrayed on the night Durbridge went hurtling down the circular stairs.

I jumped to my feet. Ugly memories had no place here, and not through me must my mother be reminded of them. Nor must she learn of Durbridge's reappearance. Life was being more generous to her now than it had ever been; let it remain so. I stammered something about being late, of leaving at once, of finding a cab, and Magnus Steel said calmly, "No need. I can drive you. I called for my sister, but can return for her." And then we were outside, and standing beside the curb was the trap I remembered so well.

Climbing into it was like renewing acquaintance with an old friend, and as we bowled away I was aware that Magnus glanced sideways at me. Then he asked, in that blunt way of his, "What are you running away from, Mrs. Calder? Why the sudden desire to escape? The reason couldn't be associated with two women who love you, so it must be something on your mind, and running away won't help, because anxiety or fear accompanies a person wherever they go. It seemed to me that you suddenly recalled something you wanted to forget. What was it? What memory could upset you so much that you want to run away from it? What is wrong?''

"Nothing," I lied. "Quite the reverse. I am on my way to the Boswell Theatre to rejoin my father's company, and what could be more wonderful than that?"

He said it was splendid news, but I knew he was not deceived. My sudden desire to leave had been very obvious, but I was glad he let the matter drop.

"Does this mean you will be going on no more tours?" he asked.

"Not in the immediate future."

"I hoped you were going to say never." The words gave me a strange pang of pleasure, which immediately subsided when he added, "For your mother's sake, I mean. She misses you, Mrs. Calder."

Instantly we were back to our earlier relationship—distant, polite, poles apart—and instantly I was remembering the hints in Clementine's letter, hints that she was enjoying herself yet again in the way she liked best, and with someone new, and back came the fear that this man had at last become her lover, and this time the thought was distinctly painful.

Being back at the Boswell was wonderful. For me, the place had an atmosphere unequalled by any other theatre. I could almost sense the presence of earlier actors who had trod these boards, for many famous names had played here, some little known when first engaged by former Boswells, but achieving renown under their banner and on this very stage. To walk in their footsteps was my dream and my ambition, but even greater was a growing sense of responsibility, an awareness of the Boswell blood in my veins and the talent it had passed on to me, and the love of this theatre which it inspired. It was a heritage which demanded devotion, even though I did not bear the family name.

It was good to see everyone again. Kindly Bramwell Chambers greeted me affectionately and Chrystal Delmont was warm with her welcome; so was Willard, as proud as ever of being stage director here. Everyone, right down to Jerry the callboy, greeted me with enthusiasm.

"My, missy, but you're a sight for sore eyes, that y'are! The place ain't bin the sime wiv'art yer."

Jerry, clad in a Norfolk jacket and knickerbockers, knee-length stockings and sturdy boots, was certainly spruced up.

"You look very smart," I said. "Have you been promoted?"

He beamed. "That I 'ave! Assistant to Props, that's me now, but still callboy, o' course, an' earning ten bob a week more. Me ma ain't arf proud."

"So am I, Jerry, so am I!"

* * *

I think it was during these weeks, back at the Boswell, that I really began to grow up and to realise that one didn't become a woman merely by going to bed with a man. Life was more than the mating dance my husband had once called it. It consisted of facing up to issues, shirking nothing, working to achieve one's goals, and living every moment to the full, whether good or bad, difficult or easy. And the worthwhile things were never easy. They had to be fought for as well as prayed for, and they demanded the dedication and hard work of which my father was an example.

That he expected as much from me became abundantly clear from the moment that I took over the part of Maria, and we found mutual happiness in this hard work and dedication. I was happier onstage than anywhere else, a fact which made me almost ashamed when I returned, after a performance, to find my husband waiting up for me, or absent because he had gone to the Interval Club to seek company. He became morose, bored with idleness, resentful of my acting, and yet reminding me that he would expect me to perform at his side when the new Shaftesbury tour got under way. He never let me forget that his contract involved both of us, which made my heart sink. I hated the thought of acting away from this theatre, and, even more, the prospect of doing the rounds of second-raters in another trashy production and hearing by husband gloat because it made money.

Alternating with his difficult moods were others of supreme optimism and a certain pride in me. Sometimes he came to the theatre and watched from the wings, ignoring Willard's reminders that at the Boswell this area was out of bounds to all except actors awaiting their entrances. Other times he would be out front and, later, would criticise my performance from that angle, sometimes adversely.

"Of course, you are handicapped by Nevill's old-fashioned training, but in time we will overcome that." Or: "You are wasted in this traditional stuff, and costume drama hides that lovely body of yours. Strange, though—even in costume Clementine manages to suggest what lies beneath."

Comparisons with Clementine were more frequent than I liked, and one day I said so.

"It is useless to expect me to resemble her. She is herself and I am myself and we have never been the remotest bit alike. My father doesn't hold her up as an example, so why should you?"

"My dear love, I am doing nothing of the sort. I merely want you to make the most of yourself. As for your father, what has he in mind for you after this production? A permanent place at the Boswell? He must have plans of some sort, though I suspect they don't include your husband. He despises me for signing up with the Shaftesbury people. He resents my leaving. He thinks every actor should be proud of appearing at his theatre and be content to remain there forever, but I would only go back if he livened up his ideas. The Boswell has scope for development which he can't even see. If you ever achieve influence there—"

I laughed aloud. "Influence! *I?* Whatever do you mean by that?"

"Getting dug in there firmly."

"I thought you didn't want me to."

"I wouldn't be averse to your having an interest in the place—a financial interest, I mean. Why not? My revered stepbrother-in-law isn't likely to forget you in his will, even if only to assuage his conscience. He must die one day and leave you provided for. He has promised to. He told your mother so, remember? That could mean an income of sorts, but it could also mean much more. A share in the theatre, perhaps."

"Ridiculous. He has a wife and daughter, both actresses."

"You are his daughter and an actress too. I suspect he is gratified by your love of the place, and I must say you are playing your cards well. I am now not in the least sorry you returned. In fact, I think it a very wise move, and one day we will both be glad of it."

I protested indignantly that it wasn't any move at all and that I wasn't playing any cards, but he went straight on without seeming to hear me.

"When the day comes, be guided by me. Modernise the place, bring it up to date, get rid of that wall dividing the grand circle from the bar behind; it would open up a wide area where people could promenade."

"For the same purpose as at the Empire?" I said scathingly.

"Not necessarily. People love to display themselves and to parade their fashions. If they intermingle and drink together, it helps to swell the profits."

"And very soon the function of the promenade area would be the same as the others. That doesn't sound like the Boswell Theatre to me, and if I were in a position to oppose such an idea, I would. Not that I am ever likely to be. I am an actress at the start of her career, a member of the company, no more, and you have made it clear I must cease to be that."

"Only temporarily. Once we make money in the provinces, we can return to London permanently and do whatever we want to do. You can act at the Boswell for the rest of your life, if that is your ambition. You know you will always be able to go back, you know he will always have you. Take my advice, my love, and keep on the right side of him, as you are doing."

Conversations like this made me uneasy. I found myself incapable of reading my husband's mind. Even in our most intimate moments that feeling of oneness seemed to be lost, so that we were merely two bodies cohabiting, and sometimes, when we had finished and he turned away from me, I would lie there feeling I had merely been used and that something beautiful which had meant a lot to me was fading, and fading very fast.

But happiness came back when I was acting, particularly in scenes with my father, when that mental communion would spring between us again and everything and everyone faded into the background. At these moments life pulsated only here, on this well-trod stage, and it seemed as if all the generations of actors who had gone before were watching and applauding, and I would see the tired droop lift from Nevill Boswell's shoulders and hear life come back into his voice, and it would seem as if it were I who took the lead now and he who followed, almost gratefully. At those moments his eyes revealed an inexpressible gladness and I knew it was because we were together in this scene. Simultaneously, I knew that without me he could not have got through it, and that was frightening, because long before anyone else suspected it, I was aware that my father would not be acting much longer, and that he was aware of it too.

Time took on a feeling of urgency. I felt it important to bring my parents together, and so I took him to see my mother. The three of us frequently had tea together after that, and following these meetings, my father and I would drive to the theatre in a hansom cab, and I am sure he shared my gladness that Bernadette was not appearing in this production because we were now able to meet and talk freely offstage. Clementine, whose dressing room was always filled with admirers, was much too busy to spare time for her father, and had she been aware that during the intervals I often sat talking with him, she would not have cared. Accepting me as "her father's bastard," as she put it, had been extraordinarily easy for Clemmy, who begrudged nothing so long as she was deprived of nothing herself and was left alone to enjoy life in her own way. People were only irksome to her if they put obstacles in her path or became possessive or demanding. When that happened, she discarded them, and at discarding people, no one was quite so adept as Clementine. Rejected lovers smarted beneath her treatment, but were powerless to withstand it. Reproaches or pleas or attempts at retaliation glanced off her. Sometimes I feared for her, but she never feared for herself.

One day, after visiting my mother, Nevill Boswell said, "It is good to see Trudy looking so happy, so content. This is what she should have had long ago. Money and independence help a woman to maintain her pride. I know you think I treated her badly, but at the time, to keep her near me—you also—seemed the most important thing. But I have told you this before."

"And made up for it now, so let us not talk about the past."

"All the same, I would like to have been the one to establish her as she is now established, but she would never accept more from me. The most I have been able to do, as you know, is to provide for her after my death, when she will be unable to refuse it. In fact, I have made her promise not to. Even so, I can't help feeling envious of whoever set her up in those premises. It makes me feel . . . usurped." He moved uncomfortably. "I suppose I have no right to ask, but is there another man?"

We were driving to the theatre, and in the shadowy cab he did not see my start of surprise. I stammered the truth—that there was no man in my mother's life—but my speculation was wild. If not Nevill Boswell, then who had been my mother's benefactor, coming to her aid so providentially at a time when she most needed it and most deserved it? I could think of only one person, because she had only one other friend. Or two friends. I hoped it was the pair of them jointly, because I had no wish to be under an obligation to a man who had openly condemned my husband for marrying me in secret, and me for agreeing to it.

And so these weeks at the Boswell Theatre slipped by, filled with happiness, until Gavin announced that the right play had been found to follow *Bedtime Frills* His exuberance depressed me, because I knew that ahead lay a struggle I did not want. Nothing would induce me to abandon my father now, but to voice the reason for it was something I could not do. For his sake, I had to join in the pretence that nothing threatened the end of his stage career, but my reason for refusing to give up the part of Maria was not based solely on that, but—and this, I knew, would matter even more to him—on my love of the part, my love of the play, and my love of his theatre.

So I said no to Gavin. "I will not come with you on tour. I will not leave the Boswell Theatre, now or ever."

I anticipated stormy scenes, but there were none. He merely shrugged and turned aside.

"As you wish, but when the end comes, don't come snivelling to me, begging for a part. No one is irreplaceable, remember."

As always, my father was intuitive where I was concerned.

"Something is wrong, Lucinda. Tell me what it is."

We were driving back from the theatre. He had fallen into the habit of taking me home by cab, leaving the carriage for Clementine, but because this was a precious half-hour to both of us, I could not spoil it by telling him of my difference with Gavin.

I should have known his intuition would be stronger than my will.

"Your husband wants you to leave the Boswell—is that it? I guessed this would come. Why else did you ask for that release clause in your contract? You would never have thought of it for yourself; it had to be prompted by someone else, and the obvious person was Gavin, who needs you even more than I do. Oh, yes, he does, my dear, so don't look so surprised. I know how that man's mind works. I know what motivates him. Have you given him your answer?''

"Yes."

"And he is displeased? Good. That means you have given him the answer he doesn't want, and *that* means the answer I prayed for."

He sighed a little, and in the passing light of a streetlamp I saw his eyes close. He looked very frail tonight, almost fragile, but he also looked at peace, as if he had at last accomplished a mission and could now rest.

20

I heard the news in the worst possible way—from a newsboy shouting in the street and placards proclaiming: DEATH OF EMINENT ACTOR and SIR NEVILL BOSWELL DIES IN SLEEP.

It was the following day and I was crossing the south side of Trafalgar Square toward the Strand. I had a matinee this afternoon and, like my father, I enjoyed walking to the theatre, even though the route was long— from the Chelsea Embankment to Sloane Square and Eaton Place, round by Buckingham Palace, up the Mall, and into the Square. I had crossed over to Nelson's Column when I heard the newsboy and saw the placards beside one of Landseer's lions and stumbled to a halt, stunned by shock.

This was the first time death had ever touched me, the first time I had lost someone close to me, and although I had known instinctively that my father was nearing the end of his career, I had refused to believe it meant the end of his life, or to accept what I knew, in my heart, he had himself accepted. I still refused to, every instinct screaming denial.

Through numbed senses I heard the newsboy shouting, "*Read all abaht it! Read all abaht it!*" The sound seemed to come from a long way off and yet was deafening. Somewhere a hurdy-gurdy was playing. "*Daisy, Daisy, give me your answer do, I'm half-crazy, all for the love of you . . . Dee-dah, dee-dee-dah, dee-dah-dah . . .*" The notes jangled in my ears and mingled with the newsboy's shouts and the melancholy cries of pigeons wheeling overhead from Nelson's cockaded hat and empty sleeve. I tried to move, and could not, and the newsboy's voice yelled on, "*Actor dead, famous actor dead, read all abaht it!*" and the hurdy-gurdy changed its tune: "*Oh, I do like to be beside the seaside, I do like to be beside the sea . . .''* I saw ragamuffins dancing in time to it, and a detached corner of my mind, clutching at anything in a hopeless attempt to reject the truth, thought how terrible it was that despite these past years of social reform, children still ran barefoot in the streets of London.

Then my body jerked to life. *Mother!* I had to go to her at once. I stepped blindly off the kerb and straight in front of approaching hooves. The vehicle wheeled to avoid me, then reined to a halt. I heard a man's voice, but I paid no heed, scrambling back onto the pavement without any sense of direction, because the whole world was suddenly a blur.

The man's voice came again, right beside me.

"Lucinda!"

Through my tears I saw Magnus Steel looking down at me from his great height.

Without hesitation and without thought I flung myself against him, sobbing noiselessly, and his arms went about me. Neither of us was aware of sidelong glances or disapproving stares. Then he picked me up bodily and placed me in the ever-welcome, ever-friendly trap, after which he climbed in beside me and gathered up the reins.

"I passed the theatre as I came along the Strand. There was a board up, cancelling today's performances, and of course I knew why. I had seen the newsbills when I left the mission, and bought a paper at once." We were bowling along Cockspur Street now, heading to the West End. "I didn't bother to call at the theatre, judging that you would either have been and gone, or would be on your way there now. I know you always walk if weather permits, so I kept an eye open for you, hoping we would meet and that I wouldn't have to visit Calder's flat, though I would have had no hesitation about doing so."

I felt he was talking deliberately and for a purpose, and for that I was grateful.

"I intended to fetch you to your mother," he went on. "She will need you, so I'll take you to her now. That is what you want, isn't it?"

How did he know? And did he guess that my need for her was as great as hers must be for me? I didn't even think of my husband or feel the urge to go to him, but later, remembering this, I knew the reason. Gavin would never understand as this man understood, because Gavin hadn't the slightest idea of how much Nevill Boswell had meant to me, not only as a person and the man my mother had loved, but as the man I had at last been able to call by the name of Father. To Gavin, he had merely been the owner of the Boswell Theatre and a man whose affection for me should be traded on. But none of this occurred to me until later. As Magnus drove me to his house, tactfully avoiding the south side of Portman Square and the shuttered windows of number 47 so that no reminder should distress me further, my thoughts were solely with my mother and my own terrible sense of loss.

* * *

I soon learned a tragic truth—that women like my mother, who cannot be openly loved, cannot openly show their sorrow. They must mourn in secret. Not even my husband comprehended this when he called at the Steels' house much later that day, annoyed because I had not returned home immediately, and even more annoyed because I had sent him a belated note informing him of my whereabouts, and delivered by Magnus's man, Barker.

"The very least you could have done," he reproached, "was to come with me to see Bernadette. After all, you are my wife. To have to visit her alone and make apologies for your neglect was the outside of enough. At such a time, a widow needs the comfort of her relatives."

"Comfort Bernadette! *Me*? And since when has she regarded me as a relative? Apart from the fact that I would not be welcome in her house, *I* would not welcome the thought of going there. My only thought was, and still is, for my mother, and I shall stay with her for as long as she needs me. I sent that note merely to let you know my whereabouts and to spare you anxiety. I shall be unendingly grateful to Magnus for bringing me to her at once."

"But Trudy isn't Boswell's widow. She was nothing but his mistress, and years ago at that."

I flung back, "They loved each other! To the day of his death they loved each other. Don't you *understand*? Can't you even comprehend her grief? She never married because she loved no man but him."

"Very touching, I'm sure, but the fact remains that poor Bernadette is his bereaved wife and the pair of them hurt her deeply. You can't expect me to sympathise with a woman who virtually wrecked their marriage."

"My mother did nothing of the sort. In fact, *she* was the one who suffered most, and in silence too."

He answered curtly, "She was looked after. She was given steady employment and a roof over her head, and she knows she is remembered in his will—an added humiliation for my poor stepsister."

"For a man who has never displayed anything but private ridicule for 'his poor stepsister,' I find this sudden compassion unconvincing." Pain and anger forced the words out of me. "And since your concern for her is so great, I suggest you go back to her at once and leave my mother and me to comfort each other."

"Or to speculate on the material benefits likely to accrue from his death?"

Inflamed, I struck out at him blindly, only to have my wrist seized and forced behind my back. He held it there, so tightly that I was unable to break free.

"Don't you ever try to do that again, Lucinda. And now get your outdoor things—I am taking you home, and tomorrow you will offer your respects and condolences to Bernadette."

He dropped my wrist and I was rubbing at it and trying ineffectively to check my tears when the door opened and Magnus walked in. He looked from one to the other of us, a brief and comprehensive glance which took in Gavin's anger and my pain, although his inscrutable eyes revealed nothing.

He said politely, "I am glad you have come to see your wife. At a time like this, she needs your understanding, so I am sure you will appreciate her need to remain with her mother." He was holding the door open significantly. "Rest assured she is more than welcome in my house, and my sister and I will do all we can for both of them."

Gavin gave his consent grudgingly. "Very well, she may stay for a while, but I shall expect her home at the earliest opportunity, and most certainly for the funeral." At the door, a thought struck him and he turned back to me. "On the other hand, perhaps it would be wiser if you didn't attend that. It will be trying enough for Bernadette without public reminder of her husband's infidelity. The press is sure to be there and there might be curiosity and speculation; I understand rumours have already been flying around at the Boswell Theatre and elsewhere. And then, of course, there will be the reading of the will, in which you were given to understand you would be a beneficiary. . . ."

I choked, "I couldn't attend that, either, and nor could my mother, I know."

"To be frank, my love, I cannot imagine Nevill's lawyers being so tactless as to ask for the attendance of either of you, so I will bring any news to you after the reading. Naturally I shall be there, as his widow's nearest relative."

"Please . . . I don't want to hear anything about it."

Magnus cut in quickly, "In such an event, Calder, the solicitors will notify your wife, and I suggest you leave such matters to them."

After that, all I heard was the shutting of the front door.

The news came the day after the funeral. I was still with my mother, although she had urged me to return home, insisting that I must put my marriage first. She seemed to have shrunk these past days, looking as pale and fragile as a piece of delicate porcelain. Even so, she said—quite unaware of Gavin's lack of sympathy—"Your husband is being very patient and I promise you that I shall be all right. Life goes on and one has to go on with it, which is what Nevill would wish me to do. And you can see for yourself how occupied I am. Work is always a salvation. It will be yours also. You must get back to the theatre. It reopens next week, does it not?"

I nodded, guessing that Bramwell Chambers would take over the lead as he had sometimes done in the past, and that there would be much reorganisation, but of what kind I could not speculate. If Bernadette had inherited full control, which seemed inevitable, I guessed well enough that she would not include me in the company. I also knew that under her management the theatre would not long survive. I had given no thought to what would happen in that event, but now the question loomed large, and it seemed likely that the future would hold no more for me than a return to touring.

So the news Gavin brought, immediately following the reading of the will, stunned me. He called when Magnus was out, and it was Helen who announced his arrival. He was waiting in the first-floor drawing room, tense with excitement, and the face he turned to me was smiling broadly. He didn't even pause for greeting, but burst out, "You've done it, Lucinda! *You've done it!* My God, but you're a clever girl and I *am* proud of you!"

He seized me then and waltzed me about the room, laughing and exultant, holding me so tightly I could scarcely breathe.

"I couldn't wait to get to you, my love. Bernadette is beside herself, of course, but Clemmy is pleased, as well she might be, though I suspect half and half isn't wholly to her liking. Still, I have my own ideas about how to go to work on her. . . . You will have to pretend you are surprised, of course, to everyone but me."

He kissed me soundly, still giving me no chance to speak, and raced on: "You played your cards better than I expected, sweetheart, and I did you an injustice when wondering if you were really after nothing more than acting with the company—"

"Gavin, *please!* I don't know what you are talking about!"

"Of course you do. My darling, I underestimated you, really I did. You must forgive me for that, *and* for the misunderstanding last time I called. Now I realise why you really kept out of sight these past days—a good ploy, my sweet, and totally convincing. Everyone was surprised, and I did my best to appear so, but it was hard to conceal my gratification, because I thought at one time that he might have changed . . . I mean, I thought he might have cut you out . . ."

My husband seemed to be talking incoherently and was suddenly conscious of it, because he laughed and said, "If I am not making sense, bear with me and put it down to excitement. What I am trying to say is that I did feel there was a risk, when we eloped, that his Victorian prudery might have jeopardised his plans for you. Prudery!" Gavin laughed again. "A man who keeps a mistress and sires a bastard can hardly be accused of prudery, but you know how he liked to preserve his good name. Even so, he went ahead with his plans, thank God."

I managed to break in. "I can't even follow you. If only you would tell me what you are talking about!"

"Oh, come, Lucinda, don't pretend with me. You were perfectly aware that Nevill was providing for you."

I nodded. My mother had told me that long ago; my father also. But I had never speculated or wondered, or even hoped for much. Now, from my husband's wild excitement, I knew that Nevill Boswell had been more generous than I could have anticipated, but the full extent came as such a shock that I could only sit down weakly when I heard, saying, "I don't believe it . . . I don't understand . . . I don't believe it—!"

"Then let me repeat it, and listen carefully. You inherit joint ownership of the Boswell Theatre with your half-sister, Clementine. 'To my natural child, Lucinda Grainger, daughter of Miss Gertrude Grainger, I leave an equal share in the ownership of the Boswell Theatre with my legitimate daughter, Clementine, either of whom may dispose of the said share should she so wish, though I trust that neither will ever have the desire to do so.' Bless the man, he hadn't changed a word of it and the fact that you are now Lucinda Calder makes no difference. Your name was Grainger when the will was drawn up; that will is still valid, and you are still known professionally as Lucinda Grainger, *and* you are the daughter of Gertrude Grainger, so there can be no disputing it."

I cut in quickly, "What do you mean, 'he hadn't changed a word of it'? That sounds as if you knew already."

He laughed, then nodded with an assumed air of guilt.

"Well, to be honest, sweetheart, I did. He made that will years ago, and I saw it on his desk, entirely by chance. There it was, lying open, his signature scarcely dry. I didn't read it deliberately, of course. His lawyer had just left, and I happened to go into Nevill's study to look for him a minute or two later. He had gone downstairs to see the man off—and there the thing was, witnessed by a couple of clerks the lawyer had brought along with him—"

"So you read that far, right to the end!"

"Well, darling, I couldn't help just *seeing*. . . . Nevill wasn't too pleased when he came back and found me there, but of course I never let on that I had glimpsed a thing, much less that very important clause."

Memory went speeding back over the years. I was a small girl pausing outside that study door, arrested by Sir Nevill's angry voice and marvelling because I had rarely heard it raised in anger. "*What the devil are you doing at my desk?*" And then the young Gavin Calder's apologetic laughter and his excuse about looking for a missing script. . . .

* * *

I heard myself saying, "So that was how you learned the truth about my birth."

"Lord, no! I guessed that long ago. It's easy enough to put two and two together unless you are the wife of a faithless husband. They are always the last to suspect."

"But you knew of this bequest when you married me."

Gavin was indignant. "Is that an implication? What kind of a man do you take me for?" He sounded hurt, insulted. "Are you suggesting that I had your legacy in mind and married you because of it? If so, you are very much mistaken. I had forgotten it entirely until the will was read today. My God, it's years since the thing was drawn up! Do you seriously imagine I could remember what was in it after all this time?"

"You remembered just now. 'He hadn't changed a word of it,' you said."

"Well, naturally, I recalled the wording when I heard the will read out, but not until then. Besides, what difference does it make? I am delighted for you, not for myself. It doesn't affect *me* in any way. I am all set now as a producer and lead actor, so why should I want more? For you, it is different. You haven't a penny of your own, other than your irregular earnings as an actress. You have never had security in your life, but now you have something even more valuable. You have power, and sharing it with Clementine only means that you will have to shoulder most of it because she is so empty-headed she won't know what to do with the theatre anyway. You must aim to buy her out at the first opportunity; meanwhile, she will go along with our plans, because she hasn't the brains or the imagination to do anything else."

"Our plans?" I echoed, with a slight emphasis on the first word.

"Yours, then, but influenced by me. You will need guidance, and I can give it to you. I am more experienced in the theatre than you are. I know the ropes. What's more, you will need someone to back you up when Bramwell Chambers tries to interfere."

"Bramwell?"

"Oh, I forgot to tell you . . . my revered stepbrother-in-law conceived the odd notion of rewarding his lifelong friend with a minor investiture as a so-called 'adviser' on the theatre board. We mustn't begrudge the gesture, tiresome as it may be."

"I don't begrudge it. I am glad of it. It will be good to have Bramwell to lean on."

"You will have *me* to lean on. I shall be there, in the background; not thrusting myself forward, you know I would never do that, but supporting you in whatever you do."

"And what part is Bernadette to take in things?"

"None at all, heaven be praised, but she is more than well provided for; a substantial income, plus that house across the square, with an established fund to cover its running and maintenance forever. There is also a stipulation that she shall continue to act at the Boswell Theatre for so long as she wishes to and whenever there are suitable parts for her.'' He smiled meaningfully. ''All you need do to keep her from under your feet is to make sure there are not any suitable parts. Cast her in a difficult role, and without her husband's support she will fail; *then* she'll be willing enough to slip into a life of leisured ease. No doubt she will weep a bit when it happens, sigh for her dear dead husband, then fade out tearfully, feeling sorry for herself but not really missing Nevill at all, because she will still be a wealthy woman. Your mother won't be badly off either, thanks to all that insurance Nevill carried, and investments which no one knew anything about. No wonder he could afford to put on a shaky revival every now and then.''

''I won't play tricks on Bernadette. My father wouldn't wish it. She will be able to play Lady Macbeth and many other parts for a long time yet.''

''Of course, darling, if it's your intention to continue with Shakespeare. But remember, it will be up to you to make that theatre *pay*, and you won't have additional resources to fall back on if you fail. It is money you must aim for, not prestige.''

There was one further surprise when official confirmations came to my mother and to me from the Boswell-family lawyers, though to me it was really no surprise at all. The firm was not Messrs. Peabody, Wainright & Waring of Lincoln's Inn Fields, who had earlier deposited the sum of one thousand pounds with Coutts Bank in her name, on the instructions of an anonymous client, but a company called Huxtable & Bailey, of Raymond Buildings, Gray's Inn, who had, I learned later from Gavin, acted for the Boswell family ever since that legal firm had been established in 1834, and at no time had the Boswells used any other.

''Perhaps dear Nevill did on that one occasion, to avoid any advice or comments from the family firm,'' my mother speculated. ''Obviously, he wanted it to be kept secret, to avoid awkwardness during his lifetime.''

I said nothing, but I had my own suspicions about the earlier gesture, and resolved to act on it as soon as I could afford to. Meanwhile, life took over, the first event being a visit from Clementine a day or two later. I had returned to the Chelsea flat that morning. Magnus had driven me across London and I parted from him with regret, sorry the past few days were over, for in the friendliness of his house I had been happy, but when I tried to thank him, he had brushed it aside.

''It was our happiness to have you. It is always good to have you near, Lucinda.''

The words, and the warm sensation they left, lingered with me when he had gone. I was glad Gavin was out. I wanted to be alone, to readjust, to be quiet for a while, and Clementine's unexpected call seemed almost an intrusion.

She looked splendid in black, which acted as a perfect foil for her fair complexion—skilfully enhanced with a discreet application of *papier poudre* and absolutely no rouge at all. She fell upon me with a tragic embrace and then detached herself, saying with gratification, "I can see you approve, darling. I thought you would. Pale and suffering; *that* is what is called for, I think, at a time like this. Sorrow can make a woman look very fetching—except Mamma, of course. You were not at the funeral, so you missed her dramatic appearance; the best entrance she has ever made, I do declare, tottering into the church on Gavin's arm, well fortified with her favourite medicine and wearing a flowing grenadine dress and duchesse mantle, her face very wan beneath her widow's weeds but her head held bravely, like 'Patience on a monument, smiling at grief.' I swear I could almost hear her reciting the words! And no expense spared in setting the sacred stage; arum lilies everywhere, and people swooning from the perfume, and the most expensive organist she could hire, and St. Paul's in Covent Garden, of course; the Actors' Church. Everyone who *is* anyone attended, including—guess who?— Lord Durbridge. In a wheelchair, my dear—so tragic. I gather he had an accident of some sort. Hunting, I believe."

She was unaware of the irony of those last words. Human quarry, and the younger the better, was this man's game. I had neither seen nor heard of the man since receiving Clemmy's memorable letter, and had begun to hope his ghost had been finally laid, yet here he was again, conjured up as a respectful mourner at my father's funeral service, no longer hiding his crippled state in his Berkshire country home, but being seen openly about London in a wheelchair. Did that mean his injuries were permanent—that I and my mother between us had brought them about and could be targets for his bitterness and hatred forevermore? Then common sense told me that one might just as well blame young Jerry for the tragedy, for being cajoled into that empty dressing room and thereby contributing to the events which followed. I had never yet found out exactly how the boy came to be there. He had maintained his stubborn silence on that point ever since.

Clementine's silvery voice was running on. She had studiously acquired the fashionable soprano tones which echoed through society now, light and trilling, with a hint of a baby lisp; cooing and affected and somehow reflecting the frivolous attitude to life which was creeping in as rapidly as the heavy Victorian attitudes were fading out. England would change, people said, once the old queen died and her rollicking and lovable son came to the throne. Out would go the cumbersome clutter of

Victorian homes, the solid furniture, the smothering window drapes, the gloom, the hypocrisy, the dull respectability hiding extremes of vice like dirt beneath the carpets. Already there were hints of new manners and fashions in the frilly furnishings and flimsy *papier-mâché* tables and fragile gilt and bamboo chairs which were becoming so popular.

Everything seemed to indicate a swing away from the conventional portrayal of sombre morality. So was my husband right when he predicted a decline in theatrical values and an upsurge of empty-headed trash on the London stage?

I jerked my attention back to Clementine's ever-flowing chatter.

". . . I swear I was quite overcome. I could scarcely speak when all those dear people flocked around us outside the church. Such crowds! One could feel their sympathy outpouring to Mamma. Oh, dear, am I being tactless? You look quite strange, Lucinda. Almost angry. *Not* angry? Resentful, then? You are thinking of your own mamma, perhaps, sitting alone at home, but what else could she do? She could hardly put in an appearance, could she, nor you yourself for that matter, even though you are dear Gavin's wife, a fact Mamma will have to accept eventually, but give her time, dear, give her time. Other people too. Suspicion has always been rampant, I gather, but never more so than since Trudy's sudden departure, with her child, from number 47 Portman Square—and all confirmed now, of course, by Papa's will. It is easy to own up after one is dead; one is no longer there to face the music. Sometimes I am tempted to keep a diary so that my memoirs may be published after my death and shock the world, but alas, I would miss all the fun of seeing its reaction. What was I saying? Oh, yes. You look strange, you certainly do. What are you thinking behind those eyes of yours? Do you know, I have often wondered and never been able to make out? All my life I have seen you look at me like that, as if all sorts of secret thoughts were going through your mind."

"We all have our secret thoughts."

"I have shared a lot of mine with *you*," she reproached.

"Not since you grew older."

"Wiser, you mean. Oh, I admit you have never betrayed me; one thing I *can* say in your favour is that confidences are safe with you." She giggled. "Do you remember the things I told you about that French gardener? My dear, if you knew of experiences I have had since, that youthful initiation of mine would seem trifling."

"Experiences with Curtis?" I asked without thought.

"Oh, Curtis . . ." Her pretty brow creased. "That man really will have to go now Papa is dead. He is quite above himself these days. He even dared to suggest that I should not keep him waiting too long this afternoon because it is chilly sitting up there on the box. Such impertinence! But I could never appeal to Papa to get rid of him without giving good reason, and had I dared to do that, Curtis would have become ugly and threatening. And I doubt if it will be any easier with Mamma, because Curtis has her eating out of his hand. He can be very charming and deferential, you know, and the silly woman is susceptible to the flattery of men much younger than herself, especially handsome ones. If I tell her he has become uppish—and *that* is putting it mildly!—she tut-tuts and dismisses the very idea. I have tried to buy him off, but my allowance and my earnings as an actress barely keep me in fashionable clothes, and the sum he demands is exorbitant. I have never before found it so difficult to get rid of a lover, but somehow I shall succeed. Are you listening to me, Lucinda? Your thoughts seem miles away again.''

They were. I was thinking of Magnus and his parting words to me. . . .

Clementine piped on, "You are not resentful, are you, because you had to miss that beautiful funeral service and all those sorrowing people?''

I decided to let her think that, if she wished. How could I say that Nevill Boswell would have hated such an elaborate display, that I was thankful not to have seen it, and that my mother and I needed no such trappings of grief, our feelings being wholly private? I let Clementine prattle on without interruption as she shed an elegant sling-sleeved wrap, a fetching gauze bonnet, and long black gloves. Then, taking a black-edged mourning handkerchief from her reticule and spreading her black skirts of lustrous Merveilleux, she seated herself with the familiar ease which she had displayed on a previous visit, for all the world as if she were well acquainted with these rooms. But that was typical of Clementine. She took possession of any place she entered.

This time I gave her no opportunity to chide me for being a poor hostess, but placed a glass of wine at her elbow and poured one for myself. She lifted it and said, "I suppose we must toast each other in our new and, let us hope, profitable venture, though somehow I cannot imagine us seeing eye to eye, and Mamma is quite right in saying that you, in particular, are totally inexperienced in theatrical matters and therefore unsuited to handle them, or even have a share in them. You were not born into the theatre, as I was—''

"On the contrary, I was born in a dressing room. Next to the actual stage, nothing could be nearer to the heart of a theatre than that.''

"You know perfectly well what I mean; what *we* mean. The best possible thing—for you, Lucinda, we are thinking only of you—is for us to buy you out. Then the theatre will once more be exclusively in the Boswell family, as it should be. We would be generous, of course, and pay you handsomely. I think you will agree that Mamma and I have always been unstinting toward you—clothes, opportunities, everything.'' She waved her mourning handkerchief negligently, as if encompassing a vast

area of munificence with the gesture. "In fact," she finished, "paying off
Curtis can wait until after we have dealt with you."

I froze. So this was the object of her visit. My father had gone, and
now I could go too. For a moment I was incapable of answering, so I
sipped my wine and let her wait.

"Well?" she demanded at last.

" 'We' would be generous, you say. By 'we,' you mean yourself and
your mother?"

"She primarily, of course, because she holds the purse strings. All *I*
have inherited is this share in the theatre, so any ready cash must come
from her. She won't call on you herself, and in any case I wouldn't allow
her to. '*I* will do the negotiating,' I said, 'and spare you all that distress,
dear Mamma.' Oh, I know how to be the dutiful daughter when necessary! I admit it was her idea, though. 'We will have to buy that young
woman out,' she said, 'and the sooner the better.' Of course, she thinks
it scandalous that Papa should have been so generous to you, and I confess I was astonished that he should place you on a par with myself, but
it's no use crying over spilt milk and there's always a way round everything, even if it looks like a *fait accompli*, or so I've heard Gavin say many
a time. Money talks, he says. Money always talks."

"And you think it can talk to me?" I could feel two spots of anger
burning in my cheeks. "And do you think my husband would agree?
Have you discussed it with him?"

"Certainly not. If there is one thing Gavin has always wanted, it's a
share in a theatre. Any theatre. Unfortunately for him, the last amendment of the Married Woman's Property Act now stops him from getting
his hands on yours."

"Gavin isn't like that!"

She smiled at my vigorous protest and said knowingly, "You think so?
Well, perhaps you are right. Perhaps he is a reformed character, but I
hope not—I am rather fond of my rakish 'uncle.' I did toy with the idea
of seeking his cooperation, but common sense told me he would persuade you to do the reverse and keep it in the family, so to speak. But it
is my family who should have it."

"So you called when you knew Gavin would be out and therefore unable to influence me against the idea?" I laid aside my unfinished wine
and rose. "You have made the first mistake in this partnership of ours.
My share isn't for sale. How about yours?"

She laughed. It was a high, brittle, angry little sound. "You wouldn't
be able to raise enough money to buy mine."

"No, but Gavin might, and if you are wanting to get rid of Curtis and
can't get the money any other way . . ." I left the sentence unfinished,
not liking it very much. "Let me make this clear, Clemmy. Not for any
price would I part with my share of the Boswell Theatre. My father en-

trusted it to me and I am not going to let him down. He dedicated himself to the place, and I intend to do the same.''

"Not one hundred percent, you can't. I own the other fifty, and don't you forget it.''

Her mood was reminiscent of childish tantrums when thwarted, but more vicious. It left me unmoved. I said, "And don't *you* forget that we have a fine team—Bramwell, Willard, an experienced stage crew who have worked at the Boswell Theatre for years, a loyal team of actors, including your mother for character leads, and a good leading lady in Chrystal Delmont—''

"Whose parts *I* shall take over.''

"Eventually, perhaps, but you are too young and too pretty to do so yet.'' It was always wise to soften Clemmy with flattery. "And who could possibly replace you in ingenue roles? Not I. I am not beautiful enough. Juvenile characters—those are the parts for me, I think. I suggest we ask Bramwell to cast future productions. His appointment as adviser to the company will cover all that sort of thing and help on the management side as well. We must let the theatre run as it has always been run. I am sure that when the first meeting is held, everyone will agree.''

"What first meeting?''

"With the stage management and house management; with everyone who has a part to play in running the theatre. Bramwell says the important thing is to decide what to put on when *Twelfth Night* finishes its run. Bookings are good for some time ahead, but after that a complete contrast seems a wise choice, because, as he so rightly says, the public will associate the play with Nevill Boswell for a long time to come. For the time being, no actor could really replace him. Bramwell will do his best to fill the gap until bookings begin to fall off, but—''

"It sounds as if he is becoming self-appointed mouthpiece!'' Clementine's voice was tart. "Well, *I* will have a suggestion or two to make.''

"Naturally. So shall I. I think a Sheridan revival, perhaps. *The School for Scandal* is splendid stuff.''

"I have a far better notion than that. We must branch out into musical comedy.'' She rose and, pirouetting, began to trill from *Florodora*:

Te-e-e-ll me, pretty maiden,
Are there any more at home like you?
There are a fe-e-e-e-w,
Kind sir. . . .

"Delightful music, don't you think?''

"Very pretty, but I remember Sir Nevill once saying that the Boswell wasn't built for musicals, and surely you remember, when we did *A Midsummer Night's Dream*, that 'Philomel, with melody' couldn't reach the front row of the grand circle even when sung in chorus? And with the

D'Oyly Carte constantly doing Gilbert and Sullivan across the road at
the Savoy, musicals at the Boswell wouldn't stand up to such competition. My father always said so.''

She frowned a little, as if she couldn't get used to my referring to him
as my father, but before she had a chance to answer, Gavin spoke from
the door. Neither of us had heard him come in.

"And Nevill was right," he said. "Leslie Stewart would certainly be
eclipsed by Gilbert and Sullivan; he has always been, and so has Edward
German, despite his *Merrie England,* so the obvious thing to choose is a
totally different type of musical entertainment, the kind which relies on
being seen rather than on being heard.''

From their exchanged glances, I had the sudden conviction that my
husband and my half-sister would make formidable opposition and, almost guiltily, I felt thankful that he would have no authority, no active
say in things, and even that he would be away from time to time touring
the provinces.

He went over to Clementine now, slipped his arm about her waist, and
kissed her lightly. Surely it was only my heightened imagination which
saw something more than brotherly in the gesture?

"You look very beautiful, niece. Mourning becomes you . . .''

She pouted prettily and then pointed out, as I had heard her point out
before, that she would have him know she was not his true niece and that
he was only her stepuncle and no blood relation at all.

"I do know," he agreed. "I also know that your handsome coachman
is sitting outside, scowling like thunder, and not, I suspect, because of
the cold. Could it possibly be because you are keeping him waiting? You
should send the fellow packing, dear Clemmy. He no longer seems to
know his place.''

"I intend to, as soon as I can afford to. Meanwhile, let him wait—he is
only a servant.''

She deliberately held out her glass to be refilled, and then Gavin
poured wine for himself and settled down to flirt with her lightheartedly
while I looked on. The afternoon had almost gone by the time he saw her
down to her carriage. When he returned, he remarked that Curtis was
too insolent by half and looked at his mistress in far too familiar a fashion—"though no doubt she has brought it on herself; Clementine is a
born coquette. What a career she could have had as a courtesan at Ver-
sailles! And what brought her here, by the way? Not an unquenchable
longing to see *you,* I am sure. She has always been as jealous as hell
where you are concerned.''

"Jealous of *me?* Clemmy! That's impossible. She has always had so
much more than I.''

"Oh, no, my dear, she has not. Not your looks which, I admit, are not
the fashionable looks of today, as hers are nor your intelligence, nor

your talent, nor your body—though I also admit that the body she has is certainly worth having, and I'm sure many men have enjoyed that privilege. Anyway, why did she call?"

"She—that is, she and her mother—want to buy me out."

He slapped his thigh and roared with laughter.

"Already! And how much had she come to offer?"

"I have no idea, because I gave her no opportunity to mention it. Naturally, I refused to sell."

"I said you were intelligent, didn't I? The time to sell is not yet. We will pick the right moment for that."

"I shall never sell. I regard this bequest from my father as a sacred trust."

"A fine sentiment, my love, but see if you feel that way when the place begins to show a loss. Not that it will; I am resolved on that. In fact, as far as selling a share in the theatre is concerned, I wouldn't be surprised to find the boot on the other foot, and very soon too." He dismissed the subject and held out his hands to me. "Now, come to bed, and to hell with the time. I have been starved for that body of yours these past days. You have a lot to make up to me."

There it was again, the implication that my body should be rendered up by way of atonement. I was beginning to feel merely like a commodity designed to serve his purpose and to be taken at will.

21

I don't think anyone at the theatre missed Sir Nevill quite so much as I.

"Strange without him, isn't it?" Willard commented, and proceeded to get on with his job, as did everyone else. Bramwell moved into his dressing room, and I was glad about that because, had it remained as it was, the empty room would have reminded me of my father too poignantly. His dresser dealt with his costumes and gave his makeup and other such items to lesser players who would be glad of them, but I managed to obtain some personal souvenirs which neither Bernadette nor Clementine wanted—a few photographs in costume roles, taken at dress rehearsals and then pushed away into a drawer, forgotten; the tray on which his sticks of Leichner and other items of makeup had always been neatly set out on his dressing table and which I intended to use for the same purpose forevermore; and an antique footstool embroidered with Germanic beadwork, which he used when resting. I remembered my mother picking up that footstool for a song in the Caledonian Market, and slipping into his dressing room on his birthday many years ago, to place it secretly before his comfortable armchair.

"I can't understand why you don't throw that old thing out!" That was one of the things I had overheard Bernadette say when I was a child, but perhaps he had known, or suspected, who had put the footstool there, and had treasured it for that reason. Now I resolved my mother should have it back, together with first choice of his photographs, since she had no other personal items to remember him by.

One other person missed Sir Nevill at the theatre.

" 'Tain't the sime wiv'art the gov, is it, missy? 'Tain't the sime at all." Young Jerry sniffed disconsolately. "When I go 'ammering on 'is dressing-room door an' it's Mr. Chambers wot answers, it seems all wrong-like. 'E were a wonderful man, the gov."

"He was indeed, Jerry. We were both lucky to work for him."

"An' 'twere lucky fer 'im, missy, 'aving *you* ta fall back on 'ere at the theatre. Is it true you've come into 'arf of it?"

"Quite true, Jerry."

"An' I s'pose *she* 'as t'other 'arf?"

When I nodded, his young-old face looked knowing. "I guess 'e only left that share to 'er cos she were 'is daughter, and t'other 'arf to you cos 'e knew wot the plice means to yer. You love it, don'tcha?"

Helen Steel implied the same thing. I spent more time with the Steels and with my mother these days while Gavin was preparing for his next tour, about which he told me little. He had ceased to reproach me for refusing to join him, and how he had wriggled out of the husband-and-wife partnership clause in his contract he didn't confirm either, but he seemed well content and very much occupied, at home less and less due to rehearsals, so I fell into the habit of spending my afternoons at my mother's shop, on the days when there were no matinees, or going with Magnus and Helen to the mission and returning to their house for a meal before proceeding to the theatre in the evening. There was a happiness about these days, though I saw less of Helen due to her increasing friendship with Hugh Maynard and his children.

"Your sister is a born mother," I said to Magnus one day as we drove back from Stepney alone, at which he nodded agreement.

"That is why she is such an asset at the mission," he answered. "She loves children and they love her, so when and if she marries and has a brood of her own, I shall be pleased for her sake but regretful for the mission's."

"*If* she marries? I thought there was a distinct possibility that she and Hugh Maynard might do so. I thought they were in love."

"That is true, but there are difficulties."

"Which you don't want to talk about?"

"Which I cannot talk about, much as I should like to, perhaps." He changed the subject. "I suppose you know that your mother is turning the rooms above her shop into a flat for herself?"

"Yes. She feels she has imposed on your hospitality long enough."

"It was never that. She rewarded us greatly in so many ways, but she deserves a home of her own, the first she has ever had."

I said carefully, "You felt she deserved more than that, didn't you, when you appointed those Lincoln's Inn solicitors to act for you in secrecy?"

He was silent. I looked at his unyielding profile as he stared straight ahead.

"Silence isn't denial, Magnus, and I know I am right. You wanted her to believe it was my father's thought, didn't you?"

"Let her. Let her always. If you disillusion her, I shall never forgive you."

"I shan't disillusion her, I promise, but one day I will pay you back. We have accepted so much from you. Too much."

"One can never accept too much from friends, nor give too much, and if you attempt to pay me back, I shall be extremely angry. Remember that."

Even though I was aware that this man's anger would be something unwise to encounter, I retorted, "Don't try to intimidate me, Magnus."

"Intimidate *you*?" He laughed. "You have as much courage as your mother and as strong a will as my sister, and since life could never intimidate either of them, it would find it doubly difficult to intimidate you. And you are going to need that courage, my poor Lucinda. Friends, too, so let me stay in your life that way."

"Naturally, I hope we will always be friends," I answered, suppressing a touch of bleakness at the thought and failing to understand the reaction, because in what other capacity could this man remain in my life? I had a husband whom I loved and I had no reason to believe that Magnus had changed in his feelings toward Clementine, whom he had loved on sight. Whether any close relationship had developed between them, I had no idea. Since marrying and leaving the vicinity of Portman Square, I no longer knew what went on in her private life, nor did I want to, because the idea of Magnus being her lover proved as distressing now as on that long-ago night when, as a mere fourteen-year-old, I had walked with him across the square. And that I could not understand, either.

Unexpectedly, his hand left the reins and covered mine. The gesture was brief and unaccompanied by words, but somehow I knew that the moment was as potent and important to him as it was to me, signifying a closer understanding and sympathy between us.

* * *

Again I was glad when I reached home and found Gavin out. Even when I returned from the theatre late that night and found him still absent, I was not sorry. Of course I knew that work was the reason. I was settling down to the acceptance of our marital routine, and to the life of an actor's wife. To have expected the enchantment of the early days to last longer than this was, of course, foolish, but perhaps our separate careers were to blame for the widening distance between us.

I was nearly asleep when he came home. He slipped into bed beside me and took me in his arms. I could sense an elation about him and drowsily asked what had happened.

"You are excited about something, aren't you? I can feel it."

He kissed me then, long and hard, and promised to tell me in the morning, and to silence further questions he began to make love to me with such expertise that my body rapidly responded, persuading me that the magic of our marriage was still alive. Every rhythmic and pulsating movement seemed to confirm it.

The first meeting of the managerial side of the theatre had been arranged for ten o'clock. When I wakened, Gavin was still asleep, and I left him there, slipping quietly out of the flat in order not to disturb him.

Bramwell was waiting in the green room with Willard, but as yet there was no sign of Clementine. After a prolonged wait I was about to suggest starting without her when the door opened and Gavin walked in.

"My apologies for the delay, gentlemen, but my wife very indulgently allowed me to sleep on. You all look very surprised, but this will explain why I am here." He produced a long manila envelope and opened it. "This contains a certificate of sale, the transfer of Clementine Boswell's share of this theatre to me." He looked at us triumphantly. "Why the surprise? You all know Clemmy's love of money—it is the only language she understands."

(*"Money talks, he says. Money always talks."* Her voice echoed in my disbelieving ears.)

"You look stunned, Lucinda. Not very flattering to me, is it? Aren't you pleased to have me as your partner? You should be delighted to know that full control of this theatre is now in our hands. Clementine would have been an extremely tiresome partner, and well you know it."

Willard burst out, "Do you mean to say that your wife didn't know about this deal?"

I saw the eyes of the other two men focused on me, Willard's in disbelief and Bramwell's with a sort of questioning surprise mingled with pity.

Gavin answered blandly that it had all been settled very late yesterday. "You were asleep, weren't you, my love, by the time I reached home?"

Mischief danced in his eyes. It was Gavin at his most engaging, the Gavin I had always been able to forgive or excuse for anything at all, but now I felt differently. I felt defrauded and angry. He had hoodwinked me and had obviously been hoodwinking me for some time, because deals like this could not be settled in a hurry. There must have been discussions and negotiations, meetings with Clementine and lawyers, agreements signed and exchanged. The document he now produced with a flourish displayed a fine red seal and his own flamboyant signature above Clementine's and those of witnesses. He laid it on the table, saying, "Take a look at it, if you want to. All of you. You should be pleased. We will make the Boswell Theatre pay as it has never paid before."

Bramwell said contemptuously, "By putting on productions such as it has never done before and turning it into the kind of theatre it has never been? The Boswell has always been renowned, with fewer ups and downs than most theatres, even the Lyceum and Drury Lane, and far less than that ill-fated place in Covent Garden. But we all know your views and theatrical tastes. Do you honestly think your wife will go along with them?"

"She will have to. What does she know about theatre affairs or making them pay? Between her and Clementine the place would have fallen to pieces. Fortunately for Lucinda, she is my wife and has me to guide her. She knows already that I will do so."

I reached for the document, only vaguely hearing Willard's voice added to Bramwell's. "What of this producing job you've got? What of this tour you are going on?"

"Naturally, I am not going on any tour now, and as for the producing job, I have wriggled out of that very satisfactorily."

"I am quite sure you have, Calder. You have always been as slippery as an eel, and Sir Nevill knew it." That was Bramwell. "And don't forget that I have a voice in the running of things."

"But not a partnership. The final say in anything and everything will come from the owners—Lucinda and myself."

"Nevertheless, I am an appointed adviser, which gives me the power to oppose things if I feel it necessary."

"Do so, if you wish. Advice doesn't have to be taken. You won't be dealing with a couple of gullible young women on their own."

"I would support Bramwell," growled Willard. "I would back his judgment every time."

Gavin shrugged and pointed out that stage directors could always be replaced, but their voices seemed to retreat, flowing over my head merely as background noise, because I was staring at the date on the document and could heed nothing else.

I spoke for the first time.

"You say this was settled only yesterday, Gavin?"

His face jerked round to me. His eyes flickered. He reached out for the document but I held onto it, pointing to the date.

"A week ago," I said. "A whole week."

"What difference does that make? It is a *fait accompli,* my love. I didn't tell you until now because I thought it a good idea to wait—for a celebration, you understand, today being the day of days."

He was blustering badly, and I had no intention of coming to his rescue. I pushed back my chair and walked out of the green room, out of the theatre. I wanted air. I wanted to think.

"There's always a way round a *fait accompli,* or so I've heard Gavin say many times." Clementine herself had said that, but I knew there was no way round this one, and I knew what was going to happen to the Boswell Theatre. It would go down and down, putting on vulgar shows, shaming the name of Boswell and the whole line of that famous acting family. I could see the promenading when the grand-circle bar was opened up, the soliciting, the prostitution, the men like Durbridge frequenting the place for their own particular type of fancy, and I experienced a blinding anger such as I had never felt before, so that when my husband caught up with me in the middle of Maiden Lane and, seizing my arm, spun me round, demanding to know where the hell I thought I was going and what the hell I thought I was doing walking out of the theatre like that, I pulled away from him violently.

"Get away from me. Leave me alone."

"For God's sake, pull yourself together," he protested. "Don't make a scene in the street. Come home and we will talk this over quietly. I thought it would be a wonderful surprise for you, that you would be pleased."

"You thought nothing of the sort, or you would have told me before, privately. You have been working and scheming for this behind my back for one reason only—because you knew my ideas about running the theatre would oppose your own, so I would naturally have opposed your sharing control. Well, that *is* all you've got—a share, no more—and I will fight you every inch of the way."

"How?" He laughed. "My dear Lucinda, you are a mere sixteen and totally without experience. Against me you haven't a chance. What do you think I am going to do with the place, anyway?"

"Degrade it."

"By taking a more liberal line, a broader view of public morals? And as to morals, my dear, you need to develop a more tolerant outlook."

"Morals have nothing to do with it—not the kind you are thinking of, anyway. The question is, what is to become of the Boswell Theatre, a place built and renowned for good drama and good acting—the very best acting and the very best dramatists. The moral issue is one of professional standards, nothing else."

He took hold of my arm, saying indulgently, "Come, darling, back home in bed I will woo you over and you will love every moment of it."

I wrenched free. "I am not coming home."

"Running to dear Mamma, I suppose? Or is it to that doctor whose house you visit so often?" When I turned aside, not bothering to answer, he said, "Very well, go to your mother. It's not a bad idea. She will see the sense of our partnership. She couldn't have been happy about the joint arrangement between the legitimate and the illegitimate daughters. Stay with her tonight and have a good heart-to-heart, and by the time you come home tomorrow you will have come to your senses."

I agreed that I would stay with my mother tonight, "but only because I don't want to be with you."

He laughed and let me go. I heard him hail a passing hansom and the folding doors slam as he climbed inside. It passed me as I walked on blindly, not looking where I was going until I collided full tilt into a woman standing only a few yards away. Her voice came to me like an ugly echo from the past.

"G'morning," she said. "I've been waiting for you, your ladyship."

It was Maisie, looking shabbier and more world-weary, but shrewder and harder too.

"Don't pass me by, Mrs. Calder. You might be sorry if you do. I've been hanging around for days, hoping to catch you alone."

"What can I do for you?" I was aware of a sudden pity for the woman. Hunger looked out from those eyes; her face was pinched.

"I want work. Badly. I'm getting a bit past my other occupation." The hard defiance was still in her voice; bitterness too. "I'm not so young as I useter be, and there are too many young 'uns on the beats now, 'specially around Shaftesbury Avenue and Soho, where I've always had my own particular pitch. There oughta be a union to help the likes of us, but I s'pose there never will be."

"So you want work at the theatre? I'm sorry, but at the moment—"

"At the moment," she interrupted, "you're sitting pretty. I read in *The Era* all about your coming into a share of the place. Who'da guessed you'd strike it rich like that? Come to that, who'da guessed who you really were! Couldn't keep *that* outta the papers, could they, when Sir Nevill's will was published? No wonder you gave yourself airs!"

I pushed past her.

"Sorry," she said quickly, grabbing my arm. "I could never stop getting at you. Something about you goaded me."

"I shouldn't try it anymore. Let go my arm, Maisie."

"I've said I'm sorry and I mean it." Her tone changed to pleading now. "Truth is, Mrs. Calder, I hate having to beg, 'specially from you, but now you've got a say in that theatre, you'll know what shows will be coming on, and *The Era* this week says the Boswell will be doing something new pretty soon.''

''I don't know what, or when. It hasn't been decided yet.''

''But if supers are needed—''

''*The Era* will announce auditions.''

''By then everyone will know, and I'd like to get in first.'' Her eyes became calculating, cunning. ''What's more, I think it will be worth your while to see that I do, Mrs. Calder.''

Again I tried to move on, but her wiry body darted in front of me, barring my way.

''Of course, I *could* go along and see your husband at that office in Shaftesbury Avenue. I read in *The Era* about him being their producer and lead actor, and I know where the office is because I sometimes stroll by there when the young 'uns aren't hogging the beat, so I often see him go in and out. Lord Durbridge, too, wheeled by that man of his. Now, what's so startling about that, Mrs. Calder? Don't pretend you didn't know Durbridge had a finger in the pie, though his name doesn't appear on the nameplate by the door. No names do, other than the company's. But *his* name is kept quiet in all sorts of ways, isn't it? A lot of things are kept quiet about *that* particular gentleman, such as what happened to him that night at the Boswell Theatre.''

I stood there staring at her, and a smile spread across her haggard features and glittered in her malicious eyes.

''I've never breathed a word to anybody, Mrs. Calder. Bided my time. I didn't even drop a hint in the dressing room, did I, when I talked about young Jerry barging outa the theatre as if the devil were after him? I let it rest at that, because at the time I didn't see anything suspicious about a couple of men carrying another outa the stage door later—and quite a bit later it was, because my gentleman friend had paid me off and I was heading back towards the Duke's Head before they closed at one o'clock, and I just happened to pass on the other side of the street when out came your husband and the other man, carrying Lord Durbridge between them and putting him into his carriage. I didn't hurry so much then, so I was able to take a good look. The noble lord was unconscious; dead drunk, I thought, though he's not a drinker, as everyone knows. Then I saw his face, and it wasn't the face of a man who was drunk. He'd been injured or knocked out or something. And I recognised his carriage because I've seen it often enough around London. Who hasn't? Until it faded from the scene, that is. He disappeared for quite a while, didn't he, and I daresay you know why, since you married Gavin Calder after it happened. I have to admit I forgot the whole thing until I saw Lord Durbridge around in a wheelchair recently. Then I began thinking about your husband joining the new company that was formed shortly after all this happened, as producer *and* lead. That's interesting, I thought, and put two and two together and came up with an even more interesting answer."

When I said nothing, she went on, "My goodness, Mrs. Calder, I've got to hand it to you—you *are* a good actress. You look as if you've been struck, really you do, but don't try to kid me that you didn't know how your husband got himself fixed up so nicely. Something must have happened backstage that night that Lord Durbridge wanted to be kept very quiet indeed. So what with that young shaver running like hell outa the theatre, and knowing that particular gentleman's taste for small boys as well as big, and seeing handsome Gavin Calder, who's got his head screwed on the right way, as everyone knows, smuggling his lordship out through the stage door like that—well, it's all very interesting. What had he done—left Durbridge there while he went to fetch his manservant? Doesn't matter. What does matter is that after that you became Mrs. Calder, and a wife always knows what games her husband gets up to, or at least has her suspicions, and you wouldn't like me to gossip, now, would you? You'd be surprised how well I can hold my tongue if I'm properly looked after—which means work, your ladyship. Regular work and good pay, and I keep my mouth shut permanently."

"You are making it all up," I stammered, and somehow got away from her. I heard her shouting after me. "All right, turn your nose up, but you'll regret it, that you will!" and I didn't care that people were staring. I was almost running along Maiden Lane and across Bedford Street into Cranbourn Street; then along William IV Street and across the foot of St. Martin's Lane and into the Charing Cross Road; left into Leicester Square and past the Empire, until I reached Rupert Street, and then up there to emerge along Shaftesbury Avenue . . . hurrying, stumbling in my haste, driven by a frantic determination to know the truth, yet dreading it. And all the time I was remembering things my father had said long ago: that life in the theatre could not only be heartbreaking but very often shocking, that there were aspects of which I had no knowledge, that ignorance or innocence could be a great protection, and that it wasn't the gossip and the conventional scandal which made up the worst part of theatrical life.

He had hinted at undercurrents from which he would wish to protect me and which he had fought to keep out of the Boswell Theatre. Not only my innocence had now gone, but the last shreds of my ignorance, and all the ugliness which lay beneath the surface of this world, which had now become mine, stared me in the face. Yet I knew I had to learn the whole truth and come to terms with it.

It took me a little time to find Cathcart House, which proved to be a narrow entrance on the left-hand side, near Frith Street, with the name in gold letters on the transom above the door and a list of offices on bronze or brass plates beside it. Shaftesbury Productions were, as Gavin had once let drop, in Suite Number 6, which proved to be at the rear of the ground floor at the end of a long passage, and beside their name was a list of other activities—Visual Exhibitions; Mobile Tableaux; Artistic Displays. Meaningless titles to passersby, but suddenly very suggestive after Maisie's implication. What sort of "visual" exhibitions, what type of "mobile" tableaux or "artistic" displays? The kind for which the notorious Temple of Love was famed, and the highly expensive brothels around the Haymarket? One could not live in the metropolis at any time during Victoria's reign without knowing of the extent of such activities.

There was a bell by the door leading into Suite Number 6, but I didn't trouble to use it. I turned the handle and walked in. The office it revealed was well furnished, with a solid mahogany counter and, beyond, a receptionist's or clerk's desk, and filing cabinets and other office equipment. No one sat at the desk, and a large office clock on the wall pointed to thirty minutes after midday, so whoever normally occupied that desk had probably gone to lunch.

And left the main door unlocked? Unlikely, I thought, which meant that someone else was on the premises.

All this passed through my mind in a detached sort of way, coldly reasoning as I lifted the counter flap and walked through. I ignored the brass bell for the use of visitors. Suite Number 6 appeared to consist of only two rooms, a door to the one beyond lying straight ahead. I opened it without ceremony and looked straight across the room at Durbridge.

22

He had a tray on the desk before him and a glass of wine in his hand. Someone—that unseen assistant from the outer office, perhaps—had attended to his wants before going in search of his own. It was odd how unimportant details stamped themselves on my mind, irrelevant and distracting and yet undermining my resolution in no way at all.

I was satisfied to see that his surprise exceeded my own, but after the first startled glance he recovered quickly.

"You must forgive me for not rising, Mrs. Calder. Unfortunately, I can no longer get to my feet as I would once have done in the presence of a lady. I have you to thank for that. You and your meddlesome mother."

The voice was just the same, cultured and smooth, but now tinged with venom.

"No," I said, "you have only yourself to thank, Lord Durbridge. You should have left that boy alone."

The red lips quivered very faintly. Against the unhealthy pallor of his face they looked even more red than I remembered.

"Unfortunately I cannot usher you off the premises, Mrs. Calder, and I am not sure that I wish to until I know what brings you here. By that time my assistant may have returned, or a waiter from the Trocadero to remove my tray, or my man, Stacey, may arrive to take me home. I put in only token appearances at these offices, so you were lucky to find me here. An entrepreneur like myself works mainly from home, and since I became a cripple I find it less strenuous. It is a damnable handicap, being a cripple, but at least I can offer you a seat whilst we talk. I presume that is what you have come for, though what we can have to say to each other I cannot imagine. As a young woman you have never interested me, and I am quite sure that as a man I do not interest you. I have been aware of your dislike and mistrust since our glances once met on the corner of Oxford Street and Park Lane. But at least let me appear to be hospitable by offering you a glass of wine, though I must ask you to fetch a glass for yourself from that cupboard over there."

I declined with a shake of my head, and said bluntly, "I want to know how and why you persuaded my husband to work for you."

He laughed. It was a thick-lipped grimace more than a laugh, redness curving away from very white teeth and nothing more than a harsh gust of breath emerging.

"*I* persuaded *him?* Is that what he told you?"

"He has told me nothing."

"Then how—?"

"I knew only that a new company had been formed, and that he had been appointed producer and lead actor."

"And curiosity has only just brought you here? Well, that is hardly surprising—you are very young and Calder is very astute, though 'devious' might be more apt. And in a way it would be more truthful to say that *I* work for *him*. People who hold trump cards can control the game, and he did. Not for nothing was the Amendment Act of 1885 called the 'Blackmailer's Charter' by one eminent lawyer, as Oscar Wilde's trial revealed last year. The penalty for my kind of offence is well known, and that night's incident put me in Calder's power, because he knew precisely how I came to be in that dressing room, and why. He didn't hesitate to make use of his knowledge. I am a wealthy man and am behind various entertainments—enterprises, shall we call them?—which have made me even wealthier, though it would be hard to prove my association with them, nor to establish any link between them with the official business names displayed here and registered under the Companies Act. The books in this office bear inspection; correspondence files also. On those counts I am safe, but on other 'moral' ones I am not—though you, damn you, have now handicapped me even in those respects.''

"Then if I was instrumental in protecting small boys, perhaps it was a good thing.''

Hatred looked out of his puffy eyes.

"One day I shall retaliate, Mrs. Calder. Meanwhile, if you are toying with any idea of revealing the information I have confided about my business sidelines, you would be wasting your time, for the reasons I have already explained. Any kind of interference from you would avail you nothing, because you could prove nothing. And that ambitious and unscrupulous man you are married to would soon put a stop to any attempt you made. He knows of these sidelines, exhibitions and live performances discreetly shown in private at gatherings young ladies like yourself would never attend and probably cannot even imagine. But your husband enjoys them. It is a man's world, my dear, and men must be permitted to indulge their tastes—except men like me, who must never be found out. Your husband could have betrayed me to the police that night. You also. The boy too, as Calder reminded me. But he knew how to handle you, he said. He boasted that you had always eaten out of his hand, that he knew what tale to tell you and that you would jump at the chance to marry him, also that the boy was too devoted to you to hurt you by revealing the truth about the man you were in love with, the man who sent him up those stairs that night. Ah, I see you have guessed the rest. You look very white, Mrs. Calder. Are you sure you won't have some wine?''

The room was spinning; I sat down and saw that the red mouth was now smiling.

"You look distressed, my dear, but why? All your husband did was tell the boy that you wanted to see him, that you were upstairs in your dressing room and needed him to run an errand for you. Frankly, I didn't even suspect you were up there and, funnily enough, neither did Calder. He believed you had left the theatre and that the whole place was deserted, which suited me very well. He had even got rid of the stage-doorkeeper, leaving the coast clear for me to waylay the boy as he came upstairs—''

"Please . . . I don't want to hear any more.''

"*But you will.* You came here for that reason, so you can have the whole truth and, by God, I hope it hurts you.'' The voice shook with anger and hatred and a longing to destroy. "You got the husband you wanted and he got what he wanted out of me, and I hope that one day the pair of you suffer even one-quarter of what I have suffered. I had to finance that touring show to keep his mouth shut. You saw me there, that night at Reading, as I intended you should. I hoped the sight of me would shock you, frighten you, and it did. I saw it in your face. I planned to follow the show from town to town, to haunt you from theatre to theatre, but I couldn't continue to sit through trash like that week after week, even though I was pleased to see you degraded by the performance you had to give. I am only sorry you escaped from it, but I reckoned without Nevill Boswell."

He paused to sip his wine. I wanted to drag myself from my seat and out of this place, but couldn't, and I was forced to listen as he continued.

"To tell the truth, I didn't even know that Boswell was your father until his will was made known. Your inheritance took me as much by surprise as it did everyone else, though I strongly suspect that Calder had an idea—it would be unlike him not to. And the situation had its humorous side. I would love to have seen Lady Boswell's face when the will was read; the stupid woman always bored me. And as it turns out, I can be grateful to Sir Nevill now, because his generosity to you enticed Calder to change his tactics, which I am pretty sure he had in mind already. That is why I believe he knew of Boswell's intentions even before he married you, otherwise that scheming brain of his would have persuaded him to look elsewhere. But once you became part-owner of the theatre, he was able to raise his sights higher than being a mere producer of provincial tours—and earlier than he expected, since Boswell's death came so obligingly soon. Are you sure you won't have that wine, Mrs. Calder? I think you need it."

Again I shook my head, and he laughed.

"Nothing will induce you to even drink with me, will it? But perhaps the next piece of news will persuade you to thank me, mixed blessing though it may be. *I* advanced the money for Calder to buy out pretty Clementine, but not altruistically or because a partnership between you and Boswell's legitimate daughter couldn't possibly work. I couldn't give a damn in that respect. My only concern was myself, to get rid of Calder and his blackmail, so I had my own price for helping him to acquire the other half share of your father's theatre. He had to sign an agreement to importune me no further. So now, thank God, Shaftesbury Productions can be wound up and I can be rid of him. And if he ever, at any time in the future, attempts to spread hints about events which led up to my accident, they will come too late. They would have been heeded at the time, but not now that I have his signed undertaking to trouble me no further. That compromises him thoroughly. How could he explain signing such an agreement? And people have now accepted the idea that I met with a riding accident; belated rumours at this stage would avail him little. Even the police would ask why he didn't go to them before. 'Why wait until now to report an illegal assault on a boy? If you helped to conceal it, sir, that makes you an accessory,' which God knows he was. I can imagine their scepticism and his unconvincing excuses, his desperate attempts to conceal his own involvement *and* his blackmail following it. My dear young lady, are you leaving already?''

I was at the door, sick and shaken, stupidly turning the knob the wrong way in my desperate desire to be gone, and as I did so I looked back at Durbridge and saw him as he really was—a man without conscience, without compassion, and consequently a lonely and even a tragic man, loathsome as he was. Then I was out in the street and I knew that his shadow had been lifted from my life forever.

Instead, another shadow touched me, and it was that of my husband, walking beside me throughout my life along with heartbreak and disillusion and the shattering of all my dreams, the naive dreams of my childhood and girlhood. I had loved and idolized him; he had been my knight-errant, handsome and trustworthy, the hero of all my fairy tales. But now that figure existed no more, and the one that replaced it I did not even know.

"You are going to need that courage of yours, my poor Lucinda."

How did you know, Magnus? How did you *know?* Have you seen through Gavin all along, or merely guessed at things?

I walked aimlessly, for how long and how far I was scarcely conscious; then I went back to the theatre and rested in my dressing room until it was time to prepare for the evening's performance. And somehow I got through it, aware all the time that Bramwell Chambers was helping me; Willard too, with his sympathetic glances and his encouraging words whenever I came offstage.

Clementine greeted me happily, thrusting her head round my dressing-room door and saying, "You've heard by now, of course. Gavin told me he was going to keep it as a surprise for you and everyone else today.''

She was excited and pleased, so I knew she had profited well from the deal.

"How has your mother taken it?'' I asked, at which she grimaced and said that dear Mamma had not yet heard, and that she, Clementine, would take very good care that she never did.

"Why should she be told anything, except what she already knows—that you refused point-blank to be bought out, which enraged her. Do you think I am going to enrage her further by revealing that *I* have been bought out instead? I have been able to send Curtis packing, and that is all that matters.''

I didn't trouble to answer, because I didn't care about Curtis or any problem lover she might have. She had got herself in and out of scrapes all her life, and always would. When I remained silent she said, "You don't look very pleased, but you should be. You and I would never have hit it off as partners, and Gavin will handle the reins very well indeed."

But not in the way my father had handled them and for which I would fight. I didn't know how, but I would do it. I would never break my promise to Nevill Boswell, but I knew now that I was up against an unscrupulous husband and that the trouble between us would be nothing so light as mere incompatibility within a husband-and-wife partnership.

Clementine left the theatre early—a supper party at the Savoy, she confided. She took one curtain call only and waited for no more, which was unusual for Clemmy. I wondered if Bernadette was aware that her daughter was ignoring the accepted year's retirement from the social scene following a bereavement, but doubted it. Back at Number 47 Portman Square, the immortal Bernadette was probably consoling herself in her usual way, dramatising her widowhood and enjoying it. She was no more able to love a man deeply than her daughter was, but neither her behaviour nor Clementine's was of any real concern to me because I knew now that neither of them was capable of any real depth of feeling, so nothing would ever hurt them deeply or for long.

My mind tonight was more occupied with the thought that I would soon have to face Gavin. There would be no visit to my mother at Magnus Steel's house, no running away from issues. I would go home instead and tell him that I now knew the truth about his association with Durbridge and his dreadful use of a small boy in the course of his blackmail, and however ugly the scene, I would face it.

Even so, I did not hurry when removing my makeup and changing into my street clothes, and when George, the stage-doorman, delayed me for a good-night chat on my way out, and then Chrystal Delmont and Bramwell joined us, I discouraged none of them. I could sense that Chrystal had heard the news of Gavin's takeover share and was as anxious as the others to assure me of her loyalty, though none of them seemed to know quite how to put it into words. It was strange how actors, so accustomed to expressing themselves eloquently onstage, often found it difficult to do so when not speaking lines set for them—except those who acted offstage as well as on, like my husband.

Eventually we all said good night, and I waited while George sent Jerry to fetch a hansom for me. I gave the boy a lift home, glad of his company, enjoying his chatter about Ma and Joe and the kids, now tenement-housed and "doing lovely, thanks, missy—though I s'pose I shouldn't be calling yer missy anymore, should I, ma'am?"

Before I set him down in the Edgware Road I said spontaneously, "About that night, Jerry . . ."

I didn't have to say which one. In the light from the flickering coach lamps he looked at me in a guarded sort of way and said, "Wot abaht it, missy?"

"You never told me how you came to go up to that dressing room."

"It's a long time ago, missy. I fergit."

"I don't think you do, Jerry. Did you know I was upstairs?"

"'Course I did. I'd seen ya go up there. That was why I be-lieved . . ."

He checked, and I finished for him, "You understood I wanted you to run an errand, and you believed the person who told you, and so you went up willingly enough. Isn't that how it happened?"

He nodded reluctantly, and I knew he wanted to avoid further questions, especially one.

"But you didn't know Lord Durbridge was up there, waiting for you?"

"What do *you* fink?" he demanded indignantly. "I knew the kinda bloke 'e was, first time I ever laid eyes on 'im. Joe'd taught me 'ow to recognise 'em. D'you fink I'd've gone anywhere near the likes of 'im, from *choice?*"

"So whoever sent you up there . . ."

He was out of the cab like a shot. He looked back at me from the pavement. "I told yer, missy, I can't remember nuffink, and don't you go worrying yer 'ead abaht somefink wot 'appened long ago. *You* weren't 'urt and *I* weren't 'urt, an' that's all wot matters. So fergit it, missy. You've nuffink to fret abaht."

As I tapped on the roof hatch and told the cabby to turn and head toward Chelsea, I thought: *Dear, loyal little Jerry; loyal to me, not to my husband.* So loyal that he had resolved I would never know the truth, but his very determination to hide it had confirmed it once and for all.

I dismissed the cab within a short distance of my home and walked the rest of the way. I don't know what made me; the need for exercise and fresh air, perhaps, or the need to brace myself for the coming encounter with Gavin, or even cowardice and a desire to postpone it for as long as possible. Whatever the reason, it was a mistake, because when I approached our apartment block a figure loomed out of the shadows close to the entrance. All the horror stories of attacks on women after dark shot through my mind so that I stood still, every instinct urging me to run away.

Instead, it was the man who disappeared, slinking hurriedly out of sight, but not before I seemed to detect something familiar about him, something I could not place. Briefly he was silhouetted beneath a flickering gas lamp, then vanished into deeper shadow beyond.

I ran up the front steps, fumbling in the darkness for the lock. The building was small, housing only six flats, one of the new compact apartment houses being built toward the turn of the century. A caretaker lived in the basement, but was never around at this time of night.

In daylight, the place looked elegant, but now was as shadowy and gloomy as its smart neighbours appeared to be in an ill-lit London street, the only light coming from the flickering gas lamps standing along the Embankment wall across the road and from a few on the pavement this side. Fog from the Thames was seeping inland, enshrouding everything and penetrating to my skin as I fumbled with my doorkey; then I was indoors and hurrying up the flights of stairs to our own apartment on the top floor, and virtually falling over the threshold when I reached it. I was vexed with myself for panicking and therefore having to face Gavin in an unnerved state. This put me at a disadvantage, and once within the hall I leaned against the closed door, resolutely calming myself.

Everything was as usual, the oil lamp shining on the hall table, the door to the living room closed, the short passage to our bedroom stretching ahead, that door also closed. I unpinned my hat and laid it, with my gloves and reticule, on the console table; then I unbuttoned my coat and removed it and hung it up. I was doing everything slowly and deliberately and, suddenly impatient with myself, I walked straight into the living room to face Gavin without further delay.

It was an anticlimax to find it empty, the gas mantels on the walls unlit, the fire dying, not even an oil lamp burning to await my return. Then I recalled that I was not expected home tonight. Facing each other angrily in Maiden Lane, I had told him I would not be back, and I had meant it.

I returned then to the hall. Beneath the bedroom door at the end of the short passage, light shone, so I knew he had gone to bed and was probably reading.

I walked along the passage and opened the door. I looked straight at their naked bodies on the bed, her legs apart and he between them, reaching the culmination of their love.

23

"Get out!" cried Clementine. *"Get out of here!"*

I wasn't aware that I still stood there. My mind had recoiled, but not my body. That stood frozen, incapable of movement, and I remained like that as Gavin, exhausted, slid from on top of her, rolled onto his back and, half-raised, stared at me also. Her head remained tilted from the pillows, exactly as it had been when she caught sight of me over his shoulder, but now it dropped back and, laughing helplessly, she cried, "Oh, my God, Lucinda, you should see your face!"

I saw the sweat on his body and the gleam of it on hers, and the whole luscious abandon of her, satiated by sex. She was quite uncaring, and so was he. They had had their fill of each other, and in the satisfying aftermath it was they who were triumphant.

"Better get yourself a brandy, Lucinda. You look as if you could do with one." As Gavin spoke, he dragged himself from the bed and pulled on a robe, half-tying it about him. "If it comes to that," he drawled, walking toward me indolently, "I could do with one myself. How about you, Clemmy? You usually enjoy a drink when we've finished, though admittedly after we've had a chance to rest."

I backed away. He caught up with me and slid an arm about my shoulders, shaking me a little and saying, "Oh, come *on*, love, don't look like that! It doesn't mean a thing. Haven't I told you that life is nothing but a mating dance, so what does it matter who you do it with?"

Beyond him, I saw Clementine half-propped against the pillows, uncovered, stark naked, languid. She yawned, stretched as luxuriously as a cat, and then purred, "Jealous, Lucinda-bastard?"

I fled, stumbling down the stairs to the street and out into the darkness and the swirling fog. In the misty light of a nearby streetlamp I saw the sinister figure again, waiting.

The front door fell to behind me, and I stood there at the top of the steps, unable to go backward or forward, bewildered and helpless, trapped. I had neither latch key nor purse, and there was nothing between that lurking figure and myself but a flight of stone steps, and not a soul in sight.

Terror leapt as he came toward me. I ran, but at the foot of the steps he caught me.

"She's there, isn't she? She's up there, with *him*."

I knew that voice, even though I had not heard it since leaving number 47 Portman Square. His face I could not see; it was half-muffled with a scarf beneath a slouching hat brim. He was no longer in his smart green uniform with gilt epaulettes and cockaded hat, but he was unmistakably Curtis.

Relief momentarily overcame my terror until he shook me, hard, and repeated, "*Isn't she?* Don't lie to me, or I swear to God it'll be the worse for you."

His mood was ugly; to lie would make it worse. But now my whole body was trembling, and when I tried to speak, no sound came. I went on mouthing helplessly until he shook me again and the viselike grip of his fingers made me cry out.

"That's better. Now you've got your voice back, you can speak. You found them up there, didn't you? In bed, most likely, because there's no light in that living room in the front. D'you think I don't know the bedroom must be at the back? I've driven her here often enough, sometimes when you've been in but more often when you've not, and always I've been left to bloody well wait for as long as she pleased. You've only seen me here once, the evening you came to that window and looked out, and then her father came along and ordered me to take her straight home. There was a light in that front room then, and I saw him moving about in there too, so I know it's the living room all right—and there's been no light there since she came tonight. That means they went straight to the bedroom. I followed her from the theatre by cab. She didn't even suspect I was a passenger in the one travelling behind her—out-of-work servants don't travel in hansom cabs, or at any other time if it comes to that." He gave my arm another shake. "Tell me what you saw up there. You saw *something*, or you wouldn't have come tearing out like that."

I heard my voice stammering, but had no idea of the words. The sound I made was wild and senseless, made up of sobs and terror. His grip on my arm hardened.

"I don't want to hurt you, Miss Lucinda, but if I have to, I will. You caught them at it, didn't you? *Didn't you?* Don't tell me I've no right to know. I have every right. The bitch was mine. She came to me willingly enough. She let me think she loved me and, God help me, I believed her because I didn't think her kind let a man have her body for any other reason. Not a well-known actress with a good name to preserve! Not a lady from the upper classes!"

He turned and spat on the pavement. "Classy whores are the worst because they're so bloody dishonest. Street whores do it for money and make no bones about it, but not she—she did it because it amused her, and it amused her even more to do it with the likes of me. A servant. You can use a servant for as long as you like and get rid of him when you like; pick him up and put him down, beckon him and dismiss him, and then when you finally want to send him packing and he won't go without a murmur, you pay him off to shut his mouth; better still, you book him a one-way passage out of the country from the East India Dock, with just enough money to keep him until he gets work. That way, he's not likely to turn up in London again, making a nuisance of himself. The bitch. The fucking bitch. She thinks she's won, but by God, she hasn't."

He began to shiver, partly through cold and partly through hatred. I was cold too. I had fled without even seizing my coat, running from the sound of Gavin's mocking voice. "Divorce? Is that what you are thinking of, looking at me like that? My dear Lucinda, you haven't a hope in heaven of getting a divorce."

"I can for adultery! It's the only grounds on which a woman *can* get a divorce."

"If you imagine that, you are wrong. The law today rules that although a man can divorce his wife for a single infidelity on her part, she cannot do the same to him, no matter how often he is unfaithful to her, unless she can prove that his adulteries are accompanied by physical cruelty, rape, incest, sodomy, bigamy, or a desertion for more than two years, and you cannot level any of those accusations against *me*. As for tonight's little episode, I would deny it, and so would Clementine—wouldn't you, Clemmy?''

He had called to her from the tiny hall where I had confronted him face to face after retreating along the short passage until my back was against the wall, but there had been no answer from the bedroom. Through the open door we could both see her naked body curled up in the middle of the bed, deep in untroubled sleep, and Gavin had laughed indulgently and said, ''Marvellous, isn't she? Totally animal. Satisfy the body and the senses and then relax—that's Clemmy. A cheap little bitch, of course, but still with a shrewd streak; she wouldn't risk exposure or scandal. She can brush the truth aside, or inconveniences, and even people, without so much as a pang of conscience—''

''As you can!'' I had flung the words at him, and he had not even heard them. He had simply continued to talk in that confident, indifferent way, stifling yawns because he was as tired as Clementine, and I was a nuisance who had to be dealt with.

''So there'll be no talk of divorce, Lucinda. It would get you nowhere, not only for the reasons I've named, but because, in your case, any accusations of adultery could be regarded merely as jealous ravings—the illegitimate child hating the legitimate one and seeking vengeance with any trumped-up tale. That is an old, old story and one the courts are very familiar with. They are accustomed to illegitimate offspring making all sorts of wild claims. So don't try being vindictive, Lucinda. Just count your blessings and think of all you've got. All *we* have now got between us . . .''

That was when I finally fled, whirling away from him in total revulsion, and now I looked up at Curtis, his face white in the reflected streetlamp, the spluttering gas jet making a dancing halo about his head, and although I recognised him as anything but a saint, I pitied him.

There was a sudden chord of sympathy between us and he said, ''You poor thing, you've had a rough deal all your life. I remember that cook at number 47 telling me about you when I first went there. 'Miss Grainger's little bastard,' she called you, but I didn't believe her when she said how Miss Clementine used to taunt you. Not then, I didn't.''

He still gripped my arm, and I think it was then that I realised he had not once taken the other hand out of his pocket.

''What are you hiding, Curtis? What have you got there?''

''Mind your own business, ma'am, and let me mind mine. *She's* my business, and I'll wait here until she comes out, no matter how long, then I'll settle things with her and be on my way to the docks in plenty of time to get aboard. The ship sails with the morning tide at eight o'clock, and that'll suit me well. She'll have to be home by the early hours; she's playing safe these days because her doting ma is even more possessive and watchful, sleeping off her nightly consolation and then sending for her daughter to comfort her. Oh, I've made it my business to know everything that goes on in that household these days! For the moment, the beautiful Miss Clementine is dancing to her mother's tune because she can't afford not to, though how she wheedled the money out of her to pay me off, I can't make out. Lady Boswell likes me. I've made sure of that. She wouldn't hand money over to her daughter to get rid of *me* . If she had to do it, she would do it herself, full of tears and reproaches if she really thought I had done something wrong, but first she would want to know just what and when. . . ."

His eyes were on that upstairs window, and mine were on his coat pocket. Again I asked what he had there.

"Not a gun? For heaven's sake, not a gun!" I began to reason with him. "Wouldn't it be better just to go away and put everything behind you? Get aboard that ship in plenty of time to sail—"

"I'll be there in plenty of time, don't worry. And where would the likes of me get a gun from? How could I afford one?" Suddenly he became impatient, eager to be rid of me. I was an encumbrance, even a danger. He didn't want a witness to whatever he planned to do, besides which a light had appeared in that living room high above. I followed his glance and saw the slow rise of newly lit gas. So Gavin was there; not sleeping like Clementine, but pouring himself a drink; perhaps waiting for her to waken or, having wakened her, waiting for her to dress and then to join him before taking her home.

"What are you planning to do, Curtis? Nothing foolish; don't do anything foolish. She isn't worth it. Forget her."

"I know she isn't worth it, but I'll never forget her. You don't know what she was like, what she meant to me, what we shared." His voice hardened. "Why the hell should I be tossed onto the scrap heap? Why shouldn't she know that I've found her out and hear, face to face, what I think of her? She didn't even give me the chance to do that. There was just this envelope with a note saying 'For Services Rendered,' and the money 'in lieu of notice,' and the shipping ticket—one way, of course. And nothing in her own handwriting. Oh, no! Done on one of these new typewriting machines used in offices nowadays, with a signature which looked for all the world like her mother's—forged, I shouldn't wonder, but not by her. She's too cunning a bitch for that. I'm sorry, ma'am, but my suspicion is that your husband connived, but of course I can't prove it. Still, I can get my own back now. She'll come out of that house before long. She won't stay the night. She'll come out in time to get home and cover her traces, and by God, she'll hear the truth from me!"

Suddenly he blazed, "*Get going, can't you?* I don't want the likes of you around!"

My teeth were chattering. The damp night air was soaking my dress. Fog was in my throat and in my eyes. I had nothing with me. Nothing. No coat, no money, no purse.

"I can't, I can't," I said helplessly, and he raised the back of his hand to me, his face menacing.

"If you don't, I'll hurt you. I swear to God I'll hurt you! Get away from here. Go somewhere, *any*where . . ." His head jerked round; there was the sound of hooves and wheels approaching out of the darkness, and an unshielded lamp flickering on the top of a hansom cab, indicating that it was for hire. Curtis dragged me across the pavement, shouting to the driver to halt, and I saw the cabby automatically dowse the roof light as Curtis bundled me inside and slammed the folding doors across the front. The cabby let down the solid upper half, lifted the roof flap, and asked, "Where to, miss?" and I gave Magnus Steel's address automatically because it was the only place in London I could go to, other than back to that top floor flat and the final surrender of my will to Gavin Calder.

The light was bright, slicing through curtains which were vaguely familiar yet unfamiliar. Then a shadow came between the light and myself and a voice said, "So you're awake at last, Lucinda. Good. You fancy some refreshment, perhaps?"

I knew that voice. It was Helen Steel's, and it was her face stooping over me. Even with her back to the light I knew how it looked, plain and wholesome and smiling.

"Believe it or not, you had my brother scared—he, a doctor, scared when a woman pitches across his doorstep! But that's because he cares about you. You're more than a patient to him, more than a casualty brought to his door by a cabby who waited only to grab his fare and be off. He didn't give Magnus a chance to ask where he picked you up. Not that my brother even thought of that; his only concern was you. It was I who wanted to ask a dozen questions, but you were senseless and numbed, incapable of speech, and now I suppose all questions will have to wait until later. Poor Magnus, he carried you to his study and peeled off those wet clothes with all the concern of a big brother for a little sister before even thinking of fetching me. But, as usual, I am talking too much, and this is hardly the time for that. There . . . now I've propped pillows behind you and you can sit up, but I won't pull back the curtains until you say."

"Please do. What time is it?"

"Early afternoon." She drew the curtains, still talking briskly. "You've slept for hours, and a good thing too, judging by the state you were in. By the way, we haven't told your mother that you're here. She was in bed when you arrived and left for her shop at the usual time this morning. She moves into the flat above at the end of this month, and I shall miss her sadly. Anyway, there seemed no sense in alarming her, and by the time she comes home tonight you will be feeling more yourself and ready to reassure her. But Magnus is waiting to see you as soon as you waken."

Minutes later he stood beside the bed, looking taller than ever, towering above me.

"What happened?" he asked. "Do you feel like telling me now? You were incoherent last night, and no wonder, wet and frozen through. I suggest you remain in bed for the rest of the day, though I suppose you will drag yourself to the theatre tonight no matter how you feel. What is it they say—that the show must go on, no matter what?"

I nodded, but at the same time I thought, "Thank God for the theatre, for a job to do. . . ." Meanwhile, there was a feeling of safety here and it had more to do with this man than with the warmth of this bed and the protection of this room, which I now recognised as the one I had briefly occupied prior to my marriage. In fact, so safe did I feel that I could not only look back on events of the previous night, but talk about them. I poured it all out, holding back nothing, and Magnus listened without comment, though when I reached the part about discovering Clementine in bed with Gavin his face went very still.

I said, "I'm sorry. I shouldn't have told you that. It hurt you."

He made no answer and his face remained inscrutable. I knew then that I was right. Clementine was still important to him.

"You fell in love with her the first time you saw her, didn't you, standing in the open door of her parents' house? I remember the moment well and, believe me, I understand."

He turned away, saying rather shortly that there was no need to discuss Clementine except for the part she occupied in my husband's life, but I heard the pain in his voice and stumbled on, "Gavin says he will deny it and that she will too. There is nothing I can do. The situation is trite, isn't it, in these times? To divorce a husband for infidelity is apparently very difficult for a woman to do, and when she can, she very often can't afford to because her lot can be much worse alone, and whatever inadequate allowance he is forced to pay her all too often fails to be maintained. So then she has to recourse to the law again, which has little sympathy for wives who turn against their husbands, particularly for things which are regarded as mere peccadilloes which a wife should ignore, as poor Princess Alexandra does."

"Unfortunately that is all too true, but you have independence now, a career as an actress, a share in a theatre—"

"The other half owned by my husband, who will be my antagonist, not my ally."

"I refuse to believe the day won't come when you will be rid of him. If I hadn't believed that since he carried you off, I couldn't have held on to hope as your mother has done."

There seemed to be nothing more to say and I couldn't permit myself the luxury of being buoyed by his words, which were no more than those of an anxious elder brother, so I turned my thoughts to more practical issues. The most I could do was to leave Gavin's roof, but as business partners we would still be tied to each other. In the circumstances, I cared little about being branded as a deserting wife, but I would be doubling my difficulties at the theatre, because he would undoubtedly pay me back in every possible way.

All right, I resolved. I would have to fight all the harder, develop as much cunning as he, and rely on the support of all those at the theatre who were on my side—for so long as they remained. But who could blame them if, eventually, they left the Boswell Theatre to work for a management less divided?

It would be a fight to the finish, that I knew. I was challenged by it and yet afraid of it. I wished I were older and wiser and more experienced. I also wished I could talk more intimately with Magnus, but the shadow of Clementine was between us.

The door opened, but not to admit Helen with a tray. My mother entered, her face pale, her expression taut. Behind her came Helen, saying, "Trudy has returned unexpectedly. I met her coming in and had to tell her you were here . . ." But I didn't hear the rest of the sentence because my mother was handing an early-afternoon edition of the evening paper across to Magnus, telling him to read the stop-press column.

"*You* tell her," she stammered. "You tell her, Magnus. I can't . . . I can't . . ."

But I reached out and took the paper from him and read the horrifying news item for myself.

Stunned as I was, I went to the theatre as usual. No one tried to dissuade me. Perhaps they knew that to carry on with the routine of living was the best thing for me and, dazed as I was, I knew this too, but I was glad when Magnus came with me and announced his intention to remain backstage throughout the performance, then to bring me home. Because my mother still lodged in his house, it seemed the most natural thing in the world for him to refer to the place as my home, and for that I was grateful.

Neither of us referred to the thing uppermost in our minds—that the police would inevitably call on me, and soon.

I was alone in my dressing room when Clementine arrived. I had not yet achieved the status of having a dresser to myself, nor even aspired to one, which was all to the good because she wanted to talk, and came to the point at once.

"About last night, Lucinda—I will say nothing when the police question you. I will protect you. You can count on me."

If anything were needed to shock me out of numbness, it was that.

"*You* protect *me*? From what, pray?"

"From being arrested, of course. A jealous wife waiting outside her home in the dark to stab her husband in the back—you are the obvious suspect."

When I stared at her, speechless, she went on, "Darling, I know just how you felt, really I do. Inflamed by jealousy. Only, of course it was someone else you saw in bed with him, not I. You cannot prove it was I. I expect the police will question everyone at the theatre, and when it comes to my turn I shall tell them the truth—that I left the theatre before you did and went straight home. Dear Mamma will back me up. She will have to. I have already told her that she was fuddled and asleep by the drawing-room fire when I returned and went straight up to bed. Luckily for me, she didn't waken until after I had let myself in and slipped between the sheets, and then, as always, she came stumbling up to my room—and it was quite true, she *had* fallen asleep by the drawing-room fire. Hawkins hadn't even bothered to waken her; he never does now. He just leaves her there, and so does Kate. When she wakens she becomes plaintive, and then comes fretting to me to comfort her, and that was what she did in the early hours today and, as usual, I had to take her to her room and undress her and put her to bed. So she hadn't a suspicion that I had not been asleep for hours, and no one can say otherwise."

I had just finished applying the first coat of greasepaint, my usual light number 3, and had picked up a stick of number 5 to blend on the cheekbones and chin, but now I laid it aside very slowly, very precisely, on the tray my father had used before me, and then I looked straight at her in the gas-lit mirror and said, "*I* can, Clementine. I can say a lot."

The silence was no more than a split second; then she gave her tinkling stage laugh and said, "What, for instance?"

"That it was Curtis who waited outside to waylay you. That you had paid him off and supplied him with a one-way passage on a ship sailing from the East India Dock on the early tide. They will be able to check which vessels left at that time and where they were bound, and which carried passengers. I will tell the police how I talked with him and how I learned about the note of dismissal he received, and the money in lieu of notice, and the signature which appeared to be your mother's—traced from an old letter signed by her at some time, perhaps? They can pick him up at the first port of call, and I have no doubt he still has that letter. Curtis isn't a fool. He seemed very intelligent to me, working everything out for himself—but dangerous too, as you once said he could be. Ugly and dangerous and out for vengeance. But I thought all he planned was to face you with the truth, to let you know he had found you out and what he thought of you. That was what he said, and I believed him. Then he thrust me into a cab and got rid of me, and I had no resistance. But somehow I think my story will be believed, not merely because it is true, but because Curtis will probably be traced.''

"And did anyone see you talking to him, anyone who could identify him or you? I can see from your face that no one did, and if you imagine that a cabby picking up a fare on a foggy night would even notice a passenger's features, don't be silly. Nor would he have seen Curtis's, because the man's hat was pulled down over his face, which was why neither Gavin nor I recognised him until he was upon us. And since you were not there when Gavin and I came out, you didn't see a thing that happened, so one way and other you haven't much of a leg to stand on, have you? And even if Curtis is traced, he will be convicted of robbery amongst other things, because I have already explained his sudden disappearance to dear Mamma by telling her that he decamped with money— cash I had drawn from my own bank account, which is true and can be proved because the bills would be numbered and would match any found on him. What can't be proved is that *I* handed the cash over to him. His attack on Gavin will appear like robbery too, and nothing to do with jealousy over a woman. In fact, it *was* robbery, though when I looked back as I ran away and saw him stooping over Gavin's body I didn't realise what he was up to, but the late edition of the *Evening Chronicle* reports that Gavin's pockets were empty, and his dress studs and cuff links missing. Diamonds, they were, as I very well know, because they were presents from my dear doting mamma years ago, and so was his gold watch, which Curtis apparently also took, since there wasn't a thing of any value left on his person.''

"I am surprised Curtis should make such a mistake. That watch has Gavin's name engraved inside the lid, but of course Curtis couldn't know that. If the police find him, it will be additional proof of his guilt, so don't come to my dressing room with the idea of frightening me into silence. I have nothing to lose by speaking the truth, but you have.''

"You will find it difficult to prove *any*thing, Lucinda Grainger. It will be a case of your word against mine.''

She spun away from me, flung open the door, then turned back.

"Damn you,'' she spat. "Damn you again! You have everything now and I have nothing, not even the share my father left me in this theatre. With Gavin's death, you get that too!''

She was beside herself, unaware her words could now be heard clearly in the passage outside. She stormed on, *"That* is additional motive for stabbing him. To get your hands on the other share and full control of the theatre. The place has always been your passion. Do you think I'll keep *that* from the police?''

It wasn't something that had occurred to me. I had given no thought to the share which Gavin had laid his hands on by supplying the money to get rid of Curtis. My only realisation was that I had been freed by that desperate man in a way I could never have wished for anyone—death by violence, stabbing in the back. Vengeance on a faithless mistress by killing her current lover.

I turned my back on Clementine and saw her reflected in the big mirror surrounded by naked gas jets. She was framed in the open door of my dressing room, staring at me with hatred—and Magnus behind her in the passage.

He said in a voice of stone, "As a matter of medical evidence, Clementine, it is not unknown for women to kill with the knife, but normally a stab wound deep enough to slay a strong man would need the power of an equally strong man behind it. I too have seen the evening papers. The police doctor's report mentions the force and depth of the stabbing.''

She whirled round, stared at him aghast, then cried, "So you are against me too, you of *all* people!''

"You know I have never been against you, but I can't stand by and let you frighten Lucinda.''

I could not understand the glances they exchanged—inscrutable on his side and questioning, almost frightened, on hers—but the implacability in his voice was undeniable.

Without a word, she pushed past him and fled to her dressing room, and I saw the distress in his face as he looked after her. Then he turned to me.

"I knew you had it," he said. "That courage I spoke of.''

But reaction was setting in; reaction from shock catapulting on shock. Reading the newspaper account of my husband's death had left me stunned and disbelieving, but this scene with Clementine had sent it leaping into reality. I had to clench my hands to control their trembling.

"I am not so brave as you think, Magnus. Not nearly . . .''

Automatically I reached out for my stick of greasepaint again, but as I picked it up, my hand shook.

He came across and took the greasepaint from me and laid it aside.

"Then you must be," he said gently. "You will have to be, young as you are. And in a way, you are still piteously young.''

With compassion he cupped my face in one hand, but I knew the action was meant to be no more than comforting.

"Once, like your mother, I wanted nothing so much as to get you away from this life, away from the theatre, but I know now that it would be wrong to even try. You love it as your father did and, like him, you will never be able to give it up, and you will run away from nothing, not even the responsibilities of having this theatre on your young shoulders. I think your father knew that as much as I. He isn't here to give you his support, but I am. I have as much faith in you as he had. Remember that."

Gratefully I turned my face and kissed his palm, knowing that what he said was true. This was my world. Uncertain, unpredictable, heartbreaking and even violent, but unique and stimulating and beautiful too; a world totally removed from the world of Magnus Steel, but bridged by his understanding and friendship. I envied Clementine for being loved by such a man, and as I prepared for tonight's performance and wondered what time the police would arrive, I also wondered if such a love would ever come my way—even if I would be capable of loving again. I doubted it. My heart was too raw. I was sixteen and had endured enough of love's torment. Henceforth the theatre would be my life, my all, and as I picked up the stick of greasepaint once more and lifted it to my face, I was even more convinced that what Magnus said was true, for the smell was as strong in my nostrils as it had been at the moment of my birth.

Six

Clementine

24

Sometimes I long to escape from this house. Since Papa's death three years ago the atmosphere has changed, and not for the better. All our original servants, except one, have gone; not because we cannot afford them, but because the ungrateful creatures deserted us.

Hawkins went first. "I am leaving to better myself, ma'am. The Earl of Wittersham has long sought my services." Liar. I know for a fact that Wittersham is practically impoverished. Who should know that better than I, who had to reject his proposal of marriage for that reason? I don't look for wealth in lovers, but a husband without money is out of the question. Wittersham was forced to exchange his town house in Cavendish Square for modest rooms in Albany long ago, where Hawkins is now his only servant. Call that bettering himself, after being head of a household the size of ours? Yet scarcely three months after being answerable to Mamma instead of Papa, Hawkins went.

"It's the old story of men refusing to take orders from women," Mamma had declared pettishly. "Well, *he* won't be missed."

But he is. And so is Mrs. Wilson, who couldn't get on with any succeeding butler (four, since Hawkins) and marched out indignantly one day after some quarrel belowstairs which, I have no doubt, Kate instigated.

"Servants are becoming too independent, dear gel. The trouble is, they are too highly paid, but Wilson won't get the wages she earned here, mark my words. She will be begging to come back, you'll see."

But what I did see was Mrs. Wilson installed in the Driscoll household when I called on Penelope one morning for one of our friendly gossips.

There the woman was, on her way to the morning room with the day's menus in her hand, and how proudly she smirked when she saw me! "Here I am in an *earl's* household, miss. What do you think of that?" She didn't say it, of course. She didn't have to.

I have never spoken to Penelope Driscoll since, nor will I ever believe she was not responsible for stealing Wilson. Often she had remarked on what a treasure the woman was and how her mamma would dearly like to lay her hands on such a good cook, and unfortunately she witnessed a scene after luncheon one day, when Mamma sent for the woman and rated her soundly in front of Penelope and myself because her pastry had not come up to standard. (But Penelope was only a girlhood friend; it wasn't as if the scene had taken place before a whole galaxy of guests, so Penelope need not have looked so shocked.) Yet it seemed significant that only a few days later Mrs. Wilson upped and left.

Now we have a woman whose cooking is diabolical, but after a succession of others we have to put up with her for the time being. Kate abominates her. "Do you know, Miss Clementine, she actually expects us to call her Maisie! I soon put her right about that. 'Cooks have the courtesy title of Mrs.,' I told her, 'and if you'd ever worked in a good household, you would know that.' I can't imagine where the mistress got her from, really I can't."

I can. From the theatre. An ex-super who wormed her way into Mamma's favour by stepping into the breach as a dresser one day, during one of Mamma's now rare stage appearances, and then into our household as lady's maid, and then, when Mrs. Wilson's latest successor had followed her out of the servants' entrance, found even more favour by stepping into the breach again when Kate declared it was not part of *her* duties to cook a meal even in emergencies. So there she is—Maisie Stockwell. *Mrs.* Stockwell now, and quite legitimately, it would appear from the imitation-gold band on her finger. Stockwell, I gather from Kate, "journeyed to the Elysian Fields many years ago."

"Or so she says, Miss Clementine—if she ever had a husband, which I doubt. I can tell from the look of her what kind of a woman *she* has been in her time."

And I daresay Kate is right. As always, she knows everything, and what she doesn't know, she finds out. The only thing she never discovered was my affair with Magnus Steel, and that is something I don't like to look back upon, ending the way it did. Lucinda was to blame, of course, and never had I hated my father's by-blow so much.

It happened following that meeting at the theatre, the night when the police came and Magnus had found me in Lucinda's dressing room and sided with her against me. Hurt and angry, I had slipped across the square in the dark later on, and down the area steps, determined to cover things up and to maintain his love for me in the one sure way a woman always can. So I descended the area steps with confidence—and received the shock of my life.

He had locked the door against me.

It was easy to guess why. Lucinda had told him about finding me in bed with her husband, and why Curtis had lain in wait out there in the fog, and I knew with dreadful finality that Magnus would never open his door to me again.

From that moment I resolved to pay Lucinda back, no matter how long it took. I am still awaiting the opportunity, but know I will succeed in the end.

Kate is the one remaining servant of our original household and the one whom I would dearly like to see the last of. When Papa died I thought her hold on me would slacken because she could no longer betray me to him. Mamma I didn't worry about, being the stupid woman she is. I have always known how to pull the wool over *her* eyes. But to my horror Kate had then adopted another tack, becoming even more bold. Until now, she had dealt only in hints. This time she came out in the open.

"I suppose Master Gavin will take your dear pa's place now. Being your uncle, he will feel responsible for you and, I'm sure, very concerned about what you do. I imagine he'd be shocked if he knew about the familiarities Curtis has taken with you. I'm sure he would urge your mamma to dismiss the man, and tell her why, and Curtis wouldn't like that. He has quite a nasty temper, has Curtis. Besides, you've hurt him, trying to put him in his place again the way you have. But you can't do it, Miss Clementine—not when you've permitted intimacies. No servant is going to feel like a servant after that, but don't deny that you're trying to make him. He hasn't told me, but I can tell. I've seen the way you look at him and heard the way you speak to him, but don't worry, Miss Clemmy, I won't tell Mr. Gavin a thing—unless I feel it my duty to. What a lovely bracelet you're wearing! Gold, isn't it? I've always admired it. . . ."

So the retainers continued, the "subs" which, by silent consent, need never be paid back.

All things considered, it had really been a relief when Curtis killed poor Gavin, because when I recovered from the shock I realised that Kate could hold nothing over me anymore—not my affair with Curtis nor my affair with Gavin, which, I am pretty sure, she knew about and reported to Curtis and so caused all that terrible trouble. I truly believed I could now get rid of her once and for all, and how I was going to enjoy doing that!

But there I was wrong. She had poor Mamma under her thumb by then, and still has, indulging her weakness secretly so that Mamma is dependent on her. If I so much as suggest getting rid of our precious parlourmaid, Mamma is aghast.

"Dismiss *Kate?* Dear Kate, the only loyal member of my staff and my good, *good* friend!"

It is useless to try to convince Mamma otherwise. She won't hear a word against Kate, and she certainly won't countenance her dismissal. "Only *I* can dispense with servants, and I'd have you remember that, Clemmy. Besides, why should I? Give me one good reason. Just because you dislike her isn't enough. And why do you, anyway? Kate has been a loyal servant ever since she came with us to this house when she was fourteen and you a mere three-year-old, and certainly she has been the most loyal since your dear papa died."

Loyal to herself, I want to say. That is the only person Kate is loyal to. But how can I say it? How can I prove it? Only by revealing the pressure Kate has submitted me to these past years and thereby my own indiscretions. Not that Mamma would believe either. "You are making it all up, dear gel, just to frighten me. It's a way you have. *So* unkind to a mother who has always loved you. If only you had married! And I can't think why you haven't—you have had every opportunity, every advantage, and lots of men in love with you. Surely you could have landed *one* of those eligible suitors? It isn't too late now, you know, and with the old queen rapidly declining, the Prince of Wales's circle will be admitted into the highest society—not all of them titled, by any means, and not all respectable, but *all* undoubtedly rich. It is the industrialists and the Jews he goes for; they have helped him financially, as everyone knows, and he values them. A rich husband, even without a title, could still be yours."

I have heard it all before and I'll hear it all again, and I won't say there isn't a lot of sense in Mamma's outlook, and I would certainly enjoy a beautiful white wedding at St. Margaret's, just as much as I enjoyed my beautiful white coming-out ball at the Savoy, and perhaps one day I will think about it seriously, but still the whole idea of having to go to bed with the same man, night after night, week after week, month after month, and year after year, lacks as much appeal for me as it ever did. The joy of going to bed with different men is the variety of it. There's never any sameness, never any real repetition. You'd think that with men doing the same thing every time it would *be* the same thing, but it isn't. They have all sorts of individual quirks and kinks, which gives it a constant element of surprise. And if they don't satisfy or please me, I can discard them and turn to another.

Gavin, for instance, was a very adequate lover, but somehow more exciting after he married Lucinda. He came back to me, as I had known he would, and I revelled in it every time, thinking of her, with her big grey eyes looking so trustingly on the world, and imagining how she would feel if only she *knew*. And someday, I hoped, she would. That would be my moment of triumph because, by God, it would hurt her *and* it would pay her back—sweet Lucinda-bastard.

Gavin also found this renewal of our affair doubly stimulating. "It's the added deception which makes it all so much better than it was before, Clemmy. We weren't cheating anyone then."

"I was cheating my parents—"

"—which never worried you in the least. In fact, it heightened your enjoyment, because you knew they would be shocked if they found out. You were doing everything you had been taught not to do, which added spice."

So it wasn't Lucinda who had turned him into a more passionate lover, thank heaven. It was a relief to know that, because for a while I had actually wondered. He hadn't invited me to his rooms or anywhere else for quite a time after he married her. Of course, they had been on tour for some weeks, but he did keep me dangling even so, and that had made me as angry as his marrying her. No one could have guessed how I felt about that, but he did. *He* knew, all right, and told me not to be a fool.

"Marriage has to have a motive, Clemmy darling. Think on that and you will understand why I did it." But I couldn't see any motive for his marrying Lucinda until Papa's will was read and I guessed, from his face, that it was exactly what he had expected and hoped for.

"You wretch, Gavin. You scheming wretch. You married her because you knew she was going to inherit a share of the theatre, and you have coveted the Boswell always, haven't you? Be honest, now—*haven't* you? You have criticised it and ridiculed it and scorned the way my father ran it, but, oh, how you have longed to get your hands on it! Even a share would do. Well, I was inheriting a share too. You didn't realise that, did you?"

"Oh, yes, I did. Fifty-fifty between the pair of you. I was well aware of that for years."

"Then you might just as well have married *me*!"

"Marry my niece? Your parents would never have agreed."

"We're not blood relations."

"So you often remind me, but there's a kind of relationship there, all the same, an accepted uncle-niece relationship, living in the same household for years as we did. Not wholly acceptable by conventional standards, with all sorts of nasty inferences and interpretations, should anyone care to invent them."

"Let them!"

"Why should I? I don't intend my name to have even a trickle of mud on it when I reach the position I aim for. Besides, I didn't want to marry you any more than you really wanted to marry me. Let's both be honest for a change. I *would* have married you if a more propitious match, offering the same advantages and possibly more, hadn't been available. Lucinda could bring me exactly what you could bring me—as you say, a 'coveted' share of the theatre, though as yet I cannot lay my hands on it legally, thanks to this stupid revised legislation in favour of married women and their property, but even had I been allowed to marry you, your father would have taken good care that I *never* got a look-in. He would have tied up your share so hard that I could never touch it. But Lucinda—she's a different proposition altogether. So is so malleable that I can manipulate her with ease, and as her husband I am in a stronger position than Nevill ever was as her natural father. I have only Trudy to contend with on the parental side, and that woman has been too cowed by life to battle effectively, though she did try. As for you, minx, only your vanity is wounded.''

He was a cold-blooded devil, except in bed, and so I had waited, but in the meantime, turned back to Curtis. And why not? Curtis was always a good standby, and returning to him stopped the man's sulks and threatening glances. Also, it was good to be back in that room above the coachhouse, made snug and comfortable thanks to me. I have never been avaricious where lovers are concerned. All I want is plenty of physical enjoyment, and if men can have as much of it as they want, why shouldn't a woman?

Slipping round to the mews was always easy and well worthwhile, and for this reason I shall miss Curtis. I *do* miss him. And I am glad he got away that night.

Three whole years and they have never found him, and that, ironically, is thanks to Lucinda, who answered only the questions put to her by the police and volunteered no more. I was there too, so I know. I made sure of being there. I went back to her dressing room when Magnus Steel had left it, and I told her point-blank that I would deny any story she told about finding me in bed with her husband or that I was even in the vicinity of Chelsea that night.

"You will have to prove every word you tell them, remember that. You'll have to *prove* that I was there and that Gavin left the flat with me, which means you will have to produce evidence, and you can't. You didn't even see us again after you went storming out of the flat, and you have no witnesses. It will be your word against mine."

"So you have already said."

"And you won't find it so easy to pin guilt on Curtis, since you weren't there when the accident happened."

"Accident?"

"Of course it was an accident! Gavin was so angry when Curtis began shouting and waving a knife in my face, threatening to disfigure me for life, that he tried to seize it. They both went down and the knife went into Gavin's back, and then I ran away. I ran all the way to the King's

Road and picked up a hansom there. So there isn't even a cabby in London who could say I was anywhere near the Chelsea Embankment. It's a well-known fact that London cabbies are hand-in-glove with gonophs and footpads and buzzers and are too afraid of the underworld mobs to report anything to the police. Their cabs would be wrecked and their skulls too if they so much opened their mouths—which ensures that the cabby who drove you away from the scene would never be prepared to admit it, even if he were traced."

Lucinda knew that what I said was true. She could produce no evidence, no proof that she had met and talked with Curtis. So all she said was, "But *you* looked back and saw him stooping over Gavin, robbing him."

"It was the newspapers that revealed he had been robbed, not I. For all I knew, Curtis might have been stooping over Gavin to see if he were still alive."

That was true. And then the police had come, and during the first interval, they questioned us in the green room.

"Please," I had begged, taking the police sergeant on one side beforehand, "I would like to be with my sister—my half-sister—so tragically widowed and younger than I. Naturally, I feel protective. You will let me be with her when you talk to her, won't you?" And the big, burly policeman had melted at once, the way men do when I want them to. "I beg you not to harass her, Officer." (He was a sergeant, but being called "Officer" made him expand.) "Ask her as little as possible, please, but feel free to ask *me* as much as you wish."

So I, as her close relative, was allowed to be present, and thanks to me the questions put to Lucinda had been few. Had she been with her husband when he was attacked? No. Presumably he had been on his way home at the time, and the robber had either lain in wait for him or conveniently met him in the dark and attacked from behind, a real gonoph's job, so if she had not been with him it would appear that he had been returning alone? She agreed.

"Then where were you, Mrs. Calder? The flat appeared empty when the police called. No one answered the doorbell."

"I was spending the night with my mother."

"Did your husband know you were going to stay with her?"

"Yes. I had told him."

Very few questions, and none at all to me, but I mentioned casually that I myself had left the theatre immediately after the performance, without troubling to take more than one curtain call, otherwise I would have shared a cab with Mrs. Calder to Portman Square.

"But I was anxious to get home to my own mother, who has been distraught since my father's death. George, the stage-doorman, ordered a hansom for me. He will confirm that, also that I went straight home. He

gave the address to the driver for me." (That I redirected the man later
was my own secret.) "Since losing my dear papa, I have naturally given
up all social life and go straight back from the theatre to keep my poor
mamma company every night."

Then to Lucinda came one last question. Did her husband have any
enemies? Her reply was rather good, I thought. Didn't all men have enemies, particularly popular men, popular actors?

"I dessay that's true, ma'am, but can you name anyone in particular?"

I remember holding my breath at that point, although if Curtis were
traced and brought to justice it could really mean nothing to me except
the embarrassment of any story he might tell, which would surely be dismissed as lies—a well-known actress, daughter of Lady Boswell and the
late Sir Nevill, the mistress of a thieving coachman? Ridiculous! Of
course there would be the embarrassment of that dismissal note signed in
my mother's name, which he would surely produce, and the shipping
ticket bought on his behalf, but none of that could implicate me because
Gavin had handled the whole thing, and Mamma's incoherent denials
and protests would have been heeded very little, because at that time she
was really going hard at her medicine.

But when Lucinda was asked if her husband had any enemies, it
seemed to me she was on the point of naming someone, and then decided not to. I concluded that the reason was that no one would believe her
if she said her husband was hated by anyone so menial as a coachman, or
that such a man had been his amatory rival, but I was relieved when she
merely shook her head and said no more.

When we were alone I remarked, "You were going to name someone,
weren't you? Curtis, I suppose."

Her answer took me by surprise. "No. I was thinking of Durbridge.
He was my husband's greatest enemy. At least, he hated him enough to
be." But on that point I could get no more out of her.

The verdict at the inquest had been robbery with violence and murder
by person or persons unknown, a common-enough event in the streets
of London despite all the efforts of this century to enforce law and order.
Then the case was filed away as one of those unsolved attacks on respectable citizens which occur every night of the week. Not until then
did I ask Lucinda why she had not mentioned Curtis.

"What use would it have been? You would have contradicted everything, and without proof that you were the reason for his waiting outside
our flat, anything I said would have been discredited and a waste of time.
If they catch Curtis, they catch him. If he gets away, he gets away, and
perhaps he deserves to."

"*Deserves* to? A murderer!"

"A madman. Temporarily, at least. Poor Curtis. I saw his face and will
never forget it. The man had murder in his heart, but if anyone was re-

sponsible for Gavin's death it was you. You tormented Curtis and you drove him to that deed, whether it was an accident or not."

That was nonsense, of course, but Lucinda has always been over-dramatic. She has dramatised everything since childhood. Many were the times when I saw her secretly acting, and I always thought her odd, even when small. Quiet and secretive. Gavin always declared she was a shy, sweet little thing whom I shouldn't torment. As if I ever did! I was kindness itself to Lucinda. Even when I began to sense Papa's preference for her and began to wonder what prompted it, I went on being kind and generous to her, though I did sometimes enjoy teasing her. Then as she grew up, all thin and gangly and with that long straight hair which she didn't even attempt to frizz in the fashionable way, I knew she wasn't worth bothering with, not even worth teasing. But the shocks she gave me, getting round my father to coach her for the stage and then eloping with Gavin like that! Naturally a girl in her position, and not in the least attractive to men, would jump at the chance of marrying a man like Gavin, whom she had always secretly adored, as I very well knew, and it was then that I became convinced there was more to Lucinda than met the eye. And, as things turned out, I was right.

"Like mother, like daughter," Mamma has often said, and this has proved to be one of her few sound observations, for not only has Lucinda gone up in the world, but Trudy Grainger also. The woman is a fashionable modiste now, which makes Mamma livid, but not me. I've always quite liked Trudy (or as much as I've been able to like any other woman), though naturally I can't forgive her for bringing Lucinda into the world.

The fact that my father had had a mistress never worried me, but the fact that he produced another daughter still rankles, because my whole life would have been different, but for her. There she is now, queening it at the Boswell Theatre, when it is *I* who should be. What is more, she has become an actress with a growing name, but dedicated to the theatre and her career to the exclusion of everything else. It is her whole way of life, but what an existence! Where do all the hard work, the learning of lines, and the unending rehearsals get a woman? What do they bring her? Fatigue and exhaustion and lines on her face.

I have never shared Lucinda's passion for the stage. Being born into it was bad enough, with all that tension and rivalry between my parents, that awful dependency on their partnership (at any rate, on her side), and Mamma's jealousy of Papa's tremendous talent. And he *had* tremendous talent, as I have reminded her many times since his death, when she has been struggling to perform without him, but all she says to that is, "Well, dear gel, it would have been very strange if he had not, coming of a great theatrical family as he did. It was *I* who had to work for success, not he."

I don't bother to argue with Mamma when she starts ranting like that, looking back at the past with bitterness and resentment and yet with a yearning she is unable to hide. Without Papa, she cannot act at all. She fails miserably and then starts blaming everyone else in the cast for spoiling her performance, for deliberately upstaging her, for not delivering her cues correctly and so making her miss them, for masking her, and for every other fault a player can be guilty of.

"If only dear Nevill were here, he would take you all to task and very probably replace every one of you!" This stormy reproach is commonplace now, and always followed by the stupid tears oozing from between her blackened lashes and down her raddled cheeks. She is forty-two and looks fifty-two and hasn't the slightest suspicion of it. She sees herself only as she was, never as she is, and what she *is* is a tiresome bore, a woman I long to get away from. I give her a wide berth at home and recently ensured this by insisting on owning more than a bedroom at number 47.

"I need a sitting room, too, Mamma—a place of my own in which I can entertain friends. A successful actress needs the right setting. How do you think it looks, my having only a bedroom in my mother's house, as if I were a mere lodger? I'll tell you. It makes *you* look mean. Mean and possessive. So if you won't let me have my own suite upstairs, I shall have no choice but to leave home and set myself up somewhere."

"*No!* You couldn't do such a cruel thing to your mother, who loves you, and besides, no respectable single woman lives alone. What would people *think?* Oh, you can't mean it, you can't! You are teasing me, Clementine. You have always been a tease. . . ."

"I do mean it, Mamma. If you want me to stay in this house, you will give me what I want."

I was bluffing, of course, because I could no more afford to run an establishment of my own on the money I have, which somehow disappears on clothes and all sorts of things, than I could fly. Several men have offered to set me up, but I have declined, not through any silly moral scruples, but because to accept an establishment from a man would tie me to him exclusively, curtailing my liberty and restricting my pleasures. So even if I do sometimes long to escape from this house, I stay where, on the whole, my bread is best buttered, and after a particularly disastrous dinner party to which Durbridge came, when Maisie Stockwell served up the worst meal of her life (and ours), Mamma conceded defeat, and since then I have had my own suite on the second floor without any of the expenses to meet. There's a lot to be said for living comfortably with someone else paying the bills, even a tiresome mother, and I don't entirely ignore her. I am a good daughter to her. I visit her whenever I can spare the time and occasionally invite her up to my sitting room (but never when I have guests), so she knows her darling gel is still under her roof and that makes her feel I still belong to her.

This new arrangement has the added advantage of keeping Kate at bay.

"I wouldn't dream of encroaching on your time now, Kate. I know how busy you are, you have often told me so, virtually running this large house and caring for my mamma as well. So Maisie will relieve you of any duties for me. She will occupy the attic at the top of the house, the one Miss Grainger had. It is still furnished with the same things, as I am quite sure you know, so Maisie will be very comfortable besides being close at hand to look after me. You will have no reason to come up to my rooms at all, which will relieve those aching feet you moan about so much."

"Maisie Stockwell live *abovestairs?* Maisie Stockwell in Miss Grainger's old room! Why, it's better than mine!"

"Not now, Kate. It can't possibly be, with the things I have given you and the things you've been able to buy for yourself as a result of my generosity. You will find life a lot easier, with only my mother to be responsible for."

"And who is to do the cooking, may I ask? Who is going to prepare the meals?"

"A new cook. An excellent woman Lord Durbridge found for us after sampling that terrible dinner the other night. We are about to enter a new regime, Kate. Maisie will keep my rooms clean and wait at table when I have my own private dinner parties up there. At other times I will dine and take afternoon tea with my mother in the usual way, and those will probably be the only times that you and I will ever meet except for passing in the hall. The new cook is married to a very experienced butler, and he will be supervising the household just as Hawkins did. I am sure you will be glad to know that you will be relegated entirely to the duties of parlourmaid again, but to my mother only."

Kate's mouth set sullenly. "A divided household, eh? Strange way of living, if I may say so."

"You may not say so. You may return to your duties instead."

And so I dismissed her, and enjoyed it, but at the door she had the audacity to turn and say, "One day you'll get your comeuppance, Miss Clemmy, you mark my words."

I won't say I actually *dislike* being an actress, only certain aspects of it. I enjoy the applause and the adulation I receive, but grinding hard work has never appealed to me, and since the widening policy at the Boswell now includes plays by Pinero and Wilde and a new dramatist called Bernard Shaw, all of which means learning new lines and constant study, life is not so easy as it was when Papa's stock productions, familiar to me since childhood, meant no more than rehearsing for the purpose of refreshing one's memory.

Mamma was scandalised that despite Oscar Wilde's public disgrace four years ago his plays should be performed, but when she protested, both Willard and Bramwell Chambers and Lucinda herself calmly announced that his plays were classics.

"Classics!" gasped Mamma. "The man was regarded no more highly than Ouida when *I* was young. At one time in his career he even became the editor of a magazine for females called *Ladies' World* which he promptly renamed *Women's World* so that the working classes could imagine that it catered for them also, as it apparently did because its circulation promptly trebled!"

"I am not surprised," Lucinda had said. "Servant girls and shop girls and factory workers and cleaners are women too, and entitled to be catered for. We are reducing our gallery prices to ninepence for the front six rows, sixpence beyond them, and threepence at the back, for this very reason, so that poorer people may be enticed into the theatre and away from the music halls, where prices meet their pockets. *Lady Windermere's Fan* and *The Ideal Husband* and all of Wilde's plays will appeal to rich and poor alike, and I guarantee we will play to packed houses, from the stalls to the gods."

"And who are *you*, gel, to answer me back like that?"

Mamma had lost none of her aversion for Lucinda, but Lucinda displayed none for Mamma. She was now quite indifferent to her snubs. She met my mother pleasantly and courteously and got on with the job of working for the theatre, but of her private life, at this stage, I knew little and cared less. The Boswell appeared to be the centre of her existence and I had cause to be grateful to her when Mamma turned to me that day and demanded to know why I didn't put my foot down on this matter of Wilde's plays. Before I had a chance to answer, Lucinda simply pointed out that no individual person at the Boswell now decided which plays should go into production, but that the decision was made by a majority choice of the board, thereby helping me to conceal from Mamma that I no longer had a say in things. Mingled with my gratitude was resentment, of course, but at least she spared me a tirade from my mother. Even so, I passionately wanted to regain that share left to me by Papa, and had begun to wonder, more and more, just how I could go about it.

It was rare for Mamma to drop into the theatre as she did that afternoon, but sometimes she would take it into her head to sail in during rehearsals, ease her girth into a seat on the front row of the stalls, and interpose loud comments and advice, to Willard's fury. Since she was not performing in the current production, she had actually no right to be

there, but no one would have been so ill-mannered as to question her arrival. She was endured out of courtesy to her late husband, but when her
interference became too much, Willard would turn to her and demand
icily, "May I ask, Lady Boswell, who is stage director here—myself, or
you? And may I remind you that Sir Nevill would never have dreamed of
interfering when rehearsals were being conducted by me?"

Somehow I feel there must be an easier way of winning admiration and
applause and being paid for it, and that one day I will find it or it will find
me. Meanwhile, I continue to act at the Boswell despite the modest salaries it now pays, thanks to the team running it—Lucinda, Bramwell,
Willard, and Montgomery, the house manager, who keeps his eye on every penny. These four are more concerned about making the theatre pay
its way than they are about the cast being able to. Audiences might drop
until the company re-established itself firmly. Increases in salary would
have to wait, it was announced when the theatre went into production
again after my father's death. There was a lot more talk about everyone
pulling together and upholding the theatre's reputation, and three years
later the talk is still the same and I am still waiting for the promised salary
increases. Mine, anyway. Lucinda is all right, of course, owning the place
and taking all the profits.

The day following my mother's unexpected visit and the argument
about Wilde's plays, I tackled the girl. "*You* are sitting pretty with your
hand in the till, but what about me? My father wanted me to have an
equal share in this theatre, and that is what he left me in his will."

"With the freedom to dispose of it, if either of us wished, and you
did."

"But he didn't intend you to have *all* of it!"

"Nor did Gavin. Remember?"

"I consider you should hand my share back to me, for dear Papa's
sake."

Lucinda gave me that level glance of hers and said that for his sake she
would do so without hesitation if she could trust me not to dispose of it
again. "But that is precisely what you would do, I'm sure. You don't enjoy the hard work of acting, only the limelight, and if anyone came along
who again offered you a nice lump sum for your share in the theatre you
would take it. I can't run the risk of your selling to an undesirable purchaser, someone none of us would want to have at the Boswell."

"Such as?"

"Durbridge. You are friendly with him, I know, and he is an entrepreneur with plenty of money. Oh, no, Clementine—you can't have
your share and sell it twice. As for my hand being in the till, Montgomery deals with the financial side, and I have nothing to do with it. I work
on salary, like everyone else, but when the theatre reaches a certain per-
centage of profit, I will take what is due me."

"It must be showing a profit now. We are not playing to empty houses by any means."

"That is true, but we have set ourselves a target, and until we reach it, whatever profit we make is being reinvested in the company. All sorts of improvements are needed if we are to keep ahead of others—electricity throughout, and new stage sets for new plays for which old sets cannot be merely repainted and disguised. Bramwell has forgone his fee as adviser for the time being and is even carrying on at his old supporting-lead salary despite the fact that he has taken over my father's leading roles, and although Chrystal Delmont could do with an increase even more than you, she's not complaining."

"What a noble band of saints! The Salvation Army should look to its laurels."

Her gaze didn't flicker. She looked at me in that calm way in which her mother used to look at mine, and it was then that I realised how startlingly like her mother she had grown and remembered how Gavin had predicted she would. I hadn't believed it then, angular and gawky as she had been, but I have the evidence of my eyes now. Lucinda has her mother's figure, but taller, and where she had once been skinny she is now slender. Although by today's standards she lacks the desirable voluptuous curves, I have to concede that she has achieved a certain grace of form and that her face—well, if you like that kind of a face I suppose you could call it beautiful.

And she certainly knows how to dress, thanks to her mother. She was wearing a checked tan gown that day, trimmed with a yoke of shot silk in a deeper shade of tan, on which were lines of amber velvet embroidery. Around the yoke, wrists, and on the crossed waist band was matching ornamentation, and I recognised Trudy's touch; she had toned down the elaborate trimmings and embroideries which had been fashionable for so long and introduced much more restraint and simplicity. The result was very effective and I resolved there and then to do what I had always wanted to do—have my clothes made by Trudy even if my mother raged and ranted against the idea. I could keep it a secret, though Trudy Grainger's designs were becoming recognised about town these days.

Her premises had expanded to include the adjoining shop and the floors above, which had been made intercommunicating, until the two places were one complete building. Before I quarrelled with Penelope Driscoll I had gone along with her one day to watch her being fitted for a new gown, and had been decidedly impressed. I scarcely recognised Trudy. She had a vitality and a sparkle which had never been part of her personality in the old days, and she had greeted me entirely without embarrassment.

"Clementine, how nice to see you. I trust you are keeping well?" She might have been a society hostess receiving me in her drawing room.

Lucinda had appeared then and invited me upstairs to the rooms she shared with her mother above the business premises. These surprised me too. A flight of thickly carpeted stairs ran up from the private street door at the side of Trudy's salon, painted white to match the whole façade, and these stairs terminated at another white door sealing off their living quarters, which occupied the two floors above, plus attics. This door had its own brass knocker, a replica of the one facing the street. From these private stairs, at a halfway landing, a door opened onto the workroom floor above the salon, divided into fitting rooms and, beyond them, the premises in which Trudy's staff worked. But in the Graingers' home above, the two worlds were remote from each other. Not even I could hide my surprise when I entered it.

"Well, well, Lucinda . . . you *have* gone up in the world, you and your dear mamma!"

"Is there a *double entendre* to that remark?" Lucinda had laughed, closing the white entrance door from the stairs. I was glad she made light of the moment, because it enabled me to do the same and to say how pleased I was by this evidence of her mother's success.

"And to think that my dear Papa was responsible for all this! He financed her, of course."

"On the contrary, she was able to establish her business prior to his death, as you very well know, and received no financial support from him until his will provided her with an income."

"*Some*one must have put up the capital. Another lover, perhaps? I think dear Trudy has always been a dark horse. I wonder who the man was. . . ."

"Not a lover," said Lucinda in a tone which brooked no further discussion, to my regret. I would have enjoyed finding out the truth. If another man had come to Trudy's rescue, it would interest my dear mamma profoundly. It could possibly prove advantageous, even helping us to upset my father's will, though I couldn't imagine how. But still, a hint here and there that Trudy Grainger had traded on other men besides my father to finance her independence—well, hints like that might be useful as well as amusing to spread around, and they could conveniently lead to further suggestions that poor Papa had possibly been blackmailed into leaving half-ownership of the Boswell to her daughter, and that Lucinda had then been equally cunning in persuading her husband to wrest my share from my grasp.

But there I had to tread carefully, because I had successfully hidden from Mamma the fact that I had sold out to Gavin, and why. Lucinda had kept quiet about it too, and so had those at the theatre who knew the truth. Naturally it paid them not to talk, and no doubt they preferred to forget whatever they had learned on the day dear Gavin died, believing that the less they knew, the better.

"What's past is past." I could almost hear Bramwell saying it, patting Lucinda's shoulder to comfort her in that fatherly way of his. Right from her childhood he had been fond of Lucinda; right from the days when she had sat in a corner of Mamma's star dressing room. That room is mine now, with the silver symbol still on the door, though I know perfectly well it should be Chrystal Delmont's dressing room, since she has taken over Mamma's lead roles more or less permanently, which is why I moved in before she had a chance to, daring her to make a fuss and knowing perfectly well she would not. Chrystal is too ladylike for that.

But remembering Lucinda as she had been when a child, sitting quiet and subdued in that corner, it seems impossible that she should have grown into the blossoming creature she now is. The stage crew is devoted to her, particularly Jerry Hawks, who is now ASM, a nattily dressed cockney who dislikes me thoroughly, though he never actually shows it. But I can tell. I am waiting for him to make just one slip, to be rude to me just once, but he never does and he never is; always he has that cheerful cockney smile which seems to differ in no way from the smile he bestows on everyone else. But something lurks behind his eyes when he looks at me, and I know perfectly well what it is. Dislike. In return, of course, I dislike him, but as far as a mere ASM goes I can bide my time, just as I bided my time when Lucinda was a docile child.

How I had longed to goad her into naughtiness! One scene caused by her, one petulant wail, one disturbance, and she would have been banished upstairs to Wardrobe, and a good thing too. It had always been a source of regret to me that it had never happened, and I used to remind her of how privileged she was to be allowed into the great Bernadette Boswell's dressing room regularly and how generous it had been of my dear mamma to admit her.

"She had no choice," Lucinda had startled me by saying one day. "She would never have had *my* mamma as her dresser otherwise. It was my mother's stipulation, not your mother's kindness."

That made me seethe, and still does in remembrance. Lucinda had been twelve at the time and I fifteen, shortly to depart for the convent. Before I went she needed to be taken down a peg or two because she was obviously becoming a shade too confident, and that happened very effectively when a trinket of my mother's was found in Lucinda's coat pocket. If I hadn't brushed against the door and dislodged the coat from its peg, the trinket (a brooch, I remember) would never have fallen out in full view of Mamma, who was naturally horrified. I was filled with concern for Lucinda, but all my pleas on her behalf were unheeded beneath my mother's spate of reproaches.

"Your child is a thief!" she hurled at Trudy. "And to think I have trusted her and favoured her all her life!"

Of course, she was banished from the star dressing room after that and had to sit quietly by the SM's table in the prompt corner, a cold and draughty spot which, to my chagrin, she didn't seem to mind. She even appeared to enjoy it, watching the performances starry-eyed and my father in particular. No wonder she had got round him so cleverly! The adoration in her face had been obvious to everyone.

Naturally, I told her it was thanks to me that she was permitted to sit there. Only stage crew were allowed to be present in the wings, or members of the cast when awaiting entrances. "And it is only for your mamma's sake that you are admitted to the theatre at all now. Poor Trudy—she must be heartbroken over what you did."

"I didn't do it, Clemmy, as I think you know."

"If not, then who?"

"I think you know that, too, and so does Mamma."

I avoided Trudy after that. I didn't like the way she looked at me. Anyway, I was off to France and a life which I expected to be dull, but which turned out to be quite the reverse. . . .

But now that is all in the past and mercifully forgotten. I admit (but only to myself) that I had played a joke on Lucinda, but not for a moment had I imagined it would misfire and cause such a hullabaloo, with my father springing to Lucinda's defence and a quarrel between my parents because of it. A bit of fun is a bit of fun, and I did try to smooth troubled waters and make everything right for her. It wasn't my fault that I failed.

Funny that the memory of all that should return to me when I entered those upstairs rooms in George Street. It was as if the tables had been turned on me completely. The place outshone my own suite (if such it could be called) in my mother's house. The Graingers' home consisted of a spacious drawing room and an elegant dining room, from which I glimpsed a roomy kitchen and a maid's sitting room beyond. On the floor above were two charming bedrooms and a bathroom I would have dearly liked to possess. From that floor a short staircase led to an attic, no doubt comfortably converted into a maid's bedroom. The elegant bathroom particularly took my fancy and I decided there and then that Mamma should install one exclusively for me. A bedroom and sitting room of my own were not enough. But when she suggested that I myself should pay for it, she certainly took me by surprise.

"There's a single room at the top of the house, the one that gel used to occupy. You can have that converted, if you wish. You can surely afford it, being part-owner of your father's famous theatre. I cannot think why you are always coming to me for money when you already have a good allowance, plus your earnings as an actress *and* fifty percent of the theatre's profits."

I dodged that by saying that Lucinda's old room was scarcely big enough to accommodate a bath, let alone a toilet. "I would be ashamed to let my friends use it, *or* to let them climb stairs to the attics. The room above the hall, on my own floor, corresponding with the one of yours which has already been turned into a bathroom, is far more suitable.''

"Then take it, dear gel. It will be a more costly conversion, but you can well afford it, whereas I, alas, have only the income left me by your father.''

"A very substantial income, Mamma, plus this house and an established fund to meet all expenses. The new bathroom for me should come out of that.''

"This house was left to *me*, Clementine, and the fund along with it. It was to house and shelter me for the rest of my life without anxiety, and that will be a husband's responsibility toward *you* when and if you have the sense to realise it.''

When my mother grew testy like that it was a sure sign that she needed her medicine. She seemed more and more disinclined to act these days, which wasn't surprising since she had been adversely criticised in the press for every performance she had given since Papa's death.

She blamed the new management for that, and particularly "that gel" (she had never referred to Lucinda by name since the parting of the ways). "That gel is determined that I shall fail." "That gel is trying to oust me and imagines I don't realise it, but I will outwit her yet!" "That gel chooses all the wrong plays and does it deliberately, making sure there is either no part for me at all, or only a bad one, and it puzzles me why you, as her partner, don't put your foot down.''

It was like being caught in a trap; I couldn't argue because it would reveal too much. I merely pointed out, as Lucinda had done, that all decisions were reached by the theatre board, letting Mamma still believe I was a member. Hoodwinking my mother might have been entertaining if the whole business had not been as irritating as she was herself. I had ceased to find Mamma amusing a long time ago. She is now nothing but a burden, a liability, and I wish I could be rid of her.

Sometimes I think I shall marry just for that reason, but that might be going from the frying pan into the fire. A possessive husband wouldn't give me the liberty I manage to get at number 47, so I continue to put up with dear Mamma, making sure she doesn't invade my privacy when I need it. Maisie helps me there. Maisie has turned out to be quite a treasure and, thank heaven, so has the new cook, together with her husband, the butler. They appreciate their joint accommodation, plus that sitting room which used to be shared by Hawkins and Mrs. Wilson, and the Graingers too, once upon a time. How long ago that all seems now! Anyway, the new couple have settled in nicely and we are indebted to Lord Durbridge for finding them.

Since Papa's death I have seen Durbridge occasionally, although after that first meeting at the Driscolls' house he never again made his interest in me quite so obvious. Inviting him to my coming-out ball had been the clever ruse I had intended it to be, for not only had I won an acceptance from one of London's social lions, but my triumph was increased by the knowledge that he had declined invitations to almost all others, including Penelope's. On the night of my ball I knew instinctively that one day this man would play an important part in my life, and the feeling never left me even when he disappeared from the social scene for so long. I always felt that one day he would return and take control in some way. I now believed that culmination to be imminent and, with judicious manipulation on my part, that I could even hasten it.

Part of Durbridge's fascination was his inscrutability and my own inability to penetrate it. This made him all the more challenging, and the dark undercurrents which, I felt, lurked beneath the surface, even more compelling. I was not in love with the man, he aroused no sexual desire in me, but I was drawn to him because I knew he wanted me to be. It was as if he held out a forbidden cup which, until now, he had kept just beyond my reach and that he would allow me to drink from it only when he decided the right moment had come.

So when he wrote to me after Gavin's death, nothing could have been more welcome, particularly since I was then smarting bitterly beneath Magnus Steel's rejection.

> I know how attached you were to your mother's stepbrother, [Durbridge wrote]. Everyone regarded him as your uncle—except you, perhaps?—so please accept my condolences on the occasion of his death and I trust I may be permitted to call upon you one afternoon, either at your home or at the theatre. You have only to send word, dear lady. You are no doubt aware that I am now tragically crippled—incurably so—a spinal injury which has robbed me of the use of my legs. Consequently my social life is limited and you would be doing a lonely man a great kindness in receiving him. I am, alas, confined to a wheelchair, but have an able man to attend me and to negotiate stairs when necessary, but this only serves to remind me of my helpless state and I am therefore happier when faced with level areas along which I can propel myself with as much dignity as such a sorry state permits. Therefore, if I may suggest it, dear Miss Boswell, to be received in your dressing room would perhaps be a happier choice than your home. I am sure your gentle and compassionate heart will understand and indulge my sensitivity.

Poor Durbridge—my heart did indeed go out to him and I hastened to invite him to take tea with me after a matinee. The man was charm itself and I could see no reason for Lucinda's dislike of him. I thought she would be lucky indeed if a man of his wealth were instrumental in providing further financial backing, and I had no doubt at all that in such an event she would jump at it, urged by her small coterie of supporters at the theatre, so not for a moment did I believe her excuse for not returning to me the share I had inherited.

From where Durbridge got his wealth I had no idea. Gavin's dark hints about its source had never been enlarged upon, which convinced me that he had been making them up. Obviously, Durbridge's riches were inherited and all Lucinda's talk about him being an entrepreneur of some kind was nonsense. The man was a charming dilettante, interested in all forms of art. I knew of no fewer than two young men whose careers as artists he had sponsored, another whom he had launched as a musician and still another in whose career as an actor he took a personal interest.

So even if I did manage to lay my hands on my share of the theatre again and even if I did resell it, Lucinda would be lucky indeed if Durbridge became the purchaser.

Lingering over a spendid champagne supper with him at the Savoy one night I confided in him; not my idea of selling out to him if I had the chance—it was a little premature for that—but how my papa had left me inadequately provided for, which was a good lead-up to the subject.

"Everything except the theatre went to dear Mamma. Not that I begrudged her one penny, I do assure you, but where Lucinda Grainger was concerned I felt differently. Was it really fair to treat a by-blow as if she were on a par with a legitimate daughter? It was a shock, dear Lord Durbridge, a most terrible shock; the whole story of my father's association with that dresser, and the child she had borne him, and the way they had come to live in our house, and *then* to provide for the girl in exactly the same way that he provided for me, as if there were no difference between us, was humiliating to a degree. I ask you, Lord Durbridge, was it justice? Mamma is financially secure; in fact, she is extremely well off, but I have only my earnings as an actress and not a penny besides."

"Surely you had an allowance in your father's lifetime and it continues?" Durbridge murmured, and I wondered if he had heard about the income settled on me when I departed to the convent in France. It had been increased when I made my bow at court and again by my father's trustees when I reached the age of twenty-one, by which time it had reached its maximum, but of course Durbridge couldn't possibly know about any of that. People just naturally assumed that a young lady in society had her own settled income or a very generous allowance from her parents, but it did no harm to let him think otherwise, so I shook my head and smiled bravely.

"Only my earnings as an actress and not a penny more," I repeated. "When the will was read I made no complaint, of course, though dear Mamma was aghast. I assured Lucinda Grainger that I was delighted for her, but in order to hold up my head and deal with tiresome creditors I was forced to dispose of my share in the theatre, which, I am sure, would have grieved Papa sorely."

"Which is why you sold it to your stepuncle."

I was surprised by his knowledge and guessed that Gavin must have revealed it. How like him to betray a trust! The man had never possessed a conscience, and this, to someone like myself who has so much of it, always seems profoundly shocking. However, I concealed my reaction, merely saying that in the circumstances it had seemed the best thing to do. "That way, I believed I was keeping it in the family and not letting Papa down. But then poor Gavin was tragically killed, as I am sure you heard."

"Ah yes—by some cutthroat at dead of night."

"Precisely. And never traced."

"Unhappily, footpads rarely are. Our police force is undermanned so can hardly be blamed for failing to solve all the crimes in London, apart from which they have enough on their hands trying to cope with the vast problem of prostitution amongst both sexes, including children, of which our leading cities have the highest numbers in the world. The situation is little better now than it was earlier in the century, despite all our social reformers. Even Dostoevsky was horrified by the thousands of prostitutes flocking the streets of London, and that man was a widely travelled and seasoned sinner, and since our railways spread to the outer suburbs, the trade has expanded to the stations there, and beyond."

"It sounds as if you have made a close study of the subject," I said lightly, wishing he would get back to my own problem, but he persisted by confessing that he did find it interesting.

"Even amusing," he added, "since our Victorian age is so straitlaced on the surface that I suspect the word 'Victorian' will go down in history as synonymous with narrow-minded bigotry, thanks to the veneer of middle-class respectability which dominates the nation—not provided by so-called society, but by our Honest John citizens, the merchants and shopkeepers and factory owners with their Bible-thumping and prayer meetings and patriarchal home life. Underneath all this moralising, a man who has the money to pay for it can enjoy any perversion, any sado-masochistic experiment, and any sexual deviation or, as some would call it, degradation. But still the law frowns on activities not regarded as 'normal' and brands them illegal. Am I shocking you, Miss Boswell? I doubt it. The theatrical world is known for its immorality, and many theatres have links with nearby places of doubtful repute. Even the Lyceum is rumoured to have an underground passage leading directly to a brothel, and that Irving's famous mistress may have something to do with it. Perhaps she has—who knows? The fact remains that actresses are notorious, and on the whole justifiably. Many rank amongst the most highly paid courtesans in London. Being in the theatre yourself, you must at least know this, even if you have never participated—as I am sure you never have.''

Was there mockery in his voice? I couldn't be certain, so changed the subject by saying, ''We were discussing my affairs . . .''

''Ah, yes. Forgive me. What finally happened to the share you sold to Calder?''

''Inherited by his wife, who is avariciously holding on to it. Poor Papa would be grieved and disillusioned if he knew she had robbed me of my inheritance, and in refusing to give it back to me she *is* robbing me. After all, it was not *she* I sold it to,''

''I can understand your wish to get it back, dear lady, and of course anyone with a generous heart would comply in the circumstances. Perhaps unaccustomed power has gone to the young woman's head?'' His sympathy pleased me, but his next words did not. ''However, she is quite within her legal rights. Anything inherited from her husband is hers, and the best way to wrest it from her is to appeal to her heart and her loyalty.''

''She has neither heart nor loyalty as far as I am concerned.''

''But your father? She was devoted to him, I understood. He was her idol.''

''How do you know that? Did she tell you?''

''Indeed, no. I scarcely know the young woman.'' His eyes seemed to go quite cold—his voice too, as if to even discuss Lucinda Grainger chilled him. Durbridge could switch from warmth to ice in the most uncanny fashion, but I knew instinctively that the ice, at this moment, was not for me. His white hand, with its thick coating of black hairs, moved across the table and covered mine. To my surprise, the palm was moist and warm; not in the way a man's hands could be at intimate moments, but like the damp paws of some strange animal, softly padded. There was something mesmeric about the touch, compelling me not to withdraw.

''If you cannot play upon her loyalty to your father and a consideration of his wishes, my dear young lady, you must bide your time until you are in a position to buy back the share. There I may be able to help you. Meanwhile, be patient and, above all things, show no animosity toward her. No two young women could be more different than yourself and Lucinda Grainger, but don't emphasise it. Be her friend, or appear to be. You could win her trust that way. In some ways she is very naive.''

''Not now. She has grown up since Gavin's death. The shock, I suppose.'' I refused to admit, even to myself, that Lucinda's personality could have changed overnight as a result of walking into that bedroom at that particular moment. . . .

Durbridge was repeating, ''And don't forget, if you need help, come to me.''

"Help in what way?"

"Any way at all, my dear."

The fleshy paw still covered mine; the warm, damp pressure increased, but still there was nothing sexual about it. It didn't stir my blood. What kind of man was this? Different from others, I knew. I had recognised years ago that Durbridge was far from run-of-the-mill and that he could teach me things and introduce me to things which I had still not experienced. The thought excited me, but the touch of his flesh didn't, and there the oddness lay, because even so there was something meaningful in the pressure of his hand.

I said in shocked tones, which I hoped were convincing, "If you mean financial help, you must surely realise that I would never take money from men."

I couldn't see why this declaration of virtue should amuse him—if the slight quivering of his red lips and the hasty lowering of his heavy eyelids indicated amusement. The reaction was fleeting, and when he answered his tone was solemn.

"Of course not, my dear Miss Boswell. I would never insult you in such a way, but if you ever need an ally, you can count on me. To tell the truth, I have never taken to your half-sister and it would please me to help to outwit her. Meanwhile, a young woman with your looks could supplement her income very advantageously if she were not so highly moral."

"What do you mean?" I withdrew my hand deliberately. The time was not ripe to reveal that in certain ways I lacked conventional scruples. It was still important that he should think me as virtuous as I had appeared on the night of my coming-out ball, when he had compared me with the flowers that bedecked the ballroom. "Pure and unsullied, white and virginal," he had murmured as we danced, giving me the same odd feeling that he gave me now, that somehow there was a double meaning in everything he said, but his admiration then, as now, had seemed genuine enough. All the same, what did he mean by my looks enabling me to supplement my income? It seemed to me that only one interpretation could be put on that.

As if reading my thoughts, he said hurriedly, "Don't misunderstand, darling Clementine. That name suits you better than sedate Miss Boswell, though I should hate you to be lost and gone forever, like the lady in the song." He was speaking facetiously now, lightly and flirtatiously, removing any hint that he regarded me as anything other than a pretty and desirable young woman, and certainly not as one whose physical attributes could be turned to monetary advantage. Even so, I felt disinclined to let him off lightly.

"I dislike the implication, Lord Durbridge, so please do not try to change the subject. Women who supplement their incomes by trading on their looks do it in only one way—the profitable trade you discussed earlier."

"There you are mistaken, my dear. A woman doesn't have to sell her body to men in order to profit from its beauty, and someday, if you wish, I will show you how."

I was intrigued, but didn't say so. Something told me to play a waiting game with this man. Nor was it wise to appear too curious or too eager, so I smiled very sweetly and thanked him for an enjoyable supper and said that poor dear Mamma would be worried if I stayed out too late.

He made no demur and as if by some unseen signal his man, Stacey, arrived to wheel him away from the table and the new hotel manager who had succeeded César Ritz was bowing low, and nothing so vulgar as the presentation of a bill or the passing of money took place, Durbridge being the type of man to whom credit was automatically extended. He ran accounts at all the best restaurants, I had heard, which suddenly reminded me of that long-ago night at Romano's.

Perhaps the champagne had loosened my tongue tonight, because after I stepped into his carriage and waited whilst Stacey and a doorman lifted Durbridge's wheelchair and anchored it within the vehicle, with a special device installed for the purpose, I said without thinking, "What *did* happen that night, Lord Durbridge? The night you gave that supper party at Romano's, I mean. We all missed you so much."

He made no answer, and it could only have been in my imagination that I heard the brief intake of his breath, because in the light from the hotel's entrance I saw his face clearly and it was absolutely composed. So was Stacey's as he tucked a rug about his master's knees, yet I could have sworn that between the pair of them a sudden sharp awareness had been exchanged. Then Stacey was calmly closing the door and climbing up on the box and we were bowling out of the Savoy's courtyard in silence, and I was still wondering why a simple question seemed to have caused such a strange reaction.

However, by the time we reached my front door he was all affability again, kissing my hand with his moist red lips and saying, "We must not lose touch, Miss Boswell. And don't forget, if you need help in the matter of regaining your share of the theatre, I will be glad to assist you." Then his eyes ran over my body, assessing it in the way he had done at our very first meeting, like an artist summing up the attributes of a model, after which he smiled and murmured, "We could be of use to one another, you and I. For instance, I could help you to earn a great deal of money."

"By investment, you mean? But I understand little about stocks and shares."

"You are being deliberately naive. You know I am no city broker and *I* know that you are no innocent. The virginal white gown and garland of camellias you wore with such charm at your coming-out ball deceived everyone but me. Even Magnus Steel was taken in, which speaks much for your ability as an actress, which, forgive me, you employ better offstage than on. Don't look so ruffled. Beauty alone ensures you success, but it could be exploited more expertly. However, that is digressing. I was referring to Steel's enslavement and the tribute it paid to your capacity to deceive. Believe me, that man normally has a disconcering ability to see through people."

"I deceived him in no way at all!"

Durbridge's only comment was that the worthy doctor was an idealist at heart, and when an idealist met someone who appeared to embody his ideals, he could be wholeheartedly duped. "No doubt he saw you as the personification of pure young womanhood." The idea seemed to amuse him, but I failed to see why.

"He saw me as I was, as I am," I answered coldly.

"Oh, no, my dear, he did not. Only I saw that. Is the man still enchanted by you? Did he become . . . part of your life, shall we say? I ask only because if the day ever comes that Steel does get to know the real Clementine Boswell, he may take it hard. Idealists do when disillusioned. I have no doubt that coming into daily contact with the raw side of life has only intensified his desire for the wholesome and the good. Now, I am no idealist. I am a shrewd observer of life and people; at one time an active participant, now merely an onlooker, but I am learning that a great deal of enjoyment and even satisfaction can be the lot of the spectator, and there are even ways in which a crippled man can console himself."

"I don't know what you are talking about, Lord Durbridge."

I saw the tip of his cigar glow within the shadows of the carriage; then he exhaled slowly and said, "You will, darling Clementine, when I take you to Babylon. You are startled, but why? You know the area in London where Babylon exists, and with your insatiable appetite for experience I am quite sure you have often wanted to have a peep behind the scenes. Be patient. I will take you there in my own good time."

25

I suppose I should have been insulted, but I was not. I was excited beyond words. How often I had begged Gavin to take me to that area around the Haymarket and rich St. James's, Bond Street and the Burlington Arcade, all of which were so eminently respectable by day that sedate matrons and well-brought-up young women could go about their shopping without even suspecting that it was anything but the elegant area it appeared to be! But Gavin had always refused, although I knew full well that Babylon was one of his favourite haunts. All he had ever said was, "It is no place for you, Clemmy, though I wouldn't be surprised if you found yourself there one day. But *I* won't introduce you to it. For one thing, I can't afford to, because the pleasures I seek there are too expensive, and for another, many of the pastimes are not the kind in which you could participate. And for yet another, if a man wants a woman, he goes there to find one, not to take one."

Consequently the place held an increasing lure for me, and this unexpected promise of Durbridge's served to whet it.

Only at night did Babylon come to life, discreetly concealed behind exclusive façades and flourishing, as all such places did in high or low areas, despite the Amendment Act of 1885, which made every variety of whoremongering illegal, but had proved totally ineffective. Babylon was the haunt of titled noblemen, wealthy industrialists, rich merchants, successful courtesans, and actresses who preferred to be the toast of vice dens rather than struggle along like the Chrystal Delmonts of the theatrical world, with reputations high and bank balances low.

One could not live in London and not know about the expensive brothels, divan houses, accommodating restaurants, and cigar shops with their "acquaintance rooms" at the rear. A well-dressed gentleman would stroll in to buy a cigar, linger awhile, and soon a well-dressed woman would stroll in after him, or already be chatting to the assistant behind the counter, and their next steps would not be out into the street again, but through an unobtrusive inner door.

I had known, of course, that Gavin often wished I was not so well informed about his activities, but very early in life I had found out how he spent those "temporary loans" he had wheedled out of his silly, doting stepsister, loans which both he and she knew would never be paid back. After one such rewarding visit to my mother's dressing room I had followed him out of the theatre, seen him pick up a woman in Maiden Lane and take her down the alley which ran from there along the side of the Boswell Theatre direct to the Strand. From this alley were vast sliding doors opening directly into the stage wings, through which scenery could be admitted or removed, and inset into them, when closed, was a smaller one which the stagehands used when they wanted to step into the alley for a quiet smoke between scene changes. This entrance was close to the prop room, that cluttered but somehow orderly place which housed all sorts of things—Grecian columns, Roman arches, flights of steps, tables, chairs, screens, sofas—anything and everything needed for varied productions.

I didn't follow Gavin and his woman through this side door from the alley. I went back the way I had come, checked that Mamma had only just reached the stage of removing her makeup, which meant she then had to embark on the application of her increasingly heavy street make-up and then dress to go home, so I wandered nonchalantly toward the stage, now deserted. The performance was over, all stagehands gone, and when I tried the door of the prop room I couldn't open it. It remained locked as members of the cast emerged from their dressing rooms and went home, and soon I was the only person lingering in the darkened wings. I heard my father's voice calling good night to his dresser as he left his room in the main corridor beyond the stage and then his footsteps as he went along to see if Mamma was ready.

Knowing she was not, I still had time to linger, and as it happened, luck was with me. Just when I estimated that I would soon be called, the door of the prop room opened and Gavin and the woman came out. She was buttoning up her skirt beneath her opened coat, but had not even had time to put her hat on again.

"My, you're a fast one, ducks! I never knew a man do it so quick, but surely you don't have to hurry me outa the place half-undressed!"

"Unfortunately I do, or we'll be locked in the theatre all night. Be off with you—and go by the same door."

She merrily kissed a gold coin in her hand. "That's the quickest sovereign I've ever earned, dearie. Generous, too. You could've had me for ten bob!"

Beaming, she stepped through the narrow door into the alley and was gone. Gavin locked it after her, went back to the prop room, took the key from the inner side of the door, and then locked it from the outside. Then he placed the key on the rack above the SM's desk and as he did so I heard Mamma calling my name from the stage-door passage.

"Clementine! Clementine, darling, where are you? Time to go home!"

I stepped out of the shadows and called sweetly, "Coming, Mamma!"

Gavin stopped dead in his tracks.

"Good God, you little brat, how long have you been there?"

"All the time, Uncle Gavin. And I am not a brat. I am thirteen. And I thought members of the company were not allowed to bring visitors backstage except by special invitation on first nights, or with permission from the management. The sovereign you gave the lady pleased her, didn't it? I wonder what Mamma would say if she knew. . . ."

I got one myself, just for keeping quiet. Perhaps it was that incident which first gave me the idea there must be easier ways of earning a living than by memorising long dreary passages of Shakespeare and attending endless rehearsals. And now Lord Durbridge was hinting the same thing and promising to take me to the forbidden world which beckoned so invitingly. In some ways, Durbridge was the most exciting man I had met since Curtis, because he dealt in hints and innuendo, whereas Curtis had been blunt and to the point. "A cat may look at a king," he had once said, "so why shouldn't a coachman look at a queen, especially when her eyes invite him to?"

Poor Curtis—so attractive, even intelligent, and yet unable to realise that my favours had been bestowed on him as royalty might condescend to single out a courtier, and that such favours could be withdrawn, leaving him still a servant. Not for a moment had I intended him to take it seriously, or to imagine it could last.

I found that I could now remember Curtis with some regret, but where Magnus was concerned my feelings were more difficult to analyse. There was anger, of course, for the way in which he had dismissed me, and yet a kind of challenge for the same reason. It would give me the greatest satisfaction to make him want me again, to possess him again. But had I ever really "possessed" the man? In recollection it seemed that in some way there had always been a sort of barrier between us, a reserve on his part which I could not penetrate, as if his mind was really far removed from my own. I knew well enough that bodily unity did not necessarily mean mental unity; otherwise my ill-matched parents would never have begotten *me*.

Looking back, it seemed that Magnus and I had never drawn so close to each other or communicated so well as at our first moment of meeting. I can remember him now, standing on the pavement outside our home. I knew then that he had fallen in love with me and I knew it again at my coming-out ball, when he danced with me as often as possible, which, with so many tiresome duty dances to perform, was not as often as either of us wished, and I knew it when he came round to my dressing room in the interval on that memorable first night. The place had been crowded, but his eyes had said volumes as he stooped over my hand.

I tried to jerk away from nostalgia and back to my more promising future, but the recollection of that first night came sharply into focus. That Magnus had not been included in the supper party at Romano's had been disappointing. Whose fault had that been, I'd wondered, Mamma's or Durbridge's? I was fully aware that Mamma did not consider a doctor from an East End mission as *quite* socially acceptable, but Mamma considered nothing less than a title as socially acceptable anyway—hence her delight with the attention Durbridge paid me and with his idea for a special supper party at Romano's as a later celebration.

What an awful night *that* had turned out to be, and how much more enjoyable would have been the fight in Marylebone between Battling Bruce of Bermondsey and the pugilistic doctor. To watch Magnus Steel in action would have been far more exciting than that disastrous supper party and the awful scene in my home which followed.

I have never been able to forget that night and I still wonder what really happened to Lucinda to make her mother lose her self-control. Even now I can remember Lucinda's discoloured face, deeply scratched with blood drying on it, and Trudy's incoherent babbling, which brought our whole house of cards tumbling to the ground.

Of course, Lucinda would never reveal a thing, even when I taxed her about it at the theatre next time we met.

"I tripped over an angle rod backstage," she said, "and you know how rough those floorboards are." That was her story and she stuck to it, but I have never believed it. A fall backstage which merely disfigured her daughter's face could never have been responsible for Trudy's wild ramblings about "something terrible happening to our darling child," and that although "she had always striven to protect her, that night she had failed." I even wondered if Durbridge's failure to turn up at Romano's had had anything to do with it, then dismissed that idea because I could not believe he had tried to seduce Lucinda. It seemed out of character, she being so conventional and ordinary in those days, which Durbridge most certainly was not.

"You are very quiet, Miss Boswell. I trust I have said nothing to upset you?"

I returned to the dim light of Durbridge's carriage almost with a sense of shock, realising that we had been sitting outside my home for quite a time. In the faint glow from his eternal Havana and the flickering of the carriage lamps I saw his pallid face, red lips revealing very white teeth. A fascinating and compelling man. Some women might find him repugnant, but not I.

He said quietly, "You smile. At what, I wonder? You find me grotesque, perhaps?"

I hastened to reassure him. "I was remembering what you said about Magnus Steel being enslaved by me. The idea is amusing, because I believe he actually dislikes me now."

"Dislike can play a strong part in any attraction. You could be his Achilles' heel. Even the strongest men have them."

Nothing could have pleased me more than those words. Magnus's rejection of me made me want him even more, and though I knew my growing desire to win him back was largely based on the frustration of losing him, Durbridge's pronouncement was gratifying. Could it be possible that Magnus was still aware of me, still wanted me? To finally conquer a man like Steel would be different from conquering Curtis, who was wholly but gloriously animal, or the exploratory Pierre, who, I realised now, had enjoyed sex only if it satisfied his quirky desire to initiate the uninitiated, and with Gavin, of course, it had been no more than satisfaction of the senses. But Magnus was a different propostion. He al-

ways gave me the feeling that sex, to him, was an expression of something deeper and that I would never know him completely until I used it
to express the same thing.

Preparing for bed that night, I stripped and stood before my cheval
mirror, studying myself critically. My body was beautiful, and I wasn't
surprised that men enjoyed it. It had the curving hips they loved to lie
upon, and full thighs which sent them wild, and voluptuous breasts
which had known their share of passionate devouring. Before he ever
saw my body I had known that when Magnus looked at me he saw everything which lay beneath fashion's concealing garments, because, thank
God, he was one hundred percent male. It now occurred to me that his
inspection had always differed from Durbridge's for that very reason.
Magnus never observed me with the cold, professional eye of a mere
connoisseur.

However, Magnus was out of my life for the present and Durbridge
was back in it, and because optimism has always been part of my nature, I
took hold of it now. Durbridge's reentry was full of boundless promise,
and I knew that, through him, a whole new world was to open up before
me, which I could scarcely wait to embrace.

This promise could not have come at a more opportune moment, for
life had been bleak and empty of late. Despite the fact that there were
always plenty of admiring men hanging around stage doors, the real pick
of them prefer the Gaiety. I know I would fit in better there than at the
Boswell, which doesn't attract the same kind of male audience, but when
I approached the management of the Gaiety (unbeknownst to Mamma or
anyone else) I was received with nothing but scepticism. The offspring of
a renowned theatrical family, already playing prominent roles in the
straight theatre, seeking to join a chorus line which had no more to do
than look delectable and enticing? They wouldn't even take me seriously.

Equally irksome was the new policy at the Boswell of varying Shakespeare with other classical dramatists, both past and present. It was
shortly after my supper at the Savoy with Durbridge that we went into
rehearsal for *The Rivals*. Not since my childhood had this Sheridan play
been presented at the theatre, and I had never taken part in it. I was
therefore unfamiliar with any of the lines, so Bramwell Chambers cast
me in the minor role of Lucy, the maid.

"A rank insult!" cried Mamma. "My darling gel should play either
Julia or Lydia Languish, and nothing less. Refuse the part, Clementine.
Refuse it immediately."

"How can I? Bramwell is in charge of casting, and you know perfectly
well that no one can go against the casting director."

"We had no such thing in your dear papa's day!"

"Because he was actor-manager, but those days have gone."

"We will soon see about that. *I* will speak my mind at the first rehearsal."

And so she did, her fury further incensed when discovering Lucinda was to play Lydia to Chrystal Delmont's Julia. Mamma herself was cast in her old part of Mrs. Malaprop, but since she had already taken that for granted she expressed no gratification. In view of Papa's stipulation that she should continue to perform so long as she wished to do so, and so long as there were suitable parts for her, and since she had played Mrs. Malaprop many times in her career, she obviously could not be omitted from the cast now.

"More's the pity," I said to Lucinda. "Everyone will regret it. Mamma has deteriorated, and you know what I mean by that."

"Then I hope being occupied will help her. She was always very professional, able to cover any defects when acting. And we must never forget my father's wishes."

It always jars on me to hear Lucinda refer to Papa that way. *"My* father," as if he had not been mine also. I could not resist pointing out that I had a greater right than she to call him that, since I was his legitimate daughter, and bearing his name. She flinched a little at that, showing she was as sensitive as ever beneath her poise. She used to flinch in such a way when I taunted her in childhood, but now she recovered quickly and said, "Since I think of him as my father, which he was, it comes naturally to me to refer to him that way. You call him Papa, which is natural too, since you were brought up as his lawful child, so we each have our own particular name for him, haven't we?"

She spoke without resentment or malice, leaving me with no answer, and I remembered Durbridge's advice about appearing to be her friend and, above all, to show no animosity if I hoped to win her trust and so lay my hands again on my lost share of the theatre. "Until I was in a position to buy it back," he had said, but would I ever be unless he fulfilled his promise to help? I had heard no word from him from that day to this and was growing impatient, because regaining my rightful share in my family's theatre was becoming more and more of an obsession with me, my resentment against Lucinda for holding on to it, deeper and deeper.

Even so, Durbridge's counsel was wise and I followed it now, smiling very sweetly as I answered, "So we do, Lucinda dear, and why not? Dear Papa meant a lot to both of us and it makes me happy that you respect his memory the way you do. But to get back to Mamma, I fear she will be a nuisance and everyone will wish she was not back in the company."

I was right. She began to cause trouble right away, sailing majestically onstage at the first rehearsal call, marching down to the footlights, and demanding of Willard, waiting down in the auditorium for the cast to assemble, "Just *why* has my precious gel been given the paltry part of Lucy, the most unimportant of the four female roles?"

"You must ask Bramwell, ma'am. He does the casting. Here he comes now."

Bramwell had followed my mother onstage. Everyone was gathering now. There were eight male parts in *The Rivals,* and since the stock number of resident actors and actresses in a company consisted of leads, second leads, character leads, and juvenile leads, four outsiders had been engaged for the other, supporting male roles, but the adverse impression Mamma was making on these newcomers worried her not a bit. In fact, she enjoyed "throwing her weight about," as Gregory, the stage manager, sarcastically put it.

"You heard my question, Mr. Chambers, so I need not repeat it. Your explanation, *if* you please."

With his customary calm, Bramwell replied that since her daughter had never acted in the play and therefore knew not a line of it, Lucy would be the easiest and the quickest for her to learn.

"And you know very well she isn't a good study. You hate learning lines, don't you, Clemmy? You are much happier in parts you have been familiar with since childhood."

"Neither has that gel played in *The Rivals,*" Mamma shouted irately, "yet you cast her as Lydia, with as many lines to say as I have, and possibly more! If *she* can learn them, my darling gel can do so equally well."

"Lucinda knows them already. She is word-perfect."

I could see the light of annoyance in Bramwell's eye. He always reacted that way when my mother refused to call Lucinda by name.

"Oh, you would champion the gel, of course. You have always had a soft spot for her."

"That has nothing to do with it. Lucinda will be admirably cast and give a splendid performance."

"As *my* daughter would, and probably better!"

"We won't enter into an argument about that. The fact remains that Lucinda already knows the part and probably much of the other female parts as well, for the simple reason that your husband set her to study Lydia as part of her training, added to which she has devoured dramatic works ever since she has been able to read. I doubt if there is a Sheridan play she hasn't read over and over again and therefore knows almost backward."

"My Clementine is just as knowledgeable! She used to spend hours, literally *hours,* reading plays aloud with her father, so close was the bond between them."

That wasn't true, but I didn't bother to say so. My pride was insulted by being cast as Lucy, but apart from the fact that I hated being involved

in one of my mother's awful scenes I was secretly consoled by the fact
that I would at least have less studying to do, which would leave more
time for pleasure. Those sessions from my childhood and girlhood, when
Papa had tried to encourage me to read aloud with him, had never been a
great success because I had found them frankly tedious, even though he
used to say that it was the finest way of studying drama.

"Constant reading means constant memorising, and this makes line-
learning almost effortless. It also means that if ever the day comes when
you are cast in any such part, rehearsing will be more enjoyable. You will
already be so familiar with the words that you can concentrate on devel-
oping the character."

I would then answer dutifully, "Yes, Papa," or "I understand, Papa,"
and escape as quickly as possible, but Lucinda-bastard had evidently in-
gratiated herself with him by adopting his method and was now reaping
further benefit. And it was true that she was maddeningly word-perfect.
Even at the first run-through she rattled off Lydia's frantic instructions to
her maid in Scene 1, when hearing that Mrs. Malaprop and Sir Anthony
Absolute were on their way upstairs, without even referring to the
script.

"Here, my dear Lucy, hide these books. Quick, quick! Fling *Peregrine
Pickle* under the toilet . . . throw *Roderick Random* into the closet
. . . thrust *Lord Aimworth* under the sofa . . . cram *Ovid* behind the
bolster . . . there . . . put *The Man of Feeling* into your pocket
. . . so, so, now lay *Mrs. Chapone* in sight and leave *Fordyce's Sermons*
open on the table!"

"Well done, Lucinda," called Willard from the stalls. "You're one of
the few actresses I have ever heard reel off those titles at a first rehearsal
without making a mistake!"

And what had I, as Lucy the maid, to say in reply? Nothing but, "O
burn it, ma'am, the hairdresser has torn away as far as *Proper Pride!*" and
what did I come out with? "O tear it, ma'am, the hairdresser has burned
away the whole of one side!" which sent Willard into such a towering
rage that I was thankful when I could return to more mediocre responses
such as, "No, indeed, ma'am," and, "Lud, ma'am, here is Miss Mel-
ville," with a few variations such as, "O Gemini! I'd sooner cut my
tongue out!" and, slightly more ambitious, "Ha, ha, ha! . . . let girls
in my station be as fond as they please of appearing expert . . . commend me to a mask of silliness and a pair of sharp eyes for my own interest under it!" I scarcely cared about committing such nonsense to memory and was prepared to ad-lib even if it made Willard tear out his hair,
which it almost did.

"My God, Clemmy," he yelled, "*you* don't need any bloody mask of
silliness—just be your natural stupid self!" Whereupon Mamma
screamed abuse upon his head, halting the entire rehearsal.

"If my poor Nevill were alive, he would dismiss you on the spot, and I would it were in my power to do so now!"

"Sir Nevill never dismissed anyone on the spot," Willard snapped back. It took all Bramwell's diplomacy to calm them both.

But Lucinda restored Willard's good temper with her rendering of Lydia. She always came vitally alive onstage. Even the crew would gather in the wings to listen to her, and cleaners out front pause in their labours, leaning on brooms and mops, spellbound. *Well, let her enjoy it all,* I thought, *since there is nothing else in her life. No lovers, no pleasures apart from the theatre, no other ambitions or amusements.* I would not exchange my life for hers, dull though it was while waiting for Durbridge to fulfill his promise to contact me again.

I was growing impatient for the promised visit to Babylon. Meanwhile, I felt no envy for Lucinda's talent, nor for the admiration of the stage crew. Who wanted either? Let that cockney Jerry Hawks be her slave, and benign Bramwell her fatherly friend, and even shrewd and exacting Willard proud of her professionally. He liked directing her; I had heard him say so frequently. She might represent competition for me onstage, but none whatever in my private life, and most certainly not with any man. That she was content to live with her mother again proved that.

To my astonishment she had disposed of Gavin's flat on the Chelsea Embankment, saying she had no desire to occupy it. *I* would have had the good sense to keep it. A place such as that would have been a tremendous asset to a woman who was free and unfettered, but Lucinda had rejoined her mother like a homing chick. Pleasant little dinner parties in those charming rooms above Trudy's shop might be all very nice, and from what one heard, Trudy Grainger and her daughter were earning for themselves the reputation of being charming hostesses, but where did it get them? What did it bring? Plenty of orders in Trudy's books from her fashion-conscious friends, perhaps—though I still smarted under her polite refusal to make anything for me; when I had decided to order a gown from her, all she said was, "But I know you are dressed by the House of Worth, and I would not dream of competing with them," which was a polite refusal if ever there was one.

But what social success had her daughter achieved? Since Gavin, no man had even wooed her, and I could not believe that one unfortunate experience in her life could have made her discourage other men or lose interest in them. When one man was behind you, the sensible thing was to find a replacement as quickly as possible. I would certainly never understand Lucinda, and in the circumstances I felt I could afford to ignore her as I had done when young, but somehow she still managed to get under my skin.

To find out one adverse thing about her, even one trivial thing that could be used to her detriment, would give me great satisfaction, be-

cause the very least she could have done, the night of Gavin's death, was
to keep quiet about my part in it. To tell Magnus, as she obviously had
done, that she had found me in bed with her husband was a very mean-
spirited thing to do, in my opinion, and I was convinced she had done it
out of spite, aware that Magnus had become my lover, and wanting to
destroy our relationship solely for revenge.

Oh, no, she wasn't the amiable creature she pretended to be, and how
I would enjoy embarrassing her as I had years ago with that accidentally
discovered trinket! But the damnable thing was that she was never involved in any scandal, her name was never linked with any man's backstage, and never had she been known to visit any actor's dressing room.
Never, in fact, did she put a foot wrong.

My mother was not too pleased about Chrystal Delmont being cast as
Julia, but she could hardly complain about that, since Chrystal had
played the part years ago and was still good-looking enough and youthful
enough to carry if it off. Chrystal was as slim as a reed, which was an asset
behind the footlights these days, because fashion seemed to be decreeing
less voluptuousness in the female form (though I was convinced that men
would always love it). My mother's majestic proportions suited her well
for Mrs. Malaprop, and the lines she had to speak guaranteed success for
any character actress. When playing with my father, Mamma had been
good in the part; it was therefore expected that she would be equally successful now, but in playing opposite Bramwell she seemed less happy. I
knew the constant scenes she created at rehearsals were all building up
into one grand and glorious row, but little did I expect that Maisie would
be the eventual cause of it.

In her services to me at home, the woman was proving very useful indeed. When entertaining friends she would clear away after we had
wined and dined and then retire to her attic, and if she heard anything or
guessed anything, she kept both her eyes and ears shut.

Of course, Mamma was never included in my private little dinner or
late supper parties. "Darling Mamma, you know you have nothing in
common with young people today; you will be much cosier and happier
down here, and Kate will bring you your medicine whenever you need
it."

Nor was Durbridge included, as yet. Apart from the problem of negotiating endless stairs, which could have been overcome with the aid of
Stacey and the butler, the greatest deterrent to inviting him was that
Mamma, had she heard that "dear Durbridge" was to be there, would
have turned up as an uninvited guest. She even now cherished the idea
that I might become Lady Durbridge, whether his lordship had been rendered impotent or not. ("A woman can always take a lover in such cir-

cumstances, so long as she is discreet about it, dear gel.'') All of which showed how stupid dear Mamma continued to be.

Never at any time had she realised that Durbridge, even when able-bodied, was not the marrying kind, but I had guessed it by now. Whether his tastes ran to men or to unorthodox practices with women I had never been sure; the latter, I had hoped, because there were still experiences which had not come my way, but of course I would never know now. Handicapped as he was, I couldn't see how he could indulge in sexual activities with anyone.

But the real reason for not inviting him was that I knew instinctively that I should make no move until he took the initiative. So I filled in my time with flirtations, with passing liaisons, with frequent yearnings for Magnus, and even more frequent yearnings to be avenged on him—but also, very much to my surprise, to wondering where Curtis was and if he had been successful in the East. And at that point nostalgia always took over.

After his disappearance I had stripped those rooms above the coach house, selling the furniture I had installed, just in case dear Mamma took it into her head to inspect the place prior to engaging a new and older man. Parting with the beautiful feather bed was painful, because it brought back such memories.

The passing liaisons I now consoled myself with never seemed to amount to more than hasty retreats behind closed doors at fashionable bohemian parties, and there was not a man in my life who stirred in me any desire for more—except Magnus, who now represented a challenge constantly thwarted, but who, said Durbridge, must have his Achilles' heel.

Sometimes I would see him driving around Portman Square in that modest trap of his, and if he saw me he would raise his hat politely and pass the time of day as he drove by, without even troubling to rein. Occasionally he called at the theatre for Lucinda; I would see him pass my dressing-room door after a performance or rehearsal, sometimes alone, sometimes with Trudy or his sister, and I would skillfully find out, without appearing to, the reason for the visit.

There was a grapevine of gossip between theatrical dressers, and Lucinda and I very conveniently shared the same one, a garrulous woman who needed no encouragement at all. I would let her pursue her running commentary when she attended me, prattling about this and that member of the company and tidbits she had heard—idle stuff, but sometimes interesting.

"Miss Lucinda doesn't seem to have much social life, does she, Miss Boswell? None that she talks about, anyway. Just events with her mother and occasional suppings-out with friends—that Dr. Steel, f'rinstance: and sometimes his sister and a gentleman friend. They all went to the

Carlton last night—Miss Lucinda's birthday. Very popular place, the Carlton, I hear tell, since the famous Ritz left the Savoy to go there. Oh, yes, I'm well up in society details, even if I can't afford to mix in such circles!'' This was said with an arch giggle which jarred profoundly, but had to be ignored if I wanted to hear more, and one never knew what gems of gossip dropped from this woman's lips.

"A nice man, that Dr. Steel, and her very good friend for many years, I understand, so there can't be anything in it, otherwise they would have made a go of it by now, don't you think, Miss Boswell? Sometimes he just calls to take her home from the theatre, but only if he happens to be passing this way from that surgery he runs in the East End. Not very romantic, thinks I, but of course, an actress doesn't spend her whole life in the theatre, she has a private life too, so maybe . . ." A shrug and a wink then. "Very reserved is Miss Lucinda. Doesn't talk about herself much. Spends most of her time offstage just reading in her dressing room, and when men send flowers—"

"*Do* men send her flowers?"

"'Course they do. She's a very popular actress, isn't she, and a good one too, and she looks real lovely out front. Have you ever seen her from out front, Miss Boswell? You really should. Gawd knows, she's pretty good-looking offstage, but out front she's a raving beauty. The way she moves and walks and talks fair leaves you breathless, and as for acting—well, when me and my husband have been in on my free comps I've seen people out there shedding real tears when she's been playing tragedy. But as Lydia in this new show she's going to give a real joyous performance. Seems to be able to play anything, doesn't she—comedy *or* tragedy."

I wasn't interested in backstage theatre critics and stopped the woman's spate by asking what Miss Lucinda did with the flowers she received.

"Sends polite notes of thanks, that's all. If there's no address on the card, then I have to go along to George at the stage door and ask him to pass on her thanks to the sender, because sure enough, he'll be lingering, hoping to be invited to her dressing room."

"And they never are?"

"Never. Miss Grainger is a very retiring young lady. Pity, really."

Stupid, thought I, who made many a useful acquaintance by responding graciously to bouquets from admirers. If the donor turned out to be dull, at least he was good for a supper at the Savoy, and if he was amusing, then more besides. If he was rich, even better. But I couldn't see the part of Lucy in *The Rivals* bringing me much in the way of flowers or gifts or invitations, with Lucinda stealing the limelight as Lydia and Chrystal Delmont getting her fair share of it as Julia. A lesser part meant lesser attention *and* lesser pay, and as always, I needed and wanted money, which still seemed to trickle through my fingers like water. Regain my share of the theatre? Earn enough money to buy it back? What a hope! Durbridge had obviously forgotten all his promises.

It was at this stage of my life, steeped in lethargic boredom and unaccustomed depression, that two things happened, both on the same day. First came my mother's demand to have Maisie back as her dresser, which I promptly refused, and then, at last, came Durbridge's invitation to Babylon, for that very night, which I promptly accepted.

My refusal to release Maisie sent my mother storming home from rehearsal in a towering rage. She summoned the woman immediately, and I stood by while she did so.

"Ha, Maisie!" she cried as the woman appeared. "You will be returning to the theatre as my dresser."

Maisie gawped, lost for an answer, and turned instinctively to me.

"She will not, Mamma."

"*I* pay her wages here!"

"Which I supplement. You didn't know that, did you? But Maisie does. I don't think she would be prepared to forfeit that extra money to accept a mere pound a week as a theatrical dresser again."

Maisie nodded vigorous agreement, and dear Mamma's face went quite purple. Before she could attempt to dismiss Maisie on the spot, I pressed home my advantage.

"If you are thinking of docking Maisie's wages as a member of this household, or even of dispensing with her, do so by all means. I will then employ her myself." Turning back to Maisie I finished, "You can come back to the theatre as *my* dresser and continue to live here and serve me. What is more, I will pay you for both tasks. The choice is yours."

I thought with relish that it would be quite like old times, when Trudy Grainger served my mother in the double capacity of dresser and lady's maid, but not for double pay. In the face of such an offer I knew my mother was vanquished and, as I expected, Maisie's choice was inevitable.

"Lady Boswell, ma'am, I appreciate your offer, really I do, but I've grown used to serving Miss Clementine now. I know her little ways."

I didn't like that. Nor did I like the slightly conspiratorial glance she sent me, which I chose to ignore

"Then that is settled," I said firmly. "Another dresser will be found for you, Mamma, and you will be totally relieved of any financial responsibility for Maisie—which means, of course, that you will be unable to call on her services in any way at all. They will be exclusively mine."

The double financial outlay was a nuisance, but I had no choice if I hoped to ensure Maisie's loyalty, and with Durbridge's invitation dangling before me something told me I was going to need that loyalty very much indeed.

Mamma was gasping for breath. If she ever achieved the opening night as Mrs. Malaprop I would be amazed, I thought, and hoped devoutly that she would not. However, she was one of those indefatigable women who went on forever and, faced with the last ditch, she now stormed, "I will have my dressing room back, at least, you ungrateful gel! And don't you dare remove that star from the door."

"I wouldn't want it. Papa always considered it tawdry."

Not for the world would I have let her see that I cared, but care I did. That star on the door never failed to boost my sense of importance, but I had known I would have to vacate that dressing room anyway, since the part of Lucy was not a lead role. The thought of being relegated to a room inferior to Lucinda's displeased me too, but I had other things to think about at this moment, chief amongst them the gown I would wear tonight.

Durbridge's invitation, delivered by hand this morning, had been characteristically autocratic, making it plain that any prior engagement must be cancelled forthwith. "I will send a conveyance for you at ten o'clock this evening. We may then sup at leisure and proceed to Babylon when that fascinating world begins to come to life."

It was a royal command—one I was only too pleased to obey.

26

I wore an evening gown of eau-de-nil satin bordered with sable round the hem, the sweeping skirt with a semi-train further enriched with bead embroidery of matching eau-de-nil in an iris design. The pointed waist then draped low across the bust, with a jabot falling between branches of similar bead embroidery. Sable shoulder trimming completed the square décolleté, with short puffed sleeves of dotted mousseline de soie under ruffles of beaded satin. I was tempted to order Maisie to remove the ladylike sleeves and jabot and so reveal more of my arms and breasts, then decided against it. I did not want to be mistaken for one of the ladies of the town, nor, I felt, would Durbridge wish me to be. The gown was sufficiently revealing for my first visit to this notorious part of London, and I completed the picture of elegant refinement with a fan of sable-coloured lace appliquéd on a film of transparent tulle.

Such a fan was always a useful accessory. It could be used as shield or invitation. It could conceal or reveal. It could emphasise a provocative glance when covering the lower part of the face or, when snapped shut, sharply reprove a roving hand. It could also, used judiciously, dislodge the shoulders of a gown so that they inched slightly lower and lower as mood (and response) demanded.

Durbridge sent his carriage promptly at ten. It was the same impressive affair, crested in gold with his initials entwined beneath. I remember Papa once calling it ostentatious. Many noble families, he had pointed out, never indulged in such display, but personally I liked it and so did Mamma. However, I was glad she was unaware of its arrival and knew nothing of my appointment with Durbridge tonight, though she would no doubt hear of it from Kate, who happened to be emerging from the drawing room as I descended the stairs.

The new butler was holding the front door ajar and the carriage could be seen clearly in the light from the iron lampposts attached to the railings at the foot of our steps. I saw Kate's eyes slide toward it, taking in every detail, noting that the carriage was empty and that it had therefore been sent to fetch and deliver me to its owner's house. And she would know who the owner was, for Durbridge's carriage not only bore his insignia but had brought him here as a guest in the past. But what did I care? If Kate told her, I could silence Mamma's curiosity by saying that Durbridge had been giving a private supper party in his home and that many guests had been invited. She would resent being excluded, but she would believe my story and her hopes of a rich match for me would flutter again.

Maisie accompanied me downstairs, holding up my semi-train, and Kate's eyes slid from the open front door to take in every detail of my appearance. I gave her a gracious smile and said, "You will see my dear mamma safely to bed, won't you, Kate? I know you look after her so much better than any personal maid."

She nodded, but that was all. Since I had firmly disposed of her she had never shown any affability toward me, which, to my mind, proved that she knew she had met her match. Then I saw her give a disturbing little half-smile at Maisie and I jerked my head round sharply to see Maisie returning it. Had those two ceased to be antagonists then? I didn't wholly like the thought, though no doubt it made for greater peace belowstairs, where Maisie still took her meals and carried out such personal tasks for me as laundering and ironing. I was always more easy in my mind when I knew that Maisie was safely in her attic room, but of course I could not compel her to spend every hour there. She was still a servant in this house and therefore belonged in the servants' hall. But the exchanged smile between these two disturbed me. Gossip was less likely to be bandied between people who were on unfriendly terms.

Outside, Maisie held my gown slightly higher to avoid any contact with the pavement, but when Stacey stepped forward to hand me into the carriage, she stopped dead. It was left to him to spread my skirts carefully about my feet and then to see that my costly cloak of sables (not yet paid for) was well wrapped about me. The night was chill, autumn rapidly giving way to winter.

Glancing through the window as we departed, I saw Maisie standing on the pavement, transfixed. I could not think what had come over the woman. Anyone would have thought that the sight of this particular vehicle, and the man who drove it, had been a shock to her.

Lord Durbridge's house in Grosvenor Square bore testimony to his wealth. The place was magnificent, with a sweeping marble staircase spiralling up on the right-hand side of the hall, the floor of which was also of marble. There was a Fontainebleau touch to these sweeping stairs, also in the elaborate ceiling moldings and baroque decoration. A further touch of grandeur was provided by the splendid wrought-iron banisters, featuring a scrolled design of intertwined leaves, birds, and wood nymphs all delicately picked out in gold leaf.

A less sophisticated woman than I might have been awed by this spectacular entrance, but my predominant feeling was one of relief because I had chosen my gown so well, for despite all the grandiosity, an overdressed woman would have struck a jarring note.

I could see that Lord Durbridge approved of my appearance, although his heavy-lidded eyes did not blatantly study me. He was waiting in his wheelchair at the head of the stairs, and as I ascended, sweeping eau-de-nil satin trailing splendidly behind me, I knew that he assessed me from head to foot. His man had relieved me of my sable cloak, but somehow I knew Durbridge had noted that too as, from above, he had watched me enter his house.

I enjoyed his scrutiny. To have been accepted with indifference would have been far from flattering. When I reached him I held out my hand, palm down, to be kissed. He unbutttoned my silk glove at the wrist, turned the palm up, and his thick red lips touched the exposed skin.

"Admirable," he murmured. "I applaud your taste, Miss Boswell. To have chosen something more elaborately décolleté for your first visit to Babylon would have been too . . . obvious, shall we say? You will be noticed, but favourably, because it will be immediately apparent that you are not an habitué—yet."

"You think then that I shall become one?"

"I am resolved upon it."

He had propelled his way along a wide marble landing until we reached double doors leading into a drawing room, where he braked to allow me to pass through first. Invalidism had not robbed this man of his courtesy, but I knew, as I preceded him, that he was studying every line of my back, from décolleté neckline downward, and I knew that, as always, there was a detached assessment about his glance.

We lingered over champagne before proceeding to supper, served in an adjoining dining room an hour later. Meanwhile I had time to observe the magnificence about me, the valuable furniture, porcelain, and pictures, the luxuries only wealth could buy. The man appeared to be a collector of works of art, displayed with a lavish hand. Would Papa have considered this room flamboyant too? I brushed the thought aside. Dear Papa was dead, but I was very much alive. Lucinda might cling to his standards and share his views, but I was entitled to my own. And why did I have to think of my illegitimate sister at this moment? I knew the answer to that—because I had discussed her with Durbridge the last time we met and revealed how she was obstructing my repossession of what was rightfully mine, which had led to his promise of help in regaining it. I wanted to ask if this visit tonight was linked in some way with that promise, and when embarked on my second glass of champagne I hesitated no longer.

"You offered to help me, Lord Durbridge. You said you could put a lot of money in my way. Does the offer remain?"

"Of course. That is why you are here. But be patient. We have hours before us, and not a moment of them will be ill-spent."

"I am curious, nonetheless."

"Your curiosity will be satisfied, young lady, when I decide that it shall be."

Maddening man. Infuriating man. I had to play his game, but I refused to become lightheaded through too much champagne, because I felt this was part of his testing of me. When I put the remainder of my glass aside, I knew he approved.

Throughout supper the conversation remained light and impersonal, but even impersonal conversation from this man had motivation behind it.

"You are between productions at the theatre now, I know. That is why I waited until your evenings were free. What plans are afoot at the Boswell?"

"A production of *The Rivals*."

"And whom do you play—Lydia or Julia?"

"Neither. I am cast as Lucy, the maid."

"Good God, what a waste! What is the idea behind that—to keep you in the background?"

I had only to tell him that it was Bramwell Chambers' choice since he was responsible for casting, but a shrug was a more effective answer, implying much.

"Then it was the decision of your half-sister—though she cannot be called that legitimately, not being entitled to the Boswell name."

Another shrug. Let him think what he liked. I would devote myself to this excellent meal and let him form his own conclusions.

"A part like Lucy cannot bring you much money."

"No more than a drop in the ocean, considering my needs."

"Such as the sable cloak. Has it been paid for?"

I smiled. Nothing fooled this man, so I answered indifferently, "Not yet. Fortunately the Boswell name still commands credit at the best establishments . . . except," I added lightly, "that of a certain modiste in George Street."

"You mean the Grainger woman? Did she actually refuse you credit?"

"She did more than that. She refused an order from me on the grounds that it was unethical for her to encroach on the House of Worth."

"Ridiculous. There is no form of ethics governing the clientele of any fashion house, and the woman in George Street is nothing but a jumped-up backstage servant who happens to be a skilled dressmaker."

The vehemence of his reply astonished me. Durbridge rarely revealed anger, but it was there now, and rather more than anger, I felt. There was unmistakable venom there, but when I looked at him in surprise the hooded eyes and pallid face were as impassive as ever.

Supper was over and so was the lingering, the dallying, the suspense. Stacey appeared as if by magic, withdrawing my chair and then wheeling his master from the table. Durbridge said, "There is a bedroom on the floor above, Miss Boswell, immediately facing the head of the stairs. There you will find everything necessary for a lady's needs."

The strange thing about that essentially feminine bedroom was the feeling it gave of never having been occupied by a woman, though there was every feminine toiletry imaginable, and a bathroom leading from it complete with luxury accoutrements. My sable cloak had been brought upstairs and laid upon the bed, and when I was ready I descended, to find Durbridge waiting for me in the hall.

My next surprise was the carriage outside, a plain, unornamented affair which would not attract a second glance. So Durbridge intended that his presence in Babylon should not be noticed; a plain black carriage could wait in some side street without advertising its ownership. The man was discretion itself, I thought admiringly, and a quiver of excitement ran through me. There was a delicious touch of the illicit about this night's adventure.

"Where are we going first?" I enquired.

"So you have guessed that we shall take only one step at a time? Truly you are wasted in playing a minor theatrical part of a servant girl, which, apart from its poor financial reward, can win you no attention whatsoever." His hand reached out and patted my own, but he said not another word. Nor did I until we pulled up outside a modest supper room at the Haymarket end of Jermyn Street. It had a single name above it, BOLLARD'S, but anticipation ran through me. I had heard of this establishment, but had never plucked up courage to enter as, I knew, many unattached women did.

Its appearance was unprepossessing—a plain brown Victorian façade, windows veiled in lace. Respectable women shoppers would pass it during the day, when its doors were closed, without even noticing it, and even by night its presence was only advertised by the flicker of light issuing from behind drawn blinds and the hum of voices from within. In appearance it was uninspiring, but the interior was the reverse.

The drab, brown-painted doors opened onto a saloon brilliantly lit with gasoliers and walled with mirrors in heavily gilded frames. Across the centre ran a wooden barricade about four feet high. In the middle of this barricade was a small gate which could apparently be opened only from the inner side, for the moment Durbridge appeared a waiter beyond the barricade leapt to attention, unlocked the wooden gate, and allowed us to pass through.

This inner sanctuary was wider than the side onto which the street door opened, and soon I realised why. From the table which appeared to be reserved exclusively for Durbridge I was able to survey the entire premises. On our side of the barrier was a lengthy, well-stocked bar, with waiters hustling to and fro bearing laden trays, but on the other the only furnishings consisted of a long row of chairs against the wall. These were occupied by ladies who could buy no service whatsoever, not even a glass of wine or a cup of coffee.

"They pay five shillings to enter, to sit there, and to hope," Durbridge told me. "If you watch the procedure, you will find it both edifying and amusing. The section we are in is reserved exclusively for men. Those sitting with lady companions have either brought them here, as I have brought you, or summoned them across from the other side, the latter being more common, since that is what both sexes come here for."

"And what have you brought *me* here for?" I asked, faintly annoyed. "To witness the hire of prostitutes? I suppose there are rooms at the back—"

"Supper rooms, my dear, which serve excellent meals and to which I would not hesitate to take you as my guest had we not dined already. Beyond the supper rooms . . ." He shrugged expressively. "There, I admit, I would not take you. As for my reason in bringing you here, it is merely as an aperitif before taking you elsewhere. Meanwhile, a glass of wine while you savour the atmosphere of this place? You were eager enough to visit Babylon, and at Bollard's we are merely standing at the gates.''

And so I sipped, and watched. Communication between the sexes was easy and the procedure ritualised. The row of women, varying in ages and attraction, sat quietly waiting, but they were not permitted to make the first advance. Each kept her eyes on the milling crowd beyond the partition, watching for a man to raise his glass or to indicate in some way his wish to be acquainted, then both would stroll to the boundary fence and chat awhile, after which the lady would be admitted through the wicket gate to join her admirer or to return to her seat if politely dismissed. All the men were top-hatted and in evening clothes, their hats rakishly tilted at varied angles or pushed negligently to the backs of their heads, and none troubled to remove them when speaking to a woman. Only when they proceeded toward the supper rooms were toppers and white silk scarves handed casually to the waiter.

"Five shillings for a night's unsuccessful vigil seems a high price," I commented, at which Durbridge again shrugged and said that a woman could always come back another night.

"And if successful," he added, "five shillings is a modest outlay for an evening which could earn up to fifty pounds or more. Come, it is time to move on. For one thing, I dislike the way that American tourist over there is eyeing you.''

"How do you know he is American?" I asked, already aware of the man's interest. He stood out because he was the only man present who was hatless. In the brilliant light from the gasoliers his mane of greying hair, beard, and heavy moustache left little to discern of his features. I also noticed he made no attempt to beckon any of the hopeful women beyond the barriers.

"How do I know he is American?" Durbridge echoed. "Because only an American would dress like that. His evening clothes have not been tailored for him, though no doubt he is rich enough to equip himself in Savile Row before he returns to his native heath, and he is obviously here as a spectator to study the seamier side of Victorian England. If he journeys deeper into Babylon tonight his pockets will be emptied without his even being aware of it, and serve the man right for having the impertinence to stare at the only lady in the room—or," he added with a teasing note, "the only woman who looks like one and is dressed like one.''

He signalled to Stacey, who was waiting impassively just within the main door.

"We will waste no more time on places like this," Durbridge continued. "There are entertainments far more amusing, including a new establishment modelled on the notorious Kate Hamilton's, which was closed by the 1865 Act, but for fifteen years she ruled her palace of debauchery like a bloated empress. Rumour has it that the new Roman Temple behind Bond Street is hers, although her face is mercifully never seen there. Even when young she was hideous, and now she must be even more so in her dotage."

"And what goes on at the Roman Temple?"

"My dear, need you ask? Roman health baths, as they are called in order to qualify as spa premises; regularly inspected by the authorities, too. One section for ladies and another for gentlemen, rigidly separated—until the dividing walls slide back. The secret of how they operate has never yet been discovered by the police, who have raided the place many times, only to find everything seemingly in order. Other pleasures are Roman massages, Roman feasts, and, of course, Roman orgies when one has penetrated to the inner depths of the place. Some other time I will take you there. Even a crippled spectator can enjoy the nude bathing of other people and partake in ensuing pleasures. However, much depends on . . ."

He did not finish the sentence because Stacey was placing my sable cloak about my shoulders and then wheeling his master to the door. Outside there was no sign of the carriage.

"We will sample some culture now, dear lady, and since it is within walking distance, Stacey can wheel me and thus avoid the tedious business of heaving this cumbersome vehicle in and out of the carriage. You need fear no molestation so long as you stay close beside us. Stacey is agile and I myself am not as useless as I appear. Since being reduced to my present state I have developed much skill and strength in my arms. "

His hand touched the inner side of his chair and I noticed a deep pocket in the leather upholstery, slightly bulging.

I said lightly, "Don't tell me you are armed, Lord Durbridge! What have you concealed there? A derringer twenty-two? That is small enough to hide conveniently."

He smiled. "A lady's pistol, to my mind. I carry nothing remotely resembling it, nor any pistol, for that matter."

"Then not a knife, I hope."

"You shudder. You must be remembering the night your unfortunate stepuncle was stabbed."

I let him think so, though in truth I had not thought of that incident for a very long time. When I remembered it at all, it was only to wonder how Curtis had managed to get away, and in what part of the world he was now, and then would follow an inexpressible yearning for the times I had spent with him.

I also pretended that I was shuddering at the sights around us.

"Dollymops and harlots and pimps and ponces, my dear? Surely you knew what to expect? No doubt you have only glimpsed London's nightlife from within a closed carriage on your way home from the theatre, and I expect your late father would have insisted on the coachman avoiding this area at night. However, we will walk, Miss Boswell, and enjoy the pageantry of London's other world, which the police are incapable of controlling and not averse to ignoring when it is made worth their while. Who can blame them? No police force in the world could handle such trafficking as this. London is a thriving market for cash copulation."

I scarcely recognised Jermyn Street, in which I frequently shopped by day. Heavily painted women moved along in droves, waited in doorways and at the corners of side turnings, while smarter lorettes seemed to be heading for their regular resorts from which came bursts of light and snatches of ribald music as doors opened to admit them; child prostitutes dodged after clients, plucking at their sleeves, or were offered to passing men by mothers or bawds, and there was a continuous stream of well-dressed men and women descending from broughams and hansoms.

At last the seething streets of the Haymarket area were behind us, and though fascinated by this close-up view of what was only a minute section of London's squalid nightlife, I was glad when we emerged into St. James's, the focus of smart and competitive harlotry. To my surprise, we halted at the elegant door of Harris's Art Galleries. I had passed this door many times and seen its bow windows displaying fine pictures and *objets d'art* for sale to a discerning and wealthy clientele. My surprise was because I had not suspected that Durbridge had real culture in mind. I had imagined him to mean entertainment of some kind, because it was well known that Babylon abounded in varied entertainments of dubious taste. Even Gavin had admitted that its lewd performances must surely rank amongst the worst in the world, and although performed by women as well as by men, no females were admitted amongst the audiences in some of the establishments because there were certain sights and scenes which only men should witness, and indeed wished to witness only in male company. I had therefore presumed that Durbridge was taking me to some form of entertainment suitable for both men and women, even if in doubtful taste.

Therefore entering the select portals of Harris's Art Galleries came as an anticlimax. Nor did I realise that the establishment opened its doors after closing hours. However, we were admitted by a man impeccably tailored, with all the dignity of a resident butler. He ushered us along a thickly carpeted hall to the main art gallery and invited us to spend as much time there as we wished, and promptly left us. I saw a sign indicating that rare porcelain was displayed on the floor above.

Stacey wheeled his master slowly along the room, and it was almost as if Durbridge had forgotten me, so absorbed did he become in the fine selection of paintings.

"Harris has some new acquisitions," he commented. "I must come in

daylight for a closer inspection. It is some time since I added to my col-
lection, and one cannot get a true impression of colours by gaslight. Tell
me, Miss Boswell, do you appreciate art?''

I assured him that I did, but suppressed a yawn, whereupon he
laughed and told me not to pretend.

"It bores you, I can see. You must forgive me, my dear. I am passionately devoted to the arts and tend to forget that others may not share my
enthusiasm. Come, we will proceed upstairs. Harris' gallery is as noted
for its fine porcelain as for its paintings, and we are privileged to be able
to view them after their doors are closed.''

I felt that both his voice and his eyes were mocking me, and began to
feel uneasy. But I was in his hands. I could not venture alone into the
streets in the vain hope of summoning a cab to take me home, for any ve-
hicles prowling the area and picking up a solitary woman passenger
would, more likely than not, take her to any destination but the one she
asked for. I could be dumped into a den of vice in any quarter between
here and dockland, if I had not already been cornered by a squad of top-
hatted and intoxicated mashers out to seize hold of a woman and convey
her to some room in a side street and use her, one by one, for their pleasure. In my eau-de-nil satin and sables I would be a target for attack of
many a kind, the sables stripped from my back, my jewels and money
snatched, my body used and cast aside.

Enduring this unexpected turn of events with Durbridge would be better than that, boring though the evening was turning out to be. Did he
actually think that a paltry glimpse of life's immoral side at Bollard's, followed by an unpleasant walk amongst massed prostitution, was sufficient
excitement or sufficient novelty?

I decided I had overestimated this man, and when he then subjected
me to a tour of the porcelain showroom above I was convinced of it. We
reached this floor by one of the newest electric lifts, which only rich establishments could afford to install, proof in itself of Harris's highly respected success.

Durbridge again took his time, noting several pieces he decided to
purchase, then despatching Stacey to fetch someone to take his order.
Stacey did not return, but the impeccably tailored gentleman did, and it
was after he had respectfully noted Durbridge's requirements (by which
time I was yawning for my bed) that instead of seeing us off the premises
he calmly walked to the end of the room and touched part of the molding
in a panelled wall. To my amazement the entire panel slid back, revealing
a passage, at the end of which appeared to be nothing but a solid wall.

Without even glancing at me, Durbridge propelled himself forward
and I followed. The panel closed behind us soundlessly. A dim light
overhead revealed that the walls and the closed panel were thickly padded, but I had no time to linger because Durbridge was gliding smoothly

ahead of me and saying over his shoulder, "I promised you culture, darling Clementine, and now you shall have it."

It seemed that in some way a section of the wall ahead of us was automatically timed to slide apart as we approached, for we were abruptly
confronted by a blaze of lights and the sound of voices and laughter
accompanied by lilting music.

"Welcome to the Salon of Art, my dear."

I could have imagined nothing like this in Babylon. The room was an
art studio, filled with students of both sexes, seated at easels. The easels
were arranged in circles, and in the centre of each circle a naked model
posed. Then I noticed that to each group of male students the model was
a woman, and to each group of female students the model was male. It all
seemed very innocent, because, as everyone knew, all artists were taught
to paint from the nude in life classes.

It was only when I glanced at their easels that I realised none had any
ability to paint, nor ever would have, and were not in the least interested
in acquiring the talent. Even more indicative of what they had come for
were the individual sketches. Not one easel showed a full-length figure,
but only a particular section of the body (though some of the men concentrated on the breasts as well). Nor did there appear to be any art
teacher, except a tall and good-looking woman who sauntered amidst the
students, chatting amiably. She wore an artist's smock of transparent
material which revealed very plainly that she wore not a stitch beneath,
and it was she who, from time to time, changed the disc on the phono-
graph. Although harsh in recording, the music was sensuous in the extreme.

At the far end of the room was a small stage, the tabs closed. Durbridge explained that it was used for group modelling and that the sessions for such tuition would follow the present individual life-study class.

"You see, even Babylon has its serious side, its cultural side. I must
introduce you to Anna, who supervises. In fact, it is very important that
you should meet her, if you hope to earn enough money to repurchase
your share in the Boswell Theatre."

"So you hadn't forgotten!"

"Of course not. That is why I brought you here. I told you, didn't I,
that your beauty could be exploited more profitably than in the legitimate theatre, and far less strenuously? The models are highly paid. They
earn more than many respectable actresses, and in their spare time too.
You could supplement your earnings very lucratively in this highly cultural setting, and a body like yours deserves to be displayed."

"And is that all I would have to do—pose in the nude?" I was disappointed, because I was ready to savour greater excitement.

"That is up to you. Further steps are not compulsory, though of
course more profitable and, human nature being what it is, I have never

known anyone not wish to go further than the initial titillation of these art classes. The frustrated and frequently titled ladies from respectable Kensington and similar districts, who enroll for tuition, really come here to enjoy the services of the male models, and vice versa. And now here comes Anna—handsome, is she not? A graduate from Bollard's—and all for an initial outlay of only five shillings. She is now very well off. The rich and titled gentleman who beckoned her across the partition the first time she ever ventured there was in the process of setting up this exclusive establishment and was seeking the right woman to act as hostess. One glance and he knew he had found her. Good-looking, respectable (in those days), and shrewd into the bargain. He engaged her at once, installed her in a smart villa in the part of St. John's Wood which is *not* inhabited by London's most famous courtesans, and neither he nor she has regretted the arrangement. I shall introduce you merely as Diana, which I consider a most appropriate name for you—Diana the Huntress!" His laugh was teasing and I had to share it. "However, you will find a surname useful, so what about Portman? Diana Portman. That will help to preserve your anonymity. Anna, my dear, come and meet my guest."

I liked her and she liked me. We had a lot in common and both of us knew it instinctively. I wondered who her rich lover was and resolved to find out one day, because I knew very well that I was going to belong to this Salon of Art and that I would enjoy every moment spent in it. If I ran the risk of being recognised as an actress from the London stage, it would not matter, because the members of this group of so-called art students would never wish to reveal that they patronised the place, nor would they acknowledge each other should they ever meet outside it, particularly the respectable women to whom it was so essential to retain their virtuous reputations. The men were of similar kind and would be equally anxious to remain anonymous, which was their chief reason for coming to a place like this instead of the more blatant pleasure houses whose red-lit front doors advertised a man's reason for entering. The students' academy, skillfully concealed at the rear of Harris' Art Galleries, was designed solely for discretion.

Anna's experienced eye ran over me approvingly. She guessed why Durbridge had brought me here, and when he left us together she came to the point without delay.

"The fee for posing individually is ten pounds for each session of twenty minutes between eleven P.M. and three A.M., which is very much higher than other establishments pay for nude posing, but they are not so fastidious about the type of models they employ. Ours *must* be ladylike. You may take part in as many sessions as you wish or . . . rest, shall we call it, if you desire to earn over and above the basic fees? There are comfortable rest rooms for this purpose. I know how to investigate every man's financial state, but how I do it is a trade secret. If he fails to qualify, he is not admitted here. The only variation to this rule applies to American tourists, who are always loaded with money and therefore a highly profitable passing trade. They come to watch the group posing onstage and for 'participation' later, of course."

"But this place is so well concealed. How do they discover it?"

"Word passes round. One tourist tells another. I have known Americans make this their first port of call when arriving in London, having heard about it from acquaintances at home. As to the additional fee you can expect for the pleasure of your 'company,' I will arrange that, the minimum being fifty pounds, and during the course of the night, if you are enterprising and give satisfaction, you can earn five times that amount, and more. And the maximum fee can be very much higher, depending solely upon the versatility of your talents."

I knew precisely what she meant and was both amused and titillated by her discreet wording. I also knew that my own "talents" were already versatile, but that this bohemian salon could teach me a great deal more, which I was eager to learn.

The woman continued blandly, "The evening commences with individual tuition in painting from life, as you can see"—her smile became wicked—"but since no model can be expected to remain absolutely still for longer than twenty minutes—indeed, a medical client who comes here regularly insists that it is not only bad for the circulation but bad for the heart—we have lengthy breaks in between for refreshment and for getting to know each other in private or here in the studio as a group. Group activities—and I can see from the light in your eye that you know what form *they* take—tend to increase as the night progresses, until even the modelling demonstrations onstage attract no more attention. You will see an example of these demonstrations in a few minutes. Artistic tableaux, mobile displays, and all extremely tasteful."

"Performed in the nude?"

"Naturally," She glanced down at her transparent smock. "I will be performing there myself tonight, and I hope you will enjoy it, also that you will learn much from it, because I think you would be particularly adept at the art. I have an excellent male partner. He means nothing to me personally, but he does to Durbridge. He is that handsome youth wheeling him into one of the rest rooms now. Poor Durbridge, his tragic accident deprived him of much pleasure, but he has his own methods of making up for it, as you probably know."

I didn't, but as Durbridge disappeared I saw his hand slide down into that inner pocket of his wheelchair, but what he took from it I did not see. The door had closed behind them by that time.

Anna said calmly, "I can tell you are not easily shocked. Durbridge must be aware of this, otherwise he would not have brought you here. I take it you *are* going to join us—Diana, didn't he call you? Diana what?"

"Diana Portman."

"And have you any other profession? You look pretty enough to be an actress. We have a number on our books, and this supplementary work after nightly performances proves highly profitable to them."

"And what of your own name, Anna? Since you know mine, shouldn't I know yours?"

"Why not? I have never hidden it, but it will mean nothing to you. It is Maynard. Anna Maynard."

I don't know why I was so startled. There could be hundreds of Maynards in the world.

"Miss Maynard?" I queried.

"No. Mrs. But a long-forgotten and no-longer-used title, except in my private life. I am simply Anna to everyone here. Not even Durbridge has ever asked about my marriage."

"Why should he?"

"Because he employs me. He owns this place, just as he owns Bollard's, where he discovered me. Little did I dream, that night I plucked up courage and paid my five-shilling entry fee, that I was buying freedom from domestic drudgery, from irksome motherhood and the equally irksome duties of wifehood to a man so unambitious that he would never press for payment from patients who couldn't pay their bills. It didn't matter if *I* couldn't make ends meet. 'It is a doctor's duty to serve humanity, and we are not starving, my dear.' Philanthropic fool! The day after he said that I packed a bag and walked out of that depressing house in the wrong end of Fulham and never went back. And all it cost to buy my freedom was a paltry five shillings—but quite a gamble when all I had in my pocket was ten! You must come and have tea with me one afternoon, Diana. Durbridge installed me in a very pleasant villa and, of course, with a man like that no strings are attached, except to retain an air of dignity and respectability, to which the right address contributes. That is essential, since I conduct the business side from there and the police would never think of searching that quiet suburban address for evidence."

"And what of your husband? Did he never try to trace you?" (It *had* to be the Dr. Maynard whom Helen Steel was in love with. Were there likely to be two doctors of that name in the wrong end of Fulham?)

Anna laughed. "I am quite sure he did, but do you imagine a hard-up and unimaginative doctor would dream of looking for his suburban wife in Babylon? For one thing, he couldn't afford the price of admission to most places, and scouring those streets outside would never yield a glimpse of my face. For another, Hugh knew me well enough to know I would never turn to streetwalking, though God knows I might have had to, but for the luck of being seen by Durbridge. I think even that would have been preferable to remaining with a man I no longer loved and being mother to a couple of brats I never wanted. Motherhood was never part of my nature. So . . . here I am in Babylon, thanks to God and Lord Durbridge, though I doubt if Durbridge's name should be linked with the deity!''

She laughed merrily and continued, ''Anyone who wishes to disappear effectively has only to go to ground in this area or any other part of London's underworld. Even the police rarely succeed in tracing missing persons in this warren, and my eminently respectable husband knew I had not been abducted. I left a note telling him I had departed of my own free will and, for the sake of Kathy and Julian, not to try to get me back. I knew that if I mentioned the children it would work, because *he* knew they would be better off without me. I was never a good mother. They irritated me, got on my nerves, drove me mad. Why am I telling you all this, I wonder? I have never told anyone before, but we are two of a kind, you and I. In my circumstances you would have done exactly what I did—gone after the thing you wanted. In my case, freedom. In yours, I think it would be another man, though I doubt if you would remain faithful to any.''

As Durbridge said, she was shrewd, but I didn't mind her summing up of me. I was vastly amused. I thought of dull Helen Steel eating her heart out for this scandalous woman's husband, and never being able to have him because even if his wife had left him forever, he was still tied to her. Could a man divorce his wife for desertion? I neither knew nor cared.

Anna Maynard said, ''My dear, your eyes are sparkling with excitement. You look vastly entertained, too. But for real entertainment, wait until you see my performance when those curtains part.''

It was everything I expected it to be, as were all ensuing performances during that extraordinary night, but when Durbridge eventually returned he showed not the slightest interest in what was going on. He merely propelled himself across to me and announced that we would now leave. I was disappointed, because I very much wanted to remain, but, alas, I had no choice but to obey.

When we emerged into St. James's, there was Stacey with the carriage. We drove back to Portman Square in silence. Durbridge seemed too exhausted to speak, but I was determined to make him. Discovering his ownership of Bollard's and the Salon of Art (and how many other establishments?) made me feel I was entitled to know something more.

''It seems to me, Lord Durbridge, that if you cared sufficiently about helping me to buy back my share in the Boswell Theatre, you could have offered to lend me the money. Why didn't you?''

''Because this way you can earn it for yourself without paying the very high rate of interest I would undoubtedly charge. I am not a philanthropist, Miss Boswell, and apart from being an asset at the Salon of Art, you can serve me in another way. You recall my saying that we could be of assistance to each other? In return for the rich rewards you will undoubt-edly earn by methods which, I can tell, you will have no scruples about employing, plus the opportunity to reacquire your share in the theatre, you will then sell that share to me. I will pay you double the figure for it that Calder paid you."

"But you don't know how much that was."

"On the contrary, I do, since I supplied the money."

I was too astonished to answer, but now I realised that behind Dur-bridge's apparently friendly interest in my welfare there lay a much deeper motivation, and one I could not comprehend. I wasted no time in asking how Gavin had extracted the money from him. What I wanted to know was why he was prepared to pay me double the amount in order to lay his hands on part-ownership of the Boswell Theatre.

"If you want it so much, why not let me have the money now and we can complete the deal more speedily?"

"Come, my dear, isn't it obvious? Your bastard sister would immedi-ately wonder where and how you obtained the money, knowing the state of your finances. To sell it to her husband in the first place she must have guessed you needed money badly. You have also told me that you begged her to give the share back to you, and she refused. The fact that you have not offered to *buy* it back is sufficient indication you cannot raise the required sum, so how could you explain a sudden windfall? Be-sides, a waiting game is a shrewd one. To be able to go to her eventually with proof that you have valiantly saved up to buy back the share will be admirable testimony of your desire to respect your father's dying wishes, and of your remorse for betraying them. That will touch her heart. She won't refuse you then. So . . . take your time. You can easily earn enough money at the Salon of Art, and I am sure Anna indicated how quickly and easily it can be amassed."

"Lucinda will know perfectly well that out of my salary from the theatre I could not possibly save so much."

"Of course. The girl is no fool. So you will tell her the truth—that you have worked for it in your spare time."

"Tell her *that*?"

"Don't be silly. You have been giving tuition in elocution and deport-ment to wealthy daughters of society. Anyone would be prepared to pay high fees because of the Boswell name. You couldn't have a more con-vincing story."

It was brilliant, of course, and the prospect of eventually doubling my money was tempting, but I could not forget Lucinda's statement that she would not return my share because of her conviction that I would resell it, and to this very man. Then I told myself that that only applied were she to *give* it back to me. In the event of a repurchase, surely a resale would be no business of hers?

In any case, I reflected, tempting as Durbridge's offer was, in the long run I might fare better by holding on to a fifty-percent share of the theatre. The new management seemed to be working well.

I said, "When I have it, I may decide to keep it, no matter how much money you offer me."

"That you will not, darling Clementine, and I advise you not to try. If you do, the story about giving costly elocution lessons will be revealed as false, and the true story of how you earned the money will most certainly become known. It would be one of the greatest scandals in London. Every newspaper would feature it. I am powerful enough to ensure that without my name being involved. Anna has dealt with inquisitive members of the press before. She knows them well and they respect her. She can contact them at any time and bring about your disgrace very effectively—and will, if you oppose me. So when you get that foothold in the theatre again, as you will, you will resell it to me, and I am being very generous in my part of the bargain. Do I make myself clear, darling Clementine?"

All too clear, I thought sullenly, and answered, "And what if I decide not to return to the so-called Salon of Art after tonight?"

"An idle threat. You know you want to. If any woman is eager to belong to that world, it is you, and just how greatly you want to regain your share in the Boswell was equally apparent when you first told me about it. Even more obvious is your need and desire for money. You can satisfy neither, so quickly, in any other way. Gifts from men? They could only be intermittent, and you have no ability to save. That is why your earnings at the Salon of Art will be put aside for you. Anna already has her instructions to hand them over only when the required amount has been reached. You look surprised. Did she fail to tell you that no money changes hands between clients and 'models'? An oversight, I am sure. Payments are made direct to the management, and after deducting the usual commission, the balance is then passed on."

"You think of everything, don't you? It seems to me that only one thing is unexplained—precisely why you want this foothold in a theatre which can never make money on such a scale as places like the Gaiety or the Empire or the Alhambra."

He answered quietly, "I want it because I have a score to settle, and settle it I will."

27

The Rivals had been running for a month, at first to mixed notices. Favourable to Chrystal Delmont and Lucinda Grainger, but slightly less favourable to Bramwell Chambers, who, declared one critic, "is not yet equipped to step wholly into the late Sir Nevill's shoes, fine actor though he is, but time will tell. . . ." Time did. Audiences began to warm toward him rapidly, and soon the same critic was predicting a long run and commenting on Bramwell's increasing stature as an actor.

The critics, on the whole, were kind to me, some saying that the part of Lucy was an inadequate one on which to judge an actress's performance, though the stringent and increasingly influential Max Beerbohm commented that my father would have been less than pleased by his daughter's performance, since "it relied more upon pertness than talent."

Worst of all, which didn't surprise me, were dear Mamma's notices, of which Beerbohm's was a caustic summing up: "Just as an aging woman should learn to grow old gracefully, so should an aging actress learn to retire gracefully, which lesson, it is to be hoped, the once-illustrious Bernadette Boswell will now take to heart."

She took it to heart so violently that her understudy had to step into the role the following night, Mamma being prostrate at home. She was the only person not to realise that her acting days were over.

"I have the migraine," she wailed. "How *dare* that man be so insulting!"

Thanks to her medicine, her migraine was to last several days.

"Don't reproach yourself," I said to Lucinda sweetly. "Even Papa must have known that as an actress she could not survive without him."

Nor did she. She rejoined the cast some days later, gave an even worse performance, and was booed off the stage. She stormed into the wings, vowing never to return. Willard and everyone else stood by helplessly, but not I. I put an arm across her buxom shoulders and said, "You have made the right decision, Mamma. You are grossly unappreciated by today's audiences, so why waste your talents on them? Let the world remember you as the great star you were when acting with dear Papa. Together you were a partnership that will go down in theatrical history, so let the memory of it be preserved. You could write your memoirs. The world would rush to read them, and your name would be immortalised forever."

"I didn't know you had so much tact," Willard told me. "*I* could not have handled her so well."

At that I smiled sadly and said that I could not bear to witness my dear mother being so badly hurt.

The truth was, I was glad to have her out of the theatre, because she expected me to return home with her every night, which meant waiting for the play to end since Mrs. Malaprop was involved throughout, whereas Lucy made her final exit at the end of Act II. Once home, I then had to slip out of the house again in order to get to the Salon of Art before things really began to warm up for the night, which meant sending Maisie out to fetch a hansom for me and thereby arousing her curiosity. I had to remember that there was much of Kate in Maisie's character, though so far she had remained loyal to me. Of course, she was older than Kate, and after a rough life she appreciated the security of a roof over her head, food in her mouth, and regular money in her pocket.

Even so, I never let her hear the address I gave to the cabdriver, and her curiosity about where I went night after night, and from where I returned morning after morning, had to remain unsatisfied. However, once Mamma retired from the cast, I was able to leave the theatre at the end of my final lines and go direct to the Salon and earn far more money than I had ever dreamed of, enjoying every moment into the bargain.

But Maisie did eventually remark that I was tiring myself out. "You can't burn the candle at both ends forever, Miss Clementine," but she said it in such a motherly way that I could not interpret it as anything but real concern.

She was delighted to be back in the theatre. "It's in my bones," she explained. "I first trod the boards in panto when I was no more than a nipper. But if I may say so, Miss Clementine, it seems all wrong to me that you, being a Boswell, should have a less important dressing room than Miss Grainger, *and* be playing a smaller part, in a theatre which bears your father's name."

I always felt that Maisie didn't like Lucinda very much, which was all to the good. I was also glad that I had engaged her privately as my personal dresser, because that ensured her loyalty. She owed nothing to the management, only to me.

Things began to be more friendly between myself and Lucinda because I was working really hard at making sure that they did. Whatever type of a man Durbridge might be, he was at least a wise one when it came to advice on how to handle people. As he predicted, Lucinda responded until we almost reached the stage of intimacy we had shared as children, though perhaps "intimate" was hardly the word to describe our present relationship, because I would certainly never confide certain details of my life to her now, as I had done when returning from the convent.

And, of course, she was reticent by nature, rarely talking about her own life except insofar as it touched on her mother and her friendship with the Steels, whom she always referred to jointly, so I hadn't the slighest suspicion that she saw a great deal of Magnus until Maisie told me.

"They're close friends, aren't they—Dr. Steel and Miss Grainger, I mean. I see them together a lot, and I know they meet in the square gardens sometimes. I suppose that's when his sister is at home and he wants a bit of privacy from her. She's a right busybody, that one."

"The Steels and the Graingers have always been friends," I said negligently. "The doctor has never regarded Miss Grainger as anything more than a little sister."

"Not so little now."

"She is dedicated to her career and to this theatre."

"But it is yours too, isn't it? Your dear father did leave it to the pair of you, didn't he?"

"And how do you know that?"

"Everyone knows. I remember the papers making quite a feature of his will, and I remember thinking it wasn't really fair to you, to treat her the same way as his real daughter."

I could not miss the ingratiating note in Maisie's voice, but merely shrugged.

"If you've been in the theatre nearly all your life, Maisie, you must know it is not so conventional as the world outside."

"That's true enough! Attracts all sorts of queer folk, don't it? That Lord Durbridge, f'rinstance. He used to chase the chorus line, the men in particular, when I was a chorus girl myself. Of course, that was before he had his accident. Tragic, weren't it? And to think that the very night it happened he were backstage in this very theatre. . . ."

I jerked to attention and asked what she meant.

"Why, nothing much, Miss Clementine—only that I saw him at the champagne party onstage that night, the first night of the revival of *The Only Way*. I was one of the supers then, and when I came down those stairs from the women's dressing room on my way home—number twenty, 'twere, I well remember—he was as hale and hearty as ever, but later. . . ." She broke off, almost biting her tongue, but I knew she was dying to continue all the same.

"Go on," I encouraged. "Go on."

"There's no more to tell, reelly. I mean, I didn't actually *see* anything happen, only something *must*'ve done to put the fear of God into that Jerry Hawks. He was callboy then, and I saw him come pelting out into the street as if the devil were after him and go tearing off down the alley at the side to the Strand. Comes right out near Romano's, where Lord Durbridge was giving his supper party, except that he didn't turn up for it."

"And how do you know that?"

"News gets around. Besides, I heard one of the actors talking about it next night. Being only a super, I couldn't talk to a lead player, but I could've told him why his lordship didn't turn up. He were carried out of here by that man of his, and handsome Mr. Calder. Drunk, I thought."

You didn't think anything of the sort, I reflected. *You want to tell me more, but wonder if you ought to.*

I encouraged her by saying, "I have never known Lord Durbridge to drink too much."

"Then he must've been hurt, right here in this theatre. Come to think of it, the two of them were carrying him very carefully. But how could he have been injured backstage at the Boswell? Doesn't make sense, does it, because guests only have to walk from the stage straight off to the wings and then along the corridor direct to the stage door. No steps to trip over or anything, so he must have been drunk for once in his lifetime."

I found it hard to believe. For all his vices, of which I had now learned much, insobriety was never one of them. Durbridge was abstemious in that way at least, and had nothing but contempt for people who drank to excess, maintaining that only fools stupefied themselves with alcohol.

My mind raced on. The night Maisie was talking about was the night when Trudy had ranted about something terrible happening to her darling child, and Lucinda's face had been a frightful mess, though she had dismissed it as trifling. I now recalled that she had shared that supers' dressing room at the top of the circular stairs, which made me believe, even less, her story about tripping over a prop. But how else had her accident happened? A fall down those treacherous stairs would have resulted in greater injuries than minor facial ones.

Injuries as great as Durbridge's. . . .

My heart gave a leap. Could it be possible he had visited her in that faraway dressing room and met with a tragedy afterward; a fall, but not when out riding as he had claimed? I could not credit it because I could not imagine Durbridge attempting to seduce the girl Lucinda had then been. Besides, I knew his sexual tastes now.

One person seemed likely to know the truth—the boy who fled from the place—but I knew that if I tried to question Jerry Hawks now I would get nowhere. Cockney kid though he was, he had a disconcerting ability to retreat into a kind of dignified withdrawal when he felt so inclined. I could imagine him saying politely, "I don't know wotcha talking abaht, Miss Boswell. I don't even know wot night yer mean. Can't even remember that far back, though if anyfink outa the ord'nry'd 'appened, I'd be sure to remember, wouldn't I? Sorry I can't oblige, Miss Boswell, ma'am." And that would be that—a quiet and very firm rejection.

He was a deep one, young Hawks, though Lucinda didn't consider him so. "The nice thing about Jerry," she always said, "is his honesty. If he has made a mistake in any way, he owns up. He doesn't just wait to be found out; he goes straight to Gregory and tells him—and he never makes the same mistake twice. That is why Gregory has made him ASM, though the boy is honest enough to admit he wants to aim higher, and because the SM's job isn't likely to fall vacant in Gregory's time, he has asked if he can learn all about lighting in between ASM-ing. With electricity taking over in theatres now, he sees big things ahead, big changes. And he is right. With electricity, the whole business of stage lighting is going to develop in all sorts of ways, and there will be bigger and better jobs in the lighting department than on the SM side, where it's a case of waiting for the SM to retire or go to another theatre or, alternatively, to try for a job elsewhere himself. But Jerry swears he will never leave the Boswell because the place is a real home to him. So in between performances he is putting in time with Lights, who is only too glad to encourage the boy's interest. Too many technicians are afraid of the new innovations and the use of so many switches and fragile bulbs. Magnus is paying for him to attend classes in electrical training two mornings a week."

"Magnus? Why Magnus?"

"Because he wants to. Jerry is a protégé of his, and Magnus is as proud of him as I am. He will go far in the theatre, will Jerry."

No wonder the boy was so devoted to Lucinda, with all the interest she showed in him and the encouragement she gave him, and in the face of such devotion any attempt to pump him would be a waste of time, so I abandoned the idea and turned my attention to Maisie again, who was saying, "There, now, Miss Clementine, you're all ready to go home, and I hope you *are* going home tonight, because you're beginning to look very tired, if I may say so, and that there Kate is getting curious."

"*Kate?*" I demanded angrily. "Why Kate?"

"She has a gentleman friend at the livery stable I've been ordering your hansom from every night—or did until your mamma stopped acting and you haven't had to travel home with her and then slip out afterwards."

My God. Kate. And Maisie too? What lay behind all this gossip, this show of devotion and loyalty? I remembered the half-smile they had exchanged the night Durbridge sent his carriage to collect me and Maisie's astonishment when she saw it. She had recognised it, of course—also Stacey, who had helped that unscrupulous stepuncle of mine to carry Durbridge out of the theatre.

In all this bewildering spate of information my chief concern was for myself. I recalled that it had always been the same cabby who drove me to Harris's Art Galleries, and that after the first night or two it had not even been necessary for me to direct him there.

"Are you trying to tell me the driver of that cab was a 'gentlemen' friend of Kate's?''

"Well, *I* didn't know he was, Miss Clementine. How could I? And he only told her that he took you to a high-class art gallery somewhere, so of course *I* told *her* you have some very exclusive and cultured friends and that no doubt the art gallery belonged to some of them. And, if I may make so bold, Miss Clementine, I'm very glad I haven't seen Lord Durbridge's carriage calling for you again, because there are all sorts of stories about him—''

"You shouldn't listen," I told her sharply, "and what is more, you should neither listen nor talk to Kate. She has been a member of our household since I was tiny, and I know her well. She is untrustworthy. It is my mother who insists that she remains. If I had my way, she would go, and so would all servants who gossip.''

I saw fear flicker in her eyes, and was satisfied.

"I would never betray you, Miss Clementine, whatever you did.''

"My dear Maisie, nothing I ever did would be worth betraying. As you say, my friends are cultured and very select.''

"Indeed, I know they are. The likes of you would never mix with people who weren't. But . . . please forgive me, Miss Clementine, but I can't help worrying about you, because you really are beginning to show signs of tiredness. I hope you'll be home before the early hours tonight? I can't help hearing you come upstairs, and somehow I can't settle until I know you're safely in bed, London being the sort of place it is at night.''

I was not deceived by her assumed air of concern. If she dared to try Kate's tactics, out she would go. I said abruptly, "You worry unnecessarily. Whatever friends I happen to be visiting or supping out with see me home safely by carriage, and only drive through the most salubrious streets. Besides, it won't last much longer. The winter season is always crowded with parties, but when the spring comes. . . .''

I broke off with a jerk, because Lucinda had entered.

"When spring comes," she said, "I hope you will take a rest, because we will be between shows then. Forgive me for walking in unannounced, but the door was open and I want to talk to you.''

I couldn't refuse, though I hated being delayed. I looked forward to my visits to the Salon of Art, where I had quickly become popular and where I was earning a great deal of money very rapidly. Fatiguing it might be, but I could always sleep late in the morning; therefore it was nonsense for Maisie to say that I was looking tired. Moreover, the food and drink there were excellent, and I enjoyed both, particularly the food, which was superb and expensive, as was everything in that temple dedicated to art. But the patrons paid for it, not I, so I always took my fill. My mother's partiality for drink had discouraged my taste for it, but nothing in the world could discourage my taste for food, despite Anna's warnings that it would make me fat. Me, fat! Men loved my curves. They always had and they always would, and if my clothes were becoming a little tight, Maisie could always let them out.

I had been a "model" now for more than six months, and the money was accumulating in Anna's carefully kept accounts, which she was honest enough to show me whenever I asked. For this, I had to visit her villa in St. John's Wood, where she handled business matters from behind an admirable screen of respectability. I was aware that in a few more weeks I could reach my target. Never had I dreamed that so much money could be amassed so quickly.

As I signalled to Maisie to leave us alone, I noticed that Lucinda was looking very lovely tonight, but, as always, too thin in my opinion. She would not have attracted many customers at the Salon of Art, but I had to admit that she wore clothes well and her gown was beautiful.

"Going somewhere special?" I asked.

"Supper with Magnus, that's all."

"That's all? It means so little to you, then?"

She coloured slightly. "I didn't say that. One says 'that's all' merely colloquially, when an event is part of one's life."

Part of one's life? Part of *your* life? A regular, accepted part? I thought of Magnus's rejection of me and smarted beneath it, as always, but I had been too busy in recent months to give him a great deal of thought. Not that I had forgotten my intention to make him regret it somehow, or even to win him back someday in some way, if only to prove that I could, but there was time enough for that, I decided, even if supper parties with him *were* part of Lucinda's life now. Habits could be broken, and that long friendship between the Steels and the Graingers contained no threat. Had it done so, I would have sensed it long ago.

Something made me ask, "And how is Helen Steel these days? Still doing her good works?"

"Of course."

"And the worthy doctor she is in love with? Still pining her heart out for him? I always think it such a waste of time to fall in love with a married man."

I had expected that to take her by surprise, but it didn't. All Lucinda said was, "One cannot control the heart in these matters."

"So you know he is married?"

"Of course. I have known for some time. Magnus told me long ago that there were certain difficulties, and later he told me what they were. Poor Helen, and poor Hugh also. Life deserves to be kinder to them and I hope it will be one day. But that isn't what I want to talk to you about. Bramwell and Willard both asked me to have a word with you, and frankly I have been wanting to myself because I am feeling worried about you. Not only are you looking tired, but your performance is suffering. Are

you feeling unwell? Bramwell says it can't be due to overwork, because
the part of Lucy is anything but demanding, but is there anything wrong?
Or anything I can do to help? Would you like an understudy to take
over? You will remain on full pay until the end of the run, which is not
so far off. After that we will be doing *The Importance of Being Earnest,* in
which you and I will play Gwendolen and Cecily, equally lovely parts and
equally important, you'll agree. That should make you much happier,
and we can study our parts together. That is a wonderful way of learning
lines.''

She was absolutely sincere. Her concern was genuine and so was her
anxiety for me. I think it was at that moment that I saw Lucinda's character clearly for the first time, or perhaps acknowledged it for the first
time. She was too honest to be capable of guile. That didn't make me resent her any the less, but it did give me a golden opportunity to appeal to
her, because guileless people could also be gullible.

"Well, to tell the truth, Lucinda, I *am* feeling tired. I have been working so very hard and must continue to because things at home aren't
easy. Mamma isn't a good household manager, and the part of Lucy car-
ries such a small salary that I have had to supplement it by teaching elocution in every available spare moment. I have a large number of pupils
from the wealthier classes, so I am able to charge very high fees—the
name of Boswell counts for something still. But the work is exhausting
and consequently I am fatigued when I get to the theatre. Still, I need
the money for a very specific purpose—to buy back the share Papa left
me. I have always been so ashamed about letting it go. He would have
been hurt had he known, poor darling. I intend to give you back the
money Gavin paid me for it, and then everything will be put straight,
won't it, and everything forgiven and, I hope, forgotten. That is really
why I have been slogging day in and day out.''

She was aghast.

"Oh, Clemmy, if only I had known! Coupled with nightly performances and matinees, you are wearing yourself out.'' She put her arms
round me spontaneously, and it was just as if there had never been any
animosity or rivalry between us. At that moment she wasn't even remembering how Gavin and I had hurt her. Had she actually forgotten
that moment when she found me in bed with her husband? Right now
she was certainly not thinking of it. She was happy solely because I was
sorry about letting Papa down.

She insisted that this extra work should stop. "It *must* stop, because
there is no need for it. I am going to do something which I know my father would want me to do. I am going to give you back your share, because what you have just told me would have made him very proud. He
always admired people who were prepared to work hard. I have to admit
that when you simply demanded to be *given* it again, as if taking for grant-

ed that it should be, I felt one inevitable reaction, particularly as circumstances were at the time. But this! There could be no better proof of how sincerely you regret parting with his legacy. We must start again the way he wanted us to, sharing the theatre between us. As for buying back your share, I won't hear of it—no, don't protest! I mean it. This is something I want to do for my father's sake. I know he would wish it. I will put the matter in hand at once.''

She kissed my cheek spontaneously and I am quite sure she thought my smile was one of gratitude, not of gratification. When she had gone I let rip, collapsing into a chair and laughing until my sides ached. *Durbridge*, I thought, *you're a genius! She swallowed the whole story, and it touched her heart just as you said it would!*

Then I sobered. On no account must I reveal to Durbridge that she was giving my share back to me. He must believe I was buying it, because only that way would I get double the amount out of him. Already I had almost earned the basic figure; I would pocket that from the Salon of Art *and* Durbridge's double payment when making the share over to him. In that way I would not part with a penny, but make a handsome profit.

The thought of Durbridge becoming Lucinda's partner entertained me, knowing how much she disliked him. Nor would she be able to get rid of him by buying him out, because somehow I knew that once he had a foot in the door nothing would induce him to withdraw it. I could not understand his passionate desire to be involved with the Boswell Theatre, but hadn't he said something about wanting to settle a score? And could it possibly have something to do with that story Maisie had told me?

Meanwhile, the theatre was spending lavishly on extensive new lighting equipment, not only for stage effects but throughout the house, and replacing seating which had been installed when the theatre had been built originally, also on redecorating the whole of the auditorium and foyer, not to mention staging entire new productions, which meant new scenery and costumes. Lucinda could have spoken nothing but the truth when saying she had not yet reaped her share of profits, so heaven only knew when I would get any tangible benefit from a fifty-percent share, even if I tried to hold on to it. A substantial sum of cash in hand now seemed more desirable than waiting for any fine-feathered bird to fly out of the bush.

Feeling decidedly optimistic, I went to the Salon of Art on air that night. When I entered I saw several of my regular patrons and a quick estimate of how much money they would yield heartened me even further.

Anna met me with the news that we had a rich American tourist tonight.

"He must be," she said, "to buy his way in without an introduction. The charge for that is more than high. And he paid without even raising an eyebrow. He simply flashed a fistful of sovereigns and there could be no magic wand more powerful. I will point him out to you. This is to be *your* night, remember, so make the most of it."

I knew what she meant. Focus on the rich American. She scarcely needed to point him out, because his clothes gave him away. Besides, I had seen him before. For a while I could not remember where; then I recalled the greying-haired man with beard and heavy moustache that night in Bollard's, the one who had stared at me and at no other woman. That night seemed so long ago I was surprised he was still in London. Tourists' time was usually limited; a rip-roaring fling and they were gone.

"A strange man," Anna went on. "So far, he has just sat over there like a spectator, talking to no one, just quietly drinking, which isn't the way Americans usually behave. They drink, all right, but never alone. They make a beeline for the models. With so much money on him we must make sure this one does more than drink all by himself, and if anyone can succeed at that tonight, it will be you, Diana. Once he sees you up there . . ."

She gave an expressive glance toward the stage and moved on.

Reminding me that tonight was to be my benefit night meant that I was to pose up there in the nude, alone. Not that I needed any reminder, because I was looking forward to it. I was avid as ever for new experience, and this was my first chance to give a solo performance, and a "mobile" at that. Anna had had new lighting effects installed, lamps shining through revolving coloured slides, spotlighting me in exotic shades. This was a big step-up from posing for the so-called life classes, and even from posing with a group, and the evening would result in a great amount of money both for me and for the establishment. Anna had also taught me movements that were sensuous in the extreme. "Look upon it as merely an act, dear, because that's all it is, and being an actress, you are accustomed to being onstage and will take it in your stride, I know."

But I had never performed like this on any stage. I could imagine poor dear Mamma having a stroke if she knew about it.

However, it was all an enormous success and when it was over men rushed to congratulate me, to touch me, to fight to have me, bidding against each other in such high figures the other models were plainly jealous. I was laughing, loving every moment, until someone pushed through the little knot of men and I saw the grey-haired, bearded tourist staring down at me. Then he took off his jacket and covered me, and for the first time I heard him speak.

"So you have sunk as low as this, have you . . . Miss Clementine?"

28

I couldn't believe it. The voice belonged to Curtis, and so did those penetrating eyes beneath the mane of grey hair. There was a new intonation in his voice, a new accent, but the tone was unmistakably his, and at close quarters, between the heavy moustache and beard, I saw the mouth which I had once found so fascinating.

"Go and put your clothes on," he ordered, giving me a push toward the side of the small stage.

Oh, yes, it was Curtis, all right—he had never missed a thing, and tonight he must have seen me disappear behind the curtain which concealed the cramped wings of the stage and guessed rightly that I had shed my garments there.

I could not take a step. I was shaking. I stood clutching his jacket to cover my nakedness, because somehow he made me feel self-conscious and ashamed. I didn't understand why I felt that way because no one was ever embarrassed in a place like this.

"Go on," he rapped. "Do as I tell you."

Anna glided up. "I must point out, sir, that visitors to this art studio are not allowed to bully the models. I am afraid I must ask you to leave."

"You don't have to. I am leaving and taking her with me."

"For the exclusive companionship of a model, the fee is substantial, sir."

He pulled further sovereigns out of his pocket. They seemed to be stuffed haphazardly on his person, as if money were immaterial to him. Anna beamed and said to me, "Hurry, Diana, you mustn't keep the gentleman waiting. I will give you a hand."

Behind the curtain she almost bundled me into my clothes. "The chap must be a millionaire. You've done well tonight, dear. When I've counted this money I am sure you will have reached the figure Durbridge stipulated you were to earn. . . ."

I wasn't listening.

"What's the matter?" she demanded. "You look as if you've seen a ghost. You'd better have a brandy before you leave. A man like that isn't going to settle for a wilting flower."

She was gone and I was alone, dressed and ready for the street. But I could not pull back the curtain and face that man with Curtis's eyes and voice. Beyond the stage was a concealed rear entrance for the convenience of those who wished to enter and depart unseen. I had only to slip away . . .

The curtain was ripped aside.

"So you're ready." He took hold of my wrist and led me away. His grip was viselike, and to try to escape, impossible. Nor would the scheming Anna allow me to. Offend a rich customer? Never! And there she was, brandy glass in hand. We walked right past her and out of the place.

Shock still gripped me, and I still remained silent. He had a hansom already waiting outside, the driver half-asleep on his box and the top light dowsed to indicate the vehicle was booked. He jerked awake when Curtis opened the folding doors across the front, lifted me bodily inside, then joined me. Evidently the cabby already had his instructions because he didn't open the hatch to ask for them. He let the top door down to give us the privacy he thought we wanted, then whipped the horses into action and headed up St. James's toward Piccadilly. Only then did I find my voice.

"Where are you taking me?"

"To my hotel."

"And if I refuse to go?"

"You won't refuse a good supper. You were always fond of your food, and judging by the weight you've put on, you still are. We can talk across a supper table, and that's all I want of you tonight."

"You've . . . changed."

"The hair, the moustache, the beard? You'll know me better when I shave them off and have the hair cut shorter, the way I used to wear it. The greyness I can do nothing about. I'm not one of your fancy men who dye their hair."

"You're thinner, leaner . . ."

"Not surprising. I went through a lean time after I left England—*not* on that ship from the East India Dock. You didn't really think me fool enough to board that vessel, did you? I knew I could be traced if I did. I wouldn't have put it past you to give me away to the police, accusing me of having run off with money. Besides, I'd spilled a few beans to Lucinda Grainger, though I trusted her more than I did you. So I got rid of the shipping ticket in the safest way—struck a match in a side alley and burned it. I enjoyed rubbing the ash into the gutter. Then I got myself to Tilbury and onto a cargo vessel sailing along the coast to Southampton. Any vessel needing an extra hand would have done, any destination. I wasn't going to buy a passage on any ordinary steamer with some of the money you'd paid me off with because the banknotes could have been traced—"

"And of course," I interrupted pointedly, "you had the things you'd stolen from Gavin Calder."

"Those too, I admit, though robbing him was an afterthought. A safeguard. I didn't mean to kill the man."

"Then why the knife?"

"To put the fear of God into both of you. I was so insane with jealousy that night I could have slashed your pretty face. By God, you bitch, you'd treated me rottenly. That's why I'm back. This time *you* are going to find out what it's like to be another person's slave.''

"Let me out of here!" I reached up, banging on the roof hatch and shouting to the cabby, but Curtis merely laughed.

"You're wasting your time. The man has already been told to head straight back to my hotel without stopping, and nothing speaks louder than money—except perhaps Britain's gold hoards in the Bank of England. The richest country in the world with the richest society and the greatest poverty! I wonder what will happen to it when the old queen dies and overseas expansion begins to die with her, though maybe that began when England lost her American colonies. That's why I headed for the States. A man can do what he likes there, provided he's ready to work and grabs his opportunities—or makes them. There's many an immigrant climbing to the top. It doesn't matter what a man's background is or even if he has come up from the gutter. It's his success that matters. I have got it, and will get more.''

The vehicle drew to a halt and the cabby jumped down and opened the doors. The hotel was not far from Portman Square, and a good one, an exclusive and expensive one. And Curtis had spoken nothing but the truth—he didn't take me up to his room. There was a table already reserved in the dining room.

"You were very confident I would come," I said when we were seated.

"Not confident. Determined. You hadn't any choice, had you? I would have raised hell in that so-called Salon of Art, and the last thing that Madame wanted was a scene. All discretion and good manners, isn't she, but I could read her like a book. Who is she answerable to? Some racketeer, or what is known over here as an entrepreneur, though I don't know if I've pronounced the word correctly. Anyway, there are places like that in uptown New York, behind all the grandeur of Fifth Avenue and Washington Square. There are mansions along Fifth Avenue equal to any here on Park Lane—"

"*In* Park Lane," I corrected automatically.

"I'm not an Englishman anymore, so I don't speak like one."

"You certainly do not." I had recovered my poise now, thanks to the good food and wine and the tone of this restaurant, which was the sort to which I was accustomed, but had never dreamed of visiting with Curtis. "You have an American accent now."

"I *am* American now. An American citizen legally. The country has given me more chances than this one ever did, so I reckoned I owed it my loyalty.''

"Then why come back?"

We were between courses, and while waiting for the next, Curtis astonished me by lighting a cigarette and then even more by saying, "I came back because of you. I've never been able to forget you. Never got you out of my system."

I laughed. That seemed to be a mistake, because he frowned, and his eyes narrowed as he leaned toward me and repeated the words with emphasis. "I . . . came . . . back . . . because . . . of . . . you."

A drift of smoke made me cough, and I fanned it away in disgust.

"Gentlemen do not smoke between courses."

"They do in America, so you'd better get used to it."

I stared, amazed by his impudence. I stared for so long that he burst out laughing. If anything was finally needed to convince me this man was really Curtis, it was that laugh. It had not changed a bit. It sent me winging back into the past and the happy times we had had in his rooms above the coach house; after loving me he had often been boisterous. "God, but you're marvellous," he would say. "You make me feel on top of the world! I'll bet there isn't a man in London, not a single one of your fine gentlemanly friends, who wouldn't change places with me!" And he would laugh for the sheer joy of it, and I would join in.

But now I couldn't even summon a smile.

"I don't know what you are talking about," I remarked icily. "I am never likely to visit America, unless to perform in one of New York's finest theatres."

"You'll never get a chance to, if you act the way you do in that part you're playing now. You're terrible in it. I've seen the show more than once and almost felt sorry for you, but you've never liked hard work so I expect you have only yourself to blame. You've let Lucinda Grainger get way ahead of you. She's grown into a fine actress, that one, and a beauty too. And take that jealous look off your face. You've always resented her, even when you had no cause. Now it seems you have, and it serves you damn well right."

I said even more icily, "Kindly summon the waiter to fetch my wrap. I wish to go home."

"You'll go home when I'm ready to let you, and not before. I haven't hung around London trying to get you to myself all these weeks just to have a chat for old times' sake."

I suddenly wondered why he had not called on me at the theatre, and said so, at which he laughed again, but not with mirth.

"Would you have received me? Of course you wouldn't. If the stage-doorman had announced that your onetime coachman Curtis had come to pay a social call, you wouldn't have believed it, or else you would have been as alarmed as you were tonight when you realised who I was. Terrified, weren't you? Shocked because a murderer you thought you'd got rid of had come walking back into your life. Except that I'm not a murderer. An accidental killer, yes. That was why I pilfered Calder's pockets, to make it look like a stab-and-run robbery. It was a quick decision, and a good one, because that sort of a crime happens in cities after dark all over the world. Leaving him there dead, with all his possessions on him, would have made it look like deliberate murder, and then there would have been a real police hunt on. So I took everything, including his gold watch and diamond studs and cufflinks, and his wallet and all the cash in his pockets. Leaving no identification on him gave me more time to get away. I knew that by the next day, at least, Calder would be recognised. My mind worked fast, I remember. It had to. I didn't attempt to pawn the diamonds until I reached New York. They set me up when the time came, though the fence gave me only half their value—"

"Fence?" I interrupted. "What is a fence?"

"Pardon me, ma'am, I quite forgot. You're too ladylike to be acquainted with underworld terms." His voice was laden with sarcasm. "A fence, sweet innocent Clementine, is a receiver of stolen goods. Theft has never been my line, though I've knocked about the world and done all sorts of things and been almost down and out sometimes, but for the first time in my life I was in possession of stolen goods and intended to make use of them. They were to be my ticket to success; without them, I would have been another down-and-outer in New York, which is as bad as being a down-and-outer in London or Paris or any other great city. I threw Calder's gold watch into the Thames as soon as I discovered his name engraved in the lid. I wasn't going to carry around anything that could associate me with a well-known actor found dead on the Chelsea Embankment."

"And at Southampton you booked a passage to New York?"

"Not likely. That would have taken every penny of your Judas money, and I was going to need the rest of it when I got to the other side, so the best way of crossing the Atlantic was to work my way. You forget I'd had seaman experience. I still had my seaman's ticket to prove it, and I got a job belowdecks on a ship going to New York. If I'd tried to buy myself even a steerage passage, I could have been noticed. I would have had to mix with passengers and immigrants, but working down in the bowels of a ship and being fed and paid into the bargain suited me well, because seamen rarely ask questions about each other. Too many of them don't want questions asked in return. They work and eat and sleep, and either remain in the job because they like it or because they don't want their wives to find them, or else they do what I did— scarper at some port of call."

"You still use cockney words, I notice."

"Why not? 'Scarper' applies exactly to what I did. Then I found a flophouse in the hellhole part of New York, where a man can hide and learn a thing or two into the bargain—such as how to find a fence, the right fence. A dollar here and a dollar there buys information, but a bit at a time, because it isn't wise to flash too much money around downtown in any city, nor was I going to give an inkling of what I'd carried hidden on me ever since I left England. Not once had I had all my clothes off for that reason. One of the first things I did was to buy a bar of soap and some disinfectant powder and find a bathhouse where, for a dollar, I could have a bath to myself and lock the cubicle door and keep an eye on my clothes while I cleansed myself. That dollar was my first investment in the future, and after I was clean and shaved again I walked up Manhattan Island all the way to uptown New York. Hours it took me, and every minute well spent, taking in everything from the start of Fifth Avenue at the Washington Arch till I reached the rich part of Park Avenue around Sixtieth Street, and I made a vow there and then that one day *I* would live uptown. And now I do.''

I was on the final course now, delicious *crêpes suzette*, but Curtis ate nothing more. Glancing at my plate, he said brutally, ''If you're not careful, you'll be the size of your mother one day, and then no one will employ you to flaunt your naked charms.''

I blazed, ''Many an actress supplements her earnings in artistic tableaux and posing for artists—''

''Not *my* wife.''

''Your . . . wife? You are married, then?''

''Not yet, and not sure that I ever will be, though maybe I had it in mind when coming back. Or maybe I only wanted to show you how well I've done without you, and seeing what you've become, I consider my success far greater than yours. 'For better, for worse' with you would be decidely 'for worse.' Though not in bed. That part was always good between us, wasn't it, Clemmy? I've never forgotten it—and never found it so good with any woman since. Always I'd be remembering and comparing and wondering who you were doing it with now, but God knows I never expected to find you posturing the way I saw you tonight.''

''Posing,'' I contradicted feebly. ''There is a difference between posturing and posing.''

''Not the way you were doing it. I was ashamed for you. When I got the address of that art gallery, I was puzzled. Classy sort of place by day, and no lights showing behind its swanky shop front by night, but apparently the cabby had taken you there regularly after you'd returned from the theatre with your mother. A livery stable sent a hansom along to take you to the same address night after night.''

I dropped my fork with a clatter. The noise attracted attention from nearby diners, but Curtis's face remained impassive. I tried to control mine as I said, ''How did you know about the livery stable, how did you hear of it?''

"I didn't. I merely found out that a regular cab had called for you from an establishment nearby, and a gentleman friend of Kate's happened to be the driver. That was how she knew the address."

"*Kate!*" I hissed. "You questioned Kate about me?"

"I didn't need to. She was only too willing to talk."

"How did you meet her?"

"By the simple method of ringing your front doorbell when the butler was off duty. I've been watching the house discreetly, wondering how to contact you. I saw you in a place in Jermyn Street the first night after my arrival. Couldn't believe my eyes. How could any man have such a mighty stroke of luck so soon? But you didn't even recognise me, which wasn't surprising, I suppose. When you left the place with that man in a wheelchair and I followed, I lost sight of you in the crush. A man is pestered and waylaid every other minute in that quarter, and after a while I gave up. It seemed obvious to me that someone in a wheelchair would have been transported by carriage, which meant that you had too. I went back to Bollard's and asked for the man's identity, but every lying bastard said they didn't know—which told me they did. I went back time and time again, but you never appeared. Then I discovered this new hotel quite close to your home and moved in. After that my daily vigil was to keep an eye on your house. Sometimes residents in the square are careless about locking the garden gates, especially nursemaids with children, and I would sit there watching number 47 until I knew when the butler was on duty and therefore likely to open the door; also that Kate answered it when he was off. Once or twice I even caught a glimpse of you leaving for the theatre, so I knew you still lived at home and not with some man legally or otherwise, but by the time I'd hurried out of the gardens to accost you, you had driven away. Besides, I didn't really want to approach you in the street. I wouldn't have put it past you to cry out for the police—there's a flatfoot on the beat in the square regularly. I didn't relish the idea of being accused of molesting a lady in public. So I had to bide my time. Then one day I rang that doorbell when I knew Kate would answer. She did, and I asked for you."

"And she recognised you? *That* was why she talked?"

"She didn't know me from Adam. It was dusk by then, and I had my back to what little light there was, and I took the precaution of making my American accent real strong. She didn't talk voluntarily, either—not Kate. I had to grease her palm with the age-old lubricant. For a pound she was ready to tell me anything I wanted to know, which was where I could find you."

"A pound! If I know Kate, she would have talked for five shillings or even half a crown."

"For a pound she really opened up, so it was worth it. 'You mean *after* the theatre, of course, sir. She goes to a very select art gallery in St.

James's, sir. A friend of mine from the livery stables round the corner used to drive her there after she and her mother got back from the theatre, but since Lady Boswell retired from the stage I suppose she goes there direct, because she still returns in the early hours, same as ever. Harris's Art Galleries, sir. I don't know the street number, but I expect you'll find it. It's very well known, I believe.' That was last night, and I wish to God I'd got hold of her before. I would have had you out of that place before you sank so low.''

I couldn't speak. Rage choked me. *I'll kill Kate for this*, I vowed. *I swear I'll kill her.* I looked at this hard, determined stranger and wanted to get away from him fast.

"Don't you want to know how I've become so successful, Clemmy? I'll tell you, all the same. I am a restaurateur. Sounds grand, doesn't it? And it is grand. I started with a cheap chophouse downtown and moved slowly nearer and nearer to the area I aimed for. The chophouse was launched on the proceeds from Calder's diamonds, but most of the money went on a large gaming room at the back. This did so well that soon I had a bigger and better one, because Americans love to gamble. I suppose it's in their blood, because they've had to gamble in business and in every other way to get to the top, to succeed, to get rich, to build a nation. They had to start from the ground up, and that's the way I started too. From there I graduated to a better-class steak house, because those were the only things I knew how to cook, plus trimmings, but it was the gaming saloons that made the money. I worked all day and every day, all night and every night, until I was making enough money to employ a real chef and the whole tone of the place promptly went up. The big spenders and the big gamblers who also appreciated good food replaced the steaks-and-poker crowd, and then I sold those premises and moved right up to the Washington Square end of Fifth Avenue, and not only did my regular customers come with me, but new ones too. It is now one of the smartest places to eat and to gamble, but never at any point along the line have I had rooms at the back for whores, like some of the New York eating places.

"Food and gambling, tone and discretion, plus brains and a helluva lot of work, and in something under four years I've made it. And I'm still on the way up. I've made a bid for an uptown hotel now, and I'll get it too, even if I have to outbid all others. It will be the first of a whole chain of hotels. One day, and not so far distant either, to stay at a Curtis Hotel will be *the* thing to do.''

I was impressed, as he meant me to be, but I wasn't going to let him see it.

"Congratulations," I said indifferently, but my mind was racing. A woman could do very well for herself with such a man, in such a country, with or without the blessing of the Church, and he could do even better with the right woman beside him—a woman who knew how to greet people, how to talk to people; a woman with my own background and a well-bred English accent. I had heard that Americans liked an English accent so much that they even employed English butlers. I found that vastly amusing, but resisted the temptation to laugh this time in case Curtis thought I was laughing at him again and asked why. So I thrust the whole idea aside, also the recollection of what a marvellous lover this man had been. He could have lost none of the art. He never would. Determinedly I reminded myself that I was a London actress and intended to remain one. Even if I planted in his mind the idea of linking his life with mine again, in his newfound success he would expect me to be subservient to him, and I would never be any man's slave.

I yawned significantly, and he made no attempt to deter me. A casual lift of his hand brought the waiter at once, and soon my cloak was being placed over my shoulders and we were walking out of the restaurant with everyone bowing and smiling (Curtis obviously knew how to tip), and he didn't even suggest going upstairs to his room.

We walked out into the night and he said, "It's only a few steps to Portman Square. It won't ruin those dainty shoes of yours to walk." And so we walked. This time he lit a cigar, and on the night air the drift of its smoke was rich and pleasant.

"What made you take that minor part you're playing now?" he asked "I remember, when your father was alive, you played more important roles. I felt proud of having a well-known actress for a mistress."

"I am still a well-known actress," I retorted icily. I was not going to admit I was playing the part of Lucy because I had had no choice. "What is more, I am buying back the share my father left me in the Boswell Theatre, and nothing would ever induce me to be anything *but* an actress. I have a name here in London."

"If you go the way you *are* going, you'll lose it. And I didn't know you'd ever sold your share of the theatre. I knew about your father's bequest, because it was in all the papers at the time, but why sell it?" He broke off, stopping dead in his tracks. "Good God, did you sell it to get rid of me? Was *that* how you raised the money?"

When I made no answer, he said bitterly, "That makes it just so much worse—that you would sell what your father left you in order to get rid of a lover."

"You wouldn't have gone otherwise."

"You're dead right, I wouldn't. But who is better off now, you or me? We're equal, anyway. I'm no one's servant anymore. I'm an American citizen with the rights of an American citizen. I can afford to come over here and flash gold in people's faces and have them open doors to me without question. Like the gentleman at the art gallery and that madame who runs the place behind. By the way, who did you sell your theatre share to?''

"Gavin Calder.''

For a moment I thought he was never going to utter another sound; then he bellowed with laughter.

"So *she* got it all in the end—Lucinda Grainger, Calder's little widow! It does my heart good to think of it. No more than sixteen, wasn't she? I always felt sorry for her. I'm glad she has come out on top, as I have.''

"She won't remain so. We will be partners again soon. She is selling my half back to me at the price Gavin paid me.''

"More fool she, though I could always tell she thought the world of your father; *her* father too, of course, so I suppose that is why she's doing it. On the other hand, she can't be such a fool or she would do what I could well imagine her doing—*give* it to you for his sake. That's the kind of young woman I judge her to be.''

I made no answer to that and we didn't speak again until reaching number 47, when I thanked him for inviting me to supper, said politely that I had enjoyed it, held out my hand, and wished him well.

He took my hand, but didn't release it. His grasp was as hard and strong as in the old days, if not more so. He was lean and hard and strong all over, and I knew he was as capable of arousing me now as he had ever been. But go to that unknown country with him, a place inhabited by immigrants from Ireland and Scotland and every nation under the sun, a hotchpotch community in which I would never feel at home? Act as hostess in an uptown New York establishment dedicated to food and gambling? Whatever made me think of such a thing?

He said bluntly, "If you imagine you are seeing the last of me, you're wrong.''

His arms went about me swiftly and I felt his mouth press hard on my own, and it felt just as it always had, despite the moustache and beard.

"That's just to remind you what it was like,'' he said as he put me aside, and I answered in a voice which I tried to keep steady, "I wish you would shave all that off.''

"I will tomorrow; then when I call, you will know me instantly.''

"*Call?* You mustn't come here!''

"Why not? Because you told some pack of lies about me to your mother, and she believed them?''

He was too shrewd for my comfort. I walked away up the steps, fumbling for the latch key I had insisted on having and which Mamma had opposed. Unmarried young ladies living at home never had latch keys. Servants had to wait up to let them in. I had overcome that obstacle by helping myself to Mamma's own latch key without her knowledge, aware she would not miss it because she never used it. Never would the great

Bernadette Boswell demean herself by unlocking her own front door and closing it behind her. But times were changing, and nothing confirmed that more than my dining tonight with an ex-servant. I insisted on thinking of him as that rather than as an ex-lover or even a future one.

From the foot of the steps his voice came up to me.

"Don't imagine you are going to escape me, Clementine. You were my woman once and you will be again, but this time for as long as *I* decide, and *when* I decide. What's more, I can afford to make my visit a lengthy one, so I can take my time. You have no more forgotten what we meant to each other than I have."

29

Lucinda was as good as her word. She put the share transfer in hand without delay and brought the document to my dressing room before curtain-up at a matinee a week later.

"What ages lawyers take just dotting the i's and crossing the t's," I said, scanning the laborious copperplate handwriting which all solicitors used, but going no further than the opening lines, because reading legal mumbo jumbo was always so tedious and made even more so by their irritating elimination of punctuation. So the contents of those opening lines were good enough for me, confirming as they did that she, Lucinda Grainger, residing at number 10 George Street in the district known as St. Marylebone, et cetera et cetera, did hereby transfer to Clementine Boswell, residing at number 47 Portman Square, et cetera et cetera, a half-share in the ownership of the Boswell Theatre situate in the Strand . . . the said transfer to be free of all purchase fees. . . . *That* was all that mattered to me, and I thrust the document back into its large manila envelope, well pleased.

Lucinda said, "I had it drawn up on lines suggested by me. If you and your own lawyers approve, it can be signed as soon as you wish, but I expect there are points you will want to raise or have amended."

"Heavens, what unnecessary delay! I will accept it as it stands. Why do lawyers like to make everything so long and wordy? To spin out their charges, I suppose. I don't intend to employ a lawyer anyway. I can't see the point in both of us running up legal bills."

"As you wish, but aren't you going to read it through?"

"Later. We're on in five minutes. Besides, I see it confirms the essential detail, that the transfer is a gift to me and not a sale, and that is all I am interested in. I appreciate it, Lucinda, really I do."

She looked as pleased as I did. Lucinda seemed very happy lately. She smiled more than she used to and that intense seriousness which had settled on her after Gavin's death had eased considerably. She had dedicated herself to the theatre and to acting from that day forward, so perhaps her new relaxed air was due to the success she had achieved. I could see no other reason for it.

But I had little thought to spare for Lucinda. I couldn't wait to see Anna and to demand the money owing to me, nor to get a message to Durbridge telling him I had the deed of sale from Lucinda and was ready to sign it just as soon as I could produce the necessary down payment. The document was mine and therefore not for him to see, and should he ask to, I had only to say that it had been sent on to my solicitors pending signature. That sounded rather good, I thought, and legal documents *were* strictly private. He need never find out that the deal had been a gift in the form of a transfer. The only legal document he would ever be concerned with would be the one confirming the sale of my share to him on the agreed terms.

Immediately after the matinee I took a cab out to Anna's house in St. John's Wood. I had not been to the Salon of Art since the night Curtis had come back into my life, for the simple reason that he forbade it, threatening to drag me out of the place if I dared set foot in it once again. And I knew Curtis well enough by now to know that he fulfilled his threats.

He had called at my home the following day, just as he had said he would. Minus beard and moustache and with greying hair neatly trimmed, he had an air of distinction and, with the acquisition of money, an even greater air of confidence.

When the butler announced that there was a Mr. Curtis calling upon her, the name had at first meant nothing to Mamma. I was with her in the morning room, and of course, at that hour, she was in full possession of her faculties. Even so she said, "Curtis? Do we know a Mr. Curtis, dear gel?" and I had answered evenly, "Of course, Mamma. You will remember him as soon as you see him. . . ."

So Mamma had given instructions for the visitor to be shown upstairs to the drawing room, and after the usual inspection in the mirror she sailed up to the first floor to receive this forgotten acquaintance, and I went with her.

I knew what would happen and had no intention of missing it. As soon as she saw him she would realise who he was and give instant instructions for him to be shown out. An ex-servant who had reputedly decamped with money and then had the audacity to pay a social call upon a former employer could expect no other treatment, and after the things he had said to me I would enjoy witnessing his discomfort. That I had "sunk low" indeed! That our old relationship should be renewed because *he* intended it to be, and terminated when *he* decreed! That he should have the overweening impertinence to cross the Atlantic for the express purpose of flaunting his success and trying to prove that he was now my equal! Well, Mamma would soon put him in his place again, and very much would I enjoy it.

These were the thoughts I clung to as I followed her to the drawing room. I would not allow myself to remember last night's impassioned kiss and the memories and desires it had stirred. In the cold light of morning it was easy to reject that one betraying moment.

But when I saw him standing with his back to the hearth, clean-shaven and handsome, I was aware only of his magnetism. He was thinner-faced, his features more sharply etched and striking, and even those outrageous clothes made no difference. Curtis had acquired the air of distinction which goes with success, and when he bowed to my mother she positively preened. Sailing across the room, she extended her hand, palm down, so that he was compelled to kiss it, which, I knew instinctively, he had fully intended to do. I remembered how he had always been able to twist Mamma round his little finger, but could he do it now? It seemed not, for the moment he raised his head and smiled down at her, she was immobilised by shock.

"Curtis! *That* Curtis! I did not realise . . ."

And now, of course, he would be shown the door, and I would enjoy his humiliation. Of course I would enjoy it. To feel this extraordinary desire for him to be accepted and forgiven was irrational—so was my sudden longing for him to stay.

"Lady Boswell, ma'am, I see that Miss Clementine did not tell you of our recent meeting. Perhaps she wanted to keep my arrival as a surprise for you? I can see it is a surprise, and understandably, but not an unpleasant one, I hope? Even in my humbler days, before I achieved my present success in America—I am a rich man now, Lady Boswell, a very rich man indeed—even then I was aware of the kindness of your feeling toward me, your consideration, your courtesy, so typical of the very great lady you are. So it was natural that when holidaying in Europe I should wish to see again the one woman in London whom I most greatly admire and hold in the greatest respect."

Beneath his spate of flattery her astonishment changed to gratification and then to the most gracious acceptance. Rich, he had said . . . very rich . . . The words acted as a charm, and when he drew a jeweller's case from an inner pocket and begged her to accept this small token of his admiration, "which he had held eternally in his heart," total victory was his. The gift was a brooch of rubies, and the jeweller's box bore the name of Tiffany, which was as impressive as Asprey.

He had bought his way into our house with complete success. If Mamma remembered the reason I had given for his disappearance, she forgot it now. Begging him to be seated, she then ordered refreshment. "A glass of madeira, perhaps, Mr. Curtis?" When he replied that since living in America he had become accustomed to coffee: "Then coffee it shall be, dear man."

I marvelled that he had left this house through the back door in disgrace, and reentered through the front door in triumph.

"I always knew you would make good," Mamma declared fondly. "I used to say to my dear Nevill, 'There is a young man not born to occupy a lowly position! He has fared ill at the hands of fate!' "

"True, Lady Boswell. Fate had indeed treated me badly, but it has atoned now."

"And rightly! I predicted that also, to my dear Nevill. 'Mark my words,' I used to say, 'one day he will come into his own and occupy his rightful place in the world.' And now, I can see, you do. Pray tell me, how long will you be remaining in London? Sufficient for us to have the pleasure of a further meeting, I hope? Clementine, my darling, you were a very naughty gel not to tell me of his arrival."

"I had no knowledge of it, Mamma. It was as great a surprise to me as to you."

"Then I am even more surprised that you did not tell me of your meeting!" She gave me a playful tap in reprimand. "When and how did it happen?"

"I called on Miss Boswell at the theatre," Curtis put in quickly and easily, "and she received me as graciously as you have done. I asked for permission to call this morning, and to that she also graciously consented."

Mamma could not withstand him. Nor could I, but as I drove out to St. John's Wood my mind was not so full of him as it had tiresomely proved to be these last few days. He had called every morning, and when I emerged through the stage door at night, there his hired carriage would be waiting, he inside, and we would go on to supper somewhere, and always to an exclusive place frequented by equally exclusive patrons, never to more popular places where I would be greeted by flyabout members of society who recalled meeting me at wild all-night parties. In the places Curtis chose I was recognised by fellow diners only as the actress daughter of the late Sir Nevill Boswell, and because I was a member of the straight theatre (a branch of the theatrical world which was becoming respectable), their glances were admiring but never familiar.

I think it was then that I realised what a wonderful source of escape this man could be, if ever I needed one, and back came that earlier picture of myself at the side of a successful man in a rapidly prospering country. As the wife, or even as the mistress, of a prominent restaurateur, I would be greeted with respect, particularly if it were known that my father had been a titled Englishman and one of London's most revered actor-managers. Any link with a title was impressive in a country which lacked them. Snobbish? Why not? A successful businessman should use every asset he could lay his hands on, and if and when the right time came, I would certainly suggest it—but subtly, of course. It was wise to think ahead, even when things were going well—as they were for me now that I had manipulated Lucinda so adroitly and would do the same with Durbridge.

Meanwhile, Curtis made no immediate advances. He took his time, as he had said he would, with all the brash confidence which now typified him. I had to accept that it was all a part of his scheme to pay me back in kind, to use me as I had used him. It was painful to realise that this was the only use he had for me now, and on those terms I was resolved not to submit, rich and attractive as he was. Two could play at this game and, thank God, things were now going so well for me I knew I was going to win all along the line. Curtis was in for a shock when he realised that coming to London with the sole intention of getting even with me was to sadly misfire, even though he had won my mother over so successfully.

On my way to St. John's Wood to visit Anna, I reflected that this brief respite between the matinee and evening performances was almost like a reprieve. I knew Curtis would be taking tea at number 47 Portman Square with dear Mamma, and that he would be expecting me to return between the matinee and evening performances. It would do him good to be disappointed.

The document now in my possession gave me a feeling of defiant independence. It represented my first step toward freedom, not only from Curtis's domination but from the Salon of Art. Much as I had enjoyed the place, I didn't want to go back. It had all been so fatiguing, catering for man after man, besides which it had prevented me from enjoying the social life I had known before. Friends were demanding to know what had happened to me and why I had dropped out of things.

"Parties aren't the same without you, Clemmy darling!" they would coo, dropping into the theatre to see me and trying to entice me to go on somewhere after the curtain came down, which I had to refuse. "She's having an *affaire*," they concluded. "When it is over, she'll come back to us again. . . ."

Anna Maynard received me with surprise. The house was familiar to me from previous visits, but today it impressed me even more with its air of sedate respectability. Springdale Avenue was in that part of St. John's Wood where well-bred ladies called and left cards, had their At Home days, and held up their hands in horror over the latest scandal. I doubted dear Anna even joined in these neighbourly activities. However, I was wrong, for I arrived just as a group of suburban ladies was departing, and there was Anna, in a dignified tea gown, standing in the hall bidding them farewell.

The hansom which brought me had been forced to halt beyond the line of broughams and landaus at the pavement, and after instructing the driver to wait, I had walked along select Springdale Avenue to Anna's front door, noting the trim gardens and impeccable paintwork, the spotless steps scoured and whitened daily, the shining brass doorknockers and snowy lace curtains. Anna's house was exactly the same. No one would have dreamed that behind the door of number 18 lived a woman who, by night, became the madame of one of Babylon's most expensive and notorious pleasure houses.

Her surprise faintly displeased me, and I realised her reaction was due to my arriving at an inconvenient moment. Didn't she want her respectable neighbours to know that she had an actress friend? The thought ruffled me, and I was glad when the departing ladies eyed me with mixed expressions of curiosity and envy. Not one was so elegant as I, not one so pretty, and not one was introduced to me. Anna carried off the moment with a rush of chatter.

"My dear Miss Portman, how nice of you to remember my At Home day, but how unfortunate that you should be late! The traffic, I presume? Really, one cannot *move* in London these days, can one, with all these new electric tramcars as well as horse-drawn omnibuses and more and more people, even tradespeople, driving abroad in their carriages. As for these noisy, smelly motors, I declare they are a danger on the road, but now the Prince of Wales has become addicted to the craze I fear we shall see more of them. Did you hear that his motor suffered tyre trouble the other day? And no wonder—it is said he was driving at fifteen miles an hour! The joke is that he had to call at a bicycle shop for aid. One does not have that kind of trouble with horses, does one?"

Her trilling laughter followed her guests from the house, cutting off immediately the door closed behind them.

"Why didn't you let me know you were coming?" she demanded, her voice low. "You know Durbridge installed me in this house for the express purpose of maintaining a respectable front, and that, my dear, means identifying myself with the people around me. Here I can keep his account books in perfect safety—"

"Which is why I came," I interrupted. "I know the balance entered to my own account has reached the stipulated figure, so I have come to collect it."

She silenced me swiftly. An immaculate maid had emerged from the front parlour, carrying away the remains of afternoon tea. This reverse side of Anna Maynard's life amused me, but I guessed how important it was to her and how she treasured it, for she lived well and without encumbrances of any kind. No wonder she deferred to Durbridge's wishes in all things, running the Salon of Art with discretion, keeping his sordid secrets, filing all accounts and records in this quiet suburban house in the most sedate part of St. John's Wood. Springdale Avenue did not even touch the outerskirts of the famous courtesan quarter that must give Anna's respectable visitors so much to gossip and gasp about.

As she closed the parlour door behind her I said with a laugh, "I suppose they imagine you are a widow?"

She didn't laugh in return, nor invite me to sit down. Nor did she seat herself. She stood there, coolly regarding me.

"Naturally. Do I look like a spinster? I am a mature woman and a good-looking one. To pose as a spinster would be unconvincing. The only tiresome part is having to keep amorous husbands at bay."

"And what if any of those amorous husbands turned up at the Salon?"

"No fear of that. None could afford to. This is an area where husbands work to keep their wives and families comfortably. That leaves little money for visits to expensive establishments in Babylon. No doubt they make do with milliners' back rooms provided for dollymops." She glanced at an enamelled fob watch pinned to her bodice. "Pray state your business again. I don't think I heard correctly."

"You certainly did. That was why you silenced me when the maid appeared, but to make it quite clear, I will repeat it. I have come to collect the money owing to me."

"And you imagine I can write a cheque without Lord Durbridge's sanction? It is he you must approach, not I."

"But you handle all cash transactions."

"Cash, yes. I pay it into a certain bank account, but not in my name. These things are complicated and take time. Certain arrangements have to be made, besides which you have not been near the Salon since the night that rich American carried you off. In the circumstances, I suspect that the debt is now on your side. You met that man on the premises and were permitted, by me, to spend the rest of the night with him—"

"He paid you well! I saw him do so."

"For that one occasion only. How many more have there been? Come, girl, I am not a fool. He hired you for the rest of his stay in London, did he not? That is why you have not returned. Durbridge is aware of it; I made sure of that. We are entitled to commission on all money you received from him, and I know Durbridge will refuse to release anything to you until that is fully accounted for."

I blazed, "I haven't received a penny, and that is the truth!"

"You will be declaring next that you have never seen the man again, and that is *not* the truth. You have seen him every day. He has called at your house every day. Maids can be persuaded to gossip. All we had to tell them was that we were after the man for an unpaid hotel bill. Naturally I did not call myself. A messenger was used, looking like a discreet enquiry agent.''

I sat down slowly. I had never suspected she knew where I lived, or who I was, but of course she was in Durbridge's confidence about most things. I should have guessed. And which maid had been persuaded to talk? Kate, or Maisie, or both? Maisie would not know Curtis's identity, but Kate did, and since removing his beard and moustache, I knew she had recognised him. Not that that was important. What was important was Kate's gossiping tongue and her acceptance of bribes.

Anna said in dismissal, ''I will speak to Durbridge on your behalf. I will let him know you called. And now you must excuse me. I always sleep at this hour—''

''—and rise and go out late at night, without *your* maid being suspicious?''

''She comes daily. I take care not to have anyone living on the premises. There she goes now, leaving by the area steps. She will let herself in tomorrow morning at eight, when I am back in bed and asleep. She will bring me my breakfast tray at nine-thirty, and my quiet, well-regulated day will begin. I don't employ her on Sundays. I need that day to deal with my extensive household accounts.''

She opened the parlour door, ushering me off the premises. *You bitch,* I thought. *That doctor was well rid of you.* I wanted to have the last word, but all I could think of was, ''Tell Durbridge I expect to hear from him, and soon.''

She answered amiably, ''I have already promised to tell him you called. I will send a message at once. I cannot do more than that, can I?''

Her voice followed me across the doorstep. The hansom had drawn up before the gate, and I stepped inside and drove back to the theatre. I was in no mood to face Mamma, and certainly not Curtis. That man could sense my moods too well. I would have a tray sent over from Rule's. In the quiet of my dressing room I would compose myself before curtain-up. It was the first time in my life I had ever wanted to be alone. After my encounter with Anna Maynard, I felt obscurely frightened.

The curtain speech at the end of Act I was mine, and the longest I had in *The Rivals*. Most of it was confined to reading extracts from a list of Lucy the maid's trafficking in bribes, which seemed to be a characteristic of servant girls, I thought as I read aloud tonight:

''*For abetting Miss Lydia Languish in a design of running away with an ensign . . . in money, sundry times, twelve pound twelve. Gowns, five. Hats, ruffles, capes, etc. etc. . . . numberless!*'' It was Kate all over again. ''*From the said ensign, within this last month, six guineas and a half . . from Mrs.*

Malaprop, for betraying the young people to her, two guineas and a black padua-soy. . . ."

I had never read these lines with great attention. All that had mattered to me was not having to memorise them, but tonight they went right home. Lucy could be Kate or Maisie or any of their kind—and just what had Anna Maynard been threatening me with, behind that icy composure? I felt uneasy and depressed as I walked back to my dressing room. I could not imagine why life was so unkind to me. I didn't deserve it. What unkindness had *I* ever inflicted on anyone?

When I re-entered my dressing room I was surprised to find Durbridge there. A glance from him sent Maisie from the room. His face looked even more pallid than usual, and his red lips parted in the mockery of a smile. There was a look in his eyes I could not fathom. To try to was like peering into an ice-cold well of bottomless depth. He did not trouble to return my greeting, though I made it as radiant as always.

"So you want money," he said without preamble as I seated myself before my dressing table. "I gather from Anna that you believe you have earned it."

"So I have." I dabbed idly at my makeup. "And I have done more than that, which should please you. I have won my way with Lucinda. She is selling back to me my share in the theatre and I have the document to prove it."

"I presumed that was why you demanded money, but let me see the document first."

"I cannot. It is with my solicitor. Naturally I sent it on to him to examine. When finally approved, I will sign and so will she, and you know what the next step will be."

He was not in the least gratified. He sat quite still, his hands on the arms of his wheelchair, looking at me until I shifted beneath his gaze. Then he spoke.

"You lying whore."

My head jerked round, and what I saw in his face actually frightened me. I mouthed stupidly, trying to think of an answer, and finally gasped, *"What* did you call me?"

"A lying whore, which is what you are. Your solicitor doesn't have that document. I have."

I snatched up my reticule, but before I opened it he was holding up the manila envelope and then, very slowly, extracting the paper.

"How did you get that?"

"With the aid of a paltry five-pound note. I don't think your dresser has ever seen one in her life, judging by the way she goggled at it. And merely for handing over your reticule so that I could put a small present into it as a surprise for you! That was what I told her; then I sent her along to the stage to see how far the action had progressed. I know *The*

Rivals well; therefore I knew that in Act I the maid is the last to leave the stage. I estimated that Scene 2 should have quite a way to go yet, and I was right—Julia had just made her entrance, I learned. Your dresser was most considerate and offered to fetch refreshment for me from the Duke's Head across the road. 'A nice glass of port, sir?' I had no desire for it, but since I desired her company even less and the opportunity to read this document even more, I suggested she should nip across and have one herself. I rather fancy she now considers me the perfect gentleman.''

"Which you are not, God knows. No gentleman steals property from a lady's reticule."

"And no lady lies about what is in it. 'With your solicitor' indeed! Even worse, that Lucinda Grainger had agreed to *sell* to you!" A rush of angry colour suffused his face. "You made the worst mistake of your life when planning to hoodwink me, darling Clementine. Lucinda Grainger is giving you that share, but you intended to conceal that fact from me."

I answered with bravado, "I am sure *you* have thought it wiser to keep your own counsel on occasion. And in all fairness, you must admit that whether I buy the share or not is no concern of yours. The important thing is that I get hold of it so that you may buy it eventually. I don't know why you have set your heart on getting a foothold here at the Boswell, but I can give a guess. You want to oust Lucinda. You want to own the place eventually and so get the better of her. You bear her a grudge. You want to pay her back for something. Did she resist you that night you met with an accident here? I thought you didn't fancy women."

My throat went dry. I had gone too far. I had never seen such a look on any man's face. With one deft movement the wheelchair spun toward me, and in a flash his arm shot up and struck me a blow across the cheek. I sagged back in my chair, dazed by the strength behind it. But the blow did more than shock me; it stung me to fury.

"*For that, I won't sell to you.* I swear it, Durbridge, I swear it!"

"Don't be a fool. You know you can't anyway. Or haven't you read beyond the first paragraph? I wouldn't put it past you to lack the sense. You really are the most stupid creature, darling Clementine. All body and no brain. You thought you were being supremely clever, didn't you? You planned to get money out of me to buy something which you were not going to buy at all, and then sell it to me at double the mythical price. That was the idea, wasn't it? But how did you propose to overcome the final stipulation?"

I mouthed almost incoherently, "What final stipulation?"

"As I thought—you haven't even read that far. Your bastard sister is not so naive as you think. She *is* giving you back your share, no doubt through some sentimental loyalty to your father, and you *are* entitled to sell it should you ever wish to or need to—but with one reservation.

That you only sell to one or more existing members of the theatre board—namely, Bramwell Chambers or the stage director, Willard, both of whom 'have the interests of the theatre at heart and have expressed their willingness to purchase the share either singly or jointly, depending upon the asking price.' But to no outsider. Which means me." He held out the document. "Read it for yourself, if you don't believe me."

I took it with a nerveless hand. Every word he said was true.

30

I heard the callboy shouting, *"Act II—overture and beginners, please!"* and thanked God I was offstage for the whole of Scene 1. I needed time to recover from this latest shock.

When Maisie reappeared, Durbridge said, "I think you should fetch your mistress a brandy. She is feeling unwell." He handed her a pound note, adding that she could keep the change, and she departed with alacrity and great concern. I heard and saw all this as if from a distance, because my mind seemed to be numb.

Neither of us said a word until Maisie returned with the brandy and began to flutter over me, suggesting I should lie down in the green room, where there was a "comfy sofa" and she could cover me with a rug. I dismissed her with a feeble wave of my hand and Durbridge said, in that smooth way in which he could change from mood to mood, "Your concern does you credit, Maisie. Miss Boswell is fortunate in having you as her dresser, but she will be all right in a moment—won't you, my dear? If she needs you, I will call. Meanwhile, just wait outside."

From a man so generous she was ready to take any order, even though she knew what he was. Quite apart from knowing about his sexual tastes, she had been in the theatrical world long enough to recognise the truly corrupt, and she had hinted as much many times. But I had had enough of Maisie and Kate and Durbridge, and that untrustworthy bitch Anna Maynard too.

The brandy did steady me. At least it enabled me to say, "All right, you win, but I am entitled to the money I asked Anna for. I earned it, God knows."

"And you may have it, provided you do what I ask."

"Stipulations from you too? Why should I listen?"

"Because it will be to your benefit. Because if you cooperate you can not only have the money put by for you, but the sum I promised for this share of the theatre. You will therefore arrange for Lucinda Grainger to meet you here at some time when the place is deserted. You will say you wish to discuss this agreement before signing—that the legal jargon is confusing and needs clarifying. When you meet, you will then ask her to change that final clause. Point out that your father made no such stipulation, nor that such a stipulation is binding on *her*, so why should it be on you? You will come here alone so that she will believe you are unaccompanied, but I will follow—and then join you. If she is stubborn, I know how to make her see reason. When is the theatre most empty?''

''Saturday morning. Sometimes a few of the stagehands—Props or the master carpenter or Lights—come along to check things, to retouch the scenery and do repair jobs where necessary, but that is during a long run and they are confined to the workshop area immediately offstage.''

''And toward the end of a run, such repair work is unlikely anyway?''

''That is true with *The Rivals*, which is coming off in two weeks.''

''In that case we can safely suggest this coming Saturday morning. Speak to the girl tonight. I will send Stacey back to the theatre after he has driven me home, and you can give him a message. The green room is a good place for private discussions, is it not, and well away from the stage in this theatre?'' He put out his thick moist hand and patted mine. ''There, there, my dear—you have nothing in the world to worry about. Everything will go according to plan.''

''If it doesn't,'' I said stubbornly, ''I am still entitled to my earnings from your 'cultured' Salon of Art.''

''But of course! Surely you don't imagine I would cheat you out of them?''

''And what if I refuse to cooperate at all? What if I sign that document just as it stands and take what is rightfully mine at this theatre, and hold on to it?''

''I fear you would regret it. An actress's name is so easily besmirched, because they are considered beyond the pale in most circles in any event. And, indeed, the majority deserve to be. The day when acting is accepted as a respectable profession for women is long distant, despite your father's worthy endeavours to preserve the good name of his wife and daughter and every member of his company. He chose his players with care, but even the respected Chrystal Delmont would be toppled if scandal touched her. It would be even worse for you, being his daughter. Don't forget that Anna is a very clever woman, working solely in her own interests—which means protecting mine. One slip, and she could lose all she has. *You* have already slipped, my dear. You have been slipping for years. What a field day the press would have with your story . . . and I would be no more than a member of the great British public, reading about it at home.''

He had propelled himself toward the door. Did he really think I was going to rise and open it for him?

I finished the brandy, staring morosely in the mirror. In it I saw his reflection, and it no longer seemed fascinating as it had done long ago. He had me trapped, and knew it. For one wild moment I thought about Curtis—could I appeal to him for help? Never. He was no longer the amenable man he had once been, clay in my hands. In his way he was as ruthless as Durbridge, but concerned only with building his business empire across the Atlantic. He would have no part in anything like this, no truck with London's underworld. He would wash his hands of me once and for all.

Magnus? What about Magnus? No—it was useless to appeal to him, because he was Lucinda's friend. He had defended the Graingers always and wasn't likely to switch sides now. No doubt he would think Lucinda's stipulation very fair, knowing of her devotion to the theatre and her desire to carry on the traditions set by Papa.

I felt I hadn't a friend in the world and that it was a very unjust place, particularly to me.

"All right," I said. "I will do as you ask."

But still I would not open the door for him. I reminded him that Maisie was outside and he had only to call for her. "Though I am sure you are strong enough to reach out and knock on the door. You reached me easily enough." My hand went up to my cheek.

"You must bear me no resentment for that, darling Clementine. You deserved it. You will forgive me when I help you in this matter on Saturday. I shall be righting an injustice on your behalf. Think about that, and I am sure you will agree."

I did think about it, and I did agree. Lucinda's action was indeed an injustice. I could not forgive her for it, and the more I thought about it, the more indignant I became, but by the time I was called for my entry in Scene 2, I was composed enough to be able to say to her the exact words Durbridge had put into my mouth. We met in the wings, and she agreed to meet me at the appointed time, as he had known she would. Perhaps, after all, everything would come my way.

By the time I left the theatre I felt more optimistic, and when I saw Curtis waiting in the darkness of his carriage I joined him quite happily, making no resistance when he took me in his arms and kissed me.

He had not attempted to do so since that first night. He was certainly fulfilling his vow to take his time about making me "his woman" again. Did he imagine these delaying tactics would provoke or tantalise me? His kiss succeeded in that, at least. The desire it stirred remained with me throughout supper, taken at his hotel tonight. Despite my disturbing day, it was enjoyable and we were both very relaxed and happy.

"You are not going to that place anymore, are you, Clemmy?"

"Never," I answered truthfully. It was good to be able to speak the truth without dissembling, but so often in my life the truth would have led to complications. I did not add that I had decided never to return to the Salon of Art because I found it so difficult to lay my hands on my earnings there.

All he said was, "Good," and smiled at me across the table. It was almost like old times, except that our positions seemed to be subtly reversed. Now it was he who called the tune, he who would summon or dismiss. I hoped he would summon me tonight. I hoped he would take me upstairs.

He did not. He walked me home and said good night in the most polite fashion, and I saw his handsome features smiling down at me, thoroughly amused. Damn him. He read my mind too well. He had been teasing me, tempting me all evening, just as I had teased and tempted him once upon a time. And now he turned away as casually and indifferently as I had ever done.

Lucinda and I had arranged to meet in the green room at ten o'clock—an ungodly hour, in my view, but she explained that she was going along to the mission at eleven.

"What on earth do you do there?" I had asked in surprise.

"All sorts of things. Any things that need doing. If you can't manage ten o'clock on Saturday, we can leave it until later—between the matinee and evening performances perhaps?"

But that would not do at all. Durbridge had stipulated total privacy, and with a theatre full of people backstage, such a possibility was remote. There could be interruptions even in one's dressing room, and especially in the green room, where visitors had to wait to be received, and were sometimes entertained.

So ten o'clock in the morning it was. I arrived promptly, but Lucinda was already waiting. She wore a blue serge gown which was remarkably becoming. I would never have chosen such a dull material myself, but the gown had Trudy Grainger's stamp. She could make the most unlikely things supremely elegant. Lucinda had removed her hat of matching blue trimmed with cock feathers glinting with the same colour. A bright red rose or two would have added a fetching note, I thought, but Lucinda seemed to have a taste for plainer clothes than I. Her cloak of dark red velvet had also been laid aside.

"You are very elegantly dressed for a visit to an East End mission," I commented.

"I wear overalls when there. We all do. When I first attended the mission I used to wear the oldest clothes I could find, then discovered that many of the women delight in seeing pretty gowns. Now we are teaching them how to make them—Mamma, Helen, and I."

"And how can the poor afford to buy materials?" I asked, not really interested and wondering how to lead up to the point of this meeting.

"They don't. We supply them."

"Out of your own pockets? You must be mad!"

"We budget for it. Mission funds won't run to new stuff, so we add what we can. The bulk of the work is renovating clothes which are given us. If you have any to spare, they would be welcomed."

"You of all people know how generous I have always been with my old clothes," I reminded her.

She ignored that. Nor was she the least put out by the remark. We fell silent then, each waiting for the other to make a start. The theatre seemed very quiet, apart from distant sounds—cleaners in the auditorium, no doubt.

Lucinda laughed. "Why are we waiting? You have a query about the transfer. I can't really believe you fail to understand the legal jargon, as you put it. That was an evasion. Say what you want to say, Clemmy, and let us settle the matter."

Was that a movement outside? Footsteps? Stacey's soft tread behind his master's silent wheelchair? One glance at Lucinda's face told me she had heard nothing, so perhaps it was my imagination. In one way I wanted Durbridge to come; in another, I didn't. He had frightened me the other night, and I had no desire to sample his anger again. If Lucinda would merely agree to changing that clause, all would be well and I might even get away from the theatre before he arrived.

"You haven't been quite fair," I began.

She answered serenely that she had expected me to say that. "You don't like the stipulation at the end, do you, the one governing any possible resale? Let me explain. I promised my father I would do all I could to uphold the standards of his theatre. At the same time, remembering that he willed the shares to us with the proviso that we could sell them if we wished to, I felt that in giving your share back to you I should at least do the same, but take a certain precaution. You see, that promise to him means a lot to me, and his standards too . . . but somehow I don't think they do to you."

Had the door opened a crack, or was that my imagination again?

"I always admired Papa," I protested. "You know I did."

"Not enough to think twice about letting an undesirable man get his hands on your share. I mean Gavin. Looking back, I see him as he was, totally. I have accepted the truth about him for a long time and been all the happier for it. When the scales fell from my eyes, I was able to see someone else . . ." She broke off, checking her words. "Let us just say that recovering from Gavin was a wonderful release. I grew in confidence from that moment. I began to live from that moment, to *feel* again . . ."

"I can't see what all this has to do with the present situation. Gavin is dead. I am glad you have recovered from his loss and are happy, though God knows you seem to lead a very dull life to me, with all this dedication to the theatre and your career."

"Oh, there are other things in my life too," she said happily. "Things you know nothing about and would not understand."

"Like doing good works at a mission." I shuddered.

"Like having people in my life who love me."

"Well, I am glad of that." I was impatient, anxious to get the business over and done with. "All this talk about Gavin is wasting time."

"But it happens to be relative to things now. I don't want anyone like him, in any way at all, to be involved in this theatre, destroying my father's dreams for it. I have told you that already, so you should have been prepared for the precaution I took. It isn't right for me to forbid you to sell your share again, should you ever need or want to, but it *is* right for me to fight for Nevill Boswell's ideals."

"Suppose I give you my word, a verbal promise, will you alter that clause then?"

"No."

I protested, "You are very dictatorial! Success has gone to your head. I *must* have the right to sell as and when I please, and to whom I please."

"No."

"My God, I didn't know you could be so stubborn."

"About some things, I can be."

"Don't you *trust* me—I, whom you have known all your life?"

"No."

"For heaven's sake, stop saying no to everything! Why shouldn't you trust me? Tell me that."

"*Because* I have known you all my life."

The coolness of her, the calm assurance and determination of her, made me want to scream. I heard my voice rise. "It is no business of yours, you cannot dictate to me about what I can or cannot do! You can't name specific people to whom I must or must not sell!"

"I have done so and I am sticking to it. I know perfectly well that you would sell to Durbridge, and for this reason my stipulation must remain."

She turned to pick up her cloak, and as she did so the door was pushed open very quietly and Durbridge glided in. The door swung to behind him, but failed to close entirely, so she was unaware of his presence until he spoke.

"And how do you know that I would be the purchaser, Miss Grainger?"

She spun round. She stared at him and then at me.

"You came together," she accused. It was rare for Lucinda's voice to be raised in anger, but it was now.

"Not actually together," Durbridge told her. "Just about the same time. I commend your punctuality, darling Clementine. I was half-afraid you might be late, knowing your natural laziness. But you have not answered my question, Miss Grainger. How do you know that I would be the purchaser?"

"I guessed, and rightly it seems. Why else should you be here? You have come to add your pressure to hers, I take it."

"Not if you are sensible and make it unnecessary."

She flung her cloak of dark red velvet about her shoulders. It brushed his knees, and he snatched at it. I heard the sound of violent ripping as he tore it away.

"You are not leaving yet, Miss Grainger. You and I have some business to settle."

"I have no unsettled business with you, Lord Durbridge." She picked up her damaged cloak and said with grief, "My mother made this for me. It was part of my—"

He interrupted, "You will amend that clause in your agreement with Miss Boswell, giving her complete freedom to sell to whomsoever she pleases."

"Never."

He revolved the wheels slowly, and she backed away at his approach. Then she tried to sidestep, only to find him blocking her again. His hands were adroit and, I remembered, strong. They could move as quick as lashes. His thick white fingers spun the wheels with unerring precision. Soon he had her pinned against the wall, and I saw her face go pale.

I could do nothing but stand there, mesmerised. I was astonished that a man so handicapped could so swiftly and inexorably trap an able-bodied person. The metal footrest of his chair made a relentless barrier, but before she could push it away he snapped on the brake, then released it and braked again; in this way, vicious jerk after vicious jerk, he rammed her against the wall until, despite the thickness of her skirts, she cried out in pain. Then he stopped and asked in a voice which revealed nothing but idle curiosity, "Just why are you so averse to my owning even part of this theatre, Miss Grainger?"

Through tight lips she said, "You know why."

"But I am a successful entrepreneur, Miss Grainger. Such people are valuable to any theatre."

"Not to this one. A producer of indecent displays and worse besides! Do you think I don't know the things you are responsible for?"

"You consider the naked body indecent? Are you a prude, then? I find it hard to believe, because I clearly recall your running around this theatre stark naked on one occasion."

That did startle me. I knew then that something had definitely happened between these two and that as a result of it they hated each other.

Lucinda managed to answer, "The human body can be very beautiful. Degradation of it is not."

Another jerk, another cry. Teeth clenched, she gasped, "Help me, Clemmy! Get him away!"

But how could I? How *could* I risk another blow across the face from an upswung arm?

"My dear Miss Grainger, you can release yourself quite easily. You know how. You have only to agree—"

"*Never!*"

It was a wild and defiant and agonised declaration.

I burst out, "Lucinda, be sensible!" I wanted to help her, but what could I do? Surely she didn't expect me to grapple with that wheelchair? "If *only* you would be sensible!" I pleaded, and of course I was pleading for her sake, not my own. This whole scene was unpleasant and unnecessary, and the sooner it ended, the better.

I saw her big grey eyes staring at me in disbelief. She was white to the lips.

"You want me to give in to a man like this?" she cried. "I will never have such as he involved in my father's theatre!" She almost spat at him then: "You are evil and I have known it from the moment I first set eyes on you!"

He rapped out, "*Stacey!*"

Swift and silent, the man appeared.

"Unfasten her bodice," Durbridge commanded, and as he spoke I saw his hand slide to the inner pocket of his chair, just as it had done when that handsome youth had gone with him into that inner room. The thing he took out was a whip with a silver handle.

I was rooted to the spot. I could not have moved had I tried to. I saw Lucinda trying to ward Stacey off, her arms flailing helplessly.

"*Clementine . . . help me. . . . Fetch—*"

The yoke of her gown ripped, exposing her camisole beneath. I took a hesitant step forward, then retreated when Durbridge cracked the whip in the air between us. Another sound of tearing and her bare flesh was exposed. In pitiful defence her arms folded across her breasts, and still she cried, "*Clemmy . . . fetch—*"

Fetch what? Fetch whom? There was no one here, the theatre was empty except for those distant cleaners in the auditorium, who would scatter in fear if I dared to run to the stage and call to them for help. What could I say? That there was a madman backstage whipping a woman? I wanted to run away myself, and when Stacey seized Lucinda's arms and half-turned her body so that he could pin them behind her, and the first crack of the whip lashed out sideways and cut across her shoulders, I did so. Lucinda's piercing scream followed me to the door, increasing my terror. What if Durbridge turned on me? In the state he was in, he might easily do so. I had to get away, fast.

I had the door wide open when Stacey grabbed me.

"I . . . I'm not going to fetch anyone," I stammered. "Truly I'm not! Let me go, please let me go! I am not going to interfere in any way, I promise!"

A second scream echoed through the open door and along the bare corridor outside, flung back from the stone walls and rolling along the stone ceiling, amplified into a continuing stream of agonised sound. Stacey pulled me back into the room, and the sound waves from the corridor seemed to be merged with others, coming nearer and nearer, louder and louder, heavier and heavier, but no one in this room even heard them. Lucinda's body had sagged and her head had fallen forward. I could not see her face because her hair made a curtain over it, but with Stacey's release of her arms she had instinctively crossed them over her breasts again.

"Stacey, you fool, hold her up!"

The man obeyed. Lucinda's head lolled back as he jerked her arms behind her again, twisting her body from the waist so that it screened himself but left her exposed to Durbridge's attack. Her eyes were closed and her face deathly. I saw red streaks across her flesh and I promptly began to whimper. I have always been too sensitive to bear the sight of pain or blood. I had to bite hard on my knuckles to stop myself from crying aloud. It would have been perilous to draw attention to myself.

Durbridge's face was twitching with pleasure, and there was elation in his voice as he shouted, "My God, how I've waited for this! But for you, you interfering bitch, I would never have been crippled! Do you hear me, Lucinda Grainger? *Do you hear me?*"

The whip snaked across her flesh with a louder hiss and a more savage crack, and when another line of blood appeared, he laughed aloud.

"Do you think I give a damn for the Boswell Theatre? It is *you* I was after. Punishment . . . *punishment!* I made that vow when you brought me to this state!"

His frenzied arm raised again, and I closed my eyes because I could not bear to see any more, but when no sound of lashing came, but only that of thundering feet and a man's shout of rage, my eyes jerked open, and to my astonishment I saw Magnus Steel clutching Durbridge's upraised arm with one clenched fist and punching him in the face with the other. It was a boxer's knockout blow, and the fleshy, twitching features were knocked senseless. Then in one swift movement Magnus released Durbridge's chair and sent it spinning across the room. He caught Lucinda's body as it fell.

I saw the look of horror on his face as he carried her to a sofa. "*Water,*

Jerry . . . a bowl of water, quickly!'' To my surprise that cockney boy was there, and the chief electrician too. The boy streaked off and the man shot across the room to grab Stacey.

"Oh no, you don't! You're not getting that bloody sadist out of this building until the doctor decides what to do with him."

It was Durbridge's servile manservant who looked white now.

Magnus was pulling off his shirt and ripping it into shreds; then he was leaning over Lucinda and gently wiping away the blood. "Thank God, the cuts aren't too deep . . ." He didn't seem to be talking to anyone, only to himself, and his voice sounded frantic.

I wondered if I could inch toward the door and slip away unseen, but Jerry Hawks reappeared at that moment, blocking my path. Water slopped from a bowl in his hands, and to my amazement he was crying. Sobbing his heart out. As he set down the bowl he gasped, "She's goin'ter be orlright, ain't she, Doc? Say she's goin'ter be orlright!"

"I promise you that, boy. We got here in time. Now, fetch some drinking water . . ."

Jerry shot off again. I heard his steps go racing down the corridor, his sobs echoing with them.

I didn't wait a moment longer. The last thing I saw, as I fled from the place, was Magnus Steel's face as he bathed Lucinda's body. It had a look I had seen in no man's face before, but none of this registered until I was safely home in my bed. Dear God, what an experience, what an escape! I had to ring for Maisie to bring me a brandy to get over it.

I really do wish I were not so sensitive.

31

Well, of course, after such an upsetting morning, I could not be expected to go on that afternoon, so I sent Maisie to the theatre with a message that I was unwell and that my understudy would have to appear instead. Frankly, I felt I never wanted to set foot in the place again. Whenever I passed the green room I would remember that dreadful scene and imagine how terrible it would have been had I really been caught up in it. I found myself looking forward to Curtis' arrival for tea this afternoon. That would take my mind off things, and by Monday, being a true professional who would never let her fellow players down, I would go on again even if I were still suffering from the shock of it all.

I hoped there would be no scandal involving the good name of the theatre (and mine), but I didn't really see how Durbridge could fail to be in trouble, though on what charges I didn't yet know. Causing grievous bodily harm, perhaps? I didn't imagine for one moment that Magnus would let the man get away with it, for I could still see that look on his face, the horror and anger of it, the rage as he sent the man's wheelchair spinning, the desperate anxiety in his eyes as he stooped over Lucinda's unconscious form, and the infinite tenderness with which he ministered to her.

Of course, he would be equally concerned for any of his patients, I told myself, but all the same I knew that his outrage this morning was not something that would blow away like a puff of smoke. As for Jerry Hawks, I could imagine him turning on Durbridge like a wild young animal, given half a chance. And the chief electrician—there had been disgust and fury in his face too as he prevented Stacey from getting his master away.

Three people, besides myself and Durbridge's manservant, knew what had taken place in the green room, so all could be called as witnesses. I knew the others would testify more willingly than I, because naturally I didn't want to be involved in any unpleasantness and many things might come to light about Durbridge in the process of a court case. Therefore anyone involved with him in any way would be wise to steer clear if they could.

Somehow I would have to do so myself—plead indisposition, sickness, anything. It might even be a good idea to forget about that money owing to me from his Salon of Art, just in case the existence of the place was discovered, but on the other hand I didn't see why I should be defrauded of what was rightfully mine.

I decided to wait and see what happened and to plead total ignorance if necessary, though I could hardly claim not to have been in the green room when Durbridge attacked Lucinda, since I had been there when Magnus and the other two arrived. Not for the first time in my life I wondered why things could never go smoothly for me. Fate was very unkind, really it was.

I had scarcely any appetite, but forced myself to eat some luncheon because I had to keep up my strength somehow, and a good meal was always sustaining. Mamma commented, "You look slightly wan, dear gel. You are not feeling well, Kate tells me." (And who told Kate? Maisie, of course.) "You are wise to skip the matinee, and I advise a good rest until Mr. Curtis comes for tea as usual." He was always *Mr.* Curtis now. Mr. Curtis, the wealthy New Yorker. That he had ever been a coachman was entirely forgotten.

So after fortifying myself with soup, followed by saddle of lamb and only one portion of my favourite chocolate soufflé, I took Mamma's advice and lay down. I was glad Maisie wasn't hovering around, as she had been intent on doing ever since Durbridge's visit to my dressing room the other night. I knew she wondered why he had ordered a brandy for me and that even now she would be wondering why I had needed another today. Perhaps it would be wise to get rid of her, but I had other things to worry about at this moment, chief of which was how to keep myself out of any involvement with the Durbridge affair.

It was then that Kate came tapping on my door to announce that Dr. Steel was downstairs, wanting to see me.

"Didn't you tell him I was unwell?"

"Of course, Miss Clementine, but he said that seemed all the more reason for seeing you."

Reluctantly I told her to show him up to my sitting room.

"If you're not well, Miss Clemmy, mightn't it be better for him to see you in bed?"

Was that a smirk on her face, an insinuation in her voice? I ignored both, and after I had heard her bring him upstairs I washed off the rouge which I found so necessary these days, and though I was reluctant to let any man see me looking as pale and shadowy-eyed as I had become in recent months I thought it would stand me in good stead now. I dragged myself through the door, running a shaking hand through my hair, certain his heart would be touched by the picture I made.

"Oh, Magnus, how good of you to come! I imagined you would be too concerned about Lucinda to spare any concern for me."

"You were right. *You* weren't injured this morning. You were standing there watching and blubbering instead of going for help."

"I wanted to, truly I did, but I thought the theatre was empty."

"You could have taken the trouble to find out. Surely it's a natural human instinct to run for help in terrible circumstances? Out into the street, for instance, since Lucinda apparently didn't tell you that I had come with her. Even to seek outside help might have occurred to you."

"But I had only just arrived . . . I saw nothing. It was all happening before I—"

"*Don't lie.* You were meeting Lucinda in the green room at ten o'clock, and because I had promised young Jerry to see a lighting demonstration he had worked out with the chief electrician, I accompanied her. She went to the green room to wait for you. We were early because Lights wanted to start at a quarter to ten. He and Jerry were waiting for me in the wings. Furthermore, I know the reason for your meeting with Lucinda—"

I interrupted with annoyance, "She seems to tell you everything!"

"Naturally she does." I couldn't see why it should be "natural" to confide everything even to a long-standing friend, but it was plain that he took it for granted, because he went on, "I know about her handing back your share in the theatre. What I *don't* know is how Durbridge came to be on the scene, though, God help me, I now know why. I heard the

man's frenzied words toward the end. I vowed long ago that one day I
would learn what happened that night, and I told Lucinda so at the time,
but she has never referred to it since. Now I know the truth about everything, because at last she has been able to talk about it. That alone makes
me even more determined to see that the man gets his deserts, and *you*
are going to tell me how he knew Lucinda was to be in the green room at
ten o'clock this morning.''

"She can tell you as much as I," I muttered.

"Even if that were true, I'm not going to badger her with any more
questions. She is sleeping now. She will be all right because I reached
her in time, but Durbridge might have killed her . . .''

He seemed to choke on the words, which surprised me, because I
thought doctors had to remain completely unemotional about their patients. He turned away and stared through the window, and I saw his
hand clenching and unclenching behind his back, and before he could
ask any more awkward questions about how Durbridge came to be in the
green room I said in a tone of relief, "Well, I am glad to hear she's going
to be all right. I suppose Jerry Hawks let them know at the theatre that
her understudy would have to go on?"

He spun round, blazing. *"What the hell does that matter?* All that does
matter is Lucinda, and that Durbridge is brought to justice and, before
God, I shall see that he is, but not through her. She has suffered enough
at his hands. I'm not going to have Lucinda put into any witness box or
involved in any way with his filthy name. I shall get him on other charges,
and he knows it, *and* he knows I'll make them stick. I had time to tell
him that much at least before I got Lucinda home, but of course the man
laughed—or tried to. He is insane in his belief that he can't be brought
down because, megalomaniac that he is, he believes himself invincible.
Knowing you as I do, Clementine, I believe you can help me. You *were*
responsible for the man being in the theatre today, weren't you?"

I dodged that by saying, "Knowing me as you do, Magnus? That is intimately, remember? We meant a lot to each other. You loved me—"

He cut in impatiently, "Oh, that. I've forgotten it. I was besotted, in-
fatuated. It was easy to forget because it meant so little. That sort of
thing never does. There have been plenty of men in your life since, I am
sure. Men you have met through Durbridge?" When I made no answer,
he changed his tone abruptly. "Put on your outdoor things. I am taking
you somewhere." When I hesitated he rapped, *"At once."*

"I . . . I don't feel well . . . Kate must have told you—"

"There is nothing wrong with you. Nothing at all. I'll give you two
minutes to put a coat on, or take you out of this house as you are, without one, and I don't give a damn if you freeze."

* * *

That shabby old trap which he still used was waiting outside. He handed me into it and drove at a brisk pace from Portman Square along Wigmore Street and across Cavendish Square into the environs behind Oxford Street. I was astonished at the speed we made, and more than puzzled about where we were heading, because I had imagined he was taking me to George Street to face Lucinda and her mother, and further questioning from Trudy, which I did not want, so when he headed in another direction, I was thankful.

Then I thought of Durbridge. Was he taking me to him? Was the man under arrest at some police station, and was he taking me there for questioning? My thoughts ran wild because I knew Magnus Steel would stop at nothing to get at the truth, but the nearest police station to the Boswell Theatre and the Strand was Bow Street, and we were not heading in that direction either.

"Is Durbridge under arrest?" I asked. "Did you hand him over to the police?" I remembered Lights stopping Stacey from getting the man away "until the doctor decides what to do with him," so what *had* he done with him?

At my question, Magnus shook his head. "I let him go, chiefly because my concern at that moment was Lucinda, but also to lull him into a false sense of security, but that man of his wasn't deceived, which means that he will squeal when the time comes—and that will be sooner than either of them expects."

"Then where are you taking me now?"

"You'll see."

But what I was beginning to see, I didn't like at all, and I liked it less and less the farther east we drove, through an endless sprawl of slums, the like of which I could never have imagined.

"For goodness' sake, Magnus, take me home! What ghastly place is this?"

"You've just come through Rotherhythe, and now you're in Stepney. These people you see are inhabitants, and the women are prostitutes, driven to it by poverty. You will meet some face to face shortly."

"I don't want to! I won't, I won't . . . I refuse!"

"Squeamish, Clementine? But not squeamish about looking on while Lucinda was whipped by a man who trades in prostitution? Not this kind of prostitution, because there is no money in it for a man who deals in it on his scale. This isn't Babylon—this is the other side of the coin, the result of starvation wages and harsh conditions. Do you know what a woman is paid for sewing collars and wrist bands onto shirts? Twopence-ha'penny for each shirt. How many a day do you think she can do to earn enough to feed herself, let alone her family? Why do you think these tragic creatures are queuing up for sailors coming ashore? They are driven to it through hunger and poverty and seeing their husbands and children starve. For many it is the only way to survive, and if I were to tell them that you have enjoyed yourself in Babylon, and even by looking at you these days I can tell you have— (How? I and others from the mission have rescued many a tragic child from its streets, so the stamp it leaves on a woman's face is recognisable) —and if I were to tell them of the ways in which you have enjoyed yourself, they would probably spit on you. And Stepney is a drop in the ocean compared with the size of London, its population merely a handful. A handful of thousands, and all in the same boat. Look, Clementine, *look*. You are seeing yourself as you would have been, born into such conditions."

"You are trying to frighten me!"

"I am indeed, and I am telling you things and showing you things I have wanted to tell you and show you for a long time. You are a high-class whore who has never given a thought to anyone but herself, never done another human being a good turn, never loved anyone or cared for anyone. Your way of life makes a mockery of all that is wholesome and beautiful. It may surprise you to know that that is what a physical relationship between a man and a woman can really be. I don't wholly condemn you for your appetite for men. There's a word for women like you, though you may be unfamiliar with it. Nymphomaniac. A woman with an insatiable appetite for sex which one man alone cannot satisfy. In that way you are to be pitied. What I don't pity is your selfishness and cruelty and dishonesty and viciousness. And now here we are at my mission and you can see where Lucinda and her mother and my sister come to do what they can in any way they can, and I hope the sights you see awaken in you some spark of shame."

I have always wanted to forget that afternoon, but sometimes it comes back to me like a nightmare. He spared me nothing—the children, the mothers, the aged, the wrecks, the alcoholics, the worn-out drabs, the gaunt faces, the skeleton frames, the cavernous eyes. I was thankful when Helen Steel quietly took me away from it all.

"The first encounter is always a shock," she said gently. "I will get you a cup of tea and then take you home. I am due to go off duty soon; time to pick up Dr. Maynard's children from school. He will carry on for me at the clinic. My brother will stay, and the two men will travel back together late tonight." She opened a door, and Dr. Maynard was there. "You remember Miss Boswell, don't you, Hugh? She called one Sunday when you and the children and Trudy had come to lunch."

He rose to greet me, and I sank gratefully into the chair he pulled forward. I even thought, remotely, what a kind smile he had. Then I thought of Anna, living in her comfortable house in St. John's Wood, thinking of no one but herself, caring for no one, loving no one—just as

Magnus had accused me. I would never forgive him fo. that, but I would show him how wrong he was, and already I knew how I would accomplish it. I would get the money owing to me from the expensive Salon of Art, and I would donate it to this mission—*that* would prove how generous I was, but of course he would never know where the money came from. He would think it came out of my own pocket, which, in a way, it would, of course. That made me feel really virtuous.

When Helen returned with the tea she said, "I was expecting Lucinda this morning. She often puts in an hour or two before a Saturday matinee, but I suppose something prevented her. I must ask Magnus."

I wanted to cry, "Don't! Don't ask him anything!" but then I knew she would be sure to hear anyway. Apart from the fact that the Steels and the Graingers seemed to have no secrets from each other, the world would hear a lot of things in the near future because Magnus would see that it did, and it was all going to be quite, quite dreadful and I could not imagine how anyone so sensitive as I was going to face up to possible involvement in it.

When I reached home, Mamma told me reproachfully that Mr. Curtis had been for tea as usual and that it was naughty of me to have gone out, especially when I had been feeling unwell. I told her I had needed air, but that I was now going to bed for the rest of the day and would she please apologise on my behalf if he called again tonight. And it was the truth. The more I thought of those terrible sights in the East End, the worse I felt. There was nothing to do but go to sleep and forget about them. That was what I always did when I wanted to escape something unpleasant.

Next day, Sunday, I remembered that Anna spent the day at home "doing her household accounts," so I decided to call on her again and to be very, very firm this time. I would tell her that Durbridge was threatened with exposure and she would realise just how much could come out and how many people could be involved, particularly herself.

I had everything neatly planned in my mind and knew that nothing could go wrong, so after Mamma and I had been to Mass as usual I said I would take a drive through the park and along the Ladies' Mile, which she knew was now quite a respectable thing for me to do, since Rotten Row had been cleared of its scandalous parade of courtesans riding on splendid mounts in splendid habits and never going at more than a trot, because no inviting male glance should be missed, nor the chance to ogle any passing man, whether accompanied by his wife or not. So while Mamma had her aperitif, as she called it, before lunch, I told our elderly coachman to drive me out to St. John's Wood.

Springdale Avenue was deserted at this hour. I could imagine all the

respectable inhabitants preparing to sit down to their roast beef and
Yorkshire pudding, having returned from Matins or Mass, and I could
imagine Anna looking very surprised when she saw me.

She did, but my own surprise was greater. She looked haggard. She
was about to shut the door, but somehow my foot was inside, and then
the other one followed.

I said, "I can see by your face that you have heard about Durbridge.
There is going to be trouble, real trouble, though no doubt he doesn't
believe it. But Stacey does. I suppose the man got word to you. I have
merely come to tell you I intend to have the money owing to me, every
penny of it, and that I don't believe you can't arrange it. All the other
models will be demanding the same."

To my utter astonishment she answered, "My dear Miss Boswell, I
don't know what you are talking about. You are not one of our models.
Your name isn't even on our books, so how can you claim that we owe
you money? You *are* Clementine Boswell, the actress, aren't you?"

When I got my breath, I had to admit it. "But you know me as Diana
Portman. That is the name you registered me under."

Haggard as she was, she still had her wits about her.

"We may have someone named Diana Portman on our books, but no
Clementine Boswell, so I am sorry, my dear, but you can't come here
demanding money. We only pay to registered names."

She thought she had won, and for the moment, she had; then I realised that, in a way, *I* was the victor. When the crash came, my name
would not be involved at all! When Durbridge's unsavoury activities
were uncovered, there would be no Clementine Boswell listed anywhere.

The thought was a profound relief, but even so I would hit back at
Anna Maynard, and hit hard, because she had swindled me, cheated me,
and if there was anything I hated being cheated out of, it was money.

After lunch, I walked across the square to Magnus Steel's house.
When I rang the doorbell, there was no answer, but I knew the gymnasium door might be unlocked, and it was.

Barker was there and, as before, he came hurrying across.

"Ma'am, you can't come in here, you know you can't."

"Even when no gentlemen are present?"

I looked around. There was no sign of Magnus, so I went toward the
door opening onto the stairs.

"I'm expecting some gentlemen for a special class at any moment,
ma'am, and if you want to see Miss Steel—"

"I tried the front doorbell, but received no reply. I presume she is
out, so I will leave a note for her upstairs."

"You'll be wasting your time, ma'am. Miss Steel doesn't live here now. She has a place of her own down near Fulham."

That stopped me in my tracks. *Well, well,* I thought, *how very interesting!* Not that I blamed the woman. She was in love with Hugh Maynard and he with her, so why shouldn't she live near him? I could help her achieve more than that, and *then* Magnus could never accuse me of not doing anyone a good turn and of thinking of no one but myself.

"I presume your master is at home?"

The man nodded. "Yes, but perhaps I'd better announce you, ma'am."

I brushed past him and went upstairs, and as I climbed I was aware of a pleasurable feeling of anticipation. So Magnus was living alone now; this was a bachelor's house. I wished I had known before. My spirits lifted as I pictured him taking back every unkind word when he heard what I was prepared to do for his sister. How could his heart fail to soften toward me then?

Behind all this was a picture of Anna Maynard's face, and I relished it.

The ground floor was empty, the morning room with a deserted air, and his study similarly. Books had been closed, papers put away. It was Sunday, of course, so he would be upstairs in the drawing room, reading the Sunday papers, sitting beside the fire with his slippers on. I could not have called at a more pleasant time.

To my surprise, the drawing room was empty also, but a fire burned in the grate. Obviously, he must be somewhere around, and Barker's suggestion about announcing me confirmed this. The drawing room occupied the whole of this floor, running from front to back, so I went determinedly up to the next one and opened the first door I came to, and saw them in bed together.

32

The slashes on her body had been dressed, and these dressings were the only things she wore. He was cradling her very gently, cherishing her. Her eyes were closed, and on her face was a look of peace and contentment. I also knew that he had not been loving her physically for fear of hurting her wounded body, but that even so she was aware of the depth of his feeling for her and of his longing and desire and his willingness to wait until he could love her bodily again.

I wondered how long they had been lovers, and at the same time I realised that the relationship between these two was something outside all my experience, because this man loved Lucinda in a way he had described to me only yesterday. What had he called it? "Wholesome and beautiful." From the look on his face it seemed to me that it was also sacred, and that puzzled me, because nothing had ever been sacred between myself and any lover I had ever had.

When he saw me he slipped off the bed very quietly. He was wearing a robe, and I remembered Gavin Calder sliding off a bed a long time ago, casually tying one about his nakedness, and sauntering across the room callously and indifferently, laughing as he did so. Magnus behaved quite differently. He simply came across, took me by the arm, led me from the room, and quietly closed the door.

Then he said frankly, "You know, Clementine, I would have expected even a woman like you to have more tact than to walk into the bedroom of a married couple."

"*Married?*" I don't know how long it took me to get the word out, but it seemed a very long time indeed. "You and *Lucinda?*" I added disbelievingly.

"Some weeks ago. Very quietly. Just her mother and Helen and Hugh Maynard at the church. We wanted it that way because it means a lot to both of us, something very personal and private and important."

Into my memory flashed a picture—Lucinda looking at her red velvet cloak with grief and saying, "My mother made this for me. It was part of my—" I hadn't even dreamed that she was about to add the word "trousseau."

Magnus was saying, "I have waited a long time for Lucinda, but she is my Achilles' heel, so what else could I do? I waited for her to grow up, to get over the man she married, and then to have room in her life for something more than the theatre. I used to hope that one day she would want to have no part in that world, but I learned to compromise, to understand what it means to her, to realise that I can play my part in it too by protecting her from its worst aspects. That is what I will be doing when Durbridge's case comes up. He is being charged with corruption, corruption of all kinds; and on whining Stacey's evidence and all the others who will squeal in self-defence, plus evidence I have collected against the man bit by bit, he will be found guilty—and that will be my vengeance on him for what he did to my wife and for what he has done to others."

He led me toward the stairs. He was sending me on my way. I felt wounded and resentful and bewildered. I was faced with something I could scarcely comprehend and did not want to believe. It was as if Lucinda had vanquished me without even trying.

Magnus said good-bye and turned back to the bedroom, then stopped abruptly and asked, "Just why did you come here?"

I had forgotten until that moment, so I told him Anna Maynard's address and about Harris's Art Galleries and what lay behind them, and how the woman was employed there.

"But if you want to know *how* I know, I won't tell you. My name must be left out of it."

He promised that it would be and, being Magnus, I knew he would keep that promise.

"My sister's happiness means a lot to me, and Hugh Maynard deserves his freedom. He will get it now, thanks to you. This was a kind action of yours, Clementine, and makes up for things to a certain extent."

I let him think it *was* a kind action. In fact, I thought so myself, but as I left his house and walked back across the square, all I could see was Anna Maynard's face, twisted with fury, and it delighted me. I clung to that picture for another reason also—because I didn't want to recall the one of Lucinda, lying in bed with Magnus Steel, looking more beautiful than she had ever been.

Curtis was waiting for me. He had been shown upstairs to my sitting room.

"I asked to see you, not your mother," he explained without any preliminary greeting. "I have to return to New York. There's a battle going on for the hotel I bid for, and I'm determined to be on the spot to win it. So it's good-bye, Clementine."

I felt as if the last door had been slammed in my face, and I realised then that the idea of using Curtis as a source of escape if things went wrong had been growing at the back of my mind. But now that escape route was being cut off—if I allowed it to be.

I rallied instantly, and summoning all my ability as an actress I put a note of unconcern in my voice as I said lightly, "What a pity! How soon do you have to go?" but I made it obvious that the words were spoken with an effort.

"As soon as possible. I've been to the shipping office and booked a passage on the first transatlantic liner available. Meanwhile, I have telegraphed a higher bid."

I moved closer to him.

"I shall miss you, Curtis."

"You'll soon forget me, leading the life you are leading now."

"I am not leading it anymore. Not since you returned." A step nearer this time, a softer note in my voice. "With you in my life, I don't need any other men, and you know it."

He shook his head, a wry smile on his lips.

"You'll soon go back to it, Clemmy. You like the easy life. Why else did you become part of that place in St. James's? And you have greater ability in bed than you have as an actress. You won't have a stage career

as renowned as your mother once had, because there is no one to prop
you up the way your father did her. I doubt if your chances of marriage
are still great, either, with the reputation you've been earning. Don't
look so astonished—I've had my ear to the ground since coming back,
and a name that is bandied around loosely is Clementine Boswell's.
You're out of the marriage stakes now, unless you can find some doddering old fool to hoodwink. Face the truth, Clemmy—you've had your
chances and you missed them, and I guess all those once-eligible bachelors are blessing their luck now.''

Oh, God, I was going to lose him! I couldn't let it happen! I *wouldn't*. I
needed this man badly.

I cried out on a note of pain, "If you think so little of me, I'm surprised you came to say good-bye. Why did you? Why bother? Why not
simply return to America and forget all about me?''

We were standing so close now that he could see the hurt in my eyes
and I could see the response in his, the awareness of me, the stirring of
desire.

"I tried to," he admitted, "but, God help me, I couldn't.''

I laid a tentative hand on the lapel of his jacket as I whispered, "Because I belong to you, that's why. We belong together. No man has ever
been able to take your place, nor ever will. We're two of a kind and have
always been. There isn't even any social distinction between us now. As
you so rightly pointed out when you returned, we are equals.''

I had touched the right chord there and drove the point home by adding, "I have become more and more aware of it every day. I have been
proud to have you as my escort here in London, and I don't think you
have had cause to be ashamed of me—I have seen approval in your eyes
when you've called to take me for a drive, or out to supper after the
theatre. Admit it," I coaxed. "Admit it.''

"You dress superbly, I admit that . . . and, yes, I've been proud to
be seen with an elegant woman.''

"*And* one who knows how to conduct herself in public. So don't condemn me altogether, Curtis. Remember my social assets, at least, and try
to forgive the rest. And I hope you find a woman in America who will be
as great an asset to you. A man in your position needs one.''

I moved away from him then, but not before he had seen the sad smile
on my face, the brave-little-woman accepting the inevitable.

"Think of me kindly now and then," I pleaded, "as I shall think of
you. You have held a mirror before me, showing me what I am—no,
what I was in danger of becoming. For that, I am grateful, because you
have saved me from my own folly. I thank God you came back, but I cannot thank him for taking you away.''

He took a step after me.

"Clemmy . . .''

"No . . . don't come near me!" I held up a beseeching hand. "Don't make it harder for me to say good-bye!"

It was touch and go, and I knew it. Had I overplayed my hand? Suddenly my world seemed very shaky. I thought of Anna Maynard, who was even now hiding apprehensively behind her lace curtains, unaware that even if she were lucky enough not to become notorious through the coming Durbridge scandals (which she undoubtedly would), her respectable neighbours would be drawing aside their skirts at her approach—a widow who was not a widow, but (infinite disgrace) a divorcée. So what price her freedom and independence now? She would lose that house and she would certainly lose the husband she had once despised. She couldn't go crawling back; she could only go crawling down.

I felt almost willing to crawl to Curtis in return for the escape he represented. Not that I was now in any danger of being implicated in the Durbridge affair, but life had little to offer me other than slogging away in the theatre until I was eventually booed off the stage as my mother had been.

Curtis was right—I wasn't ambitious enough to become a successful actress. All my father's talent had been inherited by Lucinda, not by me, and I didn't really mind, because I would have hated to have to work as hard as she did. I could not share her enthusiasm for playing either Gwendolen or Cecily in the coming production, because either part would necessitate the learning of endless new lines. Bramwell Chambers was right in saying that I was not a good study. I was tired of the theatrical grind, but I would never tire of the limelight and I could get plenty of that as the mistress of a successful American hotelier.

So if I won this final round, I knew what I would do with that document from Lucinda. I had held on to it after Durbridge thrust it before me in my dressing room. I would sign without further objections and, later, I would write from America and offer it to either Bramwell Chambers or Willard or both. With his business acumen, Curtis would advise me well on what sum to ask. By this means I would at least get *something* out of the Boswell Theatre, then part from it without a pang.

But first I had to make sure of Curtis, so now I gave a little sigh and said wistfully, "What a pity your success lies in New York instead of London! Together we could have gone such a long way. I could have given up the stage and helped you get right to the top, because I am just the kind of woman you need at your side. And I am the right woman for you in other ways too. . . . But I mustn't think about that, I mustn't remember how things were between us. They *were* wonderful, weren't they, those hours we spent making love?" I let a quiver come into my voice then. "Perhaps it is a good thing you haven't taken me to bed since you returned, because had you done so, I am quite certain I could never have let you go like this."

"*Clemmy!*"

I was in his arms. It had worked, it had worked! I felt more than passion as I returned his kisses. I felt triumph. But when he put me aside, holding me by the shoulders and looking down at me with that expression I remembered so well—determined, possessive, suspicious—my triumph became tinged with apprehension. Had he realised I was giving the performance of my life?

"If I thought you were fooling me—" he began.

"How could I ever fool someone like you? A man who achieves all you have achieved cannot be hoodwinked. Besides, you said yourself that I am no great actress. But in any case," I finished, wide-eyed and innocent, "you are leaving me behind, so why should I pretend that I am not the loser? You know full well I am."

I sensed his satisfaction, his feeling of conquest, of having got the upper hand over me at last, and I encouraged it by looking up at him very humbly indeed, whereupon he said reflectively, "There's much in what you say about the right woman being an asset to me, and that woman could indeed be you, provided you were prepared to come to America with me."

(America! That new world full of opportunities and, I had heard, almost as many millionaires!)

I answered meekly, "I would go anywhere with you, you know I would."

He became masterful then.

"There would be conditions, mark you. I wouldn't be prepared to share a mistress with any other man, as you have good reason to remember."

I nodded, my eyes downcast.

"And what about your mother?"

"Oh, she'll be all right. This house is hers for life, with a trust fund to run it and a substantial income to live on."

"And no one to keep her company even occasionally. No one to look after her or keep an eye on her, except that untrustworthy Kate. You can't abandon your mother to a fate like that. She is your responsibility. Left alone, you know what would happen to her. So I'll tell you what I'll do —I'll arrange for her to follow later, after this house is sold. I'll see an agent on her behalf before we leave. With the money from the sale, and the trust fund which will be made over to her, plus her income, she can be set up very well in New York. She can have her own swank apartment and queen it in social circles as the titled widow of a renowned Shakespearean actor, and that is something she will love."

(Well, at least she wouldn't be under my feet so much. . . .)

"But what if she refuses to leave London?" I said, devoutly hoping that she would.

A broad smile spread across his handsome features, making him devilishly attractive.

"Believe me, Clemmy, she'll be eager for New York by the time I've gone to work on her. I could always twist your dear mamma around my little finger, you know I could. And I'll have her put on a cure when she arrives, and intermittently after that if and when she needs it, but perhaps with a new life and new interests and being made to feel important again, she won't want to drink so much. You have as great a weakness as hers, anyway. A weakness for food, and *that* will be controlled too. A fat woman would be no ornament to me. I need one who not only has tone and class, but wears clothes well. One more pound on that body of yours, and you won't be able to, in which case you'll be *out*. Remember that, Clemmy. Cease to be a credit to me, and I'll have no further use for you."

Oh, yes, you will, I thought. *You will always have one particular use for me, and I for you, so long as it suits my book.*

He continued magnanimously, "Be all I want you to be and do all I want you to do, and I might even consider marrying you, but only because 'my mother-in-law, Lady Boswell' sounds rather good and could be a further lever in my line of business."

One man, one bed, forever? I turned away from such a thought and said with a shrug, "What's in a title? You haven't become a snob, I hope?"

"Better to be a snob than a slave," he retorted, and I heard anger and passion flare in his voice as he finished, "I know what it's like to be a slave, a woman's slave, and by God, Clementine Boswell, the time has come for you to find out what it is like to be a man's."

Has it, indeed? I thought as I dropped my eyes in submission and went meekly into his arms. I could feel his self-congratulation even in his embrace, and I let him think the victory was entirely his as I hid my secret smile in his shoulder.

Who said I could only hoodwink a doddering old man?